ANGELS

ANGELS

— BOOK 2 OF THE CYBER SERIES —

LEN GIZINSKI

Polestar Press

To all the Kellys, and their families.

I also dedicate this book to my siblings, who have spared no level of support and encouragement as they faithfully waited for me to complete this work.

Lastly, as always, to you, Dear Reader, especially to those who have read "The Metal Within" and have (sometimes gently) encouraged me to get this second book out the door.

It's been a long time, and it's good to be back. So, Ladies and Gentlemen, start your engines,

And as always,

Enjoy the Ride!!!

"Long is the way and hard, that out of Hell leads up to Light."
—John Milton, *Paradise Lost*

*"Found out that we cannot have nice boys, cuz
we're the ones nice boys are told to avoid."*
—Wonder Truly, *Kids Like Us*

"It might look cozy, but really it's death."
—Jessica Pratt-McConnel

TABLE OF CONTENTS

Life in these Divided States xi

I. FREE RIDES AIN'T FREE 1

II. RESEARCH AND DEVELOPMENTS 69

III. INTO THE RABBIT HOLE 123

IV. MAKING THE SCENE 353

V. OF PITS AND PENDULA 509

EPILOGUE 651

Acknowledgments 661

A Personal Word 663

ALL RIGHT, CHOOMS, let this little lady tell ya how it is. Books can only fit so much of what all actually happened between 2020 and 2045. Stuff gets dropped. Sometimes they want it dropped. Sometimes they want it rewritten. Sometimes they want to focus on something else, and there just ain't no room. Any which way, it's gone. So, for those who only heard what they taught you in your college history classes, let me get you caught up on the lay of the land…

They used to say that it's always darkest before the dawn; now, people are saying it's always darkest after the last flicker of light burns out completely. And the lights of civilization started flickerin' like it had hotwired itself into the ATLAN Energy grid and never expected the megacorp to send its heavies to collect.

The 'Rona pandemic hit in 2020, wiping out several thousand around the globe. Panic ensued, both from the disease itself and the government's expanding controls over what used to be private lives. Second, third, and fourth waves of the virus proved the vaccines weren't the magic bullets the pharma corps and bureaucrats billed them to be. Amid the rising chaos, Iranian extremists tried to nuke any nation they deemed undesirable; not all the missiles actually went big-cloud, but places got leveled, and people went ghost. Within minutes, global leaders fired back a devastating counterstrike that reduced much of Iran to a 200-mile-wide crater of black glass we now know as The Bowl.

Not that that was the only problem we had at the time; a worldwide lack of government accountability led to several other global crises. Like for one, even without the Forty Minute War, the depletion of oil reserves threatened to cripple economies on a global level. Between the pandemic, the missile strikes, and the oil shortages, society's immune system couldn't handle much more. So, of course, Mother Nature, annoyed as she was by all the pollutin', strip minin', and deforestation, up and decided to haul off and give humanity a swift kick to the rib cage while we were down. It might have been the fallout of the nukes from those Iranians and every other country under the sun. It might have been the oil running out in enough farms that they couldn't keep their crops right. Or it might have been some new kind of GMO that got out of the development pens. More likely, a combination of all three. What mattered was that somehow a grain blight hit pretty much the entire planet. Though nobody that I know of figured out the exact cause, the effects were all too familiar to everybody. Grass died, livestock that ate the grasses died, then food reserves died. Mass starvations. Food riots. Civil wars after people completely lost confidence in their governments. It was a miracle any civilization survived at all.

Now, it might be true that it's always darkest after the last flicker of light burns out, but mankind's got a rebellious streak that just wouldn't let us go down without a fight. So, when Mother Nature up and had her hissy-fit, humanity played one of our strong suit cards with a vengeance. Everything in society was failing, but ironically, our propensity towards greed kept it from dying altogether.

It was the megacorporations that, however unforgiving, were able to preserve any semblance of society beyond a local level. See, society was no longer bound by any national allegiances, but profiteering still required order and infrastructure. Contracts were to be made, and once made, honored. Corporate wars took on a whole new meaning that few could have ever imagined two generations earlier. The smaller companies and local governments usually either got goinked by the heavies or just simply starved out. Competition was both aggressive and fierce among the bigger sharks in the tank, but the order was maintained. That order required commerce, commerce required deals, and deals required the dance of biz. Biz required communications and the roads. The corps that survived started working together to cover the infrastructures that used to be supported by the now-defunct governments. The most successful of these megacorps grew large enough to become city-states within themselves, some even true international entities. International corporate conglomerates, or ICC's, were born.

And that oil problem? Well, it's still a problem—but then, we still got our rides, right? Well, the development of high-performance electric engines and miniaturization of both electronics and weapons tech ushered in the desire for heavily armed and armored vehicles. Corps had already begun toolin' up their suit's vehicles for protection. Seeing new profit avenues ripen, some corps assimilated auto design specialists to develop factory-produced weaponized vehicles for the commercial market. Even highway construction crews armed and armored their vehicles to the teeth and had local police and militia support. After all, just cuz biz needed the roads didn't mean raider gangs wouldn't wanna yoink their stuff.

Oh, one more thing happened during those years. Now, the ICC's bought or hired their own static armed security forces, but they didn't really care about the devastation unless it directly affected them. I mean, life was all relatively safe and cozy if you happened to have sold enough of your soul to the corp; you got to live on corp archology grounds, eat corp food—you could even get them to sing the corp anthem at your funeral if you ranked high enough to have corp-sponsored funeral insurance. But most areas outside the archologies had little to no protection of any sort. Since nobody else was either willing or able to help the common citizen fight against the outlaw raiders, people started hiring out wheelmen— professional vehicle combat specialists—to combat the new threat.

And Time marched on—yeah, they still say that one. And I could try to tell you that life marched on right along with it, but let's be real—after life got jacked from behind by the blight, it was more of a low crawl. Besides, when greed is your savior, you know life ain't gonna be worth much no matter where you're at in the spectrum of "Haves." But we had one last card—a trick card, a hidden Ace—that few knew about: the last vestige of a collapsed government that was so secret it kept on going, continuing in the shadows that had birthed it. The covert agency, mostly *not* known as the Cybernetically-Enhanced Response Force, is also mostly *not* known as CYBER.

You see, a few years before the federal government went belly up, unseen powers that create unseen agencies created CYBER and gave it authority to conduct clandestine operations to protect its citizens from what the U.S. was becoming. Now, CYBER's whole method of operation was different. For one, rather than the typical centrally-governed hierarchy, CYBER deployed autonomous teams of about five to eight, with the leader of each team responsible for training and provisioning the team. For another, it was by far the most technologically advanced organization in the government's plethora of technologically advanced organizations. But the biggest difference was that, unlike most of the other organizations, they didn't focus as much on the tech as they did on recruiting the people who were integrating with it. CYBER was effective where other agencies bogged down—not because they enforced any doctrine or policies better, but because they all felt the same deep sense of personal integrity. They understood that it wasn't the metal inside the agents that made them special. It was the mettle within that proved the makings of a good team.

After all, I oughtta know. Blaze's Fist is one of the tightest crews CYBER's got. And I'm Blaze.

I. FREE RIDES AIN'T FREE

"Life gives us a flair of awareness in the breeze of our daily journey and offers a free reign to explore what we are, to experience what we are not and to find out what we may become: a free ride until everything melts down into the indistinct and indefinite, while walking up to the ultimate gate of non-existence."

— Erik Pevernagie, *Living on Probation*

1. Witch City Blues...

Nighttime in Witch City was nowhere to be on the run. She pushed on though, half skipping, half hobbling, wincing with each step, fires of agony flashing in her eyes. She couldn't let herself cry; they would hear her.

She stumbled and fell as heavily as her undernourished frame would allow. At least she was getting closer. Closer to her freedom. Closer to being reunited with her family. *Family*—just the thought of the word brought renewed strength of purpose. She crawled onwards, no longer able to walk. It just hurt too much. Earlier she had gritted her teeth, picked up the piece of metal she found in the alley and gouged out the RFID chip they had implanted in her right heel. The pain was unthinkable, but if she didn't do it, they'd just track her down like they did the others who tried to run. She didn't want to end up like them.

Something crashed down the alley ahead of her. She covered her mouth with her hand and stifled the scream that would give her away. She wasn't far enough away to let herself scream, or cry, or express any other human reaction to what she had been through. She couldn't afford to be human just yet. Maybe, if she was lucky, she could work on that later. For now, she had to focus every fraction of her will just to keep moving.

A dog barked in some far-off location behind her. She thought of Ferdinand, the pet she once had, and the family she once had, and the humanity she once had. She remembered she used to be Kelly. She found herself fading into a sleepless dream crafted in her mind until she caught a glimpse of herself reflected through a puddle of some unknown oily liquid. It took a moment for her to recognize that the gaunt and ragged face was her own. And with that, Ferdinand was replaced with Adolph and Brutus, the snarling hounds they kept on hand to intimidate anyone who did not obey their every wish. Her family was replaced with them, and her humanity was replaced with what she had become. Exhausted, she slapped her hand against the dirt and gritty macadam of the alley, grinding it to keep herself awake. "Stupid!" she accused herself in panged regret a second later. She couldn't afford to injure her hands now—she needed the pain to keep her awake, but she had to keep crawling.

Something stirred in the alley's darker shadows ahead of her. Whatever caused the noise a minute ago was still there. She was almost too afraid to go on, but that would mean going back. Whatever was ahead of her had to be better than what she was running away from. She dragged herself along, her fear blocking the abject pain she felt along each torturous inch. Then she saw him—a kid maybe seven or eight years old, as gaunt as she was, maybe even paler. Despite his pallor, he smiled when he saw her.

"Hi," he said weakly, like voicing that single syllable was twisting his chest inside out.

Most of her scorned him for delaying her, but she was still too human to turn him down. "Hi," she eventually said as she took a moment to catch her breath. He didn't answer right away. Maybe in her frantic state of mind, the kid was already dead, and she couldn't bring herself to deal with it; maybe she was talking to herself.

"You sure are pretty," the youth finally said with such obvious innocence she couldn't despise him for it.

"Yeah, thanks, I guess," she practically scorned. She paused then and tried to focus on getting moving again. "Why are you looking at me like that?" she almost jeered but stopped short when she saw him shivering. Instead, she tried her best to smile. "Your vision's blurry, kid," she said in as friendly a manner as she could muster. "How long you been here?"

"Long enough," he replied. "Guess I—won't be here—much longer, though."

She didn't have the time to stay, yet she didn't have the heart to leave, either. The kid was dying, and now another chill October drizzle began to fall. The kid coughed, the sound a clogged rasp that spoke of lung. Scanning the immediate surroundings for anything she could do for him, she dumped a plastic garbage bag of its contents as quietly as she could manage, then carefully folded it around his huddled body. "Here," she said. "At least this'll keep the rain off and help keep you warm a little."

Hollow eyes beheld her, and they would have been piercing if there was any light left inside them. He seemed to remember something, then looked at her again, his eyes widening, fearful and hopeful to equal degree. "Are you—are you an angel?" he finally asked, a slight tremor in his dying voice. The question caught her by surprise—the water that began to slide gently down her cheek had nothing to do with the weather.

"I don't think so, kid," she said, "but you'll be seeing them soon, I guess." She paused, then asked him, "And hey, when you do? Can you let them know I'm still down here?"

"I will, lady. Thanks for… my… blanket."

And with that, he fell asleep. She heard a quiet rustling from some adjacent piles of side-alley refuse. She muttered a brief apology, but despite this latest wound to her heart, it was time to go. She regained her feet in her limping hobble, lightning flashes of white-hot pain with each step on the foot of her injured heel. She got about half a block before she heard a commotion behind her. Fearfully looking back, she saw a small swarm of kids about the age of the one she had just seen die gather around the body, some a little older, reaching down, pulling the garbage bag blanket that had become the best she could do for a burial. A new panic caused her to hobble even faster as she noticed they looked up at her briefly. She risked a quick glance back a few steps later, relieved yet horrified when she saw they had returned to their task. Pain upon pain ripped her apart and caused her to openly sob as she imagined exactly what that task was—the children of Witch City sometimes went feral.

Another two alleyways later, she was close to completing her escape. She was troubled that she had lost so much time to the boy but knew that she couldn't have just left him. The rain fell in a steady drizzle now and almost gently pattered off a second garbage bag she had managed to find for herself. She began to hear music that came from somewhere ahead of her. It sounded distant, but in her tired and drug-addled mind, she couldn't be sure. Maybe the music wasn't really there at all. She'd come down hard before—maybe she wasn't really in a cold rain-splashed alley at all. Maybe she had never left and was waiting for them to return to start the never-ending cycle all over again. Or maybe this was all just a long, bad dream, and she was still Kelly—her family and Ferdinand waiting for her to awaken. Her stomach churned, harshly impaling the message through to her that this was all too real. Maybe Ferdinand was just a dream. Maybe *Kelly* was the dream, the place she went to when the Dreamers kicked in enough that the pain went away, and she could get far enough away from herself to become someone else for just a little while, the boy, a part of the hallucination, to remind her that maybe there was some way to be worse off than she already was.

Her stomach churned again, jolting her out of her imagination's escape. She was used to being hungry, but she missed the ups they used to give her to keep her from noticing just how much. Another fear grabbed at her, joining all the others she had in her mind— soon the withdrawals would hit, and if that happened before she got away, she would die. She crawled on, beginning to whimper despite herself.

The cold October drizzle now turned to a full rain. It gave her a chance to get a drink out of some oil-rainbowed puddle water and helped clear her head a little, but mostly it just felt cold and sent her shivering. With an effort that took all of her will, she pushed on, finally making it to a street that had some regular people on it, people who looked like her when she dreamed she was Kelly, like her family and friends. Like nice people.

"Please," she begged in a hoarse whimper. "Please, help me."

But the people who could have helped her had other things to do than getting involved with a drug-crazed, unkempt ragdoll of a street tramp who, in their unspoken yet all too shared judgment, had obviously brought this all upon herself. And she was *bleeding*, they noticed. Any individual in the crowd might have stopped to offer assistance, but in the sidewalk bustle, the individuals merged into its own larger multicolored organism, too disinterested in anything but itself to notice the tiny speck of humanity that lay at its many well-shod and high heeled feet. And in the security of their societal cloak, those who did notice the stray human crawling along the outside of their fungus of dulled humanity concluded she should not have been walking barefoot through the streets like the tramp that she clearly was. She didn't fit in—probably diseased, it collectively concluded—so it treated her as though she herself was the disease. The protective layers of social programming would not permit the disease to enter into it, and it was too much effort for those within to overcome the cushioning of commonality to aid her.

So, she lay there in the rain, pleading to the organism, the crowd, in this case so much less than the sum of its parts, for help. She was about to give up when a car approached, slowed, and stopped. An elderly lady lowered her window and asked, "Dear child, you look like you could use some assistance. Might I help you?" she asked, offering her a hand to get into the warm, dry vehicle.

"Please," the girl said.

"Oh, do come in. There, there." And as the girl who thought she might be Kelly got into the car, the lady reached for the car's vid-phone. "You gave me quite a scare back there," the older lady said, "but I am so glad I found you when I did." The car door closed, and the big vehicle pulled away from the curb. Free at last!! The woman applied some lipstick from a gaudy cosmetic case, closed the mirror kit, dialed a number in the phone, and looked at her almost apologetically. "You know, I'm sorry I have to do this, dear, I really am. But at my age, this is about the only way I can keep my car. It means I'm still useful to them."

The girl wailed in shock and utter despair as the phone screen came to life and a deep male voice answered.

"Ricky T. Showbiz? This is Mama Solace. I found her. She's with me now... We'll be right over... You want to talk to her? Of course, here you go…." Then, turning to the girl still moaning in grief, she continued, "Now calm yourself, child," Mama Solace advised as she swiveled the display over to point to the girl, "Sweet Trick Ricky T. Showbiz doesn't like it when his girls make a fuss."

"H—Hello?" the girl barely croaked, desperately trying not to earn any more of the wrath that was sure to come.

"Baby, baby, you shoulda known better than to try that—an' after I was so especially good to you, letting you have a juice for breakfast for a whole week straight!"

"Are you… are you gonna kill me?" By the time she finished the question, Mama Solace had the ether rag over her nose and mouth, not that the girl had the strength of will left to resist anyway.

"Nah, baby, I ain't gonna kill you," the Master laughed—not a friendly sound. Then he got so serious she felt its chill over the call, through the acrid smell of the ether as it worked its way into her system. The last thing she heard before succumbing to the chemicals was his responding, "Not yet."

The organism that was the crowd saw the girl get into the car, but it had places to go and things to do, and so it closed its collective mouth and kept it shut as though to swallow her whole. The organism then continued to shamble on with its constant flowing movement, as though the girl had never really existed at all.

2. Events

Jack "Preach" Mathews wasn't as young as he used to be, and the Cybernetic Enhancement Response force (CYB.E.R.) training event seemed bent on proving it. He had just made a tough call.

"OW!" Chrome exclaimed. Normally, Chrome expressing any sort of pain would have been monumentally shocking to everyone enough to stop the game, but for the first time, the Pride was actually winning a training event against the Hounds. Corey "Hardcore" Martin hadn't technically hit Chrome with his car—he just caused Rickshaw to hit Chrome with *his* car after Corey's Sabretooth power-slid into the Hound wheelman's Dominator.

"Yeah, Preach! *Nice!!*" Corey shouted over the Sabretooth's PA system.

"Not fair!" Rickshaw shouted back over his own PA. We're ain't s'posed to hit anyone with the cars!"

"That's right, Rick—and if you do it again, you're out of the game!" Preach called back, much to the amusement of his team.

Johnny had been standing right next to Chrome but had somehow managed not to get hit. Now that the Hound's muscle was momentarily downed, he twisted the ball from the powerful cyborg and tossed it to Susan "Lady Blackwolf" Blakeslee. Approaching the goal at a brisk trot, she caught the pass and broke downfield for the score. If she could hit here, they would win. With her augmented agility, that would have been no contest. Just as she crossed the ¾ mark, however, a looping arc of microfilament line shot past her and ensnared her ankles. The blonde gymnast fell to the ground with a *whuft!* as the line was retracted with an audible zipping sound. Araña, or Spider as he often referred to himself, eagerly waited to retrieve the ball as his grapnel rapidly dragged her back to the half-field. Only five yards away from her would-be captor, Susan thought of a way out. If he wanted to use his toys, she would use hers. She popped her cyber claws and slit the line, allowing the momentum of the line's pull to hoist her, scissor-kicking, into her Hound counterpart.

Jack had been closing in on Spider from behind to assist his struggling teammate. Spider suddenly vaulted, somersaulting over the kicks Susan tried to land on him. He somehow managed to grab her hips in mid-air and used her forward momentum to propel her into Jack. Susan exploded in laughter as she collided with her leader, reveling in the thrill and fun of the moment. "I can never get over just how fast he is!" she said between bouts of belly laughter. Chrome took advantage of the turn of events to grab the ball back from her. Rickshaw was waiting at the Hounds' own goal line 120 yards away; Chrome effortlessly made the toss. The game was again tied.

Araña trotted over and helped the crumpled rival team members off the ground. "Heard you comin', Grey—err, Preach," the Hispanic commando corrected himself. Some years earlier, Jack Mathews had been known as Greyscale, Araña's team leader. Now Greyscale was back with a new name and a new team. "Preach" was the name given to him by the street gang he had ministered to in the intervening years. His crew, "Preach's Pride", was a collection of new kids CYBER had just recently recruited. Araña took the lead over Grey's Hounds, but nobody on Jack's former team felt right about changing the group's old name.

"Sue," Spider encouraged, "that was a pretty good move you pulled. You're definitely learning." He deliberated whether he should say more and decided to take the opportunity. "You know, I heard what you told Preach. You're at least as fast as I am, physically.

You're just not used to it yet; *mentally,* you're holding back. It won't be long until you really internalize the truth of this."

"Really?" she asked Araña, glowing in his approval. He wasn't her CYBER team leader, but he had been her coach and mentor since her first day in the organization of elite agents. While her heart belonged to Corey since their escape from Pennsylvania and the Steel Jackals, she and Araña had gotten close. And in that closeness, she sensed that somehow a turning point was going to transpire in their relationship.

"Good news and bad news there, sister," he assented with a minor sigh and just a twitch of grimace. "The good news is that when you get there, you'll finally know just how fast you've really become. You will hardly be stoppable."

"And what's the bad news?" she asked, knowing she would need to probe to get the whole story.

He looked at her squarely, not wanting to tell her but wanting her to know. He appeared just a little sad, which was unlike his normal, almost happy-go-lucky self. "The bad news is that when you get to find out just how fast you are...."

"Yes?" she asked, urging him to continue.

"You'll *have* to know," he grimly stated. After another pause, he added, "And typically, when that happens, it'll be someone else who'll pay the price if you're not fast enough."

The moment of Susan's laughter faded as Spider turned and jogged back to the others on the field. In the fun of the moment, she had forgotten that these were called training events for a reason.

3. Session 7

JOSANNE INDIGNANTLY ENTERED Jack's office for yet another one-on-one session. She had been an investigative journalist before CYBER had recruited her to become a trained conversationalist. She knew all about what was coming and why before Jack ever spoke a word. She disliked the sessions, disliked Jack for holding them, and disliked herself most of all because she knew why he knew he had to have them.

"Hi, Josanne. How are you doing today?"

"Okay, I guess," Josanne replied as she took her seat in the leather chair she usually sat in during these meetings. While Jack regularly met with all his team members, this was his seventh special session with Josanne since Operation Drawbridge, when she killed one of Mahlon Atchins's joeboys in his suite. The guy had been beating on and probably about to kill her best friend Melissana when Josanne drew her laser pistol and fired, shooting him in the back and, at that range, burning a hole right through him. The guy was a thug, a *govek*, a threat to her best friend's life—and another human being. As if that wasn't enough, Josanne wasn't just the team medic. She had been trained how to read people to elicit guided responses from them as well. She knew the rest of the team thought she should be over it by now and that they were disappointed with her that she wasn't. She also recognized it was Jack's job to fix her. Not bothering to mask her annoyance, she fixed her stare on him and asked, "How should I be doing?"

Jack tried his best to smile reassuringly. "I think you're doing pretty well, given what you've been through."

"Really?" she exclaimed more than asked, her voice raising in pitch, tempo, and volume, her arms thrown wide in exasperation. "Then why are we having these extra meetings? You're not having them with anyone else on the team." She caught herself leaning forward, hands gripping the front edges of the arms of the chair. "Besides," she added, relaxing herself back into the seat's cushioning, "your smile was a little forced. Your cheek lines are slightly more pronounced when you smile for real."

"Yeah, you're right," he admitted. His boyish grin at getting caught was all too real. "The fact is, I am concerned about how you, the person Josanne, are really doing. You spotted that, huh?"

"Well, I am our conversationalist, remember? Expert-level people reading is what I do."

"Yeah, I remember," he said, glad for the break in the ice. "And that can go good or bad for our meetings. But I don't think that'll be too much of a problem for us."

"Are you sure about that?" she asked, trying to draw him out.

"I know the training you had, Josanne, but that doesn't matter. I promise you that I'm not going to try to trick you, fool you, or manipulate you. I'm not here as your boss or even your team leader. Right now, you're not Trigget, you're Josanne Sinclair, and whether you believe this or not, right now, I'm here to look out for your personhood more than your job performance. Whether you see it this way or not, I also see myself here as your pastor, and to me, that means sometimes I'm going to have to help you see the light of day when you can't make it out on your own, someone to help you find your way when you don't even think there is a way. And sometimes, I'm going to be the one to care for you, even when you quit caring for yourself.

"Oh, I admit I care about your performance—the safety of the other team members will sometimes depend on you. In fact, it already has, which is why we're having these discussions. You saved Melissana's life, and it cost you. I know how that feels, believe me. Even more, I *appreciate* how that feels. We talked about the real sacrifice we make joining CYBER after the first Matsua run, about having to deal with the tough choices so others don't have to, so I get it. I even admire you for it.

"But I don't have any tricks I'll use on you, no clever schemes, or get-healed-quick scams. I do have tools, though, that have stood the tests of time and countless trials. I have a lot of experience leading teams, God's Word, prayer, faith in God's desire and ability to heal you, and I have my integrity. So, I already know that when you look me in the eye, the conversationalist training will only verify my genuineness."

Josanne offered him a look of veiled sincerity. "My pastor, huh?" She seemed to contemplate the rich leather arm of the chair as her fingers absently traced some unknown pattern on it. "Well, didn't Jesus say, 'The light of the body is the eye,' and, 'If the eye is light, the whole body is full of light, but if your eye is dark, how great is that darkness'? That's why Shakespeare wrote that the eyes are the windows to the soul, right?"

"Yeah, He did," Jack responded.

"Then that's a problem for me," Josanne declared as she fully turned her attention back on him, the gesture almost a dare, surprising him. "Because despite me knowing about all your ulterior motives, you want me to look you in the eyes and see that you are being genuine."

"What's the matter? I'm afraid I don't see your point," Jack confessed.

"You're telling me to look you in the eyes, and you yourself don't see the problem? Isn't it obvious, Cyber-Man?" She paused deliberately, allowing time to wind more tension into her final reproof, wanting the weight of her words to hit him with the blinding force of the contempt and anger she had up to this point saved for herself.

"You had your eyes replaced, '*Preach*.' You replaced the windows to your soul with agency-provided machines."

Jack had no words to say, so he didn't even try to stop her as she got up, turned her back, and gruffly walked out his office door.

4. Sitter

THE WHIRRING OF the light motorized wheels echoed in the cold, damp hollow stillness of the nearly abandoned warehouse. The expanse of cracked and pitted concrete flooring was dotted with dilapidated shipping containers, crates, and remains of tattered pallets. Their original use forgotten, they had been repurposed long ago in the meager hope they might be useful enough to be used as potential firewood, adding a touch of dry rot to the ever-present scent of old dust. But something other than the more common rat lived in that darkened vestige against the Witch City night, sheltered at least in part from the chill October rain that had resumed its pattering against the metal roof of the ancient structure an hour earlier.

He hadn't always been in his current condition. Over a decade ago, he went by the code name Partisan, a rising star in a corporate surveillance team for one of Air Dynamix's main competitors. Then he committed the mortal sin of the megacorporate world: he switched companies. Partisan had been nearly legendary among the elite of the electronic espionage set—until the mercenaries hired by his former employers caught up with him a month after he had extracted himself. An Air Dynamix rescue team found him three days later, his back broken, his hands maimed, and his mind hung over from the joy juice they poured down his throat. That hangover lasted three weeks, and the damage it did to his higher brain functions ensured he would go into violent seizures any time he tried to use any high-end surveillance device. Air Dynamix had wasted their capital on a resource that was no longer profitable for them; his mind was still sharp but no longer megacorporate-espionage sharp.

Corporate insurance paid for the medical surgeries, but the effort for the surgeries he needed was only half-hearted and less than quarter-funded, leaving him wheelchair-bound with minimum use of his hands. Once the surgeries and minimum recovery period were completed, corporate attorneys provided him a six-month severance package and an executive motorized wheelchair, which included some self-defense systems. Their final gift was a sternly-worded notice that his business with them concluded; it was in his best interest that he disappear.

So, Partisan disappeared. Now the locals who knew him at all called him "Sitter." Those who didn't know him knew of him and of the special kind of crazy that had kept him alive for this long. He was fiercely intelligent and had a will to live that had just gotten tougher as the often painful years literally rolled on.

The electric whine of his chair across the warehouse floor stopped, choked short as he tentatively came to a standstill upon hearing the sharp click of the exterior door latch. His sharp black eyes surveyed the areas of the cavernous room with an acute awareness. A breath of cooler air confirmed his hearing was true. Being wheelchair-bound—even in his special motorized one—was never easy. In the dog-eat-dog world of 2048, his day-to-day autonomous survival was a day-by-day miracle play. Several seconds lapsed before he heard the muffled latch click of the door closing—it had been open long enough to admit more than one or two people. He couldn't see them yet, but he could now hear occasional scuffles of their footsteps padding slowly, deliberately, across the concrete. He activated a small console at his left wrist; within seconds, the camera surveillance system he had installed revealed a group of eight unkempt youths between the ages of six and fifteen, stealthily surveying the place as they advanced across the floor.

"They're quiet," he smiled to himself. "They're good right now," he thought, "but they can get better. If they would've been a little more experienced, I wouldn't have noticed they had entered at all." A gap in the heavily weathered crates provided a deep, narrow inlet—an excellent hiding place in the darkened structure. He backed into the narrow man-made crevasse and silently waited.

As the group of intruders crossed the deeply shadowed recess, he keyed a button sequence on his control panel. The chair burst from its concealed presence and fired a volley of darts that shattered a crate not twelve feet from the boys, startling them. Homemade knives and jury-rigged spears bristled from the older children; the youngest one brandished a quick shrill scream.

"It's all right, boys," he exclaimed with a chuckle. "You remembered your drills! Excellent! Never forget that just because a place was your home when you left doesn't mean it's still yours when you return. Always check the place over when you get back! But, at least for now, the coast is clear. Now line up and show me how it went tonight."

Rustles of weathered knapsacks mixed with a few clatters of scavenged goods the young explorers had managed to gather from their foray into the Witch City alleys. Food in the form of a few dead rats and scraps from one of the local diners was placed for all to see. They were a family of outcasts, all of them, and they shared what they had in equal measure. Sitter often adopted the abandoned youth of the city, becoming a father figure for them. They, in turn, became his arms and legs. In this mutualistic process, the kids not only learned how to survive, but they also learned some electrical knowledge, a certain amount of practical engineering, and a host of other skills they could never get on their own. They learned to care for each other, and they learned purpose in helping each other out. They learned Sitter was a wealth of knowledge, and in their comradery, they typically enjoyed a bit of oasis from the fundamentally dismal state of what had become Witch City.

Yet tonight, the newest of their small group moved slower, more numbly, than the rest. The others noticed, then they too slowed to a stop. A note of sadness suspended over the boys as though some invisible performer had stopped playing a familiar tune, leaving everyone to lean into the moment as though to elicit the next note.

"What's the matter?" Sitter asked. "What happened?"

"We also found this," the newest member of their small band said as he produced a tattered jacket and pair of makeshift shoes. "It was on a kid in Drogue's Alley. He was dead when we got there but by no more than only a minute or two. If we'd have gotten there sooner, maybe we could've helped him, y'know? Like you helped us."

Sitter shifted to face the oldest youth in the group. "One of ours, Nick?" he asked, his voice faltering in sadness and loss.

"Probably, judging by his stuff. I wasn't sure, at first." Nick looked upward into his own memory, considering the course of the night's events. Dubbed Saint Nick after some of his harrowing escapades on the streets under Sitter's tutelage, the oldest of the youths was all too familiar with life on the streets. "We couldn't have done much for him, though, I don't think. And there was a girl with him—a street girl. She was bent over him when we first spotted 'em."

"Robbing him, no doubt," Sitter concluded. It was not uncommon for street dwellers to prey upon each other, but he felt a definite paternal instinct for "his" kids, whether he already had them under his protective custody or not. Preying upon his kids was inviting trouble that in certain circles had begun to grow into the local underground's urban legend.

"We thought that at first," St. Nick opined, "but I don't think that was it. She was, I dunno, *caring* for him. It looked like she was trying to keep him dry, just spending time with him. Do you think maybe she's one of us?"

"Unusual!" Sitter exclaimed, his frown of contempt turning into a smile. He thought he was the last one who even considered the notion of kindness on the Witch City streets. "So, what's become of her? Is she here?" he excitedly asked, maneuvering his chair to see around the gaggle of boys.

"She bolted as soon as she spotted us. She looked like she was drugged up and scared, and the way she moved, she must've been hurt real bad."

"And you did nothing to help her?" Sitter challenged.

"We checked the kid first to see if he was okay, and then we had to find her again. Like I said, it looked like she was on the run. And she must have been..." he concluded, withdrawing into himself.

"What happened to her?" Sitter asked. He didn't think it was anything good. St. Nick was well aware of how harsh life could be, and it wasn't like him to get sullen like this. The next few seconds confirmed Sitter's unspoken apprehensions.

The normally brash St. Nick looked up, his rapid blinks betraying he was trying to hold back his emotions in front of the others. Sitter had known Nick a long while; he had only seen the youth cry a small handful of times the entire time.

"It was *Solace*," Nick confessed at last. "Mama Solace got her."

The black cold of bitter anger passed through Sitter. He spasmed, rocking his wheelchair for a moment as the cold passed up his almost useless spine to result in a glowering scowl across his face. In a barely controlled fury, he pressed Nick for one more piece of information.

"Nick, the trucks left for The Den about an hour ago. Was it before then or after?"

"This just happened about two hours ago. We pretty much came straight back."

"On the run—from them—and she still took time to help one of our kids? She must be still relatively new to the life; she's got some heart left." He internally deliberated for a moment, then declared, almost to himself, "She deserves better. We need to try to get her back."

"Sitter, the trucks left an hour ago," Nick complained. "Even if we had the firepower to stop them, they're way out of our range by now. We'll never catch them."

A nearly palpable aura of dark vengeance crossed the normally calm features of the young street gang's chairbound leader. "We're coming for you," he swore to no one but himself. "Maybe we can get you out of there. But even if we can't, I swear they'll pay for what they've done to you."

Then, pulling back on his joystick, he reversed and spun, maneuvering himself into another enclave that housed a small communications console. "Nick and T.J., fire up the generators. I have a call to make."

… …

Three trucks and their seven escort vehicles ribboned their way westbound on I-70, small shiny stars in the illumination of the night scope. If they wanted a place to hit the convoy while it was slowed down a little, this was the place. The terrain had been prairie-table flat up until the missiles that had been launched against the Air Force Academy and NORAD HQ had fallen short of their intended targets. Upon re-entry into the atmosphere, each missile launched several smaller warheads that pummeled the entire area. The multiple hits transformed the treacherously dull flatlands into treacherously winding pockets of craters and low man-made hillsides formed by the loose dirt strewn about by the blasts. Despite the devastation, most of the populace was grateful; at least none of the missiles actually went nuclear.

The night air was cold, which would help her spot if any of the crews dismounted from their vehicles. Of course, she thought, it would also help them to spot her. She pulled her jacket in around herself. It was just hardened leather surrounding some ballistic Kevlar plating, but within its folds, she found comfort against both the present cold and the coming heat. More than the physical protection against these elements, she felt the strength from the comradery of her sisters, knowing they would face whatever danger awaited them together. She adjusted herself a little smaller against the rocky surroundings of her position before high-band radioing to her fellow raiders concealed inside the eastward sides of many of the craters below.

"Mother Freya? Rogue Moon One here. They're on their way; they should be in range in about ten minutes."

"Rogue Moon One, this is Mother Freya. I heard you. Good eye. The lead truck will be all weapons to blast through anyone tryin' to resist them. The second and third will have their cargo. We don't care what happens to the first truck as long as it stops. We'll take care of the other two." Then Freya transmitted a new message:

"Ready up, sisters!"

Rogue Moon One removed her jacket, pretending to herself that she was using it as a blanket against the chill of the October night. In reality, she just wanted to take another long look at the large patch that had been laboriously stitched across the back leather that covered the Kevlar plating underneath. Looking back at her was a Norse Valkyrie, mouth framed as though blowing a saucy kiss with her left hand, her right arm raised. Besides the kiss, there were two deviations from the traditional concept of the angelic battle maidens: the raised arm held an AK-54 assault rifle in place of the traditional sword or spear, and the warrior woman in the patch wore a small dark brown beret, sharply cocked to one side. Moon briefly left her leather cocoon to recheck the wiring on the remote sniper rifle and camera. Satisfied, she again tucked in, pulled her jacket tighter around herself, and waited against the growing anticipation.

Her sisters were hidden in their vehicles, listening for the distinctive sound of Rogue Moon's rifle shot, trusting in the experience the gang's sniper had earned in the six years since they had originally recruited her. In all, 27 motorcycles, dune buggies, and cars were lying in wait, each fully crewed with a set of the fiercely dedicated all-female badland raiders known as Valhalla's Brownies. Rogue smiled as she considered the faith they put in her. She was the only one who could visually assess the situation. The gang's leader, Mother Freya herself, was half-buried under radar and IR reflective camouflaged tarps. When they rode into battle, Freya always led her sisters in person. As she sat in her own hillside perch, Rogue was palpably aware she had the trust of Mother Freya and her sisters but not their company. "A small sacrifice," she said, looking appreciatively at the large-barreled MX-79 sniper rifle. "Besides, dear Natalia, tonight I have you for my company."

Five minutes later, she popped an *X-Cite!*, adding to the already palpable tension in the air, rechecked the camera sighting on the remote rifle, and settled into her firing position.

"We will strike again soon, my Natalia," she crooned to the military-grade sniper rifle, gently stroking the main housing of the weapon. Valhalla's Brownies were about to ride.

… ……

"Yeah, Mojo, soon as we get to the Den and unload the herd, I'm gonna get somethin' ta drink, something ta eat, an' then something ta rest on! I swear, it ain't right we gotta transport all this cattle and don't get ta taste any of the meat!"

"I hear ya, Wild Bill," the lead truck's cabin gunner replied back to his driver through the helmet radios, *"but we gotta keep the meat for the buyers. Still, though, plenty o' leftovers where we're goin'! Maybe some of last haul's fillies are ready, and maybe by now, we could afford some of that!"*

"Whoo, there's an idea! I can see us at it now!"

"This is Sandstorm," a third voice cut in. *"You two keep your eyes peeled right now, or you won't make it to the Den! We're coming up on Brownie territory—keep it sharp!"*

"We hear ya, Sand," the first voice replied. *"Roger, Wilco, and, out!"*

And with that, Wild Bill cut to a different channel, the frequency passed on to Mojo by the phrase he used as he feigned acquiescence to Sandstorm.

…… ……

Mother Freya gave three chirps on Rogue Moon's comm link. Her sisters were ready. Switching to her camera, the Brownie sniper took aim between the lead truck's metal slats constructed over the bulletproof windshield and triggered the remote rifle. The tractor trailer's windshield would be heavily protected to avoid the obvious threats of most hostile fire; Moon was prepared.

The silenced remote rifle fired a round that passed between the metal slats overlaying the lead truck's windshield and popped like a large bug against the extra thickened bulletproof glass. The round wasn't designed to penetrate the hardened windshield, just to splatter its highly potent acidic contents against the reinforced glass. Rogue Moon would personally fire the real attack against the now weakened target with her beloved Natalia.

…… ……

"You there, Moooojo?" Wild Bill hailed.

"Yeah, I'm here. An' the name's Mojo, you drek for brains!"

"Well, you were born on a farm, and a name's a name, ain't it? Anyway, why, that was just plain danged rude of ol' Sandy to inter-rupt our conversation that way! I just hope one o' them Brownies does try to get the jump on us! She may not like it when I jump her back! While I'll bet...."

…… ……

Nine and a half seconds had lapsed since her first silenced shot. One half of one second later, Rogue Moon aimed Natalia and squeezed the trigger. Her pet rifle screamed its battle cry, spewing the tungsten-tipped explosive round into the weakened windshield. The effect of the tiny maelstrom of violence that Natalia punched into the truck cab's interior silenced Wild Bill before he had a chance to finish his bet.

……

With the driver neutralized and the gunner wounded, 23.2 tons of truck careened wildly out of control into one of its escort vehicles. The heavily armed tractor-trailer then jackknifed across the highway and tipped with the groan of bending metal, balefully screeching as the trailer's left-side weapon systems were eroded to jagged bits of scrap metal against the roadway while it slid, wailing in agonized metallic shrieks as it skidded to a halt. The top-mounted turret was effectively reduced to swiveling on a vertical arc, practically useless, as was the middle weapon pod located midway on the right side of the trailer. The right front and right rear weapons pods were still active, though the results of the unexpected attack left the gunners stunned and unable to effectively respond. The escort vehicles scattered in reaction to the threat, but the two remaining tractor-trailers were forced to slow down to weave around the wreckage of the first truck and the area's ever-present craters.

"*Now!*" Mother Freya yelled over her comm circuit. "*Hit 'em, Ladies!*"

In immediate response, ten armored dune buggies, four pickup trucks, and nine machine-gun-toting dirt bikes burst forth from their hiding places. Converging on the convoy from both sides, they fired wildly as they pursued the column ahead of them.

"*Railroad to Den: We're under attack! Repeat, we are under attack!*"

"*Copy Railroad. That's what we pay you for. What's your location?*"

"*Just passed Botha.*"

"*What's the problem? You got three trucks and a fleet of escorts. Dust 'em and keep rolling!*"

"Not that easy! Got a whole army of vehicles—our lead truck's already completely out of the fight. Drek!"

"What's the problem now, Railroad? Get a hangnail or something?"

"They're flying colors—It's the Brownies."

"Frak, Railroad!! Reinforcements are on their way, but they're an hour out. Get outta there, now! And above all, don't lose the cargo!"

"Oh, drek—there's more of 'em up ahead...."

A sudden silence fell over the airwaves—the radio went as dead as the drivers. The only sound the Den communications operator picked up was the sound of the muted crowd applause sound of the receiver's static. He clenched his mic in a white-knuckled grip as he canceled the call for reinforcements, then half threw it back onto his desk and grunted.

5. Conference Call

Jack's avatar electronically fidgeted as he sat in Simon's virtual office. Several months earlier, Simon had requested Jack to rejoin CYBER to lead a new team. Jack had said no at first, but then as he studied the backgrounds and profiles of the new recruits, he saw their need. Even after that, though, he still balked. He finally had a church who would accept him for who he was, and he didn't want to lose that sense of family, even though he found it at what looked to most people like the dead-end of a dead-end; the church was in the teeming Roanoke out-zone slum where the local law enforcement protection had come in the form a street gang known as the Razors. Pleading for God to affirm him staying at his church, he resigned himself to the denial God had provided. While not a complete surprise, he found that while no one wanted him to leave, they all had the same general impression. Deciding to put his faith in God over his own perceptions of stability, he had rejoined the Agency.

"Your team's vitals, for the most part, look strong," Simon began as he appeared into his office with a shimmer. The meeting had begun; Jack didn't need to check the time to know Simon started the statement at exactly 2:30.00.000 P.M.; Simon was always precisely on time.

"Corey and Susan are developing quite nicely in their new abilities, Melissana is proving to be quite adept in her grasp of virtual operations, and even Johnny is starting to integrate into the team."

"Which leaves Josanne?" Jack submitted.

"Which leaves Josanne," Simon affirmed. "Her progress report readings are quite low compared to the rest of the team."

"I'm working with her," Jack assured. "You built her profile; you knew her temperament full well before we recruited her. She wasn't all that happy about the augmentations, to begin with, but she joined. She's the team's conscience, and now she's working through the first time she's actually killed someone. To be honest, I'm glad she's struggling."

"And why is that?" Simon asked. Simon normally was quite adept at tracking the thought processes of the CYBER team members, but he sometimes struggled with logic nuances like this. She was on Jack's team, and Jack was telling Simon she was underperforming because she was going through emotional pain and discomfort. He knew Jack cared about his team members. Jack's declaration that he was glad Josanne was struggling did not conform to what he knew about Jack and, for that matter, any of the other humans Simon had ever interfaced with.

"It means I can trust her," Jack proclaimed, his voice patterns reflecting a tone that somehow, to Jack, the matter made perfect sense.

Simon was developed to know what to do, to quickly gather vast amounts of data, analyze the impacts and repercussions of the billions of seemingly unrelated factoids, patterns, and trends, and extrapolate the multitudinous volumes of potential outcomes. Given any vast array of options available, he had been created to prioritize the outcomes and render the most advantageous course of action. Simon had been there when the signs of the fragmentation of state and national governments began to appear. He saw it in the patterns of the rhetoric of the media and of the chants of protesters in the streets. He saw it in the profit-taking of corporate executives, in the government confiscation of businesses, in the gun control laws, culture control laws, and politically correct mind control laws.

The processes and subroutines Simon initiated had returned. While the individual reports were not entirely unanimous, the aggregate result of the collective analysis was overwhelmingly, "Trust Jack." What Simon could not determine was exactly why he should do so. He decided he would need to revisit this later for further analysis…

"I just forwarded you some emails," Simon announced after some internal deliberation. "To be precise, you are getting eleven of them. I've held them for you because I did not think you were ready to see them before. Now you are."

Jack stiffened in his virtual chair, startled at the apparent suddenness of the revelation.

"Oh? Why mention them here?"

"They are of consequence to us both."

Jack's avatar shifted to a series of pale blues as Jack's sigh permeated into the virtual office. "Outside", he knew and even understood the inevitability of Simon monitoring all CYBER team members' electronic communications of any form; in here, though, Simon was almost too human, and Jack felt his privacy invaded. It was an emotional response—a reflex—and a moment later, Jack's focus returned. "Both of us?" Jack replied, suddenly more curious than offended.

"I considered it best to forewarn you before passing them on."

"And why is that?" Jack challenged. Despite being back in the Agency, he was still far from trusting Simon's intentions. In fact, Jack wasn't convinced Simon could even have intentions. Simon always felt highly proactive. Deep inside, though, Jack couldn't completely suspend his disbelief that Simon was just responding to a near-infinite series of IF-THEN and CASE protocols at phenomenal speed.

"They're from a former associate of yours," Simon responded, and with that proclamation, a five-foot nine-inch mildly overweight middle-aged bald man wearing an inexpensive business suit appeared in the office. Jack started, recognizing the digital image in a cyberspace instant. As "Greyscale," the former decker and leader of Grey's Hounds, Jack had been on countless CYBER runs. He had faced death, both his own and of his teammates, in the wires before—more times than he cared to know—but he had never felt as awkwardly out of place in the net as he did at that moment.

"Ryan Elverson," Jack grimly murmured. "Last I saw him, he was telling me to get lost. What's he want with me?"

"He's been trying to contact you for some time. I've been intercepting him until you had gotten re-acclimated to give you the time you've needed to integrate into your new team."

"How long?" asked Jack.

"I noticed him searching for you while you were in Roanoke. I confounded his efforts, of course, as I concluded by the way you left us that you did not want to be bothered by your past. I have monitored your communications for disruptions to your wishes as a courtesy. It was, in fact, the least I felt I could do. At first, I did not know why he was making efforts to contact you. Over time, however, it became clear he'd had second thoughts about your time with us in the past. In short, he'd discovered he had need of your services just when you were no longer in a position to provide them."

"So, what's changed? Why bring it up now?"

"I think you are ready now—at least you are ready enough to be made aware of his efforts. Your team's performance was more than satisfactory, albeit the overall rating is somewhat marred by Josanne's extended duress over the use of her skills. Of course, this remains a concern of mine, even if that concern is not shared by you. The general success of your first mission, however, is irrefutable. You also have succeeded in getting your team to bond despite your insisting on telling them about me and showing them—in detail—the risks they've faced in joining us. Your group of recruits is now a team, and their first mission a success. But is that success repeatable? Humanity excels at doing something once, but is your team truly ready to pursue CYBER activities independently? Of course, it is up to you if you agree, but I believe your team is ready for another mission, and I believe this to be that mission."

"You said this affects you, too," Jack probed. "How so?"

"I said they are of consequence to us both," Simon corrected. "Please review the messages, along with the data I have gathered concerning them. You will know the answer to your question when you have completed that task."

Jack took a cursory glance at the top FACT sheet. The entire office turned the shade of faded blue jeans as he caught one name, then a charcoal grey as he continued reading for another two seconds. Finally, he looked up, doing his best to analyze what he knew was beyond his scrutiny.

"Simon, are you absolutely sure about this?"

Simon was checking his watch, a gesture intended to indicate to Jack that the meeting was coming to a close; Simon always knew exactly what time it was anywhere on Earth. He stopped, looked at Jack straight in the virtual eyes, and with unmistakable genuineness offered one irrefutable syllable in reply: "Yes."

Jack almost thought he sensed regret in that syllable, but of course, he dismissed the idea.

Simon smiled. "Thank you again for returning to CYBER, Jack. I missed our meetings."

With that, Simon's office blanked into a computer-grey cube, and Jack unplugged from his cyberdeck.

"A.I.'s," he grumbled to himself. Then he saw the emails and folders of data SIMON (Synchronized Independent Interface Monitoring and Observation Neuronet) had printed for him while they were in conference. Even though he could scan the data through the network quicker, sometimes Jack preferred the absorption process of studying physical paper; SIMON had somehow recognized and stored that personality factoid into Jack's profile. He sighed to himself, picked up the first of the emails, and began to read.

… …

16:45 blinked red in the upper outer edge of his peripheral vision, the implanted alarm clock informing Jack he was due for the team meeting of Preach's Pride. He fully agreed that Simon was correct about his team being ready for another mission, but he was far less in agreement that this mission was the best place to continue. Further, he absolutely despised what he surmised was Simon's reasoning that caused him to suggest it. Even more, he could not forget that Elverson had been the main driver in getting Jack ousted from his first pastorate after leaving CYBER. As he read the file, though, Jack saw the direness in Elverson's situation that drove him to seek his help. Poetic justice had been served to his former church board director in spades. Whether either of them liked it or not, Jack was probably the best chance Elverson had and quite likely the only one.

He closed his eyes and sighed. CYBER had a government mandate to help where no one else could, and Jack had a mandate from his ultimate authority to forgive his enemies. And at the center of it all was someone who was innocent of all the history between Jack and Elverson, a member of his former youth ministry who now desperately needed him. He set his jaw. If the team accepted the run, it would be a dirty one. His eye internally blinked the time again; he closed his dossiers and headed to the conference room.

6. Team Meeting

The rich sepia of the mahogany combined with the glossy obsidian finish of the conference room table had always impressed Melissana, but then most things about CYBER still did. She had no idea how many nights she had lain awake thinking about the improbability of her situation. Thrown out by her abusive father, she had somehow learned to survive on the streets as a seventh-grade child—the fact that she had survived at all was a miracle in itself. The computer skills she had learned and the way she had learned them? At the time, she had been trying just to get by from one day to the next. That her path through those days eventually led her to be recruited into CYBER was almost too much for her to track. Had anyone else told her this would happen to her while she was a low-town Roanoke P.I., she never would have believed them. Looking around the lavish room, she still could hardly believe it was all real herself—yet here she was.

And then there was Iylo, the Neon Bard, or *"Iylothien, Barde de la Nêone,"* as he had originally introduced himself to her, complete with flourished bow. Her mind drifted back to their first meeting in his virtual reality environment …

"Hello there!" she heard from a cheerful male voice that came from above and behind her. Startled, she turned the voice. She spotted a young man, slim but with the athletic build of a trapeze artist, wearing a green tunic and leggings. He had yellow-blonde hair of medium length that would have hung straight down, except—he was hanging upside down by his knees from an oak branch some 25 feet above the

ground. He wore a wide grin on his face so big and projected a boyish innocence so infectious she was almost immediately disarmed. On all accounts, he sounded and appeared friendly, but she wasn't quite buying it just yet.

"Who in the world are you?" she smiled in spite of herself.

"Please, allow me to introduce myself," he responded.

To her surprise, he suddenly let go of his perch with his legs and dropped out of the tree, doing an aerial somersault on the way down. He landed lightly and surely on his feet. It was then that she noticed he carried—a bow? Extending a hand and bowing with dramatic flair, he proclaimed, "I am Iylothien, Barde de le Neone, and Master of this Realm. And for my part, I have the finest pleasure of speaking with the Brave and Clever, the Absolutely Charming, Melissana.

"And please allow me to say, now that I have finally met you, you are Completely Beautiful…"

She smiled at the memory, her cheeks reddening ever so slightly; it still made her blush.

Online, the two had quickly shared an attraction for each other. By the time she had met him in person, she had already fallen for him enough to overcome the difficulties of their physical situation; they could meet online in their hacker environmental modules and spend virtual months with each other doing nothing but walking in digital parks together if they chose. Their bond was tight, their training frequent—he the virtual ranger/bard, she the mystic electron sorceress—the two of them together, a formidable pair of elite hackers that, given enough time to prepare, could crack even international corporate conglomerate megacorp ICE. Her smile broadened a little, then fell. For all of their virtual prowess, Iylothien was still stuck in his physical prison; freeing him to actually do any of even the simplest of those things together was impossible.

As if on cue, Corey and Susan walked into the room holding hands, leaning into each other in their closeness and smiling at each other. Melissana looked at her own hand and almost reflexively squeezed, just a little, wanting to feel Iylothien's hand in her own but feeling nothing in the motion except a longing accompanied by a slight pang of jealousy. She resolutely pushed the emotion aside as she waved hello to the couple—it wasn't their fault they were normal.

Next came Johnny, sauntering into the room in his typically aloof style. He didn't do chems, but what he craved was the edge that cut both his skills and his luck to the quick. Reality itself was his ultimate audience, held spellbound by the death-defying dance displays of his particular skills. CYBER training was good, but it wasn't *real*. Johnny wasn't wired to settle down, and she saw in his demeanor he was getting bored. He openly yawned when he sat down, reminding her of when Susan had shared her initial impression that Johnny had been recruited into CYBER to impersonate cats. Melissana had grown up on the streets and seen his type before; she saw far more truth in that offhand quip than Susan dared to guess. But Johnny wasn't some guy impersonating a cat; he was far more like a back-alley tom impersonating a human: hunter instinct, slinking stealth, nine lives, and all.

Still, Simon had seen something more in the highly talented youth of the street, as he—*it*, she corrected herself—had somehow done with each of them. Johnny was more than just a back-alley scrapper tom, Corey and Sue were *definitely* more than "normal," and even she herself—the survivor, the street-raised private investigator, and hacker persona Queen Vixenn—was more than the small-time slewfoot she had been before. Simon had seen something special in each of them and somehow used Jack to pull it all out of them— even Josanne, she mused. In the pinch, her best friend was the only one who could have gotten Mahlon to talk.

In the end, Josanne had come through for them all, though the mission had cost her deeply. Of all of them, Josanne had been the most reluctant to join the elite cybernetic agency; it pained Melissana that she didn't seem to have the words to help her friend work through the consequences of that decision—the necessary body alterations, the violence, and the end result: Josanne, the most innocent of them, was forced to kill a man on the team's first mission. Ever since, Josanne's conscience was tearing her apart inside. Her act had saved Melissana's life, but the detective just couldn't find any words appreciative enough to help her friend get past the guilt of killing. So now Josanne's healing was up to Jack, too.

Next to enter the room were Spider, Chrome, and Rickshaw from Grey's Hounds, the mentors of the newer team. Melissana sat up a little straighter, suddenly more alert. It was unusual for them to be present for their internal team meetings—and if the three of them were here, then… Melissana glanced up to the wall-sized display screen in acute anticipation, rewarded by seeing the upper left corner of the screen frame an image of an electronic forest, a light but athletic youth clad in forest green riding a giant locust towards them from some far-away location. Nearing the virtual camera projecting the scene, he lit from the beast with an aerial somersault, landing perfectly in center screen, long golden hair falling exactly into place despite the aerial tumbling maneuver; Iylothien had arrived.

"Good evening, Team!!" he cheerily hailed. Then, turning to face Melissana's seat, he flamboyantly bowed as he continued, "And hail to you, Queen Vixenn!" She would have been embarrassed, but she recognized his location as the tutorial level of Randolph & Emerson's "Ultimate Fantasy," the environment simulation where they had first met. In response, she simply smiled and returned the greeting with a wave. By the time everyone had finished their mutual greetings, Josanne and Jack had both entered the room. Jack closed the door, and with it, the polite conversations.

"Vacation's over," he announced. "Simon has a run for us if we take it."

"About time," Johnny pronounced, leaning forward in sudden interest. "What megacorp do we bring down this time?"

"This isn't that kind of operation," Jack replied. "It's a search and rescue."

"Well, Preach, that leaves me out. S and R isn't exactly my skillset, if you don't mind me saying so. In fact, I don't know that it's any of ours."

"It's an *urban* search and rescue, Johnny," Jack clarified. "I have no doubt in my mind that all of our skillsets will come into play before this is done." He set his jaw firmly and braced himself against his confession. "And it's personal."

7. Kelly

Thunderous applause roared past the stadium and echoed into the streets beyond. Entrust Arena was holding a Battle Hockey event. It was a close match, and Air-Dienamix, the home team, had been only marginally ahead. The home team's Attack Forward had just intercepted the puck and broke through the opponent's lines to score, extending the margin of victory and also managing to break the leg of the opponent's star defensive back in the process.

"What you getting excited about, ho?" Sweet Trick asked her just as she started allowing herself to get caught into cheering for the home team. "You're here to work, so get to it—I expect at least two grand out of you tonight. You'd better get on it, or I'm adding your wasted time to your tab. And oh—one more thing—what's your name, ho?"

"Kel—Shimmer," she whispered as though in confession. "They call me Shimmer, 'cause I'll make your night magical," she half-whispered in as sultry a manner as she could, hoping he wouldn't hit her for reflexively almost using her real name.

"Girl, if this wasn't a big night, I'd smash your face in!" he roared, barely checking his backhand smack. "I don't ever want to hear you using that stupid-frak old name you think is you. As it is, I'm just gonna have to fine you your first night's trick so you can get it right. Now get me my money, govek!" he yelled as he forcibly shoved her out of the car and into the crowd of onlookers.

"With any luck, the Dienamix will win," she thought to herself. Either way, the fans would be extra rough on them. They always were, after the sporting events. They were pumped up on the violence as well as the adrenaline surges that came when the wage slaves caught the vicarious thrill of victory as if it had been them who had somehow triumphed just by watching the game. They often went delirious in the mayhem they had exposed themselves to. If the home team won, though, at least the johns wouldn't be angry as well, taking out the anger of the shared loss and reminder of their true insignificance on the girls they'd be renting tonight by the half-hour.

Another roar of the crowd indicated something was going well for the Entrust team. "Well," she thought, remembering there were always out-of-towners at these events, "at least most of them won't be angry." She inwardly shuddered as she smiled at a group of older guys who were starting to look her over. Tonight, she would be 'Shimmer,' which in a way would be a good thing—the trauma would have driven Kelly insane. She slipped into Shimmer's mindset, casually approaching the men who were old enough to be her father and who should have known better. Their leers told her they didn't...

8. The Mission

Prior to training with Foxfire, Josanne automatically would have rolled her eyes at the statement. She checked the motion, letting Jack continue uninterrupted.

"Iylothien, Simon downloaded a set of satellite images with some radio transmissions. Synch 'em up and play them out for us, okay?"

"Sure thing," Iylothien replied. Within a few seconds, the rest of the team caught images of wrecked vehicles, three tractor-trailer trucks jackknifed, one on its side, bodies and burning across the entire scene. Susan coughed as though she could smell the heavy, oily smoke as it wafted across the camera view; the scene was similar enough to what happened to her hometown that she relived the smells through her memories. Corey's brows furrowed, his jaw and chin locked in grim determination. Melissana stood and leaned in towards the screen. Rickshaw rubbed his thigh. Chrome was impassively quiet; Araña let out a low whistle. After some time, their senses registered the broken transmissions coming in…

"Drek! They's on us!"

"Scorpio! Scorpio! Come in! Can you hear me?"

"Bridgette, Hilia, Frida! Stop that frakkin' second truck," a female voice yelled over her comm circuit.

"Charger here," a male voice hailed. *"I gotta pull over. Got some sorta pink goo all over my windshield, and my escorts are taken out. All gunners engaged."*

"Ha! Got one! Hit…" <sound of the nearby blast, then static>

"Charger, this is Sandstorm. Do NOT stop. Your cargo's got to get through. Clean your windshield, or whatever. Wild Bill's already dead, but if you stop here, I swear I'll shoot you myself!"

"But I can't… oh, drek!" <sound of rubber skidding on gravel, metal groaning, a blast, more screeching, sounds of two girls cheering> *"Sandstorm, I'm ditched. We're…"* <sounds of close gunfire, followed by more static as the radio cuts out>

"Den, this is Sandstorm. Where's that backup? Where's that…" <radio goes dead one last time>

After fast-forwarding through a time-lapse covering ten minutes, what sounds like Sandstorm's radio transmitted again, but with a female voice coming over the system.

"This is Mother Freya with Valhalla's Brownies…" <much victory-cheering along with occasional gunshots heard in the background > *"I got your precious cargo. You want it back. I dare you to try any time. You got our number. We ride the 70. Eastbound, Westbound, makes no difference to us. You can have your drivers back, but they don't work the same now that they're dead. And one day, we'll come for you and turn your own cargo against you, I promise. Valhalla's Brownies got the kiss of death for you goveks."*

And with that, the transmissions ended.

"What you have just seen," Preach began, "was an all-out assault on a three-truck convoy and their small fleet of escort vehicles. The trucks were armed for bear, and from the look and sound of things, the escorts were heavily armed and experienced. They were chewed through to a man in just thirteen minutes. Simon picked up on the mayday call for help to someplace called The Den and turned a satellite to get the rest."

"So, somebody's hitting truck convoys." Corey grimaced. "Looks like a big bike gang, but not as big as the Jackals. We've done this before."

"What do we know about these 'Valhalla's Brownies'?" Melissana asked, her mind in gear. Her upturned eyebrows and hand poised mid-air indicated something wasn't adding up to her.

Josanne caught the gesture without a thought, kicking in her own conversationalist training. Jack wasn't Jack right now; he was in "Preach" mode. He was fully engaged with his team, but there was more. Iylothien cut in on her thoughts.

"They're an all-female biker gang operating in the Midwest. Not the horde Corey and Sue faced down, but respectably powerful. Err—umm, it seems they prefer each other."

"Not a gang I've ever met who liked outsiders, Iylo," Josanne stated rather dryly.

"That's not what he meant," Melissana replied.

"Oh…" Josanne stated. She felt herself blush.

"But what was that they said about using the cargo against them?" Rickshaw pondered. "This wasn't a random hit for loot."

"No, there's more," Josanne concluded. "Jack's holding out. He hasn't told us everything yet. So, what's the rest of the story?" she asked, almost as a dare.

"You're right again, Josanne," Jack replied. He ignored the challenge for the moment, but he would need to address her developing attitude soon. Instead, he hit a button that showed a new video. This one was crisp, clear footage of an overhead camera zoomed in on the aftermath of the scene they had just watched, the sound captured by a hyper-parabolic microphone that had managed to pick up the slightly muffled conversation. Valhalla's Brownies were claiming their loot. A stocky, tough-looking brunette in full biker gear, surrounded by her other leaders, approached the back of one of the tractor-trailers. They trained all their weapons on the doors as they carefully inspected for traps, then they readied themselves to blast any resistance inside and quickly heaved open the armored trailer doors.

The CYBER teams expected to hear howls of glee at some newfound weaponry, some whoops at grabbing some new tech, or some wild cheers at the bounty that could be sold for lucrative profit. Instead, Mother Freya openly howled in anguish and wept, handing the heavy bolt cutters she used to the two Brownies closest to her. The two entered the trailer and emerged several seconds later, helping a procession of half-starved young girls, what clothing they had torn and ragged, out of the truck. As the young women stepped out, shielding their eyes against the brightness of the open sky, Mother Freya herself carefully hugged each one, the other Brownies very tenderly providing the girls with food and care.

"What in the name of...." Susan began, too overcome by the scene to continue.

"Holy—" Melissana exclaimed. "It was a convoy of slavers—sex traffickers, by the looks of those girls."

"So, this time, the biker raiders are the good guys?" Corey asked in surprise.

"You wouldn't want them to hear you say that," Jack replied. "You're only half right, and they'd take definite issue with the analogy."

"That was one heavily-armed convoy they took down. It's gotta belong to a major operation," Johnny added.

The video resumed. Another one of the Brownies approached the group, carrying what appeared to be an old paper book. "Bring up the sound," Jack commanded.

"Mother, I found a list of names and brief descriptions. Might be their cargo invoice. They were headin' for the Den; after that, they'd be split up and shipped off to Utah, the Wash, Cali—all over. O'course, some of them they'd keep at the Den. Hey—looks like they're one person short!"

Mother Freya looked over the list, eyes darting from the book to the girls who were now in a straggled line, wolfing down some of the rations the Brownies had looted from the trucks.

"Frakkin' goveks—they haven't fed them anything in a week," she complained with a scowl. A tall, long-haired brunette with a long-barreled rifle left the feeding line and approached the leader.

"Woah, look at that," Chrome exclaimed. The others turned in surprise to look at him. Not even Araña had ever heard him comment on a girl like that before. "An MX-79—that's hers? If she can use that thing the way it's supposed to be used, and if the rest of them are like her, they'd be enough to mess up anyone's day."

The group collectively shrugged, returning their attention to the video. Johnny stifled a chuckle. The video resumed.

"One of the girls says there was someone else who was supposed to be with them, but she somehow escaped them in Witch City. She was pleading with us to find her before their masters did."

Freya swore. *"The one who escaped—did you get her name?"*

"The girl I was talking with lapsed into unconsciousness, but she mentioned it before she passed out. The pimps give them all hooker names to make the girls harder to trace. Most of the girls comply, but the missing girl had such a hard time letting go that the dreks repeatedly beat her senseless in front of the others to make an example out of her."

"What was it?" Freya asked, looking at the roster of names in her hands.

The female sniper paused, but even across the expanse of all that distance, the entire CYBER group could feel the hatred and disgust palpitating from her.

"The one I talked with had been too drugged up at the time to remember the escapee's street name, but her real name was Kelly something."

The one called Freya sighed heavily, the sound picked up by the satellite microphone and transmitted to the team of observing CYBER agents.

"Well, that's just dandy!" she complained to herself. *"All right, Rogue, thanks. Do me a favor, will you, Hon? Have Brigga radio Sitter back. Tell him we intercepted their convoy. The rest of the girls are banged up but relatively safe."* She sighed again before continuing. *"Tell him, though, that his bird wasn't in the cage—she never got out of Witch City."*

"I wouldn't want to be Sitter right now," the tall brunette said.

Freya smiled for the first time. *"No, Moon, honey, you wouldn't want to be anyone on one of his lists right now."* Her mood forcibly brightened.

"C'Mon, my raiders, my Valkyrie! We have much to celebrate today! We have freed our sisters from the bondage of Men. Tonight, we celebrate!"

And with that, the satellite video zoomed out back into the stratosphere. Before the microphone withdrew, however, it picked up howls of glee at some newfound weaponry, some whoops at grabbing some new tech, and some wild cheers at the joy of keeping the pimps' bounty from being sold for lucrative profit.

"Oh man," Melissana said while punching one fist into another. "I wish I could've been in on that raid!"

"You may get your chance, Melissana," Jack said. "The target of our search and rescue was taken by the people running that convoy."

"Who is she?" This time it was Susan who asked. Jack breathed a quiet sigh of relief it wasn't Josanne before responding.

"Her name is Kelly—Kelly Elverson," Jack stammered, eyes softening.

"You—know her," Josanne surmised. "How?" she asked, simply, softly. Jack had been a pastor for several years. He recognized this was not her conversationalist training kicking this time; it was true compassion. He was more relieved because of it.

"When I left CYBER and became a pastor, the Elverson's attended the first church I served at. In fact, Ryan Elverson was the head of the church board. Kelly is his daughter—she was in our youth group when she was eight. She was one of the sweetest kids in the group.

"Anyway, one evening, I ended up sharing about where I really came from with some of the church leaders. I didn't go into our missions or capabilities. I just felt like I wanted them to know more about my background."

"Only that didn't work out too well," Chrome inserted with contempt at those who wronged his former mentor.

"No, it didn't," Jack affirmed.

"What'd they do?" asked Josanne.

"Elverson called for an immediate board meeting," Jack replied, visibly hardening as he continued. "They told me that even though I had done a good job in their church, they couldn't have someone who sold out on God, accusing that my willingly altering my body to do what I did amounted to blasphemy and that they couldn't have me in their church—especially in a leadership position, let alone as their pastor. Not everyone felt that way, of course, but to avoid a big split over it, I voluntarily left.

"Anyway, Simon just informed me before our meeting today that Elverson's been trying to reach me since his daughter went missing some two years ago. There was some evidence she'd been abducted, and he didn't know who else to turn to. Simon added 'Kelly' and 'Elverson' into his monitor search patterns."

"Wait," Susan interrupted, "you said she was abducted two years ago? And that she was only eight when you were at their church?" She did some quick counting on her fingers. "That would mean she was abducted when she was only about twelve—and put her current age at around 15!"

"The slavers like younger girls because, grossly enough, most of their customers eventually end up liking them that way," Melissana answered her. "Sick jerks keep driving down the ages all the time."

"But that's just *horrible*! Who could do something like that?" Susan returned.

"Well, it's not just your bikers and outlaws," Johnny chimed in. "Plenty of twisted screws work a cube. Just Johnny Wage-slaves all day long, likin' a little action on the side. Helps them to feel tough since all they have to live on is sippin' on the straw of their boss's drek an' callin' it chocolate all day."

"A few weeks ago," Jack cut in, resuming the briefing, "Simon picked up on some transmissions making a connection between a 'Kelly' and a reference to a den somewhere. Quite by accident, he picked up the emergency broadcast from the convoy requesting backup from someplace called 'The Den.' The large-scale raid against a well-armed convoy drew his interest, so he monitored the battle. Once Simon discovered what the 'cargo' really was, he cross-referenced the new additional transmission and email references and somehow concluded Kelly would be in the convoy.

"Is this what we do, Jack?" Johnny asked. "I mean, don't get me wrong, I want to help as much as the next guy, but first there was Angie, and now Kelly? Is this our gig, rescuing damsels in distress that are somehow connected to you?"

"You gotta admit, Jack, the kid's got a point," Rickshaw added, causing Corey's eyebrows to rise. "There's gotta be hundreds of operations like this going on. You and Iylo know Simon better than any of us. Why this one?"

Jack's shoulders slumped as he let out a breath he hadn't been aware he was holding.

"It's Kelly, on one end. Simon is aware of my personal connection and wants to ensure she won't be used to gain leverage to compromise me."

"So your connection to Kelly's on one end," Chrome mentioned. "What's on the other end?"

"On the other end, Simon has been monitoring a certain party that gained his interest when we were recruiting the Pride. Over the course of several intercepted calls, emails, and financial holdings analyses, evidence indicates said party is running large-scale smuggling and trafficking operations—international if you include Utah and certain megacorporations from Central America up through Canada.

"Simon cross-referenced the satellite images with projections of what Kelly would look like, but she wasn't any of the girls rescued here. So, if we all accept the run, we're going to find out where that convoy originated from, go get her and anyone else with her. In the process, we're going to shut down their organization." As he looked around the room at each of them, he added, "With prejudice."

"Wait a minute. You said whoever's running this show gained Simon's interest when you were recruiting us?" Corey exclaimed.

"Who's this interested party? None of us knows anyone with that kind of reach that could be that devious."

"Actually, Corey, one of you does. And quite frankly, that's the other end of the test," Jack replied, resolved to tell all he knew. If the team rejected the run, Kelly was doomed, but he would not compromise his standard of openness to the team. They had to know. *She* had to know, even if it broke her. She was still struggling from the last mission; this might shatter her completely. And what really frustrated Jack the most was that Simon, of course, knew that. He turned and squarely faced Josanne. "His name is James Sinclair."

9. Ruminations and Decisions

ALCOHOLS OF VARIOUS distillations combined with the smoke of cigar and cigarette, providing the air at the Facility Lounge the peculiar aroma reminiscent of a hospital on fire. At this time of night, the CYBER lounge was a combination of dim lights and brilliant minds, sharp music and the numbing drowse of tight comraderies forged by sharing tough times. Jack didn't come here often, but he knew this was the best place to bring his closest friends for the conversations they wouldn't have anywhere else. As he had predicted to himself before he had walked through the doors, the afternoon's meeting ended badly. "In the multitude of counselors is safety," he quoted to himself with an inward sigh; tonight, he needed the input from the people he trusted the most.

"So, what do you guys think?" he asked.

"I don't get it, *Jefé*," Araña volunteered. "I mean, first you tell them everything about Simon and Iylo before they join up, and now you tell Trigget—who's barely hanging on, I might add—that the op Simon put together is specifically targeting her brother? I don't get it. Are you trying to get them to quit?"

"Chrome," asked Jack, "if Spider held back that kind of info from you, how long would you follow him?"

"Guess I never thought much about it," the Hound heavy hitter reflected. "Probably long enough to make sure he stayed down," he concluded with a mirthless smile. Then turning to his new team leader, he added, "You wouldn't hold out on us with anything like that, would you, Bro?"

"That's different," Rickshaw interjected. "We're seasoned, but that little girl's gonna crack if she doesn't start getting over what happened. And maybe that's Simon's point."

"That's the way I'm seeing it," Jack rejoined. "Simon's testing me to see how I'll handle Kelly at the same time he's testing Josanne's resolve."

"At the same time, *it's* testing her resolve, Grey," Chrome corrected. "And that's cold—machine cold."

"Yeah," Rickshaw added. "Machine efficient, too."

"So, Spider, you wouldn't hold out on us like that, would you?" Chrome repeated.

"No, I wouldn't," Spider admitted. "I'd feel like I'd be lying to my own team."

"And the Pride is Greyscale's team," Chrome affirmed. "Let him handle them. By all accounts, he's doing at least as well with them as he did with us when we first started. You got my vote, Grey. They're your team. You lead 'em." Chrome made a show of finishing his beer, slamming the glass back down like it was a judge's gavel. "Well, ladies, I gotta take a nap," he offered in parting. "Assuming your people decide to take this job, we'll have to start prepping up tomorrow.

"By the way, if this one does work out, it probably means you guys can cut out on your own; you won't need us anymore." And with that, Chrome got up from their table and wandered off, apparently trying not to break anything as he shuffled out of the Lounge, his friends watching with both some bemusement and concern.

"Man, how much has he had?" Rickshaw asked. "I didn't think he could even get buzzed."

"He can't," Araña responded. "He doesn't like the way the conversation turned, so he's faking it, at least in part. He doesn't like what Simon's pulling, either."

Jack didn't challenge that assessment, but inside he wasn't so sure. Of all his former teammates, Chrome's comments about machine cold seemed out of place. Maybe Chrome didn't like what

Simon was doing, but maybe there was a part of the armored cyborg that somehow empathized with Simon's lack of empathy. In the end, though, Chrome's human side seemed to approve of Jack's sensitivity to his team. In this situation, Chrome's approval seemed to count the most out of all of them. He decided to shift the subject.

"Either of you guys ever hear of this Den before?"

"I don't remember ever hearing about anything like that," Rickshaw responded, "though I've only been through the Midwest a few times. Mostly to the South."

"Me neither," Araña added.

"Well, I guess if the run is on, tomorrow we'll start to find out."

The remaining Hounds settled their bills, made their farewells, and left. If the team agreed to the job, tomorrow would be a long day for all of them. Jack left for the privacy of his own room. At times like these, he really missed Rita Williams, but he still had one more person to check with. Having received the perspectives of the others, he would invest the next hour or so ruminating over all of them in the presence of his closest friend.

… …

"Half cred for your thoughts," Susan offered hopefully in mid-brush.

Corey had been silent for the rest of the day, brooding over the aftermath of the team meeting. By evening, Susan was confused, almost desperate to help him open up and talk with her about what was bothering him. She hadn't seen him like this since their first meeting in that same conference room during their initial recruitment.

"Hey, what's going on in that fuel-injected mind of yours?" She put down her hair brush to flash him a smile, then lightly prodded him further. "You know, you'd better let me in," she quipped. "When you're not in your car, I can take you now. And I can give quite a tickle now, you know."

Corey visibly relaxed and looked up at her, seeing both her beauty and her concern. Caught up in her presence, he smiled. "Yeah, I bet you can," he replied.

"So, what's going on, Corey?" she said as she took a seat beside him on the bed.

"That's just it, Sue. I don't know. We're drugged and kidnapped into this CYBER thing, we go through the surgeries, and we do a mission. We're all good. Then this comes along, and I almost feel back to square one."

"What do you mean?"

"Half-information, the ways our missions are chosen, working for an A.I.? You can't tell me you don't think this sometimes doesn't feel weird—like we're somehow part of a bigger game than we were led on to believe...."

"I have to admit I don't always understand the bigger picture." She hesitated, then continued. "Sometimes it seems too good to be true, sometimes it seems too weird to be true, and sometimes it just seems too big to be true."

"And maybe it is," Corey cut in. "There just always seems to be something they're hesitant in letting us know, some game Simon is playing to keep us just on the edge of either quitting or giving up."

"But I think they're trying to do the right thing. Besides, if it wouldn't have been for their help, we wouldn't have survived Iron Mike. And Jack seems like he's really watching out for us. He's going out of his way to tell us everything. You don't have to be a conversationalist to see he was disclosing things that some of the others weren't comfortable discussing. I think we can trust him, at least."

"Yeah, maybe you're right," Corey admitted. "I guess part of it all is that it's kind of hard to believe that an organization like this would consider people like us."

"Oh, I don't know, Corey," she said, leaning in to give him a caress. "When I think of who you are and who you have been to me," she continued, searching out his eyes, "it makes perfect sense that they would choose you."

In her mind's eye, Susan suddenly caught flashes of the raid on her hometown, Iron Mike capturing her, his leering at her, her gagging reflex being triggered at the memory of his odor. Her mind flashed again, seeing the girls being led off that truck, mostly starved and completely terrified after being subjected to the terrors Corey had spared her from. She recoiled away from Corey, breaking the mood of their intimacy.

"Susan—what's wrong?"

"I want to say, 'nothing,' Corey, I really do," she said between gasps, trying her best to catch her breath. "But I can't. I just remembered seeing those young girls stumbling out of that trailer. They were saved from a living hell by that Valhalla bike gang, but if Simon's right, there are so many more." She took his hands in hers. Corey knew her well enough to know some tears might soon follow.

"Corey, you saved me from Iron Mike, and I can never thank you enough for that." She looked at him, imploring him with an intensity of commitment he knew must be consuming her …

"We have *got* to do whatever we can to save those girls."

He looked at her in rapt awe. He had once saved her from a bike gang that had destroyed both of their hometowns. Since then, he had seen her passion for saving others rise up again and again, despite the risks to herself along the way. He gently towed her into himself, embracing her, allowing her to feel the complete unabashed sincerity of his commitment to her.

"We will, Honey. Yeah, what Rickshaw said was true—there are definitely a lot of other operations like this one out there. But looking at it, I guess what it all comes down to in the end is that you and I now know about this one. Besides, you're right about Jack, even if he doesn't seem to be the kind of guy to fit into an operation like this. It's messed up with Trigget, but it's what we signed up for. And if going after this operation is something you really want to pursue, we'll do whatever it takes. I promise."

… …

"Wire-girl's not online with Iylo? What's the matter?"

"Oh, nothing, Johnny. We were just talking, and now I just need to think a while," Melissana responded between reaching for a Soy-da and closing the refrigerator door. "How about you? What are you up to?"

"Oh, every once in a while, I just come down here to reflect, myself," He silently smiled at the memory of his first night's talk with Blaze. "I guess you can say that this was the first place I started thinking this really could feel like a home." Snapping out of his memory, he came back to the present and thought of how different this conversation was. "Here, let me open that for you." He took a glance at the bottle and, with a sharp swing, dashed the neck against the countertop. The inner lip of the metal cap caught the edge just right, ricocheting off the wall into his waiting hand for the catch, the artificial cola inside fizzing to crest just at the neck's surface.

Melissana couldn't help but laugh. "How do you *do* that?" she asked, beaming in admiration.

In spite of himself, he smiled. She was Iylothien's girl, and despite the nearly impossible obstacles stacked against the relationship between those two wire-runners continuing, he had enough compassion for the girl's absentee mentor to leave them be. More than that, he had a lot of respect for Iylo—the young decker's struggle to survive possibly beat anything that even he thought he could have survived. Plus, Johnny had a front-row seat when Iylo single-handedly hacked an entire megacorp major headquarters. The hacker had even worked out a way for Johnny to watch what was going down in the Matsua complex while the skilled luckster basically babysat the front gate. No, he respected Iylo, even though the very attractive raven-haired CYBER detective was standing just a few inches away from him, laughing at one of his stunts. *He respected Iylo…*

"Just lucky, I guess," he shrugged, resuming his distantly nonchalant stance.

"No way," she denied—the affirmation of his talent almost a tease. "The way I hear it, you're so lucky you appear skilled, or so skilled you appear lucky—that's your tag line, anyway." She smiled, leaning in just ever so slightly, "So, which is it?"

"Pretty much a blend of both, actually," he admitted. "I think it was Thomas Jefferson who once said he was a great believer in luck and that the harder he worked, the more of it he seemed to have." He reached into the fridge and got a bottle of his own, using the conventional tool to open it. Catching her surprise, he sat down, smiled, and with a shrug said, "Luck is something you only want to push when you need to." He took a sip from his bottle. "So, what's on your mind that dragged you down here?" he asked, not so much to change the subject as to move it along.

"It's the mission, or whether we should take it," she responded, taking the seat across from his own. "Iylothien is definitely for going in after them. Evidently, he and Simon have kept tabs on James Sinclair since he put the contract out on Josanne. The guy's been looking dirtier and dirtier with each passing day, and now that they've connected Sinclair to the traffickers, Iylothien's ready to put that member of the Sinclair family out of action for good. What do you think about it?"

"It's something to do. I dunno, the way they were carting those girls in those trucks? It's definitely a worthy cause. Weird, though, how Trigget's brother and Preach are both tied in with it. You've known her for a while now, what do you think? If we do take the job, do you think she'll be able to handle it?"

"That's what Iylo and I were discussing. It's been about a month now since the Matsua run. She's taking quite a bit of time adjusting, but of all of us, she's the one who's had the most to adjust to." She sighed across the top of her bottle, causing a puffy whistle. "To be honest," she admitted, biting her lip, "I don't know."

... ...

She walked alone in dream-fog blackness, a soft breeze that was neither warm nor cool, causing a billowing ruffle in the black knee-length cape she was wearing. She wasn't aware how she got here; she had been alone in her room pondering, now always pondering, feeling alone, now always feeling alone. She knew how the other team members felt about her. She felt distant, like she couldn't really talk with any of them—not even Melissana—anymore. In her conflicted state, she became aware that she couldn't even talk to herself. Over the last couple of months, she had made so many deeply conflicted decisions, fundamentally understanding both sides of each one at a core value level, that she had isolated herself from her *self*, and in the process, had become her own enemy. She spent a long time fitfully tossing in her bed, physical evidence of the internal struggles against her own thoughts and feelings in the darkness of her room.

As Josanne allowed her mind to stray down this newer, even darker line of thought, she drifted into the exhaustion of depression and found herself walking in a blackness extending out until it ran into the even blacker oily haze of her dream. As she walked, she began to wonder if the team was trying to save her because she was a part of the team or if they were perhaps just trying to destroy the part of her that could be a threat to the team. She knew Simon was testing her—so even a machine could grow impatient with her, she realized, passing through the shadows of dark thoughts in an even darker background. She continued walking.

The scene eventually faded into the blackness of a sleepless dream she would not remember having. The images played like some grotesque slow-motion film in surreal jerky movements, as though filmed under strobe lights flickering under various incompatible frequencies, portraying the memory of her shooting Atchins's minion in the back with her laser pistol, over and over again burning the silvery hole through the thug's entire chest. Only in each loop of the recurring pattern of her dream, a computer in the room began to maniacally laugh as it grew hands that pointed at her, singling her out from the blackness enshrouding her. And in each loop of the recurring pattern of her dream, when the thug turned, the face didn't belong to the guy who had been beating Melissana to death; as he turned, she realized that the man she had killed was her brother…

… …

"Good morning, Team!" Jack greeted them with an energy he inwardly didn't completely feel. He had been up until 3 A.M., praying whether they should take the mission. It's not that he didn't want to—he genuinely cared for the young girl and was horrified about what had become of her, despite the history with her father. The question was whether or not he should. Again he would be risking the lives of his team against an unknown but powerful enemy, with additional risks imposed by both his own emotional involvement and Josanne's entanglements. He knew far too well that if the devil couldn't get someone to fall for something inherently evil, he might sometimes try to get him by tempting him with something that seemed to look good. So, before each mission, and especially with this one, Jack sought advice from others and then spent the rest of the night praying about what to do. He was tired from his vigil, but having arrived at his decision, he was at peace with whatever would happen next. Judging from the tired expressions and bloodshot eyes as the group—Trigget especially—assembled for their midmorning workout in front of him, he could easily see he had not been alone.

"All right." He tried to grin. "Looks like we all had a long night. We've had a lot on our minds—the nights before deciding on runs are almost always the worst. Well, we've all got too much on the mind, right? So, I'm going to help you all with that and provide a distraction. I'll tell you what. We'll skip this morning's training event."

"Oh, thank goodness!" yawned Melissana.

Jack smiled for real this time. He had been wondering if he was making the right decision by canceling the usual routine this morning; now, he was sure of it.

"Instead, we're doing a fifteen-mile formation run. He looked meaningfully at where the Hounds were sitting. All of us."

"What?" exclaimed Melissana, "You know that some of us don't have mechanical legs?"

"Running ten miles? And how is that going to help my driving?" Corey chimed in, surprising Jack. Corey was, by both nature and build, athletic.

"It's fifteen, Corey," Jack responded. "Sometimes, you'll be outside your car. And even so, the tech we wired you up with is only as good as the mettle of the person inside it. We can't have you atrophy just because you're our wheelman."

"Well, what about them?" Melissana pouted, pointing out Chrome, Araña, and then belatedly, Susan.

"Yeah," Johnny complained. "This is gonna kill us, and to them, it'll be a walk in the park."

"I hate to say it, but that's not true," Chrome cut in. "Yeah, my legs are machine, but my cardio and breathing still need endurance workouts like this every once in a while. Think of the shape Rickshaw and Corey would be in if they sat all day inside their vehicles."

"And trust me," Araña added, "for me and Susan, running ten miles in formation takes just as much focus for us not to pull ahead and finish the race as it takes willpower for you to keep going." Susan nodded in agreement.

"I think most of us slept in," Rickshaw said in the middle of a somewhat sleepy stretch. "At least you caught us before breakfast."

"Come on," Jack concluded. "We'll meet up at the practice yard in twenty."

As the group filed out to prepare for their run, Jack noted that the only one who hadn't joined in the protest was Josanne. Instead, she just sat there, silently, then without fanfare or saying anything to anyone, she quietly slipped out of the room with the rest of them to get ready. "Lord," he silently prayed, "help me to know how to help her." Then he yawned, stood, and stretched as he got up from his seat. Fifteen-mile runs weren't easy for him, either, but it would be good for him to have something to focus on other than his thoughts.

... ...

Three hours later, the group returned to the Facility's conference room after their run. Physical tiredness had replaced their mental exhaustion, but now that they were cleaned up, their natural endorphins had kicked in. They were in about as good a mood as they were going to get; it was time to have the final discussions about the mission and conduct the vote.

"OK," Jack began. "Time for any last-minute questions, answers, and conversations about the proposed run. Just to remind you, this is not a majority rule. We either *all* agree to the job, or there is no run. This one's no exception. We are way too emotionally involved to goad anyone against their judgment. CYBER just doesn't work that way. Anybody want to go first?"

After a slight pause, Corey lifted his hand. "Sue and I talked about it. To be honest, I'm not completely sold on how we get these proposed missions; I mean, this one sounds like Simon is playing us like guinea pigs. But like I said, we talked, and we're ready to go forward on this one. Whoever is doing that to those girls has got to be stopped, regardless of how you and Josanne are somehow connected to all of this."

"Josanne," Susan added, "I know it's going to be hard bringing your brother in, but as we were talking about it, we figured that maybe at least this way you can be there to make sure it all goes down the right way. If something had happened to your brother and one of the other teams did it, would you ever really believe that team did everything they could to avoid it? So, for the safety of those girls *and* for you, Josanne, we're in. We'll do it."

"I said it once before," Johnny chimed in. "If there's anyone to stop the choobs doin' this, it's you guys—except now, I guess it's us, ain't it?" he added with a wry smile. "Search and rescue? Sure, I'm in," he declared with a nod.

"Josanne?" Melissana asked as gently as she knew how. She waited before her friend looked up to her, eyes far distant despite their physical closeness, brows and cheeks lowered in forlorn concern. "I'm in if you're in. How do you feel about it?"

"How do I feel about it?" Josanne sneered. "How do you think I feel about it? According to our 'briefing,' we're going up against my own brother! I mean, we all thought it was oh so horrible that he would send assassins after me, didn't we? So, tell me: what makes what we're doing any different? Answer me that one, and I'll consider it. And oh yeah, it's a big loyalty test. Is the next mission from 'The Great Computer in the Sky' for Corey and Sue to take out that Handsight guy in Hagerstown? Or will it be an arena duel between Chrome and Araña?"

"Josanne, that's enough!" Jack sharply rebuked, to everyone's surprise. The unexpected chastisement stopped her cold; while she stared at him in anger, doubt, and fear, he recognized that he at least had her in a place she could listen. After he took a moment's pause to calm himself, he quietly continued. "You want some answers? Fine. Having doubts and second-guessing yourself? I've been there, I get it. Mad at yourself for all of this? We told you before you signed up that there would be a lot of days you'd wished you would have gone the other way.

"You don't believe in yourself, and you're taking it out on the others, including Melissana, who hasn't done anything to deserve any of this. It's not Melissana's fault you killed that guy who was beating on her, and it's not yours. You took action that you would only have taken in a life or death decision. It hurts. Again, I get it. But it was his fault, not yours. You saved the lives of those kids. You saved Melissana's life. So, since you wanted to save the life of your friend, wouldn't you want to be her friend now that she's still alive? Just think about that for a while.

"Regarding going after your brother, did you hear any of what Corey and Sue said? This is the initial phase of the investigation. If James isn't involved, the investigation will clear him. If he is involved, we'll stop his operation and bring him in, but we're not street assassins."

Jack stopped to take a breath, and Chrome took up the pace. "We'll stop whoever's behind this, but like we said before, there are tolls on our consciences when people die. You think you're alone in what you feel? You think the only one Jack meets with each week, is you? Corey and Sue still have nightmares from some of the stuff they've been through.

"You might not trust Simon yet, but Iylo has seen the effort Simon puts into matching team profiles. You can be sure Jack didn't want to come back, and Simon ran multiple profile scans to find someone different to take his place. Came up Jack every time, and you guys all need someone with his faith in his God and in each of you, plus his abilities to coach you through the startup. If Simon wants to assign this op to us, he's got his reasons. It has a higher regard for human life than you give it credit for.

"But I get that I've been around Simon a while, and you haven't. I get you not trusting the machine. I get you not trusting us, too. I can even get you not fully trusting Jack yet since he has a past affiliation with all of us. But what I can't get is why you won't at least trust the people who are taking the hits alongside you—especially the person who's been your best friend for years.

"Oh, and about all of this, 'Nobody wants me here because I'm too different' crap. Look around you, sister; if you let yourself off that horse you rode in on, you'll see you're no different from any of us. Not even me." he concluded with a slight shrug and twist of a derisive smile.

"OK," she finally said, shoulders only slightly sagging. "You're right—you're all right. I'm sorry. I thought I was the only one having the extra meetings with Jack. When we were first recruited, I almost got us into trouble by my turning a blind eye to my brother's activities. And, well, I went ahead and signed up, but then when that guy was hitting Melissana, I… well, I *wanted* to kill him! That's what has me so afraid. I don't want to turn into a cold-blooded killer; it's not how we were raised! But I was so angry at him for hurting you, Melissana, I wanted to shoot him!

"I guess that's why I was so angry with you; I didn't like what I didn't want to see in myself. And Jack, you were just an easy target. But then, having to confront the likelihood of James being caught up in all of this?" Tears began streaming down her face. "What happened to him? Is that what's happening to me?" she openly sobbed in front of everyone.

Melissana was the first one to approach her, wrapping her in a hug. "Hey, it's okay," Melissana comforted her. "We'll go in together and find out either way. And if James somehow is connected to any of this, we'll do our best to see he comes in peaceably and unharmed, okay? And don't worry, Trig—you're nothing like your brother, and all of this proves that."

"Josanne, are you sure you want to do this?" asked Jack, concerned. "If this actually does go south, we could be forced to take him down hard."

"At least I'll know we did what we could—that I did what I could," she affirmed. "And maybe I need to get back in the game to help me get over myself a little."

And so it was that Josanne "Trigget" Sinclair agreed to try her best to get herself back on track with the team and also opted to join the mission. With the unanimous agreement, the run was a "Go." The other members of Preach's Pride and Grey's Hounds gathered around Josanne to welcome her back, reassuring her after her open, soul-bearing confession. Surrounded by her friends and teammates, Trigget smiled, a picture of healing, hope, restoration, and rekindled trust. And along with all those sentiments she outwardly displayed, there was one additional thought that she left unexpressed:

Foxfire had trained her well.

II. RESEARCH AND DEVELOPMENTS

"The boldness of asking deep questions may require unforeseen flexibility if we are to accept the answers."

— Brian Greene

10. The Mean While

"You haven't found her yet?" Sitter asked the group of boys gathered in the chilled abandoned warehouse. His current focus was on a restored console screen displaying the territory normally scavenged by the ragtag group of street urchins.

"Haven't seen any sign of her anywhere," one of the younger boys responded. "We been lookin', she just ain't been around."

"Maybe they colored her hair since we last seen her. It's one of the things they kinda do, so nobody can recognize her," another youth offered.

"They would have already done all that before we first spotted her," Saint Nick disagreed.

"Then maybe they don't normally work her in this part of town. Maybe that's why she ran here."

"That could be," Sitter contemplated. "Then let's go past our normal neighborhoods. If we don't find her soon, she could be lost to 'the life' for good."

"Sitter, she could already be dead after runnin' like she did."

"If she's not, she probably wishes she was," the group's mentor responded with a sigh, then his features hardened. "It's like this," he suddenly declared, spinning his chair to face them directly, driving in the intensity of his resolve on the matter. "We won't know if they've moved her out of the zone until we find her, we won't know if we can do anything to help her until we find her, we won't know how much time she has left until we find her, and we won't know if she's alive or dead until we find her. What that means is there is only one thing I actually do know before we find her: we are not giving up until we find her!"

"Sitter?" It was again Saint Nick who was asking, trying to frame the question in a way that wouldn't agitate his mentor any further. "You know that girls like that just disappear every once in a while," he ventured. "Do you think maybe she's disappeared like some of the others?"

"Well, Nick," Sitter stated in a calmer yet more determined resolve, "if that does turn out to be the case, then I know two things: One, we will be looking for a long time; two, we're going to step up our game against Ricky Theodore Showbiz and his crowd. She jeopardized her rescue to take care of one of our own; she lost her chance to make a break for it to help someone who had no chance at all. I expect us all to do whatever it takes to take care of her. We owe her, and I swear we're gonna clear that debt, one way or another. I want you to try to find her like she's your sister."

… …

"Well, Sister? How are the girls?"

"They're traumatized, Freya," Rogue Moon responded. "Most want to go home, some don't, quite a few are jack scared we brought the wrath of that pimp and his gang down on 'em and that somehow he's gonna capture them again. Too frightened to move forward, too scared to go back, too nervous to stay here, too unsure to go anywhere else. Put 'em all together, and ya got just too much 'too,' y'know what I mean?"

"Yeah, I guess I know somethin' 'bout that," Mother Freya grimaced. Noticing a lizard making its way across the desert rock, she took aim and spat, barely missing the reptile as it darted by. "Do me a favor, will ya, Hon? Round 'em up for me, into the theatre; it's about time we had a chat."

… …

The combination of veteran bikers and rescued teens packed the town's old theatre, creating a room full of eyes looking forward in anticipation, backward in shame and regret, upward in hope, and (for some) awe. The panel of four Valhalla's Brownie leaders on the stage returned their gazes in a combination of respect for their fellow Valkyrie comrades and compassion for those they had recently rescued. A tall redhead, complete with thickly braided hair and Viking-styled horned helmet, stepped forward and offered a loud but overly-ladylike "Ah-HEMM!" into her hand-held microphone to gather the room's attention.

"*Ladies and ladies*," she began in true ringmaster style with a smile. "Yeah, that's right—there ain't no gentlemen here. In case we haven't already met, my name's Ingrid. I'm pretty much in charge of accommodations, but today I'm here ta make ya a promise. If any men, gentle or otherwise, do show up, we'll soon show them the error of their ways! Trust me, there's not a man within a mile of here—well, not a living one, anyways." Various hoots and cheers rose from the more experienced Brownies. Even some of the timid girls smiled.

"That's right, sisters, laugh it up—it's all right! The beasty men are gone, and they won't be comin' back. Put *that* in your thinkers!" She stooped down from the stage to be more at eye level with the rescued girls, offering her compassion to the recently rescued slaves.

"Young ladies, it's true," she said in as much of a reassuring calm as she could muster. "More than any mere thing I could give you, I want to give you a 'think' to put in your thinkers: 'You're really, finally, free.' Now that's a very special think, so breathe it in a little. We know you came from horrid backgrounds and that the men did horrible things that shouldn't be done, what might be too much to even think about sharing with someone who hadn't already seen it or been through it. You're free now, though. It's true. An' if there be one think we want you to keep in your thinkin' through all this, and beyond, it's that it's really, completely true. You. Are. Free." She let the statement hang in the air a moment, both to let the girls take another moment to realize what she had just told them and to gather her vocal strength. She then launched herself back to full height, right arm raised in grandiose flair, left hand holding the microphone to her mouth as she raised her voice back to ringmaster volume and with infectious optimism asked, "So how 'bout *that*, eh ladies? You… are… *FREE!!*"

The cheering was thunderous, resounding off the old theatre walls. With a bow and a wave to an almost equally tall blonde on the far right of the podium, Ingrid handed off the microphone and walked off stage to take her part in the audience sea.

"Hello girls, I'm Bridgette," the blonde greeted with a wave as she advanced to front center stage. "I'm in charge of logistics and communications. For you new girls, that means we're trying our very best to take care of you for a while. All you need to do is just rest up and heal. If we missed anything, or if you need anything, please let me know. I'm in the building right by the old gas station down the block from here. If I'm not there, just leave a note or something, and we'll see what we can do. We're really doing our best to make you feel at home while you're here. In the meantime, any questions?"

A girl barely sixteen raised her hand. Bridgette remembered her. When the Valhalla's Brownies radio expert first laid eyes on the young girl, all she had to wear was a t-shirt that had been badly torn and an old pair of boxer shorts. A veteran biker from way back in the day, she inwardly cringed when she spotted the burn marks and severe bruising on the young girl's face, arms, and legs. A few of the bruises were from the rescue, sure, but most had been deliberately inflicted upon her by her captors and their clientele. She had immediately closed up shop for the girl; her top priority had immediately changed to providing the young survivor some half-decent clothing to protect her body from the desert Sun and, maybe even more so, what was left of the girl's dignity. Now a few days later, the bruising did appear to be slowly going away, as was,

Bridgette hoped, the constant looming PTSD panic in the girl's eyes. "Yes, Crystal?"

"First, I—I want to say, 'Thank you' for everything you've done for us," Crystal began. "S—so thank you. A lot." Bridgette smiled, waiting for Crystal to continue. "And I mean, this is all really super nice, but what are we supposed to do now?"

"I'm glad you asked," a not-so-tall, stocky brunette stated as she approached center stage. "I'll handle this one, Bridgette, thanks," she said as she received the mic. She looked across the theatre and waved to the assembled crowd. "Hey there, girls. I'm known as Mother Freya around here. I'm the Leader and First Consort of Valhalla's Brownies, the band of brave heroines who rescued you from your former masters." She took a few seconds to make a joking display of self-appraisal. "Yeah, I donated my height to Ingrid and Bridgette, and they, in turn, donated some of their weight to me." Some of the girls laughed—their masters had always shamed them for what was in their shallow minds the slightest imperfections the girls might have had. Mother Freya's flaunting her own foibles helped to lower the anxiety levels of the girls. She was an expert leader, grateful as she saw her attempts to break the ice with the girls had paid off—if even just a little.

"To answer your question, where you go from here is up to you. I don't know where you all are from; some of you may not know yourselves. If any of you have family and want to go back, we can offer you safe passage within the limits of our territory, but I'm sure you understand we can't give you all rides back to your homes. Bridgette can try to help you contact your families, and if they're able to get to our territory, we can arrange the meets. They are free to bring donations or expressions of gratitude to our little group, sure, but we are definitively not charging any kind of ransom, rescue charge, finder's fee, or anything that might indicate to them that we're holding you hostage. We acted to free you because we knew we had to. The way we feel about it, if we don't do anything about this problem, we're actively contributing to it.

"I also realize that some of you may want out but don't want to go back to your families. Believe me, I get it that sometimes the family dynamic is messed up. From what I heard, some of you were even sold to that govek Sweet Trick Ricky by your own parents. Others of you may have been taken so long ago that you don't know who your own families are. If that's you, talk with Ingrid, and let her know where you want to try to go. Again, we can't guarantee you safe passage beyond our own borders, but we can sometimes get a reliable truck driver—a female one, of course—to get you that one step closer to where you want to be.

"Oh, and there is one other option. I like saving the best for last, so I'll let this little honey on my left explain it. She can do a better job at that than me. Besides," Mother Freya added with a smile, "she's taller." And with that, Mother Freya made a joke of hobbling down the theatre stage steps into the audience, joining the friends and family of her own.

A tall, lavishly black-haired woman took to center stage, the only one on the podium visibly armed. Slung over her shoulder was a heavy-looking rifle that was so long that, as tall as the woman was, she had to sling it diagonally to avoid scraping the weapon's muzzle across the floor. The woman took a moment and looked over the group, almost as if she was daring them to confront her. Freya appeared tougher, but to these girls, she was, all in all, the single most dangerous-looking woman they had ever seen. The black-haired woman smiled at them, a subtle blend of nod and challenge in equal measure. She saw their rapt attention and knew that whatever directions the rescued slaves would go, they would take her message of regained strength with them wherever they went.

"Greetings," the tall woman began. "I want to introduce you to a friend of mine," she continued while reaching her hand back, unslinging her rifle. Then, holding it in a pose that someone once described to her as statuesque, she continued her introductions.

"This is my dear friend, Natalia, and I am Rogue Moon. We've been together for a couple years now, have spent many a night together. On our latest date night, I fired the two opening shots that took out the lead truck of the convoy that held you prisoners, signaling the start of the raid that freed you." She paused for effect, allowing the young girls to absorb that Rogue Moon, *by herself*, had taken out one of Ricky T. Showbiz's heavily armed war rigs. She used that time to pan the crowd of recently freed victims, ensuring she made eye contact with every one of the rescued girls. She had a good sense for this type of thing—the girls were captivated. Now for her punch line.

"Six years ago, I was one of you." She again waited for the words to sink in, catching the startled gasps from many of the rescued girls before continuing.

"I want to let you know about that third option. If you want to pay back Sweet Trick Ricky T. Showbiz and those like him in a proper way, you are each welcome to ride along with us. If you lack experience, we'll train you up; no worry there. And our doors are standing wide open...."

... ...

The door was standing wide open, but Kelly didn't move one inch towards it. She hurt too much: physically, emotionally, and even spiritually. Several times after dragging her back into her pen, they had left the door open and left the room. And each time she had approached the open door, they returned, sometimes in two's, sometimes in three's, one time in five's. Each time she scrambled to retreat back into her pen, but they somehow always knew she had edged closer to the open latch. Laughing as they forcibly dragged her from her cage, they took turns forcing themselves upon her in every way they could imagine, each time beating her to within inches of her life.

Eventually, she learned her lesson. The open door meant danger. She must never approach it unless they were there and demanded that she come out. Huddled in the corner farthest away from the opening, she shivered, suddenly panicking that maybe they thought she was trying to escape again. She pushed herself further into the wires that formed the back wall of her pen. Once, they had overheard her praying, whimpering for Jesus to do something, anything, to help her. Their jeering taunts intimidated her, but their threats that they'd go back and do the same things to her family if she didn't shut up cowed her into a submission that was fearful, mute, and total. She shivered in a cold darkness that was both physical and psychological, afraid of the dark, afraid of the open door, but most of all, afraid of Sweet Trick Ricky T. Showbiz.

11. Passive/Aggressive

"Allright, it's been four days. What do you have for me?"

"Nothing much, Preach," Melissana responded, using his new moniker for practice. "By Simon's coordinates from his satellite communications he fed us, and from the highway Freya broadcasted, the convoy hit happened in Kansas near the Colorado border. We also got a load of history on trafficking from searching through some old-net archives. Seems that back in the last century, there were quite a few campaigns to legalize prostitution, trying to label it as a 'victimless' crime. Man, if they ever knew."

"What do you mean?" Johnny asked. "I mean, it was a way for a girl to make a quick buck. Not such a bad gig, I guess, for the most part. They come in, do their thing, then leave, right? It's just these traffickers that take girls against their will—those are the bad guys."

"No, Johnny, that ain't how this rolls. Iylo and me have been hitting all the data stores we can think of. Prostitutes, porn videos, 'net sites—we can tell from the data that they're all connected. And they're all sourced by trafficking."

"No way that's possible. All right, I can see a maybe couple of the back-alley places taking the girls for their kick, but—"

"A couple, Johnny?" Iylothien cut in, obviously agitated. "How many's a couple? Three? Four? Two hundred?"

"I don't know, Iylo, maybe a couple hundred. There were a lot of girls that got outta that truck, and that was only one truck. I mean, I'm not sayin' it's okay; why are you giving me all this grief about it?"

"Because, Johnny, the data's been there. People have known about this since back in the 1990s. There have been organizations that had tried to get the word out, but nobody wanted to listen. If they did, they'd be forced to admit to themselves that it was there, and they were deliberately choosing not to do anything about it!"

"What're you getting at? Know about what?"

"It's the numbers, Johnny," Melissana desolately responded. "They've known since the early 2000s. The number of slaves being trafficked into prostitution isn't a couple; it's not twenty, it's not two hundred. The number of slaves fed into prostitution, porn videos, and 'net cam sites is higher. Much higher. It's been proven and made public. And they knew about it since the turn of the century, but hardly anybody did anything about it."

"Johnny," Iylothien resumed for Melissana, who lost her voice to her emotions, "there were statistics that indicated it was as high as 66 to 70 *percent*."

"What are you talking about? I mean, that's impossible!"

"Vixenn," Jack interrupted, obviously pained by what they had just relayed, "are you sure about those numbers?"

"Grey—sorry… Preach," Iylothien corrected himself. "We ran the numbers through more than a few times. The statistic tracking died along with the rest of society back in the meltdown, but there are records out there indicating 89% of the girls involved wanted to get out but couldn't. There were counter-intel ops to put out that the number of trafficked 'sex workers' were inflated, but even those had to admit that at least 10% of them were either maneuvered, coerced, or outright forced into it. Not everybody who was trafficked was because of the sex trade—turns out forced labor didn't originate with the corp wars we have going on now—but forced prostitution accounted for anywhere between 30% and 75% of the human trafficking, depending on the year. The information was available, but evidently, the media was too caught up in trying to influence elections to care."

"What kind of data, Iylo? Who was doing the tracking?" Jack persisted.

"*Lots* of people!" Melissana answered, irritated to the point of pacing. Their discoveries clearly agitated her. "Before the turn of the century, they'd bust the girls and let the pimps go almost scot-free. The girls got sent to jail if not prison."

"Eventually, some people started talking with the girls," Iylothien inserted. "I don't know exactly how it started, but somehow people started getting the real stories."

"But by the turn of the century," Melissana rejoined, "people started putting it all together. The girls were brought in, turned to 'the life', and from there, where could they go? The cops? They'd bust them. Then the girls would get a record, so their chances of getting out were made even more remote."

"And that's not counting the times the cops were actually involved in the rings, flashing their badges to let anyone coming around know that they were actually the watchdogs guarding the place."

"*¡No me lo creo!* Lethal force backed by blind authority?" Araña interjected. "Maybe things haven't changed all that much after all," he sadly added.

"Well, back then, that was the exception, but it happened often enough," Iylothien replied. "To answer your question, Preach, eventually enough noise was generated that congress members, government law making and law enforcement agencies, and even some nonprofit organizations started collecting data. National trafficking hotlines were set up, and they kept statistics, and the old FBI also started tracking the statistics. In 2017, the national trafficking hotline reported that 71% of their trafficking calls involved sex trafficking."

"Yeah, and those were the ones who were left alone long enough to place the calls," Melissana interrupted. "Think about it—3,418 people—in one year!"

Iylothien resumed. "There was even a global trafficking database with dozens of maps and statistics available for anyone who wanted to get involved."

"That's what gets me the most," Melissana seethed. "Not many did. They just didn't frakkin' care! They had the information available in infographs—over half a million different ones—it was there. Even if you barely knew how to read, you could follow the things! Broken down by state, age, gender, what specific venue or industry. Hotels? Massage parlors? Residence-based? Escorts? You name it, they had it by the numbers. The masses just didn't care."

"And even when they cared enough and worked hard enough, things still *weren't* enough. I found records of a case where a girl was kidnapped by a husband and wife team who got her hooked onto drugs and forced her into prostitution for over four years. Eventually, she got freed, with enough hard evidence to get an arrest. Luckier yet, the case goes to court. The good guys won! They even got convictions on them both!

"Now, here's the punch line. The guy gets 18 months in prison with another three years of community time. The wife didn't do any time at all. The court's reasoning was that the wife had to watch her kids."

"So she could do *what*?" Chrome growled.

"Yeah, she had other kids in the house, her own kids, and the courts thought it'd be okay for her to skip jail time for kidnapping and forcing another girl into prostitution so she could take care of them. Guess they thought the girl had it coming because she had run away from home before the two creeps caught her."

"And it was a non-event," Melissana added. "No media outrage, no protests, no notice. No Child Protective Services. In an age when prisons were making allowances for mothers giving birth in prison, she got off. And people didn't want to know, and for an industry that brought in more profit than three of the most recognized corporations of the day *combined*—in one U.S. city alone, illegal sex industry was said to bring in over $290 million a year—well, I guess that kind of money buys a lot of hush."

"Okay," Preach said, looking distractedly off into some far corner of the room, but actually deep in thought, "you've done your homework. Those people had no excuse, and I can only guess things are even worse now. But now we're here, not those people back then. It's our watch; we won't be guilty of turning a blind eye to the problem.

"I'll run down this Sitter they mentioned, find out who and where he is. Iylo? Queen? Find this slaver operation. Find a way in. Set up a decoy inside a tar baby."

"Tar baby?" Josanne asked.

"It's a decker program that draws people in but kind of keeps them trapped in the system for a while so they can find out where the signal's coming from and the ID of the person we're talking with," Iylothien answered.

"Oh."

"Anyway," Preach resumed, "play the game, draw them out. Be passive; let them come to you. If you rush it too much, you'll tip them off, so just lead them on a little and see if they give you anything we can use to find out where Kelly is. If she's in the same condition those other girls were in, she's running out of time. Trigget, you listen in on Vixenn and Iylo. Build up psych profiles on the johns and see if you can figure out how we can target this ring. Also, work with them to help them tune their techniques to draw more perps.

"Chrome, Spider, Rickshaw, and Hardcore: review the old maps and narrow down where this is all happening. The Brownies said they were operating on an eastbound/westbound 70. It's probably along the old I-70, but often different states had their own connecting state roads. There's an old 370 North of here a little, but we would have heard of this den if it was this close, and the satellite coordinates place the raid happening somewhere in the Midwest. We need to know which '70' they're on and where.

"The rest of you, start training up and get ready for anything. These guys are dark streets, but we're going to light 'em up. Now, if you'll excuse me," he said, standing, "I need to go pray a while. It's our turn now, and I can tell you one thing: we're going to end this." With that, Jack turned and resolutely made his way to the door.

Araña whistled. "Not every day you see that!" he exclaimed. "I haven't seen him that edged since 'Frisco."

"So, he's just going to pray about all this?" Josanne challenged. "He sounded like he was all worked up a second ago."

"Oh, he's worked up, all right," Rickshaw commented. "Remember, he knows this girl, and he knows what kind of trouble she's landed herself into."

"So, he's taking a prayer break?" Susan asked, just as confused as Josanne. "I don't get it."

"You guys better start training up," Rickshaw commented. "You can be sure these guys aren't just gonna fold up and run away. But I can promise you that neither will Jack; he's dead-to-justice serious about this one. Somebody'd better get some popcorn—situations like these are where Jack really shines, and as of the moment we made our decision, Valhalla's Brownies are the least of the slavers' worries.

"And I gotta tell ya," the Hound's veteran wheelman admitted, grimacing towards the satellite images of the girls getting out of the trailers, "I don't have one bit of sympathy towards any of the goveks for the wrath he's going to bring down on 'em." Chrome's scowling nod reflected his assent.

"I don't get it," Corey confessed.

Observing the perplexed looks in the eyes of each remaining member of the Pride, Araña tried to explain. "That's because you don't know Jack like we do," Araña asserted. "You all better figure on being along for the long haul on this one, because when it comes to saving victims from their tormentors...,"

Chrome cut in to finish Araña's thought. "You see, especially in situations like these, the cross isn't just some squeamish little bridge

Jack uses to invite nice people to Sunday church—it's the battering ram he uses to obliterate the walls of Hell."

The two teams dispersed in a resolute calm, fully aware that they were about to engage in a no-holds-barred war against an unconscionable enemy. If they didn't die in the process, they would bring this one slaving operation to a definitively permanent end.

… …

Six days had lapsed since their last full team meeting. Jack fidgeted in the once comfortable leather executive chair, his body language indicating some sense of his frustration to the others. Kelly needed him, and here he sat, stalled in some office conference room.

"I'll go first," he began, uncharacteristically terse, as the CYBER team members were still taking their seats. "It's been six days, and I haven't been able to locate any traces of the mysterious Sitter. Not even Simon has picked up any other communications from or about him since that raid last week. I'm doing everything I know to do, including praying my eyes out," he admitted, "but I got nothing so far." He sighed, looking around the conference table to the others. "So, anyone got any good news?"

"Vixenn and I got some hits," Iylothien reported in, "but nothing directly related to Kelly, Sitter, or the raid."

"Frakking perverts is what they are!" Melissana practically gagged, "There are some twisted puppies out there," she seethed. "But the worst ones..." The former private investigator started to spit in disgust but checked her impulse for the sake of the conference room. "Some of 'em have kids no older than the girl I'm playing, still trying to score and acting like it's no big deal—it literally makes me sick sometimes."

Jack grimaced, then glanced towards Chrome. "How about you guys? Do you have anything for me?" He stopped himself and glanced downwards. He wanted to add, "or did you strike out, too?" He had gotten uncharacteristically emotionally wrapped up in this mission and had already been shorter than he wanted to be with his team. And while a measure of emotional investment was good, if he wasn't careful, he'd have them all as off-balance and wound up as he was. But when he looked back up at his team, he noticed that Chrome, just as uncharacteristically, had broken out into a grin.

"I think we found 'em, *jefé*," Araña reported. He didn't wait for Jack to ask before continuing. "Yeah, there were a lot of 70s to look through, but Valhalla's Brownies only ride one of them, and the satellite coordinates confirm it. Bring up the map, Iylo."

"Turns out they ride the old I-70. Their turf is about 50—75 miles each way across the old Kansas/Colorado border," Rickshaw divulged as the wall screen displayed a section of flatland prairie with a 100-mile radius circle superimposed over a point near the bi-state border. The center dot read, "Limon," the thin east-west line bearing the US highway emblem showing I-70.

"Zoom out," Jack ordered, and the details of the map grew smaller as the area expanded. "A little more... more... more..." he said, his cybernetic eyes zooming in as the image expanded. Without realizing it, he had jumped out of his seat, shoving the heavy executive chair backward as though it was a cheap fold-up. "There!" he shouted.

What is it?" inquired Corey, who had been going over the same maps for days but hadn't seen anything to get excited about.

"The Den," Jack declared, pointing triumphantly to the map in front of them all. "It's not a club..." he began.

"It's a city!" Corey finished for him, having finally caught Jack's drift. "The Den is their tag for Denver, Colorado!"

"And if that's the case," Rickshaw added, "and you got The Den over here, following I70 back through Brownie territory, and you get...."

"Witch City," Jack concluded. "More commonly known as Wichita, Kansas."

"Ouch," Rickshaw exclaimed. "Corporate headquarters of Air Dynamix. If they're involved in this...."

"I don't think so," Preach replied. "The convoy would have had air cover. At the very least, that particular convoy was not corporate."

"Makes total sense, Grey," Iylothien inserted, not even trying to correct himself this time. "Wichita's been the crossroads for human trafficking across the U.S. of A. since before any records were kept."

"How's that?" Susan asked. Everyone knew the danger of slavers, but the former inhabitant of the Pennsylvania small town was never really aware of the details of their operations.

"I see it!" Corey exclaimed, noting to himself that the study of the road maps was paying off after all. "70 runs east-west, practically across the entire continent, and I35 runs north-south from the western edge of Lubric ICC territory where Texas used to be, all the way up through Minnesota." He turned to Susan with a grin that was more a grimace than a smile. "And guess where they happen to meet."

"You got that right on the money," Rickshaw concurred. "While they actually touched in what used to be Salina, truckers will lop quite a bit of drive time cuttin' the triangles if they're going either left or right. And if you're either coming from or heading south, Wichita is the place to do it."

Araña started researching the city ever since the name came up, and now he had his own information to add. "Says here Wichita has always been a central hub of traffic, going back even to the old cattle trails of the 1800s."

"Guess old habits die hard," Johnny sighed.

Chrome shook his head in disgust. "Well, let's go and help them with that," he muttered with a glance back to the team's luckster.

"We can't just go in there and blow up the whole town!" Josanne exclaimed. "And don't roll your eyes at me just yet; hear me out," she added, tensed in frustration.

"Listen. I get that we all want to get the bad guys. I do, too. Nobody should be treated the way those girls were, and after the last couple of days we spent profiling these goveks, I've heard enough to make me want to put them all away. But we can't go in there yet, because both Denver and Wichita are big places. We still need to find out where they're holding Kelly, and…," she purposefully looked directly at Jack, "the others."

"That was always part of the plan, Josanne," Jack assured her.

"But how are we going to infiltrate them when we don't know anything about them?" Susan asked. "I mean, we know a little about them, but we don't really know them or their customers. If we can't get in soon, we'll either lose her, tip them off, or both."

"You're right, Susan," Josanne responded. "I have some of the johns' profiles down, and I think some of the girls, but we need to learn a lot about what really goes on from the inside before we can even hope to get close enough to infiltrate."

"You're all absolutely right," Jack admitted. "How about you, Johnny? You ran that Yakuza sting a couple years back—you ever have associations or run into anyone with those kinds of connections?"

"Sorry, Preach, not really. I mean, I dated a girl once, but she wasn't trafficked. She just did it for extra cash. I never really got that close to anyone in that kind of business."

"Well then," Jack sighed, feeling the emotional body slam of getting so close only to be reminded they still had what looked like an infinite journey ahead of them, "I guess we go back to what we were doing. Josanne, I think you should—"

"Wait, I have an idea!" Melissana blurted, then took a few seconds to process her flash of inspiration before she continued. "It'll be hard for her, and she might not agree to it, but there is someone we can call who can probably give us a good run-down on the inner workings of the industry."

Josanne looked up, shocked. "You mean…"

Susan caught on to what Melissana was suggesting. "Melissana, are you serious?"

"Yes," the former detective affirmed. "Right now, I think she's the only one who can help."

Corey, too, looked down at the floor, obviously conflicted, if not embarrassed, by the thought of Melissana's idea.

Jack looked around at the group. He wasn't a conversationalist, but he was getting to know his team. Corey's expression iced it for him; he got the picture. His mind raced through a dozen scenarios weighing the pros and cons of Melissana's proposal, weighing repercussions on the guilty, the involved, the freed, and the innocent. It was a gambit that could get very messy for them all without helping them one bit. It was a long shot, but maybe it could help, if only a little. He considered a dozen options, a score of outcomes, and hundreds of details and ways this could complicate the mission. He inwardly sighed as he was forced to admit to himself that there was no other way to learn what they needed to learn in time. He glanced at each of the CYBER team members in turn and saw that they all shared the same concerns. They were on hold, awaiting their leader's decision. And he was their leader.

"Make the call," was all he said.

12. Old Friends

THE LUXURY APARTMENT safe house was an unexpected but necessary expense. CYBER could not conduct the interview at Facility without revealing the base's location. The interview subject was a friend of theirs and a prominent corporate persona; they would not even consider blindfolding her. Even if they did, the likelihood of implanted tracking devices as a precaution against someone abducting her would have rendered the blindfolding useless. Similarly, neither party would enjoy the attention that would be drawn by gathering both CYBER teams into the subject's ICC penthouse. Meeting in a restaurant was also out of the question; the nature of the conversation was too personal. In the end, each member of Preach's Pride contributed proceeds from the previous run to rent a penthouse apartment for a year, establishing a meeting place that was both secure and neutral for both sides.

"Company's coming," Rickshaw reported from his Dominator. He had followed her since she left her corporate archology, ensuring nothing would happen to her en route to the meet. While her husband took her security seriously, today, her regular security team would have extra support.

- *"She's in the building,"* Iylothien announced.

- *"All right, Iylo, thanks,"* Preach sub-vocally replied. *"Rickshaw, come on in. We'll all need to hear the details from her if we're*

91

going to have a chance to pull this off. Spider, you and Chrome are up."

- "Lobby's clear, Preach," Araña updated. "We've introduced ourselves to her and her security staff. Nobody on her team acted like they recognized us. Of course, Chrome and I weren't wearing suits when we last would have met. And you were right; she's wearing a locator chip. What's weird is that one of her team has a listener bug on him as well, but I'm scrambling it."

- "The joeboys are coming along for the elevator ride," Chrome added, "but they'll stay outside the penthouse. Well, they might not know that part yet," he said with a twist of a grin.

- "Burn the muscle's bug, Spider," Jack commanded. "We can't afford kinks, and we don't have the time to figure out side angles. Chrome, I want you in here as well, and we need to play this close to the vest. If the joes give you any grief about staying outside, don't waste time babysitting them; take 'em out. No permanent damage, though—ideally, they'll be driving her back to the archology."

- "Understood," Chrome silently radioed back, puzzled. Normally Preach would avoid any display of force unless absolutely necessary. He shrugged, guessing it would be necessary if the interview was to be everything they needed it to be. "We're here," was all he replied.

The penthouse door opened, admitting a five-foot-seven blonde woman. In honor of their corporate celebrity, both teams were dressed in business suits and formal wear, but professionalism fell by the wayside as Melissana burst out of the luxury executive chair she had been seated in to joyfully rush their guest for a hug as soon as she entered the room.

"*Elaine!* It's great to see you again!" she practically squealed. "Thanks so much for coming!"

"No, it's fine, Melissana," Elaine Martinez returned. "You all have helped me and Justin so much, and if I can help someone else get out of the living hell I've been through… Well, I don't have super powers like you all, but I'll do what I can."

"Mrs. Martinez, I believe some introductions are in order," Jack opened and introduced her to the rest of the two teams that she hadn't already met. After the ice was broken and some refreshments served, they were ready.

"OK," Elaine began, leaning forward and getting to business. "What do you need to know?"

"Everything," Jack sighed. "I truly apologize for making you relive those days, but this girl and the others with her are in deep, and if we're going to infiltrate the underworld circuit to save them and end this operation, we need to hear it all."

"Okay, then," she said, bracing herself against the memories she began forcing herself to recall. "Here goes…"

13. Full Reverse Reverie

"I GOT STARTED at a young age," Elaine began, then quickly checked herself. "Well, I guess almost all of us did, though I started younger than most. I was really scared, but it wasn't that bad at first. My job was running. After a couple months, the things I had to do got… harder," she faltered and decided to take a few moments, distracting herself by pretending to pick some lint or something off her jacket. She gave up with a frustrated sigh and looked straight at Melissana, suddenly angry at the memories. "You've been on the streets. You've seen us—you know what it's like!"

"Yeah, I've seen some things," Melissana smoothed, taking Elaine's hands into her own. "And I had my low moments, don't get me wrong, but… I've been spared from that. I knew some girls, but I never really knew what they went through. They never told me; even when I asked to try to help them, they just smiled really sad and told me I had enough problems of my own. I think a couple of them thought if their pimps—well, they called them managers— knew I was hanging around, I would've been their next target. To be honest, I don't know how I avoided it."

… …

He had been wondering, hoping against hope that had not happened to her, the records being too vague to know for sure. Upon Melissana's confession, over two hundred thirty miles away in a subterranean research facility's basement, three very real tears of relief escaped Iylothien's left eye, slowly rolling down his temple to be absorbed into his pillow.

… …

"I'm sorry," Elaine resumed. "I didn't mean to…."

"It's okay," Melissana reassured, "it's okay."

"You know, it's not like I haven't said all of this already when I first went public," the wife of Justin Martinez admitted. Then she looked directly at Josanne and added, "But this is somehow so much more *personal*."

"How about if I reconduct our interviews when you did first go public?" Josanne suggested. "Do you think that might help you?" With Elaine's nod, the former journalistic reporter that had first told the story returned to her persona as an interviewer for the Roanoke media station, when she had conducted Elaine's exclusive breaking interviews of the princess wife who had such a tragic beginning.

"You said that at first, you were running—I'm guessing that meant you were dropping off packages?" Josanne began.

"Yes, that's right," Elaine responded. "Small packages, handwritten notes, that sort of thing. I guess part of it was so I could learn the streets, part of it was because nobody would suspect what I was doing due to my age."

"And what about after that?"

"Soon enough, they started the videos. They'd bring me into this one room that was really nice, you know, like a movie set. It had a nice white bed with some stuffed animals and stuff. They always kept it really clean and were careful to keep the floor around it super well swept, and I got to take a shower every time it was my turn to go into the room.

"The first time or two, they just let me play in it for about fifteen minutes, but after that, they began filming. They'd tell me to say stuff like I was talking to a really nice man, but it always ended up with me having to take my clothes off and lay down in the bed like I was going to go to sleep with the animals. I felt really awkward and confused about that, but I always had to smile and pretend I really liked that part. If I didn't get it just right, they'd start hitting me, so I always tried really hard to get it right…

"But the porn vids are their gold mines. They hijack your dopamine levels, then package them back into twelve-year-old girls and sell them back to you, one half-hour at a time. What they're really selling isn't the meat. It's the fantasy that she really wants the guy who's raping her, that she'll want anybody else who does the same." She took a sip of water, coughed once to clear her throat, and continued.

"It doesn't take a genius to figure out the movies got worse over time. I found out later they had a variety of different movie sets ranging from a little girl's bedroom to dungeons. The only thing that really stayed the same in each of the rooms was the requirement that I had to pretend that I was doing all of those things because I truly wanted to." She cast a smirk in a realization. "Actually, the little girl bedroom was probably the hardest for them to keep up; 'Dungeon' wasn't too far from our normal conditions."

"Mrs. Martinez, please forgive me for asking," Josanne probed, "but what were the pimps like?"

"Mostly scary," Elaine responded, huddling into herself as she must have done so many times before. "And sly. I mean, at some level, you think they're all gangers, coyotes, or mobster types, but it's not always that easy. Sometimes they're foster parents, aunts, uncles, friends at school—it could be anyone. They just have to be dirtbag enough to be okay exploiting others for profit." She shuddered at an old memory. "Believe me, there are more out there than you'd think.

"For me, there were like ten guys I was sold to, almost all of them real mean, always complaining about something we did or threatening us in one way or another. One guy was okay, but then there was this other guy, Damen, who always stood up for me, told the others to back off." She relaxed her shoulders, just a little, as she said the next words. "He protected me, even threatened them once, and was going to get in a big fight with them, over me. I knew that as long as he was around, I'd be safe." She sighed, hung her head, and resumed her study of the patch of carpet, smoothing her hair to hide that she brushed away a tear that had formed on her cheek.

"What happened?" Susan asked, totally drawn into the story. "Did they—hurt him?"

"One day, we got a couple new girls into our family." The CYBER members picked up instantly on her use of the word. "And I thought that they should come over to where we were, so Damen would keep them safe, too.

"I was wrong. When one of the new girls started to come over, he started yelling at her and took a swipe at her. He even got up, took off his belt, and started storming over to the other girl, threatening to beat her senseless if she wouldn't mind her own business. Then a guy who was one of the meanest to me stepped between them and told Damen that if he didn't back off, he would put Damen in his place permanently. Then he walked over to the two girls, squatted down to their level, and told them not to worry, that nothing was going to happen to them as long as he was around.

"That's when I realized the whole thing was just a game to them. They'd take turns protecting the new girls. It was how they built up a sense of loyalty. Eventually, I could tell who a new girl's master was going to be; it was the one who would stick up for her.

"And that was just the start of it. The total financial dependence, the lack of any identification, the mind control, the fear, the being kept in dog kennels, the physical torture, the beatings, the rapes, the threats against your family members, the threats against the other girls if you got out of line or made a mistake… How much do you want to know?"

"Frakkin' *drek*, Preach!" Melissana swore. "I mean, I'm sorry. I grew up on the streets and didn't know things got that bad." She impulsively rushed up to tightly hug Elaine but checked herself as she realized Elaine desperately shrank back from any physical contact related to the events, even after all those years. Instead, the former P.I. just sat back down, embarrassed by putting Elaine on the spot like that.

"I am so sorry! You are such—I don't even know the words. How could you possibly get through any of that? I can hardly bear to hear you talk about it. How can you speak about these things?"

"Well, Melissana, first you try denial, then drugs. The drugs are easy enough to get; the masters use them to increase your dependency on them and to increase your debt, so you'll never buy your way out. After that, you might try suicide unless you're caught. You don't ever want that to happen!" She sighed, looking down at the same patch of carpeting on the floor she had evidently been trying to memorize, then continued. "Eventually, you accept that's your purpose; that's the reason you were born." She then made sure she had eye contact with them all before she added, "And I promise you, talking about it isn't easy. The only reason I'm doing it now is for you to get that girl and any who might be with her."

"Thank you for your time and help, Elaine. This is a super brave thing you are doing here by sharing all of this with us. I have one more question, if I may," Josanne asked, almost hissing in her breath through clenched teeth.

"What are the girls going to be like? How will we need to approach them, and what will they need once they've been freed?"

"What will they need? Confidence, tons of patience on your part. They'll be streetwise in a lot of ways, but many of them won't have a clue since they haven't had any independence or done anything on their own, ever. Think about it—good parents raise their kids so they can live out on their own. The last thing a master wants is extra work making sure someone can't walk away. Materially, they'll need toothbrushes, toothpaste, lip balm, soap for both regular and sensitive skin, the things you would pack if you were going on a trip: socks, gloves, over-the-counter headache stuff, and bandages."

"Elaine," Johnny chimed in, "I don't mean to be negative, but it ain't like this is 2022—we can't just walk up to the corner grocery and buy this stuff in a bag. How are we going to get all this stuff?"

"Relax, Johnny," Jack responded. "We can find it easily enough if we look. We can't just waltz into an archology and simply buy all the stuff they'll need, but we're government, and I ran an urban ministry in three different cities long enough to know how to find necessities for the homeless. We can't provide everything for everybody, but we can make do where we can. Anything else, Elaine?"

"They won't trust you at first, and rightfully so. They need to know you're on their side. Don't take pictures of them, don't introduce them as victims, but as your friends. Love them where they are and let them move forward. Remember, they're all too used to being pushed in one direction and then another; don't ever try to let on that just because you rescued them, they owe you anything— not even their gratitude or friendship. They're used to being bartered for, and they can smell it a mile off.

"By the way," Elaine added, "while we're on the subject about letting them make their own decisions, I'd better warn you now. Don't be surprised when at least some of the girls won't want to be freed. They're all different, and they'll all have their reasons. For some of them, as bad as it is, it's all they've ever known, and they've been indoctrinated into believing that's all they'll ever be good for. Some have been fed so many lies about how anyone else would ever treat them that they'll be afraid to leave. Some are terrified because of threats made against their families, while for others, they either have nowhere to go or are afraid because it was their families who sold them in the first place. Some will be so afraid of their pimps they'll be too scared to leave, and others will believe their pimps truly love them and fight to defend 'their man' to the death.

"Above all, just remember; each one is an individual girl, not just some non-citizen in a disenfranchised social class. Every time you talk with any of them, remember that each one is very much a human being. I got lucky, chip-truth lucky, the day I met Justin. Any one of the girls you are going to meet could easily have been me." She squared herself, looked each of them in the eyes, and made the declaration her audience couldn't dare forget. "The fact is, they're *all* Kellys."

The group sat still, moved to motionlessness. Josanne, who had been trained to empathize in order to facilitate relationship-building as well as to detect deceit, was overwhelmed by the sheer volume of sincerity behind the torrid tale Elaine had narrated. Melissana realized that, despite her own tragic childhood, her life could have been much worse. Susan shuddered, memories of the terror she felt in those moments with Iron Mike graphically ripped from the distance her mind had put between them. Corey was pacing, Rickshaw studied the floor; as men, they felt too ashamed to look directly at her. Spider reflected the same emotion, but he had shifted his gaze to the ceiling while Johnny was reflecting inwardly, looking nowhere at all. The typically boyish Iylothien, who had been monitoring the discussion, remained silent. Chrome twitched once, then dove even deeper into his inner self. Glancing about the room at each of them, Jack was praying silently for the right words to say in response. None came. Everyone's emotions were too raw for words; he would have to let silence coach them through the processing of what they all had heard. In the end, it was Josanne who broke the silence once more.

"You said you started younger than most. How long were you—I mean—how old were you when you started?"

"Remember when I did the series of interviews, Josanne? I lied to you. I wasn't seventeen like I said I was." Her hand visibly shaking, she took a sip of water, pretending to look at each of the CYBER team members. Josanne could tell, though, that Elaine wasn't looking at anyone around her, but more like the spaces in between, where the people weren't. She read that Elaine was trying to convince herself that it wasn't her fault—that maybe if she just came clean and told them the truth, they would understand.

"That is, the first time I was sold…." But not even her Justin knew this part; it had always been too difficult for her even to try to explain. She finally gave up trying to be unashamed, averting her eyes from each of them and just looking down at the carpeted floor in front of her.

"I was four."

The atmosphere inside the room instantly grew as tense as a flash-frozen pane of glass; air pressure dropped as each member of the CYBER teams sucked in their breath out of shock. After a moment's hesitation, Josanne stepped up to continue the interview. Anywhere in the conversation was better than where they all were now. At least that's what she thought.

"Is that—typical? I mean, how do people get into that kind of situation?" she asked.

"No, not typical," Elaine replied, still looking at the floor. "The average of a lot of the girls who I knew were recruited between fifteen and seventeen." She slumped her shoulders in complete shame, hanging her head like a scolded dog drooping its tail between its legs. "My mom said she needed the money."

Melissana swore. Araña broke out into a fast-running litany of ghetto Spanish. Somewhere in the room, glass broke—Susan had subconsciously popped her claws, destroying the tumbler she was holding. Chrome wheeled in a tight circle, looking for something he could hit as hard as he wanted, knowing that whatever he did strike would not resist his blow enough to be even vaguely satisfying. Rickshaw crammed fisted hands into his jeans pockets and hunched his shoulders forward, clearly struggling to avoid blowing out altogether. Corey hadn't had enough experience to match Rickshaw's control; in the parking garage, his Sabretooth flared to life, revved its engine, and fired three High Explosive rounds into the row of cars in front of it. The effects of the emotional intensity filled the atmosphere of the room so quickly that Josanne felt like she was being hit by xenon strobe lights; she barely had a chance to quickly sit back down before the emotional flash-bangs threw her senses into a complete whiteout. She even heard Jack let out with a muttered "Jesus Christ!" only she wasn't sure if he was taking his Lord's name in vain, calling on Him for help, or maybe some combination of the two. Several seconds lapsed before the air was clear enough to even hope to continue. Ironically, it was Simon that brought the team back to life again.

- "Preach, or any other member of the Pride or the Hounds," Simon called. "Your bio-readings are proverbially and almost literally off the charts. Authenticate and give me an immediate verbal assessment of your status. You have seven seconds to comply before I mobilize two other teams to respond."

- "Simon, this is Chrome: 'seven - x-ray - lima - three - two - niner - fife - whiskey.' I repeat: 'seven - x-ray - lima - three - two - niner - fife - whiskey.' We are in no danger. Repeat, no danger. We just heard some very bad news that happened to a very good person. It hit us all pretty hard, but we're okay."

Chrome then leaned over and whispered to Jack, "Preach, you better do something—Simon almost went nuclear on that one."

Jack gathered his courage along with his breath. Some days were just plain hard, but they were all looking to him to lead them.

"Elaine," Jack finally offered, "if we were to try to infiltrate the circle, how could we do it?"

"Well, that depends. As a john, it's easy: go to a sporting event, a bar, or cruise around at night. Sporting events are huge.

"And don't just go by attire. Not every hooker is being trafficked, although the odds are high that it's either happened or will happen. Look for girls who look new in town, disoriented. Look for nearby guards—they aren't there to protect the girl; they're there to keep her from making a break for freedom. Above all, look for fear—fear of strangers, fear of people they know, fear of whatever security they have out there, fear of their pasts, fear of their present, fear of no future, fear of the future that's likely to be, and fear for a future that will probably never be… a future where they can stay home at night and go to bed just to get some rest.

"Show the creds and look lonely," she said, then added. "Of course, getting in as a girl is the easiest way. Just let yourself get caught—trying to get back out again is somewhere you don't want to be, though, so I wouldn't recommend it. If you're trying to play a hustler, don't try to go it as a local—they're too organized for that and would spot you right away. Play as someone from out of town, maybe trying to move in and set up a new business. You'll need to know some names from the location you're supposed to be from; like I said, they're more organized than you'd think."

"Yeah, so we've learned," Johnny remarked with a pointed look at Josanne. The reference to her brother's involvement hit home; she attempted to shrug it off but failed to completely mask the glare that the hurt and anger had, however briefly, etched on her face.

Jack noticed her expression as well, wishing Johnny hadn't thrown the taunt; he had enough trouble keeping the novice team from fragmenting as it was.

"Would you be willing to provide us with some names to start with?" he offered as a distraction. "Even if we only had a couple names, we could gather a list of players and probably get enough on them to be able to fake it."

"I can give you quite a few johns and hustlers, sure, but my info's quite dated by now."

"Not likely to be a problem, ma'am," Spider offered with a warmly polite smile. "It'll take some time, but we should be able to build a current list from the info you give us."

"Well, okay," she replied, slightly confused. "Although I have no idea how you can pull that off. That would take months of research."

"Well, we have a pretty good research team," Melissana offered, placing a comforting hand on Elaine's arm. "And any lead is a start."

"By the way," Josanne asked, "are there any 'insider' signs, jives, lingo, or postures we should know about—to either help us fit in or at least not to give us away?"

"That depends on the area. Different places will have different, shall we say, 'customs.' Where are you going?"

As a group, both teams looked to Jack to see whether he would answer. It wasn't normal to let anyone know the location of an upcoming run—the potential to tip off the bad guys, even accidentally, made it too risky. Yet time was precious, and Jack also had to know how big a mess the team was getting into. He decided to try something. He cleared his throat and looked at her square in the eyes.

- "Trigget, pay extra attention for any reaction."

"Where are we going?" Jack continued. "We're not exactly sure. But they call it Witch City."

Josanne didn't need to be cued to catch Elaine's reaction; it was plain enough to everyone when she fainted. Sharp raps on the penthouse door a few seconds later interrupted their reviving her.

"Her security team picked up her blood pressure drop on her implant," Araña reported.

"They responded in no time flat," Rickshaw muttered as he headed for the door. "They're good." Then he called to the bodyguards outside, "She's okay, don't kick—" The door withstood the first two kicks of the men outside, but they were an ICC security force protecting the wife of their Director of Research, and their monitors indicated she was in danger. The DoorBuster charge violently blasted the door open, flinging the forty pounds of now misshapen bulged metal into a wobbling, spinning arc that could have decapitated Susan and those behind her if her reflexes weren't wired faster than the door turned clumsy shuriken; she couldn't absorb a full blow from the heavy structure, but by matching the door's rotation speed and using the momentum of the door to provide the propulsion, she diverted its path up and away from causing harm to others. The door's flight ended as it embedded itself into the far wall just above the penthouse window, the resounding crash accompanied by a series of loud bursts and screaming whistles of the Shrieker flashbang explosives the agents had applied before blasting the secure penthouse's entry.

One point five seconds later, Elaine's two bodyguards were through the aperture in a flawlessly executed low/high maneuver. The Hounds had sprung to full alertness. Chrome stepped slightly forward protectively; he would be the most likely to survive the leaden storm of a small-arms attack, so he wanted to draw their fire. The members of the Pride were only slightly less quick in their response. Johnny reflexively drew his weapons; the high man swung his weapon at the slim gunslinger and squeezed the trigger to mow him down with a burst of automatic fire but mysteriously, his gun jammed.

"What the—?" the bodyguard managed to get out before Corey moved forward, his hands raised.

"Just *WAIT!*" Corey bellowed in a panicked shout. Miraculously, everyone froze except for the bodyguard, who had gone high, intently focused on clearing his jammed magazine. The low man held back, apprehensively examining everyone in the room as he covered them. As he scanned the entire group, something he saw clicked in his mind. He peered at Corey for a moment, then Susan. His weapon lowered, only slightly, but his left hand went from cradling the weapon's short barrel to a gloved point at the Pride's wheelman and Susan.

"I remember you!" he exclaimed. "You're those two Cryo-Jaegers from Hagerstown who rescued Martinez from that quarry incident. Jim, this guy was his driver for a while. And you," he added, pointing to Josanne, "you were the one who covered the story." Then, back to Corey, "Wait—are you still with FoodTech?" Confused, he concluded, "I thought you all died."

The ice broken, everybody relaxed as much as they could, given the circumstances. Jim gave up clearing the weapon jam long enough to study Corey, Susan, and Josanne for himself to verify his partner's thoughts. Corey exhaled.

"Yeah, that was us," Corey admitted. "And what you heard wasn't far from the truth. The thing is," he continued with a nod towards Elaine, who was just starting to revive, "we're in deep cover, so we'd like to keep that illusion going."

"We know you'll need to include some of this in your reports," Araña added to enhance the spin, "but don't let it get out."

- "Iylo, intercept their reports when they come in, and purge them of any details or descriptions. If you can, work up some kind of small attaboy recognizing their action. Nothing big enough to warrant anyone to really notice, just let them feel that their discretion is appreciated," he added subvocally.

By that time, Josanne had revived Elaine, who thanked her security team and assured them that everything was all right. She let them know that she was almost ready to leave but also that she wanted time alone with her hosts to wrap things up. Feeling more confident that Elaine was with proven FoodTech security teams and her former bodyguards in deep cover, they acquiesced.

The moment her escort team left for the elevator, a desperate, haunted look etched itself into the features of the normally placid Elaine. Her face pale, she tried to bring a glass of water to her mouth, but her hands started shaking so much that she ended up spilling almost a quarter of the drink onto her dress.

"What is it?" Melissana implored.

Elaine looked up at the former detective, pure pain reflected in her eyes.

"I was there," she said at last, through gasps that threatened to turn to sobs any moment. "I thought I had forgotten. It's one of those things that, you know, you just kind of put out of your mind.

You see, I wasn't originally from North Carolina. I was grabbed from my hometown in Washington. We were just trying to survive day-to-day—we didn't know the I-5 corridor was a huge trafficking conduit."

"Yeah," Melissana nodded at the all too familiar pattern. "Everybody knows it's out there every day, but somehow everybody always thinks it's happening somewhere else."

"The point is, once the girls are picked up, they're all too often transported out of their hometowns to cut them off from family and friends. And if that transport goes far enough, they'll go through Witch City." She shuddered again at the mention of the name. "And Witch City is bad."

"I don't mean to be impolite, Mrs. Martinez," Johnny began, "but we've seen some bad stuff in our day. We're just looking to…."

"You've seen some bad stuff in your day?" Elaine asked, tone and temperament rising. "Boy, I don't mean to be impolite, but I don't think you're hearing what I'm saying!" She visibly struggled to hold her emotions in check and evidently had won by giving up. "You know, there's really no way to explain it to you. Let's just say that if Hell had a dungeon level, it'd be Witch City. There's no imagining the evil that goes on in that place, all under the noses of the civilized society that allows it to flourish!" At that, Elaine's sobbing began in earnest, shoulders heaving as the details of her former captivity broke free from whatever bottle she had imprisoned them.

"Why?" she finally wailed, slumping her head into tightly-gripping hands as she started slipping from the control she had over her emotions. "Funny, isn't it? How you want to know what I know, but you can't imagine, and I don't want to know it at all, and now I'm stuck having to remember?!" She looked up, teary eyes imploring, as though she wanted to ask more; her mouth, reliving long-lost grief freshly remembered, framed some words she was trying to say, but no sound came out. After several seconds, she finally quit trying and just hung her head as her shoulders heaved in tortured sobs she no longer had the will to control.

Melissana and Josanne both glared at Johnny like they were going to kill him, and Johnny, his own shoulders slumped and hands in pockets, looked like he would have welcomed it. Araña contacted the security team and let them know Elaine was still all right, but then looked at Jack and shrugged in resignation.

- *"That's all I got, Preach."*

Preach became keenly aware that that was all any of them had. CYBER training was the best; tactics, operations, team building, leadership. It was all premier training that normally only ICC execs could have afforded had it been offered on the market, but it couldn't cover everything. But Jack was a Christian, a pastor, and had some very definitive experiences in being completely out of his league. He closed his eyes, inwardly sighed, and, letting Elaine literally pour out her grief through her eyes, silently prayed. *Lord, please give me the words. She needs help, they all need my help, and I need Your help. Like Araña, I got nothing, but I know You, and I know You always have everything we need, so please lend me some of that. Thanks.* After that, he felt he could either wait for an answer or trust that God would answer his prayer. After a short while, though, the silence, reinforced by Elaine's crying, had gone on long enough; he had to act.

He slowly knelt on one knee in front of the wife of the Deputy Director of Research at an ICC that was keeping the world fed, to be face to face with her, on her level. She had it all and still needed so much it almost frightened him. He sighed, out loud this time, at the paradox. "Mrs. Martinez?" he began softly, tenderly, hoping his words could pierce through the walls of despair that were trying to surround her like a locked and barred fortress. She looked up at him, saw the deep sorrow in his own eyes as they shared her grief, but still said nothing. Jack sensed her struggle and decided to go on.

"Mrs. Martinez, I am sincerely sorry for both what you have gone through in your past and that we are bringing all of that back.

And words alone are never going to be enough to express that—for any of us," he added, glancing back to Johnny, who slowly nodded his acknowledgment. "But there is a girl out there who's maybe fifteen, living out the very same things that happened to you, and there are other girls like her that we don't know about yet. And they are in Witch City right now, and we're going to do whatever we can to save them. And Elaine? Right now, you're the only one we know who can help us get to her. We're trying to figure out a way to find her and get to her, and the only reason we came to you is that you're the only one we know of who can help us in time." He looked at her, and she felt, even behind his curious eyes, the weight of his sincerity. "So, Mrs. Martinez, can you help us to help her? I know we're asking a lot of you, and you've given so much already, but she is running out of time. I'm really, really sorry I have to be the one to ask, Mrs. Martinez, but she can't ask you herself." He made sure they had eye contact as he concluded.

"Please, Mrs. Martinez… You're her only hope."

Steeling herself against the pain of her memories, she took a deep breath and exhaled forcefully. Drying her eyes and coughing once, she looked at Jack first, then at the others.

"You're right, you know. And after all that all of you have done to set me free from my own past, it would be very selfish of me to even consider refusing." She took another sip of water, leaned back, and contacted her security team. "Everything is all right, even though my biostats have probably fluctuated. I don't like talking about my past, and these people are here to help out with some of my former… involvements. I may be here a while longer, though, so please feel free to relax for a while."

Receiving nods of encouragement from Melissana and Josanne, she leaned slightly forward, squared her shoulders, and glanced around the room to each of them.

"Before I go any further, don't forget to be careful yourselves," Elaine warned. "Where you're going, over half the population are raw street survivors, and over time quite a few of them turn feral;

sometimes we could hear them outside," she shuddered. "I have never seen or felt anything like it since we left." She took another sip of water. "Now, what more would you like to know?"

… …

"I would like to know how the Brownies knew we were coming," the hologram image said as though musing to itself.

"What makes you think they knew? They raid convoys all the time," Sweet Trick Ricky Theodore Showbiz replied, although even as he said the words, he squirmed, as though his body was telling him the truth his mind didn't quite take in yet.

"Oh, they knew. This wasn't some random hit. They were lying in wait, dug in. They slowed and stopped the trucks carrying the cargo—they knew what we were carrying. And don't forget the message they sent afterward. They knew what we were carrying, they knew where we were coming from, they knew where we were going, they knew the route, and they knew when. Somebody tipped them."

"Wasn't nobody on my crew," Ricky T. Showbiz postured. But this time, it wasn't just a show; he didn't have even a hint of doubt. He believed in his crew. They'd banded together to get by ever since the big breakdown hit when they were kids. They drew blood and bled, together. They'd joined and crossed a dozen or so other gangs on their way up, yeah, but they were climbing their way to the top. Witch City was the central oasis of all North American skin biz, and Sweet Trick Ricky Theodore Showbiz and his crew owned the skin biz in Witch City. Now they got their cut of almost every trader that passed through. He let his thoughts drift, musing over their success. It was a hard-fought climb, but he and his crew had each other's backs all the way up. If the Brownies were tipped, there was no way it was one of his.

But then he stopped as a new thought crossed his mind. That suit's operation, now that was something relatively new to him. A voice on the phone, the occasional order of a couple girls… And who knew what they were doin' with them? Whatever it was, they never came back. Not like he cared, of course—the suit certainly paid well, and the creds were always good—but he never really heard whatever happened to any of 'em. Ricky T. Showbiz mentally shrugged. He could deal with the suit having a dark-perp streak himself, as long as the creds rolled in. Still…

"How 'bout you, Suit-man?" Sweet Trick finally voiced. "Got any wires on your side? Gotta admit, if my chummers talk, it'll be them takin' the dirt nap. Your choobs, not so much."

The holographic image almost rolled its eyes as it sighed its disappointment. "I can assure you, Mr. Ricky T. Showbiz, it is no one in my organization. If it had been one of mine, I would have already known about it."

"So you say, Mr. Suit."

"So I *know*, Mr. Showbiz. May I remind you that, while you are a self-hailed 'king' in your Witch City, comparatively speaking, you are still only the biggest fish in a somewhat limited pond.

"But I digress. I know it was no one in my organization, and you are just as convinced it was no one in yours. Presuming we are both correct, that leaves only one other option. Somehow, someone outside both of our organizations became aware of that particular shipment. Who could that have been? And before you even start to suggest such a thing, no one on my team has talked; to do so would be… unprofessional. Nor am I suggesting, for the moment, that one of your team did. But the convoys do leave from your location. Was there anyone who could have known about that convoy?"

"Just the choobs who charge and prep the trucks and escorts. But I don't think they'd sell us out."

"Oh? You bet quite a bit of stock on the loyalty of your people."

"Nah," Ricky T. Showbiz replied, flashing a diamond-toothed grin. "Ain't nothin' like that!" He let himself laugh at that one, then locked his eyes on the hologram in utter seriousness. "It's all about the fear. They wouldn't snitch me 'cause they know better."

Something about his laughter stirred a memory. The last time he had laughed like that—"Hey, hold on one minute…." He cocked his head to reflect on the memory.

"What is it, Mr. Showbiz?" The time was slipping by, but it seemed to the hologram man that this glorified pimp might actually have an idea.

"There was Shimmer. She ran on the night of the convoy."

"It wasn't her," the hologram disagreed.

"Why not?" Showbiz asked, perplexed.

"If the girl knew she was going to be rescued, don't you think she would have made sure she was on that rig?"

"Yeah, I guess you're right. But maybe she said something to someone."

"You said she was only gone for a few hours. Do you actually think she made a random contact with one of the Brownies in the brief time she was out?" The hologram made a show of checking the time, then reconsidered his position. "Still, we have few other leads to go on. Maybe she somehow did contact someone. Question her. But try to be gentle on the poor lamb. We may want to speak with her ourselves. And if we do, we will want both her body and her mind in working order."

14. The Plan

One of the best things Corey "Hardcore" Martin loved about CYBER was the fruit. It was always somehow there whenever they had a meeting, and each time he ventured to try one, he found the very real taste too good to imagine. They had lived on algae substitute foods for so long that it took him a little while to believe something could be that flavorful without some lab doctoring it in some way. Even as he considered that, though, he knew CYBER vehemently avoided doctoring food plants here; they wouldn't risk a second blight.

He also had a great sense of pride in being part of a group that brought down the Bad Guys that no one else could—or would. CYBER was unique in its reach. International Corporate Conglomerates, or ICC's, were more powerful than the struggling governments that remained. Who would stand against an ICC when one of *them* got out of control? Who fought for the little guy in the small towns, guys like his father, whom he buried before spending weeks rebuilding his Dad's Sabretooth? His eyes flashed, and his lips parted in an involuntary grin. *He* did. The proud grin softened to a smile of gratitude. Sometimes CYBER saw to threats like the Steel Jackals and Valhalla's Brownies, too. After all, that was how he and Susan had first gotten acquainted with the covert government agency. The second best thing about CYBER was the *ridiculous* tech. He silently chuckled at how Blaze's Fist had introduced themselves in that first meeting. His forearm suddenly itched as he recalled Fuser rolling up his sleeves and electronically opening and exposing various compartments and devices in his arms like an aircraft checking flight controls before takeoff. The young CYBER gadgeteer had appeared so casual about the whole thing! And who would have ever thought the technology would exist for him to have a direct neuro-link to his Sabretooth, let alone having a miniaturized fusion reactor enough as the car's power source? The only word he had to describe it all was just plain ridiculous.

But the best thing of all about CYBER was the bond of camaraderie between them all, despite their differences. Chrome was the typically dour walking tank that had been part of Preach's former team, and Johnny had been as distant as they came when CYBER had first recruited him into Preach's new team, the Pride. Not everybody was like them, though. Spider's ready smile and friendly demeanor always made him feel welcome, and Iylothien was a boyish swashbuckler. Of course, he could hardly think of Iylo without thinking about Melissana, the outwardly tough street detective who had a surprisingly tender heart. The way she always perked up in any team meeting where he appeared on the screen spoke volumes of their relationship, even though her only connection possible with the young hacker was via the environmental modules they used to simulate data networks in virtual reality.

Just as puzzling to him was her real-world connection to Josanne Sinclair—or Trigget as they called her when they were on a mission. The two came from opposite sides of the tracks—Josanne was a wealthy heiress who had taken to journalism after her brother ousted her from the corporate scene. Josanne's ground-breaking interview with Elaine Martinez had propelled her to a media personage only a few weeks before CYBER had recruited them all. The only other thing he knew about her was that she was hard to get to know. Josanne and Melissana evidently had somehow connected in Roanoke and had become best friends over time. Exactly how, he could not imagine. He inwardly chuckled; after considering Melissana's kinship with Josanne in the real world, it wasn't hard to imagine the virtual romance she had with Iylothien. And thinking of their relationship, as impossible as it was, brought him full circle to the gratefulness he felt for his own with Susan Blakeslee.

Also known as Lady Blackwolf, she was the close combat specialist of Preach's Pride. They had met as they were forced to flee a biker horde that had destroyed their home towns, but over the course of time, had fallen hard for each other. The young couple had drawn the attention of CYBER and now were even more inseparable than they had ever been.

Lastly, of course, there was his own mentor, Rickshaw. Always good-naturedly affable when not running a mission, when he operated as the Hounds' wheelman, his normally congenial nature turned to a stony professionalism that both impressed and chilled the young Sabretooth driver to an equal degree. Over all of the others, Corey felt honored that Rickshaw had accepted Corey as a valuable member of the team and hoped he would someday be just like the veteran driver.

Even as he thought this, though, he remembered working on the Sabretooth with his Dad:

"Son," his father had instructed, "the car and the gear are nice, but never forget it's the reason for the car that's important. Protecting people is the 'why' behind all of this." Corey had agreed at the time, but that was before Iron Mike and the Steel Jackals massacred his hometown, wiping out his entire family in the process, before he and Susan had taken on the Road Ragers in the quarry shakedown, before the Matsua run, and before he knew that Elaine Martinez, the very gracious wife of a friend of his, had been sold to sex traffickers at the age of four years old.

"Dad, protecting people might be the why," he thought to himself, "but saving lives isn't quite what I have in mind right now. Because, if me and my team are going to help save lives, we're going to have to put some people down." As if on cue, the other team members gathered to finalize the strategy for rescuing Kelly and any other girls they could find from the living hell of Witch City.

… …

"OK, so how are we going to do this?" asked Jack as he entered the room and set the meeting into motion.

"Well, we still have a number of things to find out," Melissana began. "We know Witch City is an area in Wichita, but we have no idea where, and it'll take time to find out."

"Good point, Mel. Iylo, why don't you bring up a map of Wichita? And we'll build up a whiteboard." The high-level map took up a spot center left of the conference room wall screen gone blank except for an outline map of North America and its component territories.

"Then there's that Sitter guy," Rickshaw continued; Iylothien obliged with a question mark, bottom right.

"And Valhalla's Brownies," Josanne offered. "Somehow, they fit into all of this." The Valhalla Brownie logo appeared left and slightly above Wichita.

"As does James Sinclair, don't forget." Jack winced—the remark came from Johnny, who was taunting Josanne again. Iylothien replied with an "All right, already," but posted the picture of Josanne's brother to the far right over Massachusetts. Most of the team leaned in to study their nemesis; some subconsciously took second glances at Josanne and nodded at the resemblance.

Furrowing her brow, Melissana added, "Back up a sec—*is* Sitter a guy? I don't think we have evidence of that, and the connection to the Brownies might indicate otherwise."

Jack nodded. "I studied the satellite interceptions long enough when I decided to find him. The pronouns they used were 'his' and 'him.' Sitter's male."

"We got the Den, too." Chrome stated; with that, Iylothien placed a map of Denver onto the whiteboard, further left and again above the icon for Valhalla's Brownies.

"What about Kelly's parents?" Araña asked. In response, a photo of a middle-aged couple appeared, anchored in Texas just northwest of the Lubric border.

"That's quite a list of pieces to this puzzle," Corey lamented.

"And in the center of it all," Jack concluded, "is Kelly." The photo of a thirteen-year-old girl, sent in one of Ryan Elverson's emails, took the center spot and expanded to a life-sized image.

"I wish the General was here right now," Susan muttered to herself, referring to the young member of Blaze's Fist who had come up with their first mission's plan to raid a corporate archology.

- *"Trust your leader, Blackwolf." Araña, who had heard the remark with his heightened hearing, encouraged. "Remember what I told you. Jack shines in situations like these."*

Absorbed in trying to take in all the facets to the problem, it was several minutes before anyone spoke again.

… …

The quiet lingered for several minutes, as though the constantly settling dust seen in the slivers of light that filtered through the cracks of the factory walls absorbed any sound. But as the late October sun began its retreat behind the Wichita skyline, several sniffles of choked back tears arose from somewhere in the group of huddled bodies. Sitter sighed as he noted their ramshackle clothing, cheap footwear that could barely pass for sandals, and helpless stares.

"Twelve of them—a whole new batch. Where'd you find 'em, Nick?" he finally asked after he completed his survey of the unkempt youths.

"Kung spotted 'em. While he was scavenging near Corpland, he heard a large door clang and seal shut. Made his way over to Egress 19 just in time to see a couple dogs show up from the alley for a feeding time."

"Glassed one of 'em with my spear before they knew I was there!" Kung, who had been one of Nick's scavenging party for the night, triumphantly declared. "Got the other one when it sprang for one of the newbloods."

"Yeah, you did," Nick approved. The youngster basked in the senior boy's affirmation. "The kids panicked and started to scatter when I arrived," Nick resumed his narrative. "If the others hadn't surrounded 'em, they would've lit, and we'd never been able to find 'em all."

Sitter circled the group in his chair, noting that some assumed protection for their little group by how they kept themselves between him and the others while some huddled helplessly in the center of the circle. He probed them a little further, testing their resolve, their temperament, their discipline, and a host of other measures in his psychological tug of war. "Not a bad batch, all in all," he surmised.

"Good work, Nick—All of you," Sitter proclaimed to his self-styled gang of impoverished youths. They had all done well, but Sitter was proud of Nick's making sure everyone received credit for the evening's work. He couldn't keep from smiling, despite the night's turn of events. Then he quickly spun his chair to face the group of newcomers as he had done many times in the past.

"Hello," he began simply, calmly, in as friendly a manner as he could manage. By now, he had almost enough practice greeting new members into his fold to perfect his technique. "I know you're confused, scared, cold, hungry, and feeling just about every kind of misery. You miss your parents, you're wondering what you're doing here, and how you messed up so bad that you ended up here." He noted more than a few nods subconsciously offered as the different boys had their rawest emotions of the moment identified. Sitter continued. "And I know that some of you feel threatened by Nick, Kung, the others, and even myself," he added, catching more nods.

"The simple fact is, you're all new to the streets of what they call Witch City, and those dogs you ran into in your first ten minutes of getting here are the least of your worries. The slightly more complicated fact is that we didn't capture you; we rescued you." He paused for effect and then added, "We know what you're going through; all the boys here went through the same thing you just did. We don't expect you to trust us for a while yet, but if you let us help you, you might survive.

"For starters, let's all get something to eat."

"What are we having?" one of the newcomers asked.

Sitter rotated his chair to make sure the youth saw the seriousness in his face.

"Let this be your first lesson," he replied. "This is Witch City. You eat whatever tries to eat you." Then he turned away from them, trying to portray confidence instead of the guilt and sadness he felt at having to teach such a gruesome lesson to kids who just got here. "Tonight, we celebrate. We're cooking our meat!" he added before anyone else could break in. "Kung, they're your trophies. You get to light the fire."

He moved a joystick forward and rolled away, hoping to appear jubilant and very pleased with himself, but Saint Nick knew his mentor wondered where he could come up with a sustainable way to provide enough food for all of them with the additional dozen newcomers. He hoped the noobs would get their heads together early enough to be able to help.

…… ……

"I hope we get our heads together early enough to be able to help," Susan whispered to Corey. "There's just too many different pieces for us to put it all together."

"Put it all together?" Corey asked in a hushed reply. "I just hope those different pieces won't pull us all apart."

"What'd you just say?" asked Jack, turning to focus on his wheelman. Corey suddenly felt like he was back in grade school and his teacher just caught him passing a note. Jack had been extremely focused and just a little off baseline. Maybe Johnny might have been lucky enough to have gotten away with the comment, but Corey was afraid he might have pushed his own luck too far.

"You heard that?" Josanne asked her team leader. "I know your specs—I can see Araña hearing flies in the next room, but how did you—?"

"Later, Josanne, I promise. Not now. What was it you said, Corey?"

"Well, Susan said we can't put all this together, and, well, we've been having some team conflicts over this. So, I told her I hoped it doesn't pull us all apart."

Jack examined the whiteboard map once again, pointing first at this map, then at that photo, then staring, apparently at some blank patch of white that yet remained on the board. Crossing his arms, he withdrew into himself so far it appeared he had forgotten they were all there. Rickshaw and Araña looked at each other and nodded. Chrome expectantly grinned. Grey's Hounds had evidently seen this behavior in their former leader before. He continued for another minute or so, then spent another two minutes with his eyes squeezed tight, lips barely moving in what the Pride concluded was either some method of channeling Simon or intense silent prayer.

He finally came out of his trance and smiled, then looked around the room at each of them as though to see if they were all still there. "I think I have a way," he announced to them all. "Thank you, Corey, I think I have a way."

"As to how I heard Corey," he said to Josanne as if the last several minutes hadn't occurred at all, "I didn't." Jack continued with a smile, "But with more of my systems back online, I can lip-read someone across the street and down the block if I need to."

"Good to know," Josanne thought to herself, being very careful not to so much as twitch her jaw muscles.

III. INTO THE RABBIT HOLE

"When the going gets tough, the tough get professional."

— Lorie Manix, *to the first responders, 5/5/2017*

"I'm telling you, that's the most difficult color to maintain! Everything's attracted to it—mustard, ink, lead…."

— Robin Spisak, *on wearing white, 5/10/2017*

15. A Parent Issue

The people began their exit from the pristine sanctuary, shaking hands with the 60-something-year-old black-clad speaker as they stepped out of the alcove into the Dallas, Texas sun. Josanne remained seated until the small crowd had filtered out. Then she finally stood, glancing around with a puzzled expression on her face portraying that she was new in town, or new to the faith, or just plain new. The speaker noticed her; she knew and recognized the instant flicker of hope that was quickly extinguished, as though he was hoping she was someone else he had been waiting to see for a long, long time.

An usher approached as the crowd continued to thin, and it was time. "Excuse me?" she asked, drawl as thick as the honey she was trying to spread. "Why, I do believe that was a wonderful sermon! Ah'm new to this city, but ah am so glad I came! I have some questions for your pastor, might ah ask you about one or two of the finer points, maybe in private?"

"Well, young lady, may I be the first to say, 'Welcome to Dallas.' I am delighted you took such interest in the message today. Let me find my wife, and I'd be delighted to talk a bit."

"Honey? We have a visitor today!" he called to an adjacent room. Approaching footsteps told the young lady that his wife was on her way.

"Why, who do we have—here?" A woman just beyond middle-aged asked. The visitor was quick to note the same intensity of hopeful near-recognition and shattered aspiration. Then the courteous smile came back into play. "I'm sorry, miss, for a moment, you reminded me of someone else."

The visitor returned with a smile of her own as she replied, "Oh, that's okay. That happens an awful lot in the places ah go."

"She has some questions about the message today. I thought we might get her a coke or a water. My name's Roy Elverson, and this is my wife, Alicia. What was your name, miss?" Roy asked.

"Oh, most folks just know me as Miss Trigget," she replied with a glance to the ushers and others still lingering in the building. "Mah ride is waiting for me outside—ah believe you're expecting us?"

Roy Elverson was visibly shaken by her announcement. Josanne could see the immediate tension in the man's demeanor as he portrayed his internal conflicts through a series of outward micro-expressions. His wife, Grace Elverson, had reacted as well but quite oppositely of her husband. Her quizzical expression disappeared, replaced by a relaxed smile combined with an instant excitement; it was like Josanne had just revealed she had the cure to a terminal disease Roy's wife was suffering from. Of course, she thought to herself, Jack seemed to have that effect on people. It was as though he was a vaccine of hope for just about everyone he came into contact with. She briefly wondered why he didn't have that effect on her but almost immediately rejected the notion. She figured her conversationalist training heightened her journalistic skills to make her a geometer of conversation; because she knew all the lines and angles, they wouldn't work on her.

She walked the couple to the vehicle where Jack sat and waited; he got out as they approached. Roy Elverson put on a southern smile as he stuck out his right hand in greeting, but Josanne noticed he stiffly buried his left hand ever deeper into his pocket as he did so. The conversationalist read shock, fear, guilt, shame—and under it all, threatened to be extinguished by all the other emotions—a slight flicker of hope. Mrs. Elverson excitedly almost ran up to Jack, hesitated as she glanced at her husband, then openly rushed him with a heartfelt hug, almost collapsing into his arms as tears trickled down her face.

"You came back!" she exclaimed as she hung on him. "Thank you, God, thank you!" She paused for breath, then looked at him through very wet eyes and summed up her emotions. "I wasn't sure you would come," she said. "But you came back! Thank you, Jack! Thank you!"

Eventually, Roy approached the couple. Still grasping for words, he eventually turned, facing eastward and casually scanning the distance.

"Ya know, the western border of Lubric extended out past Longview to the Terell Outpost," he began, not quite knowing what else to say. "Border tensions between Texas and Lubric are still pretty touchy at times, but things quieted down some after Lubric's initial expansion. They'd've taken Dallas, too, but you know them Fort Worth boys. They wouldn't let 'em have it. We got the wall now between Lubric and Dallas with about ten miles of no man's land in between, but commerce is opening us up a little…." He cleared his throat in preparation for the real conversation. "So, you've been waiting outside all this time?"

"I waited outside so you wouldn't be distracted during service and also so the others wouldn't notice my return. We could've waited at your house, but I didn't want to make anyone too uncomfortable." Jack noted that both Elverson and Josanne seemed caught off guard by his sensitivity.

"Dang it all, Jack," he outburst, no longer able to maintain his stoic cool. "I'm sorry. We thought we were upholding truth, but we acted out of fear. Fear of what others might think if they found out, rather than what God already thought. We hurt you and our congregation when we—scratch that; *I* hurt you and our congregation when I—asked you to leave. I heard it said you can break every commandment in the Bible except Galatians 6 verse 7: 'Whatever a man sows, he will also reap.'

"And I have reaped!" he released, breaking down in an anguish he could no longer control. "So, I beg you, Jack, please forgive me, and maybe God will lift this curse I have put myself and all of us under!"

"Roy," Jack softly replied, laying a hand on the man's shoulder after a slight hesitation, "the Bible also says, 'All have sinned and come short of the glory of God.' That 'all' includes me. What you did hurt—a lot—and I have to confess I'm still working through some of it. But I've got nothing against you that Jesus hasn't already paid for. Roy, I chose to forgive you before I came back here; it's already done.

"This is Josanne," he said, both to introduce her and to move the conversation along. "She's one of the people on my team who are going to get Kelly back. But we need your help. You need to fill us in. What happened here?"

"That's going to take a while," Roy responded, once again looking to the ground as though asking the dry Texas dirt to forgive him. Alicia knew the posture all too well and instinctively lifted her hand onto his shoulder to console him, seeking solace for herself as well as for him; she couldn't comfort her lost daughter, but it somehow seemed to help her when she could comfort her husband. "C'mon," Roy said as he turned to his vehicle. "The Sun's gonna scorch us if we stay out here. Let's head back to the house. We can talk in the cool."

…… ……

"So, Roy? What happened, and when?" Jack began once they were all seated in the Elverson's living room.

He and Alicia sat closely together, absently wringing intertwined hands. Josanne wondered how many hours or days this couple had sat together just like they were doing here, doing nothing but waiting to hear from their missing little girl.

"I guess it all started soon after you left. Kelly was upset that you'd gone. We knew she would be, of course, but we had no idea how much." He took a sip of his drink, but seeing an angry intensity of Jack's stare as the former pastor set his drink down way too deliberately, he quickly continued. "When she found out I was the main driver behind your removal, well, I lost connection with her. And because she grew more distant, Alicia and I didn't notice when Kelly had made a new girlfriend." He sighed.

"Eventually, that friend introduced Kelly to a guy. Kelly grew even more distant, isolated. We were trying to give her some space, but that guy used all of our love against us, poisoning her into thinking we didn't care about her. Eventually, the guy groomed her—set her up."

"She told us one night that she was going over to her friend's house for a sleepover," Mrs. Elverson picked up the story. "I said, 'Kelly, I don't want you staying at that new friend's house,' and she just laughed at me and said, 'Well, that's all right, Momma, I ain't stayin' with her.' I thought then that maybe she was staying over at a different friend's house…." And that was where Alicia's voice gave out, and she gave in to a bout of weeping.

"The fact is, Roy resumed, "she went to stay with him, and that was the last we saw of her."

"We tried everything we could," Alicia resumed. "We even tracked down Kelly's new friend."

"What happened then?" Josanne asked, sensing and trying to interrupt Jack's rising anger.

"Her parents were getting ready to find us," Roy concluded. "Their girl went missing the same night Kelly did. We found out a week later the girls were loaded into a vehicle that was last seen leaving town on I-35 Northbound."

"So, if you wouldn't have fired me, Kelly would be okay?" Jack accused, standing up and beginning to pace. "God knows what a struggle it already was for me to come out here, and now *this*?"

Josanne had never seen Jack so enraged before. She was suddenly concerned he would start beating on Elverson.

Elverson broke down, weeping, acknowledging that was all true, and began literally begging Jack for forgiveness, for Kelly's sake. Josanne saw it wasn't fear that had incapacitated the man but guilt—he didn't even flinch when Jack raised his hand to strike the failed board member away from him. The CYBER team leader managed to check his swing with visible effort, lowering his arm as he slumped back into the couch. Josanne watched the drama and realized there was more to Jack's background than she had ever given him credit for—especially when Jack, still struggling, again forgave Elverson and promised to do his best to bring Kelly home.

Josanne was released from having to stay, but they all felt it. With true repentance on Roy's part, true hope on Alicia's part, and true forgiveness on Jack's part, the three of them decided the best thing they could do for Kelly was to pray for her, together, in unity for the first time since before the tragedy began. While they all asked that God would protect Kelly, Jack had an additional request: to find the girl but also to bring everyone involved to a justice that was certain and true.

…… ……

Elverson gave Jack and Josanne a ride to the friend's parents the next day. He introduced the pair as special investigators he recruited for help. Both girls had disappeared two years earlier, but maybe the parents might know or remember something useful. They all knew time was against them, so they had no time not to be thorough.

In time, Jack and Josanne—now fully in Preach and Trigget mode—were able to work together to interview enough people in the chain of events to find out the name of the local pimp who sold the girls online to some suit in Connecticut. The pimp didn't know who the buyer was, but the suit had money, so he put the girls on a truck headed northbound. The last thing the flesh peddler said before getting his jaw broken and hauled somewhere out of town was that some guy called Kanker vouched that the credits were good, so what did he care where they came from?

16. Two for the Road

THE OSPREY VII lifted off the rocky Arizona mesa, the VTOL craft's launch blasting out a horizontal hailstorm of small rocks and sand. Two figures remained in the wake of the mini sandstorm and awaited one more mission clearance after the final pass of the transport plane verified that they were safe for the immediate moment. Rumor had it there was significant bike gang activity in the area; they were there to verify those rumors.

"Okay, gentlemen," the Osprey pilot hailed, *"you're clear and on your own from here. Good luck."*

"Roger that. Thanks for the ride."

They finished suiting up and mounted their own motorcycles— the smaller mounted his Yashuba-made Desert Knight, the other his Morrison-Hayley Highwayman—and began their 35-mile ride southwest to Highway 19, where they would turn south for the next 200 miles on their trek. They stopped 25 miles out from their destination when they spotted low clouds of smoke that wafted up from a smallish fortress town ahead of them. Each nodded his awareness to the other. They were prepared for battle; after wordlessly confirming their mutual assent to continue, they rode on.

After riding another 20 miles, they caught the eye-searing flash of the Sun reflecting off a shiny surface above and ahead of them. Two seconds later, a small piece of the rocky surface just ahead of them chipped with a loud *crack* and spiraled away from their line of sight. After another three seconds, a pair of red dots appeared on each of their riding jackets that, once applied, managed to stay unerringly on target despite the riders' attempts to shake them off. The duo swerved their bikes into a roadside ditch away from the snipers and dismounted to assess the threat. The snipers occasionally fired shots here and there, keeping them pinned until the two heard the shooters' recon team approach behind them.

"OK, you two. Just raise your hands, and keep 'em up." a voice calmly, almost politely, instructed them from behind. He wasn't yelling, not shaky, not struggling for the control he already knew he had over the dismounted cyclists.

The pair turned to see they were at the center point of a concave arc of about a dozen bikers, each one armed to the teeth. In the center of them all, a forty-something tall man with grey-black hair and about two weeks of unshaved growth some might mistake for a beard commanded them again. The arms of his armored leather jacket would have creaked as he adjusted his weapon if it hadn't been so road-worn.

"I ain't gonna tell ya again, up with the hands," he ordered in the matter-of-fact manner of someone casually asking them to pass the algae salad at dinner. Both men complied.

"Now that's better," he drawled. "You two look like you're pretty geared up. Mind my asking what you're doing here?"

"We're looking for the Paladins," the leaner of the two men replied.

The "sna-katch" sounds of bolts slamming forward with loaded rounds accompanied the distinctive snap-clicks of safeties disengaged. "Well, you found us," the team alpha replied as he flipped the lapel of his motorcycle jacket to display the white Templar-style cross on a blood-red field. "Now, who are you, and why are you lookin'?"

The larger rider sighed, looked down to the ground, and slowly shook his head in resignation.

"We're looking for Small Eddie," the other man said. "He still ride your colors?"

"Small Eddie? You expect us to just up and take you to him? He's a much sought-after man. A lot of people would love to have the bounty he's got on his head. So, I can figure why you'd might want to see him. Question is, why would Eddie want to see you?"

"Ask him yourself," the bulkier man replied, growing tired of the delay. "Tell him that where most people see things in black and white, the Hounds work with Greyscale."

After a brief radio confirmation involving Small Eddie quite audibly expressing his enthusiasm, the leader of the recon team asked, "Well, he sure seems happy to hear from you. He wants to know who all is here."

"Just Spider and Chrome," Araña responded. "The others are busy elsewhere."

"Well, a pleasure to meet you," the man said, lowering his weapon. He broke into a grin as friendly as he had been serious. "I'm Luke," he greeted as he shook both their hands. "Eddie's sure excited to hear from you! C'mon, let's get you an escort into town."

Eventually, they arrived at what they had originally appeared as a mini fortress town. As they drew closer, it turned out to be just a small village with a wall around it. Wrecks and smoking buildings radiated the heat they collected from the Arizona sun; brokenness and ruin revealed a battle had been fought and only recently completed. It was too hard to tell if anyone had won yet or if there was just a lull in the combat.

Small groups went about assigned tasks. Some moved slowly, evidence to the newcomers that many of the survivors were still processing the intense shock of their first real firefight. Others moved with the mechanized deliberateness of hard-won experience. All about the small town, people were repairing walls, towing or scrapping vehicles, tending to needs here and there so they could be ready for the next round, whenever that might be. However novice or experienced, each person worked with the growing awareness that if they didn't do the sometimes gruesome chores now, they wouldn't be ready when the next attack came. A man who stood about five-foot-six was at the center of it all, coordinating, prioritizing, directing, and most of all, encouraging them all to continue. As the formation of bikes approached, he left all that behind to greet the new arrivals, breaking into a genial smile as he saw the two men.

"Hey—*Heyy*! Chrome! Araña!" he broke out into an even bigger grin as he approached to swap hugs with the two newcomers. He paused for effect as he neared the bulky crew-cut cyborg that was almost a full nine inches taller than him, then with abandon exclaimed, "Aw, c'mon, ya big guy, I won't hurt ya!" and lunged forward to finish his greeting. His mood was infectious—even Chrome smiled and allowed himself a brief laugh.

"Small Eddie," Chrome greeted in turn. "How are you guys holdin' up?"

"We're doing okay," he said, a little more distantly, glancing around the smoking reminders of the recent battle.

"So, what's happening?" Araña asked, noting the activities. "Seems you guys have a situation here. Everything okay?"

"Yeah, they'll be all right," the biker leader off-handedly spat, punctuating the statement. "We were ridin' through when we noticed this small town here. The village folk were tryin' to get by. We decided to set up and try to help 'em out: dig for water, help 'em with some of their building projects, that sort of thing. We were also holding some church meetings, the kind they used to do back when they had short-term mission trips—except now they're needed pretty much everywhere we go. Turns out, they'd been coming under attack by some group of whack jobs who smelled easy pickin's. We were all holdin' meetin' when the raiders returned.

"Y'know," he added with a far-off look in his eyes and a displaced, taut-jawed frown, "I really would rather turn the other cheek, and I tried to warn 'em... But sometimes these types don't leave you no choice," he concluded. "No choice at all." He paused a moment to recover himself. "But there ain't no law out here; nobody else was goin' to protect these people, and from the way we saw things, they wouldn't last if we didn't do somethin', and these people had nowhere to run to.

"So, the Paladins did what we had to do like we always do," he concluded with a sadness combined with just a touch of pride in his family. "I mean, we certainly don't look for trouble, but in this day and age, somebody's gotta protect the oppressed."

Chrome nodded his approval. The Paladins weren't weak-kneed types who hid behind church doors to keep the reality of the world outside. They had begun as a group of born-again bikers that, in their early days, used to ride together for fun. After the country went to pot, they stayed together. They initially banded together for mutual support in an effort to help spread the word that even in this day, Jesus still cared. They quickly developed a reputation for lending assistance wherever they could. Over time, they found themselves needing to defend more and more who were being ravaged by others who didn't share their moral outlook on life. Now with several chapters, some over three hundred strong, the Paladins committed themselves to the reality of carrying the cross to the lost—which was just about everyone, Chrome thought as he too surveyed the village. In a way, they reminded him of Jack; he smiled at the thought.

"So, tell me something," Small Eddie mused. "I haven't seen you two since you guys helped us out in the Scottsdale incident. What have you all been up to—and where are Jack and the others? Everyone okay, I hope??"

"Well, that's why we're here," Chrome responded. "We need your help."

17. Puppet Practice and Fishing Trips

"I'm just saying, Corey absolutely hates this idea," Susan muttered more to herself than to either Johnny or Melissana. The fact that she also hated it had been an argument she had already lost. "Besides, I look ridiculous. Who would ever go out dressed like this?"

"Fifteen-year-olds who are forced to," Melissana reminded. "When you're doing this, you can't think about yourself; you have to think of them. This is optional for us—we're doing it to help them. And without us getting involved, they have no way out."

"Aw, come on," Johnny interrupted, "I mean, I know it's happening with Kelly—and whoever is running this operation…."

"Josanne's brother," Susan bitterly interrupted.

"We know he might be involved somehow," Melissana defended, "but he's not the one holding the girls in Wichita. Even if he's in the food chain somewhere, maybe he doesn't know how bad things are for them."

"Yeah," Johnny mocked, "and maybe all we need to do is call him, and he'll say, 'Oh gee, I'll just let all the girls go and give each one a couple million creds to show them how sorry I am.' Because he's such a nice guy that when we were being recruited, he put out a contract on his own sister." He smirked at his own cleverness, then stopped, the smile on his mouth transferring itself up to become a furrow on his brow. "Drek, no," he said to himself, so lost in thought that Melissana wondered if he knew he said it out loud.

"What is it?" she asked. "And skip the argument that it was nothing."

"I just had a thought. It's not like CYBER recruited any of us using traditional means," Johnny began. "What if Trigget's right and her brother's not involved?" He looked at her with rising suspicion. "What if SIMON made up the story about the contract, just to pull us in?"

"Do you think—?" Susan asked.

"No. I'm not buying it." Melissana cut in. "Iylo was the one who told me about it; he and SIMON were monitoring James for a while. Iylo would've told me by now if it was a hoax."

"If he knew," Johnny persisted. "Iylothien's sharp, but SIMON's an AI. Maybe it planted the data for Iylothien to stumble across. For that matter…" he paused again, considering a new thought. *Johnny respected Iylo…*

"What is it now?" Susan asked. "And if we're going to continue this conversation, can I please get out of this—*costume*—and into regular clothes?"

"You're right, Susan," Johnny said, grateful enough for the interruption that he'd say anything just to drop the conversation. He knew if he'd have said another word, he could have damaged their relationships beyond repair. "Okay, girls, let's practice the walk again."

From what he gathered, Preach came back to CYBER after being reunited with his once-lost protégé, Iylothien. Melissana was won over to CYBER after Iylothien melted his way into her heart online. Josanne was brought into CYBER largely because SIMON and Iylothien produced documentation and clips "proving" her brother had put a contract out on her. Corey and Susan, he remembered, had gotten emotionally involved with CYBER because of trying to save Josanne from that same threat. And each of them, including Johnny, had been moved by the revelation that the free-spirited wire-runner was actually physically imprisoned within his own body, completely incapacitated except for the direct neural network connections SIMON had worked out to save the young man after he had gone comatose. *Johnny respected Iylo…*

Did he? Did he really respect Iylothien, or was he just being fooled? The questions crept within the suspicions of his mind and started to itch.

He sat down heavily and asked for a break, chilled by the thought that was thickening from the tenuous vapor of apprehension into a solid wall of doubt. SIMON was an AI, after all, and who could tell what was going on inside that thing? Did Johnny really respect Iylothien, or was it possible that, just maybe, he had been conned? In their meetings, SIMON projected itself as the sharply dressed, suave yet paternal fifty-something man in his grand office with the two United States flags. Granted, it was possible that maybe SIMON didn't fabricate the evidence for Iylothien to find. But maybe SIMON fabricated something else, something deeper. And even more sinister.

Maybe SIMON fabricated Iylothien...

... ...

"Where are we heading tonight?" she asked. They would have to travel on foot once they got close, but if she had an idea of where they were going, she could open a portal and teleport them to somewhere closer.

"Well, now that we know where Witch City is, I thought we'd take a stroll through to scout out the area. Maybe we can find a lead that we can trace back to a different location, scout out that area, and get you enough local intel that you could all reasonably impersonate someone from that area."

"Hey, that's pretty smart!" she exclaimed in approval.

"I am the smartest," he replied with his warm, friendly, and admittedly to Melissana, totally cute smile. "So, my dear Queen, care to open the gate?"

"With pleasure, m'lord," she said with a smile that was all too genuine. Queen Vixenn had come a long way in a very short time. She launched Chrysallis, her new daemon program, to watch their backs. Her former daemon, Dog, was modified to focus more on sniffing out system back doors and passwords. She extended her arms high over her head, palms outward, and gracefully extended out and down, opening a portal that would connect her to the local traffic node for the region. As she was doing so, Iylothien, Barde de la Nêone, summoned his locust, which now was long enough to seat two. Together they would ride the net in Randolph and Emerson's Ultimate Fantasy, the environmental module invented by Iylothien and Simon. Once again, they would be spending hours working together, finding and hacking bad guys for the data they would need to bring them down. It was fun, it was justified, it was usually successful, and it was the two of them, linked mind to mind, together. For her, it was Heaven.

Even in The World, her face wore a delighted grin.

... ...

"Hey, baby, like what you're lookin' at?" Melissana crooned after their training resumed the next morning. "It can be yours, y'know. C'mon, why don't you try some?"

"Almost perfect, Melissana," Johnny approved. "Except for the 'it can be yours' and not 'I can be yours.'"

"I did that on purpose," Melissana countered. "The guys we're dealing with don't want the baggage associated with having the actual girl to take care of, just the fantasy that she really wants to have him. Trust me—I've seen it enough back home. I just didn't know about what was really going on."

"All right, I guess," Johnny relented. Turning to Susan, he said, "And what about you?"

"What about me?" Susan returned.

"You don't really look like you're trying very hard."

"Well, I'm sorry I'm not as good at this as Melissana—I've never done this before!"

"And what is that supposed to mean?" Melissana shot back. "I don't like doing this any more than you do if that's what you're implying. I'm just trying to get out of my own head long enough to try to save some kids!"

"Susan, you have to try harder." Johnny agreed. "It just doesn't look right, and they'll spot us a mile off."

"Yeah, well, that's easy for you to say," Susan replied. "I mean, all you gotta do is stand there looking like a pimp. It's not like you're part of the show."

"Actually, he is" Melissana countered. "And he's not doing any better at it than you are."

"What do you mean by that?" Johnny asked, suddenly bewildered.

"Johnny, you're treating us like we're your friends. You'll have to do better. I know you've seen way more than you're letting on about all of this. If you don't get into your role, we're done. From now on, if Susan doesn't act the way you want her to, especially if we're out there, well, I really don't want to even say it," she said, sadly looking at Susan, "but it's important."

"Then what?" Johnny asked.

"Then hit her," Melissana dispassionately stated.

"I'd like to see you try!" Susan flared, her right hand flying back as if rearing to take a swipe at him. They all noticed Susan's claws extended out; whether the action was intentional or reflexive, not even Susan could tell. Everything stopped as each considered which case would have been worse. Melissana shrugged, then took the risk that Susan was in better control of herself than she had been a few seconds earlier. Besides, the CYBER close combat specialist had to get it right, or she would jeopardize them all.

"And if she still doesn't get the message, kick her. We have *got* to look like the real thing."

Johnny's shoulders slumped. "Melissana's right, Susan. Believe me, I don't want it to come to that, but we can't screw this up."

"You know you'll never be able to land it," Susan said with a furious glare, "You'd better not even try." Everyone though, including Susan, breathed in relief when she sheathed her claws and lowered her arm.

"Hey, what's going on here?" asked Rickshaw as he and Corey entered the room.

"Uh, we were just trying to practice a little bit," Johnny replied. *How much had they seen?* "What brings you guys down here?"

"We're getting ready to head out," Rickshaw explained, "and lover-boy here just wanted to come down here to kiss you all goodbye. I don't get it," he chuckled. "Who decided to call this guy 'Hardcore'?"

The three offered a little laugh, but it was nervous and forced.

"Okay, really—what's going on?" Rickshaw asked. "I'm just a wheelman, and I ain't trained in all this psych mumbo jumbo like Trigget, but even I can tell something's not right here."

"This isn't going to work," Susan admitted. "I just can't bring myself to do it. I've been trying. I have," she said with a glance for some sort of affirmation from Melissana. "But every time I even think about it, I go back to what happened with Iron Mike, and I…." She then just gave up, hanging her head. "I know I just told you a minute ago that I've never done this before, but the truth is that I came far too close to exactly this same thing. I am trying, honest. I just *can't*."

"I'm sorry, Susan," Melissana said softly as she stepped in and put her arm around her friend. "I didn't realize you were reliving that episode every time we asked you to… I can see it now, though, and I am really sorry."

"Great!" Johnny exclaimed, taking a seat. "It would have been hard enough already to take on the tough guy pimp attitude with her before. There's no way I'll be able to hit her, knowing what I know now."

"To do what?" Corey asked incredulously, balling his fists and stepping forward.

"The team's compromised," Rickshaw stated, raising his arms outward as he calmly maneuvered himself between Corey and Johnny to separate the two. "The team's compromised," he repeated, "by the plan. It's a good plan, except that it's unworkable; we need to adapt the plan to the team."

"Can we do that?" Susan asked.

"Lady Blackwolf," Rickshaw grinned, "you have joined CYBER. The one thing we do, all the time, is adapt our plans as we go. We all get paid to think on the run. We just communicate the changes to the rest of the team, so we're all in the loop."

"That suits me," Corey said, relieved. "I hated this idea."

"I told them you did," Susan pouted.

"Kids!" Rickshaw complained lightly, rolling his eyes for effect. The tension broke, and the group lightly laughed for real.

"Well, c'mon lovebird, we gotta roll."

"Wait—you're leaving now?" Johnny asked as Rickshaw turned to go. "What do you want us to do about the change to the plan?"

"Figure it out," Rickshaw called back without turning. "You're CYBER now. Empowerment's not just in the new gear and body parts we gave you; it's the freedom to use them, and even more, your minds. If we didn't trust you to be able to come up with something when things get jacked all kinds of ways south, we never would have recruited you in the first place."

… …

"Okay, so what exactly are we doing again?" Corey "Hardcore" Martin asked his mentor over the vehicle radio.

"We're heading to Denver," Rickshaw's Dominator answered.

"I get that, but why did we come over I-80? 70's quicker."

"Preach doesn't want us risking making the wrong kind of contact with the Brownies. Yeah, there's bound to be bandits up here, too, but we won't have to worry about diplomacy as much."

"So, what's the plan when we get to Denver?"

"Well, then we get to the work of looking like a couple johns out to score. We'll work it from there to try to find out about those convoys. Outside of that, well, there really isn't much of a plan—except, since I'm more familiar with this section of the country than you are, try to let me do the talking when we get to town."

"OK, got it—hey!" Hardcore shouted as he felt a sudden pinch in his right leg, *"I just took a hit in the rear fender!"*

"Roger that, Hardcore, no need in fighting if we don't have to, open her up, and let's see what your Sabretooth's got!"

The duo's pursuers had nothing on the powerful engines and superior machining of the elite government agency, and soon the gap between the two widened considerably.

"Active scanners are online," Corey's Sabretooth informed him. *"Potentially hostile targets detected 1.3 miles ahead."*

"Immerse!" Corey mentally ordered, initializing the transformation from driver to what he simply called, 'Unity.' There were three ways to drive a CYBER wheelman vehicle: as a regular human driver, remotely via neuro-link, and in full immersion mode, where he transferred his very consciousness to the car. In a tenth of a second, his conscious awareness imploded away from his five physical senses, then exploded, expanded beyond his own into those of his car. His immediate sensations were the steady thrum of power he felt in his chest coming from the car's powerful engine and supercharger systems. Almost immediately after, he felt the slight tingle of the tires racing across the unlit highway and enhanced vision from the Sabretooth's headlights. A moment later, his vision further expanded into the infrared and ultraviolet systems, RADAR, and heads-up map overlay. The exponentiation of his senses completed as his hearing was augmented by the car's radio, SONAR, and satellite communications. A second or two after

processing these transformations, he flexed his arms, neck, and back, testing the vehicle's various weapons systems.

Several teams of CYBER neuro- and nano-surgeons had interwoven cybernetic implants and neurolinks that tied his nervous system to his Sabretooth. The forward-facing machine guns and grenade launcher, turret-mounted recoilless rifle, antipersonnel mines, and series of rear-mounted weapons responded in perfect accord. He instinctively knew his mentor, Rickshaw, had done the same with his Dominator.

"OK, kid," Rickshaw stated through the Dominator's radio. *"Good spot on what's ahead. There's a road that cuts right just ahead of the blockade; how much do you wanna bet that's the way they want us to go?*

"So, when we get to the blockade, we fake right, then punch it through and try to get around it on the left. We're miniaturized, but we don't carry unlimited supplies of ammo; I'd rather save what we've got for the real show."

This is pretty much the real show right now, Hardcore thought to himself, but he tried not to think it too loudly—he was still working on fine-tuning his responses after the parking garage incident on the day the team met with Elaine.

- *"GOOD EVENING, GENTLEMEN," scrolled over a message feed atop the map overlay. "YOU HAPPENED TO HAVE RUN ACROSS A CLASS 2 LOCAL/REGIONAL THREAT…"*

- *"Aw, caltrops!" Rickshaw complained, "I know what's coming next."*

- *"ENGAGE THEM. SIMON CLEAR."*

"What'd I tell ya, kid?" Rickshaw said as he spun a tight 180-degree spin, waiting for Hardcore to catch up before charging their pursuers. As soon as the younger driver did, they both revved

their engines three times, then peeled forward as their attackers approached. *"We're CYBER—changing plans is what we do. Just because us wheelmen are seated doesn't mean we don't spend most of the time thinking on our feet...."*

... ...

As Hardcore and Rickshaw had navigated through the Den's litter-strewn streets, they wondered if they were on the right trail. Their attempts to make contacts with the underground over the last few days had brought them here. From what they had gathered from the locals that would talk to them, this seedy fixer bar was their best shot at getting a job that paid good enough to get them out of this down and out urban dumping ground of spent humanity. The night-time precipitation was just enough to add a rain-slicked veneer that collected the neighborhood's dust into gritty micro-puddles but not quite enough to actually rinse any of the grime away. Now that they were finally looking at the run-down hole-in-the-wall, they felt it; this was the place.

They paused a moment outside the brick and stone dive to take in the pulse of the gritty, beat-down slum, their efforts rewarded with the sounds of alleyway rats burrowing into a refuse pile and an out-of-sight derelict retching up the remains of his last binge. The flickering neon sign over the thick steel doors read Poor Odds, or occasionally Poor Odd's when the sign managed to flicker just right, the glowing d's a pair of dice that had come up snake-eyes. Their anticipation heightened as the steady throbbing of the music, joined by the cacophony of humanity that emanated from within as the door security someone opened the door to enter the place, seemed to confirm it. Rickshaw shifted the load of a duffel bag he had slung over his shoulder, and they each took one more breath as though preparing to go for an underwater swim. Both wheelmen wanted one last lungful of relatively fresh air before they entered the likely mix of who-knew-what smells, odors, and out and out stenches they would find within.

Crossing through the inch-thick steel doorway, they were not disappointed. A heavy volume of cigarettes, cigars, and a variety of smoked chems filled the place and assaulted their nostrils as soon as they got through the entrance; the hanging cloud was the most prevalent feature of the indoor weather system, constantly attended to by the establishment's clientele. The music, they discovered, was live; local cybergoths sporting stiff multicolored mohawks had been performing ATG but had just switched to bit-grunge after announcing they were going to do some new stuff. That conversation still continued over the volume of pops, chirps, and other noises of whatever local band Poor Odd's had let onto the stage was a testament to either the persistence or the depravity of the human spirit. Down and outers, last chance cowboys, hackers, low-end mercenaries, muscle, dealers, and hustlers all crowded the pool tables, gambling machines, bull rides, and in the center of it all, a well-used fight pit that was currently between rounds.

"Used t'be a dogfighting pit," Hardcore overheard someone explain as they worked their way to the bar. "But eventually, the staff got tired of cooking algae! And b'sides, human fights'll do just fine if ya give 'em the proper motivation." Corey decided then and there that, no matter what, he would not eat any food in this place.

"Newcomers, huh?" the bartender asked in a whiskey-induced permanently guttural voice that sounded to the Pride's wheelman like a combination of burly rasp and sore throat. Corey stopped cold, surprised to see the man had to be no more than four and a half feet tall, stocky, with a frazzled thick beard. Since he wasn't tall enough to tend the bar on his own, he was standing on a platform that ran behind the length of the bar. "Don't remember seein' either of you here before. What bring's ya ta Poor Odd's?" He then leaned across the bar into Corey's face as he added, "Ain't polite t'stare, kid," he almost growled, "I ain't inclined t'serve impolite guests in this establishment."

"N—No, I mean, I'm sorry, but...."

"But what ya mean t'say is that I look like a *dwarf,* and now yer thinkin' it all makes sense somehow that I'm up to my ears in beers and ales?" At this point, he yanked down a hand microphone that hung suspended from the ceiling, and with the flick of a switch, overrode the band and practically everything else in the bar.

"Hey, we got us a couple of newcomers here! Let's give 'em a round of applause."

- *"I don't like this at all," Rickshaw grumbled.*

- *"Yeah, like you think I do?" Corey returned.*

- *"Yeah, well," he suggested with a sigh of resignation, "better roll with it."*

Rickshaw held out both hands, and with a smiling nod, glanced around and said, "Yeah, that'd be us," he drawled. "Ain't never been here before, and we're kinda new in town, so we asked around," he said while glancing around the room. He found himself *really* wishing for Chrome to be there.

"And what were ye askin' fer," asked an oversized, muscular man wearing torn overalls and a black t-shirt. By his expression and demeanor, the wheelmen presumed the man was the joint's bouncer. He was big—Corey hoped they would get thrown out and not simply killed, beaten to death in this freakshow of a bar.

"We were askin' about work," Rickshaw flatly replied, apparently unruffled by the behemoth's attention.

Corey remembered the cold professional that had hailed them over the radio when he and Susan had first met the veteran driver. *"If we get through this,"* Corey thought to himself, *"I'm going to be him someday."*

"Work?" the bartender resumed, "I don't need janitors. What kinda work are you two lookin' for?"

"Well, it's like this," Rickshaw began, then held up his finger as though he just had an idea. "Wait one sec, if you don't mind," he said as he began to reach behind his back. The surrounding bar patrons brandished a small wave of firearms at the gesture, the movements of the individual draws so cohesive that Rickshaw momentarily wondered if they practiced the effort for hours under a drill instructor.

"I been shot before," the bouncer declared with a weird kind of smile. "It usually makes me mad."

"And believe me," the dwarf grinned, "the two of you don't want to make Monty mad."

"Got it," Rickshaw nodded, "but that ain't where I'm going." Then he slowly hefted the large duffle bag onto the bar and dumped out a couple bumper plates, two steering wheels, and a helmet—all marked with the insignia of the bandit gang that had attacked them the night before. "Y'see," Rickshaw continued a little louder, "we had a delivery we had to bring from back East. We came out from just under Chicago, and we ran into these guys on our way down the 80. Our business is going to keep us here for about a week, then we're headed back east some. We figured we should probably find a different way back, and well, with this here bein' the wild west an' all, why go back empty if we can maybe score a job for the way home?

"Besides," Rickshaw added with a sheepish grin, "from what we hear, there's female problems on the 70, and I'd rather not cross that bunch with just the two of us. I'd like to steer clear of 'em if I could, but that adds days goin' southbound that I don't have. So, we asked around to see where we might pick up an extra job for the way back, an' this place came up as the best bet."

Corey squirmed a little at the mention of the Brownies, but he didn't say anything. The dwarf noticed.

"What's yer problem this time, kid?"

Corey sagged his shoulders—he'd been caught. "That's not why we're here, Rickshaw!" he accused. "You told me that after the

Denver job, we'd get hired on, easy, so we could avenge Cousin Donnie. You promised me we'd get a chance at that Freya cow!"

Rickshaw sighed and, upturning his palms as he shrugged an apology, nodded at the bartender. "Yeah, that's the truth of it." Then he turned to Corey. "Kid, I told ya, you make this personal, and nobody's gonna give you the job. And now, after all this work, we're done. We ain't even met the contact we're supposed to make, and you done blowed it like this," he said, sadly shaking his head.

"I know that group you crossed on your way into town," the bartender commented. "That's an impressive set of credentials ya got there. Who is it you're supposed to be contacting?" he disinterestedly asked as he began to wipe a glass.

"All we were told was there's a fixer who works out of Poor Odds who can find us a job for our way back east," Rickshaw replied.

The bartender glanced left and right, lowered the glass, nodded, and reset the switch as he announced, "OK people, let's get back to what we were doing." Immediately the music and other bar noise resumed, although the band seemed to have changed songs to something a little less sporadic.

"My name's Odd," the bartender stated. It wasn't quite an open greeting, but it was progress. "Poor Odd's is mine, and yeah, kid, before you make it obvious, it's already a long-time joke that I was always a little Odd. All I heard growing up was 'poor Odd' this and 'poor Odd' that until it became my name. Made sense to everyone when I opened this place, and no, I ain't really all that poor anymore.

"So, you had a delivery to the Den?" the bar owner asked, giving Rickshaw a sidelong glance as he pretended to wipe down another glass. "What'd you deliver, and who'd you deliver it to?"

"Well, that was our business that brought us in here." Rickshaw non-answered. "I learned a long time ago not to talk about jobs to those who aren't involved. A close friend of mine taught me that once, by talking about a job to those who weren't involved."

"Consider this an interview question," Poor Odd stated flatly. Hardcore felt the scrutiny of some people standing behind them.

"You two look like you can handle yourselves all right, and you wouldn't have that duffle of résumé if you weren't worth hiring. But I don't think you could handle all of us. So, I'm asking you again, nicely. But I gotta tell you that I'm dying to know—which means, of course, that you'll be dying to tell me." To make sure he made his point, he put down the glass, stared at them both with no expression at all, and added, "Literally."

- "Now!" Rickshaw sub-vocalized.

Rickshaw materialized a sawed-off 12 gauge shotgun from underneath his jacket and pointed it straight at their host. Hardcore produced a pair of machine pistols and spun a tight half-circle to place his back against Rickshaw's. In the process, he also made a show of the two cords that looped across his thumbs with gold rings. The bar's muscle froze as Hardcore's opened jacket revealed the explosives wrapped around his torso. A dead quiet covered the entire bar and clung to each occupant like the ever-present cloud of patron-induced smog. It was a very rare thing at Poor Odd's.

"Now, here's the thing," Rickshaw stated, matching the owner's tone. "I don't like talking about jobs to those who aren't involved. We both know that I pull this trigger and we won't make it out of here alive, we put our guns down, and we don't make it outta here alive, and my boy Hardcore here lowers his hands, and *none* of us make it outta here alive. Maybe, you have enough guys that you can grab his arms fast enough to keep him from pulling one of those cords, but I doubt it—the only way that thing gets disarmed is he takes his thumb out of those rings, and then you think you'll have us. Now maybe you're willing to bet I won't pull this trigger, that my boy and me can be lulled to a false sense of security, and he won't pull the cords.

"So, I feel compelled to let you know something else. I noticed when we came in that your door was about an inch thick of steel. Now, that's fine for stopping bullets but is nowhere near enough to stop the HEAVE rocket outside that's pointed at it." Seeing the bartender's nervous glance to his left, Rickshaw said, "Go ahead, have one of your boys check if you want." At the twitch of Odd's head towards the door, two of the crowd forcefully made their way to the front to confer with the door's security. Rickshaw momentarily turned his head over his right shoulder as though he reflexively followed the movements of the two; the Dominator's turret swiveled right and then centered back on the heavy steel door. At the same time, Hardcore risked a quick glance off to his left, and the man at the door saw the Sabretooth's turret sweep left and back again.

"There's two occupied vehicles, weapons primed and pointed right at the door," the spotter reported. "He ain't bluffin' 'bout the HEAVE rockets, neither."

"This thing goes any farther south, and people will be calling you 'Poor Odd' at your funeral," Rickshaw concluded. "We understand each other now?"

The bartender cleared his throat. His men were shaken. The clientele, none of which were strangers to threats and danger, actually looked scared. Somehow these two newcomers had neutralized the entire place. Odd cleared his throat a second time, stalling as he thought through the situation.

After a few more seconds, Odd grinned ear to ear and stuck out his hand for a shake. "What'll you two be having?" he asked. Instantly the music resumed, and life at Poor Odd's was back to whatever version of normal his patrons subscribed. "I'm the guy you're looking for," he pronounced, leaning in to avoid shouting over the reinstituted din. "We got a convoy we're hiring out for running east down the 70 to Witch City in about a week, and I don't do business with someone I never drank with."

The tension dissipated as though it had never existed; the threat was indeed over. Corey sighed, carefully slipping his thumbs out of the dummy detonator cords. He had to maintain the illusion that the cords were real while anyone still might be paying attention. He was sure his hands would eventually stop sweating.

"Witch City?" Rickshaw asked. "What's the cargo?"

"There ain't none," Odd replied with a grin. "Your friends, the Valhalla's Brownies, have been raiding our other convoys; we've lost a lot of money to those hags. So, it seems we've got us a common enemy, and you definitely have skills, so if you want, you're in. The whole purpose of the trip is to take out those abominations once and for all. The only cargo will be the Brownies we pick up along the way. Besides the payout for the gang hit, our Johnson will pay us a bonus of twice what we'd normally get for each Brownie we load up alive. Once we collect, you two can be on your merry way. We'll be swappin' out the load and then head north to Toronto, but we won't need you for that leg of the trip. There's always plenty of muscle for hire in the W.C."

18. Setting the Stage

"Moon, this is Friggia," the lookout reported in. *"I need you to come over here and get your hazels on this ASAP. We're getting company, but I've never seen anything like this."*

Minutes later, Rogue Moon was at Friggia's side, looking out over I-35 near the southern border of Brownie territory.

"What ya see, hon?" she asked.

"Down the road, about five miles past our markers," Friggia explained. "It's like a cross between a biker war party and a traveling circus or something. They were coming up the road doing about 70 or so, but about ten miles out, they slowed to what's gotta be only 15 or 20 miles per hour. It was their slowing down like they did that got me to call you."

Valhalla's elite sniper scanned the roadway in farther and farther increments from their border. Glints of light pelted her eyes like miniaturized suns as they reflected off dozens of polished suits of medieval-styled high-tech cryoplast armor. Each bike in the first rank of ten motorcycles had two riders: one steered and manned the front vehicle weapons, the other held a tall lance capped with a heralded banner. Moon reasoned the armor somehow augmented their strength; that was the only way she could explain how they could steadily maintain the load of the wind force created by the moving bikes slapping against the flags. Besides the typical firearms, they also carried ultra-tech versions of medieval melee weapons of abnormally high quality. The normally unflappable Brownie sniper turned ashen at the sight—rumor had it that the weapons belonging to the biker group's highest castes were powered.

Moon counted four ranks of the elite guard in the foreboding armor, followed by approximately thirty ranks donning the traditional leathers and body armor, followed by two tractor-trailers, followed in turn by a rearguard of another three ranks of ten bikes. Each rank rode in a perfect line, each column straight in military precision. And the bike just ahead and center of the very first rank sported the most distinguished heraldry of all: a blazing red Templar cross on a white background with a travailing serpent punctured into the ground by the foot of the cross. There was one bike on either side of him ridden by guys in black combat armor. The one on his left rode a Desert Knight and wore a full suit with a helmet, while the stockier one rode a Highwayman on the right just wore a breastplate and leg armor, sporting a blonde crew and cut content to shield his eyes with a pair of black sunglasses. Neither of them had any Paladin regalia, which made Rogue Moon think they were more like typical mercenaries than part of the group they rode with.

"I've heard of them," she exclaimed with a chill in her voice. "And the stories I've heard of them seriously freak me out. And now here they are, showing right up on our doorstep! You did good to call me on this, Frig," she said while trying to stifle a shiver. "Real good."

"Freya, this is Rogue Moon. The Paladins just rolled up on our southern border—not just a war party, it looks like an entire bishopric, maybe four or five of their parishes, or whatever they call them… No, they haven't done anything yet. They just all cruised up outside the border, slowed down, and started setting up for one of their tent meetings or something. They look like they're all armed up and ready to go… No, they're not on our land. They stopped about a half-mile out and set up three white tents.

"Freya, three of them just pointed us out and stepped up to about 10 feet off our border. Well, this is just embarrassing. One of the three

just waved at us… Holy—the guy in the center is Small Eddie himself! What? No way! I hate those… yes, Mother Freya…"

Moon stood up to full height and waved back. She would rather have just shot them all. "What do you want?" she yelled to them. "You goveks take three more steps forward, and you're dead."

Small Eddie produced a bullhorn and checked to see that it was on. "I am for peace; but when I speak, they are for war—Psalm 120:7. It was true back then, and it is still true today."

The guy on the Desert Knight on Eddie's left removed his helmet— Rogue absently noted he was a Latino—and tapped the Paladin commander on his shoulder. He said something that caused Small Eddie to pause, look back over his shoulder, and wait. A few moments later there was a commotion farther down the road, a swirl that progressed through the mass of itinerant bikers as they parted to allow a shape to pass; as soon as it did, the hastily formed space closed up again, the small void filled back in as the bikers resumed their positions, even more, energized than they had been before. Rogue Moon crouched, pulling the less experienced Friggia down beside her, and furtively moved to a different location, fearful the bikers were bringing up some sort of weapon to launch an assault. To her surprise, the shape in the swirl turned out to be a black sedan that pulled through to Small Eddie's location and dropped off a man and a woman dressed in neoconservative business before it faded back behind the army of bikers.

The newcomers' fashion clashed with the traditional leathers and medieval cryoplast armor of the bikers, but by the excited swapped hugs and warm gestures, Moon surmised that Small Eddie and the newcomer were old close friends who hadn't seen each other in a long time. The two suits apparently were also well acquainted with Small Eddie's non-Paladin escorts. After talking among themselves for a few moments, Small Eddie handed over the bullhorn to the newcomer. Still just barely peeking around from behind their new location, Moon was dismayed to note the newcomer scanned the countryside until he was looking right at them before he continued.

"We're under Truce and request a meet; we're not looking for any trouble," he said with a smile. "Please ask Mother Freya if she will agree to talk."

"About what?" Moon shouted after a few seconds delay that indicated Rogue was relaying the requests and responses over the radio. "Kinda obvious we don't have a whole lot in common!" Araña was too far away to discern if she was also guiding in a Brownie assault force, but he was the first to hear the engines of a large number of vehicles approaching from behind the Brownie liaison. "And I'm warning you now, if it's not something she really wants to hear, you'll regret coming." Just as she finished speaking, a large conglomeration of motorcycles, dirt bikes, dunes buggies, and even a few armored hovercraft appeared as Moon's backup.

The Paladins were somewhat nomadic and traveled with their families so they wouldn't have to leave them unguarded as they explored or ran their mission trips. Near the tents, several women not already engaged in the show of force scurried to protected positions with the children while others joined their men in reaching for weapons or mounting additional bikes. Small Eddie and his entourage stood their ground, although the female suit visibly twitched like she was going to run before she caught herself.

Small Eddie leaned over and whispered, "Hey Greyscale, are you sure about this? You know the Brownies hate us, right?"

"If I thought there was another way, I'd have used it," Jack replied. "But yeah, I think we'll be okay." Then to Josanne, "You ok?"

"Not really," she stated slowly, quietly, deliberately. "You guys act like you do this every week... *Do* you guys do this every week?"

"Welcome to ground zero," Chrome stated, leaning over slightly to make eye contact. He was actually smiling! "I'm working with a bunch of lunatics!" she thought to herself, not for the first time, making sure she didn't move her mouth while mentally voicing the unspoken thought.

A short woman emerged from the turret of a heavily armored hovercraft the size of a tank and stood to full height.

"I'm Mother Freya," she announced, "and like my Rogue Moon here said, this better be something I actually really want to hear, or you're all goners." A torrent of cheers, war shrieks, jeers, and insults issued from every one of the Brownies' vehicles. The Paladins, while armed, armored, and tensed, did not retaliate, a testimony to the discipline of each Paladin. Jack knew the Christian biker group. They wouldn't fire first, but that wouldn't stop them from defending themselves against the small horde now facing them if they had to. After a few moments, Freya waved her troops to cease. The air was quiet, everyone waiting on what the man with the bullhorn was going to say next. Both sides tensed like hungry leopards about to pounce at the slightest misstep of the other.

"We didn't come here for a fight," Jack began. Josanne focused in on Freya, trying with all her might how to read the aberrant biker raider clan leader standing before them, but the distance was so far she almost wished she had Jack's eyes.

"Yeah, you said that!" Freya argued. "That's not interesting…" she raised her arm, Josanne knew, to drop it sharply and start the assault.

- *"Jack!"*

"We saw your last convoy raid," Jack quickly stated. "We know you're trying to break up the slavers." Mother Freya slowly lowered her arm as Jack added, "We want to help."

"Yeah?" Freya almost jeered with her voice, but beyond the obvious signs of suspicion, Trigget and Preach both detected the faintest traces of… hope? "You and the Paladins wanna help us? How so? You know, suit, the Paladins and us don't quite see eye to eye."

"A couple weeks ago," Preach began, "you hit a convoy from Witch City to the Den, and you threatened that one day you'd come for them. You freed two truckloads of girls from the slavers, but one of the girls that was supposed to be in one of the trucks was missing. How am I doing so far?"

Freya drew her pistol, an ancient .45 caliber which Jack could see that, despite its age and apparent usage, seemed to be in prime condition. "There's only one way you could know all that," she raged. "You're one of them!"

At her gesture, hundreds of weapons were raised and aimed on both sides, with Jack, Josanne, Small Eddie, Chrome, and Araña still between the two groups. Josanne felt like diving for cover but was afraid that as soon as she did, she would draw everyone's fire. Then she looked at Jack and saw him just standing there, not even agitated, somehow calm, at peace. "How could he do that?" she wondered.

"That girl that was supposed to be on that caravan," he calmly continued, "but was missing? I have reason to believe that I was her youth pastor. Her name is Kelly, and she was kidnapped from her home about two years ago. We just got her location traced to Witch City, in no small part thanks to your assault on that convoy."

Preach smiled, looked up at her, and said, "And I'm here to get her back."

"How did you know all that about the raid, and how did our raid help you locate the girl you're looking for?"

He ventured a small step forward and offered a small recording device to her. "Listen to this," he stated while hitting the Play button. The recording didn't just include the satellite transmissions, but some of the team strategy meeting as well. She told him to play through it twice more before dismounting the war wagon. Freya then signaled for Moon and Bridgette to join her as she approached the small group. Valhalla's Brownies were still tense, waiting for something to go wrong, but the remaining conversation would be held without shouting across the distance that separated the two groups.

"This is all legit?" Freya asked. Jack nodded his assent. For several moments, the only sound was a slight desert breeze and the crackle of dirt scraping as Mother Freya walked up and down the line, studying each of them. She stopped at Chrome.

"Small Eddie, I know, but you're no Paladin, are you, tough guy?" she asked him. She began to stroke his bicep to rile him but reflexively jerked her hand back at the sensation; his skin was hard like Kevlar and warmed in the desert sun like metal. She peered at him closer then, studying him enough to determine the synthetic nature of his skin.

Chrome fixed his eyes on her and simply said, "No."

"And why are you here?" she pressed in a sultry tease, trying to dismiss the uneasiness she was feeling. "I saw you looking at my Rogue Moon. Is she to be your prize?"

"I was admiring her." Chrome flatly replied.

"Yes, I could see why you would, tough man," she said as she tried to regain her composure. "She is very pretty."

"That's not why I admire her," Chrome said.

"Oh? Then what is it?"

"She's a good shot," he replied as evenly as he had before. Looking to Moon, he added, "Not many can handle an MX-79."

Rogue Moon laughed. "These chooms aren't worth our time, Freya. This ain't an MX-79. They don't even know their weapons— we're deli truck meat if we join up with them."

"I didn't mean the .308 Kohlberg you've got now," Chrome added. "I heard a couple shots the '79 fired the night of the convoy hit; you were carrying it after the raid."

"Not bad," Rogue grudgingly admitted after Freya gave her a nod. "But the question remains, my admirer… Who are you?"

"I'm Chrome. And you are?"

"Uninterested in admirers," she flatly retorted. She didn't know exactly how he did, but she noticed something about this guy clearly unnerved her gang leader.

"Fair enough," Chrome replied with a barely perceptible nod accompanied by the slightest evidence of a grin.

"And how about you?" Freya asked, moving on to Araña. "He's the tough guy; that much is evident. Who are you, and what's your specialty?"

"I'm Araña—Spider if you prefer. I'm kind of a jack of all trades," he casually replied. He could have been meeting someone over lunch for all the concern he showed. His ease with the situation bothered Freya almost as much as how that Chrome guy felt when she touched him. She involuntarily stepped back; catching her own apprehension, she decided she had met enough of the small group for the moment. Putting her game face back on, she returned to the leader of the small party. As she approached, she noted that Small Eddie, a Paladin Bishop no less, was also following him.

"And where do the Paladins come in?"

"The Paladins are here as backup and support. They're good in a fight, and they see their lives' mission is to fight evil…."

"Yeah? Fight evil?" Freya cut in with a wave of her hand. "I've heard that one before. In fact, I've seen it before. And ain't their version of evil anyone who doesn't follow their ways? Seems like a bunch of judgmental bigots to me."

"Have you ever met any of us," Eddie joined in, "or are you just repeating something you seen on some media channel? 'Invisible biases' work both ways, you know. We came to you in peace because someone needs our help, and you seem more interested than most in doing something about this. So, forgive me if this offends you, but between the two of us, who's being judgmental?"

"Freya," Jack cut in, "your group's going to need help if you want to end this operation once and for all. I could have hired out to some mercenary corp, but there are some other things the Paladins bring to the table."

"And what are those?" Freya asked, still sorting out Eddie's questions.

"They're committed, they've got the resources to help the girls get their lives back, and most importantly, the girls will be safe with them; we won't have to worry about the Paladins turning on the girls once we get them out."

"I've never seen the man who wouldn't turn on us in a second." Freya bitterly complained.

"Until today," a female voice stated. It was so unexpected that everyone, including Jack, had to turn to look to see who had spoken; in the interchange, everyone had quite forgotten she was even there.

"What was that?" Freya asked.

"Until today," Josanne repeated, casually approaching Mother Freya, arms lowered to her sides, palm forward to show the Brownie leader she wasn't holding any weapons. "I get your concerns, and I get that you're looking out for your women. Valhalla's Brownies is your family; I get it. But I also saw what you did to rescue the girls that convoy of trucks was carrying. That was a really brave thing to do, but it wasn't enough." She stopped when she arrived two feet away from the gang leader. *So far, so good*, she thought to herself. "You're hard, and you're tough," Trigget continued, "but I heard your heart breaking when you found out that one of the girls was missing. Yeah, guys can be jerks—a lot of times! But you can believe *these* guys really are here to rescue this girl and those that are trapped with her. And if you can't believe them, then believe me."

The elongated pause as Freya internally deliberated was deafening. Eventually, Jack cleared his throat and risked moving forward with the conversation. "We don't want to throw you under the bus without any support. We're going to ask a lot. That's why we got you the backup."

"And so," Freya finally responded after pondering the situation further, "of all the crews you could've picked, you got the Paladins? You are one crazy govek." She shook her head as she studied the ground a moment longer. "But I can get along with crazy," she guardedly approved, slightly but visibly relaxing, "and this whole thing is so far-fetched it's gotta be true." She looked up from the ground to stare him full in the face as she asked, "What do you have in mind? This is far from decided, but I'll hear you out."

"You and the Paladins are going to provide a distraction. I know you got a tip about a week ago that another convoy was coming through, this time from Denver eastbound into the W.C."

"And how'd you know about that?" Freya half accused.

"My organization has been monitoring your frequencies since we stumbled onto your attack a couple weeks ago," Jack confessed. "We know you're already planning on hitting this one as well. You already know the date, the time, and the typical route they're going to take. But just to show our goodwill, here's something you don't know. They want you to ambush the convoy. The whole setup is a trap; the trucks are empty, except for the extra combat vehicles they're carrying inside. The cargo they're planning on hauling to Toronto is any Brownie they take alive that survives her stay in W.C."

"So, then we'll leave that one alone," Freya decided with a nonchalant shrug. "Thanks for the tip."

"Actually, I have a different plan, if you don't mind," Jack countered. "Hit the convoy. Hard. There'll be a fight, to be sure. Ten, maybe fifteen minutes in, though, the Paladins will come in like they're trying to help out the convoy. Instead, you'll combine your forces to take out the convoy, make it look like the beginning of a gang war between the two of you, and also make sure that no one gets into or out of Witch City once this all gets started."

"Just bottling up an entire city? Is that all? And what'll you be doing?"

"My team is going to infiltrate the city, find out where this Ricky T. Showbiz guy is, get the girls out of there, and shut down his operation for good."

"You and your team. You mean the four of you—by yourselves—against Ricky T. Showbiz…" she said in absolute unbelief. "You guys are just plain outta your frakkin' minds! You know that, don't you?"

"We've got a couple more joining us later. Besides, do you know anyone else we can take with us? We need you guys on the perimeter to make sure Ricky T. Showbiz doesn't ghost on us, and you just admitted you'll have your hands full trying to do that."

"Well, there's a problem with your plan, phallo. Witch City is the capital of the coast-to-coast trafficking operations, and in Witch City, Ricky T. Showbiz ain't just some pimp; he's the warlord of the pimps. Besides that, have you ever declared war on a megacorp? You do know Wichita's been called the Air Capital of the World since the twentieth century, pretty much since they had planes, right? Air Dynamix claims this place as their home port, and they're not going to take kindly to us blockading their turf—they're gonna dispatch their SECOPS forces as soon as they figure out this ain't a just a hit-and-run. Maybe we can cover the ground war with them, but not even the Paladins will have a prayer once they scramble their air support on us."

"They won't scramble," Jack replied. "We'll take care of the air war."

"And how are you planning to do that?" Freya incredulously bemoaned, throwing her arms to the air in exasperation.

"Three ways," Jack replied with a confidence that seemed real enough to the brazen ganger. "First, it'll look to them that you and the Paladins are having a gang fight, so your perimeter won't look like a perimeter. The locals shouldn't see this as any direct challenge to them, so you won't have to worry about retaliation; that is, as long as you stay within their acceptable loss tolerance margins. Once even a few rigs get hit in collateral damage, word should get out to keep other shipments away until your feud blows over. Dynamix might even stand to make a profit if they airlift all the goods in and out while this is all going on.

"Second, if things do start to go dicey, we'll communicate directly with Air to let them know our true target. That should get them to stand down because we'll be cleaning up their city for them. They'll probably spin it like they were the ones who sponsored the whole thing to get some PR credit for it...."

"Yeah?" Freya interrupted again. "Only that's frakkin' Witch City in there. Ever think the corps might not care about Ricky T. Showbiz running his skin biz?"

"It crossed my mind," Jack admitted. "They may even be charging him taxes to work there. But my bet is that once they realize Ricky T.

Showbiz built up this much heat, they'll see him as a liability, drop him, and leave him hanging."

"And get somebody else to take over?" Eddie asked. Freya nodded at the question—so the Paladins were just as skeptical as she was? Somehow that thought calmed her. The guy might be crazy, but what he was saying was legit.

"Maybe," Jack replied. "But even if they really are getting some kind of kickback from Ricky T. Showbiz, maybe they'll figure the game is no longer worth the play." He shrugged. "Who knows? They might want to get rid of him as bad as we do."

"I seriously doubt that," Freya commented. "What's the third way?"

"The third way," Jack replied, "is we ground their planes." He spoke it with such finality that Freya, blown away so many times already during this meeting, just accepted that, somehow, this suit who rides with the Paladins with his robot friend actually thought he could do it. Well, the risk was all his, she concluded. If any of this started to go wrong, Valhalla's Brownies would stick the knife deep into the back of the Paladins and be outta there.

"Jack," Eddie cautioned, "Lord knows I've seen you and your teams do some crazy things, and I know God is still in the miracle business, but I gotta ask… Do you seriously think you can do this, or are you on a suicide march to save that girl?"

Jack turned to face Eddie. As he did, Josanne saw a slight change in her leader's demeanor, a sadness she hadn't seen in him before, but she couldn't tell if he felt betrayed because his friend's opinions of him sank that low or because his friend had just called his bluff in front of everyone.

"It's all I got, Eddie," he replied, seemingly from far away. "But I have faith in God, in my teams, and in you, that we can really pull it off. Just keep the city bottled for us. We've taken on worse."

Eddie started examining the toe of one of his boots for a few moments but reluctantly nodded. "Okay, Jack. If you say so, you say so. Gotta admit I feel just a little like the apostle Thomas."

"Because you're doubting?" asked the former pastor turned CYBER team leader.

"No," Eddie replied. "More like the time when Jesus declared to his followers He was heading for Jerusalem, and Thomas told the others, 'Let's go and die with Him.' But it's a fair plan, a good cause, and we all prayed about this before we got here, so okay, let's go. Freya?"

"All right," she said with a slow nod. "We're in, for now. What's the next step?"

"The first order of business," Jack stated, "is to get your Brownies and the Paladins to be able to work together. We've only got a couple days to get this all ironed out."

"And to that end," Small Eddie continued, "we'd like to hold a moot. Preach has some connections, and with his help, we'll provide the food. Hopefully, we'll all be able to get along that long, 'cause after that, we'll be working together."

"Crazy cult freaks—and backed by action suits!" Rogue Moon cursed under her breath. Despite her objections, a few minutes later, she relayed to the rest of the Brownies that Mother Freya would indeed meet with the strangers under truce. Moon didn't like it. To her, the whole thing smelled worse than her first encounter with a deader. While she despised suits, she hated cultists more than anything else—and the Jesus-freak Paladins were at the top of *that* list. Considering the thought, she realized there was only one thing she hated worse. The only thing she hated more than the cultists at her doorstep was the army of Witch City slavers they were going to take on.

…… …

The third day of the moot saw a sullen tension hanging in the air between the Paladins and the Brownies. Jack and Small Eddie had been praying for at least a working harmony between two gangs, but the CYBER forces heard complaints and small arguments breaking out no matter where they went. Plus, while Jack's team had the solid support of the Paladin leadership, beyond that, they were almost complete strangers to the rank-and-file of both sides. At least there were positive signs of relations forming between the three factions in the leadership circles. Jack hoped it would be enough, but on midafternoon of the third day, Araña called for a brief team meeting.

"Preach, I don't know if this is going to work," he began. "I mean, we pulled off that thing between the Razors and the Brotherhood, but at least they both thought the same way enough to at least have a basis for understanding the other side's point of view. These two groups, I just don't know. Their whole thinking is diametrically opposed. You know as well as I do that once the shooting starts, there won't be any mock battle—this thing's gonna blow up on us, *Jefé*."

"The problem is," Josanne added, "they don't have anything to really get them to see beyond their differences. They're so afraid of who's on the other side of the table from them they're not uniting."

"Trigget's still getting her head in the game," Chrome began, "but she's right on this one. You're trying to overcome generational hatred in two days, and outside of the senior leaders, both the Paladins and the Brownies are seeing themselves as being played.

"Maybe you should get them together and admit to them that you need to come up with another idea. They can't work together. Right now, the only thing both sides agree on is that when the mock battle starts, it's going to be a slaughter, and each side thinks they're going to be the victims."

Jack reflected upon what his team had just relayed to him. He knew the plan had always been a longshot at best, but it was the best he could come up with. He had been so focused on saving Kelly that he just didn't have room for the groups not to at least temporarily get along. He had prayed about it, and he had run by the plan with SIMON before leaving. Even now that the longshot was fading fast, it was still the only plan he could come up with. But, he admitted to himself, Chrome was right. Both sides saw themselves as the victims in this, and they'd be firing on each other for real in minutes.

- *"You guys better get over here," a Paladin voice hailed over a radio. "Small Eddie and Mother Freya just broke into a fight."*

Jack almost swore. This was the last straw. If the biggest leaders of the two groups couldn't keep it together, what chance did they have?

"What are you two *doing*?" Jack yelled at both gang leaders as he approached. "What in the world is so important that you two are risking everything we've been working for?"

"I told her we're having a tent meeting to pray before going out in the next couple days and asked her to invite the Brownies," a seething Small Eddie began.

"And I told him that him and his Paladins can all go to Hell!" Freya shouted.

"So, what did we do this time?" he complained, exasperated.

"Stop judging my crew, getting into their heads, and always trying to make them feel guilty!" Freya commanded, equally frustrated.

"Come on, Freya," Eddie protested. "You know as well as I do how this works! You ask us to do something, and you rail on us if we don't want to join in. We have our services without inviting you, and you claim we're sanctimonious and exclusive. We invite you to our services, and you say we're being self-righteous, holier-than-thou hypocrites. You say we're judging you, but if you really thought about it, you know you'd have to admit that you spend more than your fair share of time judging every little thing we do—or don't do, if you can't think of something we're actually doing wrong.

"If we don't say anything, you're saying that we're stuck up and that we don't consider you worth caring about. We hear your girls always telling each other to go to hell and laughing it off, yet the minute we try to say to someone that they don't have to go to hell, we're labeled as judgmental?"

"I know your kind!" Mother Freya retorted. "You Paladins have been throwing your 'Hell this' and 'Judgment that' around since the beginning of time! You think everybody should just think all the ways you do, and I've seen enough of your kind to know that most of you are really just waiting for us to be dead and in hell so you'll never have to deal with us again. Well, I got a question for you, holy man: What's to say that any of us would actually want to spend a week with any of you, let alone an eternity, 'cause my version of Heaven doesn't have a bunch of self-righteous goveks calling all the rules!"

"I agree!" Jack cut in before Eddie got another word out of his mouth, causing everyone who heard him, including his fellow CYBER agents, to do a double-take.

"Wait—what?" Eddie and Freya said, almost in perfect unison.

"I agree," Jack repeated, more calmly than he felt. "And if I heard Eddie right, I think he does, too."

"What do you mean by that?" Freya asked. At first, she felt vindicated in her argument against the Paladins; now, she suspected a trap.

"Are you aware of what happened when Jesus came? It's a long story, but in short, He got along with the lost and disrespected in society: lepers, diseased, women, and kids—all were held in very low regard by the society people of His day. And they all loved Him for it, even though He challenged quite a few of established notions— He told them to love their enemies, get along with the Romans— he even made a half-breed Samaritan the hero of one of His most popular stories. In fact, the only people who really had a problem with what Jesus was doing at the time was the religious right, who were all about the rules and actually had very little in common with what God really had in mind."

"Well, if that's true, then these Paladins sure got a lot to learn," Freya accused.

"We're not trying to keep you out of Heaven," Eddie replied, now calmed considerably. "We want you to be able to go! God has no desire to see anyone go to hell. It was created for Satan, not for people. That's why Jesus died."

"Oh yeah?" Freya re-engaged. "Even your Bible says God wanted Pharaoh to go to hell; that's why he hardened Pharaoh's heart."

Small Eddie shook his head and smiled. "That word used there doesn't mean God made Pharaoh's heart hard, although a lot of people think that's what it means. The word used for 'harden' was used in other places, one of them being the Ten Commandments…."

"Oh, here we go with your commandments," Freya interrupted. "Like thou shalt not kill? What do you guys do with that one?"

Josanne was watching Jack see his world fall apart in front of his own cybernetic eyes. Foxfire had trained her well: too well for her not to notice that however misguided CYBER was about her brother, Jack was really *all* in about saving his former youth group member. She wished she could say something to help, but it seemed like everyone was so worried in their imaginations about becoming the next victims, they completely forgot about the very real victims they were supposed to be saving. And then she had an idea, and despite how it horrified her, she knew it might be the only way this could work.

- "Jack?" she hesitantly sub-vocalized, "I have an idea."

She had to collect herself when he turned to her. She didn't know his eyes could still cry. After she explained the concept, he simply looked at her, smiled, and told her a simple, kind, "Thank you." She had too much conversationalist training to miss that he meant it intensely. There was something else in knowing that, which gave curious rise to how she felt about his response. And, she recognized, that something else had not so much to do in her conversationalist training as it had in her being a woman.

… …

By 7:30 PM, the theatre was completely filled with both Valhalla's Brownies and Paladins. Backstage, Jack, Josanne, Small Eddie, Mother Freya, and Rogue Moon were doing some last-minute conferring before the show started.

"Gotta hand it to you, hon," Mother Freya told Josanne, "if there's anything that'll get our minds off of our pasts and focused on where we need to be, this is it."

"I wish I could have thought of something different. I feel like I'm using them," Josanne replied.

"It's okay," Moon affirmed. "You're right—I lost sight of what we were doing this for. I talked it over with 'em, and all forty-five who are coming forward are willing to. Actually, even more, were willing to come, but we didn't want to run too long. Probably only ten of us will actually speak; the rest will be there for moral support and to show that it's not just ten or twenty girls we're talking about. The fact that Kelly is still back there is providing them a lot of motivation."

"Well, God Bless you for going ahead with this, if you don't mind me saying so," Small Eddie assured the Valhalla sniper. "For what it's worth, it's a very brave thing you're doing."

"Hell," Freya replied, "you Paladins are the ones who rode into the middle of our turf to allow it to happen, and not a lot of people would've agreed to do that. Err, no offense," she quickly added.

"None taken. By the way, back to that 'thou shalt not kill' question and the hardening of Pharaoh's heart… We defend ourselves, and yeah, we defend others who need our help, but despite the tools we need to do that, we don't enjoy the bloodshed. But the command I was referring to was 'Honor your father and mother.' It was the same word, and it was used in a bunch of other places the same way. That word—translated that one time as 'harden'—really means 'honor.' God doesn't want you to go to hell, but He will honor your decision in the matter. Freya, we don't hate you. We just hate the direction you're going because we believe we're going miss you."

"Never heard it that way before," Freya conceded. "Thanks for that."

Applause sounded from the theatre audience as the lights came down, a single spotlight illuminating the center stage.

"Don't mean to interrupt things," Moon interrupted as she headed forward to the curtain, "but I'm on."

"Break a leg," Jack reassured her.

"Oh, she's good at that!" Freya quipped, but the sniper had already taken claim of the spot-lit stool and brought a microphone to her mouth.

"Hi. I'm Rogue Moon," she announced to the crowd. She sighed, set her eyes on some imaginary focal point in the back of the room above the crowd, squared herself, and continued. "Six years ago, I was rescued from slavery in Witch City. This is my story...."

By the time the tenth girl, a frail blonde no older than sixteen, took her turn at the microphone, both sides had forgotten their differences and had squarely fixed their minds on the real enemy. Josanne found Jack kneeling in one of the darkened corners of the theatre after the event was over, practically sobbing his eyes out as he prayed for the success of the operation and thanking God for sending her along with him despite her misgivings about the mission. Josanne began to approach him to see if there was something she could say when she overheard him also praying for help in winning her trust. Struck by his sincerity, she remembered the sessions they had back at Facility and how many times she had thrown everything he was trying to tell her back in his face. Suddenly ashamed, she turned around as quietly as she could and withdrew. Still mulling over what she had heard, she realized just how quickly Jack's prayers were being answered...

19. Insertion

JOHNNY'S IMPRESSION OF Wichita's eastern entry checkpoint was that it was pretty much like any other fortress town large enough to handle an ICC archology and surrounding franchise territories. After the team meetings and Elaine's stories, he had expected the whole city to be nothing more than a cesspool of debauchery; he was surprised that, from what he could currently see, most of Wichita was just like every other city he had ever been in.

A pair of SF-73 Interdictors, Air Dynamix's latest premier strike fighters, once again flew over the line of vehicles in the checkpoint line. Johnny involuntarily ducked at the freakish howls their engines made as the aircraft descended to a mere fifty feet above the ground to buzz the line of traffic awaiting entry. Immediately afterward, both pilots simultaneously pitched their planes into near-vertical ascents and lit their afterburners; anyone within the resultant ground carpet of the twin pairs of sonic booms experienced the equivalent sound blasts of cannon fire at close proximity. The pilots, having sated their immediate sense of fun, leveled off their climbs to resume the normal combat air patrols around Air Dynamix's territorial perimeter.

"Okay," Johnny said to himself, "so Wichita checkpoints aren't exactly like every other fortress town."

- *"What was that?" Melissana asked through her transceiver.*

- *"Air Dynamix—they have aircraft patrolling their perimeter."*

- *"That could complicate things," Melissana noted.*

- *"Simon said it would handle it," Johnny somewhat dourly responded.*

- *"That wasn't Simon," Melissana corrected, "Iylo said he would handle it."*

"One and the same, Mel," he thought, but he checked himself before he said it out loud. He wondered what he should say in response, but at that moment, the checkpoint guard waved his car forward.

- *"OK, time to still up and hold your breath. We're on,"* he said, *somewhat grateful for the interruption.*

The checkpoint staff waved off the first two cars ahead of him, but a red light flashed as Johnny approached the scanner, and he was waved to the side of the line. He pulled over, but even though he was perplexed, he didn't have to try hard to look cool and collected. He had had plenty of practice getting pulled over and evading various arrests long before CYBER had recruited him.

The checkpoint guards who approached the car were not the friendly ones who smile and wave people through the gate. Literally dressed to kill in full combat armor the color and pattern of desert scrub, one stood about thirty feet off holding a shoulder-fired rocket launcher directly on the car while the other approached, auto-rifle leveled at the driver's window as he asked, "May I see your identification, please?"

Melissana thought to tell Johnny to wave his arm and state, "This isn't the car you're looking for," but decided against it. She didn't want to take a chance on them picking up the sub-vocalized frequency, and at best, the guard sounded like he was in ill humor.

"Here you go, sir," Johnny respectfully replied with a nervous smile. "Is there anything wrong?"

"Your name, please?" the guard asked without answering Johnny's question.

"John, sir. John Sebastian, from Kellogg, Michigan."

"This your first time to Wichita?"

"Yes sir, it is," Johnny responded truthfully.

"And you're by yourself?"

"Yes sir, I am," Johnny lied.

"So, John Sebastian from Kellogg, Michigan, what brings you to the home of Air Dynamix?"

"I'd like to say to get a glimpse of your aircraft," Johnny began, purposely trying to gauge the response force's reaction to the potential threat of corporate espionage. Feeling duly compensated by the reflexive twitch of both guards, he continued, "But the truth is, Kellogg downsized me, and I'm trying to pick up somewhere far enough away that I won't have to smell them anymore."

"We don't take to vagrants," the guard began. Now it was Johnny's turn to take offense. "Whom do you think you're addressing?" he snapped. "I was the Director of Processing for those upper-echelon corporate goveks! I designed their synthesis processes and tightened up their revenue streams!"

"Oh, I'm sure you did, up until the time they streamlined you," the guard said with a significant scoff. "Like I said, we don't allow vagrants," he repeated in the undeniable tone of, "No."

"They were fools to get rid of me," Johnny protested, "and it'll take me no time at all to prove that here! Then you'll see who's streamlined...." He turned his head aside as he snuffed, "Vagrant, indeed!"

This time the guard broke into an open guffaw, leaving Johnny to wonder if the guard regretted not being able to wipe his eyes through his ballistic visor plate.

"With every statement you make, I will peel yet another layer off this onion of lies," he said with a sneer. "Open up your trunk, and let's see what you got."

Johnny wondered if the bored guard practiced that line in front of a mirror every day while getting ready for work and was secretly grateful to finally be able to use it on someone. But he obediently popped open the trunk and passively watched as his luggage was torn open and searched by less-than-concerned checkpoint guards. Melissana held her breath throughout the entire time.

"All right," the first guard agreed as he told his partner to stand down. "Your identity checks. I'll let you in, but only because it'll be fun watching you sink into the downward spiral you're about to go on. I'll enjoy that, Mr. Sebastian, so have a good day. I guess you're entitled to at least one before we end up sweeping you off the sidewalks." Then he broke to his partner. "Mitch, come on. Let's go back inside. This guy's goin' nowhere so fast he thinks he's on his way up. We're done here."

Feeling the forward motion of the car, Melissana relaxed both her breath and her shoulders.

- *"What the heck was that all about?" she asked. "You goaded him into kicking you out?"*

- *"I wanted to raise their alarm with the espionage comment, then lower their suspicion even faster. Every corp merc like that guy really enjoys it when an exec goes down, so I gave them a reason not to be afraid of me and whip us through the inevitable inspection as quickly as possible."*

- *"Skillfully done, then!" Melissana congratulated.*

- *"Luckily, too," Johnny stated. "But it makes me wonder how they smuggle all the girls into and out of the city. By the way, in case you're interested, I'm pulling up to a corner where you can work your way out from underneath the back seats. I mean, if you want some real air…."*

- "You bet I do!" Melissana answered.

It took her three minutes to wriggle out from her 18-inch-deep hideaway compartment underneath the back seats of Johnny's luxury sedan. In another ten minutes, the two had sprayed a special combination of CYBER solvents and wiped down the vehicle, transforming the one-time statement of corporate prestige into a tricked-out half-beat pimp-mobile.

20. Collision Courses

At six-thirty the next morning, Jack and the other CYBER members met in a huddle with Small Eddie, Luke, and a couple of other Paladin lieutenants, Mother Freya, Rogue Moon, Bridgette, and Ingrid. The mood of the camp had indeed changed since the previous night. Not only was nobody arguing as the groups were preparing for the coming battle, across the camp, individual Brownies and Paladins actually worked together side by side. How long the temporary truce would last was anyone's guess, but for now, the current cohesion between them would suffice. They went over the plans one last time before the group split up to get into their positions. After the last details were covered, there wasn't much more to say. It was time to go.

"Well, I guess this is it," Jack began. "The convoy is scheduled to arrive later this morning. They're running a little slower to make sure you have time to set up," Jack warned Freya. "Be careful out there."

"Will do. We're almost all dug in. Now that we have warning, it shouldn't be too bad—if the Paladins show up on time."

"We'll be there, Freya," Small Eddie promised. "If we come in too early, it'll look too staged. We can't join in right away, but we'll be there."

"Hey Eddie," Jack began, "it's late notice, but do you have a couple boys you can spare me for a couple days? I'll need someone on the ground for altar calls."

"Did you ever figure out the answer to that question I asked you a couple days ago?" he replied with a question of his own.

"Yeah, I think I did," Jack replied after he reflected for a moment. He almost visibly radiated his sense of peace as he continued. "After last night, and with the Lord's help, I actually think we're going to win this thing. Thanks for asking."

Eddie grunted, then raised his radio.

"Somebody wake up Dante and Constantine. Tell 'em they got twenty minutes to get their bags and full gear packed for a couple days and get up here. I'll explain once they're here."

The organization and discipline of the Paladins could not be questioned—both men were groggy, but each made it to the bus in seventeen minutes.

"Best hammer and sword combo I've got," Eddie disclosed to Preach. "Take care of 'em." Turning to the two men, he added, "An' you boys make me proud."

"Hey, Preach—we gotta go," Josanne interrupted. "We got a couple-hour bus ride, and we need to get there before the convoy rolls into range."

"Want to pray before we head out?" Preach asked.

"Been doing little else since we met back up," Eddie replied with a grin. After a brief round of farewell prayers, Eddie looked at them and declared, "Okay, guys, ya better get going."

"Got it, thanks. Araña and Chrome, I'll need you to stay to coordinate the convoy attack and initialization of the perimeter. Join us inside as soon as you can transition the coordination to Rickshaw and Hardcore—I'd like to have you two with us on opening night. Now's a good time to say your goodbyes. We leave in ten." Freya and Rogue were having a side conversation that was beginning to sound like a disagreement. "Ladies?" he asked, "everything okay?"

"Change of plan, Preach," Rogue declared while stepping forward, away from Freya. "You got a pair of steel ones, but you don't know jack about the inner workings of Witch City."

"Moon, no!" Freya exclaimed.

"We've been over this, Rogue," Jack protested. "We have to go inside to find Kelly."

"I wholeheartedly agree," the sniper affirmed. "And if you really do want to find her quickly, you're going to need some help. Valhalla's Brownies will also need to know the communications they're getting from you are legit, and there's no way you can learn all the signs and countersigns we've developed over the last few decades. You wouldn't stand half a chance if you had a small army—you won't stand any chance at all on your own." She picked up a small duffel bag she had brought with her to the meeting and slung it over her shoulder as she took another step towards the bus. Pausing to look over her shoulder, she concluded her announcement.

"Which is why I'm coming with you."

Araña was the first to weigh in.

- "Jefé? That wasn't part of the plan...."

- "Well, Rickshaw said that CYBER always changes up the plans." Susan offered.

- "Yeah, to adapt them to the team, not just to throw wrenches into the works for the thrill of it," Chrome objected.

- "We can't really say no without throwing all kinds of red flags that could completely wreck the cooperation we just got worked out between the two groups," Josanne added. "Besides, even Mother Freya couldn't dissuade her."

- "If Mother Freya actually was trying to dissuade her," Jack finally commented. "I'm sure Freya's interested in seeing what we have going on here that allows us to even think we have a chance at this. She might just be scouting us out. Still, Rogue Moon's points were valid; she could be a definite help."

- *"Or a targeting beacon," Chrome corrected. "Remember, she was stuck in Witch City for a while before she escaped; plus, the Brownies have been hitting Wichita targets for years. I'd lay odds they spot her."*

- *"And remember Elaine's meltdown?" Josanne noted. "There's quite a different dynamic with Rogue, but she's just as emotional; she almost seems eager to go back."*

- *"All of the above are true," Jack decided, "but we don't know that she intends any harm. She's different from Elaine. She reclaimed her spirit by taking the fight back to the enemy. Do we keep an extra eye on our backs while Rogue is with us? Of course, we do. But the bottom line is she's still right; she can help us, and I, for one, hope to capitalize on that."*

"Mount up, Rogue," Jack ordered after he had deliberated for quite a while.

Completely unaware of the subvocalized conversation, she figured the gap between her declaration and his order was just him silently reflecting on all his options. Five minutes later, he stopped the bus as he drove past Small Eddie and Mother Freya before heading onto the desert roadway that led to the city. Jack opened the bus door and leaned out as it passed.

"One more thing," he called out. "When you hit the convoy, try not to fire on a red and yellow Dominator or midnight black Sabretooth with some fancy paintwork on it."

"Why not?" both gang leaders asked in near unison.

Jack looked at them both and smiled. "They're both ours—Eddie already knows Rickshaw, the guy in the Sabretooth goes by Hardcore. That's how we learned the convoy is a trap; we planted them a week ago."

"You just take care of my girl!" Freya shouted, angry at the turn of events. She caught Eddie's sideways glance. "So what was that you were talking about before they left?" she fired more than asked.

"Whether he thought he was on a suicide run or not."

"Drek! Not with my girl he's not."

"And what are you going to do about it? Attack them? Go into Witch City after them? You're already a hot enough target for them to hire a merc band to hunt you down, remember? Well, that merc band that's on their way now! So settle yourself down and get your group ready to do what they do.

"Look," he said, calming down, "I have no idea how Jack does what he does, but I do know that, pastor or not, he's darn good at it. They all are. Rogue said he'd need a small army to stand a chance; what she doesn't know is that Jack and his crew *are* a small army."

Freya glowered at him, the rocks around them, then finally at the Sun. Suddenly she nodded at some internal thought and thanked the Paladin's leader.

"Bridgette!" she finally shouted.

"Yes, Mother?"

"Come on with me, we gotta run back to town and get a message out."

"To whom?"

"Rogue said they'd need a small army once they got into the city," she explained. "And it turns out we just happen to know somebody who has one." She genuinely smiled at him. "Thanks, Eddie. I owe you for this one." Turning away, she mounted the back seat of Bridgette's bike.

"No," Chrome ordered in resolute monotone.

She locked her eyes in a defiant glare and raised her radio to her mouth. "We'll be back in a half-hour," she radioed to her Brownies. "Don't start the dance without me, girls!" Then she tapped Bridgette on the shoulder. "Hit it, Bridg!"

The fast bike lurched forward, but Bridgette collided against the handlebars and would have dumped over them if the impact of

Freya's also awkwardly falling forward hadn't pinned her in place. Dazed, they took a second to wonder what they had driven into until they looked over their shoulders to see the Hounds' heavy lifting the back of the bike to keep them from going anywhere.

"Look, you *govek*," she fumed, "we know a guy on the inside who can help them, but I gotta get word to him. With all the stuff with the Paladins, I didn't think to reach out to him earlier."

"You mean Sitter?" Araña asked.

"Do you already have contact with him?" she asked, surprised they knew about the Witch City activist.

"We know the name—it was Sitter who let you know about that convoy raid a month ago. We've been looking for him but haven't turned anything up yet."

"You can go make your call when we get this piece under control. If you abandon your place now, you'll risk losing half the people you're leaving behind," Chrome stated flatly.

"OK, fine," she resigned. "You're probably right. It's not like I got much choice in the matter." She glanced at Chrome, who was still lifting the back of the bike off the ground with one arm. "Just put the bike down and answer me a question. This bike's armored, and there are two people sitting on it. Are all you guys… like you?"

After the motor shut off, Chrome gently lowered the rear tire back to the ground with a dry smile. "We're all, shall we say, special in some way, but lady, there's only one of me."

Araña chuckled and added, "And believe me, Freya, you should be glad of that!"

"Well, we've had our break," Chrome said to reel them back in. "We've got a battle imminent, and we need to make the most of each minute until it gets here."

"Moon says your team's well on their way," Freya relayed after getting the call from Rogue. "We'd best get ready. That convoy will be coming in the morning, and with Moon not playing, we're down our best opener."

"We can handle that for you—if you don't mind, that is," Small Eddie offered. Upon Mother Freya's assent, he got on the Paladin's own radio frequency.

"Bring up the Dragon Slayer," he ordered. "Set it up on King Hill."

Freya rolled her eyes at the naming scheme, but she had to admit to herself she wondered what kind of a thing the Paladins would call a dragon slayer. Whatever it was, the Paladins were confident it could hit hard enough to stop a convoy.

… …

After closing the door and easing the vehicle northbound to Witch City, Jack turned and addressed his teams. "We'll have to change along the way. Rogue, I hadn't planned on having you along." He dangled an ankle-length plain dress the color of a Missouri dawn's patch of mud at arm's length. "Hope this fits—out of all of us, you stand the most chance of being recognized."

"I'll have to wear that?" Rogue lamented, "I've never worn anything that ugly."

"If you want to be on this bus when we pull into Witch City," he answered, "not only will you wear it, you'll act like it's your favorite."

"Welcome to the team," Trigget murmured. She mentally added, *"At least you had a choice."*

… …

- *"Spider, the convoy's 10 minutes due west of your position."*

- *"Got it, Iylo—Thanks," Araña replied through his sub-vocal mic.*

"Freya? Eddie? Let your troops know—we got about 10 minutes until showtime!"

"Cripe—how can he possibly know that? It's unnerving sometimes," Freya complained.

"He's got friends in high places," Eddie somewhat cryptically replied.

"Come on. You're trying to tell me that God is talking to that guy about the convoy vehicle movements?"

"No," Eddie smiled, "although He's done that before." He caught her confused look, then continued. "No, not quite that high, Well, with Preach, yeah sometimes, but you haven't met everyone on his teams. Preach also has a couple deckers and one of 'em's riding some redirected satellite beams to provide surveillance."

"Holy drek!" Freya exclaimed, shaking her head. "They can *do* that?"

"That's weird," Ingrid joined in, lowering a set of binoculars and pointing westward. "The locals have an old saying: 'The birds around here all died from lack of trees,' but I could've sworn I just saw a couple."

"Airborne drones," Chrome almost swore. "Well, I gotta hand it to you. You ladies certainly made an impression."

"Not as big as I'm gonna make on any choob in that convoy I get my hands on," Bridgette replied.

Chrome smiled in spite of their situation. "Y'know, Bridgett, I'm beginning to like you people."

Freya was on her own radio in less than a second. *"Get ready for the ride, Brownies. High an' tight—we got incoming."*

"You ain't bad yourself, for a phallo," Bridgett replied as they prepared for the inevitable.

… …

The shock of the first wave of drones caught many by surprise despite the warning. The drones' silence was effective; the small engines of each whispered an eerie hush coupled with silenced automatic weapons barely audible to anyone but Araña. The payload of ordinance was also muted, at least while they launched—the explosive blasts were deafening when they went off. Spider counted no less than thirteen airborne vehicles in that first wave, but due to their high speeds and trying to avoid their deadly accuracy, even he was hard-pressed to know for sure. Then a second wave came. By the time the third wave cleared, the convoy was upon them.

"By the Sword of Saint George," Small Eddie decreed over his helmet mic, *"Let it fly!"*

With a roaring *WHOOSH* that tore at the command shelter camouflage netting and every other item that offered wind resistance, a 15' long surface-to-surface missile rocketed from behind the dug-in Brownie positions at just about 40' off the ground. Every Brownie clung to the dirt in a dread panic—even Chrome cringed as the force of the shockwave pushed him forward and almost to his knees. Not three seconds later, the initial shot was accompanied by a volley of 30 micro-missiles that shrieked across the sky like a horde of harpies bent on the complete destruction of their quarry. The large missile hammered into the lead tractor-trailer of the enemy convoy, forcibly slamming it into a second trailer before the resultant blast stopped five vehicles dead in their tracks. The follow-up detonations of the smaller warheads completely disrupted whatever evasion strategies the enemy might have had planned.

"I present you the Dragon Slayer," Small Eddie announced as the female bikers gathered themselves back up. *"It's pretty much a missile-arbalest combo, but it's a one-shot. You're on your own for the next half hour or so."*

"Thanks, Eddie. After those drone attacks, we needed it!" Freya replied.

"Start 'em up, Ladies, it's our turn now," she hailed as she commanded her armored hovercraft's engines revved up to full power. *"We promised those goveks we'd give 'em comeuppance—and this... is... it!*

"VALHALLAA!!!!!" she roared as her hovercraft lurched forward, gaining an impressive amount of speed with each second of its spurred charge. And in deafening reply, the Valhalla's Brownies repeated their battle cry and rode off to war, Spider and Chrome alongside as they bore down upon the forces of the enemy convoy that were beginning to circle around the downed tractor-trailers to continue their assault.

The Battle of the Witch City Blockade had begun in earnest...

21. Opening Nights

"Hope that gate guard has a good time trying to find Mr. Sebastian," Johnny smirked. "He's about to disappear again."

Johnny and Melissana once again changed into their more colorful disguises and drove on. Like the night before, tonight's mission was to simply recon the area and get the lay of the land in real-time. This time it took ten minutes for them to find the signs of one of the higher-end tracks in the commercial zone. Girls and boys were bought and sold by men who paid for them right along with the purses and jewelry they purchased for their wives. Johnny's smirk lessened some and then disappeared altogether when they got to the edges of the warehouse district.

They rounded another street corner, taking in the dance, the biz, catching hints of credits changing hands for drugs and other wares that were still illegal in the corporate-governed lawlessness of a 2048 urbanity. They spotted the walkers first. They were easy enough to pick out—no drug, weapon, or flesh dealers could get customers if they didn't advertise. Typically, outsiders mistakenly thought the activities of underground biz were conducted in a fast keep-up-or-get-out franticness. It made for the popular vids that featured action over plot, but the fast-paced bustle of the normal grab/sell/next customer relations belonged to the safer legitimate enterprises. Johnny and Melissana had been around the real thing enough to know better. No matter what the specific vice you were looking to sate, the street deals of underground commerce were typically a much slower, more personal transaction. There were protocols to be followed, risks to be analyzed, traps to be avoided. In the reality of the underground markets, hustlers didn't really sell what the buyers were trading them credits for; they marketed trust, camaraderie, and to the truly naïve, the illusion of friendship. And while that happened to some extent at every level of commerce, from the Witch City slums to International Corporate Conglomerate banking halls, the streets took the losses to the meat level. The luxury of recovery was only available while your supplies lasted, and in the dark recesses of the shadow-ground, they didn't last long.

The dealer's dance was to convince the buyer he could be trusted, that the two were tight, or at least that the seller was necessary. The *illusion* of friendship, trust, and need was the real commodity; in some part of their souls, the buyers knew it was all a sham to fleece them of their credits, but they lined up to buy anyway. After all, the buyers tailored an illusion of their own: the drug, or the girl, or the gun would give them that dodgy sense of comfort and, if they hit the high just right, a momentary sense of fulfillment. The dealers knew any appearance of loyalty was an illusion—not that they'd ever point it out to their tight, ever-buying friends. The wealthier hustlers cultivated that misperception as much as they could, at least while their customers still had some creds left to slot into ever-eager accounts. Such was the flow of the credits. After all, blood was thicker than water, but street value for a pint of plasma these days was only 20 to 25 credits, tops.

Melissana suddenly grabbed Johnny's forearm. "Johnny, stop." Then leaning over the seat and craning her neck to review the scene before her, asked, "Do you see it?"

"Do I see what?" he questioned, still surveying the neighborhood. "I see normal people, going to shops, on their way to theatres, people just moving from one place to another like they always do."

"Look underneath what you see. See that girl with the guy by the jewelry shop? There's no hope in her, no excitement."

"So, the guy's maybe buying something for someone else, or for her just for her to wear for work, or...."

"Or she knows that as soon as she gets back to her pimp, he's going to confiscate it from her anyway," she finished for him.

"The kid who just walked past us had a bar code tattoo on her neck. And that guy halfway down the block? Those two girls that are with him sure aren't his daughters, but both are a lot younger. Looks like the one is pretty scared of him, too."

They continued their drive for another two blocks past the main thoroughfare before they stopped again.

"How obvious is that?" Johnny complained in futility. "The Single Hearts Hotel? Come on, they could at least try to disguise what they're up to. That guy on the hotel step and his joeboy are just sitting there, monitoring the traffic."

"No," the former private eye corrected, "he's looking for something. There—that car pulling up. Look! Johnny, he's literally dragging those two girls from inside the car into that dive. Geez, he just hit her—we've got to do something!" She reached for the door to confront the slavers.

"Vix," Johnny said, putting a restraining hold on her arm, "if we go now, we'll blow everything we came here to do. We can't get to them now, but bringing these guys down for good, that's the op. I don't want to say this, but we gotta get frosty this time." Two more girls walked by Johnny's car—one of them noticed him inside it and blew him a kiss, but now that he knew what to look for, he saw the sadness in her eyes. He took another glance around, pursing his lips to let out a low whistle. "Melissana, it's so subtle, so everywhere, that at first, I missed it," he admitted. "We're looking for a track in a red-light district, but now that I'm starting to see it, that's not what's going on here."

Melissana finished for him, "Witch City is all around us—these girls are everywhere."

"Seems like we found what we've been looking for," Johnny concluded with disgust. "You sure you're ready for this?"

She looked at him, and he was struck by the vulnerability he saw in her slight retreat and raised eyebrows. He had forgotten about her own past and how much of it she was beginning to relive. "You know, you don't have to do this."

"Wow," she said and genuinely smiled. Whatever personal crisis she had begun to face had lapsed forgotten, if only for the moment. "You actually care about someone?"

"Yeah," he smiled back. "The human cat must be getting attached to some of its family." As he caught her sudden stare, he added, "Oh, don't look so surprised. Sue told Corey about the comment, and sometime later, he told me. We had a good laugh over it."

"So, you're not upset about that?"

"No reason to be. In all honesty, I kinda like it." He reached out his hand, cupped her chin with his index finger, and gently lifted it to look her full in the eyes.

"But I promise you," he began, hazel-green eyes icing to a deathly serious stare, "when we get back here and start doing this thing, anybody gets outta line with you, and they're gonna find out how protective I can be."

Melissana never had a big brother to defend her before, and for the first time since they got into the city, she relaxed.

"Come on," he said, interrupting both the moment and himself. "We'd better get over to the wall."

He *respected* Iylothien—the problem was, he was no longer all that sure that Iylothien was even real.

…… ……

The thick walls around Wichita reduced most of the remote battle sounds to indistinct echoes, but to the city guards patrolling the battlement, they offered the perspective of watching from a balcony.

"Turret Three, this is Golf Eleven. How are things from your perspective?"

"Golf Eleven, this is Turret Three. They're all around the city, but they're keeping their distance. The trucks are all down, but it looks

like the Paladins and the Brownies are in a fight to the finish on this one!"

Neither of them had to say it over the radio—and neither one dared to risk severe corporate punitive measures—but every turret and wall patrol unit instinctively knew it. The Air Dynamix air patrols confirmed it. As long as this battle lasted, there was no way someone was going to attack the city. The combatants would do security's job for them. So, while it lasted, most of them just took to their posts and watched over the wall to view the auto arena shows; they didn't even have to pay this time. Whiskey Eleven was so focused on the battle playing out before him he almost hadn't noticed the flimsily dressed, petite twenty-something woman with long black hair until she was within reach of his arms.

"Hey," she called to him so quietly she practically whispered the word. She was attractive —very much so, he observed, in what he now recognized as a chic belly dancer outfit. The satin veil she wore over her face did little to hide the promise of a sensuous face underneath.

"Who are you? What are you doing here?" he asked in a somewhat dulled sense of alarm.

"They call me Bahar," she said as she approached closer to the guard on the wall. She then removed her veil, not disappointing the guard's imagination, and replied, "And I'm looking for you." An explosion in the distance drew her attention to the battle as if she was noticing it for the first time. She somehow produced a can of beer and offered it to him with an inviting smile. "Come on, honey," she crooned, leaning into him ever so slightly and raising the beer within an inch of the right side of her face. "You'd like a little drink of this, wouldn't you?"

He coughed at the question, then another explosion lit up some of the areas outside the city, and Bahar shivered at the spectacle of the night battle. "Is it always like this up here?" she asked.

"Just what are you doing up here?" he pressed, the momentary distraction enough to weaken the spell she had been weaving.

"All right," she said with a little pout. Whiskey Eleven wondered if it was genuine but decided the gesture was cute, so he settled for the possibility that it might have been.

"You're Allan, walking as Whiskey Eleven tonight, right?" At his nod, she continued. "Two of the other guards at the bottom of the wall—Jeremy and Ray, I think—had a bet. Jeremy really likes me. If Jeremy won the bet, Ray would have to pay me for a round with Jeremy. If Jeremy lost, he'd have to pay me to hook up and have a drink with you. Jeremy lost. But Jeremy made a side bet now between someone else and Ray that I can't get you to do it on the wall. If you do, I'll get a bonus at Ray's expense, and it's big enough that I can split the difference with you if you go with me on it."

"Lady, I've heard a lot of stories before, but this one…."

"Oh, come on," she insisted, sighing in frustration. "You can have me for free either way. You got nothing to lose, and besides," she said with a playful smile, "you're kinda cute. I'll definitely make it worth your while."

He grinned. He had nothing to lose, and Bahar *was* attractive.

"Come on over here, out of the cameras. You have no idea how much trouble this'd be if the shift commander caught us."

"Well, I removed my veil. Now it's your turn," she purred. Out of the camera's view and with Bahar's urging, he removed his helmet and ammo harness.

"So, how'd you get your name?" he asked as he prepared to undo his armor latches.

"A preacher told me it's based off an ancient story about some prostitute that turned out to be one of Jesus's ancestors."

"You gotta be kiddin' me!" he said between bouts of a sudden belly laugh. "That's rich!" he laughed again. "Okay, you win. Hand me that beer, sister; I am *really* going to enjoy my time with you! Jeremy and Ray, huh?" He laughed again. "I'll have to thank them both! A hooker ancestor of Jesus—too funny!"

"It's true," she said, causing him to laugh harder, but she continued. "But it's not the whole story. My name is her name backward, so there's a twist..."

At that point, a figure emerged out of the darkness behind Whiskey Eleven. Bahar cried out, "Sweet Trick—Showbiz—NO!" just before the form clubbed the unsuspecting guard across the back of his neck, instantly knocking him cold. Immediately dropping all pretense of the Bahar persona, Melissana bent over the fallen Whiskey Eleven to make sure he was out. "The twist, choob, is that I'm letting a rope down to let two spies *into* the city."

"Welcome to Witch City, our very own personal Shangri-La of Shame," Johnny greeted a few minutes later as Chrome and Spider completed their climb up the rope and made contact with him and the costumed Melissana. After some brief exchange of updates, the two Hounds skirted off to find Preach.

"You sure you want to go back down there?" Johnny asked her when even Araña was out of earshot.

"Not really, no, but with them now on the inside, I mean, so far, things are going okay, right? I guess I'm starting to feel a lot better about all of this. At least I have a choice in the matter. Kelly's in here somewhere, and she doesn't have any choices at all unless we find her." She shivered. "Besides, it'll give me a chance to change. Anything's gotta be warmer than this get-up."

"All right then, I guess we're on." He glanced back at the fallen guard and added, "We'd better go. He'll never be able to tell anyone what happened up here, but we need to be gone before they check up on him."

"And if he does decide to talk," Melissana added, "the only names he'll have are of a fictitious prostitute and a very real Sweet Trick Ricky T. Showbiz."

... ...

In the middle of an abandoned industrial park populated mostly by Wichita's homeless, an itinerant street preacher and his entourage of a technician/laborer who doubled as a musician, an usher that evidently doubled as a bouncer, and three plainly dressed young women that helped with leading songs and altar calls, waited for their second night of evening services to get underway. Two days earlier, they had arrived with a city-issued permit to conduct their crusade and set up a tent for a week-long series of meetings for the lost. The 20% cut of their gross that went back to the city as taxes was just another cost of doing business.

The first night's poor attendance didn't discourage them; they had rather expected it. After that first night's offering service, though, they fully trusted that many others would come tonight. They were grateful as they waited; in addition to the offerings, the mid-November temperatures would drop into the mid-forties and most likely encourage even more to come, if for nothing else than to warm up in the large tent's heated interior. It was all about the attendance: the "who" as well as the "how many" were both critical.

... ...

"Sitter! Can I go, too?" Saint Nick's protégé, Tag, practically begged. "If what we heard was true, Nick might need some help carrying back the haul."

"Okay, okay," Sitter acquiesced, "but follow Nick's lead. People don't hand out stuff for free unless they're going to take back more from you than you're willing to give. Keep a distance."

... ...

"Now y'all just keep your distance," Sweet Trick Ricky T. Showbiz instructed, "until they start givin' stuff away. Then, and only then, you just run up there and grab what those fools give you. An' you better bring *all* of it back right here to me, y'hear? You ho's better get somethin' right this time. I'm tired of expending myself on you worthless goveks."

"Yes, master," the girls responded in well-trained unison. Ricky T. Showbiz didn't like when they didn't get that right.

"All right then, get yourselves out there an' don't come back to me empty-handed. I want both arms full from every one of you, or you'll find out how hard my empty closed hands can hit." The girls all nodded and headed into the night as fast as they could. Each of them already knew exactly how hard Showbiz could punch. "Oh yeah, Shimmer! C'mere, baby. I got other plans for you tonight. You an' me gonna have some one-on-one time while those other girls are workin'!" He tried to make it sound like an offer, but he knew her background. He didn't want her around any of it, at least not until he knew what was going on with those goveks passing out the free stuff. The suit in the hologram had informed him of their operation in Dallas where they had gotten Kelly, and that other girl from had been in part dismantled a few weeks earlier. Sweet Trick Ricky T. Showbiz had seen street preachers before, but between the Dallas roll-up and that Kelly had been collected from some church family, he had an odd feeling about the group and didn't want to take any chances.

… …

The service had been going well. The music was a combination of tunes that were sometimes upbeat, sometimes heartwarming, always encouraging the lost who might be looking for a Savior from Heaven to care for them. And like most corporation city-states, there were always the disenfranchised who had nothing but the hope his messages bought. Most just showed up just for the chance of a handout. He sighed to the inevitable, recognizing that even Jesus had crowds that followed Him just for the free food and sideshows. For whatever reason they were here, he genuinely cared for them and continually prayed his message would bear good results. After last night's offering, the crowds would be bigger tonight than the night before. In fact, he counted on it. The worship service wound to a close, and all eyes expectantly looked to him.

Lord, please bless these people, and please don't hold me guilty for preaching your Word with more than one motive. Jack paused for a moment and scanned the mix of faces, circumstances, and lives in the crowd before he addressed the crowd.

"Thank you all for coming out tonight. We're going to switch up the order of service a little from last night and do our tithes and offerings after the message. Please be seated while we pray."

Jack prayed again, asking God to bless and anoint his words, to show the people how much He cared, and to truly touch the lives of those in this city. After that, he again scanned the face of each man, woman, and child in the crowd. The gesture took several seconds to complete but not long enough for the crowd to associate the break as anything other than a pause for effect, a transition, a brief prayer, or simply to summon the nerve to begin. No one in the crowd could have guessed that with the half-second glance he took of each face, his eyes amplified the light as necessary to magnify and record the face and its current micro-tells. Even as he continued his brief scan, facial recognition software compared each image against extrapolated mockups of the most recent photo they had of Kelly to determine whether she was in the crowd.

Some were there the night before and had returned with friends. He found no direct matches for Kelly, but his heart sagged when he spotted a cluster of girls that bore the telltale signs they suffered patterns of habitual, significant abuse. He remembered Elaine's words; while none of them were Kelly, every one of them was a Kelly. He vowed to reach out to them. If nothing else, maybe they had run into her and could provide a lead. The crowd quieted, waiting for him to begin. Jack cleared his throat.

"I know that many of you have heard differently, but to this day, the Bible remains the most historically true text of all time." Some in the crowd booed the statement, but most were willing to at least hear him out for a few minutes.

"I get it. A lot of people object to the Bible, saying it's now out of date and doesn't apply to a technical world. The fact is, there aren't a lot of discrepancies between science and the Bible. There have been some differences over the years, like those who had denied civilizations mentioned in the Bible never really existed, or the arguments that the world wasn't round like the prophet Isaiah said it was around 450 B.C. Eventually, though, science caught up. Most of the controversy wasn't because science and the Bible contradicted each other. At least, not once due scientific process was applied and evaluated through facts rather than commonly taught opinions. No, the argument wasn't between true science and the Bible, but the moral application of science. Humanists have often contradicted the Bible's moral standards, stating they never apply, or at best, no longer apply.

"So let's test that theory out. How many people would be okay if the person next to you took your stuff when you left? Anybody? No hands? Okay, so when God says, 'Don't steal,' that still applies. How many of you would be okay if someone killed one of your friends? Still no hands? Okay, so 'Don't commit murder' still applies. You guys—is it cool for some choob to stare down your girl like he's salivating all over her? Or you girls, when someone trash-talks your man behind his back because they're too scared to confront him directly? Because Jesus went on record saying that lusting after a woman was like sleeping with her, and hating someone in your heart was like killing them, even if you don't have the guts to actually pull the trigger. And on and on we can go.

"In the Bible, God calls doing those types of things, 'sin.' And the Bible says in the book of Romans, chapter 3 verse 23: 'All have sinned and come short of the glory of God.' Romans 6 verse 23 goes on to say, "The wages of sin is death, but the gift of God is eternal life through Jesus Christ."

"Our message is clear," he proclaimed to the surprised crowd of attendees, "God created hell for Satan and demons, not people. But God's Court is inviolable. We've all fallen short because, at some point, we've all decided to reject God's ways to follow Satan's pattern of pride and selfishness. God the Father is the Judge, but He didn't want to send you to hell. Jesus, the Word of God, knew you were guilty, but He didn't want to send you to hell, either. The Holy Spirit witnessed all of it; He doesn't want you to go to hell, but His nature compels Him to tell the truth, too. In fact, the only one in all of this who wants you to go to hell is Satan. So, what could they do? We were stuck.

"So, God holds Court. Satan accused us and still does today. Jesus is the defense attorney (the Bible calls this your advocate), and the Father is Judge. Satan has one card. Since he has to go to hell, then God wouldn't be just if we don't have to go, too. That's what this is all about—Satan taking as many of us down with him as he possibly can. And he had us all.

"Well, here's Jesus's play. Court's in session, Satan has all his paperwork ready to argue his case that you're guilty. The Judge asks how you plea and Jesus stands up and pulls a surprise move by just openly admitting you're guilty. And you're shocked, maybe even offended, but it's the truth, and you know it. This is not a sham court; there's no hiding here.

"Then Jesus continues. He suggests a trade. Satan pipes up that no trade can be made. No amount of money can buy off the Court of God. Jesus goes on that He meant a sacrifice, a real offering of at least equal value. Satan again countered this time that no sacrifice is equal to the value of a human soul, and then in his mind cements the deal by declaring that since all the humans have fallen, no one else can satisfy the sentence. He shows off his files; like a megacorp senior accountant, he's got a thick file for every person on the planet…

"At this point, Jesus smiles, although there's a sadness behind it. He thanks the D.A. for making His point, pauses and then makes a second surprise announcement: He Himself is innocent, and if it pleases the court, He will substitute Himself for you. The crowd in the courtroom is in shock. Satan frantically hunts for Jesus's file, but he doesn't have one. Jesus explains that He will not buy off the Court with a bribe, but He willingly offers to pay off the fine: He will go to hell for each of the defendants. The Father, tears in His eyes, says the Court accepts, then looks at you and tells you that you need to take in what just happened here because if you make light of what just happened here, you fully deserve the sentence and will have no other recourse than the full fury of the Court getting thrown against you.

"And where's the Holy Spirit in all this? He's here, right now, moving across you, God's creation, just like He did in Genesis chapter one. And He's being the witness of all of this in your hearts, right now, that this is all true.

"So, we know where God the Father is, we know where Satan is, we know where Jesus is, and now we even know where the Holy Spirit is. The only question in all of this is…

"Where are *you*?"

"Think about that for a moment. Where are you?" He waited to let his words sink in. As he prayed for each of them to make the right decision, he again scanned the crowd, this time without the image capturing. This was a holy moment, and he would let them have their privacy. Despite his earlier misgivings, he immensely enjoyed this part of the service. He left the stage to walk among the people as he continued.

"The Bible says, 'Behold, now is the day: this is the acceptable time: It also states, 'This is the day the Lord has made; we will rejoice and be glad in it.' If any of you do want to take Jesus up on His offer to have an eternity with Him in Heaven as opposed to an eternity in a hell never intended for you, it's as simple as turning away from those things that were getting you in trouble anyway, and just asking Him to forgive you. Think about it—He's already done the hardest part for you.

"If you don't know what or how to pray, here's a start. Close your eyes and picture yourself standing before Jesus, and just start talking to Him like this: 'Dear Jesus, this is me. I know I've done some bad stuff in my day, but today Lord—this is your day, and I give myself to you this day. Thank you for dying for me on the cross, thank you for coming back to life, and thank you for forgiving me and choosing to live in me. Amen.'

"Now, I'm not even going to try to make any of you come up here, but if any of you want to come up and talk with one of us about what just happened here, or if any of you have any questions you want to ask us after the service, you're welcome to please come up here in front of these railings while we conclude our service for tonight."

After several minutes, a small crowd had moved to the front of the service tent and crossed over to be immediately in front of the stage area. When the area was settled, Jack let his eyes scan each one, praying a silent prayer for them. He smiled warmly to each of them and nodded. Constantine and Dante integrated themselves into the small crowd, praying for the people who had come forward.

… …

"Nick, can I go up there and pray?" Tag asked his lead.

"Nah, y'better not." Nick answered. "In the first place, we only came tonight to see if the rumor was true, and so far I ain't seen it. For all we know, they're just gonna take all their stuff or something. You know what Sitter said—nobody just gives stuff out for free unless they're gonna take more that you don't wanna give."

The younger boy sighed, gloomily looking down to his feet. "All right," he glumly acquiesced, "I guess I'll just stay here for now."

… …

Twenty minutes had elapsed before Jack again took up the stage and announced, "And now it's time to worship God with our tithes and offerings!" he announced. "Will our ushers please come forward?" Some people reached for what valuables they might have, many scoffed, and some actually got excited and cheered. Chrome rolled his eyes, Araña smiled, Susan, Josanne prepared for the storm, and Rogue Moon stared disdainfully at Jack.

"I see some of you were here last night!" Jack called to the crowd, smiling.

"Ahh, you're a fake!" someone called out. "Talk us into feeling good, calling us God's sheep. Brace yourselves, everyone—here come the money-buckets for the fleecing! Well, I got news for you, preacher. I used to work for Dynamix before they downsized me outta my home. I know how much of a kickback you guys pay to pull off these stunts. Well, I ain't got nothin' left! How's that for your bank accounts?"

…… ……

"I don't know why you go through all this trouble. They're just a bunch of low-lifes," Rogue had complained two nights earlier when Jack had shared with her what they were going to do as they set up before their first meeting. "You could get what you need without all this show." He had replied this way was probably a lot quicker, that it was an opportunity to do good, and besides, for him, it was fun. "You're different, man," she had said, tossing her head to look away in resignation.

"Blowing all the stereotypes?" he had asked her.

"Not all of them," she had replied, emotionally distancing herself as she spoke. Jack couldn't tell if it were a compliment or a rebuke.

…… ……

Jack just looked at the man and warmly smiled. "I see you weren't here last night," he said calmly, quietly. "I'm really sorry you lost your job—and no, not because you don't have something to give me.

"You misunderstood what I said," he continued, quietly addressing the man before him, giving the heckler his respect. "And that's okay. It happens a lot with us." He put something in Rogue's hand and said something to her. She looked at it, quickly jerking her head to stare at him for a moment, looking for some sort of confirmation that she understood him correctly. He nodded, and she turned down the platform to approach the man in the crowd. When she reached him, she stretched forth her slightly trembling hand and simply gave him a credstick with 25,000 credits on it. In almost perfect duplication of Rogue's actions, the man looked at the object to see what it was, then just looked into her eyes, his own eyebrows raised into wide arches and eyes tearing. In a barely audible voice, he asked her whether what he saw was real. She was a tough biker, the elite sniper of Valhalla's Brownies, and the most she could offer was a quick nod as she tried to hold her own tears back, afraid they would open the way for her to cry openly as he impulsively reached forward and hugged her. Rogue had never done anything so generously positive and nice for anyone before. The act melted her.

Jack resumed center stage and continued.

"Our message is clear: God loves you, and so do I. Writers share an old adage: 'Show, don't tell.' God showed His love for us by making us in His image. After we blew it, He showed it again when He left Heaven to die on our behalf. And now the Spirit works in us to conform us to the image of His Son." Jack paused, again scanning the crowd. "I said a couple minutes ago, it's time for us to worship God with our tithes and offerings. By that, I meant *our* tithes and *our* offerings." Turning to Chrome and Araña, he smiled as he loudly proclaimed, "Ushers, with everyone seated, please administer the offerings!"

The music resumed; those who had already sat quickly urged those around them to sit. Some didn't sit soon enough and got yanked down; fortunately for everyone, no fights broke out. When all were finally seated, Chrome and Araña opened the trailer doors to reveal large wrapped packages that contained a Bible, supplies of clothing, algae food products, fresh drinking water, tent supplies, medical supplies, and a host of other goods that would prove invaluable to those living on the streets. For most of the Witch City attendees trying to eke out an existence, it was survival. For Sweet Trick Ricky T. Showbiz and many others who had heard about the unusual offering service, it was sheer, ridiculous profit for the taking.

"Like I said," Preach continued, "the rule is 'Show, don't tell.' Despite your circumstances, God really does care about you, and so do we."

Jack closed the service in prayer for those who had attended, requesting they remember the kindness they were shown, and to show it to those they would meet in the future, and reminding them that the next service would be held tomorrow night.

- *"Trigget, Rogue, and Spider make your way to the kids in the back left and try to find out who they are. Chrome, you and Blackwolf get to the girls in the middle back—the ones with the joeboys guarding them like they're prisoners, which they probably are. Give them their packages, ask them if they want to stay for more after the services."*

- *"What about you?" Trigget asked.*

- *"I want to talk with them, but there are too many people at an altar for me to ignore right now. I'll go back up to the stage as soon as I can and try to monitor from there."*

22. Introduction Interdictions

- *"It took a couple return trips to get to them, but we're finally getting to that cluster of kids in the back," Trigget sub-vocally commented to Araña. Now that she was closer, she observed the gritty dirtiness of their worn-out clothing, their unattended hair, the cuts, scratches, and bruises of untold survival stories. "If Witch City is even half of what we've learned, surviving as kids on the street would be miserable on a good day, and winter's coming. How can they possibly make it?"*

- *"This stuff will help," Araña offered, "but if you want the real answer, put your training to use and study their eyes. What do you see?"*

- *"They're 'poor child' bit is definitely not an act, but you're right. The youngest one doesn't show it as much, but they're focused, not beaten, intensely determined, but not crazed. The older one is far more seasoned. He's even more than determined; he's confident."*

By this time, they had approached the unkempt street rats.

"Why hello there," Trigget greeted. "Looks like we got here just in time," she continued as Araña handed out boxes of food and other goods necessary for survival. "It's going to be getting colder out here before too long."

"Thanks, lady!" the youngest exclaimed as Trigget handed him a large box of packaged foods and some clothing. "All this? For us?"

"How much?" the older challenged.

"It's free… It's a gift," the Pride's conversationalist replied, handing him a larger box.

"Yeah, the whole 'Show don't tell' thing? I've heard hustles before. What's your angle?"

"We just want to help," Josanne replied. She needed to disarm them. "You're right to not just trust anyone, and we haven't even been introduced." She stuck out her hand in a deliberately hackneyed 'put 'er there' gesture. "I'm Trigget, and this is my friend Araña."

"What kind of names are those?" the older boy sneered. "Why do they call you Spider? Except 'arañé' doesn't even really mean Spider, it's just kinda close."

"Don't mind him," the younger boy said, "I'm David—err, Tag, and this is Nick. 'Saint Nick,' we call him."

"Very pleased to meet you… Tag" Josanne replied with a genuine smile and handshake with the younger one.

"Hey, you're really nice, like my Mom was once," the youngster noted.

"Oh," Trigget replied, off balance. "Like she was… once? Where's your Mom now?"

"I don't know," the boy admitted, saddening at the question.

"Oh, I'm really sorry to hear that," she apologized. "And she used to call you David?" The boy slowly nodded, but Trigget didn't like the way this was going. "Do you have any family?"

"He has us!" Nick interjected a little too defensively for her liking. Were they both on their own?

"Tag, are you in any kind of danger here?" she tried to ask him quietly. She was relieved to see the younger boy moved in closer to Nick at the mention of danger, although she also noted he glanced at some of the crowd on the opposite side of the lot as he did so. Tag was with Nick by choice, but he regarded those others as a nearby threat.

"Not now, no," he verbally responded. "But stay away from them," he said with a nod, too scared to point at a group on the far side that looked like a gang. "They work for Sweet Trick Ricky T. Showbiz. They're real mean. They're 'specially mean to girls."

Trigget followed his eyes to the spot they occupied and noted that Chrome, Susan, and Rogue would soon be with them. She subvocally relayed a heads up to the trio and decided to direct her next question to Nick.

... ...

"Well, all *right*!" one of the gorillas threw out as Chrome, Lady Blackwolf, and Rogue Moon approached the group that Trigget had just warned them about. "Let's see some of this milk and honeys dat preacher's been talkin' about."

"Here, gimme that!" one of the girls shouted out. Some of them grabbed at the boxes like they were food at a fire sale. The men that were with them held back, laughing at the girls, encouraging them.

Arms crossed, legs shoulder-width apart, slightly leaning back and staring down the charity workers, they bore a threatening demeanor which Rogue took as an attempt to intimidate them. By the sound of Chrome's sneering "Pfft" behind her, she didn't think it worked—at least not on him. She was surprised to see Susan was showing the same signs of masked nervousness she caught in herself, as though Susan, too, was re-experiencing something akin to what the Brownie sniper had been through. She wondered if Susan also had to focus so much from one step to the next that she wouldn't throw up out of fear, stress, and tension. But Rogue did focus; she knew all too well what it was like to show open weakness to these predatory wolves.

... ...

"He's with us? So, you two aren't on your own, then" Josanne asked. Nick sighed. He had blown it by mentioning the others, but there was no way for him to take it back. But maybe that was okay, he consoled himself. Maybe he could get a couple more boxes—the supplies would go a long way for helping the others survive the coming winter.

"Yeah, we're not really alone," he admitted, looking up to her. "There's a couple of us that are staying together. Would it be okay if we could have a box for them, too?"

Tag gave Nick a sideways look and said, "A couple? There's like thirty of us now."

The older youth's shoulders sagged as he sighed. Tag was naïve, but Saint Nick knew the real score. Outsiders disdained groups of indigents like swarms of rodents. They always seemed to think that just because the two boys weren't alone, they'd be able to find all the food they wanted. Now that Tag had blown their cover, he expected the two outsiders would wrestle away their boxes and give them to someone else in the crowd.

Instead, the woman just sat down, right on one of the boxes they were supposed to be giving out. "You mean to tell me there are thirty of you children living on your own, with no one to take care of you?"

The fact that the outsider seemed to get the reality of their situation surprised Nick to momentary silence. What he heard in that moment chilled him.

"We're not on our own," Tag blurted, beaming, "Sitter takes care of us!"

… …

- *"Jefé!" Araña sub-vocally reported. "Eyes on the group of three kids we're talking in the back left—they know Sitter!"*

Resuming center stage, Jack captured several new enhanced images of each person in the back corner of the lot. He also zoomed in on Chrome's group, who looked like they had gotten into some trouble.

- *"Spider, can we trust them?" he asked.*

- *"We can trust the younger one to be honest and the older one to be street-smart. If you put the two of them together, I'd say yeah, if you do it carefully."*

- *"Send a message, then.*

- *"Break—Chrome, you guys okay?"*

… …

"Sir, please," Susan asked after the third comment. "That kind of talk is not appropriate."

- *"I think we're okay for now," Chrome responded. Blackwolf's gonna try and handle it. This group's a real piece of work, though."*

- *"How's Rogue?" asked Jack.*

- *"Choking some. I think she recognizes one of the guys."*

"Not appropriate?" the ganger replied. His tone clearly told Susan the notion was ludicrous to him. The question that flashed through her mind was whether the bug for him was that the comment was truly wrong or that he had just been corrected by a female. But exactly why the ganger was offended was academic; the situation was escalating.

"Not appropriate? Listen, who do you think you are comin' down here all high and mighty tellin' us what we can and can't do? But to show you what an upright guy I am, go ahead, 'splain to me what makes that inappropriate? Come *on!*" he suddenly yelled into her face.

- *"Oh, drek..." Chrome transmitted.*

The crowd around them grew quiet and drew back. For some of those in the immediate surroundings, the first prayers they really prayed were for the three strangers who were doing so much to help them.

… …

"Geez, Tag!" the remaining kid angrily spoke up. He had been quiet until Tag's mention of their leader. "What the frak you think you're doin'? You're in big trouble now! You know we ain't s'posed to mention him!"

"Hey, it's okay, relax" Araña quickly cut in. "And watch your mouth." Then he softened, quietly addressing the youth whose eyes had gone wide at the mention of their leader's name. "There's really thirty of you?" he asked. On Nick's nod, Araña smiled and said as warmly as he could, "Well, I'm betting if you-know-who didn't trust you, he wouldn't have sent you." He gave them each as many boxes as they could hold and passed a credstick into the older youth's hand. "With thirty of you, you guys are going to need more than you can carry in these boxes. Come back later, and we can give you a couple more. We'll be here if you want to find us. But can you do us a favor?"

"Here it comes," Nick complained to Tag. "I told you."

"Can you take a message to Sitter for us? There's a girl we're trying to find so we can help her, and we think Sitter wanted to help her, too. She went missing a couple months ago, and he might know where she is. Can you ask him to meet with us?"

"Nick, look!" Tag interrupted, grabbing the older boy's sleeve and pointing. "They're in trouble!"

Nick glanced over where Tag had pointed and sized up the situation. Something in what Sitter's Saint saw gave him clarity of purpose. Suddenly they were gone, almost immediately melted into the crowd of older, bigger people.

"They left their boxes," Trigget muttered. "They just abandoned them. They took off fast; maybe they figured the boxes would only slow them down," she pondered.

"Well, if it's any consolation," Spider mused, "he kept the credstick."

… …

"Leave her alone," Rogue murmured just barely loud enough to be heard by anyone other than herself.

JoeRay's nostrils flared, and his eyes burned with new intensity. The girl's voice was quiet—little more than a mumble—but it was another source of defiance in front of his crew, his peers, those around him, and especially, his women. If he let it go, it might spread to them, and that was the last thing he wanted.

"What'd you say?" he snarled.

- "Preach, I know you like peace and quiet, but this ain't working out so well," Chrome transmitted. "The girls are striking out, trying to be nice. I guess it's my turn."

Chrome looked the macho thug in the eye and followed through on their behalf. "She asked you to leave her alone," he said evenly. "She didn't mean to make any fuss. You're just making the ladies uncomfortable," he reasoned in a polite voice.

- "Not bad, Chrome, I'm impressed" Preach and Spider both sub-vocally congratulated, somewhat surprised by his diplomatic attempt to de-escalate the situation.

"If you were a real man who knew how to talk to a real woman," the armored cyborg continued with a smirk, "you'd have already figured that out by now."

"Y'see boy?" the tough seethed but smiled wide, leering at the girls. "Do you even know who you're talkin' to?" He stood up to full height and knocked the boxes from one of his girls' arms. "But I can be generous, too, so I'll educate you," he bragged as he struck a gaudy pose.

"I'm JoeRay. This is my block. These people you think you're helping belong to me. And I am done bein' told what to do by you people. But if you're worried 'bout your girls being comfortable, I got some ideas on how to downright make 'em feel real good." He reached out to brush Susan's cheek, but she withdrew. "Baby," he chided, "when JoeRay reaches out to touch a woman, he expects her to let him touch her."

"I wouldn't try that again if I were you," Chrome flatly intoned.

"Boy, what are you *up* to? You challengin' me? Now you be a good altar boy, an' maybe we won't take you along with your sisters here." He turned to the others and ordered, "Come on, grab 'em. I can take these two and use 'em to take up some collections of my own."

Eight gangers stood up and surrounded the trio, producing knives, pipes, and firearms. One of the girls they had come with shrieked, earning her a backhanded slap. Huddled together against the terror of their pimps' rage, they shrank back as far as they could. Araña and Trigget were on their way over but working against the crowds retreating away from the scene slowed them down.

"Now here's that part where you start to beg the Lord to have mercy on your soul and beg me not to hurt you," JoeRay chided Chrome with a wolfish grin.

"Well, JoeRay, you're probably right," Chrome replied, rubbing the back of his neck as he studied the ground in front of him. "I guess I should forgive you and turn the other cheek." Then he slowly shook his head, shrugged, and looked up at the pimp, revealing another twinge of a smile of his own. "But you see, well," he added with his arms half-raised in a shrug, "I'm kind of new to all this."

JoeRay drew and fired. The first round hit Chrome square in the solar plexus; the next two glanced off his forearm as the armored cyborg stepped in and grabbed the ganger's pistol, crushing the weapon shut. The blocked barrel caused the fourth round to get stuck in the barrel, and the fifth exploded into the lodged fourth. The ruptured handgun rocked violently in Chrome's locked grip. The force of the back-blast broke JoeRay's index finger against the pistol's trigger guard.

"Now, see what you made me do?" Chrome malevolently grinned at the shooter. "Perfectly good pistol, and now I broke it."

JoeRay was at least temporarily out of the fight and failed miserably at his attempt to not show any pain as he attempted to extricate his finger through the damaged handgun. His friends, while not quite sure of what they had just seen, were professionals in their own right. Chrome had expected to draw the fire from those who had the firearms. He had expected the girls to flee. He was wrong on both counts.

Following the lead of the one who was likely the second in command, the gangers had instead trained their weapons on Susan, Moon, and some of the nearby crowd. Araña and Trigget had just arrived but stopped short when they observed the standoff.

"What you ho's waitin' for?" JoeRay ordered more than asked. Without a word, the girls obediently swarmed up and formed a human shield between the pimp and the stranger who had somehow managed to hurt him. Once the wall of humanity had been formed, the gangers aimed at the girls. JoeRay offered Chrome a triumphant smirk. "Aww, look at that face. I bet you thought you was something, coming in here with your bulletproof vest and all ready for the ghetto. Well, now you know where the real power is." He leaned back to make his sneer visible and raised his left thumb to his chest. "It's with me."

"Let them go," Chrome threatened.

"Or what?" JoeRay shot back. "Besides, where would they go? Just a bunch of ho's. You think somebody's gonna give any of them a job? Nobody's gonna give 'em the time of day or jack anything else, and they know it. So, they gotta work. Got news for you—we all do. Life's tough that way. Even these girls, dumb as they are, know that much. Besides, we're the only family they got and the only family they're ever gonna have. They're damaged goods; nobody's gonna want them now."

"That's not true!" Rogue Moon's voice rang out against the nodding and numbed acquiescence of the entrapped girls. "He's lying, manipulating you because right now, your fear is the only thing that's keeping his worthless butt from getting kicked into the sewers where it belongs. The truth is that you do have other places you can go where people will care. We're proof of that."

"Girl, you don't shut your mouth, I'll shut it for you," JoeRay glowered. "Bobby G, take your piece offa that tramp you got it lined up on and take real good aim at this uppity callin' me a liar."

"Hey JoeRay," Bobby G drawled, "now that I got my eye on her, don't she look a little familiar?"

"I don't know," JoeRay started to complain. "You think I remember every face I ever…." JoeRay leaned in, casual inspection gradually growing into a knowing leer. "Hey, you know what? I think you might be right." His left hand fumbled into his jacket pocket and pulled out a cigarette. With a glance, one of the girls lit it for him, and after taking a long drag of deliberation, he made an announcement.

"Hundred fiddy cred an' then some goes to the brother Bobby G," he stated, enunciating the 'G' to add a sense of extra esteem. He leaned forward, a malicious grin slowly crawled across his face, and settled there. "How ya been, Gloss?"

She was too far away to hit him, so she settled for an indignant spit. "You don't ever call me that again, or I'll slit you like the pig you are."

"Hoo-*ee*," the pimp laughed out loud. "Ho was somehow lucky to get out alive once 'pon a time, and she figures she can just walk back into Witch City and start commanding us around? Or is it that you got to missin' a brother's company, and this is your way of begging for some more?

"So, OK—you get your wish. Lot of homies will be oh so glad to see you come home. I think we might even have you as the guest of honor at an extra special party tonight. An' you too, honey," he said to Susan. "No sense in letting good food like you go to waste," he said with a twisted ogle. "And I ain't forget you, fighting man," he said with a glance at Chrome. "We'll have a little something for you too, don't you worry.

"Keep your guns trained on them. And keep a couple on the other ho's so no one gets any ideas about trying to bust away… again," he said, throwing a glare at Rogue. "Any of y'all try anything, and the guns go off all at once, we clear?" Knowing at least some of the hostages would be killed before they could help, they acquiesced. "Well, all right then," JoeRay said in self-affirming finality. "So get the frak outta my way, 'cause we're done here."

- *"Chrome, what's going on?" Preach asked. "I saw some of it, but there were too many people up here for me to track what was happening."*

- *"I got this, Chrome. Stay focused on the goveks. Preach, this is Spider. Rogue's been made. Some banger is taking her back with him, and he's got Chrome and Blackwolf with him. He's using the girls as a shield, and there are too many civilians to make a move."*

- *"Iylo," Preach called, "can you clear the streets for us?"*

- "Give me a minute…" the elite hacker answered. "Okay, I'm giving you one major star containment activity just outside your gate. Redirecting traffic in nine seconds."

"Ladies and gentlemen," Preach began over the intercom system, "we need to close services for the evening. I have just been informed that there is some corporate law enforcement activity taking place outside the northeast gate. All other exits are fine, but please do not leave by the northeast exit, or they may determine you are interfering in their response."

The locals took their cue and exited, making sure to avoid the northeast exit—not out of civil-mindedness, but any indigents found to be interfering would be summarily shot, theoretically to remove any chance of them being a behind-the-back threat. None of them liked living in Witch City, but when push came to shove, they all still liked living.

The crowds thinned behind the gangers. With a backward nod to his fellow pimps, JoeRay said, "Come on. Keep your guns on the ho's 'til we're clear of all this." Spotting Araña in the crowd, he called out, "Hey, Jesus freak. Tell your preacher we said thanks for bringin' us the honeys. Praise the Lawd, these two will bag us some *serious* cred."

The group slowly receded away from the lot where the meeting had taken place. Though the chance of random bystanders being drawn into danger lessened, the CYBER forces were still hampered by the guns trained on the girls. Susan saw enough terror reflected on their painted faces to know the pimps would pull the triggers without a moment's hesitation.

They had just cleared the lot entrance, where a small group of street kids had just rounded the corner and crouched to play some kind of gambling game across the street from a homeless person curled against the shadows of a brick wall.

"That's not fair!" one of the urchins shouted.

"Is too!" another yelled back. "Wanna make something of it?"

"Yeah! You stole it, ya cheat!"

"Hey!" JoeRay shouted at the boys. "Y'all shut the frack up and get outta here. Man's gotta think!"

The first kid looked at the cluster of people, but if he noticed the guns, he didn't show it. Tears welling up in his eyes, he clenched his fists and screamed in a fit of tantrum, "That's not fair!"

"Aww, look at the baby crying!" the other boys joined in, frenzied by the youth's tears like sharks by blood in the water.

"Stop it! I am not!" the first boy protested, but it was a lost cause. In the seconds that followed, the playmates turned savage competitors, pushing and grabbing at the outnumbered boy.

"Alright," JoeRay said with a dismissive wave of his hand, "let's let 'em be and get outta here. Hey!"

In just that moment's timeframe, the small group of boys had swelled to a mob of about twenty, pushing, pulling, throwing punches, kicks, and each other as the scuffle grew to a full-on rumble that blocked the street ahead of the retreating pimps.

"That's it!" he swore. "Shoot them little goveks. That'll clear the rest of them!"

The gangers swung their weapons off the girls and onto the knot of kids. As they selected their targets, four small metal cylinders bounced once on the street between them and the kids. Before any gangers had a chance to fire, two of the cylinders exploded with a loud bang, emitting a series of bright white flashes that forced the shooters to hide their eyes. The other two emitted fogs of smoke—one the typical grey, the other flashing pastels.

CYBER-wired for speed, Susan was the only one who had seen him do it. The homeless man had flung two of the four canisters in a burst of speed that approached sleight of hand. Then she saw nothing but the after-images of the smoke-enhanced strobe flashes. The homeless man was gone, transformed into a grim figure of smoke-induced shadow. That figure slowly, deliberately approached the group. Teary-eyed thugs were reflexively firing at the threat. The slim apparition easily sidestepping the blind shots. A staff appeared from behind his back and whistled twice as it landed. Two blows landed across the rear-most ganger with the shotgun, felling the brute. The second target had an auto-pistol pointed to the vicinity of where the youths had played their dangerous game; the first blow cracked against the man's firing hand, knocking the gun downwards where it was a simple matter for the newcomer to grab the off-balanced man's hand, direct the weapon inward upon its owner, and squeeze the trigger finger shut. The resulting burst of fire dropped the pimp. Permanently.

By this time, the flash-bangs had worn off enough to allow the gangers some semblance of organized resistance against their assailant, but to little avail. The newcomer somehow continually danced around them in a street ballet, always keeping him positioned so they weren't able to bring their firearms to bear. Knives and clubs were brandished, but he weaved and dodged between the blows, sometimes using his plated duster to absorb the blows, often parrying with his staff, forearms, thighs, and shoulders.

- *"Preach, Iylo here. I got a street cam recording this if you can't already see it."*

- *"I can, Iylo, but I'm not sure I believe it. Keep the camera rolling; I want to analyze this from the different perspectives when we're done."*

- *"Geez, Preach, he's just a kid—he can't be older than twenty-one!"*

By this time, the gang of younger kids had closed in on the gunners, swarming two of the thugs, pulling them down to their level as they threw enough of their weight on the toughs to bring them down. Once down, the youths frenzied, and the thugs succumbed to the street kids as readily as if the urchins had been rats of their size. JoeRay was attempting to fire on them despite the likelihood of hitting his own, but Chrome was again there to yank his arm back in a merciless twist, snapping the wrist of the already injured hand. Lady Blackwolf also joined into the fray, her heightened reflexes easily dispatching three more of the gangers once they had been lured away from their hostages. While Rogue Moon was not directly partaking in the fighting outside of squarely kicking JoeRay in the mouth, she was involved in trying to keep the terrified girls from scattering.

Another minute later, the fight died down, the smoke dissipated, and the various victors studied each other.

"I saw you take a couple shots," the homeless man turned hero declared to Chrome. "And she's pretty fast," he said with a sideways nod to indicate Blackwolf. "But picking on JoeRay by yourselves when there are hostages around is pretty stupid."

"Noted," admitted Chrome, "but we're new in town. I take we get no credit for learning curve?"

"And where does life offer learning curves?" the newcomer asked bitterly. "Sure as hell, not here."

- "Chrome, is this a younger incarnation of Johnny, or what?" Susan asked.

"So, who are you, kid?" Chrome asked. "Gotta admit, you got bad mojo all over you, in a good way."

"No way!" one of the younger kids interrupted, pointing at the homeless newcomer. "For real?"

While unnoticed at first, Susan caught the other kids staring at the young street fighter in rapt awe. She smiled as she commented, "Chrome, look at these kids."

Seeing their open-mouthed staring, Chrome asked, "Yeah, so who is this guy? You're acting like you're gonna worship him or something."

- "Easy, big guy," Araña sub-vocalized. "We were just talking with some of these kids before you made contact with JoeRay.

We thought they bugged out. Turns out they must have rallied a bunch of reinforcements and counterattacked on your behalf."

"You don't know who this is?" Tag asked, incredulous that somebody could not know the distinctive figure standing before them, wisps of smoke cloud still slightly billowing behind him, as though that was part of the deliberate effect. The young man seemed to grow almost statuesque as the youngster finished his wonder-struck announcement.

"That's Stang! Stang Steffan!"

And, as if on some cue, a few of the kids actually did kneel before him.

… …

- *"Iylo?" Preach commanded, "Run it—who's Stang Steffan?"*

- *"On it, Preach!" A few seconds later, Iylothien relayed the rundown to the rest of the team. "One Steffan, Stang—yeah, that's his real name—exact age unknown, probably between nineteen and twenty-three. First appeared on the grid back around 2040, picked up for vagrancy—not that vagrancy was a rare thing those days, but he was squatting in a corporation warehouse. The only reason the corp security didn't kill him had been because they couldn't catch him. Couple years later, he busted up some older small-time gangers who were picking on some guy in a wheelchair. Evidently, the two became friends because there's a couple pieces of surveillance footage showing the two of them together...."*

… …

"Hey, Stang," Rogue slowly approached the urban tough, her smile and poise causing him to relax, if just a little. "You remember me, right?"

"Gloss! You—you got away..." he stammered. "I don't get it. Why'd you come back?"

"A lot's been happening," she said softly. "For one, I'm Rogue now. Rogue Moon, okay? A girl's in deep drek, and I believe these choobs are the ones to bust her out. For good. Maybe even shut down Showbiz and whoever's pimping her out...."

... ...

- *"A couple years go by, seems they found a few more street kids to join them—the two evidently started a fagin operation. Three years ago, the kid shows on the grid like a Robin Hood guy. Looks like he graduated and is now flying solo."*

- *"Iylo!" Preach exclaimed, laughing over his sub-vocal. "You said a guy in a wheelchair?"*

- *"Yeah, why?" Iylothien asked, then seemed to catch himself. "Oh, man! You can't be serious!"*

- *Chrome smiled wide, which looked more than a little weird to Susan.*

"But Stang," Rogue concluded, "we need to find Sitter."

... ...

"Well, there's a problem there," Stang admitted with an exaggerated furrow of his brows. "I don't know where he is." He paused, gently looking at the kids gathered around him. With an approving clap of the oldest kid's shoulder, he added, "But Saint

Nick here does, don't you? Nick, why don't you see if Sitter wants to meet with these guys?"

By this time, Preach and the others had approached. "What about these girls?" Araña asked.

"That'll be a problem," Preach admitted. "We had planned to use the revival services to rescue as many refugees as we could. We'd empty out the truck of goods and smuggle out any girls who could make it."

"Wait a sec," Stang interrupted. "You're the preacher, and you're in on this?" he asked, incredulous.

"Babe," Rogue smiled, "he's the one who came up with the plan. They're all in on it."

"Nobody outside of us saw what happened here," Susan offered. "We have enough food from what we planned on handing out; we can hide the girls towards the front of the trailer, and they can hide behind the crates for tomorrow night's services."

Spider smiled. "Not a bad idea, rookie. It'll take a little while to shift the crates around to create the hiding spot, but...."

"Wait!" Rogue suddenly cut in. "There were fourteen girls here with the group; now there's only thirteen!" Turning to the recently rescued hostages, she asked, "Where's the girl with the frazzled red hair?"

"You mean Rainbow?" one of the girls responded with a scoffing laugh. "That girl think JoeRay was her loverboy. She ain't never had the sense to see past his sweet-talk. Prolly went down to some dealer to dope out her woes."

Preach had a sudden look of concern. "Or get revenge," he concluded. "Time is not ours to lose. They'll know we had something to do with the gang's disappearance. Load any girls up who want out into the truck—it leaves tonight if we want to get them out of here without any trouble. What about you, Stang?"

"He'll be okay," Saint Nick bragged on behalf of the fighter. "They've been hunting him for years, and they never got him yet."

Stang bowed slightly. "Too true, fanboy," he affirmed with a grin.

"What about Kelly?" Rogue asked. "We're really just going to leave her here?"

"Not a chance, Rogue," Jack assured her. "But here's where we're going to part company."

"What do you mean? I'm not leaving you guys now!"

"You have to," he insisted. "We're staying. Dante and Constantine will drive the truck. You need to stay with those girls. They seem to know you, or at least have heard of you, and if you don't go with them, they're going to freak the entire way. You'll also need to introduce them to Mother Freya and Small Eddie once the truck gets outside. If you're not on the truck when it meets the line...."

"Okay, I get it," she sighed. "Freya goes nuts. But I want to help."

"Then keep the line open and warm up Natalia," Chrome stepped in and answered for his leader. He lifted his arm and gently laid his hand on her shoulder. "We just might need to hear her singing for us when we bust out of here."

"You're such a phallo," she lightly accused as she attempted to move his hand away. She smiled, though, when the mechanical arm didn't even budge. "But okay, you got yourself a chorus line on your way out."

"Well, come on," Saint Nick sighed as he turned his back on the group and headed down a darkened side street. "Won't take nobody too long to get some guns up and blow this place clear to the other half of hell." He nodded to a pair of the younger boys who eagerly ran up to their leader. "Take a couple others with you and bring home the rest of the boxes they gave us. Tell Sitter what's happened here and let him know I'm taking these chummers to Safehouse One. It sounds like they're trying to help the girl we spotted that night in Drogue's Alley. Oh, and tell him Stang's also involved and probably would've said hi if he'd thought about it."

23. Hittin' Streets

"Well, Johnny-boy, here we are, back at our little corner," Melissana bemoaned as she glanced around the darkened block by the Single Hearts Hotel and shivered. "How did this place get even creepier?"

"Hey," Johnny responded, "aren't you the girl who took on a whole biker gang in a quarry, by yourself?"

"Yeah," she sulked, "but it's different when you're in a car."

"You want to back out?"

She looked at him, eyes wide with a barely controlled fear. "Do decks have slots?" she asked. "But then, where would Kelly or those other girls who were dragged into that filth hole be?" She scowled at the memory. "I hate that we couldn't do anything for them earlier."

"Yeah, about that," Johnny resolutely smiled as another car pulled up to the flea-bitten hovel of a slummer's hotel. That grin was a grim thing she had only seen once, the day after he had discovered how Angie had died in Roanoke before their first mission together, "Now that we're here, you wanna do something about that?"

"What do you mean?" she asked. "I thought we were supposed to infiltrate the underworld posing as a new pimping operation from out of town."

"Right," Johnny agreed, "but now that we let Spider and Chrome into the city, if we're breaking 'Thou shalt not infiltrate' anyway, we might as well break 'Thou shalt not perpetrate.' And I see some goveks over there that I would sorely like to perpetrate upon."

Now it was Melissana's turn to smile. "Johnny, I would love nothing more," she exclaimed, then hesitated. "I wish we would've thought of this when Susan was with us. There's gotta be at least five guys there. I can probably handle one or two hand-to-hand, but I'm not wired for street combat." She looked at him earnestly. "Do you really think you can handle the rest?"

"I'm guessing there's nine of 'em: probably four inside, the spotter, the two at the curbside, and the two guarding the door. But remember that night in the kitchen when I told you there are times not to test your luck?" After she nodded, he again flashed that malicious grin. "Well, this ain't one of them times."

And with that, Melissana went game face, and Queen Vixenn stepped out of the car into the Witch City streets.

… …

"Now listen," Rogue addressed the girls, "I know this feels creepy as hell for you since you probably came here locked in a truck, but please trust me. We're getting you free and clear of this place."

"Were you really one of us before?" one of the girls timidly asked.

"Yeah," she spat. "My street name was Gloss, tricked for a phallo who called himself Kenny Cash. Met Stang a couple times. We liked each other, once upon a time. About six and a half years ago, he saw some guy startin' hitting on me, and I don't mean propositioning. Well, Stang jumps in and goes reckless on the guy. That guy turned out to be one of Kenny's up-and-coming pimps in training, and I was dead unless I got out. So Stang introduces me to Sitter, who underground railroads me out of the city and connects me to Valhalla's Brownies."

"Well, what about us?" one of the girls asked. "And how do we know you're telling the truth?"

"You saw Stang and me talking!" Moon practically swore in frustration. She sighed then, remembering how hard trust was and how much these girls had to overcome just to get from one second to the next. Paranoia was as natural to them as breathing. "Sorry kid, my bad," she confessed. "Here, I got something to show you." She then reached behind the pallets and pulled out her hardened leather jacket, taking a moment to smile once again at the large patch on the back. She took a moment to put it on, to show the other girls that the fit could only mean it truly belonged to her. She then rummaged around the back of the truck some more until she found her weapons stash and some of the other firearms the group had thought to store in case of emergency. Though they were still tense and extremely furtive, the girls visibly relaxed as they realized she really was one of the famed bikers.

The girls at least temporarily settled. Moon pounded the front trailer panel and yelled into her radio, *"Come on, phallo's, what're ya's waiting for?"*

"Just for your word that y'all are ready for the ride, sister," Dante responded. A blast faintly sounded nearby, somewhat muted by the density of the vehicle's armor. Several rapid sharp pats of small arms fire walking the length of the trailer sounded as the truck moved forward with a sudden lurch. *"Glad you're tucked in though—we got ourselves some company already."*

... ...

Queen Vixenn slowly sidled up the sidewalk on her approach to the Single Hearts Hotel, carefully trying to keep her step as she navigated the cracks and dints of the concrete in the nagging discomfort of her still somewhat unfamiliar stiletto heels. She had practiced in them before they left, of course, but that had been on even floors that failed to completely replicate the reality of the cracked and pock-marked cement of the rundown neighborhood sidewalks. She had passed a few girls and one guy on the way; some sneered, two spat at the new and unknown competition, but the others just silently expressed empathy for the newcomer. The Queen tried to mirror the disdain of the harder girls and establish herself as the top sheet of her affluent pimp, but it cut against her nature so deeply that she knew the one she was probably hurting the most was herself. After the minute or two that seemed like an hour, she was within earshot of the men on the steps.

"Tha's close enough, ho'," one of the pimps ordered as he rolled a toothpick across his mouth with his tongue. "We don' know you—who you workin' for?"

"Workin' for me," she stated, boldly looking at the pimp directly. "Me an' my man, Johnny."

The pimp's lips parted in an amused grin, showing teeth that were entirely gold-capped. The toothpick pointed sharply upward as a brief wisp of a chuckle escaped him, and he slowly shook his head side to side.

"Well, y'see now, honey, that ain't how this here works," he explained with the tone of a growling dog. With a nod, two of the pimps lighted off the stoop railings and walked behind her, cutting off her retreat. "Now we ain't never heard of any Johnny workin' girls on these streets—like as not he's dumped you here because he's tired o' your attitude. But you know, we're always lookin' for new talent, and you look like maybe I'd give you some lessons myself. Grab her."

"You wanna give me lessons?" she asked, looking him up and down with an indignant stare as she struggled against her captors, "I dunno. You got enough cred? Johnny don't like me doin' no charity work, and between you an' me, I'm tempted to charge extra." Across the street, a girl popped a bubble from her chewing gum.

BAM!! It had taken him two steps to reach her. She had expected a slap, maybe a backhand; instead, he punched her in the side of the head, which dazed her and knocked her to the ground with a loud ringing in her ear. Maybe that was why she didn't hear Johnny's arrival.

"Hey," he said, nudging her with his boot. "Damaged goods already? Get up."

"You Johnny?" the pimp asked, perturbed.

Johnny nodded, glancing from one of the pimps to the other. "Yeah, that's me," he smiled.

"So, Johnny, I don't think I ever heard of you. You got a last name?" he asked, rolling his toothpick.

Johnny smirked and made a show of selecting a toothpick of his own out of an outer forearm pocket of his ankle-length duster. Flashing his arm out to full length, he flicked the toothpick backward into the air, catching it in his mouth before nodding.

"Gifted," he said, "Johnny Gifted." The girl popped her bubble gum again. "I'm out of old Louisiana in the Lubric zone, figured there's some room for me to operate out here."

"Well, Johnny Gifted, you been in the business long, or is this your first shot at night school? You do know the rules, don't you?"

"Yeah," Johnny said. "1: Thou shalt not snitch; 2: Thou shalt not infiltrate; 3: Thou shalt not perpetrate. You want me to keep going, or are you satisfied?"

"You can stop there. You see the trouble I have with you just struttin' down here while I'm tryin' ta do business?"

"Well, you see," Johnny stated coolly, "you're a guy who knows the rules and all, so I didn't think there'd be any problem." He turned his attention to Melissana, who was still on the ground but looking like she was recovered. "Get up, Vix." The two men grabbed her again as soon as she was back up. Johnny glanced at them and slowly shook his head with a sigh, then put his hands into his pockets and resumed addressing the street toughs. "Because I know you're all men of the rules, and since this is my street now, I know you boys won't give me any troubles trying to infiltrate or perpetrate my zone."

The pimp laughed out loud as all nine men drew their weapons. "You best get your Louisiana punk self outta here while you still can," he threatened. "We're keeping the ho'. Consider it a business loss for your impudence. You don't deserve her anyway. She's got more testosterone than you do."

"That your final answer?" Johnny asked. "You move on now and I'll let it slide, but since you're giving me this trouble, you owe me 800 creds for Vixenn's downtime."

As the gangers raised their weapons, Johnny stepped back with his right foot, raised his left forearm in front of his face, and braced himself against the shotgun blast and several rounds of pistols that were fired over the next several seconds.

"Johnny!" Queen Vixenn screamed as the murderous volley of fire pronounced its death sentence on behalf of the gang of pimps. To their surprise, the new pimp in their midst was still standing. He simply lowered his arm.

"My coat's armored—pretty new stuff. Thanks for the field test—to be honest, I wasn't quite sure how it would work. Now I know," he said with a grin. "Let's see if yours is as good." A pair of auto-pistols instantly appeared from inside his duster as if by magic. Before the surprised gangers had a chance to react, Johnny fired a short burst with his left hand followed by a quick burst from his right. The pistol-armed scout on the far left jerked violently, as did a second ganger with a knife who tried to sneak up on Johnny from the other side. Both hit the ground at the same time.

A second later, another volley issued forth from the remaining enemies; Johnny was already on the move. He somehow sidestepped right of the greater force of a second shotgun blast; then, with his right leg extended horizontally, he flipped in a wheeling hop as though he had rolled his back over an invisible fence and caught himself on his right leg. With the pimps finding it utterly impossible to line up a shot, he used the forward momentum of his body to execute a forward roll, ending the maneuver with both of his arms extending forward, delivering a double burst of .9 mm rounds into the shotgun-toting threat. He kept the twin weapons firing as he stood, arcing outwards to incapacitate the other members of Toothpick's crew.

"Louisiana!" Toothpick exclaimed, voice trying to show control while his widened eyes hinted more at panic. "I do believe you got a soft spot for this ho', and I believe my two boys can find a soft spot left on her," he threatened with a callous chuckle and a seemingly appreciative nod at the two thugs who still held Melissana captive.

"Not on your life, chummer! They call these stilettos for a reason!" Melissana swore as she stabbed the razor-honed titanium CYBER right boot heel downwards into the inner calf of the captor on her right, slicing through denim, flesh, capillary, vein, and artery. As he reflexively let go of her arms to grasp his lower leg, she used the solid grip of the captor on her left to add extra power to the knee she suddenly flung into his groin, boxing his left ear and grabbing it to pull his head downwards into another quick but solid jab of her right knee into his cranium that, until then, had protected his temporal lobe. The action left him definitively concussed. Less resistant now, she used her left arm to smack him backward and down against the Witch City concrete sidewalk to finish the job. Toothpick was isolated.

"Y'all didn't think I was serious, did ya's? I mean, we're good—I get it, you want me to move on, right?" Toothpick begged in a desperate plea for his life.

"Well, since you hit Queen Vix here, I got other plans," Johnny said as he leveled both auto-pistols at the head of the pimp.

"Johnny, no!" Melissana begged. "We render justice. I got that part, but murder, even of this scum?" She approached Johnny slowly, deliberately. "I can't agree with that."

"You sure?" The luckster simply gazed at his captive and cocked an eyebrow. "And what about you, tough guy?" he asked, and with the pimp's hurried nods of assent, Johnny lowered his weapons and made them disappear back into a pair of unseen holsters embedded in the interior of his trench coat.

"Okay, my Queen," he said with a bow to Melissana. "But if you think I'm letting this govek get away with what he did, you have another thing coming!" he affirmed with a slap to the captured pimp's head.

"Aw, come on!" the pimp begged. "Even your woman says to let me go!"

"Yeah?" Johnny quipped, "well, what about the ninth commandment? 'Thou shalt not ho' speak,' isn't that it?" Toothpick slumped, defeated. "What," Johnny provoked, "suddenly you've got nothing to say?" He paused and reflected a moment. "But you know, my man, and I do use the term *very* loosely in your case, you actually just gave me an idea." The CYBER gunslinger turned his head to Melissana. "Vixenn, please gather the young ladies inside to the first floor lobby. And please make sure you get the two girls they dragged out from the car earlier tonight.

"Now, you slimy excuse for a govek," Johnny bitterly proclaimed after Melissana had left, "we'll see how you handle the treatment these girls got."

The former pimp's pleas and screams for mercy were lost to the Witch City streets as Johnny locked the door behind him. Melissana felt just a little satisfied after she administered the first kick to show the girls they really were truly freed.

…… ……

"Preach, this is Dante. We got a problem here. They're all over us. We're heading for the East gate, but right now, it's a gauntlet. They've got a bunch of people set up in the buildings—most of 'em only have small arms, but some have rockets and mini-missiles, and we've taken out three machine gun nests already. The bad guys are also rallying a bunch of pursuit vehicles and are using some to set up blockades. We've plowed through a couple roadblocks already, but we lose momentum each time. We might get stalled out altogether."

"Dante, this is Spider. Backup's on the way. Break: Iylo, you copy Dante's last?"

"Dante? This is Iylothien, Barde de la Nêone, Patron Saint of the Wires, and Guardian Angel of your truck full of refugees. I'm wired into the local security network—let's get 'em outta here."

A series of police turrets created to guard intersections suddenly barked to life as Constantine hit the accelerator pedal to ram through another blockade, scattering the blockade defenders and weakening the structural integrity of the vehicles. With an explosive blast, the truck roared through, barely slowed. The girls in the back of the truck lurched, but not as badly as before. Constantine grinned as the truck began to pick up speed. Four police drones picked up oversight over each corner of the truck, detecting and interdicting any hostiles in the buildings.

"*Iylo?*" Dante replied, "*I didn't know you were in on this run—gotta say it's good to hear your voice!*"

"*Constantine, this is Johnny. Can you swing down 97th and make a pickup? I got another twenty girls who are going to need a lift out of town.*"

"*Are you kidding? I'll have to circle around and back through town again!*"

"*Iylo, you cut it pretty close with that last blast, don't you think?*"

"*Wasn't me, Dante. The apartment complexes on your right are launching a lot of small fire. It won't hurt the truck, but the drones on that side are starting to take some hits. Drek! One of them just went down. Wait! Someone's running interdiction from inside the building, just took out somebody lining a LAW on you. Holy Mother Source Code!*"

"*What is it, Iylothien?*" Preach cut in, voice edgy with concern about the fate of those in the truck.

"*Preach, you're not going to believe this—that Stang kid just blackjacked a guy who had another rocket and fired it at our next blockade. He's somehow moving from building to building, covering the truck from their own perimeter!*"

"*Listen, you goveks!*" Rogue Moon cut in, "*I didn't mind sitting here keeping the girls company while you all did your thing. But if Stang is out there by himself, you'd BETTER find a way to get me into this fight, or I'll kick the back doors open and start firing back myself!*"

"That's suicide, Moon," Dante replied. *"The truck door armor is the only thing keeping you and the girls safe. Use the rear top hatch. I'll release the set of controls for the Vulcan in the rear turret once you let me know you're ready. I'm trying to cover roadside to rooftop on both sides as it is; I sure could use your help with the pimp-mobiles behind us."*

"Iylo, Vixenn here. I'm disconnected. Can you provide coverage? Another gang of flex is inbound; if we stay, we'll be bottled up ourselves. These girls need help, and we can't just leave them—remember what she said? They're all Kellys."

"I can cover, my Queen. Constantine, you up for the ride?"

"The truck's taken some hits but, if you can cover, we'll take the chance. Why have faith if you're never going to use it, right? Dante's updating Moon so they don't freak out."

"Constantine, take the next left," Iylothien directed as the turrets one block ahead of the truck opened up on an enemy the truck drivers could not yet see. *"Johnny, we'll be there in about twenty."*

"What about the kid outside?" Dante asked.

"Keep going," Iylothien responded with a chuckle. *"When he saw you start your turn, he broke into an oblique run to catch you. Yep, I see him. Constantine, you've got a boarder."*

"Iylothien, save the footage," Preach reminded the elite hacker.

"No need to say it, Preach. I want to watch these a few times myself."

"See you in twenty then, Dante," Johnny reported back, refusing to acknowledge Iylothien.

… …

A series of three cracks sounded, and splinters flew from the doorframe immediately to Johnny's left. Another group of gangers came into view; at least one of them carried an M18-X9 automatic rifle.

"If we can hold out that long," he mentioned to Melissana.

"Wait a minute," she responded with a smile as she loaded some weapons they had confiscated from the slavers. "Aren't you the guy who spent his whole life taking on bio-corporation security and Yakuza?"

"I see you've overcome your jitters," he mused back.

"This is street ops—we're a little upscale with the action, but I'm actually pretty used to this."

… …

"Johnny? Dante here. Where you guys at?"

"We're about a block south of the Single Hearts Hotel—yeah, that's its real name. Just pick up the girls. We found one of their weapon caches—we'll provide some cover fire while they load."

"What about you?"

"Well, we can't give you cover from inside the truck, now can we? Don't worry, once you guys are clear, we'll rendezvous with Preach."

"Well, if you're planning on giving us cover, you should be aware we're coming in a little hot."

"That's real nice," Johnny reflected. *"Because with the firestorm we're in right now, we could use the reprieve of just a little hot."*

They had never met him before, but both Dante and Constantine imagined Johnny was smiling.

… …

Saint Nick had a brief conference with Tag upon the younger boy's arrival at Safehouse One. "Looks like your troops are lightin' up a quarter of the town," Saint Nick told the CYBER agents. "Tag says with all you got started, some of the people are talkin' maybe it's time for a real change. Some of them are doing more than talking. All in all, Ricky T. Showbiz lost four lieutenants, just tonight. So, I guess you guys at least you might *appear* to be legit." He hesitated, evidently struggling with the pathway he was about to take.

"Come on," he relented as he again turned his back on the CYBER team, "Sitter cleared you; doesn't mean I'm happy about it, but I guess it's time to meet."

Once outside the safe house, the group slowly made their way through side streets and alleyways, carefully avoiding contact with any outside their group. The way was supposed to appear deserted, but Jack spotted along the way

- *"Heads up," Jack reported. "Infrared's showing picking up several small clusters of street urchins concealed in refuse-laden hidey-holes. They must be monitoring our progress and looking for any signs of hostility."*

- *"I got 'em, too," Araña responded. "SONAR and magnetic scans don't show any of the smaller kids carrying metallic weapons, but the older ones have knives, spears, and some have low-grade firearms."*

- *"Thanks, Spider," Jack acknowledged. "I'm scanning ahead with magnification and light amplification. Seeing some of the kids with what must be rather effective compound crossbows."*

- *"If they know how to use them, be careful," Chrome advised. "They reload slow, but they'd be lethal even against medium-armored targets if they connect."*

They eventually approached a manhole cover leading to a sewer. The out of towners had all gagged at one point or another, but they were only underground for about 20 minutes. Finally, Saint Nick approached a metallic ladder that was not quite as rusted as the others they had passed.

"Up," Saint Nick ordered as he produced a small weighted cylinder from under his jacket. With a flick of his wrist and a sharp *SNAP*, the cylinder he held expanded and telescoped to the length of a walking stick, the weighted end spasmodically bobbing to the rhythm of some weird unheard tune. Others in the group also drew similar weapons; Preach and the other CYBER agents suddenly found themselves surrounded by a half dozen desperate street kids wielding the bobbing cudgels. Behind them, those who had provided armed cover for their route assembled at angles that provided cover for Nick's group and supporting fire for each other without endangering any of the other cover positions. Araña let out a low whistle, himself admiring the setup; Chrome surveyed the situation and gave an approving nod. For the second time that evening, the CYBER team raised their arms in surrender, although this time, it was simply a gesture of diplomacy.

"Up," Saint Nick repeated, striking the metal drop plate at the top of the climb. White and blue sparks flashed as the metallic tip of the extended walking stick contacted the metal plate, startling Trigget and causing her to jump.

… …

"When I say 'Jump,' I don' want you to ask me how high, I want you to *jump*! Don't come here cryin' ta me 'bout your ho friends stuck wit those holy rollers at the religion show!" Sweet Trick Ricky T. Showbiz continued yelling, smashing his fist into Rainbow's already injured side. The girl thought she was getting away from trouble when she fled the scene of JoeRay's demise; she suddenly fully realized the tragedy of her mistake. She yowled in pain, heaving as she grasped the knife wound he had inflicted upon her a few moments earlier. "An' when I tell you ho's to shield JoeRay when he's up against someone, I expect you to shield him," he added more quietly, more evenly, more deliberately. Rainbow tried to brace herself, but she wasn't expecting the kick; she barely heard him through her pain, his slow drawl of breathy chuckle that was more methodical than emotional. He surveyed those gathered in the room that served as his headquarters.

They were all there—his remaining lieutenants, their right hands, and a small group of dealers, the hacker club who kept his online porn sites running, and a cadre of street snitches. He sneered and gave a sideways glance to a group of his newest muscle. "Take her out back," he ordered. "I don't care what you do to her, just make sure she ain't breathin' when you're done." Then he drew back and smiled, just a little, as he added, "And take your time. Get it all recorded. Upload it for all the 'decent' folk who stream it from the privacy of their own homes." He leaned into within two inches of Rainbow's face. "Don't worry, ho' Rainbow. We'll make good cred off your final trick."

"Mr. Sweet Trick Ricky T. Showbiz," one of the cowboys interrupted his thoughts, "you want us to re-run that vlog from Anita about how the girls really want this kind of life and the violence is all exaggerated?" Showbiz considered the suggestion—the kid called himself Sonny Thatch, and the master pimp noted he had a talent for the biz; he looked forward to teaching Thatch the finer points of the trade. He shook his head but indulged himself by taking a moment to coach the younger pimp to be.

"No point," the master pimp shrugged. "A lot of the people who pay for this kind of stuff have already convinced themselves it's all fake anyway. The rest don't care two creds as long as it ain't happening to their own women—and even then, some of those home-johns are so addicted to this stuff they'd pay to watch it anyway."

As the gangers dragged the screaming girl into the other room, Ricky T. Showbiz returned to the rest of the audience he had summoned. The night had been rough and was beginning to get expensive. What started off as a way of grabbing loot from some crazed traveling street preacher had turned into the loss of one of his organization's most prominent leaders and half the guy's stable.

"I wanted you all here in person so that y'all know you heard it from me. Allow me to spell it out. Y'all know Valhalla's Brownies are the ones attacking our convoys. Well, JoeRay and his boys went out to that street preacher's give-away, and who does that travelling circus come into the gates of my town with? None other than Gloss, one of my former girls who, once 'pon a time, managed to break away from here and got hooked up with Valhalla's Brownies. JoeRay had the situation under control, even managed to get Gloss back and take an extra honey or two for the trouble.

"Now, here's where it all gets interesting. The Bible thumper and his friends got away and disappeared after they got helped out by a clot of crotchlings—and Stang. Now, that preacher show's truck is making a break to get out of town with some of JoeRay's girls. Stang is still with the truck and somehow corporate enforcement's providing cover fire for them." He spat between his teeth. "Valhalla's Brownies, Gloss, Stang, the street rats… it seems I found our intel leak. My old friend Sitter's in on this up to his beady little eyeballs."

One of Ricky T. Showbiz's strong-arms entered the room and motioned he had an update. He approached and whispered his briefing to the king pimp of Kansas. Ricky's eyes flared at the news, then gave the messenger a fifty-credit tip.

"Seems we got a new problem. My man tells me some out-town upstart's been heatin' it up, trying to muscle in on Pick's turf at the Single Heart's Hotel on 97th. The punk's already taken out Pick, and according to the word on the street, Smokey-T is only barely keeping the guy contained. We'll pop that blister in due time, but this biz with Sitter comes first."

He stood and began to walk around the room. He wanted, no he demanded, their attention for what he would say next. He approached the center of the table and dumped out a bag onto the desk. The clatter of the credsticks clacking against the wooden tabletop spoke for itself, but Ricky T. Showbiz wanted everyone to be sure.

"I'm spottin' two million creds to someone who tells me where to find Sitter, with another quarter mil if they get it to me before sunrise." He glanced around the room, watching them look at the money as they contemplated the offer they had just been promised.

He finally snapped with an angry backhand swat against the pile, scattering it across the floor. "So, what y'all standin' around here for?" GO!!"

24. Connections

"Come in! Come in!" a slightly tenor voice cheerily greeted. Each of the CYBER members climbed through the small hole at the top of the ladder, only to step into an intensely brightly lit circle created by a ring of floodlights that blinded everyone except Jack. "Since you can't see, please allow me to explain you are surrounded by some of the steadiest shots in Witch City." Jack observed the somewhat misshapen figure check a series of readouts that were mounted in a sturdily-built automated wheelchair. "Interesting…" the man said as he studied the CYBER team. "Nick reported what he saw, but I confess that I didn't believe him.

"I apologize, Nick, but to my credit, these individuals are truly unique. If it wasn't for the scans, I'm not sure I would've noticed." He flicked a switch on his console. A muffled humming began somewhere underneath the flooring; two seconds later, a high-pitched whistle tone played in the CYBER team's sub-vocal receivers. The team gripped their ear and doubled over, trying to mute the noise that was coming from within their own heads. Even Chrome was incapacitated, though he managed to stand completely stoic except for the slightly twitching grimace.

"You see, Nick, they're cyborgs."

- "Preach," Araña's subvocal transmission sounded distant and garbled, "I can't get any readings—he's jamming my sensors!"

After the initial shock, Rogue removed her transceiver and took a step forward, but checked herself as she saw about ten kids had their homemade crossbows and other weapons trained on her.

"Sitter!" she exclaimed. "You know me—these are friends! This isn't the time for your paranoia. They came here to help. Ask your kids; they saw firsthand!"

"Oh, I meant no offense," Sitter passive/aggressively replied, "and I mean you no harm if you really mean us no harm. But this is Witch City, and trust is one of the few commodities that our citizenry typically don't deal in. I'll cut the jammers, but I want you to know that if anyone tries anything against me or one of these kids, I won't hesitate." He flicked a switch, and the whistling stopped, although it would take a few minutes for the team to recover fully. "And regarding my state of shall we say 'heightened security awareness,' Gloss—er, Rogue, please excuse me—just because they call you paranoid doesn't mean they're not really out to get you. Not all of us have had a six-year break from the City or the hard lessons she has taught us. You say they want to help? Help whom?" he asked, his voice slightly rising. "Me? My kids? Because starting a firestorm for a night or two and then disappearing for the aftermath doesn't really help us all that much!"

He paused, making a visible effort to settle himself down. "Now, Nick tells me you want to meet." He made a gesture of spinning a full circle, his smile wide and open. "I'm the one they call 'Sitter,' obviously enough. Nick and Tag you've met, along with several of the others." The smile disappeared as he leaned forward, scrutinizing the newcomers before him. "But who are you? And I don't just want your names—it's clear you're not with Ricky T. Showbiz, and I seriously doubt you're with Air Dynamix, but tell me, who *are* you working for?"

"Go ahead," Rogue said with an extended arm to Preach in a half shrug. "You need him, and if this is about winning trust, you're gonna have to go first. The way I see it, he's right. He's got a lot more at risk in all this than you do, and the W.C. is a harsh schoolmistress.

Besides," she said with a twist of smile, "I thought faith was one of your specialties."

"OK," Jack began. "Introductions: You already know Rogue Moon, and her story, and that she rides with Valhalla's Brownies. I'm Preach. To my right is Spider and Chrome. On my left are Trigget and Lady Blackwolf. We're with a government agency that has—"

"Wait a minute," Sitter interjected. "You're telling me you're from the government, and you're here to help? Hooray! My tax credits at work!" He spun his chair in mock celebration as he falsely cheered. He suddenly stopped and faced Jack directly. "Forgive me if I laugh out loud at the obvious joke, but let me get a short list together as to why I might be skeptical. For starters, which government are you from? There's not much of any left that I know of. Air Dynamix runs whatever's legal in this area, and Sweet Trick Ricky T. Showbiz runs the rest. Second, whenever the governments we used to have started mucking around in peoples' lives, they never really were all that helpful. They mostly either bloated themselves on red tape or got people so hopelessly reliant on them that they couldn't function on their own if they tried. The megacorporations are hard, and I'm not saying they don't squeeze the life out of everyone they can, but at least they produce something other than power for themselves. Third, no government's collected any taxes around here for some time, so where does your funding come from?" He fixed a scoffing sneer at Jack, then with a huff, continued. "But if you're really from some caring government I haven't heard from in a while, what I'd really like to know is where've you all been the last twenty years or so?"

"Man, you are one witless *bendejo*," Araña retorted on Jack's behalf. "There's a lot more to this country than this one urban playland you call home—maybe you haven't noticed, but we've been stretched a little thin trying to keep the rest afloat. But if you're so happy with the status quo, then maybe we should let you keep it.

"I'll leave you with a little history lesson, though. The government wasn't supposed to be just *for* the people; it was also supposed to be *of* the people and *by* the people. Only thing was, most waived that right by failing to step up and be a part of the process—it was easier just to complain about someone else not doing their job than for the complainers to do it themselves. Even before the missiles hit, the only finger most of them ever lifted was the middle one to crying about whatever the media told them they weren't getting for free! Now can you help us, or are you just gonna be one more critical govek whining about all the stuff we didn't do for you when we're asking for your help to get something done?"

A bowstring twanged and four crossbows *thwapped* as Sitter's kids, enraged at the defiance of their mentor, fired on Araña. The CYBER agent dodged three of the missiles and caught the remaining two in mid-air to elicit a chorus of astonished gasps from the young crowd. Sitter's hand edged to flick a switch on his console, but the sharp eyes of the Brownie sniper detected the movement.

"That's enough!" Rogue commanded. Knowing his element of surprise was blown, he visibly struggled for self-control but stopped, his glare blazing on the lead Hound.

Lightning hung suspended in the air between the two men. All conversation had collapsed into a stare-down, both sides justified in their conviction about the other, both sides knowing the other side was at least partially right, neither side willing to back down—and at that point, there was nowhere to back down to except further into the stony silences that had somehow spread across the entire warehouse. The click of an opening door latch and approach of padded feet belonging to one of Sitter's small scouting groups was almost deafening as it interrupted the palpable tension in the room. The newcomers furtively glanced from Sitter to the strangers and back.

"What is it, Toby?" Sitter commanded as he maintained his piercing glare on Araña. A young child who was evidently old enough to lead the group slipped close to his mentor, sent a darting glance at the strangers, bent in close, and whispered something in Sitter's ear. Sitter jerked his head to look at the youth, asking,

"More? Now? Are you sure?" The youth solemnly nodded, Sitter's shoulders collapsed in defeat. "We don't have time for this right now," he confessed to the CYBER team members as he spun his chair to face his lieutenant.

"Nick, I'm taking your word that these guys are on the level. Take a group and head to Drop 5—we've got another group to pick up."

"More?" Nick replied, echoing his teacher's dismay as he spread his arms in a helpless shrug, "Sitter, I want to help, but we're kind of full already."

"They need our help, Nick; we can't just abandon them. Go out there, find 'em, and bring 'em in." He subconsciously glanced around the warehouse setting. "We'll figure something out," he said with an assurance he himself didn't quite feel. He then reverted his attention back to the CYBER eavesdroppers, hoping to divert everyone's attention away from the waver in his tone that Trigget had immediately detected.

"Sitter," she asked, "what's wrong?

"I have a name, you know!" he suddenly exploded. He turned away from the team and stared at the floor. "I have a name, you know."

"That's not the problem!" she snapped back. "You're masking!"

- "Trigget," Jack said via their comm devices, "if he's masking, it stands to reason that whatever's getting to him just caused a deeper issue to surface. Address the deeper wound while it's exposed, or we'll lose an opportunity to really reach him."

"Whatever else is going on, though, I didn't mean to offend you," she offered in genuine apology. "I thought that's just your street handle—y'know, like they call me 'Trigget' when we're on the streets."

"He used to go by Partisan," Nick explained as he shouldered his knapsack and took point in front of a small knot of youths. "Sitter's what *they* called him. Because of his chair. He decided to own it cuz he babysits us until we're good enough to make it on our own, like Stang. Once Gloss made it outside to the Brownies, she told them, and it stuck. He might never shake the handle, but outside of us, he doesn't like it."

Preach squatted down to meet the wheelchair-bound mentor's downcast gaze. "I apologize; we didn't know."

"There's a lot of stuff you don't know about Witch City," Sitter quietly murmured in disgust.

"You're right," Araña offered, "but there's still a lot we've got to do while we can, and a lot we need to get caught up on."

- "He's stabilizing," Josanne subvocally informed the team. "His shoulders relaxed, his breathing's slowed, and his pupils are going into normative response proportions."

"Can we start with the basics?" Preach ventured.

"What do you want to know?" Sitter asked. He had only begun to regain his composure, but the fight had left him. "But we have a lot going on ourselves right now, so make it as quick as you can."

Preach looked the man in the eyes. "First, before anything else, what would you like us to call you?"

The urban survivalist looked up, surprised and pleased that Preach was even considering the question.

"I liked Partisan," he replied; a slightly boyish grin and brief sparkle in the furtive eyes added a nonverbal exclamation point. But both the grin and sparkle faded just as fast as he added, "But that was a long time ago, before all this."

"Partisan—'A supporter of a group or cause who has an emotional allegiance.' It fits," Lady Blackwolf reflected.

"They're also irregular forces that harass and sabotage an occupying army," Chrome added.

"In that case," Preach declared, gently clapping the Witch City resident's shoulder, "Partisan, I'm Preach. I'm glad we could finally meet," he added, hoping this thing was finally turning around. "And you're right—there's a lot we need to learn down here."

With the newfound recognition and some of his old self-respect regained, Sitter/Partisan straightened and seemed to sit a little higher in his chair. "So, how can I help?"

"We're looking for a girl. She was supposed to be in a convoy that the Valhalla's Brownies 'liberated' after you alerted them about a month ago. Her name's Kelly. She's about 5' 6, blonde, probably a petite average. Have you seen her?"

Partisan called Tag and shared the description. "Does she sound like the girl we've been looking for?"

The youth's face contorted as he tried to remember the night that seemed so long ago. "I'm not sure. It was dark, and she wasn't close by."

"Well, it's an honest answer," Partisan shrugged. "Plus, the Witch City industry has a way of making young girls age fast." At least Tag thought there was a semblance. Just enough to interject a weird, swirling combination of hope mixed with regret.

"I myself didn't see her," Partisan recalled, "but I remember that night. It was October. Nick led a foraging group, and they spotted a girl who was on the run. She stopped long enough to help one of my kids who was dying in an alley. She got picked up not too long after. That convoy left in the meantime—she's the reason I risked calling it into the Brownies, but she wasn't on the trucks. We've been looking for her ever since, but we've only spotted her once or twice since then and couldn't get close enough to contact her. She belongs to Sweet Trick Ricky T. Showbiz, a particularly aggressive and powerful pimp. He keeps real close tabs on her since she ran off from him. That's probably why she wasn't at your show.

"Kelly, huh?" Partisan mused. "Pretty name—it fits her. You'd never find her using Kelly, though; she doesn't go by that anymore. Ricky T. Showbiz always renames his girls, beats them pretty bad if he ever catches them using their given names." He shuddered in disgust at a memory. He paused and tried to give the team a consoling smile, but the gesture was somewhat dissipated by his experience and their knowledge. "You know she won't look like that picture if you find her—and there's no real promise you will."

"No, I can't promise I'll find her," Preach replied with sober resolution. "But even if we don't, I do promise you one thing..." Preach assessed his team's collective mindset and drew from the mood of the entire group's aggregate heartbeat; he knew he was speaking for them all. He thought of Kelly's fate, and of the fates of so many Kellys, just like Elaine had exhorted them. He sighed, the sound somehow a confirmation of the finality of his commitment. He looked Partisan in the eyes and, in a seriousness and determination so resolute it was physically palpable, he finished his promise. "We will find Sweet Trick Ricky T. Showbiz."

Partisan was too scared to do anything other than offer a small nod of assent. A bead of chill perspiration had formed in the back of his head began to slowly roll down the hollow of his neck, but he didn't dare shiver. He hadn't noticed the odd details of the newcomer's eyes until the pupils contracted to pinpricks and briefly flickered an intense beam of bright red; at that instant Partisan felt an intense burning sensation just between his eyes at the crest of his nose. The sudden heat made the point clearer than a hundred sworn declarations. Sweet Trick Ricky T. Showbiz had made a powerful enemy, and for the first time since he could remember, he hoped that the group who was looking for the animalistic pimp would find him, and that hope renewed his courage.

. . . . . .

Simon launched a small host of diagnostic and analytical subroutines as it noted the surge. Jack "Preach" Matthews had activated his lasers for the first time since his return, but there was no indication of any imminent threat. It wondered if it had perhaps reactivated the rest of Jack's enhancements prematurely. It did take some solace in the fact that the rest of the team's monitors registered a higher-than-normal level of emotional stress at the surroundings, and no one other than Araña and Trigget had shown any notice of inappropriate activity from their leader. The last returning subroutine reported the gesture had, for some reason, actually calmed Chrome. Simon logged the return call values of the other subroutines after that and returned its attention to monitoring Hawk's Flight in Oregon and Blaze's Fist in old Miami.

. . . . . .

"Well," Partisan declared to the group, "it's settled then. While you're looking, you'll need a place to stay, hide out, and keep your ears to the ground." He spun a slow circle, showing off the warehouse building he and his thirty-some charges called home. "It's not much," he offered to the group, "but you're welcome to stay here as long as you keep your heads below radar comin' and goin.' After everything that's happened tonight, your heat's so high nobody else would touch you if they could scrape gold off of you."

"You sure you want to do that?" Chrome asked. "I overheard you're getting more kids in from somewhere, and there's still gonna be a couple more of us coming in before this is all through."

"Nah, we'll be all right," Partisan responded, new hope taking root in his old frame. "We've got room, and thanks to your boxes and credstick, we'll have provision enough, at least for a while. Besides, it'll be good for the kids to have other adults around that aren't a threat to them—especially since we're getting in another group tonight. You can help me get them settled in."

"Partisan?" Susan asked as she surveyed the warehouse and ramshackle mini-housing the kids who lived there had already constructed. "There's something I don't understand. From the looks of things, you already have over thirty kids here, and you're getting another group tonight. Where do all these kids come from?"

He stopped, wheeled an abrupt spinning turn to face her. Anger briefly displayed on his face. Once again, he regained control of himself before he responded. "You'll find out soon enough." He coughed a sad half smile as he looked at her, giving her his full attention as he responded. "For now, we'll just say there's more than one reason this place is called Witch City. I'll explain it once all my kids are back."

… …

"No wonder this place is called Witch City!" Dante complained after a rocket slammed into the back of the trailer with enough force to cause its axles to lift off the ground and slam back against the city street. The impact caused the tractor trailer to skew 26 degrees from its forward path. "Rogue, you gonna quiet that guy down?"

"Vulcan's almost out of ammo," she called back. "We thinned the herd, but there's more of 'em out there that are taking the chase. Stang, you okay?"

"Barely—we all got thrown on that last one," he replied from inside the trailer. "I'm looking for more ammo, but I guess the plan was never to take on the entire city on the way out."

"The hotel's ahead of us, five blocks to go," Constantine advised. "There's some guy standing in the middle of the road staring at us. I'm accelerating—if he doesn't move, I'm cutting him down."

"*Don't fire!*" Iylothien cut in. "*I spotted him with the drones. That's Johnny—he's one of ours!*"

"*Iylo, we still got at least five cars behind us, and he thinks he's gonna take them on himself?*"

"*Just keep going!*"

The truck sped towards the lone figure who resolutely stood his ground in the center of the street. The luckster calmly raised a shoulder-fired rocket he had slung behind his back and sidestepped left twice. The large vehicle's draft tugged wildly at Johnny's duster, but as the cab passed, he raised the launcher and snap-fired into the pack of pursuing vehicles, dropped prone, and yelled through his comm device, *"Vixenn, NOW!"* The rocket hit the front of the lead car on the passenger side. The blast totaled that vehicle and caused it to skid sideways into the others behind it just as a line of several satchel charges that had been stretched across the street exploded underneath the remaining oncoming cars. The wrecks and resulting series of follow-up collisions created a pileup that blocked the road on the far side of the intersection half a block from where he stood.

- *"Did it work?" Melissana asked from the hotel. "I heard the blasts from here, but I couldn't see anything."*

- *"Couldn't have gone better," Iylothien affirmed. "I caught it all from the drones, even though I lost one in the explosions. Nicely done, Johnny! We'll add this to your video collection."*

- *"Dante, glad to see you guys made it," Johnny called. "Bring the truck up so we can get those girls loaded. If you have any ammo on board, I'll need to reload—we've been pretty busy out here, and I used the last of my bang I brought with me in my car to make the traffic jam. Once we're resupplied, you guys head on out."*

- *"You got it, rocket-man!" Dante replied. "But we're gonna need some repairs."*

- *"No time for that here," Iylothien replied. "Those blasts solved our problem with the chase vehicles, but now the stars are on the way. I've been keeping the system jammed down, but they don't need their computers to tell them where all this happened."*

Three minutes later, a small knot of girls ages 14 through 20 emerged from the Single Hearts Hotel. Some looked frightened, some looked relieved, all looked exhausted, hungry, and small against the harsh glare of the flophouse's signage. Huddled together and shivering against the chill of a Wichita November night, the girls boarded the outbound truck as the two teams were preparing to part.

"Stang," Rogue asked, "we're leaving. Why don't you come with us?"

"It's tempting," he replied, "but I gotta stay here. Sitter still needs me, and besides, this is home."

"You punk," she chided, then leaned into him for them to hug their farewells. "Take care of yourself, and remember me, okay?"

"Remember you?" he asked with a confused look. "I've never forgotten you." They hugged again. "You know, when this is over, let me know when you're in the area again." Then he helped her into the truck.

"You guys sure you're staying?" Dante asked the CYBER duo.

"Yeah, we're staying," Queen Vixenn replied as she and Rogue were assisting the girls. "We've definitely seen a little more action than we planned, but we're not done yet. We still need to find Kelly, and there's a lot of city left to search."

One of the girls stopped. "You're looking for a Kelly? About five and half feet tall, had blondish hair and some kind of southern accent?"

Johnny and Melissana exchanged glances. "You know her?" they asked in sudden anticipation.

"Could be. She's one of Showbiz's girls. I met her, once, when I was being auctioned. She accidentally used her name in front of him, once." Her voice wavered as she glanced down to the street. "That's not a good idea; he made her pay for it. He renames the girls, does anything he can to strip away their own identities." She sighed and looked down. "They all do."

"What name did he give her?" Vixenn asked as gently as she could.

"Shimmer," the girl sadly replied. "He calls her Shimmer."

The truck pulled away, leaving Johnny, Queen Vixenn, and Stang standing by Johnny's sedan. Iylothien had been screening and misdirecting the local law enforcement, but the trio could now hear sirens approaching from several blocks away.

"So, you two are with that Preach guy?" Stang asked. On seeing their response, he added, "Yeah, I met him—he's okay. We met outside his revival scene, and last I saw, they were going off to meet Sitter. Follow me. I know where he is."

"I have a better idea," Johnny offered. "Hop in. Show us the way, and we'll give you a lift. It'll be a little faster."

"Man," Stang exclaimed as he took in the gear stashed inside the vehicle, "if you guys are all like this, Ricky T. Showbiz might finally gonna get his *due*."

… …

"The group from Drop Zone Five is overdue. I don't like it," Partisan worried.

"There's a lot of extra heat out there," Araña responded, concerned because Partisan was concerned. "We started this— where can we go look for them?"

"Timmy?" At Partisan's call, yet another youth peeled off from the group of urchins, now ogling the tough role models standing before them. "Take your group to go with these chummers and show them where Drop 5 is. I imagine you'll be safe with them," he said with a nod toward Araña that was acknowledged and returned. "But stay close and show them the city along the way. If you meet up with Tag and his team, just come back, okay? We just want to make sure Tag's okay."

"Okay, Sitter," the child acknowledged, puffing his chest as much as his young frame would allow. "You can count on me."

"Okay then," Partisan smiled. He was always proud of his boys, but this was one of Timmy's first times leading a group—Partisan knew the CYBER troops would physically care for the young man, but he was still proud knowing the government troopers relied on a kid less than half their age. Especially as the youngster proudly slung his sack over his shoulder and called to the government veterans,

"Well? You noobs comin'?"

Josanne shook her head, and Lady Blackwolf simply shrugged, but Chrome unsuccessfully stifled a laugh. "You know, Spider?" he announced very much out loud as he retrieved his M18-X9, "I kinda like this place. This is really my kind of home!" And with that, they followed the young leader.

Outside on the streets, Timmy's youthful demeanor changed considerably. They would have been much faster if they had skipped the crouch/hide-from-line-of-sight/hide stealth routine, but every street instinct the CYBER troops had deterred them from raining on the youth's parade. Partisan had been right—once the teams left, the day-to-day struggles of the street would continue, and the young trainee would need to keep his reflexes sharp.

It wasn't until they were waiting at Drop Zone 5 that Partisan sent the call that he dispatched two more groups of kids to other drop zones. Stretched thin, the remaining CYBER members split up to accompany the younger forces. It was clearly an extraordinary night, even for the W.C.

25. Sitter's Stand

The group sat together in a sullen huddle, each one silently reflecting on some inner thoughts as the muffled blasts from outside the city comingled with the somewhat nearer sounds of gunshots and explosions that echoed from within the confines of the city walls. The silence of their immediate surroundings loudly contrasted against the sounds of the various firefights around them, the sense of peace in their immediate area an irritant that screamed at them that their situation was false.

"It's been over an hour since we've linked up," Araña disapproved. "Are you sure this is the right place, and they meant tonight?"

"Yeah!" Timmy asserted, "I've led pickups before." He came out of their hiding spot and waved his arms in a sweeping gesture. "Drop Zone 5, all around you. Trender's Pawn and Go, Cutter's Market, and the back end of Plaster's Bar. But the biggest clue is right in front of you," he said as he pointed to a high, heavily graffitied metal wall. Araña studied the wall closer, but Chrome spotted it first.

"The 'Flavor' tag of the big lips—the V is a little different."

"Yep," Timmy agreed, "Sitter told me that a long time ago a bunch of old people used to think thagt the letter V was a number. It mark's the doorway into the wall. I mean, it doesn't have a handle or anything, and it's really hard to see, but that's it.."

"Something's not right," Spider pressed. "Are you sure they're coming tonight?"

"Of course, I'm sure!" the young squad leader protested. "You think I'm dumb or something?"

"It's not you, kid," Chrome assured. "We believe you, but Spider's right—something's off. He glanced around, noting the still quiet that settled on the neighborhood. "Spider? Pretty quiet for being just outside of a bar. You getting anything on your scanners?"

"It is quiet," the Hispanic commando replied. "I'm not picking up anything hostile. Maybe they're just running late. We'll give it one more hour before we head back."

"If you say so," Chrome responded, shifting uneasily in his hiding spot. "But something's off—I can smell it."

- "Spider? Chrome? What's your status?"

"Preach?" Spider responded. "We're still waiting. So far, no kids have shown."

The leader of Grey's Hounds glanced at his team's discontented strong-arm. Chrome was, by far, the most stoic of all the Hounds, especially when it came to times of waiting. Spider considered Chrome's instincts as well as his own experience a moment, then cocked his head at a sudden realization.

- "Preach? How can we communicate now? Sitter's—err, Partisan's—lair was shielded against any commo not going through his tech."

- "We went topside," Preach responded. "Since the kids were getting thinned out, and with all the commotion, we decided to go with them to back them up."

- "Preach, who's left with Partisan?" Spider asked.

- "We're all out, except for a couple of his newest recruits. Sitter left his safehouse and took them back to his main place on the

corner of 13ᵗʰ and Mosleyᵗ to get more supplies. They were getting tips about kids getting dropped all over the place tonight—that's why his kids are stretched so thin."

Araña turned to Chrome, his face a reflection of acute awareness of guilt and horror. The armored cyborg missed Spider's expression, though; he was already up and halfway down the first alley on his way back to the chairbound youth mentor.

- "Stay with the kids," Chrome radioed back to his lead. "Whatever happens, cover them."

… …

The silence was deafening as Partisan and his small band of charges returned to the warehouse that served as their home. Something felt off. He hesitated, remembering his own advice to the kids about the home they left might not be the same home when you return. His sharp eyes darted back and forth across the darkened warehouse floor; listening for the typical background noise of rodents scurrying among the decrepit pallets yielded nothing. Slowly, as though trying to avoid being seen, his hand nudged the activation switch for the warehouse camera systems. His screen flickered, then faded to amber, then completely died to the screen's original grey. He ordered his kids to scatter; a moment later, he heard booted footsteps approach him from behind.

"Well now, if it ain't my old friend, Sitter," a deep voice sneered. "You missin' a couple pieces of your precious tech?"

Partisan flicked a control on his console and lobbed a small projectile that blasted the area the chairbound mentor thought Ricky's voice was coming from. The explosion flung stacks of crates and semi-organized clusters of random stockpiles that dotted the spacious interior as he raced forward out of sight. Without his camera system, he couldn't be sure he took out his opponents. As the dust cleared, the silhouette of a massively built man flanked by a small horde of his followers stood outlined in the hazy glow of the remaining light fixtures.

"Sitter!" roared the giant over the din of smashed wood and debris settling into place.

A small voice coughed several times to the left of the gathered men. Showbiz signaled, and one of the gang broke off to find the source of the sound. Defiant protests of "Let go!" indicated a stray youth had been found. "Shut up!" the ganger yelled from behind a stack of pallets. Hidden among the large wooden crates, Sitter cringed as he heard a loud smack. The coughing protests gave way to a chill silence.

"Sitter!" the master pimp again bellowed. "You better come out now, or I swear I'll wade through the blood of every one of your precious little kids until I find you. Get out here, *now!*" The invaders fanned out, quickly catching two more of the smaller youths who had hidden at the initial blast. The men returned to the pack and presented the captives to their alpha. "Last chance, you coward," he roared. One of the children began to cry.

"Don't do it, Sitter! He ain't worth it!" the other kid shouted in a rage. He glared at his tormentor, turned to face Sweet Trick Ricky T. Showbiz, and spat.

Showbiz laughed, a sound completely devoid of mercy. "You know, Sitter, I think I'm gonna keep this one. If he survives his training, in a couple years he'll be a great addition to my organization." Then he looked to the crying child. "This one's weak, though—nothing worth saving. You get out here now, or I'll feed him to my dogs."

He would have engaged his remote defense system, but somehow they were offline. He was in trouble, and he knew it.

"Stand down, kids," Sitter faintly hailed from deep within the safehouse interior. Motorized wheels quietly whispered across the concrete floor until the youth mentor emerged from somewhere within the maze of crates and industrial supplies. He traversed the floor to an open area in the center of the cavernous room, then nonchalantly rotated to face the intruders.

"Sweet Trick Ricky T. Showbiz," Partisan placidly acknowledged with a shallow smile. "You know, you could've knocked." He briefly paused to gather his strength before he continued. "Let the boys go," he said resolutely. "Neither one of them means anything to you."

"All right, all right," Witch City's grand pimp acquiesced. "Neither one of 'em's gonna stand a chance without you, anyway," he smirked.

"So, what's this all about, Showbiz? What'd we do to you?"

"Ahh, I bet the real question you want to ask is how we found you. You see, one of your new friends called one of my old friends. Then I caught one of your rats, who liked the deal I offered him. Don't worry, though, I didn't pay it. Once he told me where you were, I sold him to an associate of mine.

"You see, it's all a balancing act—a reckoning of accounts, so to speak." Sweet Trick grinned. "Let me see if I can explain how this works. Your kid brought in a pretty price for me, plus he saved me the bounty creds I offered to find you, so I've adjusted your account some. But you see, you still fall short of the balance due, on account of those new associates of yours. Maybe you want to tell me where they are now? That would go a long way to settling your accounts."

"I don't have any accounts with you."

"Sitter," he practically purred as a slow smile played across his face, "everybody in this city has accounts with me. Right now, you most of all. So, my old friend, where are they?"

"I don't know what you mean. Where are what? All I got are my kids."

"Well, you have a few less kids by now, but you and I both know you sheltered that out-of-town circus after they crossed with JoeRay, Bobby-G, and their crew. Oh yeah, that reminds me—Stang and some of your kids were directly involved in that mash-up." He grinned cruelly. "That'll add to your debt."

At the flick of another control panel switch, Partisan's chair launched a cloud of sharp darts that tore through the flesh of Ricky T. Showbiz's unarmored soldiers, with enough power left over to shatter several of the aged crates behind them. Backing up, Partisan hit another control and began firing a pair of MP-12 machine pistols, the steady stream of alternating tungsten-tip and hollow-point 9mm rounds adding further to the needled mayhem he had unleashed a few seconds before. Eight went down in the onslaught, but twenty-three were still left. Ricky T. Showbiz was one of them.

"You done?" Ricky T. Showbiz asked, calmly, with menace. After a moment's pause, his mouth opened, grinning widely. "I think he's done," he announced to the others. "Go dig him outta his burrow and bring him to me."

With gloating whoops and jeers, Showbiz's thugs hooked ropes around his chair's front wheels and dragged the now hapless mentor before the master pimp.

"Now what you gonna do?" Ricky T. Showbiz leered. The master pimp sauntered up and slapped Sitter across the back of the head. "Your kiddie boys ain't here—you can't even reload yourself, can you?" He reared back and laughed, slapping the defenseless man several more times. "So, you traded away your boys for some new friends." He laughed again. "And to think everyone around these parts thought you were so smart, with your traps, and your mysterious ways, and your invisible spy network—you were the talk of the town, the Urban Legend, the Untouchable." He slapped Partisan's head again, eliciting a groan from his helpless captive. "Not so untouchable now, are you?" Ricky T. Showbiz grabbed Partisan's hair and pulled his head back against his chair and leaned within inches of his face, his eyes flaring in anger. "Now tell me, you frakkin' cripple, where are they?"

"I'll never tell you," Sitter defiantly proclaimed. "You've come this far, so go ahead, finish the job."

"Oh, I'll finish the job, all right," Ricky T. Showbiz threatened as he gripped one of the sides of Sitter's chair. "But first, *tell* me, where…

they… ARE!" He bellowed the last word as he gathered his strength and heaved upwards, dumping the inner city youth leader to land hard onto the concrete floor. Partisan fell heavily, with no means to catch himself. Shards of white pain seared through the helpless invalid; the November cold of the concrete added to the crushing weight of his incapacitated body, his head dazed as it smacked against the cement flooring. Partisan had little enough voluntary control over his muscles; they began to spasm involuntarily, his body trying to find some sort of equilibrium against the pain.

"I won't tell you anything!" he screamed through tears of pain he could not conceal. Long-buried memories from his capture those many years ago replayed in sharp detail and added to Partisan's fear of the very present danger. His voice sank to a whimper. "I'm not going to tell you a thing."

"Well now, Sitter, or should I maybe call you Heap, since evidently that's all you are right now?" He briefly chuckled at his own joke, then his face turned deathly grim. "Anyway, we're not done yet." He unsheathed a knife and leaned down in front of the fallen youth leader, dangling the blade in front of his eyes. "Maybe I should just…" He was interrupted by the loud clang of a metal door that slammed shut from a catwalk high above the floor level. A moment later, a heavily muscled man with a blonde tight-crop wearing a black t-shirt and sunglasses loomed over the walkway railing, taking in the entire scene.

"Who are you?" Ricky T. Showbiz jeered. The only response the man in the flat black sunglasses offered was the sound of slow, heavy footfalls deliberately descending the open grated steps of the metal stairway, each stair creaking a straining groan under the weight of the booted feet. The brawny newcomer paused on the last step to take one more survey of the grisly scene before him. He focused a sunglassed stare at the apparent leader of the group, the one who had been doing all the talking when he had first arrived—the one, he noted, who had unceremoniously dumped Sitter out of his wheelchair onto the concrete floor. The scene somehow reminded him of a night in San Francisco just over six years earlier. Normally stoic beyond any expression, he was only barely in control of himself, and he knew it; he stepped off the last stair onto the main floor and resumed his deliberate, singularly focused approach.

Chrome cracked his neck as he slowly stalked across the main floor, looked Ricky T. Showbiz straight in the eyes, and produced a maliciously grimacing type of grin. "You know," he stated flatly, "there's a special place in hell for goveks like you. It's called the knuckles of my right fist."

"You're one of them." Ricky T tried to intimidate the man, but he backed up a step despite himself. "This loser's got 'Crazy' with a capital 'C' tattooed all over him!" he remarked to his gang, then returned his attention to the still-advancing menace before him. "Well come on, then," he dared. "Come get some." Laughing, several of Ricky T. Showbiz's men opened fire on the grim man, but he resolutely continued his steady advance, unaffected by the small arms fire that was obviously hitting him. In response, Chrome, maintaining the steady stride of a hunting panther, unslung his M18-X9 and fired seven three-round bursts in rapid succession. Five shooters dropped, each with at least one round buried in his head.

"Rush him!" Ricky T. Showbiz yelled, and the remaining gangers descended on the advancing Chrome with bats, knives, pipes, and a variety of other melee weapons. Showbiz regained his smile as Chrome slowed to a stop under the load of the dogpile.

"You must really think you're something," the pimp chided as he picked up a bat that had been dropped in the grapple. "Well, ain't no never-mind to me." He turned briefly to Sitter and jeered, "So you don't know where they are, huh? Well, once I finish with him, I'll pick up where I left off with you." As the large pimp finished his sentence, he stepped back onto his right leg and gripping the bat with both hands, swung with his full body weight like a baseball player slugging for a home run, smacking Chrome in the head with a loud CRACK!

Chrome's head wobbled, then he sagged; the men who had been holding him dropped under the sudden heavy weight they hadn't realized they had been supporting.

"Chrome?" a female voice called from the warehouse's street entrance. "*Chrome?*"

Ricky T. Showbiz grinned, turning to face Melissana and Johnny, who visibly started when he saw the Hound's tank sprawled on the floor.

"Ahh, and what do we have here? Must be two more flies coming home to rest. And you brought Stang with you!" He again glared at Sitter, still on the floor in a convulsing heap. "You told me you knew nothing about any of this, and now look where we are."

"Sitter!" Stang cried. The sight of his former master so heinously treated tore at any self-control the youth had, but Vixenn held him back long enough for him not to burst headlong into the group of awaiting hoodlums.

The kingpin pimp of Witch City raised his bat and pointed it at the three newcomers. "Get 'em."

As the group of thugs approached, Stang produced his quarterstaff. Johnny produced a grin. "Vixenn, get word to Trig. We need her here—*stat.*"

That was all he had time to say. Vixenn ducked behind a few crates, freeing Stang to swing his quarterstaff in a wide arc at the heads of the nearest assailants. His temper was getting the better of him, though—he was expending way too much energy on wild strokes that were easily dodged by the gang of professional thugs. Johnny had recovered enough, however, to recognize Stang's swing had caused the right side of the assault to slow down for a few seconds, which gave him his chance to attack left.

The ganger's half expected the apparently unarmed man to flee. Instead, the CYBER luckster took a step forward and launched into a parkour leap, his right foot lifting his body against a crate to his left. At the height of his arc, he spun in a counterclockwise twist, adding his entire body weight to the gravity-enhanced velocity of the sharp right haymaker he planted squarely to the top of the foremost aggressor's cranium. After a squishy-sounding crack, the ganger crumpled to the floor instantly, the CYBER agent falling with him to land on his left side just in front of the next thug. Before the surprised linemen had time to react, Johnny swept his left foot out and forward just enough to hook behind his next victim's right heel and kicked his other foot violently against his victim's right kneecap. With nowhere for the tough's lower leg to go, the knee bent backward with another audible snap.

Stang took his cue from the CYBER forces and mustered the discipline that had kept him alive in the streets of Witch City for so long. Taking advantage of the distraction Johnny had provided for him, he utilized his martial skills to keep the intruders in relatively open areas. It was knives and pipe lengths against his quarterstaff, and Stang's greater reach proved far more effective than the shorter weapons.

By that time, Queen Vixenn had enough time to crack Sitter's security protocols and take over the remote security devices. Just as importantly, she intercepted a radio message letting her know she was no longer cut off from the outside world.

- *"... truck is away, pigeons are safe. Rickshaw and Hardcore dismissed the remaining pursuers with prejudice as they transferred at the gate on their way in. I've dispatched them to the coordinates you provided on Partisan's location. Iylo out."*

Iylothien? In a flood of relief, Melissana realized she could broadcast their distress call to the teams that had been falsely dispatched to gather incoming pickups.

- *"Trigget and Preach, this is Queen Vixenn—return to Partisan's, stat. He needs medical treatment, and..."* She hesitated, *not knowing if they would take her seriously if she said it.*

- "Vixenn, this is Preach. We didn't copy the rest of your transmission. Partisan needs treatment and what?"

She exhaled sharply and decided she had better let them know.

- "And Chrome is down."

There was a brief chill of silence. Even the sounds of the ongoing street battles and windy draft momentarily went quiet, as though the whole world rocked at the news. Or maybe it was just them.

- "We're on our way."

Hearing the remote defenses spinning to life gave Ricky T. Showbiz pause. A quick survey of the grisly battle scene revealed he had lost over half of his original raiding party to three newcomers and Stang. And by what he had just heard, more were on the way. He swore violently.

"I haven't killed you yet, Heap, but your day's coming." He spat at the downed CYBER agent who had cost him at least seven men— the sunglassed gorilla somehow managed to kill two more while they grappled him. "Took you out, though, govek," he said more to himself than anyone who overheard him. He again pointed his bat against Sitter's remaining friends. "There won't even be enough for the rats to feed on when I'm done with you all," he threatened. "Come on," he ordered, summoning his remaining forces. "Let's get back to the pen and regroup. We know what we're up against now. They're down one, and we'll have more when we get back.

"Enjoy your peace while you can," he threatened. Then he turned and led the remnants of his raiding party back into the dark of the Witch City alleyways.

26. Sitter's Source

"I NEVER TOLD them," Partisan's softly repeated in a faraway voice, more to himself than anyone else gathered in the warehouse. "I never told them about you."

"We know," Preach reassured as he gently clasped the other man's shoulder. He and Trigget arrived a few minutes after Ricky T. Showbiz and his gang had left. Johnny and Stang were trying to help Partisan back into his chair while Melissana tended to Chrome. Trigget quickly moved in to treat Partisan's injuries and gave him a full checkup before allowing the others to help him back into his chair. "You gave it everything you had—none of this was your fault. In fact, you were right; if we hadn't shown up, none of this would have happened."

"If you hadn't shown up, he'd still be running around here, trafficking those poor girls with total impunity, contaminating everyone he meets." Partisan corrected. A chill November gust blew through the shelter as Rickshaw's Dominator and Hardcore's Sabretooth backed into the warehouse. Sitter shivered, but neither Preach nor even Trigget could tell if it was because of the draft, his trauma, or just plain anger. "I'm the one who was wrong. He has to be stopped."

… …

"Hey. Old boy," Iylothien playfully chided. "I know we all really want you to have your beauty sleep, but—easy, now—time to wake up. Come on," he continued, "let's see those eyelids flutter."

"What the—hey—I swear I'll…" Chrome struggled and kicked feverishly, but little was done except to stir up small wisps of iridescent flowers. After a few moments, he settled down.

"Easy there, big guy," Iylothien hushed. "You've been out for a little while. We were kind of afraid of what you'd do if we just woke you up cold. Then Preach thought we might want to wake you up in here first. Gotta say, from watching you kicking around the way you did, it was a good call. We didn't have any of the V.R. training hoods on us, though, so Trigget somehow rigged one up and bypassed it through one of your other system implants. Whatever her other faults might have been, she's done you good. After that, we just had to route the signal, and here we are in the tutorial level of the environmental module." Then the elfish ranger glanced over his shoulder to a stately female figure with almost impossibly long raven hair wearing an elegant, freely flowing robe. "He should be okay after a minute or two."

The female figure hovered over the fallen cyborg; obvious concern etched across her features. "Chrome, are you all right?"

"Him, I'd know anywhere," he half coughed his response, "but who are you?"

"I'm his protégé," she smiled the kind of smile people use to mask bad news when visiting loved ones in a hospital. "Don't you remember me?"

"Mel—err, Queen Vixenn—is that really you?" He smiled in spite of himself. "No wonder he likes you," he murmured louder than he intended. "Drek—did I really say that?"

Queen Vixenn softly laughed. The sound filled the small grotto they were in as distant wind chimes pleasantly singing in a gentle breeze. Iylothien's laughter was a little coarser but just as comforting, the sound of a hunter returning home after a long hunt.

"Yeah, he's still groggy," Iylothien assessed. "Possibly concussed—good call to wake him up in the hood first, or he could've taken out some of the good guys."

"Concussed?" Queen Vixenn exclaimed, "I thought he was dead! I saw the blow he took—how is he possibly alive?"

"He's got armor plating for his armor plating. What I want to know is how he got laid out in the first place."

"Come on," she said while putting her virtual arm around his waist and leaning into him for support. "Let's go for a walk, and I'll fill you in. Trigget needs to wrap up her medical assessments and systems diagnostics, and after everything that's happened over the last couple days, I just want to have you close for a while."

"Okay," he said. "Chrome, old buddy, we're going for a walk. We'll be back in a couple minutes, then we'll get you out of here."

After Chrome's assurances that he'd be fine, the young couple held each other close for a moment, then walked off together arm in arm, their physical bodies 2000 miles apart.

… …

"So, the containment of the city is working, at least for the moment," Rickshaw reported. Now that the sub-teams were reunited, they were using the hiatus to compare stories and notes with each other, Partisan's organization, and Stang. "The Paladins and Valhalla's Brownies will continue to work together."

"The early rescue results were good," Hardcore added. He had, naturally enough, been physically close to Susan since the pair had reunited; he remained yet closer—his arm protectively around her— since the details of the revival came to light. "Nobody really expected we'd be sending out 37 girls so quickly, so they're committed more than ever—especially since Freya got Rogue back and both Dante and Constantine have returned to Small Eddie."

"We've lost some social capital at the gate crossing, though," Iylothien chimed in remotely. "We're committed. I don't think there will be any more magic tricks to get anybody else in or out until this is over."

"So, coming back to inside the city, it seems most of the pimp gangs travel in cells consisting of about nine gorillas with about three girls per gorilla," Araña summarized, etching ash notes on the concrete. Burnt crate wood and the warehouse floor served as an improvised whiteboard.

"Okay," Preach picked up the narrative, "we also now have a layout of their organizational structure, at least on the street level. There has to be more to it than that, given the scope of their reach. Sweet Trick Ricky T. Showbiz might be the underground mayor, but in the scheme of things, he's just a middleman. This is only the center of commerce at the crossroads; we have to follow the strings to the ends to find out who's pulling them."

"Wanna bet who we find when we get there?" Johnny asked while casting an accusatory glance at Trigget.

Josanne was about to reply, but Melissana beat her to it. "Johnny, that's enough! I get it. You're tired, you hurt, and after what we had seen in our urban adventure, you're disgusted with all of it. So am I! I'm also just as mad that this has been going on since before I was born, but I've been blind to almost all of it. But it's not Josie's fault, so knock it off, already! We've got enough problems without you adding to them!

"I'm sorry," she half-apologized to the team. "It's just been a really long night, and I really need a break." She took another glance at the concrete whiteboard, shook her head, and walked off to find a space in the stack of shipping containers that wasn't already in use. Trigget followed her away from the gathering, then turned off to check on Chrome.

"All right," Preach admitted, "it has been a long night. With the loss of so many girls, several of his cell leaders, and what must be a good portion of his personal army, Sweet Trick has to be hurting." He paused to survey the warehouse interior one more time. What was the body count? He remembered 17 to 20 at the warehouse alone, not counting the aftermath of the revival, Johnny's and Vixenn's operation at the hotel, the truck chase. "My guess is it'll take some time for him to shore up enough numbers to come back and try this again. But we all have our limits, too. Let's take a break and come back to it after we've all gotten some sleep. Iylothien, I'd rather not leave this to chance in case I'm wrong. You got eyes up?"

- "I can monitor the sensors," came the reply, "but it'll help if Partisan can have some of his crew keep a physical look out as well. Get some shuteye, boss."

Jack nodded, forgetting for a moment that the gesture was lost on the Hound decker. He turned to Partisan, who numbly agreed.

"You okay?" Preach asked.

"I've been much better," the mentor replied. "It's not just me—I lost ten kids today. *Ten.* While I just sat here, helpless."

Stang reached out as broken sobs began to come forth from the chairbound leader. "Go ahead," Stang told Preach. "No offense, but you can't help here. I've been a part of this practically my whole life. This is my job—our job," he acknowledged as Saint Nick approached.

Jack wanted to say more, to say something, but he knew Stang was right. If anyone could relate to Partisan and alleviate his burden, it would be some of his own. Replaying the evening's reports, he reflected on Partisan's warnings. The Witch City resident was right. The sounds of gunfire were constant—their presence had transformed the urban sector into a series of war zones. True, Ricky T. Showbiz had to be somewhat weakened by the night's activities, but at what cost? On top of that, Jack's own team was now cut off and isolated in a hostile city with his biggest gun somehow out of the fight. 'How had that happened?' he pondered, bewildered. He stood there, lost in his thoughts, until he felt a gentle tug at his jacket sleeve.

"Sir?" Tag interrupted his drowsy reverie. "Thanks for looking out for all of us tonight. Come on. We've got a place set up for you." And with that, Jack allowed himself to be led off to get some rest himself.

… …

It was early evening before any of them awoke. Trigget's first action was to check on Chrome, who was still fading in and out of consciousness under the improvised hood. Her next task was to check Partisan. The man had taken a beating with no means to fend off any of it. Her blood ran cold as she thought of Ricky T. Showbiz and his goons dumping him out of his chair, conceding it was a minor miracle he came through as well as he did. As she tended to his various bruises and once again checking for any internal injuries, the youth known as Saint Nick approached and whispered something to his street father. She could have read the expression across the room. Heck, she told herself, she could have predicted his reaction. As it was, she felt the injured man stiffen against the news. He looked up, eyes darting back and forth between Nick and Tag, a baleful expression across the whole of his features.

"Boys," he said, his voice shaking, "are… you… *sure*?"

Both nodded, adding that they had triple-checked and cross-referenced their sources.

"Tomorrow night? You're sure?"

- "Something's up," Trigget sub-vocalized to the rest of the team.

Again, both boys nodded their affirmations.

Partisan slumped in his chair. "Give me a minute," he said, dismissing the two.

"Partisan," Preach asked as the CYBER teams formed up on the fallen leader, "what's going on?"

He looked up at them, eyebrows lifted in obvious concern. "I'm worried," he confessed. "There's supposed to be another batch of ten to twelve kids getting dropped off tomorrow night, and for the first time since I've been doing this, I'm scared. Is this another trap? Nick and Tag have promised me they've checked all the angles, and this is a legitimate drop, but even if it is, where am I going to put them?"

"Partisan," Jack began, making a seat out of an old crate, "we started to talk about this once before. I want to help you—we all really want to help you—but we need to know something first.

"Partisan, where are all these kids coming from?"

The urban mentor backed his chair away from the group that was now clustered around him and made a pretense of clearing his throat. He studied the floor a few seconds, then each one of them, before he responded.

"I'm not really sure, to be honest, but I have my suspicions. I can't tell you exactly why, or how, and it doesn't exactly follow a specific schedule that I've been able to figure out. But once, sometimes twice every couple months or so, we get a tip that a new bunch of kids are going to be dropped off at a semi-random designated location. At first, I thought they were coming from all over the city, but I've managed to track them down to fourteen sites."

"But where do they come from?" Susan asked. "That's a lot of kids."

"And they're always boys, or do the girls stay somewhere else?" asked Trigget. "I mean, I don't see any girls around, or even anything that a girl might want to have."

"Well, we don't have a lot of extra credits for luxuries, Miss Trigget," Partisan replied somewhat snidely, then sagged. "But you do happen to actually be correct. For whatever reason, it's always boys. As for your question, Lady Blackwolf, I can only offer you my wildest guess. If you plot each of the drop points, to the best of my knowledge, there's only one common element near enough to make each point worthwhile. Again, it's only my guess, but I've been doing this a long time. And I don't know why—they're perfectly good kids."

"What do you mean?" Preach asked. "What exactly is going on?"

"The kids come from Air Dynamix. They're throwing the kids away."

"They're doing *what*?!" Araña interjected.

"They're throwing the kids away," Partisan restated. "Like dumping trash onto the curb. The kids are evidently born and raised inside the Air Dynamix archology. One day everything's fine, but the next day they're called out of class at school, picked up from home, taken for a doctor's appointment, or whatever. The next thing they know, they're falling asleep; when they wake up, their memories are foggy, as in their entire upbringing is a blur, and they're unceremoniously ushered out of one of their tunnels into the Witch City alleys. At least there's someone in there now who is kind enough to message us when and where the next batch is coming from. I don't know who it is, and to be honest, I really don't care. With the paper-thin clothes and crude sandals they're issued before they get tossed, none of them stand a chance if we don't get there before the slavers, or the crazies, or the alley dogs, or this time of year, the weather.

"And we've got another batch coming in tomorrow night." Partisan shivered and subconsciously darted his eyes around the complex interior. "And before then, we need to figure out a new place to hole up, because Ricky T. Showbiz will be back as soon as he gathers more of his muscle."

"No, he won't," a familiar voice coldly assessed, drawing everyone's attention. "I think the world has had enough of that govek—I'm going to find him and serve him up a knuckle sandwich so good it'll show him exactly what the term 'pound of flesh' means coming from a quarter-ton cyborg."

Chrome was back.

27. Scouting Parties and Puddle Ripples

Echoes of blasts and automatic fire resounded through the Witch City streets as Valhalla's Brownies and the Paladins continued their mock battles outside the city walls. The nearer sounds of the rebellion beginning against the tyranny wrought by Ricky T. Showbiz's street thugs augmented the din. Inside Partisan's warehouse, however, the only thing anyone could hear was Melissana's gleeful shout as she rushed the armored giant for a hug.

"Chrome! It's great to see you!"

"Are you okay to be up and around, big guy?" Rickshaw asked. "From what Vixenn and Johnny said, you really got clobbered."

"Trigget cleared me a couple hours ago, but then she gave me a sedative just to make sure I'd wake up without thrashing the place. I'll be back to my old self in about another 30 minutes or so."

"How did you survive?" Partisan asked incredulously, "I saw how hard he hit you. You should be *dead*."

"Chrome's a little harder-headed than most," Araña stated with a small laugh. Then he turned serious for a moment. "Listen *titanicus rex*, I know you're tougher than iron, and you're our heaviest hitter outside of the cars, but are you sure you're okay?"

"Trigget says I'm okay, and outside of the sedative, I'm feeling fine. Besides," he added, "that poor excuse of a street rat broke my sunglasses."

"OK then, but once we get onto the streets, I'm having Simon keep a watch on you."

"Chrome might have more down time than we'd all like," Preach interrupted. "We can't take the fight to Sweet Trick if we don't know where he is. And if we don't know where he is, we'll never be able to find Kelly."

"Shimmer," Queen Vixenn sullenly corrected. "Ricky T. Showbiz renames all his girls. She goes by Shimmer now, under penalty of beatings and… and worse."

Stang looked up at the group, a quizzical expression on his face. "This girl you're looking for goes by Shimmer?"

"Her name is Kelly," Susan responded, the poorly hidden edge of anger dripping from her voice.

"Well, I don't know any Kelly's," he defended, "but I just saw Shimmer walking her beat a couple days ago. Ricky T. Showbiz has been keeping her on an especially short leash ever since she tried to make a break for it in October." At the mention of the escape, Preach and Partisan exchanged excited affirmative nods.

"The timing fits," Partisan beamed.

"That's got to be her," Preach agreed. "At last, some good news."

"Come on Stang, get in," Corey cheerily said as he pulled out his car keys and clapped the Witch City survivalist on the back. "Let's go for a ride and pick up a girl. We get Kelly, bring her down here, ask where Ricky T. Showbiz is hiding out, and Chrome gets to serve sandwiches."

Stang was all for the idea, but Partisan urged caution. "And after everything that's happened, and everything that still is happening, do you think it'll be that simple?"

"Well, maybe not as simple as that, but we've got to do something soon. Just because Kelly's still alive doesn't mean she's out of danger. Besides, there's a really good chance he's seen all of you. Rickshaw and I are unknowns; and between the two of us, I'm the one who looks the least likely to be associated with you all."

"You're right on all points, Hardcore," Preach intervened, "but Partisan's also got a point. We've had the place locked down the last couple days. While Johnny's ride might be spotted and recognized from the hotel, your cars are brand new to the city, which could be equally conspicuous."

"And don't forget," Rickshaw added, "we put some flex against some of these boys at the gate on our way in. Any of them spot us; they'll remember what we did."

"It's not a bad plan, Hardcore," Johnny offered in a rare compliment, "but I don't know that you're the guy for this."

"Well, it can't be you," Hardcore rebuffed. "They'd spot you in a clock tick."

Johnny cocked an offbeat smile and turned to Partisan. "First question: do you have a couple gallons of water?" The Witch City mentor nodded, an uncertain expression etching his features. "Good! Second question: have any of your kids ever washed a car? It's a lot of fun," he smiled. "I'll be back in a minute," he said, slightly stooping and sloping his shoulders, "Mr. Sebastian left his bags in the car."

"And what makes you think you'll get through and find her?" Stang asked.

"I don't know, kid," Johnny turned and flashed a grin. "Maybe I'll just get lucky." And with that, he leisurely turned and began his stroll to his car.

… …

Partisan was bewildered. As soon as the young man Johnny made his daft statement, every other member of the team simply accepted the matter as settled. Araña approached some of the boys and asked them for some buckets of water while Chrome asked Rickshaw about reloading spent magazines. Partisan thought the black-haired girl would stay with Johnny, but instead, she asked to access his facility's computer systems. The young driver of the black car with the fancy paint job stole away with the blonde girl who came in with Preach. Preach himself mentioned a debriefing he had to do and went off with the girl who had laboriously tended over Chrome. *Just 'business' as usual*, he thought to himself. He summoned Stang, Saint Nick, and Tag.

"You boys watch these people," he ordered. "Watch how they interact, how they behave." Despite the events of the night before, Partisan genuinely smiled. "I am truly beginning to enjoy this."

Two minutes later, Johnny returned in a beat up pimp-mobile.

"Hey, Chrome," he called, "I got a couple dents back at the hotel. Do you mind?"

Partisan beamed as Chrome shook his head but shuffled off to the vehicle. He traded jibes with the younger man, then nonchalantly reached behind each of the dents and twisted parts and, using his bare hands, simply pushed, pulled, or tapped the dents out. The heavy muscle commented that someone called Fuser would be better at the welding. After that, Johnny put something in the water buckets, and the kids went to work while he went to change behind a shipping container. By the time the kids were done washing the car, it looked to be a standard street vehicle; when Johnny reappeared, he looked twenty years older and stoop-shouldered—the picture of a spent businessman looking for a way to add a thoughtless act to a thoughtless life in an effort to justify both. In short, he looked like the kind of guy who would pick up a young girl and pretend she actually enjoyed being with him. Preach looked him over and gave an approving nod. John Sebastian climbed into the machine, but before he started the engine, Preach opened the back door.

"Well Stang," the CYBER team leader asked, "you going?"

"You want me to go with him? What if they spot me?"

"You saw Kelly last week, so you know where she walks. You know what she looks like. And the glass is designed so nobody can see through it. Getting spotted ain't gonna happen, kid."

Stang looked to Partisan, who nodded. "I have a feeling you will be in superlative hands, Stang," the mentor counseled. "Plus, he's right. They need you."

And with that, Stang got into the back seat. Partisan was only slightly surprised when the youth seemed to disappear as the door closed. The windows weren't merely tinted, there was some sort of overlay that interacted with the environment. Partisan could see into the car, through the car, and outside on the opposite side, but somehow Stang was invisible. Even in Witch City, boys will be boys, and Partisan's kids proved to be no different. They all gathered around and enjoyed playing the small game of "Find Stang" with the tricky car that turned colors and made people invisible.

Then the moment passed. Preach and his team came out to bid their agent a safe and successful trip. To Partisan's surprise, nobody objected as Preach offered a prayer for the safety of the pair and for God to lead them to find the long-missing girl. After that, there was nothing more for the team to do. They silently disbursed away from the vehicle, and Johnny backed out of the warehouse into the Witch City night.

… …

"I understand you're having a bit of a… situation, Mr. Showbiz?"

"Nothin' I can't handle," the overlord pimp stated with a sneer and dismissive wave of his hand.

"Oh? I find it interesting that you should think so. Allow me a moment to summarize: the convoy attack on that wretched biker gang has failed miserably. The only thing that saved that debacle from becoming a complete waste was that it drew in those equally reprehensible self-righteous Paladins. Hopefully they'll kill each other off.

"Then there is the matter with that street revival and your apparent new competitor."

"No need for you ridin' my shotgun, Mr. Suit, I…"

"On that point, we are quite agreed, Mr. Ricky T. Showbiz," the man in the hologram spoke with icy distaste. "There is no need for me to 'ride your shotgun,' as apparently half of Wichita is doing that already."

"City's goin' a little crazy, yeah, but I got it covered. We found out where Sitter is and paid him a visit. He had some hired joeboy with him; the govek could take some hits, but we plugged him good," Ricky T. Showbiz bragged. He was careful to leave out how much of his own muscle he had lost in the attempt.

"You have it covered, do you?" Somehow, the sneer carried through the hologram. "Remind me, Mr. Showbiz, of what happened at the hotel?"

"An upstart pimp tried to muscle in on my turf by shootin' up one of my places. It happens, from time to time."

"Yes, it does happen from time to time," the hologram said dismissively, "but how often does the out of town upstart survive— in Witch City?"

Ricky T. Showbiz couldn't conceal his contempt. "Never happened before," he sullenly admitted. He was getting angry. Angry at the upstart, angry at the preacher, angry at Sitter, and now, angry at the Man who was obviously trying to school him, like he was just a stupid kid from a back-end alley.

The Man somewhat discontentedly continued, "Valhalla's Brownies attack, an armed street revival makes contact with Sitter, and an out of town upstart gets the better of you—all in the same week. And you have it covered? Do you even know what 'it' is?"

"What do you mean by that?" Ricky T asked, his already rising anger flaring.

"Perceive the obvious," the hologram replied coolly. "It's a takedown operation. Do you really think the attack on the Single Hearts and the street preacher are a coincidence? They're related. The truck from the revival—with the protection of Wichita Security Force turrets and Air Dynamix drones—was the same truck that picked up the girls from the hotel. And Sitter's the common ground."

"Sitter's holed up in an old warehouse with Stang, and as soon as I get some of my guns with me, we'll wipe out his entire show. It's been an expensive night, but by the end of next week, it'll all be paid for, the Brownies will be weak enough for us to take 'em out ourselves, Sitter'll be gone for good, and the biz will be better than ever."

"Indeed, they had better be," the hologram replied. "I do dislike sifting for new associates. But do be well, Mr. Showbiz. I hope to hear an update on the final status of this problem in two days."

"Yeah, goodbye," Ricky T. Showbiz started to say, but he realized the connection had already been cut.

... ...

James Sinclair didn't like the sound of Showbiz's report at all. The word 'coincidence' had a distinctly disconcerting hollowness to it. Someone was going to great lengths to unseat his Wichita middleman, but the buffoon was nothing more than a street-smart kid from a back-end alley and could barely see the traps someone was emplacing all around him. At least those infernal Valhalla's Brownies would be taken care of... Yet, there was even something there that nagged at the back of his mind. He paused, reflecting on the situations that were unfolding, taking in the course of events over the last week. And there it was, yet another thread of a cocoon of activities being woven around its victim. Valhalla's Brownies were, of course, linked to Sitter. And Valhalla's Brownies would attack the convoy—Sweet Trick Ricky T. Showbiz and James had made sure of that. That was no coincidence.

What was a coincidence, he noted, was the arrival of the Paladins.

"This is James Sinclair," he stated sharply to his secretary. "Get me Chief of Security at Air Dynamix." He lit a cigarette, took a deep drag, and exhaled sharply. "Yes, I'll wait."

... ...

"James Sinclair has noticed the activity and has attempted to contact someone from Air Dynamix," Simon reported. "Iylothien, watch for any corporate intervention."

289

"He has direct contact to someone in the archology? I thought he was just connected to Showbiz," Iylothien replied.

"This whole thing gives me the creeps," Queen Vixenn stated with an involuntary electronic shudder that caused the environmental module they were in to slightly ripple.

"There is a 7.28 percent chance that is not true," Simon replied. "His communication was with the maintenance chief of the drones that protected Constantine's and Dante's truck. He is vested, but it is possible he used his position to check on the functionality of the drone's circuits and logic paths."

"I don't get it," Queen Vixenn admitted. "Why would he do that?"

"He's finding out if Air Dynamix was directly involved in the operation," Iylothien explained, "but it doesn't necessarily mean that the guy he talked with knows that. He may have explained his involvement to ensure the drones were not posing a threat to the citizenry of Wichita."

"Be that as it may, alert the teams that Sinclair is watching." Simon checked its watch—the telltale sign that the meeting was at its end.

"Simon, before you go…" Queen Vixenn blurted, "how is Chrome?"

"By all Trigget's reports, he is doing fine." Simon smiled the smile of the iconic suave British secret agent director, back when iconic British secret agent directors existed. "Well, I really must be going," he stated with some semblance of regret. Then he was gone, leaving the Bard de le Nêone and the electron sorceress in a solid and completely featureless white cube.

"But Iylothien," she asked with just a tinge of fear, "how is Trigget?"

"Whoah, Lady!" Iylothien exclaimed. "What on Virtual Earth brought that on?"

"It took me a while to notice, and maybe it's because we've been apart for a while. But something's just not right."

"I don't know what you're talking about, Vix. Ever since we decided to take this mission, Trigget's been performing beyond reproach."

"That's just it, Iylo," she explained. "I've known her for years. We've been best friends since she first moved from home. She's not herself…

"She's performing."

… … …

"She's performing," the street pimp dourly told the slump-shouldered and slouched suit in the car. He peered closer. "I don't know you, never seen you 'round here before."

"Oh no, sir," the man squeamishly emitted, "I just got into town last week—I'm from Michigan." His shoulders slumped even further as he ducked at the sound of more distant gunfire echoing from the next neighborhood. "Is it always this… *noisy* here?"

The pimp laughed in open disgust. "Man, what you doin' down here? Pick a girl or get your privileged self back home before I light you up myself."

"Th—Thank you. I—I think I'll come back later," the man stammered. He had just fumbled his seat belt on and prepared to drive off when the pimp knocked a couple times on his window.

"Hey," the pimp began, "I just got a girl freed up and ready for you." As he said this, another member of his cell thrust a woman's head within a few inches of his window. Her blackened eye and swollen cheek declared she had just been through a beating, and the out-of-towner from Michigan noticed the thug maintained his hold on her by gripping her bedraggled hair taut in a fist-curled grip. The pimp must have thought it was especially funny to give the woman to the mamby-pamby jellyfish while she was in this state. "She's a little worse for wear tonight, but I'll tell you what. You can have her for two hours, and she'll be a lot cheaper than Shimmer." His smile was broad and mocking as he added, "Tonight must be your lucky night." The girl, face now pressed against the window glass, looked at the driver, her eyebrows raised in vague, concussed surprise. She squinted her good eye and had only said one word, more a question of her own state of mind, before her head was hoisted away from the window:

"Johnny?"

The sheepish customer's eyes flickered wide in surprised recognition, then narrowed. He swore under his breath and visibly struggled for control.

"You got a problem with my offer?" the pimp smugly taunted.

"No sir," the vehicle's driver stated, but as he glanced at the flesh peddler, underneath his mask of timidity his hazel eyes flashed a sense of icy dry finality. The street-smart pimp felt the sudden chill that he had glimpsed his own death in the stranger's look and involuntarily shivered. But the threat never materialized. Outwardly the stranger maintained his calm; the man's milksop demeanor quickly returned with a placid smile.

"Like you said, this is my lucky night." And with that, she got into the car, and he drove off.

"I'm sorry, sir," she frantically pleaded as soon as they drove away. "I didn't mean to call you that—you're the only man I've ever been with, I swear—please don't tell my master I said…"

The driver raised his hand off the wheel, and the girl unconsciously flinched against the passenger door. She cringed against the blow he would surely deal her, but instead, he gently lowered his hand onto her bruised cheek.

"Cleo, it's all right," he said as gently as he could manage. "You're right—it's me… Johnny. And I'm going to get you out of here." He was about to say something else, but the girl had passed out.

… …

"How is she?" Johnny asked when Trigget came out of the makeshift emergency room. She leaned against the wall, exhausted.

"She'll live, or maybe it's better to say she'll survive." Her eyes once again welled up with tears. She wanted to ask when she would finally run out of tears but was afraid one of her medical programs would kick in and actually provide her the answer, forever stripping from her one more of the mysteries that allowed her to still feel human.

"How can somebody *do* this to someone else?" she cried in frustration. "The beating was bad enough, but the drugs on top of the evident malnutrition, let alone the damage to her internal organs…" Melissana rushed to comfort her friend, who began to throw up between sobs. "How can some freak even pretend she would like what she's doing?"

"Trigget, is the girl stable?" Preach asked.

"Stable," she responded when she was able, "but not good. She needs a hospital, not a warehouse. And she needs medical supplies. I can supply a syringe or two of compounds, but I'll dry out before I can self-manufacture everything she needs."

"We off-loaded what we could before the truck left," Melissana threw in, "but we're going to need more if we find any others like her."

"Was she able to talk at all?" Araña asked. "I mean, we still need to find out where Ricky T. Showbiz is. We find out where he is, we get him, we free the girls, right?"

"She's barely able to breathe," Susan replied, "she's not talking."

"*DREK!*" Johnny swore, kicking at a crate in frenzied frustration.

"You okay, Johnny?" asked Preach. "You weren't like this with the others."

"It doesn't matter," Johnny replied, but the hollowness behind his voice screamed otherwise.

"This one's personal," Trigget interjected. "Johnny, how do you know her?"

"I said it doesn't matter!" He had snapped the comment, but as soon as it was out, he shut his eyes tightly and started to breathe in panting gasps.

"It doesn't matter," he repeated to himself.

"You're dodging emotions like they're bullets, Johnny!" Melissana threw at him. "But emotions aren't bullets!"

"I know!" he shouted back. He then sighed, looked down at the floor, and quietly added, "Emotions hit harder, do more damage."

Melissana took a step forward and asked so quietly it was almost a whisper, "Johnny, who is she?"

He didn't answer right away, mostly because he didn't know how to. Hardcore took a step forward, probably to offer some supportive gesture, but Preach stopped the team's wheelman short, both allowing and forcing the luckster to dig deeper for the answers only he could provide. After several moments, he sighed again and resigned himself to tell them all of it.

"It happened back in Louisiana," he began. "I started seeing this girl. Her name was Lisa. And yeah, she was what you'd call a street worker. So, one day I approach her and just let her know I just wanted to get to know her." He smiled at an old memory. "And yeah, she thought that was funny, made the joke of 'Yeah, I bet,' and all. But she smiled, and after she got off work we spent time together, just walks, talking—I guess the stuff most normals call simple dates.

"But eventually we got to really liking each other, and man, the sparks flew." Another smile, this one more of a grin. "Anyway, we were hot on each other, and I thought maybe she was finally someone I could take all the rest of the steps with. I know, it sounds corny, but we had serious game."

"What happened?" Susan asked, drawn into the story.

"We were getting along. She was doing her thing willingly, so I thought of it as just a job for her. But over time, she grew distant. Something was off; then one day, she was gone. She just left me a note saying that I was sweet, but there was another guy, so she was breaking up and moving on."

"You just let her go?" Melissana asked. "That doesn't sound like you."

"Of course I didn't just let her go—I searched all over for her!" Johnny reprimanded, then calmed himself down again. "I saw her with a couple guys once, started walking up to her so we could talk for a minute. As soon as she spotted me, she left the guys, stormed up to me, and told me to get lost. She didn't even give me a chance to talk; she just turned and walked back to those guys, laughed, and started kissing up on one of them.

"Anyway, Cleo was her best friend from back then. They bizzed together, and in those days, if Lisa wasn't with me, then she was with Cleo."

"Johnny?" a voice faintly hailed. The group collectively turned to see Cleo trying to raise her right arm from the makeshift cot that served as her hospital bed. "Johnny-boy, that *really* you? I thought I was havin' 'nother one o' my dreams," she said through a faint line of smile. "But you're real, ain't you?"

Johnny was at her bedside in a moment, leaning down, letting the woman sweep her hand against his face, being available to her in a way none of the team would have guessed even possible for him. "Yeah, it's really me, Cleo," was all he said.

"I heard you talkin' 'bout the old days," she ventured between rasps. "Boy, the three of us was somethin' back then, wasn't we?"

"Yeah, we sure were," he agreed. "Seemed we owned the whole world back then."

"Well, at least the city," she half-smiled before she broke into a wheezing cough. "Johnny, listen. There's something you need to know 'bout Lisa." She paused to collect her breath and regain her strength to continue. "You know that woman loved you. You need to know that."

"Yeah, I thought so—at least for a while," he glumly consoled himself.

"Boy, she loved you more than life itself," she corrected. "An' that's why she had to leave you."

"What? I don't get it."

"We started our business for creds, you know that. But eventually some fellas moved in. Bad fellas." She said with a face unintentionally contorted in demonstration of just how much she despised them. "Ruined everything. Our business, us, you, and Lisa." She regathered her composure after the memory and looked him square in the eye, "Most of all, they ruined Lisa. They saw we was makin' creds, so they just came in and took us over. Beat up some of our johns, some of our friends." She grimaced. Trigget moved in to comfort her, but she gestured her away. "Girl, I ain't got many miles left, an' that boy needs to know what I got to say." As if on cue, she began to fade out, but summoned enough energy to come back from wherever she had lapsed into. She blinked twice, then focused in on Johnny like a laser target. "They was rude boys, Johnny, and they knew you'd be trouble. So, threatened to kill you, they did, if she didn't break it off with you. She dumped you only 'cuz they said they'd get you before you'd even know they were coming. She saw no other way to keep you alive." She shook her head sadly at the memory, "An' boy, that broke her heart."

"What happened to her?" Johnny asked in a barely audible murmur.

"Well, you was her *spark*, boy. Yeah, once you came along, her whole life was about you." She sighed like she was exhaling a non-filtered cigarette. "After that, she done lost her edge."

"What happened to her?" Johnny asked, more determined than before. Trigget was surprised at the tone—she had never heard that trace of imminently explosive anger in his voice before. Cleo, weak as she was, feebly moved her hand to take Johnny's. The human alley-cat analogy came back to the CYBER conversationalist, and she wondered if Johnny would lash out at the woman who was reaching out not just to him, but also for him.

"Well, we weren't makin' money for 'em any more," Cleo confessed. "So, a couple months after you left, they sold us to some guys. I didn't like them one bit, but at that point, it didn't matter—there was nothin' we could do 'bout it. We went through hell for a while. They beat us and took turns on us for a while, just to make the point that they were our new masters now. Kept us locked up, drugged up, and put down every minute of every long week."

"But what happened to her?" Johnny pressed, "Where is she now?"

"She escaped, Johnny."

"She did?" he asked, the instant relief visibly lifting the heavy load from him. "But where did she go? Where did she run to?"

"Oh, Johnny, it ain't like that. She didn't run away. She *escaped*.

"Johnny…," Cleo began, then wheezed, using the last of her energy before passing back out beyond the rims of consciousness, "Lisa died three years ago."

Johnny didn't move, didn't say a word, for several minutes. Everybody in the room had the sense to withdraw and let him mourn in silence.

…… ……

An hour later, an intensely focused Johnny emerged from Cleo's blanketed-off room and immediately proceeded to the group's ammunition storage area. No one said a word as he silently checked every pocket, every clip holder, to make sure each was full. When he was finished, he started a second round of checks.

"Hey Johnny," Preach ventured, "how're you doing?"

"I'm gonna kill 'em all, Preach, every last pimp in this fracked-up piece of hell." He reached into a pocket and once again re-examined a machine pistol magazine. "You know, tonight there ain't no such thing as a spare clip. And when these babies run dry, I'll just pick up their guns and use their own frakkin' weapons against them."

"Johnny, you know you can't go off waging a private war."

"I *can't?*" the skillster sharply questioned, slamming the clip down on the tabletop. He paused to consider his words and turned to face his trainer. "You know how I was against corporations doing this kind of thing to civilians. This ain't no different." He reflected on the thought, then shook his head. "Actually, this is different," he said as he picked the clip back up and rechecked it to make sure it was full. "This is worse."

"Johnny," Preach began, trying to calm him down. "You can't just go out there now and take on anybody you think is involved. We're so close to finding Sweet Trick—he's the head of all this. If you go out there now, we'll never find him."

"Well, I know where the ones who had Cleo are. They're waiting for us to take her back, Shimmer's 'busy,' and we're no closer to knowing where this Ricky T guy is," Johnny summarized. Everyone stared at him; Susan's claws involuntarily flashed.

"There's no way I'm letting you take her back there," she resolved.

"Of course not!" he snapped. "But they only let me have her for two hours. I've been asking about Shimmer. They'll be waiting for me to dump her off back there, and if I don't show, they're going to connect the dots anyway!"

"Preach? Spider?" Rickshaw began to ask, "Johnny has a point. They're just waiting there for him? Now, I'm not the General, but don't you think those goveks know where Ricky T. Showbiz's hideout might be?"

"The wheel-head's right on this one," Chrome acknowledged. The Hound's heavy hitter got up and gently clasped Johnny's shoulder; Johnny visibly sagged under the weight. "Come on,

Johnny," he said consolingly, "you've got an appointment. But I think I'll come along for the ride, if that's all right with you."

- "Don't kill them, Chrome," Preach radioed as Johnny's car once again headed into the Wichita night. "We need the intel."

- "Wouldn't dream of it," Chrome replied over the car's radio.

"Not before we verify what they tell us is correct," he added offline, just for Johnny.

Twenty-eight minutes later, they had the location of Sweet Trick Ricky T. Showbiz's latest hole-up spot, plus two fallback locations.

- "Preach," Chrome radioed, "we got the location. Before you ask, yes, we left 'em alive—we're a law enforcement organization, not a vigilante group. But they won't be able to grab anyone by the hair or beat on anyone again for a while. For that matter, they won't be able to hold anything at all for a while, at least until their hands heal up some.

"The bottom line is that Ricky T. Showbiz is holed up in the Palatia, a ten-story hotel he renovated. By their accounts, he's turned it into some kind of a fortress, and he's got a secured perimeter several blocks wide in every direction. You might want to have Partisan clear the streets in the next couple hours—we've got a party coming up."

. . . . . .

"So Ricky T. Showbiz's ten-story Palatia command center is here," Preach recapped, sketching an area on the warehouse floor. "According to Iylo's and Vixenn's satellite scans of the area, plus Stang's local intel, there are sniper and overwatch positions in each of these twelve locations. Rooftops have from four to eight men assigned, the water tower has three, and the old billboards have two men each. In addition to that, he now has both mounted and unmounted roving patrols to keep an eye out for us in addition to his usual guys. Did I miss anything?"

"Yeah," Partisan said. "Let's not forget the contract he has out on you guys. Once you leave here, it's going to be Wild West."

- *"Streets should be clear of civilians," Iylothien added. "Besides Partisan getting the word out, I've played the usual 'police activity/avoid the area' messages on the local comm channels."*

"What about the real cops?" Araña asked. "Won't any of them be curious about the activity?"

"We thought about that," Queen Vixenn responded. "Me and Iylo added some corporate Black Ops messaging on their encrypted channels. If they're not specifically tasked to the area for a coded response, they are to avoid it completely, subject to extreme prejudicial disciplinary action."

- *"In other words," Iylothien explained, "if they show up when they haven't been invited to the party, they expect to die. Any corp security on the ground will be imposters on Ricky T. Showbiz's payroll."*

"Sounds good," Preach affirmed. "So, that's the plan. Any questions?"

"Yeah, I have one," Stang declared with a raised hand. "Spider's on counter-sniper duty and will also find a place where the Queen can jack into Ricky T. Showbiz's off-grid security system. Queen Vixenn trails Spider and jacks in once he does. If Iylothien can ride in with her, he goes along for the hunt."

- *"Our first goal is to find any automated defenses we can hijack," Iylothien pitched in. "Then we look for where he keeps the girls, where the roving patrols are, and then we take their systems offline before the final phase of the assault."*

"Right," Stang cut back in. "Rickshaw cruises left, assisting Spider with the counter-sniper ops, plus any opportunity engagements with the roving patrols. Hardcore covers the right flank." He looked back at Preach. "You, Chrome, Johnny, and Susan—err, Lady Blackwolf, and Johnny walk the gauntlet to the front door. But what I don't get is, where am I in all this? I mean, I feel a little left out."

"Partisan's been hit at his home base once," Preach responded. "I don't want him hit again. As much as I'd like to have you along, we need you on high bodyguard detail. Once we pass the line, they could circle back and try to hit us at here again. To put it simply, that's something we can't afford."

"And me?" Trigget asked.

"We've been reviewing everything that happened when Ricky T. Showbiz found Partisan," Araña explained with an agitated sigh. "Partisan asked how Ricky T. Showbiz had found him. Do you remember what he said?"

"Yeah," Trigget responded. "He caught one of Partisan's kids, and he told him."

"True," Melissana replied with an unusually cold strain in her voice. "But he also said that a new friend of Partisan's called an old friend of his. In other words, one of us contacted someone Ricky T. Showbiz knew."

"Well don't look at me," Trigget defended. "I certainly wouldn't have called him."

"No, you didn't. But when what he said came to light, Simon ran a comprehensive sweep of all of our communications.

"So, Trigget, why'd you call your brother?"

"I just wanted to see if he was okay," she confessed, "and to give him a chance to get out of whatever it was he thought was doing, because people were using whatever it was for trafficking."

"Be glad you're still breathing," Chrome said with such a lack of emotion, not even she could read it.

"Stay here," Preach ordered. "Whether intentional or not, your betrayal cost us, and nobody on this team is ready to trust their backs to you in the field. But that doesn't mean you're completely benched. Monitor Partisan and Cleo. Don't let anything happen to either one of them; help them where you can. You're also on reserve to give medical attention to any one of the groups who has need. Stang and Partisan's group will be monitoring your moves, as will Simon."

- *"You need to sit this out," Jack transmitted subvocally over a private channel. "Be ready, understand our own why's, and take your discipline.*

- *"Because I have to tell you that, despite what I just told you, Chrome's right."*

· · · · · ·

- *"All clear," the outpost observer reported with a scowl. He shifted the long barrel of the sniper rifle he toted over his shoulder. "We been holed up here for the last two hours watchin' the Z Street approach from Sitter's place, and nothin' even moved. Ain't nobody gonna come outta there; we'll die of boredom 'fore somebody makes a move this way. One bored ever-lovin' Echo, out."*

"Hey *amigo*," a voice quietly said in his ear, "don't you know good *Ingles*? 'Ain't nobody' means 'somebody,' my friend."

"Who—" the startled gunman began to exclaim, but a five-hit flurry followed by a leg sweep accented by an elbow jab to the man's sternum cut him short and laid him out before he had time to ask, let alone raise his weapon.

"*Alguien*, my friend," Araña answered as he stooped to secure the unconscious sniper. "I'm a *somebody*." He stood to full height and surveyed the rooftop where four other gangers lay unconscious and flex-cuffed to building fixtures apart from each other. He nodded in affirmation of his work, re-zipped his sneak suit, and set his attention on a water tower a block away. An augmented running leap carried him onto a building across the street—two running jumps later, he stood underneath the structure. He raised his right arm and fired his stiletto grapnel into the base of the tower and reeled himself up to the catwalk occupied with more armed men.

- *"Rickshaw, this is Spider," he radioed after taking out the men holding that outpost. "You're cleared to pull out. Keep it quiet, though—you've got a foot patrol headed up the block to the left of Partisan's front door."*

The yellow and black Dominator silently eased out of the gaping hole that had been Partisan's warehouse door and turned left. Spider was in mid-leap to his next target when he noticed three flickers of intense red light out of the corner of his eye. Outside of the distant gunfire from the staged battle outside the city and the distant sounds of fighting from the citizen's revolution against the warlords of Witch City, not even he heard the slightest sound of confrontation.

- *"Spider, this is Rickshaw: You've got Red Carpet Left, three blocks wide and rolling, over."*

- *"Copy Rickshaw, Red Carpet Left. Wait one..." A minute later, he was back on the air. "Sorry about the delay—there were a couple extra guys hanging out up at Delta that I had to deal with."*

- *"Status?" Preach asked.*

- *"Stoy bien," he said, "I just didn't expect the party." He scanned the area for a few seconds before continuing. "Still no alerts. We have Red Carpet left. Repeat: We have Red Carpet Left. Hardcore, you are cleared to roll out Red Carpet Right."*

Hardcore's midnight black Sabretooth silently pulled out of Partisan's warehouse and turned right, went down three blocks, then cut left to parallel Rickshaw's course. His senses, already heightened by the continued gunfire beyond the city's walls, were tensely alert as he jacked into his car's scanners. As Corey switched from infrared to ultraviolet, RADAR, SONAR, and Doppler, he found no evidence of anything larger than medium-sized dogs in the scan radius. He did not detect anyone in the area who even might have had hostile intent.

- *"Red Carpet Right, I'm even with Rickshaw's position," he finally declared.*

- *"Spider to all units: Alpha, Bravo, Charlie, and Delta cleared of hostiles. Queen Vixenn, there's a small communications console at Delta you might be able to use. Rickshaw confirms Red Carpet Left. Hardcore confirms Red Carpet Right. We have Red Carpet. Royal Party, you are cleared, proceed to Delta."*

- *"Got it, Spider, Royal Party proceeding," she replied as she stepped out of Partisan's side doorway, flanked on her left by Preach and Lady Blackwolf, Johnny and Chrome on her right. "Iylo, I'll hook up as soon as I get us connected to the tower."*

The assault on Showbiz's lair had begun.

28. Raiding the Raiders

H*E* BRIEFLY OBSERVED the flashes and spontaneous fires of the ongoing mock battle outside the city, but he didn't pause for long.

- "Spider, this is Preach. I just cleared Red Carpet Four, over."

The race was on. The CYBER team provided bounding overwatch for each other with their vehicular escorts several blocks along the way to Ricky T. Showbiz's last known position. So far, they had only crossed light resistance, the echoes of the firefights both inside and outside the city masking their own engagements. But they had too far to go not to be concerned about groups of enemy gunmen circling and attacking them from behind. Another concern they had was that Spider had cleared seven of the sniper posts. It was only a matter of time before Ricky T. Showbiz's radio checks would discover his troops were missing, and Queen Vixenn still hadn't located a network jack to Ricky T. Showbiz's private network. If they didn't find one and hack it soon, Sweet Trick would encircle them and pin them down long enough to finish the job he started with Partisan.

They had been sweeping the main route to the master pimp's lair. The fortified hotel had once been the pride of that part of the city back when that part of the city still had pride. Typically enough, Jack observed, the pride had led to decadence, and just as typically, the decadence had wound a twisting path to its current end: fear, misery, and depravity in its truest sense.

- *"Halfway there," Jack subvocalized to his team. "Keep tight, keep scanning."*

… …

They had just crossed Red Carpet Five when Jack felt a sudden twist in his gut. He took another magnified scan of the buildings to his left, shifted to ultraviolet and then infrared as he zoomed in on upper elevations of the buildings to his right. Something moved—a quick furtive motion that indicated someone was trying to remain hidden. Three more seconds of rapid scans confirmed his fear.

"Cover! Cover! Cover!" he yelled, not bothering to subvocalize. "Hostiles high, left and right!"

The team dove behind shells of abandoned cars and refuse piles, turning them into urban foxholes as the metal rain of small arms fire poured in on their positions. Windows on each floor of several buildings on both sides of the street lit up with the staccato flicker of full automatic muzzle flash. They had somehow gotten used to the more distant gunfire from outside the city, but even the less distant firefights that had broken out since the night of the revival were completely drowned out by the cacophony of blasting mayhem that was being unleashed on them not two blocks away.

- *"Red Carpet Left," Spider called, "Free Roam, Free Roam. I repeat, break Carpet and Free Roam."*

- *"Copy, Spider, going Free Roam," Rickshaw replied as he steered left, away from Royal Party, and accelerated down a side street to look for any gangers he might catch in the open.*

- *"Roger that, Rickshaw. Good hunting. Break: Red Carpet Right, break Carpet. I repeat, break Carpet. Proceed back to Gatehouse, verify Sanctuary, then link up with Royal Party. Copy?"*

- "Copy Spider, proceeding to Gatehouse," Corey affirmed as he too cut a sharp U-turn to head back down the street he had just claimed.

If all went well, Corey would be back at Gatehouse within two minutes, verify everyone there was okay, and haul full throttle down the pathway "Royal Party" had walked to make sure nobody had cut in behind them. He thought of Susan, again in harm's way. If his car's sensors were more powerful, he berated himself, he would have detected the ambush. Electric motors whining, he swore to himself he'd make Gateway in less than a minute.

… …

"Caught them goveks," Ricky T. Showbiz gloated. "Knew the 500,000 creds would grab someone's attention."

"Tell the 79th Street Wolves they got their creds on account," the underlord promised with a pleased grin. "You tell 'em, they finish the job, there's another 500k comin' their way, in whatever form they wish.

"And spread the word on their location. Tell all the others where these frakkers are. I don't care who lights 'em up, as long as they get lit. Offer a 100k per head. I want them goveks cold."

… …

- "Preach," Rickshaw reported, "I don't know what just happened, but we got mobs descending on your location."

- "Yeah, we're a little hot down here," Preach stated between a round of firing into the upper level windows. "We're taking some pretty serious fire—I'm guessing they've figured we're more than uprising riff-raff.

"Break: How are you holding up, team?"

- "Ain't nobody coming within range of my auto-pistols," Johnny responded first. "I ain't hit, but I can't hit back just yet, either."

- "Blackwolf here," Susan replied, "I can get a couple shots off here and there, but I'm pinned down—can't do my best from the middle of this street."

- "Holing up and cringin', but I'm here," Queen Vixenn replied. "Def ain't my trip—I can't wait to do something I'm actually good at. I'm okay with a street fight, but I don't mind sayin' this is way outta my league."

- "This is fun," Chrome replied over the sound of his M18-X9 firing 5.56mm fire. There was also a host of plunking, plinking, and tearing sounds of multiple rounds hammering into the armored cyborg between each shot he had taken. Out of all of them, he had taken the least amount of shelter, and the professional in him would dictate that given the situation they were in, he would make every one of his shots count. "Some of this stuff tickles a little harder than most, but I haven't had any issues yet. Ammo's gonna be a problem in a little bit, though."

- "Spider, we're pinned pretty good here," Preach radioed. "It's not in the playbook, but can you circle back and lend us a hand?"

- "Someone need ammo?" Hardcore, now in full immersion mode, called in. Three seconds later, two high explosive recoilless rifle rounds blasted apart the upper floors of the buildings where most of the fire had been coming from while a pair of linked .30 caliber machine guns raking the mid-level windows on both sides.

- "No need for stealth mode anymore," he quipped.

He brought his Sabretooth to a screeching halt just in front of a gap in the debris his teammates had been huddled behind, his remark largely unnoticed as a hailstorm of small arms fire augmented by SAW63 machine guns and other assault weapons hammered against his vehicle. Despite his previous experiences inside his cryosteel shell, the wheelman was at first unnerved by the viciousness of the attack. He calmed as he realized anew the effectiveness of the armor CYBER had applied to his vehicle—the intensity of the attack would have crippled, if not outright destroyed, other vehicles. A LAW rocket skipped across his hood and blasted into a building to his right and seven meters behind him, throwing metallic shards and debris in a fifteen-yard radius. Still too close to the others for his liking, he mentally commanded his Sabretooth to edge slowly ahead despite the leaden onslaught as he continued his scans for other targets. The augmented combat vehicle obliged and inched forward, linked machine guns firing independently on any small targets within their vertical arcs of fire, the recoilless rifle occasionally belching H.E. rounds against targets that merited the extra punch, and the forward-mounted grenade launcher firing tear gas and smoke to obscure the rest of the Pride's forces.

- "My arcs of fire can only cover the first two floors of the next two buildings," Hardcore reported.

He was the primary target now; the enemy seemed to forget the others to extinguish this latest threat. But the other CYBER members were still there.

- "Thanks for the break, Hardcore. Going left!" Johnny announced as he dove for patches of street debris to use for cover. In a series of vaults, spins, and rolls, he avoided stray small arms fire and closed the distance to the doorway of the nearest hostile

building. A flash-bang later, he was inside, taking out any op-position to clear the first floor before heading to the roof level. After that, he'd work his way back down, clearing floor by floor of what remained of the ambushers.

- "I got right," Blackwolf called as she dashed for the closest build-ing on that side in a burst of enhanced speed that showed her form as a blur. Three armed assailants appeared in the doorway but never had the time to draw a clear aim; she cut through them with an ease even she herself would not have thought possible.

Preach continued his scans for targets of opportunity and called in pockets of resistance to Johnny and Blackwolf as well as to Chrome, who was providing cover for Preach and external fire support with Hardcore.

······

Two blocks north of the defenders, three heavily modified urban dumpster trucks pulled onto the main street and turned southward. The lead reached for his vehicle mike.

"All right, boyos—the Wolves got them guys pinned down, but one o' their fancy cars is tearing them to shreds. We're going in!"

"Go for it—We'll plow 'im right off the map!"

"Let's go!"

······

The street rumbled with the oncoming rush of the three vehicles. Blades down, blasts from Hardcore's turret had little impact on the advancing trucks.

- "This is gonna hurt!" the CYBER wheelman transmitted sec-onds before impact.

The collision was deafening. Corey tried to maneuver out of the way, but the rightmost heavy dump truck caught his back fender and dragged the Sabretooth back into the path of the center vehicle. Hardcore's vehicle was lifted off its right tires and pushed several yards, the armor that had withstood rocket fire crumpled against the impact of the heavy vehicles, tires that had withstood small arms fire and caltrops shredded against their rims by the sideways weight of the vehicle. Then another explosion occurred—not as loud, but more spectacular nonetheless—as the resultant fireball consumed both enemy vehicles, their heavy steel bodies half melted by the conflagration of phosphorous and napalm.

"Eat dragon!" Corey muttered, grimly pleased that the Sabretooth's rear weapon still worked despite the impacts—then he blacked out as the sensory input he received from his vehicle overwhelmed him.

The driver of the third truck backed around the mayhem and lined up to make another charge against the now stilled vehicle when the sound of wrenching metal from his passenger side door distracted him. Mouth agape, he stared in unmasked terror at the face of Chrome who, with a decidedly fixed and wicked grin, climbed into the seat next to him.

"Time for a trade," Chrome stated. "You jacked up one of my wheelmen, I'm gonna do the same to you."

The driver would have jumped out without Chrome's help, but he landed a lot farther away with it. Chrome closed the driver's side door, jerked the large vehicle to a lurching start, circled in a wide arc to build up speed, and with a blast of the truck's air horn for effect, literally plowed the side of the center vehicle into its partners, merging it with the twisted mass of burning metal that would be a long term fixture in the middle of that intersection.

- *"Trigget! We need you up here, stat!" Preach directed.*

- *"Who got hit?"*

- "Hardcore—now move! I gotta try to get him out of his vehicle."

She looked to Stang, who nodded, then glanced aside to Partisan. "You'll be okay, right?" After he said he'd get by, Stang looked to Saint Nick and Tag. "I gotta go," he said. "Make sure and take care of him, right?"

"Will do," Nick vowed. "They caught us by surprise once," he replied, even as he gestured to several of the remaining youths. "It ain't gonna happen again." With that, Stang looked Trigget in the eyes. "Time to go," he declared.

- "We're on our way," she responded to Preach.

They left Partisan's warehouse and ran into the night, each wondering what could have possibly taken out Hardcore while he was inside his vehicle, both too afraid to ask.

…… ……

Johnny and Lady Blackwolf were slowed as Preach focused on extracting Hardcore from his vehicle. He was miraculously intact—battered, not broken—but the car's internal secondary impact defenses had spent themselves in the effort. Trigget would need to check for additional injuries the team's leader could not detect. With Preach distracted, Spider doubled his efforts to loop back and assist both Johnny and Lady Blackwolf, leap-frogging between buildings to further confuse the defenders. Within thirty minutes, the block had been cleared, small fires and smoldering remains marked locations of former strongpoints and internal bunkers. Trigget and Stang, accompanied by a desperately concerned Lady Blackwolf, tended to Hardcore after Chrome had carried him into what must have appeared to be a local gang house.

"Not bad going through those buildings, aprendiz," Araña encouraged Lady Blackwolf. "But you can be faster. Relax—let yourself be faster."

"I don't like this, Grey," Spider confided to his former leader. "First, they take Chrome, then Hardcore—our two heaviest hitters. If we can't somehow even these odds, well…"

"It's okay," Preach consoled. "We've been fighting it out the last half hour. Notice anything?"

"Yeah," he said, beginning to relax, just a little, "we're not fighting now."

"Exactly. Think about it. Between the revival, the hotel, the gates, your counter-sniper actions, the failed raid on Partisan, and whatever else is going on out there with the locals fighting back on their own, we're making a dent, and it's finally starting to show."

"Think they changed their game plan?"

"I'm not sure. I don't think they were expecting us to hit them this hard, this quick. He's used up his offense, or at least, the people he's been throwing at us are beginning to think twice. So, what would you do in his place?"

"We held our own against the offense, and we're still able to push forward. If I was him, I'd turtle, and make my enemies come to me on my home turf. But we gotta have a plan, *Jefé*, cuz I'd also use human shields if I were him."

"Hey, he's coming to!" Susan announced, very much relieved.

"Sue? What are you doing here?" he asked as he first opened his eyes. Then the pain seeped through his senses, and with it, the memory of the last several seconds of his consciousness before the trucks hit. "Where's my car?" he asked, trying to sit up to see what had become of it. The pain forced him back down with a stabbing wince he couldn't control.

"He's pretty beat up, but I don't think anything's broken," Trigget announced. "His vitals are pretty normal, given what he's gone through. I don't think he has any internal injuries, but he's definitely not going to hold his own in close combat."

"Wait—close combat? I won't need—*where's my car?*"

"Relax, hotshot," Johnny gently chided, "your ride's outside. Those trucks punched it pretty hard, I'll give them that. Chrome's been trying to pull out some of the bigger dents since he brought you in here. I think it's giving him something to beat up while we're waiting here for you to wake up. Rickshaw's still on Free Roam, lighting up—and I mean that literally—any stray vehicles or foot patrols he finds along the way."

Heavy bootsteps came up the outside steps and crossed the doorway. "You up?" Chrome asked. When Hardcore nodded, Chrome tossed him a small metallic object. "Here, you'll need these." It was the keys to the Sabretooth. "Mind you, she's in rough shape, but once we get outta this mess, we should be able to fix her up again."

Hardcore groaned at the movement of his arm, but everyone knew he was as happy as he could be. He could drive his car again.

"Hey, look!" Vixenn called out to the others. "Now we know why they fought on as hard as they did." One of the rooms that had been protected by a hallway bunker had what looked like a call center. When they realized they were about to lose the facility, the defenders wrecked the equipment beyond repair so their attackers couldn't compromise it.

"It's a shame they trashed the equipment," Susan stated bleakly. "We could've used that to crack into their systems."

"But that's the beauty of it," Melissana explained with a grin as she tugged a set of wires from behind one of the smoldering machines. The bundle came loose from the machine with a series of small snaps—the far ends running into a wall. Seeing Lady Blackwolf's puzzled expression, she beamed, held up her trophy, and continued. "We don't need the machines, just the connections to their network." She twirled the wires in a slow spin. "And I'm holding 'em."

"Even better," Preach added with a rare wry grin of his own. "If they think they've kept the facility from us, they have no reason to suspect we have access."

"Then let's get this hooked up and start the party already," Chrome complained. "I don't like being in debt, and I owe that govek a sandwich."

... ...

Queen Vixenn hooked up her deck to the pimp's network and hailed Iylothien.

A black delta-shaped cloud of flying locusts appeared in the sky above a distant forest, fanned out wide at some vanishing point in the far-off horizon. How many thousands of beasts comprised the cloud, she could not tell. It didn't matter—they were friends. At their head, like a king upon his royal charger, was Iylothien, the Neon Bard, astride his favorite flying locust mount, answering the electron summons of his Queen. The giant beast hovered, the non-gusting of his animated wings blowing her hair into fractal blurs.

"I came as quickly as I could," Iylothien offered as he reached down to take her hand in his. A second later, she too was alight, sitting behind her cyberspace mentor. "I repeated the black ops warning and monitored the security networks after that last firestorm to make sure nobody from outside was going to come in; then I had to jump back a couple hops to get back over here...

"What the—?" Iylothien began to exclaim as he took in the sight of a forbidding black castle atop a craggy cliffside that was his environmental module's rendition of Showbiz's private network and its defenses. An intense low rumbling of thunder that rolled across the virtual valley between them and the fortress cut him short. Several lightning bursts tore at the simulated sky with enough force that they seemed to threaten the stability of the module interface; the resultant thunderclaps shook them where they stood. Queen Vixenn and Iylothien braced against an expected torrential downpour, but they did not expect the pinkish-purple dome of haze that appeared and blanketed the fortress.

"Well," Iylothien grudgingly shrugged, "it looks like they're not taking chances that we're here after all. That's a lot of ICE right there, and whatever's not black is a very dark shade of grey."

"Yeah," Vixenn replied. "Now we know what they spend all their money on. I guess it makes sense, given the connections between trashy websites and net crimes like blackmail and identity theft.

"I'm guessing that cloud's gonna be pretty much impenetrable in the time we have. Any ideas?"

She summoned Chrysalis and somehow produced a digitalized crystal ball. Her daemon program immediately began to sniff out the surrounding area as she surveyed the terrain through her device. In the meantime, Iylothien dispatched a few of the locusts to scout out the area around them for approaching threats. In a few seconds, the daemon transformed itself to a dog that began barking and scratching at the hillside.

"Good boy," she cooed at her virtual pet as she peered at the area through the iridescent globe. "Look what you found!"

"Let me see what I can do with that," Iylothien offered. He focused, drew his hands together. In response, a fetid brown color shone in a circle at the foot of the hill, then grew into vines that gripped the hillside. Turning his hands outwards in clutching gestures, he slowly pulled his arms wide. The vines tremored ever so slightly, but they were held together by the hillside. He pulled again, and the grass that grew against the side of the hill began to tear. Iylothien focused more, pulling even harder. A few seconds later, the entire hillside gave way to reveal a hidden tunnel barely wide enough to accommodate their passage. Inside, the tunnel had a juncture, but the electronic couple could see that in one direction, the path had a nearby cave-in and was blocked. They couldn't see the entire way down the other passage, but an automap function in their displays indicated it wound to the left and headed in the direction of the tower.

"Here's where they cut the wires—that would be the torn connections to the wrecked computer consoles in the Real World," Vixenn thought out loud as she faced the cave-in.; Then she turned to face the long blackness of the deeper tunnel, "So, this path has to go to Showbiz's castle."

With a snap of Iylothien's digitized fingers, a will-o'-wisp appeared and floated into the blackness of the tunnel ahead, bobbing here and there to illuminate any darkened areas that could hide an enemy or trap. A series of low growls and moans echoed up from the looming dark. "Well, you know that if they had the sense to throw their net ICE up when we took this place, they're going to have a horde of defense down here as well."

"We'd better get to it then—and try not to slip in all the sleaze and moral rot they'll have in there." With that, he produced a bow and nocked a silver-tipped arrow as she created a portal between them and the tunnel. They closed together until their upper arms touched. Secure in each other's company, they nodded and stepped through, transporting their virtual personae down the wires and into the depths of Ricky T. Showbiz's internal network.

… …

With the numbers the CYBER teams had already thinned and word spreading about what happened to the Dumpsters, the rest of the approach to Ricky T. Showbiz's haven was practically uneventful—the ever-present sounds of gunfire were more distant, the evidence of the inner city flare-ups and continued demonstration provided by Valhalla's Brownies and the Paladins. Finally, Preach and his team stood just down the street from the hotel.

"So, what's the play?" Johnny asked.

"We wait here," Preach responded. "They have at least one sniper crew and an automated Vulcan turret on each corner of the rooftop; they'll obliterate us before we get to within three yards of the building. According to our satellite recons of the area, there's a heavy bunker up there to defend them. The building's too high for the vehicle weapons to take them all out, and you can bet the troops are geared up and on guard. The plan was to get Iylothien and Queen Vixenn into Ricky T. Showbiz's systems. We wait for their signal."

"But how will we know when they're ready? It's been almost an hour and…" Before Johnny could finish his sentence, they heard four simultaneous "brzrzrzrzrzrzrzrzrt" sounds of the roof-mounted Vulcans high above them, followed by the thudding *smack* and clatter of a sniper and his rifle hitting the street in front of them. Seconds later, there were other long bursts as the guns fired on each other until two of them gave way. Preach looked at Spider.

"That'd be the signal. Be careful, my friend."

"Vaya con dios, *Jefé*," Araña stated. Then he closed his sneak suit, blending into the background behind him. Bricks warbled before the team's eyes as Spider raised his right arm, aimed his grapnel at a ledge of an adjacent building, fired, and hoisted himself onto the rooftop. A few minutes later, he radioed the team that the rooftop, as well as their final approach to Ricky T. Showbiz's lair, was secure. Three minutes after that, Preach stood at the entrance of the hovel, flanked by Rickshaw's Dominator, Trigget, and Chrome to his left, Hardcore's damaged Sabretooth, Johnny, and Susan to his right.

"Mind if I borrow your sound system?" Preach asked his wheelman. In response, Corey smiled and handed him a microphone.

"*SWEET TRICK RICKY T. SHOWBIZ!*" he yelled, voice amplified by Hardcore's speaker system. "*THIS IS JACK MATHEWS. WE HAVE DEFEATED YOUR FORCES. YOU ARE UNDER ARREST FOR DRUG TRAFFICKING, ROBBERY, KIDNAPPING, HUMAN TRAFFICKING, MURDER, RAPE, AND ANY OTHER CRIMES THAT COME TO EVIDENCE AS WE INVESTIGATE FURTHER. YOU AND ANY REMAINING FORCES COME OUT, UNARMED, WITH YOUR HANDS OVER YOUR HEADS, NOW, OR WE WILL COME IN FOR YOU. IF YOU RESIST, LETHAL FORCE WILL BE USED TO CONTAIN OR OTHERWISE NEUTRALIZE YOU.*

"*YOU HAVE BEEN WARNED.*"

… …

"What is happenin' here?" Ricky T. Showbiz stormed. "*What* is happenin' here? This govek thinks he can just come in and kick me out of my own home?

"I'll tell you brothers what—those mothers wanna come and play, then okay, let 'em play! You'se already set up; I'm goin' upstairs and havin' me some honey time. You boys know how ta play, so go ahead. When this is done we'll be dining off their skulls. Oh, and you get any honey's offa this, you go ahead and take what you want, y'all got dibs." They dragged three girls and handed their leashes to Ricky T. Showbiz, who yanked them along with him to the elevator. "C'mon, you ho's, time to start my victory party."

… …

- "*Preach, Vixenn here. We can't see a whole lot inside the house. They have some cameras for making their vids and stuff, but…*

319

Wait, someone's using an elevator, going up to the eighth floor. Hang on a sec."

- "Iylo here—found some things while Queen was checking some other circuits. Floor diagrams, wiring—there! Looks like the first floor is nothing but bad guys. Time to play..."

Booming noises reverberated from inside the house as Iylothien took over the various sound systems inside the building. Lights flashed on and off at irregular intervals, and any automated devices spat off in random fits of misbehavior.

"The locusts are in!" Iylothien hailed.

"Copy, Iylo—great work, both of you!" Preach congratulated. "Queen Vixenn, now that Iylothien's got control of the system, does he still need your deck?"

"Negative, Preach. Stang spliced the wires up while we were jacked in; he's got a permanent connection now."

"Perfect! You and Stang come on down. We might need the extra hands."

"On our way," she replied. Then, giving the Neon Bard a virtual kiss for luck, she opened a portal and stepped back into her body.

"That was *awesome!*" Stang beamed as she shook off the cyberlag. "Yeah," she returned, exhilaration showing through the glowing expression on her face. "You should see it from the inside! But come on, let's go. We've got a job to wrap up."

... ...

"Vixenn and Stang are on their way," Preach yelled over the music. "Rickshaw, those doors are reinforced steel about a half-inch thick, and they haven't come out yet. I don't think they can hear me over all this noise. Why don't you knock for me?"

"With pleasure," Rickshaw replied with gusto. He backed up his Dominator a couple feet and radioed for everyone to cover their ears. Moments later, the gust of the HEAVE rocket pulled at Preach's coat. The blast completely blew the reinforced doors off their housings, converting them into flying battering rams that wreaked havoc on the gunmen's fixed defensive positions inside. Blackwolf felt a déjà vu sensation, then realized the scene reminded her of their interview with Elaine.

Preach scanned the interior, his visual sensors cutting through the smoky haze that lingered from the blast. He wasn't prepared for what he saw. The first floor was nothing but a series of fighting fortifications, and there were so many traps strewn about the floor he didn't have time to catalog them all.

- *"Heads up," he reported. "The hotel is heavily modified. Hardcore, there's a concrete bunker facing front. Take it out."*

- *"Roger, Preach," Corey responded.*

He confirmed his assent by firing a salvo from the Sabretooth's recoilless rifle at point-blank range, then reinforced it with a second HE round from his Sabretooth's grenade launcher. The first shell blasted the bunker with a direct hit; the second passed through the hole and threw high-velocity shrapnel at whatever had been behind the structure. Chrome was about to rush in but Preach called him back.

- *"Thank you, Hardcore. Break: Rickshaw, please sweep up the floor."*

- *"Copy that," The Hounds' wheelman replied.*

The Dominator's turret swiveled side to side in slow arcs, occasionally adjusting up here, down there, its laser emitting a steady beam of ruby red heat. Wooden floorboards singed black, exposed formiplas laminate melted. The beam burned through the fine trap mechanisms, either deadening them or setting them off against the defending forces. After nearly a full minute, Preach determined the effort was complete.

- *"OK Hardcore, let's not take any unnecessary risks. Pop a canister in there and gas 'em."*

As Corey fired, Preach announced they'd allow ten seconds for the gas to disperse, then they'd go in.

- *"We're taking on a Bravo class defensive structure," Preach advised. "Proceed, but keep your eyes on with caution."*

- *"Hey Preach, what about me?" Araña asked.*

- *"Stay where you are for now. It's possible we'll flush some up to you."*

- *"Roger, Preach, Delta Sierra Alpha ready."*

Lady Blackwolf was puzzled. "Delta Sierra Alpha?" she asked.

"Duck Shoot One," Rickshaw explained. "It's Spider's way of saying he's set and letting a little tension out of the situation."

It was time. When he had left CYBER, they had deactivated almost all of his cybernetics except his eyes, which they had largely disempowered. After their first mission, Simon had authorized Jack to receive his two chipskill slots: slotting one to the base of his skull would almost instantly add whatever the card was programmed to provide. Preach activated Team Admin (TADM) chipskill; similar to Blaze's combat chipsets, it was focused on oversight functionality. TADM connected him to each of his team's HUD outputs and provided him with the status of each member's health, ammunition, and IFF data. A series of nine green dots projected onto his own shell map Queen Vixenn and Iylothien had provided as they had scouted the structure during their run. As a member entered an area or room, the details would be refreshed so he could always have the most recent awareness of the entire operation. He could then share it with the rest of the team, no matter how far apart the individual members were scattered.

> *- "All right, troops," Preach said, "watch for hostages and human shields. We already have a pretty high body count on this one, and I guarantee they're going to try to make it higher. Move fast, step light, and hit hard. This ends here!"*

With that, he let out a sigh to clear his head, reminded himself that leaders lead, and plunged ahead through the blasted doorframe into the smoking ruins of the Hotel Palatia.

29. Hotel Palatia

The cacophonic pandemonium caused by the sheer volume of fire he received as he passed through the entrance overwhelmed his senses and tore at his will. He was a Christian, he was CYBER-trained, he had trained Blaze's Fist, and he had been the leader of both Grey's Hounds and Preach's Pride, but he was still human. With the *crack!* of every round, every nerve ending in his body screamed in fury to find cover—any cover—before he would be reduced to a smoking paste of spent cordite. He half-retreated, half-fell, behind the small counter once used by hotel staff to record guest stays. If he didn't think, he would panic. If he panicked, he would die. A seemingly infinite number of rounds zipped past him, splintering holes and casting fragments of debris in every direction possible and hammering, hammering, hammering into the other side of his protection until the weakened structure threatened to give way entirely. Three thoughts somehow flashed through his mind amid the leaden chaos:

Ricky T. Showbiz's forces had at least some military background. Who didn't these days?

But these guys functioned at corporate response force grade levels.

As abrupt as they were, Jack held onto them just long enough to abate the creeping dread that pinned him behind the all-but-lost hotel desk. The fire hadn't lightened up for a second, but the moment had passed. Preach had regained control of his mind; regaining control of the situation was possible. He forced his eyes open and used his enhanced optics to trace the firing angles. The second floor had murder holes—firing ports that allowed gunners on the second floor to fire freely into the first—scattered throughout. Had it not been for the CYBER combat armor they wore on this mission that had a trace layer of the same armor coating the vehicles had, there wouldn't have been enough left of him for a deli truck delivery. As it was, he was forced to stagger out of the doorway as the small arms fire continued to pour into him.

- *"Rick, Hardcore, we have heavy incoming fire from the second floor, and there's a whole series of smaller bunkers all around the former ballroom and dining areas. See if you can either neutralize them or lay some cover fire for us."*

- *"We'll do what we can," Rickshaw responded, "but even with the hole I punched through their walls when I opened the door, Hardcore's view is pretty limited from here, and I only have one HEAVE left."*

Preach scanned the first floor again and added as much of a second-floor scan as his vantage point would allow. If Rickshaw had only one HEAVE left, they'd have to use it judiciously. Steady streams of .30 caliber machine gun fire began to rain in on his position. He knew he couldn't hold there much longer, but he wasn't powerless, either.

All CYBER deckers carried them, although there were variations of the main themes, and Preach decided it was time to use one of his. He crouched back behind his cover, slung his auto-rifle, and fitted a SLAP micromissile to his sidearm. Fuser preferred the panic-inducing version that sounded like cannons when they went off. Preach knew those were fine for outdoors in a large area, but the confines of the Hotel Palatia and the safety of its surrounding neighbors discouraged its use. For this operation, he had equipped himself with the much slower, much quieter drone pistol version.

Still behind his shelter, he fired down the length of the building, then switched his vision to the camera of the aeronautically shaped charge. Under his guidance, the missile performed an in-flight u-turn and retraced its path. As it neared the second-floor position, the Pride's leader aimed it straight at one of the firing ports and increased its speed to full throttle. Seconds later, the blast poured upwards from the breached firing port and completely destroyed the position.

 - "All right team, by the numbers—let's go!

Chrome was the first one in, followed by Lady Blackwolf, Johnny, Trigget, and finally Melissana. Hardcore's rocket fire had eliminated the largest of the bunker threats, and the gas grenades he had fired caused multiple casualties. Iylothien inflicted mental chaos upon the remaining forces through the building controls. Once the CYBER raiders entered the building, the first and second floors fell quickly.

 - "Okay, Iylo," Preach hailed their expert hacker, "we've cleared the first and second floors. Please restore the building controls on level one and two."

 - "You got it, Preach. By the way, I tried to send the elevator down, but it's not budging."

 - "Well, I guess Ricky T. Showbiz isn't all that stupid. He probably forced open the elevator doorway and triggered the manual emergency lock. After we secure the prisoners on the first two levels, we'll head for the fire exit stairwells."

They marshalled their forces, reloaded, and headed for the fire exit stairwell to resume their mission, only to be blocked by a new obstacle. With elevator access denied, a dead-bolted steel plate door blocked access to the higher levels.

"Preach," Chrome advised, "you and I both know I could just kick this door right off the wall it's set into, but I'm betting they already figure that if we got this far, we'd be able to breach it somehow. They've trapped this bugger. And if I were them, I'd make it a good one."

"Any ideas?" Preach asked. "Araña can scan for electronics, but if we call him down from upstairs, the bad guys have a potential way out of here from the roof."

"I have one. Chrome, bring me one of the bad guys—a conscious one." The entire group was startled—the statement came from Trigget.

... ...

"Bring him here," the helmet-synthesized voice commanded.

"What you guys want from me?" the thug asked the group of black-cryoplate-armored commandoes he had just witnessed take out the cells he had been assigned to. "Yo's may have gotten the better of us, but Showbiz gonna take y'all out just like I saw him do on that skink he did at Sitter's place. Y'all buried that govek yet?" he said with a sneer. He crossed his arms and spat onto the helmet of his inquisitor. "I ain't tellin' you's nothin'."

"Well, you're brave, I'll give you that," the synthesized voice reasoned, "unless you're even more of an idiot than you look. But please do tell me something. Don't you ever get tired of being wrong?

"First," Trigget said as she removed her helmet, "I'm not a guy, you slovenly excuse for a pig," she declared, hatefully enunciating the last word. "Second," she continued with a nod to the person on her right, "does he look familiar to you?"

"Hi there," Chrome greeted with intoned malice after he removed his helmet. "So, you say you were at Sitter's the other night? Great—I was waiting to meet up with you guys again, to finish what I started."

"Third," Trigget added after she flexed the tip of her tongue to press against the roof of her mouth and sighed, "you'll tell us everything we ask from you." From the disdainful smells that had emanated from their prisoner after he recognized Chrome, Trigget didn't think she really needed to use the pheromones, but she wanted to get the interview over with quickly. They had only cleared the first two floors; they still had eight to go.

…… ……

Johnny had just disarmed the device. They had lost precious minutes, but they had not lost additional lives. Before clearing the doorway, Preach gathered them all for one last consultation.

"So, we all heard the twist," Preach reviewed. "The third and fourth floors are basically trick rooms for Ricky T. Showbiz's direct clients who pay extra for the privilege of having his security while they're raping his slaves. Showbiz has nine guys on staff for each floor, and there will be about twenty girls we can bet on being used as human shields. There are also likely to be some high-class johns who are willing to pay the Master's premium rates. They're not primary targets, but we should run a precis on each one to see if Simon has something else on them.

"The fifth and sixth floors are where the remaining lieutenants and their cells live. We expect up to 54 hardened troops—the heaviest fighting—on those two floors. Once we get past them, all we'll have between us and Ricky T. Showbiz are nine senior lieutenants guarding his closest girls. From everything we've heard so far, Kelly will be on this floor if he doesn't have her with him."

- *"Hey, Preach, nobody's shown up here yet. Want me to join you?" Spider asked.*

- *"Negative," Preach responded. "The floor under you is desig-nated as the primary defense of the eighth floor in case the roof was breached. The ninth floor is probably as heavily defended as the first and second; don't expose yourself to unnecessary risk. Hold there for now."*

…… ……

The door gave way to Chrome's kick, but the explosion the defenders expected to render the fire exit stairway completely unusable did not occur. The CYBER strong-arm retrieved the heavy steel plate door and used it as a shield until the team reached the third and then the fourth floors. Trigget stayed behind to tend to the girls they liberated along the way as the rest of the team proceeded to the fortified hotel's fifth level.

The Iylothien-inspired cacophony of bedlam and irregularly flashing lights continued as Preach and Melissana laid suppressive fire down the lengths of the fifth-floor hallways while Chrome, Johnny, and Lady Blackwolf cleared enemy-occupied rooms. Halfway through, however, the noise and lights stabilized—the sudden normalcy of the building interior interrupted them. The defenders also were forced to shake off the effect, which was just as jarring as the craziness that the premier CYBER hacker had inflicted upon them, only the occupants adjusted a little more quickly. They had home turf advantage.

- *"Talk to me, Iylo. What just happened?" Preach asked as a new hailstorm of lead came their way.*

- *"Sorry about that. I had run of their entire system, but their deckers decided to physically pull the plugs—their network is entirely offline, so I can't help you out any more than I have. There is one thing I can do, though. Grey, you have control of the op—do you want the lights on?"*

Jack considered his options. Of everyone on the CYBER teams, he would be the least impacted by the lack of light. From what he had already seen, the defenders had some serious gear on them and were more than willing to use it. He suspected at least some had night vision equipment on par with their own. On the other hand…

- "Iylothien, do they have backup generators?"

- "You mean their computer-controlled automated systems? Yeah, they did… before Queen Vixenn mana-nuked 'em as a side quest while I cut into the main artery. They'll have to completely replace the panel circuitry."

Preach inwardly smiled.

- "Great teamwork, both of you! Everybody, get ready for night ops—the building's going dark in less than a minute. Go ahead, Iylothien, cut the power."

- "Roger, Grey—err, Preach. Wait one… I'm into the Wichita Power & Light grid. Compared to this place, no trouble at all… non-payment alerts sent… triggering batch process, and…"

The building interior went completely black.

"Pride, hold your positions," Preach called out through his helmet microphone, not even bothering to use the radio. "Chrome, take four steps forward until you get to the end of the hall." Four heavy steps thudded down the hall. "Good, hold there and light up on anyone who tries to fire at us." The CYBER lead then switched back to radio.

- "Johnny, you have night vision on?"

- "Wouldn't leave home without it."

- *"Come up on along the wall to my right."*

- *"What you got?"*

- *"There's still about thirty of these guys. You and I are going to go for a walk. And yes, in this case, you are now officially hired to impersonate a cat."*

- *"You know about that?" Johnny asked, embarrassed.*

- *"Yep," Preach responded. Somehow, Johnny knew he was grinning, if only just a little.*

... ...

The two worked their way down the hallway. Johnny knew Preach had to be able to hold his own to be part of the elite government force, but he had always just figured their leader just did the decking thing and was more of an administrator. Spider and Chrome had told him stories, like that one about the night when the three of them faced down against the Crack City Brotherhood, but Johnny had half dismissed the tales as just that—outside of training, he had never seen just what the man could *do*. Until then.

There were guys far bigger than the former pastor, and wearing armor, but between the Pride leader's mixed martial arts and quick-fire skills, it seemed like none of them ever even had a chance. At one point, while Johnny was clearing the room on the opposite side of the hallway, some big guy got the drop on Preach from a side door and had him against the ropes, but the lead CYBER agent fired a bright flash of light flashed from his eyes that blinded the thug until Preach completely incapacitated him. Eventually, Preach and Johnny had gotten to the last corridor. The pair discovered the last cell of the criminal guerillas, who had decided to lock themselves in their rooms and use the slaves they were with as human shields;

both CYBER agents could hear muted crying through the reinforced walls of several rooms.

"Preach," Johnny whispered, "even if I was Heinlein's cat and could walk through walls, I couldn't save those hostages. The second we open any of these doors, those girls are gonna get hurt."

"You're right," Preach whispered back. "And there's no drug in existence that's going to incapacitate those guys before they're able to kill their hostages." He sighed, the sound itself a brief whisper between the two of them. "There's only one way left." He closed his eyes and began to pray. "Lord, please forgive me for what I am about to do, but if I don't do this, those girls are going to die." He sighed again and, in the darkness, Johnny watched Preach mount a silencer onto his pistol and switch clips.

Johnny continued to stare, almost not believing what he saw. Preach went into a crouch, took three silent steps forward, turned to face the right wall, raised his pistol, and fired twice. The CYBER leader took another step forward, spun to face the wall on the left, and fired once more. A girl screamed, then began sobbing. He repeated the pattern: step forward, turn right, fire once. Spin left, fire again. Take three crouched paces forward, fire. Repeat again, until he had covered the entire length of the corridor. When he got to the last door at the end of the hall, he paused, stood to full height, replaced the clip, and returned to Johnny.

Without saying a word, he opened the first door on the right hallway. Johnny was visibly stunned. The CYBER teams always billed Johnny as either the guy who was so skilled he looked lucky, or so lucky he looked skilled. But he had never before seen anything like what he was looking at in that moment. In the corner farthest from the door, a girl slumped, sobbing, still in the grip of the pimp's minion, two narrow holes drilled neatly through his temple. They double-checked each of the seven other rooms along that hallway; each retold its own version of the same scene.

"Okay, Vixenn, you and Johnny come up and try to calm some hostages they were using as human shields. The rest of the Pride quietly link up with Chrome and navigate to my position. Trigget, get ready to come on up—we need you up here to take care of more girls."

Johnny knew Preach assigned him to the rescue detail with Melissana because the two of them related so well, but what he didn't know was if he was there to support the former detective or if Preach wanted her there to support him. Either way, for a change, he was glad for the lull.

When the rest of the group had assembled at that last doorway at the end of the hall, Preach again took point after conferring with his team. Banging loudly on the door, he called, "You are now under arrest. Release your hostages and open the door!"

He kept banging on the door until a voice smugly replied, "Go ahead, keep bangin'. You ain't gonna bust through the door, an' my boys'll take you out, you keep makin' that racket. You're just telling them where you're at, you jacked up—"

The ganger's litany was abruptly cut off by an abrupt loud crash against the far wall that was immediately followed by a scream and two bumps. Seconds later, Blackwolf released the latch just in time for the team to see Chrome wipe bits of wall he had just broken through off his t-shirt.

"You're right," he told the now-unconscious thug, "we're not going to bust through the door."

… … …

They had just cleared the stairwell leading to the seventh floor and took a brief rest. They were tired and starting to wear. Their armor had served them well, but they would need to replace it once they completed the mission. Trigget had been one of the busiest of them all, trying to tend to the long-term abuse and distress the slavers had waged upon their charges. None of them welcomed Araña's transmission that from his rooftop perch, he could see the horizon beginning to lighten. If they wanted to keep the elements on their side, they'd need to go faster.

Chrome cracked open the seventh-floor stairwell exit. Despite the total darkness, a stream of 7.62 rounds cascaded against the door, adjacent fixtures, and the armored cyborg. He promptly closed the door, and just as promptly, the firing stopped.

"Well, their building's offline, so they're not automated sensors," Chrome reasoned. "That means these guys definitely have night vision devices."

"Wish we had a couple more flash-bangs," Blackwolf lamented. "They come in handy for storming the rooms, and I think they mess with most night vision gear."

- *"Iylo, I have an idea," Rickshaw called in. "How often can you cycle running the job that kills the power and paying the bill?"*

- *"Pretty quick, Rick. I can probably cycle maybe twice per second."*

"Hey Preach? Why don't we have the ole' Bar Day Lay Nêone here hack back into Witch City Power & Light and strobe 'em?" he asked, deliberately butchering the hacker's side tag.

"Rickshaw," Preach replied, "that idea was as brilliant as your pronunciation was bad," he joked back. "Okay, everybody, polarize your helmet's visors and max the flash suppression—this'll hit us pretty much the same as it'll hit them; hopefully we have better equipment." Once that had been done, he concluded...

- *"And speaking of brilliance, you heard the man, Iylo—light 'em up!"*

Once Iylothien's strobing began, the CYBER forces heard painful cries of anguish from the other side of the door. Chrome kicked the door open, prepared to take several more bursts from the squad's automatic weapons, but none came, the crews too busy trying to tear off their night vision goggles, now painfully blinding them as they magnified the building's lighting operating at full capacity. Clearing the rooms went just as smoothly; in one case, the flashing light had sent a pimp commander into a seizure. The only downside was the strobing also impacted the hostages; already drugged senseless and traumatized, Trigget could only wonder what their minds were experiencing as Susan and Melissana led the almost catatonic girls away from their former masters to a safer spot of the building. One of the masters started yelling at his girls for going along with the team, but Chrome made him stop before an enraged and worn Lady Blackwolf stormed up to slice his jaw to a permanent wide-open hang.

- *"Daylight in ten minutes," Araña reminded.*

"Okay troops," Preach encouraged, "this is it. There's just one flight of stairs separating Ricky T. Showbiz from us. Everyone ready?" Seeing the grim determination in each of them, he concluded, "Good, let's get this done!"

After disarming its traps, Chrome wrenched the door from its hinges and flung it up the stairs like a six-foot shuriken. Like its smaller counterpart, the door stuck into the wall with a distinguished "*THWAK!*" followed by the wobbling sound as the solid steel door settled. By the time the group had done the same with the eighth story door and gained entry to the master pimp's lair, Araña had called in again.

- *"Preach, I don't know what you did, but a boatload of guys just came pouring through the roof hatch."*

- *"You okay, Spider?"*

- *"Come on, Preach—I had all night to set this up!" he laughed. "I had the four Vulcans pointed their way, and as soon as I knew they were all out, I activated an electric panel to a grating I set up. We got 'em."*

The Pride searched Ricky T. Showbiz's lair. Despite the opulence of gaudy gold trinkets, jewel-encrusted tooth decals, and other truly meaningless fluff items, there was no evidence of anyone being in that level of the hotel.

"I can't believe it," Susan said with disgust. "All the trauma, all the death, torture, and pain, just so he could live in flea market?"

"Well, here's something," Melissana noted as she surveyed his various items. "Looks like a hologram projector."

"I think I just found his computer control room," Chrome reported. "His techs are all here, dead, shot in their chairs. My guess is our man has a temper issue and didn't like it when his guys lost their wargame. That reminds me…"

- "Hey, Araña," Chrome called up to his team lead, "do me a favor and tell Showbiz that if he likes his teeth, he'd better pull them out and stuff 'em in his pockets, 'cuz I'm gonna hit him so hard he'll never be able to find 'em again."

Any sense of laughter fell away with Araña's reply.

- "You want me to tell him? He's not part of the roundup—I thought you guys had him."

They all stood shocked, staring wonderingly until they all shouted it out at the same time.

"The elevator!"

30. Dogs and Kennels

THE CROWDED ELEVATOR landed onto the garage floor with a slam that jolted the booth and rattled Ricky T. Showbiz's teeth against his jawbone. Shantra screamed again, earning her another slap from his top bunk, Desiree. The third girl, a drawn and overly thin blonde, did her best to only whimper to herself a little when she collapsed against the sudden stop.

"Get up, ho!" Smoke shouted, accentuating his intent with a kick to her side. She stifled another cry and rose as fast as her frame would allow—being careful not to touch or even look at any of the males without their permission. That was not allowed.

"Wouldn'a brought any of these ho's if I din't need a hostage for the three of us," Showbiz admitted to himself in a dark murmur of thought. Out loud, he just said they should be grateful he saved them from the deputy dawgs that was raidin' the place, always trying to maintain the ruse that he was somehow protecting them from the stars or anyone else who might try to rescue them.

The descent had been difficult. They had boarded the elevator he had jammed once the power was restored, intending to flee while the upper floors were being besieged. It had all gone to hell after that—for some reason, they jerked down almost the entire eight floors while the lights were flickering on and off, the girls screaming all the way down, and the ride was too sporadic to shut 'em up. Even Ricky T himself lost the grip he had on the hand railing and got lost in the constant drop-snatch-drop-snatch of the ride down; four floors down, Smoke started to throw up and G-Bang fell over

Desiree, causing them to roll on the floor like they was doin' it in a zero-g/two-g mosh pit.

"I'm gonna get the names of the ones who pulled this drek on me—ME!" he yelled, slamming a ham-sized fist against the elevator panel to release the doors. His immediate fury spent, he relented to the present. "Well, we can't help it none now, but they just wait," he muttered as he stepped out of the elevator.

He walked out onto the familiar area of the large underground parking garage. It had once served as his central meeting area, where, as king pimp of Witch City, he had hosted so many inter-gang meetings. He had bought, sampled, and sold some of the finest slaves in the continent. He had brokered deals, waged peace, waged wars. He had held auctions, trials, feasts—"Oh, the feasts!" he remembered with an all-consuming lust that had somehow never been sated. If he could only have one more feast of food, feast of flesh, feast of feasting itself. It had been his kingdom's grand hall. The studios were through another tunnel along the west wall. The videos were the real gold mine, he absently thought. Twenty room sets dotted the area, everything from the girl's bedroom to the dungeon rooms, a little makeup, and camera equipment. To the south of the video room was another tunnel that led to G-Bang's dog pens, where he kept Adolph, Brutus, and the other four hounds they used for tracking, threatening, and disposing of their victims; and in the tunnel behind that was the pens they used to hold the girls. Even in that moment, with everything falling in around him, he openly jeered at the collective, willful stupidity of his customers who actually deluded themselves into believing their tricks wanted to live like this. Well, he concluded, their stupidity was his cash flow.

Now the underground parking lot turned court hall was empty except for a semicircle of twelve elaborate chairs set up like a council of elders, his own decadently imposing golden throne on its raised dais centered between G-Bang's and Smoke's. The rest, he thought with sudden realization, would never be filled by his original gang of friends again.

It was down to the three of them, the first three of his original crew of twelve. The rest had been taken out—there was no way they would scatter on him—and so the three ended up here.

"But don' you worry none," he told the last two friends he had on earth. "We'll rebuild. Oh yes, we'll rebuild. And when we do, there's gonna be hell to pay for the drek the stars pulled on me tonight, after all we paid them over the years to keep me safe."

"Most of the stars's just gone, Ricky," G-Bang replied. "I saw some of 'em take hits comin' up the floors before I bugged up to warn you."

"Oh, some of 'em, G," Ricky T. Showbiz darkly replied. "Only some of 'em. But we'll get the rest, don't you worry." He laughed darkly—for only a moment—then his hardness set in again.

"Let's just get the hell outta here. Right now, we're on the northeastern corner of the garage. Those frakkin' wheelmen the stars had hired are probably gonna spot us if we try to slip out the ramp along the south wall, so we'll sleaze along the north wall 'til we get to the foot tunnel. That'll lead us to the sewers. Once we get there, we can split up in the series of branching tunnel exits. Once we get to the branches, we won't need the ho's no more."

Showbiz knew Desiree thought she deserved some special treatment for her efforts in keeping the other girls in line, but she was just as much dead weight as the other two now that he'd have to start over with a brand new stable. Besides, he saw as he sent a sneering glance towards her, she was starting to get old. Maybe he'd keep that newer girl if she made sure she didn't make any more fusses.

Smoke took lead. He had made it well past the halfway point to the tunnel when they heard the squealing of tires racing down the vehicle ramp. It was hard to make the vehicle in the sudden brightness of the headlights, but its bullhorn blared, "YOU ARE UNDER ARREST! DROP YOUR WEAPONS, RELEASE YOUR HOSTAGES, AND RAISE YOUR HANDS OVER YOUR HEAD—NOW!!"

Smoke made a break for it, dragging Shantra between him and the car that had now entered the garage, blocking any chance of exiting that way. He fired a burst of AK-97 rounds at the vehicle, but the bullets didn't even chip the car's paint. The turret whined once as a bright red light that left the others with vision spots burned neatly through Smoke's head and dropped him instantly. Shantra shrieked and ran away from Ricky T's group. Showbiz spotted the car's turret briefly track her, so he broke for the tunnel; if he could make it, he'd be free. His eyes went wide, and he dove for cover, throwing his hands over his head as the vehicle launched a rocket straight at him. The rocket sailed over his head, and in the fraction of the second it took to form the thought, he believed the driver had missed. Another fraction of a second later, the rocket went off, and Ricky T. Showbiz realized what the driver had really intended—the wheelman had sealed his escape route.

… …

- *"Preach, this is Rickshaw. Be advised; they were making for a tunnel on the north side of the building. I used my last HEAVE to collapse the egress, but they just fled into another side tunnel on the West side. Looks like there were three bad guys and three girls. Now there's two bad guys. I confirm, one of them is Sweet Trick Ricky T. Showbiz."*

- *"Copy, Rickshaw. Chrome, Spider, Johnny, and Blackwolf, meet down in the garage."*

- *"What do you want me and Trigget to do?"* Melissana asked.

- *"Watch over the girls,"* he replied. *"But remember our briefing with our friend. Don't detain them. If any of them want to go, you can try to talk them into staying, but let them go if they want to."*

- *"Will do."*

… …

- *"Any movement, Rick?" Preach inquired, "We're all here."*

- *"Negative. I hear a bunch of dogs barking, and I'm getting steady heat signatures. Five in the tunnel to the west, six just south of them, and a little southwest of that, it looks like another 16 or so. That's a lot of bad guys."*

- *"And the sun's up outside," Johnny stated.*

"YOU INSIDE THE TUNNEL," Preach called over Rickshaw's bullhorn, "YOU ARE UNDER ARREST. THERE IS NO WAY OUT, AND IF ANY ADDITIONAL HARM COMES TO ANY OF YOUR HOSTAGES, WE WILL ISSUE EXTREME JUSTICE—WITH PREJUDICE. YOU'RE ONLY WAY OUT IS TO SURRENDER. THROW DOWN YOUR ARMS, RELEASE YOUR HOSTAGES—IMMEDIATELY—AND COME OUT WITH YOUR HANDS UP. IF YOU DO NOT COMPLY, WE WILL COME IN AFTER YOU. YOU HAVE FIVE SECONDS TO COMPLY." After exactly five seconds had lapsed—Simon would have been proud, he offhandedly thought—Preach turned to the leader of Grey's Hounds.

"Spider, I think you're the only one with any throwables left. Mind doing the honors?"

With his increased agility and heightened senses reporting Ricky T. Showbiz's location, Spider dropped the tear gas within three feet of G-Bang and Desiree.

"Man! That—*cough cough*—is…" the rest of the sentence was lost to even's Spider's attuned hearing.

"Fall back to the pens and let the dogs on 'em!" a deeper voice commanded. Whether he had somehow negated the effects of the gas or was simply immune to it, the CYBER team couldn't tell.

Preach just had the group hold back and let the gas do their work for them. Spider heard some locks click, but the dogs didn't like the cloud any better than the humans.

"Team, advance," Preach ordered, then cautioned, "watch your step in there."

"What is this place? Little girl's bedroom next to… manacles?" Lady Blackwolf asked in shock.

"Evidently, this is where they make their movies," Spider replied as he surveyed the array of camera equipment. He shook once in spite of himself.

"And people pay from anywhere they can reach to watch the same films, over and over again, thinking the girls actually enjoy all of… this," Johnny reflected. "I think I'm gonna be sick for a week."

Chrome didn't say a word and Preach couldn't. His heart was breaking, wondering how people could do this to anyone, and how much of it Kelly had been exposed to. The other tunnel ran south from the video studios, and though it was difficult to tell just how far away because of an echo effect, the team clearly heard the slam of a heavy metal door and the screeching of a heavy hatch door creaking shut in the distance away from them.

… …

"Ricky T, I don't like this," G-Bang complained as the dogs just paced back and forth, confused by the acrid stench that assaulted their nostrils from the bright room where they sometimes fed. "We're penned in, the dogs are just as stuck here as we are, and our hostages ain't gonna do us any good."

"What?" Ricky T. Showbiz demanded, and the dogs stopped their pacing. "I don't believe I'm hearing this! After all we've been through together, you want to bail, just because your dogs don't wanna go through some tear gas? You want to bail? On me? On *ME*?" Adolph and Brutus began a low growl that was as lost on the master pimp as his temper.

"Hit him, Master Showbiz, yeah *hit* him!" Desiree harshly lashed out, trying to make rank by making the most of the division that arose between Showbiz and G-Bang. The dogs, sensing the malice in the air towards G-Bang, began barking their disapproval of both two-legs that were threatening their Master. Shantra backed away; the ghetto dog handler fully focused on his former best friend as Showbiz drew a pistol and leveled it at him.

"You—want—to bail—on me?" the master pimp asked, his voice mirroring the growling of the dogs.

"R—Ricky T, it ain't like that! Ricky, no!" he exclaimed, "It ain't like that!"

… …

Two loud shots echoed through the tunnel. The Pride hurried down the remaining length; their footfalls drowned out by a third shot followed by the sound of crashing chain link. A woman shrieked, but it was soon lost amid the sounds of snarling barks, snaps, and biting sounds coming from the room just ahead.

By Chrome's fourth kick, the heavy door sagged enough that he was able to wrench the heavy plate off its hinges and provide access to the horrific scene that lay beyond. Ricky T. Showbiz was in the middle of the room, breathing heavily as he reloaded a machine pistol, faltering due to a harshly wounded left arm. Before him, a woman lay dead on the floor, two dogs busily rending the pieces of her that were left. On the opposite wall, a young girl was cornered against yet another steel hatchway; in a curious twist, one of the smaller dogs stood between the remaining hostage and the pimp in an effort to sacrifice itself to protect the girl hidden behind it. A ganger lay in the middle of the floor, shot twice in the abdomen. Three more dogs were snarling, in their rage state savagely pulling at their chains, lunging for the person who had just injured their master. As the CYBER force watched, Ricky T put two three-round bursts into each of the large animals as they focused on the woman's body before he faced the team and leveled his weapon at them.

"Oh, Mr. Showbiz, please do try," Chrome darkly invited as he took a step forward.

"You? That's impossible—I killed you myself!"

"Well maybe you're just not as tough as you thought," the armored cyborg replied with a shrug and darkly twisted grin. "Ever consider maybe going to a gym?"

A short burst of automatic fire resounded from behind Chrome that caused everyone to tense even more than they had already been. Showbiz dropped his weapon, blood spurting from his hand and now crippled right arm.

"He ain't worth your humor, Chrome," Johnny stated flatly as he slowly, deliberately, approached the kingpin of crime. "Tell me, *Rickety* Showbiz, do you have any idea how many lives you have destroyed?" As soon as he got within reach, the pimp took a step back to the wall, and with his left hand grabbed and activated a cattle prod the gang had used to train the dogs.

"You take one more step and I'll fry your eyes out," the flesh peddler threatened. "We use these on the dogs, but they work plenty good enough on people, too. Now you all just back away. I'm gonna grab me this pretty little girl over here," he said as he inched his way over to the girl who seemed to wither as soon as the rod was in his grasp. "We're gonna walk outta here, or I'll kill her. Now back off," he ordered, accentuating his command by waving the rod at Johnny.

But Johnny didn't back off. He tucked in and rolled forward, underneath the wild offhanded swing of the electrified weapon. He came up inside the extended reach of the rod and grabbed Sweet Trick Ricky T's left arm and wrist where the dogs had already bitten him and wrenched the instrument into his own grip. He then elbowed the pimp to push off; once clear, he turned and smacked the electrified end of the rod against the former big shot's injured right arm. Ricky T screamed, grabbed his right arm, and sank to the floor in a kneel. "All right, all right, you win! What do you guys want? My money? You want some cred? You want in on the action? You made your case; I can take you into my organization. What do you guys want?"

"Oh, for the love of poetic justice," Johnny said as he considered the prod's voltage dial. He turned the device all the way up and smacked it against Ricky T's groin, causing the pimp to yowl in pain and drop even lower to the floor.

"I—want—Lisa—back—you—worthless—govek!" Johnny yelled, accenting each word by smacking the electrified rod against the pimp's now useless arms, alternating arms with each word. Ricky T was reduced to a drooling ball of torment. "So, you like these things, huh? Do you use them a lot?" Johnny darkly asked as he took a step forward. "Ever wonder what they might *taste* like?"

- "Johnny, what are you doing?" Preach subvocalized.

"That frakker killed Lisa and who knows how many others!" Johnny angrily yelled back without bothering to use the radio. "He all but killed Cleo and destroys the lives of everyone he comes in contact with. Now that I see this waste of trash, I'm gonna put him out of their collective misery." With that, Johnny raised the electrified pole over Showbiz's head. "Come on, open that Ricky T mouth for us one more time, so we can turn your useless head into a light bulb. And if you don't burn out, maybe I'll mount you on a bookshelf for a souvenir."

Showbiz's horror reflexively forced both his mouth to clamp tightly shut and his eyes to clamp widely opened. He whimpered, kicked, and cried, but he struggled to no avail; Johnny was relentless.

"Not going to cooperate, huh?" Lisa's former lover tersely muttered to the struggling perpetrator turned victim. "Well, that's okay—I'll just ram it in through your teeth." Johnny reared back to make good on his threat.

"Johnny, NO!" Preach yelled. Something in that shout caused Johnny to pause.

"And why not?" Johnny demanded, releasing the pimp, dropping him back to the floor. He again touched the prod to the pimp's groin as he casually told the pimp, "Don't go anywhere, okay?" He then returned his attention to Preach and asked, "You don't really think anyone will miss him, do you?"

"If you kill him now," Preach cautioned, "he'll just be replaced by someone else. We need to hit the top of the chain."

"Yeah, you do that," Showbiz defied through tearful pain. "You better do what your daddy over there says, 'cuz you know he's telling the truth."

"See, there's a problem with that, Preach," Johnny countered, his anger giving way to hopelessness. "When we get to the top of this chain and pull the whole thing down, there'll be someone else to take that guy's place as well."

"Johnny, the ultimate justice belongs to God, and hell is the fate of people like Ricky T and his string-pullers if they don't repent."

"Yeah well," Johnny countered, "the way I see it, if this govek is going to hell for all eternity, sending him there a couple years earlier won't make much of a difference, will it? Except maybe to make sure he doesn't do any more harm before he goes."

"Murderers go to hell, too, Johnny, if they don't repent."

"Well, at least I'll be able to see the guy who killed Lisa being tormented."

"You might, or you might not. You might see Lisa instead, or maybe in your version, Showbiz will see you tormented. Besides, in hell there is no love, just the anger, bitterness, and despair. Even if you do see Lisa, you could turn bitter against her, blaming her for your being there and never able to get out."

"Well, if that's the case, I guess I'll kill the pimps and then repent," Johnny sighed under his breath.

"Really Johnny? A lot of people play that game, but God is smarter than that. Besides, how will you really know you've repented if that was your plan all along? How would you really know you changed your mind? If you still have any satisfaction in what you've done, no matter how justified in your mind, maybe you haven't repented."

"Isn't that just a little hypocritical of you, Preach?" Johnny challenged. "I mean, the way you went down that hallway earlier tonight? That was great! You kept those guys from murdering eight people!"

"What I did was great? Let me tell you something. You knew my eyes could see infrared and ultraviolet spectrums. I can also set them to see through walls, if they're not too thick and the materials are right. The ammo I switched out was high-speed armor piercing rounds which would easily go through anything I could see through to impact the target. There was no contest, there was no chance I could miss, and there was no defense. Yeah, I kept those guys from committing eight murders, but I committed eight murders of my own to do it."

"In the middle of all this, you're gonna have a Sunday school debate?" Ricky interrupted. "I don't believe this," he said with a sneer. "Heh! You goveks think you won some kind of good over evil thing here tonight? All this runnin' around shooting and blowing things up? You'll see—ain't nothing's changed. Oh, you cost me plenty, but my underwear's more expensive than your entire outfit. You take me in, all you'll find out is how quick they'll be to take care of me before they let me back out on the streets. And when I do get out, I'll find out where you live, who your family and friends are, where you do your grocery shopping. You want hell? You found it the day you decided to take on Sweet Trick Ricky T. Showbiz. You ain't done nothin'! An' even if you do manage to take me down, all you'll really prove is that there are twenty more already lined up, just waiting to take my place. Because the johns still bring in the rent, and as long as they're buyin', someone's gonna sell it to 'em." He jeered again as he regained his feet along with his composure. "So go ahead, big shot. You ain't got the collective sand between the both of you to kill me, so go ahead, earn your meager paychecks. Take me in. You'll see, you jus' wait. Ain't nothin's chan—"

The master pimp's head exploded as one last shot blasted the air, the distinctive sound of a Magnus Magnum .45. The round ricocheted off the ceiling before it embedded itself in the wall behind the gathered team. In an instant, they had all visually traced the line of fire back to the floor where the other ganger lay.

"It changed for *you*, you frakkin' govek," the downed kennel master managed to whisper. And with that, he too died, once again triggering the hounds tethered along the wall.

"Spider," Preach wearily ordered, "neutralize the dogs."

"Why?" Lady Blackwolf protested, jarred out of the shock of all she had just seen. "It's not their fault they were raised this way."

"You want us to let them go because this was how they were raised?" he asked, astounded. "So how does that apply to some, if not most, of the pimps and others we killed tonight? Isn't this how some of them were raised?"

Jack sighed, noting the undersized mutt that was preparing to go the distance for the girl that society never would.

"Spare the one defending the girl—it's worth saving."

Susan turned away and started to cry as Spider put down the dogs, but not even Trigget could tell if it was for the dogs or because she realized the truth of Preach's rebuke.

After Spider had completed his task, the team collected the last of Showbiz's three hostages. She was eighteen and frightened. She herself had been kidnapped, but from the mid-Atlantic area that used to be known as New Jersey. Her name—her real name, she was quick to point out—was Sharon. Sharon wasn't sure her parents would want her back after what she had done over the last three months to survive, but Josanne gave her some hope out of sharing her experience with Ryan and Alicia Elverson that her parents would not only take her back, they would give anything to see their little girl alive again.

While the others were conversing with Sharon, Chrome opened the other heavy steel door on the opposite side of the room they were in and shuddered. "Oh, drek!" he said. Then he simply froze, halted as though his internal control circuitry had short-circuited. Jack and Trigget noticed and visually checked on him, but neither one observed any apparent hardware malfunction. The strong-arm just stood there, silently absorbing the scene before him, still as Death itself. The rest of the team also noticed his reaction and attempted to peer over his shoulder, wondering what could make the stoic cyborg, who had already seen so much, pause.

Suddenly, in a barely controlled fury, eyes focused on some distant point past his teammates, he marched past them as swiftly as he could until he got to the video staging rooms they had passed through earlier. Bellowing in a rage that seemed to be the release of every emotion he had never outwardly expressed before, he let his raging fury loose on the studios, the equipment, and anything he could batter to ruinous scrap.

"Chrome?" Spider asked, concerned for his partner, "What…"

"SHUT UP!" he roared, causing the whole team to freeze.

Rickshaw looked into the room that had triggered the reaction in Chrome and just sagged against the doorway for a moment. He then took off his helmet, let it drop to the floor, and sagged against the doorframe with a sigh as heavy as his vehicle. Amidst various sobbing, wailing, and begging to be released, the team heard Rickshaw mutter over and over, "I thought they were more bad guys. I thought they were more bad guys."

CYBER had gotten to the end of the trail. The last room where the Hounds' wheelman had detected the 16 heat signatures didn't contain reinforcements, and there were far more than the 16 his scanners had detected from the street. They were captive girls, emaciated, loaded into four rows of four large dog kennels, stacked three deep. Ranging from near-feral to catatonic, some pleaded for release, some pleaded for death, some pleaded for the chance to perform any sexual favor they could think of in return for something—anything—to eat, and some pleaded for nothing, cowed into the rear corners of their cages.

"Jack?" Rickshaw said after forcing himself to inspect each of the cages further. Everyone looked up. Whatever it was he had to say, Rickshaw—while on a mission—had used Preach's real name.

"Jack," he repeated, "we've been keeping track of everyone on our way through the hotel. We have all the girls accounted for. I double-checked." he slowly reported.

"And Kelly's not here."

IV. MAKING THE SCENE

"It was scary, how right I thought I was."

— Ryan Nevin

"But we are robots, sir!"

— Teodora Stanev

31. Small Solace

Daylight was growing as Jack returned to the safehouse with some of his CYBER team and a few of the rescued hostages. The chilly morning had fully broken over the city, but the gunshots and small explosions that began the night before continued to reverberate off the town walls. Partisan greeted the group at the entrance, but he fixed Jack with a narrow-eyed look that spoke more of confrontation than congeniality.

"You know, you just brought a lot of heat to a cold November," he complained. "I thought you guys were going to be a little quieter. You hear all that? That's not your ruse you planned outside the city anymore. It's all coming from inside the city—and it's all too real." He gathered his thoughts as well as his breath before continuing. "Allow me to summarize. There are major firefights between some citizen groups trying to take back their neighborhoods, gangs are now jockeying to assume higher positions in a new pecking order, and Wichita Security Forces are mobilizing to emplace a martial law before things get worse. Apparently, they didn't appreciate that someone hijacked their emergency broadcasting systems and computer nets, let alone their turrets and drones." He suddenly cocked his head to one side and cast an off-beat grin. "There is one silver lining; somewhere there are WSF corporate executives sitting in a room with *their* execs, trying to explain what happened before Air Dynamix itself gets involved."

He moved his chair in an attempt to see around the CYBER agents. Consternation turned to concern when he noticed that several CYBER agents were missing and that only a few of the victims were in tow. "You guys look pretty beat up, and there's not as many of you as before. I see you have a few of Showbiz's victims, but I thought there'd be more." He suddenly feared the operation had failed completely and hesitated to say anything more, but he had to know. "How'd it go?"

"Partisan, as much as I'd love to chat," Jack wearily replied with a sigh. "We're emotionally and physically worn. In all, we've rescued over 75 girls. Most were glad, but many were scared. We'd been warned about this, but some were even furious and attacked us themselves, since they really believed their pimps actually loved them. The angry ones left after their attack failed, but there were about 60 who decided to stay. A dozen others were in such bad medical condition they couldn't go anywhere else and had to come with us. And since we had nowhere else to go, we had to come back to the Witch City urban rescue legend—in short, you.

"After the last few days of intense operations, we finally took down Showbiz, but in reality, he was right—not much has changed. Other pimps are only too eager to fill in the vacuum left in his absence..."

He sighed at one of the night's many memories and, seeing Partisan's concern, decided to share the story he had just revisited. One of the pimps, recognizing how exhausted the CYBER agents were, had tried to make a name for himself by going after Lady Blackwolf. But her exhaustion dulled her sense of restraint and had made her more dangerous, not less so. She laid him out before Hardcore, equally spent, could run him over.

"The other pimps would have no trouble tracking the movements of a large group of girls, and we would only reveal your new hiding place. So, we decided to smuggle the girls in small groups so the other team members could provide counter-espionage activities against anyone spying out where we were going. It's safer for both the girls and you, but the circuitous journeys will make for a much longer day than any of us really want."

"And which one of these young ladies is Kelly?" the chairbound caretaker asked. "I'm looking forward to meeting her so I can thank her for taking care of one of my kids."

Jack shut his eyes tight against the question. "That's just it," he admitted with another sigh, "Kelly wasn't with the others—we still don't know where she is."

Partisan sagged. He started to ask, "You still haven't found her?" but he checked himself when he saw the small group of refugees. "You said you have about 60 coming? Well, back when I was corporate, I'd seen some ops go sideways like that. You haven't found your primary, but you saved 60, and you're all still recycling oxygen; I'd still call that a good run." He looked over the group of survivors and sighed. "I've never had so many people to watch over at one time before," Partisan commented, devoid of any trace of either threat or revelry. "Come on," he resignedly added, "you and these girls have been through enough already." With emotional effort only perceptible to Trigget, he mentally adjusted himself and prepared against the imminent demand. Then he called over his shoulder, "Nick, gather the boys. We're getting lots of company, and we have a lot of work to do today."

…… ……

The sun began to sink behind the small high rises of the western skyline as Preach and Chrome escorted the final small parade of women and young girls through the doorway into Partisan's safehouse. It had indeed been a long day that had filled each of the CYBER agents with micro-memories: snapshots of scenes of kindnesses between the trafficked girls as they shared each other's old griefs and new hopes; Trigget rushing to respond to incessant medical emergencies along the way; Lady Blackwolf and Melissana walking together, physically leaning on each other for mutual support; Hardcore and Rickshaw always everywhere, like cowboys protecting their herd from bandits and rustlers. And throughout it all, the CYBER rescuers wondering and discussing amongst themselves in quiet whispers what might have happened to Kelly.

… …

The safehouse was packed and, for the first time, co-ed. Tag tugged on Partisan's sleeve, pointed to a girl who wasn't much older than him, and whispered. With a nod from his foster father, Tag crossed the cement floor to where he slept, retrieved the remains of a coat he used as a sleeping bag, and offered it to her. She took the makeshift blanket, gave him a blanket smile in return, then leaned into him and gave him a long hug—she had been treated well by an unknown man once before, and figured Tag had just claimed her. Tag, confused, jumped away. The girl stepped back and flinched in obvious fear that she had not pleased her new owner. Catching herself, she almost calmly braced for the beating that would teach her how to show her appreciation right.

"What are we going to do?" Trigget asked. "I can be at my conversationalist best, but these girls have just seen us take out an entire building full of Sweet Trick Ricky T. Showbiz's people right in front of them. They're terrified of us."

"You thought getting them out of his control would be hard," Partisan said to the CYBER team, "but that's just the beginning. The really hard work for most of these girls—especially those who have been in longer—is getting his control out of them. He slowly turned to face his new dependents.

"Hello," he greeted them as nicely as he could. "People call me Sitter. I'm sure many of you ladies have heard of me, and some of you might have already known who I am, but for those who don't…" He rolled his wheelchair between the former slaves and their rescuers. He smiled as some in the crowd nodded. "If you've heard anything at all about me, you know I have a rep for looking out for my kids. I've been working with these people," he continued with a backward flick of his head to the CYBER agents, "because they wanted to rescue and help you.

"Now, we're nice, but we're not stupid. Trust takes time, and you're scared. But we want you to know that you are no longer slaves to anyone, and especially not to any of us. It might feel weird, and it'll take time to settle in, but you're free. You can leave any time you want to, but we think it's a good idea for you to hang out here until the dust settles a little and you get some idea of where you want to go next. As long as you stay, you're under our protection."

He shifted his chair's angle and scanned his warehouse. "There are a lot of us here right now; we still have to rearrange some things so you can have your own section of the building away from the boys while we quite literally figure out our next move. The location that was our home is compromised, and there's no way we're going back to that hotel, so we need to figure out somewhere to go that has enough room for all of us. In the meantime, you older girls can help the younger ones to get settled in. If you need anything, let us know. I can't promise anything, but we'll do what we can. Saint Nick here will bring you a couple boxes of supplies."

The scuffing sound of makeshift-slippered feet slowly shuffling across the concrete floor quietly announced a newcomer into the group. "Girls, girls, girls, why the long pouty faces?" Cleo gently chided from behind the CYBER troops. The older girls who thought she had been killed lifted hands to mouths when they saw her. Some teared, many visibly relaxed as she continued. "This is a *good* day," she said, and Preach could see she was doing her best to smile. "These boys found me just in time—they saved me. I promise they ain't gonna hurt you none.

"In fact," she continued, "I have a special introduction to give you; yes, I mos' definitely do. Y'all remember those times together, when we'd sometimes share stories to keep us going, an' how I'd tell you all about our old days when some people would actually give a rip about what happened to us?" Some of the girls nodded, remembering the pain but along with it, the more tender memories of their bonding together throughout it all. "Well," Cleo said as she walked forward and laid her arm on one of the men's shoulders, "this here is none other than Lisa's Johnny, in the flesh, who came here with these rude boys and girls, all this way an' after all this time, to set us free." And in that moment, with Cleo's backing, the group dynamic of the girls shifted from the fear bred by their emotional poverty to a flicker of belief.

Many of the girls looked back and forth between Cleo and Johnny. Cleo nodded to several of the individual girls in confirmation before her exhaustion again overcame her, and she sagged against the cryoplast body armor he hadn't yet had the time to get out of. The group reflexively tensed and expected Johnny to either hit her or push her to the floor and kick her for touching him without him calling for her. Instead, he gently took her weight and, careful of the shredded barbs his forearm protection had become, he gently lifted her, cradled her into his chest, and carried her back to her makeshift hospital bed. When he returned a moment later, most of the girls just stared at him in awe.

- *"What'd I do? Why are they looking at me like that?" he subvocally asked, mystified.*

- *"Congratulations," Preach beamed in return. "They say a picture paints a thousand words, and the way you carried Cleo just now did more to convince those girls we are on their side than we could have tried to explain in a week. Some of them probably never even thought it possible for a guy to care for a woman the way you just did, yet they saw it with their own eyes." Preach smiled and added, "And from what I'm guessing about what Cleo told them about you, I think you're their hero."*

- *"Oh great," Johnny moaned.*

- "Now you know how Stang felt with those kids kneeling in front of him," Chrome added. He somehow managed to transmit his laughter.

… …

Over the next week, Partisan and his crews of lost boys joined forces with the CYBER members to convert the ground floor of Safehouse Three to a makeshift hospital. In their spare time, the entire team occupied themselves by taking care of their new charges. Trigget especially was completely consumed. As the team's medical staff, she treated the various physical conditions brought on by the constant abuse. As the team's conversationalist, she handled the bulk of the emotional unpacking of the now very vulnerable girls. The natural wariness of survivors taxed her even further. Despite getting medical attention and emotional support, some looked like they would make a break for it at any moment. Insular stances and frequent furtive glances at exits made it clear that some still suspected their rescuers were nothing more than a new set of captors.

Corporate media reported on the violence as simple downtown rioting and had spun the story as typical life outside their archologies—their bottom line to their consumers was that they should be grateful the corporations were taking such good care of them, or they might otherwise be living as the unfortunates where most of the fighting had occurred. Rumors abounded that Wichita Security Forces engaged against civilian structures without following due process, but rather than admit they were hacked, the WSF spokesperson simply stated they were seeking retribution against those who had started the rioting the night the events had occurred.

None of the media channels mentioned the disruption of a major trafficking operation, but neither Jack nor Partisan could say whether it was because the media was trying to cover it up or if they were simply trying not to invite the competition of new contenders for his title. Since at least a couple of girls, allowed to watch the broadcasts for the first time, recognized two of the anchors as frequent visitors, Partisan and Jack both knew the media had to have known what really happened. By the end of that week, they had all moved into Safehouse Three, Cleo had recovered enough to assist Trigget, heat from their raid on Showbiz had died down a little, and the WSF street patrols had resumed their normal non-presence. With Showbiz out of the way, Jack called off the ever-present battle between Valhalla's Brownies and the Paladins, although Iylothien would still closely monitor the city gates.

… …

"Okay, here we go," Jack opened. "We've been at this a week now. Let's go around one more time; anyone come up with anything on Kelly?"

"Me and Trigget worked closely together all that week to interview the girls," Melissana reported. "When we produced the photos you retrieved from your visit with the Elversons, a lot of the girls remembered her as Shimmer, but the girl has simply disappeared sometime before the raid."

"Well, she hasn't left through any of the city gates, that's for sure," Iylothien informed the group. "I haven't seen her on any scans, and that includes the fly-outs. And the Brownies and Paladins confirm that by their spot checks of all the vehicles leaving the city. And while their pattern looks random, they actually make sure and search every single vehicle. She's still in the city."

"Yet she's not on the streets, either," Araña stated. "The rest of us have covered every dealer, merchant, and street source we can think of, not to mention Iylo and Vixenn's hack of the street cams. We've come up a bust."

"So just like every other meeting we've held before," Partisan complained, "we're just repeating the daily chore of checking off all the places where Kelly could not be." He sighed. "Maybe we're just too late. Maybe Showbiz just simply killed her. You guys were on the right track, but it's infuriatingly frustrating because you got so close."

"I don't think so," Melissana countered. "Not about being close, but I don't think Showbiz killed her. In our interviews, most of the girls provided enough witness testimony that he always made a show of what he did to the girls. If he killed her, he would've made it a show." Trigget nodded her agreement.

"So here we are again," Jack summarized. "Despite a week of detective work, Kelly is still nowhere to be found."

"Yeah, it's weird," Saint Nick offered. "Sometimes girls just disappear."

"What do you mean?" Araña asked.

"He's mentioned it before," Partisan began to explain. "Go ahead, tell them."

"Well," Stang reflected, "it doesn't happen very often, but every once in a while, one of the older girls will just simply disappear. There's no evidence or rumor of murder, no indication the girl had been sold out of town, no word on the street of what had happened. It's like the girl just so completely disappears off the streets, it's just like she's never been on them." He paused and looked up at Jack. "Like Kelly."

"OK, here's what we do," Jack ordered. "We'll get another round of interviews with the girls. It'll go faster if we have them in groups. We need to find out if they know anything about these disappearing girls. We need to get it done tomorrow and meet back here at 6 PM tomorrow night to compare notes."

… …

"Well, we went through the interviews again," Melissana reported. "This time we focused on the disappearances in general."

"Occasionally, one of the older girls, aged twenty-two to twenty-four, would disappear," Josanne picked up the conversation. "Very quietly disappear. They didn't vanish like that during a regular auction. The most information the girls could offer was that Ricky T. Showbiz would usually splurge and give all of the girls something to eat on the day following the disappearance."

"By their reports," Melissana resumed, "it was a very rare occurrence for him to allow them all to eat the same day, but Ricky T had been in especially generous moods on those occasions."

"Finally," Josanne joined in, "one of the older girls remembered something else. We asked if she would be willing to share here, so we brought her along. Ladies and gentlemen, please meet Mishka. She's originally from the Wash, but they brought her eastbound about a year ago. Mishka, can you please tell them what you told us?"

"It never happened the day of the disappearance," Mishka began, "but I think I remember seeing somebody visiting Showbiz a few days before Shimmer—I'm sorry, your Kelly—disappeared. I saw the person once or twice before, and master would call one of us, and after a couple days they would disappear and never come back. I guess between the drugs, the fear, and the relief that Ricky wasn't calling on me, I never really thought that maybe the stranger was connected with the disappearances until today, but maybe…"

The team instinctively knew they had their first clue.

"Who was he?" asked Jack, his eagerness almost palpable. "If you don't know who he is, can you describe him?"

Mishka sucked in her breath. "I'm sorry," she said, confused. "I didn't mean to say anything wrong." Her eyes dilated in fear, and her breathing increased. "Please don't be mad at me—I'm afraid I said the wrong thing." She started looking nervously at the door.

"It's okay if you can't remember everything," Josanne calmly said as she triggered a mild dose of pheromone into the air to help the girl feel more comfortable. "Just tell us what you do remember about him."

"That's just it," she replied, somewhat afraid, confused, and feeling awkward, like she was giving the wrong answer to an easy arithmetic question, "It wasn't a guy. It was an old woman."

… …

The car had just arrived at the theatre performance when a Latino pushed a stocky man with a short-cut crew top backward against the driver's side front fender. A black-haired young man and his blonde girlfriend who had been cavorting in the Witch City streets a few yards away threw out a "Woo—HOO!" and stumbled over to the stumbled man to offer him one of their beers. In the intersection behind them, a yellow and black Dominator had just collided into a black muscle car, but rather than starting a point-blank vehicular firefight, the two drivers just got out and started yelling at each other. On the opposite side of the street, a twenty-something girl with sandy blonde hair and her raven-haired partner dressed in a belly dancer outfit walked toward the vehicles that were stuck behind the accident scene to ply their trade with the expensive car's occupants.

"Ex*cuse* me, sir," the chauffer rebuffed as he partially vented his bulletproof glass window. Three other occupants who were obviously bodyguards for the vehicle's owner got out of the car and drew their weapons with a complete lack of tolerance for pedestrians who had the insolence to fall against their ride. In less than seven seconds, two of them had been completely incapacitated, and the third had three red dots trained on his forehead.

"That's okay," the man who was pushed against the vehicle said with a grimace as he turned to face him. The red-dotted man was surprised to see the curbside adversary was wearing sunglasses at night. "But seeing's how your ears probably aren't made of Kevlar, if I were you, I'd lay down and *stay* down."

"Yer a bunch of flaming morons," the driver shouted and hit the accelerator to abandon his buddies behind. He would have gotten farther if Chrome had not grabbed the fender and lifted up the front wheel off the ground, Spider had not punctured the back wheel with a grapnel, and Lady Blackwolf had not shredded the passenger side tires with her extended claws. The driver gave up on the escape and turtled, locking down the vehicle and its two remaining occupants. It took three quick taps before Chrome smashed a hole in the glass and yanked the door completely off its hinges.

"You're crazy!" the driver shouted. "But whatever you're up to, it won't do you no good. There's…"

A second limousine pulled up and parked so close behind the first car they mildly bumped. "Oops! Sorry," Melissana and Josanne jokingly called out in unison from inside the second limo.

"A backup vehicle just a block behind," Johnny mockingly continued on the driver's behalf. "Yeah, we know," he finished, as Hardcore's Sabretooth pulled ahead and backed up against the front of the vehicle with another jarring bump. Rickshaw's Dominator pulled up alongside the passenger side close enough for the limousine to emit a groaning screech.

"Gentlemen, I have had enough!" the owner shouted as she angrily got out of the car from the unblocked driver's side. "Do you have any idea who I am?" She reached inside a small purple and gold cosmetic bag, but Blackwolf batted it out of her hand.

"Yeah, actually we do," an incensed Saint Nick accused as he approached the woman with Stang at his side—not to protect him, but to make sure he didn't beat the woman senseless before they had a chance to interrogate her. "You're Mama Solace."

"What are you doing?" she cried as Chrome squeezed on the severed door until it crushed against his fists.

"You're almost as lucky as I am," Johnny informed her. "First, he waited until you were outside the vehicle before crushing it, and second, if Fuser were here, he probably would have welded the car shut with you still inside."

"Why did you do this to my baby?" she whimpered. "I loved this car. I practically sold my soul for it, and you're ruining it!

"Well, if you really did sell your soul for this car," Chrome said as he rained blow upon blow against the vehicle's roof armor until it completely gave way, "whoever you bought it from got a bum deal."

"Besides," Hardcore pointed out, "you don't need your car tonight; I'll give you a lift."

There was no need to drug Mama Solace before transporting her to Partisan's latest hideaway; she fainted once Chrome began kicking the fenders.

"What should we do with these other limos?" Stang asked. "You guys want us to hide them or something?"

"Leave 'em," Araña ordered. "Iylo's got eyes on the street; let's see if anyone comes to look for them."

32. Confessions

"WHAT HAPPENED TO Kelly?" Jack demanded of Mama Solace the moment Trigget detected she had revived. They were in a small office inside Partisan's warehouse; it didn't take much to convert the shabby room into a shabbier holding cell for their guest.

"Who—what? Where am I?" she protested. She found herself flex-cuffed to a chair in a darkened room that was lit by a single bulb.

"You don't get any answers. Just questions. And the first question is, what happened to Kelly?"

"My dear boy," Solace calmly replied, "I don't even know who this Kelly is. Why would I know what happened to her?"

"OK," Jack seethed, "let's try it this way: what happened to Shimmer?"

"Now you tell me who or what this Shimmer is, and start treatin' me with some respect, and just maybe—*maybe*, I said—I'll tell you. If I know." She looked at her bound wrists and added, "Which right now, I'm inclined to say I don't think I do."

"Cut her loose," Jack commanded as if he found his own words were distasteful. "She can't hurt anybody here." Someone behind her removed her cuffs. As Solace massaged her wrists and tried to glance behind her to see who else was in the room, Jack threw her cosmetic case onto the small table beside her. The smack of the cosmetic bag against the tabletop drew her attention back to front. Either way, Mama Solace removed a cigarette and put it to her mouth to light it, fumbling as a glossy purple ball of crumpled metal crashed against the floor three feet in front of her chair, followed by the bulk of Chrome slowly, moodily, striding into her line of sight.

"You!" she venomously acknowledged his presence like it was an accusation. "You ruined my car."

Chrome gestured towards the ball of metal. "You mean the rest of that thing? Well, it's like the Lady LeeAnn fortune cookie machine once said, 'Sometimes when life gives you lemonade, you gotta make some lemons.' Besides, grandma, with all the drek you've been involved with in this cesspool of a city of yours," he leaned into her, showing her up close his now almost infamous grin, "what do you think I'm gonna do to you if you don't tell us where the girl is?"

"Why, you'll do nothing, Strong Man," she defied and completed the process of lighting up, making sure she blew the first exhale into Chrome's face. "Yeah, you're all tough—I heard about you. But you don't scare me none, and you know why?"

"Lemme guess," a new voice with a Hispanic accent sounded from behind. "It's because you had a tracker on you when we picked you up, and you figured your rescuers were on their way. Am I right?" She started at Araña's mention of the device but recovered quickly.

"It's not my fault," Chrome almost apologized to her with a shrug. "I wanted him to keep it on you so we can meet more of your friends."

Melissana picked up on Solace's other side, forcing the woman to turn back and forth between them all. "You found a young girl who was running for her life, and instead of helping her, you turned her back over to Showbiz. After that, you just went on your way. Is that what you do, Solace? Get the runaways and give them up to your boss-man Showbiz? Does that help you feel better about where you came from? How much does he pay you?"

Solace was shaken, but with visible effort, she set her chin and fixed her lips into a pout. "Don't make no never-mind to me," she murmured. "They let me keep my car, but you ruined it—you ruined my car." She looked at Chrome with what was supposed to be an angry glare, but to Jack it looked more like an effort of pathetic sadness. Trigget spotted it too, and decided it was time for her to move in.

"You say you don't know who the girl was," the CYBER conversationalist said in a quiet tone. "Here's her picture. Look at it. Showbiz called her Shimmer? She was the girl who ran away from Ricky T. Showbiz a little over a month ago." Trigget saw the recognition in the old woman's eyes, her chin slightly raising, eyebrows arching for just a second at the flicker of memory. Solace was good, but Trigget was better. The micro-tells of the face and hands had confessed where the captive's tongue maybe never would.

"Shimmer was in your car, too," Josanne continued. She was pressing for a breakthrough—what she got was a distant nod. "And how many girls did you sell back to him? Twenty? Thirty?"

"I can understand," Jack thought out loud, "that you brought Shimmer back to Showbiz. He's your boss, he sent you to fetch the runaways, and you brought them back. His girls didn't know who you were, so I'm guessing your boss kept you hidden away, like you were his secret agent. What I don't get is why you always managed to show up a couple days before the other girls disappeared."

"Only now you're unemployed," Chrome added. Seeing her momentary confusion, he continued. "Don't tell me it's been a whole week now, and you still don't know we busted up Showbiz's operation."

Solace regained her composure, muttering under her breath, "Ain't like that," as a scoffing frown worked its way onto her face. She hadn't intended for anyone to hear the remark. And nobody did—almost.

"So then, how is it?" Araña asked.

"You readin' my mind, too?" She was a relatively elderly lady who had survived much of the Witch City depravity, becoming a very part of that depravity in order to do so. But so much of what she had worked so hard for was now worthless, wrecked by the big, muscled man with the crew cut and his friends that just—would—

not—shut—up! She was tired, and where *was* her help? Exasperated, she finally gave up.

"I don't work for that stupid two-bit idiot who can't even keep a sixteen-year-old girl locked up! He called us—us! He had a shipment goin' to the Den that night, and one of his girls broke away. He put out one of his bounties on the girl, more than doubled if we found her before the trucks left. Well, I found her and brought her back. But she was a one-off. Truth is, I normally didn't bring girls to Sweet Trick Ricky T. I didn't *sell* girls to Showbiz," she smugly huffed, her mind caught up in the moment. "I *bought* 'em." She hesitated a moment, half-wondering why she had said that. Then with a shrug, she thought if she told them that much, she could just explain to these idiots what she meant.

"See, normally I'm sent to order the girls once they're past their street market prime, but when I saw her, I remembered we have a contract with a special client, and I thought to myself, 'Now Solace, *there's* a girl with potential.' So, I took her back to the 'King Pimp of Witch City,' but not before I sent some photos of my own to my organization. Turns out, our client agreed, so a couple weeks ago I made the usual arrangements with Ricky T. Just over a week ago—I think maybe three days before your little war—I made the pickup and moved her along."

"That's impossible!" Jack raged. He thumbed over his shoulder to some vague location behind him. "You heard all that noise outside the city? The big war between the Paladins and Valhalla's Brownies that's been going on all that time? All the city gates had been shut down, all roads blocked. Nobody got in or out since that started."

"I never said she was outside the city," Solace said, "All my contacts are on the *inside*." She took another drag of her smoke before she continued; Jack noted that as long as Chrome wasn't near her, she exhaled off to the side. "When the girls go too far, like that Shimmer, or sometimes just because, I take 'em off the hands of the pimps. I get 'em real cheap that way—the pimps sell 'em cheaper 'cause the girls start losing their value." She waved her cigarette as though to brush a thought away. "They'd wish they were back on the streets when that happens."

"Where do they go?" Susan asked. Up until then she hadn't said a word, leaving the interrogation to the experts, but she got so drawn into the story she blurted the question before she had time to check the impulse. Perhaps that was how Solace seemed to be caught off guard, or maybe the sodium pentathol and caffeine they had laced her cigarettes with was starting to take full effect, or maybe she was just done with the game.

"They're sold off the streets forever," she said, looking at nobody in particular. "The archology buys 'em. I sold her two weeks ago to Apex Premier, and once that happens, they're never seen again."

"I mean," Susan continued with a quizzical expression, "it's still a horrible existence, but the corporations have got to be better than where she was. What could be worse than working the streets for someone like Showbiz?"

Solace smiled, a cold gesture, her eyes squinting at Lady Blackwolf as she inhaled another drag, running a mental market analysis on the blonde gymnast. "Oohh girl, I coulda made a fortune off of you, an' those other girls, too," she surmised out loud, exhaling her cigarette fumes as she did so. Hardcore took a step forward, but Rickshaw restrained him. "You'll find out 'afore long, I imagine, when my employers catch up with you. You'll see. What the Witch City streets do to the girl's body, Apex will do to her soul." She stopped herself as she caught what she had just said. She paused, considered her cigarette, and allowed a sly smile to play across her face.

"Well, of course you did," Mama Solace calmly stated as she reassessed Jack with new appreciation. "You laced my cigarettes, didn't you? Oh, that's all right, I know, I know. It's a good trick—done it myself a couple times, and now you got me talkin' like there's no tomorrow." She again glared at Chrome. "An' you! You wrecked my car! You oughtta be ashamed of yourself. Ain't nobody respects their elders these days."

She stabbed out the smoldering butt against a makeshift tabletop ashtray with sharp jabbing motions and crossed her arms. A moment later, she grew more distant, withdrawing into herself, but she still couldn't stop talking. She reached for another cigarette and picked up her lighter.

"Well, it don't make no never-mind to me," she said. "You know my life is ruined, don't you? Just like my car. When the corp finds me an' knows I talked, I'm gone. Just like my car." She lit the cigarette and took another long drag, held it, then exhaled as she stared at the metallic lighter she held in front of her face. "You know, you have to appreciate the irony; I had a doctor once who always told me that smoking would be the death of me." She smiled, for real this time, but tears started to run down her cheeks as she continued to study her lighter. "I had a good ride, though; I had a good ride. I was always the cool one, kept my head," she recounted from her former years with a unique combination of pride and regret. "And now I'm talking like there's no tomorrow. Of course, I guess there's not much point of having a tomorrow if I don't have my car anyways," she mused. Mama Solace cupped her hands under her chin. It was a normal enough gesture, but Josanne felt like something wasn't right as an odd expression set over their captive's face. "Yeah, but it's been one hell of a ride," she repeated. And before anyone realized, Solace placed the lighter to the base of her throat, lifted it upward, and fired the concealed needle inside, injecting her brain with toxins that killed her instantly.

The team was silent, and for several minutes no one moved. After a time, Melissana absent-mindedly began to clean up the unused warehouse office room. Then the others filtered out one by one in mournful silence until only Melissana and a brooding Chrome were left.

"Sold her own soul, and Kelly's, too. All because of a frakking car," Melissana seethed as she walked out past the stoic cyborg.

"Poetic justice is served," Chrome muttered to himself. He gave one final glance towards the metal ball that had been Mama Solace's front fender and shook his head. Then he turned away, turned out the light, and after he had exited the room, turned the key to lock the door and close the office to all of them for the foreseeable future.

375

33. Infiltration

"Well, now what?" Susan asked the group that was assembled. "We've got about 60 girls to care for, Partisan's got more than he can handle, and while the streets are somewhat calmer than they were, we're a little used up."

"I can help Sitter guard the girls," Stang offered, "but I can't go head-on against an entire corp by myself."

"We took out a major pimp who ran a trafficking operation that spanned the entire continent," Hardcore reminded them. "Maybe one of the city bad guys will take over the local operation, but they won't be able to put the entire nationwide network back together again."

"Corey, do you really think Showbiz put that ring together on his own?" Johnny argued. "Think about it—trafficking is a huge credit-maker. I'm betting some guy in some office somewhere is sending a fixer down here now to set someone else up in Showbiz's place." His shoulders sagged as he added, "Besides, you were in on the hotel rescue from your Sabretooth, but you didn't see the way they dragged those girls into that hell hole."

"And what about Kelly?" Josanne asked. "I'm really glad we got all those girls out of there, but do we just leave Kelly behind? You didn't meet her parents—there's no way I want to go back there and tell them we gave up."

"And don't forget the mystery of where Partisan's kids come from," Susan added.

"I'm just saying, this just got a whole lot bigger than we thought," Hardcore defended.

"Did it?" Iylothien asked via Partisan's comm circuit. "We knew all along there were corporations involved."

"You told us there might be one involved, not a host of them," Johnny countered. Internally, he was conflicted. He had been about to say the exact same thing, but Iylothien beat him to it; Johnny was still too suspicious of the flamboyant hacker construct to openly agree with anything it said that might steer the mission's direction.

"Preach, it's your team, it's your op, it's your call," Araña voiced.

"I don't often quote him," Jack resolutely acknowledged, "but I'm calling Machiavelli on this one: 'You can always begin a war when you will, but they won't always end when you want.' I vote we keep going."

"Well, me and the Hounds signed onto this mission to get Kelly, or at least to find out about what happened to her. Besides, we're curious to see how this Apex Premier plays into all this. We're with you."

"We're not finished here yet," Susan announced. "If what Solace said was true and whatever they're doing to Kelly is even worse than what Showbiz did, we have to put an end to it. The only thing is, how? I mean, Operation Drawbridge was one thing—we had specific locations to target and an insider to let us in. But how do we assault a corporation when we don't even know what we're looking for? Vixenn and Iylothien have been researching Kelly's whereabouts for days now with no results. I've even reached back out to Elaine, but this time she has no idea what could have happened."

"Simple," Araña said with that easygoing smile lending confidence to them all. "We find out where the targets are."

"Yeah, but how do we do that?" Susan asked. "We can't just storm a corp and wander around in sneak suits."

"Funny you should say that," he replied. "Sneak suits is exactly what I had in mind. And while we're not going to run in and storm Apex, we will walk in and take the corporation by storm." Seeing the confused looks on their faces, Araña disclosed, "What I mean to say is, we're going to *be* the sneak suits."

"I still don't get it," Melissana admitted.

"How many suit johns did we pull out of the fifth floor of the Palatia? The fact is, there are now some fresh corp vacancies to fill," Araña said.

"Yeah, we busted some johns and put 'em on ice under the Paladin's care for a while. So?"

"So, Apex Premier is a personnel company," Araña explained. "We're getting jobs."

"See that, kid?" Chrome grinned and clapped Johnny on the shoulder as the team left the meeting. "Your wish came true—you get to bring down another megacorp after all!"

… …

"Yeah, but I have this problem," the shorter youth confided to his taller friend. The group had been waiting at a commuter station for the ride that would take them onto the Apex Premier corporate center, pretending not to know each other by listening to the two friends who were aspiring rock musicians trying to break into the entertainment field. "It's like, when I'm trying to concentrate on something, I have this problem, cuz I'm like talking to myself, and I like, *see* the words. And it's really distracting because I see the words in front of me, and they distract me from what I'm trying to do."

The CYBER team members glanced at each other.

"Yeah, well," the taller friend counseled, "you gotta learn to multitask."

Johnny was about to reply to that bit of wisdom, but just then the commuter pulled up, and it was time to board. The group disbursed throughout the vehicle, but that didn't keep sub-vocal one-liners about the pair from flying. Eventually though, each agent settled in to review the various notes and dossiers Apex Premium had provided to each of their new personas.

- *"While we're waiting," Preach cut in, "keep in mind that Spider, Rickshaw, and Hardcore are watching over Partisan's place with Stang. Dante and Constantine are running supplies with Rogue Moon and Bridgette, and Iylothien's covering our background information and cover stories as need arises for any of us, as well as monitoring for signs of Kelly. Any last questions?"*

There were no questions that they hadn't already covered several times, so the group acquiesced to the silence of non-response. Thirteen minutes later, the commuter slowed to a halt and released the job candidates to their first exposure of the Apex Premier corporate culture.

The moment they stepped off the commuter, the stark contrast between the Witch City depravity and the commercial affluence of the Apex Premier corporate plaza hit them like floodlights on roaches with an intensity that struck several members of the Pride with cultural vertigo. An animated twenty-foot-high billboard of the supermodel Lyn, blue eyes popping against the fiery auburn of her hair, greeted them to Apex Premier and encouraged the women to try the latest cosmetic line that would make their skin healthier and more beautiful.

BILLBOARD IMAGE FADES INTO A SERIES OF YOUNG ATTRACTIVE WOMEN SMILING IN THE WORKPLACE, GIVING EACH OTHER APPROVING NODS AND COMPLIMENTING EACH OTHER. VOICEOVER: "Women have come a long way since the misogynist stone age of 2000."

ENTER WOMAN IN OUT OF FASHION CLOTHING, SHARING THE NEWS WITH HER COWORKERS THAT SHE'S PREGNANT. THE OTHERS POLITELY SMILE AND EXCHANGE KNOWING GLANCES... "Your corporation has invested a lot in you."

MANAGER ENTERS THE ROOM AND SERVES NOTICE THE PREGNANT WOMAN IS TERMINATED FROM HER POSITION. "Don't let career distractions stand in the way of your success. Remember: what's best for your company is best for you."

That was followed by a "Welcome to Apex Premier" presentation, where a smartly dressed woman guaranteed a promising career that would be the best fit for both them and their prospective employers. "After all," the woman concluded, "what's best for your company is best for *you*."

The two rockers simultaneously shouted a resounding "YES!" as though the lucrative success projected by every billboard, poster, and shop window was already theirs, the hypnosis of the sheer volume of ads and promised comforts dulling the senses and contorting the sense of reality.

"This isn't a corporate plaza," Melissana observed, "it's a theme park!"

- "And just as fake," Jack warned under his breath. "Remember, this is the system that created Mama Solace. We need to stay focused on why we're here."

… …

"Greetings everyone! My name is Vanessa Browning, and I welcome you to Apex Premier Corporate Placement Services!" She was a trim 5' 7", dressed in the latest business fashion that announced she enjoyed the stylish success Apex Premier offered. She talked succinctly, but the practiced pleasantness in her voice diffused the effect of hurrying the group along.

"Now I know most of you are new to Wichita as well as new to Apex Premier, so I just want to remind us all of Apex's commitment to—well, to you." She beamed her happy smile at them, but Trigget and the more experienced CYBER members saw something else in her eyes; whether the something else was ambition, or impatience, or maybe even boredom with her job, they couldn't quite make out. "Okay, so I've been doing all the talking so far. Why don't you each introduce yourselves to our little group before we go on? Ms. Smythe, I see you're joining Apex Premier directly. How wonderful!" she again smiled to Josanne. "Well, we believe Apex Premier is the leader in Biological Asset placement, so why don't you go first?"

"Hi, I'm Jane Margarete Smythe, but I prefer J.M.," Trigget addressed the group. "I'm a biological assets researcher/administrative assistant and will be working for Berkleigh Minova." Vanessa arched her eyebrows in newfound respect, subconsciously straightening her skirt. Berkleigh Minova was one of the Apex rising stars; maybe Vanessa could latch onto this newcomer and fast-track herself along a new promotion path. Josanne glanced to Vanessa, who again flashed her professionally friendly smile.

"Director Minova? That's quite impressive!" Vanessa encouraged. "You must be quite skilled if they hired you from outside to work with her."

"Well," Josanne/JM replied, "I'm good with people and seem to have a knack for reading them." Vanessa smiled again, her friendliest one yet. "Hey! Maybe we can get together once you get settled in. I know some of the best restaurants in town."

"That sounds great," Josanne replied, "but I'll need to brush up on local policies first. Anything else?"

"No, that's great," Vanessa responded. "Mr. Sebastian, why don't you go next?"

"John, ma'am. John Sebastian, from Kellogg, Michigan. I'm in Process Control—or well, I was. To summarize: I met a gate guard when I first came into Wichita who didn't think I had what it took to make it into Air Dynamix. I guess, now, that the gate guard was right. I've been on a downhill spiral since I came into Wichita, but I tried to make it on my own. The violence over the last couple weeks scared me, so I'm reaching out to Apex Premier for some help."

"Well, we're glad you did, Mr. Sebastian. You have an impressive resume," she beamed, but Josanne saw a sideways glance to her to see if the person working for Director Minova caught what a great job she did. "We're confident we will place you in your best possible fit." Turning to Queen Vixenn, now dressed in a sharp black business skirt with a purple V-collar that extended to her lower ears.

"Meredith Bertenelli," Melissana greeted. "I work IT network support—at least I did until my former company downsized me. I got fed up and headed west to start a new life, but it's been rough. I'm hoping Apex will help me get connected in the new town."

"Yes, well I can see from your resume that you're highly qualified, and you certainly have a good eye for culture. I'm sure you'll do fine. And how about you, Cynthia?"

"I'm Cynthia Jacobs, legal secretary for hire," Lady Blackwolf announced. "I'm new to the market, but I was told I had a knack for business law and should move in that direction if I get a chance."

"Oh, well we can get you started on your way, but legal and paralegal are hard to break into right off the bat. Who provided your recommendation?"

Susan smiled to herself, knowing that of all the credential checks, hers would be the most solid; the weight of an international corporate conglomerate was the Titanium Card. "Jamie Whitmore, personal friend and legal advisor to Justin Martinez, Director of Research at FoodTech I.C.C."

"Well, I'm sure we can accelerate you into the right path after passing the basic aptitude tests and your references check out."

The introductions continued through all twenty-seven people in the room. The last two left were an average-sized man with oddly piercing eyes and the musclebound, crew-cut guy sitting in the back. She had saved them both for last. "Well, that's almost everyone," she congratulated. "Our last two are both teachers. They already have positions awaiting them, but they're here for the basic introduction and orientation Air Dynamix provides to all of its employees."

"That is correct," Jack stated. "I am Jackson Johnson, history teacher, brought on to replace a former middle school teacher who has suddenly fallen ill." Susan was tempted to add, "*Yeah, just as Meredith Bertenelli here dropped him when she caught him in the room with those two girls,*" but checked the impulse.

"Well Mr. Johnson," she professionally crooned, "with your name, I'd say you were born for the role."

"Yes, that's correct," he smiled. "Why, as a child, I was always fascinated by my names. I guess my parents instilled the love of heritage within me from my earliest days."

"Yes, it appears so," she return-smiled. "And last but certainly not least, tell us who you are, sir," she said as she turned her attention to Chrome.

"My name is James Campbell," he announced as he stifled a brief cough. "I'm a junior high school gym teacher, assigned to the same school as Mr. Johnson here." And with a glance to Jack, he added, "A mind filled with facts is no good if it's housed in a sickly body." Melissana was tempted to add, "*Yeah, like the one Cynthia Jacobs gave to your last gym teacher when she caught him in the room at the Palatia,*" but checked the impulse.

"That is true, sir," Jack replied, "but it wasn't brute force that saved our planet from destruction when the blight ruined the crops two years in a row."

… …

In the team meeting two days earlier, almost the entire CYBER team laughed when Jack and Araña had assigned the various background cover stories. Of all of them, Josanne's training would best counteract Apex's own personality manipulation and psychology training so she could unravel why Apex bought girls off the street. Johnny, Susan, and Melissana would conduct their own investigations by infiltrating the ranks of cubicle workers, administrative assistants, and technical staff; Melissana would serve double duty by learning all she could about the Air Dynamix network and any potential off-grid systems. Jack, the epitome of a walking history book, and Chrome, the epitome of the middle school gym teacher from hell, were to discover why and how Air Dynamix was dumping kids into the Witch City streets.

… …

"Okay," Vanessa broke in trying to keep the disagreement to a minimum. "Now that we've all introduced ourselves, allow me to play a short introduction to Apex Premier." She dimmed the lights, and the Apex video began…

---- *HAPPY CONTENTED OFFICE EMPLOYEES PERFORM VARIOUS TASKS: TYPING, POINTING OUT SOMETHING TO ANOTHER COWORKER; CUT TO A FRIENDLY SECURITY TEAM CHECKING WEAPONS AND GEARING UP TO PERFORM A SECURITY WALKTHROUGH* ---- "At Apex Premier," the orientation video voiceover explained, "our motto is 'All about your corporation, all about you.'

---- *HAPPY COWORKERS LOOK AT EACH OTHER AND CHEERILY ACKNOWLEDGE THE END OF THEIR FULFILLING SHIFT* ---- "We know there's more to balancing your life and career than satisfying management, and more to you than your position description."

----- *A FEMALE EMPLOYEE IS APPLAUDED AT A PROMOTION CEREMONY* ---- "Your career and life management never stops advancing—and neither should *you*."

-----*DISTINGUISHED 40-SOMETHING MALE IN SUIT LOOKS CONCERNED, TRYING TO OVERCOME A DIFFICULT TASK* ----- "Spanning the globe, Apex Premier enables and inspires the highest summit of *your* human and economic possibility. However, reaching your potential requires savvy supervisors and leaders with the necessary knowledge and know-how. Our Apex

Premier family fills this gap. We're known for our ability to develop healthy career/life balance that will ultimately elevate *your* career."

---- *SERIES OF CHARTS, GRAPHS, AND TESTIMONIALS, ENDING WITH THE APEX PREMIER LOGO* ---- "Nobody does this better than we do. From education and certification to benchmarking and best practices, Apex Premier not only sets the industry standard for your highest levels of success, but we are the *peak* of it."

---- *SERIES OF SPLIT-SCREEN AND OVERLAPPING VIDEOS SHOWING HAPPY EMPLOYEES IN A WIDE VARIETY OF PROFESSIONS AND CAREERS, BOTH ON AND OFF THE JOB* ---- "We look forward to partnering with *you* in transforming *your* career in the way *you* do business. We drive *your* growth to make *you* an integral component of how *your* company reaches global customers. Your career/life balance track can appear complex, but we are here to make it simple. As *you* develop in your corporate role, your corporate role improves your corporation, which allows it the buying power to pass on those benefits to *you*."

---- *HAPPY PEOPLE SHOPPING* ---- "Together with your team family members, partners, and customers, we are united with *you* to maximize your corporation's success. After all, what benefits your corporation, benefits *you*.

---- *END SHOT: APEX CORPORATE LOGO FILLS SCREEN* ---- "Apex Premier: All about your corporation, all about *you*."

---- *FADE LOGO AND END* ----

"Okay," Vanessa cheerily resumed after the video ended. "We're going to take a break. When we return, we'll begin our Apex Premier 'TradeMark' skill assessment exam battery. The battery will take the rest of the day, up to 8 PM this evening for some of us. Once the assessments are complete, you will be taken back to the corporate grounds entry where we picked you up, and you'll be free to go home and await your next contact. Apex will match the result sets of those seeking placement with corporate needs to determine your best future. For those of you who have already been placed, your parent corporations will contact you about your next steps.

"OK then," she concluded, casting an especially friendly smile towards Josanne. "Let's take fifteen."

34. Orientations and Life Options

"I'm Charles Vandenberg. Welcome to your new home, Mr. Sebastian," greeted the low-level manager. He reached out for the traditional handshake, but Johnny saw the telltale signs of overworked fatigue behind the forcedly wide smile. His supervisor would be all too glad for the extra help even if he hadn't been aware of the new position procurement. New full-time employee slots were rare, and Charles knew enough about management not to look a gift horse in the mouth. "We're going to give you a couple days to learn the lay of the land and get up to speed, but we're already a pretty busy team, and right now, we're gearing for another project launch."

"Sounds very exciting, sir," Johnny responded. "I'm looking forward to the challenge."

"Glad to hear it," Vandenberg practically grunted. "Because when it hits, the schedule is going to be aggressive. You married?"

"Yes—no sir," Johnny replied with a sullen shake of his lowered head. "That is, I was, but my wife left me when I got downsized. Last I knew, she was dating my former supervisor."

"Ouch, that's tough—no wonder you had such an attitude with the gate sentry when you came in. Oh, don't be surprised," Vandenberg half-chuckled when he saw the expression on John Sebastian's face. "Air Dynamix is a top-of-the-line aircraft design and manufacturing ICC. We have security cameras on the gates at all times; naturally, we accessed your corresponding footage when your name came up for a new hire from out of town."

"Really?" Johnny asked, trying to stay in character. "In that case, and I hope it's okay to say this, but I hope it'd be okay if I drove through again just to show him I actually landed this job."

"You know, Sebastian, I think I'm going to like you!" Vandenberg cracked a grin that showed mirth for real this time. "Please, call me Charles." He smiled again, but responded, "But I'm afraid that can't happen. You see, a couple weeks ago when the fighting outside first started, he was temporarily assigned to night duty on the wall and dismissed a few nights later after he was found passed out cold and, shall we say, somewhat out of uniform."

"You don't say!" Johnny exclaimed as he stifled the urge to overtly shift in his seat, recalling the night he and "Bahar" let Chrome and Spider into the city.

"Yeah, tough break for him, right? Anyway, like I was saying, the shifts are going to be long, and you won't have a chance to meet anyone outside of your coworkers for a while. Now, over-fraternization in the workplace is discouraged, and as you'd expect, Air Dynamics has zero tolerance for unwelcome advances. The women working in this building signed up for their careers, not to start families, and I won't have the extraneous drama that inevitably comes along with workplace relationships. Are we clear?"

"Crystal, sir," Johnny again replied, unsure what Charles was leading up to.

"Good," Charles affirmed, "and according to your Apex transcript, you're already aware of the availability of 'companionship' outside the corporate grounds, as well as the inherent risks of said activities. Fortunately, our ICC is equally aware of the inevitable effects of all work and no play. In fact, we have a truly unique health care arrangement with Apex, the biological assets placement agency that provided your services. Based on this conversation, I think you should check out their Premier Life Plan options when you're reviewing your health insurance paperwork tonight. My wife and I were married before the options were available, but with both of our careers, we still took the maid service when the plan became available. They also have more, shall we say, elaborate plans that match subscribed assets to young men and women who *did* sign up to start families. Maybe you should check them out."

"You don't say," Johnny repeated.

… …

"So, what do you think? Did you check out the Life Options plans yet?" Susan's fellow administrative assistant, Payce, had invited her to lunch. Now that they were eating, Payce asked in a conspiratorial tone. "Aren't they the best?"

"I haven't gone through all of them yet," Susan replied in between stabs at her algae salad, not having to worry about her facial expression betraying her doubts. "It all seems kind of weird to me. I mean, Jerry and I just got married a year ago, and I guess I was hoping we would raise kids together."

"Oh, come on," Payce chided. "You really aren't from around here, are you? Listen," she said as she poured a simulated white sauce over her simulated chicken, "the company has provided you this tremendous opportunity, along with a great salary, opportunities for advancement, and benefits—including the one-of-a-kind Apex Premier Life Options plans. The corporation expects a certain level of commitment in return. You can't just throw all that away for a couple career distractions. You better get on board soon, honey, or you'll be passed over for promotions and have other benefits taken away. And let me tell you, it's pretty hard to maintain career fashion when they cut your pay.

"Besides," she continued, again in that conspiratorial tone, "it can be a *lot* of fun." she added a wink to the line, presumably in case Susan hadn't caught the obvious meaning Payce had implied.

"Did you pick one?" Susan asked her coworker in sudden realization; Payce non-rewarded her with another wink. "Did you pick the home cleaning services?" Susan repeated.

"Oh no," Payce smiled. "Nothing but the best for your Payce, my dear," she practically crooned. "I started off with the Options Plan 1 but, after about a year, I went all the way in and upgraded to the Option 3B, or the 'Butler Plus,' as they say. It's expensive, but oh honey, definitely worth it, and no emotional distractions to get in the way of my career."

"And what about your 'butler'?" Susan asked, surprised at what Payce described so nonchalantly.

"Him? Who cares?" She paused briefly to wipe her mouth. "I have my career to think about and my manager to please, and my butler has his." Payce concluded the conversation with a lewd smile and reached for more salad dressing.

… …

"Hey there," the youngish-looking man called over to her in greeting. "You must be Meredith Bertenelli!" he said as he smiled just a little awkwardly. "I'm really excited to see you—that is, I mean, we're really glad you're here, umm, you know, to help us out."

She almost rolled her eyes—Queen Vixenn could run social rings around this guy, but Meredith Bertenelli was here to make friends, so she matched his awkwardness with a shy smile and averted her eyes to the floor instead.

- *"Wow," Melissana subvocalized, "how stereotypical can you get? A geeky tech guy?"*

- *"Well, try not to fall for him too hard," Iylothien warned.*

- *"He hasn't bowed yet," she reassured with a secret smile.*

- *"Not yet, but when he does, just remember, he can't ride a giant locust."*

- "And I'd be stranded in this role if you don't fill in the knowledge gaps," she affirmed. "I picked up what I did in the streets, but most of this stuff is way beyond me."

- "And that, my Queen, is why I am here."

- "I am most grateful, my humble Bard."

"Ms. Bertenelli?" the young man asked again. "Are you okay?"

"Oh yes, I'm fine—just getting adjusted to the new settings. Where I worked before, the floor pattern was very different.

"But yes, hello, I'm Meredith Bertenelli," she said, half reaching out her hand for a greeting. "And you must be …"

"Brant Stomwell," he finished for her. "I've been designated as your lead while you're getting accustomed to your new digs."

"Cool," she said, still looking around. "So, tell me, Brant, what exactly will I be doing?"

"Well, let's just say that if Air Dynamix was an early 20th century luxury cruise ship, our team would be the guys in the engine room shoveling the coal into the furnaces. But for now you'll have the pretty typical new start. Take a couple days to get yourself oriented, read up on the system architecture docs and I&P's, the usual. Here's your login and password—you'll get your elevated accounts once you get settled in and the clearances catch up. In the meantime, I sent you an email with several links regarding our team, current objectives, and 'state of the network' analysis. Once you've gone through them, just take a couple days to go through some online training, new employee orientation, and sign up for your health benefits and the rest of that stuff."

So much for this guy being a pushover!' she thought. "Hey, about the benefits. Can I ask you a question, if you don't mind? I'm just curious," 'Meredith' asked.

"Sure thing, go ahead," Brant encouraged.

"At Apex, this woman said we'd have some 'Life Options' choices. What are they about? From the way she started to describe it, they sound like some crazy packages." The sudden dryness in both the content and tone of his answer surprised her.

"Life Options? Don't worry about them. They're kind of pricey for us techies. I don't think we're quite high enough in the pay scale to really qualify for those. Besides, from what I hear, they're not worth it. I don't think anything could be more frustrating than not being able to share the most basic details of your workday without having to dumb it so far down you'd have to take off your socks for them to see what you meant.

"Why do you ask? Don't tell me you're into puppets," he said in near disdain.

"Puppets? I'm sorry, I don't know what you mean. I was just curious about the plans because I haven't seen anything like 'Life Options' in any of my packets."

- "Iylo, what does he mean about puppets?" she asked as soon as she broke away from Brant.

- "I'm not sure yet," he replied, "but it sure sounds creepy. Maybe the others will know when we compare notes."

… …

"Ms. Jane Margaret Smythe?" the woman asked Josanne as she entered the office and found her desk.

The woman was 5'6", stout, and dressed in a traditional black knee-length skirt, white ruffled blouse, and black loafers. Her hair, cropped at shoulder length and, except for scattered silvery flecks just a shade lighter than her skirt, even further enhanced her all-business demeanor. "I am Director Minova. Please come in and sit down," the director beckoned, her curtness indicating it was a summons and not a greeting. "Yes, close the door behind you, thank you," Josanne took her cue and obediently sat in the indicated seat. A short pause ensued, but Josanne waited, allowing her superior to go first.

"I will be blunt; I am the on-site Director of Biological Assets for Apex Premier. Before you begin to say you know this already, I will explain why I am emphasizing this because I do not wish to explain it a second time.

"I was not always a Director, but I have worked hard and sacrificed much to become one. I expect my staff to work just as hard and, if need be, sacrifice just as much as I did to keep me here. Apex Premier has rewarded your past efforts and sacrifices and provided you this career opportunity. Let me be clear that along with the opportunity, Apex Premier expects a certain level of commitment in return. In particular, career distractions are not permitted. Are we clear?"

"Yes, ma'am," Jane Margaret Smythe replied.

"I have already told you how I wish to be addressed," was the stern reply.

"Yes, Director Minova," Jane Margaret Smythe corrected herself.

"Very well," Director Minova continued. "Before you can properly represent me, you need to know a little more about who we are. You know, for instance, that Apex Premier is the premier biological assets placement company in what remains of this continent. We hold this position due to our unwavering commitment to do whatever it takes for our partner corporations, including what some might call bleeding edge placement programs that are customizable to our clients' various needs. Yesterday in the initial in-processing, you saw the welcome video. Only the most naive biological asset professional would expect that to be the real aims and goals of our company, but we do keep the real one—the one we present to our prospective client corporations—to a fairly select few. As my executive assistant, you need to familiarize yourself with the true statement. You and I will review its contents together; I do not believe in wasting time, so if there are any noticeable disagreements, I will send you on your way and find a replacement. It is in front of you—please read."

Josanne opened the binder to the mission statement and read:

> "At Apex Premier, we know that there's more to biological assets than management, more to performance than process, and more to your corporation's biological assets than position descriptions.
>
> "Biological Assets management never stops advancing—and neither should professionals or their organizations. Around the world, biological asset management both enables and inspires human and economic possibility for the corporations they serve. However, to reach their potential corporations like yours require savvy operators, supervisors, and leaders with the necessary knowledge and know-how.
>
> "Apex Asset Management fills this gap. We're known for our ability to develop biological asset talent and elevate end-to-end performance. Nobody does this better than we do. From education and certification to benchmarking and best practices, Apex Premier not only sets the industry standard, we are the peak of it.
>
> "We are essential partners in transforming the way people do business, drive growth, and reach global customers. The process can appear complex, but we are here to make it simple. We develop your biological assets, they improve in their corporate roles, their corporate roles improve your company, and the

whole world economy benefits. Together with our members, partners, and customers, we are united in our commitment to global biological asset excellence, innovation, and resilience—achieved one asset properly placed into one role at a time."

"Now, Ms. Smythe, can you tell me the primary difference between the version you saw yesterday and what you have just read?"

"The thematic difference I just read is that yesterday's version was all about self-actualization, tailored to the prospective candidate, while this version shows we're actually just plugging people into whatever roles the corporation needs."

"That is correct, Ms. Smythe. And why is that?"

"Because you are planting in the peoples' heads that they are where they want to be, as though their individual assessments and personalities make them the best candidates for the positions. They'll work harder and be more patient or endure difficult situations as a result. The corporations don't need to know this, of course, although I would venture that Apex is actually very up front about this to potential client executives—it sweetens the deal for them to know how far Apex will go for the prospect corporation."

"Very astute, Ms. Smythe, you are correct. I have only two questions left for you. Think carefully before you answer:" Director Minova leaned in to scrutinize Smythe's every micro-tell, the gaze so intense that Josanne/Smythe felt as though she was matching wits against a hostile conversationalist. Indeed, that was why she had been assigned to this particular role. Director Minova locked eyes with Josanne and completed her question. "First, are you okay with the Apex Premier approach to how we do business?"

But Josanne was a CYBER-trained and enhanced conversationalist. She paused for two seconds as she looked away to simulate a trans-derivational search, then looked Director

Minova square in the eyes and replied a thoughtful but firm, "Yes." In response, Director Minova somewhat visibly thawed before Josanne's eyes.

"Last question: You had your orientation yesterday. Tell me about the staff member who provided that training."

"Well, her name was Vanessa Browning. She was sharp, very polite, well-dressed, knowledgeable, and was the picture of someone genuinely interested in meeting the needs of the clients."

"Anything else?" the Director probed.

Josanne inwardly sighed. "She became decidedly chummier once she learned I was assigned to you."

"Good," Director Minova said with a smile. "You have passed the initial test. Welcome to Apex, J.M. For me to do what I need to do for Apex, I cannot have an assistant who is not 100% on board, nor can I afford a blind fool caught up in the naivety of false friendships who would compromise our corporate goals for a night on the town or some such.

"I see you're a little surprised by this," the Director continued. "Don't be—In fact, you should be somewhat used to this by now, as I'm sure we're not the only bio asset corporation selling the ideal workplace. In fact, we have it easy compared to those teachers that came in with you yesterday," she said as she lit a cigarette. The cigarette's odor reminded Josanne of Mama Solace.

"The teachers?" she asked, "I'm afraid I don't know what you mean."

Director Minova blew a near-perfect smoke ring before she continued. "Welcome to the upper tier, kid—you are now officially 'in the know.' I told you we were bleeding edge, right? The teachers are part of it. Education is just a secondary role of the teachers. Their primary function is actually quite different."

"What will happen to Ms. Browning?" Josanne asked, slightly unnerved and trying to change the subject.

"Got a soft spot for her?" Minova smiled again. "Don't worry. In short, nothing will happen to her. We've had our eye on her for some time, and had hopes for her eventually working her way up. As of now, though, absolutely nothing—at all—will happen to her. She will not be fired, but neither will she promote, transfer to a different location, nor transfer to a different job here. She will be kept in limbo, her career frozen, for two years. You, of course, will not say a thing to her about this."

"I don't understand," Josanne admitted. "Is this because she tried to curry favor to move up the ladder?"

"Nothing of the sort, J.M.," Director Minova replied in mildly amused surprise. "We all curry favor and nurture relationships to move up. I've done it myself, countless times; that's no problem at all. But at this level, we need people with a sense of discretion. She's not in a career freeze because she tried to curry up the ladder," the director stated with a sense of finality, "she's in a freeze because you could tell."

… …

"James Campbell and Jackson Johnson, I am Administrator Montag. Welcome to Air Dynamix Junior High—Home of the Corsairs! That's our junior battle hockey team, by the way." He crossed back over behind his desk, and with an arm wave gesture for them to join him, he sat down.

"I want to thank you for joining us on such short notice," he resumed, "and I think it only right to let you know before your first classes just what our true expectations for you are. You see," he said leaning over to cup his hands and rest his forearms on his desk, "At Air Dynamix, we are taking education to the next level.

"Think back to when you were going to school. What was the number one complaint you heard from kids once they started going beyond the merest of basics?" He smiled and answered his own question. "How about, 'we're never going to use this!' Remember that one? Especially with any math beyond basic multiplication and division. And you know what? For many of them, they were right—

especially once smartphones came on the scene. All many of them needed to know was how to push buttons. Even on their jobs, as long as they had electronics, they didn't need to think for themselves.

"And what was the number one complaint of the parents? Equally thoughtless but equally true, 'Schools are more about getting kids to pass standardized exams than they are about teaching their kids how to function in real-world society.' Of course, we had to teach in accordance with our certifying bodies—well, until the bottom dropped out, anyway.

"But no more!" he beamed. "Air Dynamix has partnered with Apex Premier to produce the true school of tomorrow. And as Air Dynamix faculty, the two of you are vital components of that process. You see, by teaching the Apex Life Options curricula at Air Dynamix, you will, on a day by day basis, literally shape the upcoming generations like your predecessors could only dream of."

"I'm sorry sir," Jack interrupted. "Teachers have always inspired young minds by piquing their curiosities, setting forth opportunity-rich environments for learning, and engaging the students where they were at while encouraging them to reach for more. What is so different here?"

"And did you say 'Life Options?' I thought that was a health care selection platform," Chrome asked.

"Yes it is, Mr. Campbell. But it is applied somewhat differently in the academic arena. You see, with the Apex evidence-based Life Options program, we can be far more proactive than we've ever been able to be in the past. Your roles have just grown way beyond merely answering student questions and making them do homework to pass some standardized test. You will literally prepare them for their futures.

"Imagine a student's relief that upon graduation they will already have a job waiting for them. A job they have been training their whole lives to be able to do. No post-graduation unemployment. Just as soon as they get out of school, they will have a job ready for them."

"That sounds nice, Mr. Montag, but that's impossible. There will always be a number of kids going into a profession they think they'll like that has good opportunities, and the ones who don't make the cut will move on to something else. History proves that there are always employment gluts and scarcities," Jack wondered aloud.

"And you are absolutely correct, Mr. Johnson; in fact, I could not agree with you more. History proves that as long as the students rely on guessing what they want to be when they grow up, there will be gluts and scarcities. Is that good for the corporation? Of course not. Key positions are left unfilled while less important but perhaps more gainful employment opportunities are oversaturated. And if we would admit it, it's not good for the students either, is it? They go from graduated to unemployed in the space of three heartbeats." He leaned back into his chair and smiled. "Again, I couldn't agree with your observation more. By letting the students and their families try to get the education they wanted, we have denied them the education we, and they, needed.

"But the future is not history, is it, Mr. Johnson? Our unique partnership with Apex Premier allows us to flip our educational history over on its heels by forging a bold new approach to education. Have you seen your student pads yet? Look at the data we have collected for each student, from pre-birth. By the time they hit kindergarten, we have a genetic analysis of what job or career families they would be best suited for. Once they get into school, the data grows exponentially. By the time he or she hits fifth grade, we have a pretty good idea of their future aptitudes.

"At the same time, we have corporate analyses that run on a daily basis, extrapolating what our needs will be by the time that crop of students graduates. The results of these two distinct datasets are merged and analyzed, and we assign the students to their career tracks most often by the time they enter sixth grade. Once that happens, the age-based classes are still maintained, but the lessons are tailored to their future jobs the system has designated. Once that happens, the teacher's primary role is to motivate and encourage the students to accept their roles, instilling in them a sense of purpose in their work so they will be productive. Remember, what benefits the corporation benefits them. But even more so, the corporation is funding the education; surely you understand that it must see appropriate return on its investments.

"So what you're telling us," Jack cut in, more annoyed with every word Montag spewed forth, "is that the purpose of the school system is not to encourage the students to discover and pursue what interests them, but to assign them some corporate career and spend the rest of the time training them for that role?"

"Precisely!" Montag confirmed. "But it's not all as negative as you seem to be making it. The science and math behind it all is very real. We save the kids a lot of time trying to—what was the old phrase, 'discover themselves?' Plus, the placement system takes into account the natural gifts and talents of each student, only the results are tailored to the needs of the company to ensure there are no gaps in either the student employment or company vacancies."

"I'm still not sure I'm very comfortable with this, Mr. Montag," Jack replied with a sigh he could not contain.

"Really, Mr. Johnson, you are a *history* teacher," he said, pursing his lips in annoyance. "Surely you of all people must recognize this is as nothing more than a simple corporate continuation of the revisionist social programming begun in the early part of this century by the governments, which grew more and more politicized and less and less truly educational with each passing year. Let me ask you this: is it 'fair' to have a young man with no architectural aptitude struggle for months or even years trying to make it in a career he will not be successful in? Wouldn't he really be happier if he was productive during those years as, say, an engine mechanic? The same with young girls. So many were raised thinking they would be best at home raising children or taking care of their families. What a waste! They could be working, contributing to the corporation's bottom line, seizing every opportunity to grow and become the young women the corporation has enabled them to become!

"Take my word for it—and over the next day or so, to satisfy your concerns, review the data on the students you have, and see if their perspective careers aren't a perfect match for them. If you disagree, then as their primary observer, you are to record your notes for potential re-evaluation. But I will offer you a word of advice. Your recommendations will also be reviewed for overall consistency with the placement system as part of our feedback on your own performance. In other words, if your findings are, shall we say, consistently anomalous, you will find your own position here in jeopardy."

"Yes sir," Chrome acknowledged, "that's pretty clear to me. Lighten up, Johnson, and give this thing a chance. Besides just glancing over these figures, it all seems to be working out so far."

- "Come on, Grey. I know you don't like what they're doing, but it's too early to blow our cover." Chrome subvocalized.

- "Wow Chrome, there's a first—you're reigning me in!"

Mr. Johnson smiled and offered to shake Montag's hand. "I apologize for seeming hesitant. I must admit the newness of this all is a bit overwhelming at first; the program truly is state of the art."

"No sir, Mr. Johnson," Montag replied with a smug smile. "It's state of the *science.*"

- "Academian nut," Chrome muttered as the two headed out the door.

. . . . . .

After a round of lunchtime introductions to the other faculty, Montag's administrative assistant rather curtly issued each of them a pre-prepared lesson plan schedule and a computerized matrix used to track and update the progress of the kids they would be teaching. She also handed Preach a paper folder of hand-written notes the last teacher had not yet entered into the system, and after pointing Chrome to the gym, she then somewhat disinterestedly led him to his classroom. He had graduated school back when they still had been run by the government, but he thought the corporate schools would have at least matched the quality of the institutions they had replaced.

"Good afternoon, kids," Preach greeted as his incoming class filtered into the classroom. The system may have already written them off, but he would do his best to give them some decency while he was here. "My name is Mr. Johnson—and yes, it's a last name, not a street handle or alias," he added, drawing a mixed collection of brief chuckles and eye rolls.

"This guy's a joke," Jack heard one of the boys say to another who sat next to him. "I bet he won't last a week."

"He'll last longer than you," came his friend's reply. Jack thought it somewhat odd, but the reaction piqued his interest.

"Shut up, you moron—that's not funny!" the first boy half whispered, but Jack noticed the kid suddenly grew tense to the point of sweating a little. "Besides, I made it this far, right?" Jack made a mental note to check with the kids what that had been about, but he wanted to engage the classroom.

"Today we're covering from 2025 through the 2030's, also known as "The Third Dark Age," an intensely volatile period of history that we are still attempting to recover from. We will also cover Air Dynamix's role in overcoming several of the crises which resulted from this very recent period of history. But, since I'm a substitute on my first day here, I'm going to give you most of the class today to read up on it before we plunge into our discussions tomorrow." The truth was that after the morning meeting with the school administrator, Jack wasn't in the mood to spin history for Air Dynamix, and the more he watched his students work to learn what their ebooks touted, the more he despised the morning's discussion.

35. Developments

"Hey Brant, can you come here a minute?" Melissana/Meredith asked her lead, "I have a question."

"Another one?" he replied. "I'm somehow not surprised. You know, when I told you to learn everything you could about our network, I didn't think you would take me so literally. Do you even go home?"

"Hey, this is my home," she returned. "After all, the company has offered me this opportunity, so…"

"You know, I'm warning you," he cut in. "If you actually finish that line, I'm going to make you submit to a battery of capcha tests to prove to me you're not a robot."

"Such a primitive term," she bemusedly scolded. "I'm a replicant."

"Too bad," he replied. "I was kind of thinking you should stick around more than four years." He almost sheepishly smiled, then returned to the focus of the conversation. "So, it's been three days. What questions do you have left?"

"Well, I was checking out the network analysis diagrams, and I found something that's pretty odd." She swiveled her monitor out to show him a list of their documented logical server drives overlaid onto a graphic of their physical servers. He raised his eyebrows but nodded his approval.

"Meredith, this is excellent work—it's like you've been working here a lifetime!"

"Well, I have this ghost in my head who helps me out a lot," she half quipped. Three thousand miles away, Iylothien mentally smiled and bowed.

"But this is puzzling," she continued. "You see these? There are three entire blades of hardware on our network that aren't used for, well, not for anything Air Dynamix seems to use them for. They're not backups; there's nothing in any business plans I've seen that have alluded to expansion into these areas, nothing. Yet there are a handful of overnight processes that run against those addresses. Outside of the job names, I have no visibility into the area, even with my elevated permissions." She turned away from the monitor to look at him directly. "So it looks like we have a very large hole in the server space and data. I'd say it's just technical debt in the documentation we need to update, but based on the rest of the system documentation, this looks deliberately dark, like a ghost drive."

"I see what you're saying." Brant furrowed his eyebrows as he further examined her discovery. "Except it's more of a ghost farm than just one drive."

"Maybe we should call CST, just in case it's hostile," she mentioned.

"You want us to call the Cyber Security Team, the internal affairs division of IT? Typically they'd call us, but go ahead; I'm not about to be remembered as the guy who said *don't* call them. Just remember something before you do," he added.

"What's that?"

"They are very afraid of ghosts."

"You mean the ghost drives? That's why we should call them."

"I meant that ghost in your head who helps you figure out the network this fast. When you call them, you're going to put yourself on their investigative radar, and they'll be somewhat indignant that you found this issue before they did."

"Yeah, but we're all on the same team, right?" Meredith asked, then she sighed. "Actually, I've seen it before. Yeah, we're all on the same team, but we all sure like to be the ones getting noticed by the sponsors."

"Tell you what," he offered. "I'll make the call and tell them we stumbled onto it as part of a team exercise in documenting the system.

"So you can steal the credit?" She meant it as a joke, but she could see he was wounded by the comment.

"Nothing of the sort. You'll see—believe me." He smiled wistfully as he looked at nothing at all except a memory. "I've had similar go-arounds with CST before; they're used to this kind of stuff coming from me. Still, I would really like to see what those servers are used for," he said more to himself than to her as he turned his attention back to the graphic. He walked over to his own computer and typed several commands, showing more frustration with each press of the ENTER key.

"You don't really think it's hostile, do you?" she guessed.

"No," he admitted after he gave up with a sigh. "My elevated account privileges won't allow me access to the area either, but I'm familiar with the process naming convention." When he looked at her, she could see his open disdain. "They're interface jobs between us and the Apex Premier systems."

… … …

"All right, who's next?" Chrome asked his sixth period gym class. "No volunteers? OK. Winner, I pick you—go on up."

"The other gym teachers always pick us to go first," Max, one of the kids slated for the security program groaned. "It's supposed to instill a sense of confidence in how well the corporation had selected everyone's tracks." A couple of his friends gathered around him to throw in their support. Now puffed with bravado, he decided to raise his claim. "Besides, you picked the slowest kid in the class—he'll never make it."

"You guys don't care about how Dynamix looks," Chrome retorted. "You just want a chance to show off in front of everybody. Next time, volunteer if you want to go first."

"But the rope is so high, Mr. Campbell," Winner complained. "Nobody could climb it all the way up!"

"Nobody?" Chrome smiled at the challenge. "Listen—you've all got names like you're rock stars. 'Winner,' 'Ace,' 'Chief,' 'Max.' Even you girls—'Success,' 'Progress,' 'Sapphire,' and the rest. Now my guess is that your parents gave you those names to inspire you to well, *winning* and *success*. But you're never going to see it if you don't push yourselves once in a while, and by once in a while, I mean pretty much every day." He let that message sink in for a moment. "So nobody can climb that rope? I'll tell you what. I'm going to prove you wrong, this one time. After that, I will demonstrate every single activity I tell you to participate in to show you it can be done. Then I will tell you to do it. And you will. Do you know why?" Nobody answered the rhetorical question, which gave him a chance to put on his sunglasses and once again show off his smile.

"Because if you don't, you will know ahead of time that somebody who can do all of the things you're afraid of doing is going to be on your sorry butts until you leave class—which won't be until I let you go."

"The other teachers won't let you get away with that," one of the Successes taunted.

"Yeah, they will, sister, and do you know why *that* is?" Again the smile. "Because they won't be able to stop me. And before you say it, if you're parents want to complain, they're welcome to, but I think that deep down inside they'll be grateful to me for doing it.

"So that being said…" He paused to deftly climb the twenty foot rope hand over hand, gave the rooftop a love tap that left the metal ceiling slightly dented, and then slid down to land with an only slightly muffled stomp, "Winner, climb the rope."

Winner climbed halfway up before James Campbell told him he could come down. He was winded, but he beamed in satisfaction.

"And *that*, kid, is what we call the feeling of accomplishment. Congratulations, Winner, today you earned your name." Chrome praised. "As for you and your compatriots, Max, since you're so concerned that everyone sees how well the corporation has chosen, you can meet me after school and give a demonstration of your fine physical prowess by running 100 laps. If any of the other students really care about your show, they can come and watch. At the end of each lap, you will stop in front of me and proudly state, 'Sir, the purpose of security is to protect its charges, not charge its protectants. Service is the greatest honor.' Got that? You'd better remember that phrase, because I'm not going to repeat it later. It'll give you time to think about it over the course of the day.

"While we're talking, I'll tell you all one more little tidbit you can take home for free. Now, I don't know my way around this place yet, and there are a lot of things here that are new to me, but I'm pretty good at getting the lay of the land, and I think some of you kids need to hear this. You sure as drek don't want me as an enemy—OK, don't tell your parents I said that," he added with a slight shrug to the amusement of his students. "But I promise you that if you trust me a little and work hard in my class," he removed his sunglasses and made a point to look at each of them, "I can also make one hell of a friend. Are we clear?"

Several heads nodded yes, some smiled, some had an 'uh-oh' look to them, but by the end of the period, every one of them had climbed at least six feet.

… …

----LYNN LOOKS AT THE CAMERA AND SMILES---- "Always remember: when you have dark eye shadow or makeup, use light on your lip color; otherwise you look like Bozo the clown," Lyn advised as part of her latest video ad campaign.

---- VIDEO SHOWS A WOMAN WITH BAD MAKEUP GETTING OUT OF A CAR, SUDDENLY SURROUNDED BY

CIRCUS CLOWNS OVERLAY MADE UP IN MIMICRY OF HER. SHE SCREAMS; THEY MOCK SCREAM AND POINT AT HER, LAUGHING. GOOFY MALE VOICEOVER---- "We get paid to look like this. What's your excuse?"

---- FADE AND CUT----

"Come on," Payce urged Susan. "Let's get over to the mall. There's a new fashion line of clothing coming out, and we want to look our best on the job!"

"Oh, I was just watching Lyn for a while," Susan replied.

"Yes well, she is gorgeous, but I'm sure she's just some stuck-up prima donna who whines whenever she doesn't get her way."

"Her? No way," Susan laughed.

"Oh, like you know her personally?" Payce practically sneered.

"Actually, yes. Well, we met when I was at my last job," Susan tried to recover. Payce wouldn't believe her even if she told her the truth—that she had worked with the supermodel for several months to take down an organized crime cartel in Roanoke. No, it was better just to change the subject.

"Doesn't all this stuff get expensive after a while?" Susan asked, somewhat exasperated.

"What do you think the company pays you for? We have a lifestyle to maintain. Come on, it'll be fun."

More like exhausting, Susan thought, but she kept the complaint to herself. "OK, when do you want to go?" She gave a small hidden wave of farewell to Lyn's projected image, now smiling and advising girls of all ages how to smoothly apply several layers of eye shadow for a special night out.

· · · · · ·

"Administrator Montag," Jack began, "I have a question for you."

"You wish to know about our programs," Montag countered. "Several of the faculty have advised me that you question our methods."

"Not at all," Jack assured, making a mental note of the political climate of the school. "I understand what we're doing for most of the programs, but I am confused by the 'Corporate Liaison' program, or at least the students you're selecting for that program. I must say that I cannot recommend these particular students for the program if I don't understand that program's purpose.

"I talked about it with Campbell, the gym teacher, to see if anyone has talked with him about it, and he didn't understand it, either. We initially thought it was some sort of inter-corporate ambassador team to develop and foster strategic partnerships and alliances. But from what we've observed of the grades and overall performance of students assigned for these paths, neither one of us would have selected those students for this role.

"We also both thought the Liaison role would carry with it a certain sense of honor, but in discussing this with other staff, we've found that the liaison role is much looked down upon—even the students assigned to the maintenance and janitorial staff seemed to have higher status. When we explained what we thought the role was to the other faculty and asked for some clarification, they referred us to you."

"I see," Montag stated with a slight hiss. "Did you talk with any of the students regarding your concerns?"

"Only briefly, on one of my first days here. I mentioned the role and remarked to the selected students how proud they and their parents must be to have been selected for the lofty path they were set on. The other students laughed a little, but the ones I addressed just looked embarrassed. After class, I addressed them separately and apologized for making them uncomfortable."

"And what did the students say when you asked them why they were embarrassed?" Montag questioned.

"They said they weren't supposed to talk about it. I told them that was okay, but I would ask you about it as well." Jack paused to look the director in the eye. "To be honest, their reactions surprised me."

"You seem to get surprised quite often for a history teacher, Mr. Johnson, but humor me. What were their reactions?"

"Most of the girls looked down, one started to visibly shake, and one started crying to herself," Jack said, not bothering to hide the anger he felt growing in him. "Two of the males balled their hands into fists, and one almost took a swing at me." In fact, the youth had taken a swing at Jack. He easily dodged the blow, but he promised the student he would never tell Montag. He was sure the administrator would enact harsh reprisals against the youth. "And one of them commented that, as the school administrator, you interviewed each of them—personally—for the role."

"I have personally reviewed their qualifications, yes," Montag clarified, but the sides of his mouth twisted upwards in a smug smirk that conveyed far more to Jack than the words themselves.

"From what I have learned so far," Jack probed, "the Company Liaisons are the only group you have ever expressed this much interest in." He again looked Montag directly in the eyes. "Why is that?"

"The Corporate Liaisons are a new role, part of the Life Options provider plans we are piloting, and as a new role, the other students might not yet understand its importance. You will find out more once you have passed your probation period—if you pass your probation period. And I must be frank with you, Mr. Johnson; so far I am not overly impressed by your performance. Now I'm a very busy man," Montag snuffed. "I don't have time to interview every student that crosses through our doors, nor do I have time for your incessant questions."

"But you would if you could, wouldn't you?" Jack pressed. "Conduct an 'interview' of every student, that is?" Jack had almost used physical air quotes, but decided that was something the history teacher he was in the role of would never have done that. His intonations made the insinuation clear enough.

"I only wish I had the capability," Montag offered in a vain effort to express how overworked he was.

Jack's eyes saw what he expected was another, darker meaning of what Montag had just said, but he would replay the interview, including the micron-measured pupil and retina adjustments and skin tone fluctuations, in front of Trigget and the rest of the team for confirmation.

The message light was on when Jack returned to his classroom. There had been a breakout of some flu over the last couple days, and a few of his students would be out of class. This time Mr. Johnson was not surprised; all of the affected kids were in the Corporate Liaison program. He tried to follow up with the school nurse, but she looked away and said she had no more information than what he had already been told. On a hunch, he contacted the parents at their home.

His surprise returned. He expected the parents would back up the flu story, or maybe tell him they were transferring their kids to a different school. Instead, without exception, the parents flatly stated they never had any children that had ever attended the school.

... ...

"Meredith, this is Ms. Santone, CIO of Air Dynamix. Please report to the Warhawk Conference Room."

"Yes, ma'am," Melissana replied, wondering what was going on. She had been uneasy on her way up to the conference room, but what she saw when she arrived outright alarmed her. Bloodied, Brant sat at the room's sizable table with Ms. Santone and some guy she didn't recognize. Four armored security troops surrounded her lead. They had obviously already beaten him, but they hit him again as Melissana entered; the blow snapped his head back and caused him to groan.

"What are you doing?" Melissana/Meredith cried out. She tried to rush to him, but the guards held her back.

"Reminding you both of the first lesson of working at Air Dynamix: what is good for the corporation is good for you," Santone coolly replied. "This is Mr. Breverton, Chief Information Security Officer for Air Dynamix." As she made the introduction, the man raised his hand in a dismissive wave. "He understands that lesson very well, and he takes his job very seriously. That is why he called me. He asked how one of my newest hires had documents that identified and outlined a classified network area that was supposed to be off the grid. I set up this meeting looking for a little cooperation, but Mr. Stomwell here was a little less… forthcoming." She nodded, and the security guard hit him again.

"Stop it!" Melissana shouted.

- "Iylo, are you getting any of this?"

- "Alerting the team we have a situation," he replied. "Hang tight, don't lose your cool."

"*I* found the network drives!" she practically growled. "He didn't do anything but report it for me."

"And you actually expect me to believe that a new hire who's been here less than a week found a secret network farm?" Breverton asked.

- "Tell him you looked for what wasn't in the documentation," Iylothien coached.

"He told me to learn the network," she said, almost visibly fuming. "I found it because Stomwell's documentation was so thorough, I noticed a gap in the firewall sequencing," she said without any hint of concealing her anger. "And I searched for the void, because *we* take *our* jobs very seriously," she said through gritted teeth. "We reported this to CST just in case there was something hostile in our system. With all due respect, ma'am, if there's anyone you should slap around in that chair," she added with an incriminating look to the CISO, "it should be whoever set up the somewhat less than invisible secret storage area."

"Well, their stories match," Ms. Santone drily pointed out.

"Yvette," Breverton asserted, "there's still his other issue; besides, I set up that area myself."

"This is not the time to be bragging about that, Gary," she chided. "We'll discuss it over dinner tonight.

"And as for you, Ms. Bertinelli, I remind you that we follow certain protocols; criticizing someone in our management is not tolerated. I will make an exception this one time, as you are new here and have not had time to adjust to our culture. Nevertheless, I have now warned you myself, and I do not expect it to happen again. Am I clear?"

"Yes ma'am," Meredith obediently answered as Melissana internally seethed.

"As for both of you, good work on your discovery. If you could find the area, undoubtedly someone else could have as well." And with that, Santone, Breverton, and the CST hit squad left the room.

"Brant, are you okay?" She asked in her rush to him as soon as the door closed.

"Yeah, I'm gonna be okay," he replied. Emboldened as he basked in the attention that she gave him, he added, "See? I told you it was better for me to report it."

"Yeah, thanks," she replied, then paused. "What was that other issue he mentioned? Sounds like you two have a history."

He pointed to the conference room ceiling projector and mouthed for her to be silent. "He thinks I'm relaying corporation secrets to outside entities," he said out loud. Silently he mouthed the words, "Not here."

. . . . . .

"We got four more incoming tomorrow night," Saint Nick relayed to Sitter, Araña, and Stang. "We're sure. Kung and Tag both got confirmations. They're coming through Gate Five."

"This will be the first drop since we took down Showbiz," Spider mentioned to Partisan. "And we still have quite a few of the girls we're watching here. Now it's your call, but from what I figure, I'm sure there's a lot of locals who figured you're somehow connected to his downing."

"Well, they're not wrong," Partisan acknowledged, "but what's your point?"

"Are you okay making this pickup? Last time we went to your Drop Zone Five it was a setup." Spider knew it wouldn't be a popular thought, but he still had to ask. Partisan tensed at the question.

"Like I suddenly have a choice?" Partisan asked. "I told you when you first got here that there would be repercussions. Well now, here they are. We're a prime target for every pimp left in Witch City—and there are still a lot of pimps left in Witch City. But there are also still kids coming in from topside, and as long as they are, I can't just abandon them any more than I could abandon any of the others before. So, what do you want me to do?"

"I want you to let us help you," Spider evenly replied. "It's the least we can do. I'll stay here with you and some of the other kids, but let me send my guys with your kids when you go pick them up, just in case anyone is waiting for them when they get there. Just to make sure."

Partisan looked away, a dark expression on his face. He clearly didn't entirely like the idea. "Okay," he eventually capitulated, "but on our terms. My kids pick the route and timing. Also, I want your guys on foot—if anything does happen, your guys won't abandon them."

Araña was about to protest on behalf of the team's integrity and explain that the men would provide much better backup if they were in their vehicles, but decided against it. Instead, he simply hailed the CYBER wheelmen.

- "Rick and Hardcore," Spider hailed, "can you come up here a minute? We've got a job for you tonight."

… …

Preach inwardly sighed as he digested Araña's report. The drop and retrieval had gone smoothly, but up until then, the Pride's leader still held onto the hope that maybe he was somehow mistaken. After Spider's narration of the night's events, Jack had relinquished any hope that what he had suspected wasn't true. By the time the photos of the four boys retrieved that night at Drop Zone 5 were transmitted, they weren't needed—Jack had seen them every day in class.

- *"Hey, Spider, you gave me the report on the boys, and I confirm they're my missing students. Were there any females in the group? I'm also missing two girls."*

- *"That's a negative, Preach—just the boys."*

- *"Can you ask them if they know what happened to the girls?"*

- *"Jefe, all I can say is, if you know these kids, maybe it's a good thing you're not here. They're so doped up and crazed they barely know their own names. Without Trigget to diagnose them, I'm guessing some combination of psych drugs, maybe reinforced with some kind of shock treatment."*

- *"Spider," Jack interrupted as he winced and grasped for a wall to support himself, "You're telling me they not only drugged those kids, they electrocuted their brains before dumping them?" He groaned internally, but he couldn't let his grief at the information infect his team. Besides, Spider was probably going through the same emotional tug of war. "You done good in getting to them, Spider—real good. So, tell me, mi hermano, any other good news in all this?"*

- *"They came up negative when I scanned them for implants and trackers, but I have no idea what they did to these kids before throwing them out onto the streets. I wish I knew who our mystery callers were so we could tell them they really saved the lives of these kids. If we weren't there to pick them up, they probably would have been dead—or worse—in a matter of hours."*

- *"Yeah, me too, me too," Jack responded. After taking a moment to consider his next steps, a smile of relief played across his face. "Listen, I have an idea I need to run down. Thanks for the great work. Please relay to Partisan and the others how relieved I am that things went well. Good work all the way around—including you, my friend."*

- *"Hey," Araña replied, "I was trained by the best."*

- *"Darned right you were, my friend," Jack retorted. "Thanks."*

Jack and Spider terminated their conversation, then he got onto his cyberdeck and hailed another friend.

… …

The office retained its opulence, as Jack knew it always would. The rich mahogany and leather furnishings provided the perfect foreground for the two U.S. flags proudly displayed behind them. The figure behind the desk had been facing the back wall, but as Jack entered, the chair swiveled; the sharply dressed man in his mid-forties stood and stretched forth his hand for a virtual shake.

"Mr. Matthews, welcome back!" Simon greeted. "To what do I owe the pleasure? I must admit it is unusual for you to visit without me first inviting you. How are things going in Witch City?"

"Well, that's why I'm here," Jack began. "You see, I need a favor, and I think you're the only one who can pull it off."

Jack reported on the operation's progress while Simon leaned back in his virtual chair, elbows resting on the chair's arms. As Jack relayed his request, Simon interlaced the fingers and raised both hands to contact with his virtual chest, index fingers extended to touch the pursed lips of his mouth as though in contemplation. The gesture caused Jack to briefly pause in a momentary contemplation of his own; in all of their time together, he didn't seem to remember the CYBER Director ever doing that before.

"You've all made good progress, and your request has merit," Simon began. "But you are asking me to trace protected logs of monitored communications of thousands of people over a six-month period to correlate anticipated cross-references with the arrivals of Partisan's children. Even I cannot do that in thirty minutes, Jack. It will take some time."

"How long?" asked Jack. "We need to bring this to a close. Time is running out on Kelly, and now there are three more girls missing."

Simon pursed his lips. "Given that I'll need to share the processing time for this request with several other activities I am currently occupied with, I hope to have some answers for you in approximately six hours and forty-nine minutes." Simon then looked at his watch and added, "If you don't have anything else, I could start on it immediately."

"Of course, sir. Thank you."

And with that, Jack unplugged from his deck, using his nervous system's adjustment period to replay some of the gestures and bits of the conversation. For one, he noted that along with Simon's new gestures, that was the first time Jack had referred to the artificial intelligence as 'sir.' After a moment, he shrugged it off. He had a few hours while waiting for his answers. It was time for the team to compare notes.

36. Putting it all Together

"Okay," Jack began once the group had assembled. "It's been three weeks since we've started. What did we learn?"

"Plenty," Johnny led off. "For one, they're really into their catch slogan about what's good for the corporation is good for them. Every one of us has heard it over and over again."

"Outside of the job," Susan complained, "the only thing I've had any time to learn about anything was the amount of culture-shopping Payce does every night. One night it's an event, then it's an activity, then bona fide quests to the malls, stores, boutiques… I don't know how she does it. For that matter, why in the world would she want to? She disdains the thought of how raising a family would distract her from her career, but she drains herself of both time and money just by all the running around she does." She sighed, exasperated. "No wonder she has a butler…"

Johnny nodded. "Now that you mention it, I kind of see the same thing with the women in my office. At first, I thought it was just the guys taking off like that, but guys have been going out after work since time began. I didn't even think whether any of them had families."

"Actually," Jack offered, "remember how we all felt when we stepped off that first commuter? You're seeing first-hand how effective all that marketing is."

"Actually," Josanne tentatively spoke up, "I think it's more than that." Seeing their attention, she continued. "I was able to get the deep story from no less than Director Minova herself. It turns out that just before the government breakdowns, some little-known power broker literally designed the Air Dynamix economy to be a huge company store system that would suck almost all of the corporation's payroll money right back into the corporate coffers. But the societal meltdown interrupted their supply lines and disrupted the previously brokered trade alliances. Air Dynamix and its subsidiaries could no longer maintain control over all the goods the people legitimately needed, so leaks developed in the credit pipeline as people began to spend outside the once nearly closed system. While the CEO and Senior Executive Leadership Committee were still making cred, they wanted to hoard as much as they could. Precious corporate money was going out the door, so they invested heavily into finding out how to plug those holes.

"And consumerism fit the bill, no pun intended. While everyone else was trying to survive, Air Dynamix used its assets to create trade partnerships and either purchase, buy out, or in a few cases, perform literal hostile takeovers of several unrelated businesses. The government was too busy trying to get people fed and supporting the martial law areas—not to mention that Air Dynamix provided the government with some 85% of its fancier combat aircraft. In short, government didn't interfere too harshly. Dynamix indoctrinated its employees that they were the defenders, of course; not only did they cut pay to fund the 'defense effort,' they set up a special payroll deduction so the employees could donate even more. Anyone who questioned the party line was replaced by someone who was more sympathetic to the good efforts Dynamix provided to keep its citizens safe."

"Josanne's right," Melissana agreed. "What's happening here isn't free market consumerism—we're talking about the deliberate mechanical engineering of the bottom line. And you see all the ads promoting women and their careers? They're not empowering women, they're commoditizing them."

"I don't get it," Susan asked. "What makes this so different from the ad campaigns that have been going on since the dawn of mass media, or the old feminist movement?"

Josanne sighed at the question. "The early feminist movement was different. In the beginning, it was about the right to vote, then equal pay and rights, and equal opportunities for advancement. It was supposed to be about empowerment, but it led to other troubles. To show solidarity, many involved with the movement pressured the stay-at-home moms not to settle for 'just' being in the house and taking care of the kids, but to get involved. Others got jobs while their kids were at school to make a little extra money—after all, the mothers were smart, too.

"Problems occurred on two fronts. Women who started taking jobs for supplemental pay would take lower pay than a company would have to pay a man who had to feed his family, so to remain competitive, men looking for work had to take a lower wage. The other front came when manufacturers started charging more for their products, since double-income families could afford to pay more."

"Which," Susan added, "eventually created the need for both parents to work. Unless the husband made bank, being a stay-at-home mom was no longer a viable option."

"With rare exception, that's exactly what happened," Josanne confirmed. "Striving for the good life, they lost the lives they had. And that's not where it ended. With both parents working, daycares became a necessity that often ate away most of the earnings of the second income. And for many of the kids, once they grew out of daycare, they were just left on their own until their parents got home from work. For almost all of them, they either got into trouble or sat and watched television—tons of television—which was sponsored by corporations bent on coaching the kids how needy they were without toy X. Of course, by the time the parents did return home, they were both exhausted from work and didn't have the energy left to give the kids the attention they needed. To compensate, they'd buy off their guilt and fail to discipline the kids, which just fed into the consumerism cycle.

"The kids grew up without more than the most basic social skills, feeling entitled, and disillusioned with life, which resulted in drug abuse and other crimes. The kids couldn't or wouldn't be hirable, so social welfare programs expanded, which raised the taxes on those who were working, which caused yet more fiscal cuts in other areas. Of course, the epitome of those programs were the government welfare kids programs, which failed so miserably we coined the term govek, or government kid, as the insult of choice to this day."

"Maybe I'm not tracking, but I still don't see the difference," Johnny admitted. "Things are still the same."

"The difference is," Josanne explained, "in the old system, there was probably some tampering here and there, but all of that pretty much naturally happened on its own. Now the Corporation sells the career line to little girls by the time they start pre-school. It's far more deliberate, insidious, and effective.

"Women pay for college and corp-sponsored business schools, and after that, the empowerment seminars that specifically target women—in addition to the other training they have to undergo to qualify for the jobs in the first place. At the same time, they sell guys the line that they need to provide for these women or they're not worthy of her—which the woman is hearing at the seminars anyway. Taught to be ever fashion-conscious, especially since they need to stay current for their jobs, these women pay for cosmetics, ever-changing wardrobes, the whole works.

"They're also encouraged to have flings without responsibility, which was at one time a very 'guy' thing. And what happens if she gets pregnant? Well, you don't need a career distraction, so you also pay for abortions, pain killers, and more distractions. On the other side of the table, abortion clinics sell harvested collagen to cosmetics manufacturers for additional research on how the clinics can further 'improve the lives of women.'

"Yeah," Susan interrupted. "But remember Payce? What's all that got to do with her?"

"Everything!" Melissana exclaimed. "Don't you get it? The so-called affluence the corporation is pushing on her is no different than the mind control techniques the pimps use on the girls!"

Everyone paused to evaluate the enormity of what Melissana had just blurted. If it had merit, the repercussions of her concerns were both fundamental and far-reaching. After several seconds of silence, Josanne continued in a quieter, almost reverent, tone.

"There's yet another side effect of the repeated abortions; they leave the women flat and disassociated from both the fathers and their own emotions. After a while, boredom, marriage problems, and a sense of purposelessness sets in, so the office productivity of the females decreases anyway. It typically hits the guys even harder; remember, the girls are brainwashed their whole lives long that their careers are their purpose. Let's face it, it takes a lot to wipe out the hardcoding of Mother Nature's biological clocks from our DNA, but the abortions and post-abortion medications mop up whatever the constant messaging misses. But the males lose both their kids and, for all intents and purposes, their wives as well, so their productivity decreases. Now here's where things take yet another twist.

"Air Dynamix contracted Apex to research why Dynamix was having issues with decreased productivity, increased illness, and other morale problems, including a sharply increasing suicide rate among its most talented and henceforth well-cared for executive staff. The corporation was concerned and understandably wanted to plug the drain of its executive pool's productivity. Apex conducted several research studies and discovered Dynamix's commercialization of humanity actually both caused and widened that gap of purposelessness. So, is the answer to butt out of messing with peoples' lives? Of course not. After all, there's a lot more money to be made in selling the solutions to problems than in admitting you yourself caused them. To fix this mess, Air Dynamix teamed up with Apex to come up with the Life Options Plus plans. The more expensive options aren't available for everyone, but only because most people couldn't afford them anyway. Your wife is too emotionally drained to take care of you? Too busy to get into a serious relationship, or maybe just plain gun-shy after the shipwrecks you've either gone through yourself or seen others have gone through?"

"Let me guess," Jack interrupted. "Their answer is to have certain kids designated as 'corporate liaisons' that the schools raise to be the next generation corporate prostitutes. Payce's Butler Plus plan for the women, and the Companionship Plus options for Charles."

"Jack," Chrome cut in, "that interview with Montag. You mean to tell me he…"

"Let me show the video before you say anything," Jack said, raising his hand to quiet the cyborg. "I want to get their unbiased impression of what he said." He then replayed his interview with Montag in front of the team. Melissana gripped her hand to her mouth in shock, Susan gave a wide-eyed look from one face to another, but it was Josanne who spoke for them all.

"Damn it, Jack! That freak is raping those kids."

"Showbiz in a school," Johnny seethed. "*Gee*, we meet so many wonderful people!"

"Montag must have been the other guy Showbiz's hologram projector linked up to," Melissana surmised. "It makes sense—how else would the pimp know when and where his girls are coming?"

"This still doesn't answer all the questions, though," Johnny pointed out. "Like why do they dump the kids on the street?"

"And why," Melissana continued, "did Solace buy some of the older girls from Showbiz when they have a supply of their own, as disgusting as that is."

"And speaking of Solace," Susan picked up the questioning, "I keep going back to that thing she said, how what the corporation would do to her soul was worse than what Showbiz did to her body. What's that even supposed to mean?"

"I don't know what part Solace played in this," Josanne confessed, "but I can close the gap on where Partisan's kids come from." She sighed and hung her head. "It's not pretty."

"We have a school principal serially raping kids to see if they're ready to become corporate prostitutes," Chrome interrupted, "and you're warning us about what's coming up?"

"Remember when I told you about Apex's research to discover the gap of purposelessness? The other day she started to gloat about how people should know better in this day and age, but many couples still hit a point when they feel like having kids. For most of the parents, it's the real thing, and the corp cuts its losses by selling daycare services, after school activities, and for kids who qualify, boarding schools." She looked at Jack and Chrome. "And as you found out, Apex is now using the schools to push a neo-caste system on the kids."

"Hang on a second," Jack interrupted. "You said for most of the parents it's the real thing. What's that mean?"

"Yeah, I was getting to that." She gathered her breath, her thoughts, and most of all, her emotions, before she looked at him to finish her explanation. "You see," she said, "for the others, it's more of a phase. They don't really want the kids, or rather, the responsibility and costs of raising them. They just want the ooh's and ahh's at Christmastime or some extra appreciation for Mother's Day. Or maybe they don't want to take time off the job to do things parents usually do with their kid—you know, like those people who buy puppies because they think they're cute."

"Only, the puppies grow up…" Susan said, mostly to herself.

"Yeah," Josanne stated softly. "Like that, only on a corporate scale. After the early toy-buying phase, the corporations push the message that the kids are nothing more than career distractions getting in their way, constantly implanting the idea that the adults are worthless without a 'career shine' that they can't maintain as an attention-divided parent. Then there's the constant promotion that raising kids is demeaning to women. The bottom line is, the whole thing is a marketing sham to keep people paying back into the system, and Director Minova knows it.

"So, if the kids don't perform, or they become a nuisance to their family, or they hit puberty, or they ask too many questions, the parents can pay one more time to literally disown them and get their life back to the way it was 'supposed to be.' The corporation takes the kids, sanitizes their memories through drugs and shock therapy for a couple days, leads them down to Door 5, and dumps them into Witch City."

"But how can they do that to their own kids?" Susan implored.

"Trust me, Sunshine, it happens," Melissana replied. Josanne caught the intonation and remembered Melissana's own story of how her father had thrown her to the streets when she was in seventh grade. She had also seen that Jack had noticed the tone as well.

"I know abandonment happens on a rare basis," Jack said, "but five to twenty every couple months?"

"And those are just the boys that Partisan knows about," Josanne affirmed. "I guess the girls are all sent to the Liaisons program."

"You know, those stories about The Bowl terrify me," Melissana fumed, "but if there was ever a place that deserved solar-powered mass destruction, this is it."

"Josanne," Jack began, "let's go back to Mama Solace for a minute. In all of Minova's bragging about how clever their system is, did she ever mention anything about buying girls off the street?"

Josanne leaned back in thought. "You know, now that you mention it, I don't think she ever did. I mean, I don't think that even makes any sense, with the supply of girls they're getting from their internal school programs."

"Now you know why I hate the corps," Johnny stated icily. "Systemic predation. They charge fees for cosmetics, fees for the prostitution services, fees for abortions, fees for painkillers and medications, fees for the birthing option, fees for the childcare, education, clothing, food, toys, and all the other expenses of raising kids, and don't forget the occasional fees for blackmailing the execs who use the prostitution services—excuse me, 'Corporate Liaisons,' as they prefer to call them."

"Jack, what are we going to do?" Susan asked.

"I don't know," Jack admitted. "They're bottom-line bottom feeding, every step of the way. And they're not going to stop any time soon."

"Well I don't know about you," Chrome almost spat the words. "But I came here," he said as he drew each of his side-arms and visually checked the clips as if to accent his point, "to free slaves." When he had completed the task, he looked up and finished his thought. "I don't think we just put down Showbiz only to walk away from something worse."

As the others nodded their assent, Jack radioed Spider and the others to prepare for another run. They would meet that Saturday at Partisan's warehouse.

… …

In the three weeks that had gone by since the group left Partisan's warehouse for "the big city," Dante and Constantine had done enough equipment drops and supply runs that the team had a well-established base headquarters to operate from. Most of the girls were through the worst of their chemical dependency withdrawals, and although it would be months if not years before they could recover from the trauma of their experiences, many of them were at least starting to realize that they really were among rescuers. Trigget and Preach were especially pleased to see some of them make efforts to support each other, a critical step in the healing process.

They also noticed fairly significant gains in the well-being of Partisan's original charges. Fed and properly clothed, some of them for the first time in years, the boys were indeed becoming the small army Mother Freya had imagined them to be. Rogue Moon had also returned, extending the extremely remote possibility that there might actually be the basis of a peace accord between the Paladins and Valhalla's Brownies. While each side had fundamentally different outlooks on life, both had worked together to bring down a mutually reprehensible menace. Only time would tell if it would last, but it was holding for the moment. Inside Partisan's refurbished conference room, however, peace was a distant dream.

Melissana threw her hands up in the air, upsetting her drink as she did so. "This is just great!" she exclaimed. "We know what's going on, and once we find them, we can raid places to free the girls. But it's only going to happen again and again to others. How do we fight the idea that what they're doing is all okay?"

"I'm with her," Johnny added. "How can we fight this? The Life Options program's already so far down the track it's in pilot to an entire corporation."

"It won't be easy," Araña replied, "and we're cutting it on the edge trying to halt it this late in the game, but it is doable."

"But how?" Corey asked.

Araña approached a large whiteboard—yet another new addition since the group had left— to address them. "A company puts something out to pilot for three reasons: one, to prove it can work; two, to see what real-world obstacles arise, and three, to evangelize the product." As he spoke, he turned to the whiteboard and wrote the words so fast the Pride members thought he might have projected them. When he was done, he turned to face the group once again. "We just need to show them it either won't work, or…"

"Or if it can work," Johnny interrupted as he caught on, "it will not be cost effective to do so."

"Exactly," Araña confirmed. "If we can cause those objectives to fail, or even if we get only one of them to fail badly enough, or we make it too expensive for them to continue, we halt the program."

"That makes sense," Susan agreed, "but how do we do that?"

"There are six steps to run a pilot, once you set the objectives," Araña explained further, again writing the points so they could take their own notes. "Set the goals, decide the timeline, choose your test group, develop the outreach and on-boarding, collect and process feedback, and finally, address any obstacles."

"Well," Josanne chimed in, "I've seen the data and the program's working. They're making credits hand over fist."

"But what are their goals? We presume they're financial, but are there others we can capitalize on to offset the financials? Likewise, we know they're using Air Dynamix as their target consumer group, but are there other players?"

"Well, we just shut down one of their suppliers," Susan replied, "so if we can keep that pressure up, they might be forced to abandon the project."

"Or they'll just use the liaisons," Johnny countered. "It's not like whoever's running this program cares."

"No," Josanne added, eyebrows furrowed in thought. "Whoever's running this doesn't, but maybe the people they're selling the plans to might, if they knew what was really going on."

"Oh," the luckster persisted, "like the johns out there who are paying by the minute to rent videos of girls being tortured for their ten-minute fantasy life? Do you really think guys, or the women for that matter, really give a frack about the lives of the people serving in these plans?"

"Easy, Johnny," Jack cut in. "She has a point. Like the videos, there's a lot of subterfuge and misdirection in the process. Because really, the Life Options plans are only a part of the problem. In fact, they're a proposed solution to the root problem of brain drain from lack of productivity and staff executive suicides."

"So we add another element to our take-down formula," Araña stated as he added the item to the whiteboard list. "If we can propose a better solution—which we'll initially define as more cost effective—they might scrap the Life Options."

"But the root problem is entrenched," Josanne complained. "These faux families are a band aid over a band aid over a band aid."

"Hold that thought for now, but we'll go back to it later." Araña cut her off to reign in the conversation but wrote down what she had just said onto the whiteboard off to the side. "Let's work through the rest of the list. Trigget, do you have any idea what their timelines are?"

"Well, they've been running the program for years—long enough to have kids old enough to be thrown away to Partisan, at least. They have some pretty good data models worked up, so they have to be getting close. I'd say maybe the next year or so they'll be offering this 'service' to any corporation that can afford it."

"Which means they're probably starting to market it to potential corporations," said Johnny. "If we don't get on this soon, we're going to lose this fight before it starts."

"So, timelines are against us," Rickshaw joined in. "What about the outreach and onboarding?"

"Well, we don't want them marketing this out to other corps, that's for sure."

"I'm not so convinced of that," Preach opined. "Remember, the key to the entrenchment Josanne mentioned was the subtlety." He smiled and added, "Spider, write down another note with Josanne's idea. 'What would happen if we accelerate the evangelism process?' This whole thing involves long-term marketing, getting people to buy into each step, one step at a time, like the proverbial frog in gradually heated water. Maybe if we spoil the surprise, we'll ruin the spin."

"OK," Araña stated as he added more on the whiteboard, "timelines linked to marketing, outreach, and evangelism. Last on the list are collecting the feedback and overcoming obstacles."

"We can't overtly mess with the data too much at this point," Melissana explained. "With the pilot running this long, there are bound to be other copies of the data they could compare against that would raise alarms that the data they're reading has been mucked with. And once that happens, everything else we do will only convince them another corp is trying to skew their results so they can market their own product."

"But we can add new data," Iylothien replied, adding to the conversation for the first time. "Utilize different metrics that may have been overlooked in previous reports, or new findings that maybe invalidate the earlier results."

"Nice thinking," Chrome complimented. "Which brings up yet another way to hamstring this operation. If we insinuate that the new data was deliberately held back, we might cause the buyers to summarily reject any future dealings with the corporation. It's also pretty obvious that anyone putting something like this together can't be exactly squeaky clean. While we're doing this other stuff, we should simultaneously work to discredit the originators, champions, and sponsors to make it seem as if this whole plan was done in self-service and had nothing to do with corporate interests. Jack, our school director is a good place to start—we *know* what he's up to with the liaisons. As bad as it sounds, I'm betting a lot of the others are right there with him." Chrome looked around the room and saw everyone staring at him.

"What, you think I'm just hired muscle?"

Jack locked gazes with each member.

"Are we all in on the fast-forward of the evangelism?" Seeing the nods of agreement, he added, "Good. I'll put in a call to Foxfire to see if she has some time she can spare to help us out. The rest of you take the weekend and find out what you can on these other points.

"Spider? Great job on the pilot takedown analysis."

"Yeah well, jefe, you know how it is."

"Well I don't!" Susan exclaimed to her mentor. "How do you know all that stuff about how to bring down pilot programs and corporate marketing?"

"Well," Araña replied with a smile, "we all came from somewhere before CYBER recruited us."

"What our friend is so humbly saying," Jack added, "is that before he was CYBER, Spider here was a top-tier product developer for a corporation that eventually went I.C.C."

Catching her look of surprise, Spider once again smiled and added, "Yeah, but that was boring. All day in an office and stuffy politics? *This* is where the action is!"

"OK," Jack said as he glanced at the time. The gesture reminded him of Simon. "We've come a long way, and we've got a lot of work ahead of us. At the very least, we've got one giant run coming up against the Apex and Air Dynamix systems to deep-plant the data. Melissana and Iylothien? I'll join you on this one; it's going to take all three of us to pull it off.

"That leaves us with the task of finding out where the liaisons are kept, but I think I have some pretty good leads that Melissana, Chrome, and I will look into. If all goes well, we should have their locations by the end of the week. If that holds, we'll run on Tuesday the week after. Spider, you and Iylo come up with an exit route."

"To get a route, I need to know where you're starting from," Araña reminded. Jack paused to reflect on his options.

"Air Dynamix Junior High—home of the Corsairs. It makes sense for a number of reasons," he decided. "There's less physical defense, Dynamix won't think the kids would go back there, and they're less likely to detect the nature of the true target since we'll make it look like we're hacking school records, not planting the fake data on the pilot program and its proponents. Besides, there's one more very personal reason, for me and those kids," he added, remembering that first meeting with Administrator Montag.

"That's where their slavery started, that's where it'll end."

37. Reunions

"MISS CANDACE? HAPPY Monday," Jack smiled to the school librarian in his guise as history teacher Jackson Johnson. Placing both hands on the library counter and leaning slightly forward, he asked, "May I have a moment of your time?"

"Of course," she smiled in reply. She seemed to be one of the few staff who actually liked him. "What's on your mind?"

"Would you maybe want to come to a picnic lunch with me this Saturday—if you don't already have plans, that is? I don't seem to be very popular around here, and I wouldn't mind the company." He raised his arm to stifle a brief cough, revealing a note he had somehow spirited onto the counter.

CAREFUL. THERE ARE CAMERAS AND MONTAG IS PROBABLY WATCHING.

She started to say something, but he cut her off with a wave of his hand and a dismissive, "Oh no, I'm okay, thank you."

When he returned his hand to the counter, a photo of one of his missing students appeared. The note had startled her, but she went completely still with the photo. After a pause, her emotions betrayed her as she gritted her teeth and gave him an angry glare. She cleared her throat to regain her composure, took a controlled breath, and then through a gritted smile asked, "What exactly can I help you with, Mr. Johnson?"

He smiled back, but warmly, trying to disarm her suspicion. "Besides the picnic? Well actually, I do have a small problem. I had a student in my class who borrowed a book from me, but I'm wondering if he may have returned it to this library by mistake."

"I'm sorry I can't help you if I don't know the name of the student," her voice replied, but he saw the recognition on her face, along with a welling sadness he had hoped would be there. He sighed another smile and coughed again, somehow scooping up the photo and replacing it with another note. She looked at him doubtfully as she read the large scrawl across the top:

DON'T WORRY I AM A FRIEND

The rest of the paper consisted of a matrix of dates, times, and three columns of phone numbers. The middle column was circled. She grasped the counter to steady herself—he could see she was speechless. The dates corresponded to the dates Partisan retrieved the kids from the archology. The number in each row of the first column belonged to the school nurse and dental hygienist. The number in the middle column was hers.

"Well you see," he said with an embarrassed chuckle, "I don't remember the name of the student, being new here and all. And here's where I should know better—there are several students I could have lent the book to, but I don't remember who I actually did loan it to. The title of the book is, '2026—2040: The Missing Years'." He looked at her trying to convey his alliance in his facial expression and tone. "It was a longshot," he added, trying to reassure her he meant no harm as he retrieved the second paper off the counter with a sleight of hand gesture. "Perhaps it will come to me." He paused, then added, "Oh, and I hope you do consider coming to lunch sometime—as a friend, of course."

"Of course, Mr. Johnson," she said with a stiffly faked cheerful lilt in her voice.

"Please, if we're going to be friends, please call me Jack. May I have your number?" He smiled as she gave him a quizzical look—he had just proven he already had her number—but then she caught on that it was for the cameras and wrote it down for him.

As he turned to part, she added, "While all of this is just a little sudden, I'd like to get *your* number at that picnic."

He turned and bowed. "To Saturday, then." He waved with a smile, turned, and left.

… …

"Hey, thanks for coming out with me on such short notice!" Melissana 'Meredith Bertinelli' Trellain shouted over the rush of air coming into Brant Stomwell's open-roofed Sharkscale-*4* sport coupe. The Sharkscale was a powerful rival for her Zimata, but his armor was a little thicker, his frame and vehicle systems built slightly heavier and more solid to sustain more of a beating than her lighter sportster's stock armor had been equipped to handle. Still, her Zimata armor was anything but stock after CYBER had overlaid it with the same coating they had used on Corey's Sabretooth. If a vehicular combat broke out, her first strategy was still to run, but she'd be in much better shape than Brant. He might have been better prepared at the onset of an ambush, but she wondered if he had the armor, firepower, and skill to get away if the attack was anything more than a random drive-by.

"What, are you kidding?" he shouted back. "Someone like you asks someone like me to go out for a drive? Heck *yeah* I'm gonna say yeah! It was pretty amazing how my schedule got cleared for this Saturday, though; I was originally scheduled to work today."

"You're kidding!" she laughed as they cruised through an almost suburban section of the walled city. They were outside the archology and looking for a place where they could just relax together. Suddenly he pulled over and stopped the car.

"So, now that we're outside the Air Dynamix grounds, do you mind telling me what all of this is really about?" he asked.

"What do you mean?" she asked as curiously as she could muster. In truth, she believed she knew exactly what he meant.

"What I mean is that Candace got in touch with me, using a different number. She told me how that teacher approached her and scared the living daylights out of her with that list he had. Then she told me how he 'invited' her to a picnic—also today. How could she say no? All that guy had to do was give that list to Montag, and we'd be dead. Then your invitation came. Coincidence that you and that teacher started at the same time?" He half-laughed. "I think not. So, what are you going to do now? Are you guys going to kill us?"

Melissana sighed. "You know, for a while there, you sounded really smart, but you just blew it." She raised her arms to help rant the full meaning of her vent. "Yes—we figured out you were the number in the third column. We figured out the relay, although we really have no idea which one of you first thought of the idea or how you managed to do it. I hand it to you; it's a genius system, whoever came up with it. The kids are scheduled to be, shall we say, off-loaded. For whatever reason the corp doesn't kill them outright, but they do go through an out-processing with medical and clean up their dental records first. But the school physician-hygienist is too old-school and still cares about the kids. Who can she go to for help? She somehow connects with the librarian, who might know someone who has a way of reaching the outside without being traced. The librarian never tells the nurse who it is, just that someone might exist. But she knows you're a good guy, and you might be able to send out a signal to someone who cares. Then I see that cyber security jerk and his goons are busting your head open, and yeah, it turns out they think you're sending corporate secrets to a competitor, in which case, you're lucky to be alive at all. How am I doing so far?"

"Pretty good," he admitted. "It's true. Sometimes, when I could, I'd deliberately bring down a port to communicate in an emergency, but I had to be careful because I knew CST was watching me. I would love to bring down the corruption in the system—we all would. But up until now, all we could do was try to get word to Sitter. But if you're not going to kill me, why'd you bring me out here?"

Brant noticed a severely banged-up gloss black Sabretooth pulled up behind them and sat idling, its hood sported what might have once been an airbrushed armored knight mounted on a rearing horse standing on an anvil, lightning bolts arcing away from its hind hooves.

"Because," she said as she drew a taser and leveled it at his torso, "we have other plans."

"Oh. So, I'm being kidnapped, then," he said as the Sabretooth's passenger door opened, and an attractive blonde girl in black meta-race body armor gracefully got out and approached Brant's car door. "Well, I can always make a run for it."

"Such a drama queen! You're not being kidnapped!" Melissana playfully chided. "But no, you really can't—make a run for it, that is. You wouldn't get very far." As she said that, the blonde leaned into the vehicle.

"Good morning, Mr. Stomwell. I'm Lady Blackwolf—it's a pleasure to meet you. Now if you don't mind, please follow us. There is a yellow and black Dominator who will follow behind you. We're heading to a somewhat rough area of town, and we don't want you getting lost along the way." With that, she turned and as Brant watched, almost glided back to the Sabretooth, which inched forward as soon as she had shut the door. The Dominator closed behind to a mere three feet or so in seconds.

"I thought you said I wasn't getting kidnapped," he complained as he pulled against his collar to relieve the sudden sweaty itch he had just developed.

"Well, not really," Melissana almost sheepishly replied. "OK, well maybe, kind of," she finally admitted. "But there's someone we'd like you to meet; I actually think you're going to enjoy this."

"Oh, you mean like, the Big Boss?"

"No," she said in her most matter-of-fact voice. She gave him a side-long glance. "We're taking you to Partisan. "

'Who's that?"

"You know him as Sitter, but Partisan's his real name. Welcome to the inner circle."

He didn't say anything, but the way he leaned forward into his steering column, eyes bright and grinning like a little boy, Melissana knew she had been right. He was enjoying the ride.

… …

Brant followed the Sabretooth as it wound its way through sections of the city he hadn't imagined had even existed. His passenger hadn't said a word after she had pronounced where they were going. He studied her through sideways glances; while he could see small glimpses of the Meredith Bertenelli he had grown to know, he observed an intensity in her that, like the poverty-driven edges beyond the corporate-guarded grounds, he had never imagined.

"So I'm guessing you're not really Meredith Bertenelli—what's your real name?" he felt compelled to ask as he followed the mysterious Sabretooth and pulled into a warehouse garage door and stopped the car. She surveyed him for a moment before answering.

"Vixenn," she finally answered after some internal deliberation. "I go by Queen Vixenn."

The Dominator that had tailed them also pulled in behind them. Brant didn't recognize the driver, a mid-forties man with short hair that was somewhat tussled by his helmet. The driver of the Sabretooth also got out along with his sleek assistant. The closeness between the pair was evident by the relaxed way they stood together—soon confirmed as they linked arms as they approached. Odd, he casually observed, how the Sabretooth's turret seemed to track his car even though the vehicle was apparently unoccupied. Glancing back, he saw the Dominator turret swivel back to cover the entrance as the garage doors closed.

"Well," Queen Vixenn offered after a group of kids aged beyond their years shut the garage doors under cover while other kids maintained cove fire for them, "time to get out and join the others."

A few minutes later, he stood with a group of 17 disparate characters around a large conference table in an office that looked like it had been paneled in digital whiteboards. He recognized Candace, the librarian who contacted him when she found out the corporation was going to spirit another group of kids away. The woman accompanying her looked professional, apparently as stiffly annoyed as Candace was intimidated. Well, he was intimidated too, he admitted to himself. He also spotted Meredith—Queen Vixenn, he corrected himself—along with the two drivers and the blonde who had approached him earlier. He wondered who the rest of them were.

They were an odd collection of pirates, he thought. One tall man with a patch of beard and fiercely alert eyes in some heavily-worn leather biker armor casually relaxed with two other men in what looked like white cryoplast armor. He detected a faint blue glow between the plates that suggested—the suits were powered? He looked again and saw the crimson Templar-styled crosses on their chests and shoulder crests. He had heard of the Paladins, of course, and had even done some research on them when the media channels began reporting them as a bunch of hateful bigots. His independent study seemed to shed a different light on the group, but now that he saw them up close, he felt discomfited just the same. Not too far from them was a tall black-haired girl who had the appearance and authoritative aura of a statuesque gypsy wearing a Kevlar-plated jacket that sported the patch of—but that was just impossible—it just couldn't be. A member of Valhalla's Brownies inside the city? Hadn't they and the Paladins been at war with each other outside the walls just a couple weeks ago? The others—an easy-going Latino with an afro, a very muscular man with a blonde crew cut who was wearing sunglasses, some guy with short black hair and hazel eyes, absent-mindedly juggling a pair of pistol clips, a girl with sand-colored hair and green eyes that seemed to study each of the others at the table, and a thirty-something man with short hair and piercing eyes that seemed to flicker across the room as though he noticed everything—were also a mystery. But despite all of their differences, by their demeanor, it was clear they had achieved a level of familiarity with both the surroundings and each other. He wondered which one of them was Sitter.

"Hello Candace," he offered to the librarian with a nod, then turned to the professional woman next to her. "And you must be the other person in our little information pipeline. I guess the jig is up, as they say." He waved his hand in a polite and completely ineffectual greeting, "Hi, I'm Brant."

The woman was about to fire a retort, but Candace wouldn't allow it. "Please," she said to the unknown woman, "we're in enough trouble as it is. Please don't make things any worse."

"Lynda," the man with the flickering eyes said with a measured calm, "please don't be alarmed."

"Well, Mr. Johnson," she snapped, "it is clear you rounded us up into this—ghetto prison. Just what is going on here?"

Flanked by two ragged but dangerous-looking youths and an enigmatic young man in his early twenties, a fortyish-looking man in a wheelchair entered the room through a previously concealed entrance.

"A ghetto prison?" the man almost angrily asked, "This is my home!" Regaining his composure, he added, "Well, one of them. I have a few others just like it, you know."

"Brant," Queen Vixenn smiled, "meet Partisan. To his right and left are Saint Nick and Tag, and the young man behind him is Stang Steffan."

"Sitter? *And* Stang?" Brant's voice practically quivered. "*The* Stang? I heard about you, but I thought you were some kind of comic book character." And to Sitter, "I am grateful and honored to finally meet you. I never thought it possible."

"Well, that might be nice for you, 'Brant'," said Lynda, "but why should I… Oh my Lord!"

Stang gestured when Lynda began speaking. She stopped as two youths entered through the office door. They might have forgotten their names through the drugs and electroshock, but she never would. "Chance! Victor!" she cried, openly weeping as she rushed to the boys to shower them with hugs. "Oh my Lord, you're safe, *both* of you!" The librarian also started crying silent tears, her own combination of pain and joy colliding within her like storm-tossed ocean waves breaking against the sandy beaches of her resolve.

"Lynda," Sitter began, "I want to thank you for taking a stand against what Apex and Dynamix are doing." As he spoke, he swiveled to make sure he was facing each of the three newcomers. "If it wasn't for your courage and cleverness, most of my boys would have died."

"Please allow me to explain," Mr. Johnson began now that both the ice and emotions were broken. "Since we know who you are, it's only fair that you know who we are and more importantly, what we're doing here. My name is Preach, and this," he said, gesturing to those gathered around the table, "is my team." He first introduced each of his team members, which included Iylothien, who was evidently working remotely. Brant's observations proved correct; somehow, the group that 'Preach' worked with was influential enough to get the Paladins and Valhalla's Brownies to work together—no small feat!

Preach then relayed their mission from the beginning and summarized their progress along the way. He left out references to Elaine and Kelly's pre-capture identity, but he did divulge their plan to have Valhalla's Brownies and the Paladins cordon off the city while they sought out the missing girl. As he continued, the three lent their rapt attention to the exploits of the CYBER teams as they converged upon and eventually conquered the king pimp of Witch City, how Kelly once again proved elusive, and of their eventual discovery of and infiltration into the Apex Premier/Air Dynamix partnership.

"That is absolutely incredible," Brant offered after Preach concluded his narrative. "I won't dare ask how you did all that, but why did you risk bringing us here?"

"For two reasons," the former history teacher, now known as Preach, replied. "First, we need your help. You see, we've traced your information pipeline from Partisan's records. Lynda finds out who are getting dropped into the streets, she contacts Candace, who calls you, and you send out an anonymized data burst to Partisan so he knows when and where he can rescue the kids on the other side. But these are just the boys; we have no idea where the girls go. And from what we now know, there's no difference between what Showbiz did and what's happening to them."

"And from what we've been told by that Mama Solace character," Lady Blackwolf reminded with a shudder, "what those girls are going through is somehow even worse."

"We could try to find out on our own, but that'll take time," Trigget picked up where Lady Blackwolf had left off. "We hoped that since you guys already had the intellect, fortitude, and compassion to figure out how to communicate out what was happening with the boys, you might be able to help us track what's happening to the girls…"

"And where they're kept," Preach concluded.

"I can help with that a little," Lynda offered. "You see, I have been directed to order special—medications—for the girls once they are separated." She hung her head in shame. "Not all of them are for killing just pain." Then she looked up, determined. "I'm not sure exactly where the girls are held, but the destination codes are always the same."

"Meaning they're all held in the same place, at least at the beginning," Rickshaw stated.

"Iylo, if the girls are moved after that, can you follow the medication trails?" Spider asked.

"Sure thing, once I get the prescriptions, a couple names, and that first location code. Lynda, do you mind typing them into this form? I want to make sure I have the exact spelling."

"Not at all." She smiled to Candace and added, "You owe me a soybeer. I *bet* you there'd be a packet of paperwork somewhere in all this."

"Iylo?" Preach asked, "How long will it take to run down the location code?"

"Already on it, Boss," came the digitized reply. Brant visibly started as he saw the animated Barde de la Nêone navigate to one of his corporate grids turned dungeon gate, then open a hole and walk through like it was all some kind of computer game.

He glanced at the woman he once knew as Meredith and saw her rapt delight. And that's when he realized how she had gotten their network diagnostics as quickly as she did.

"You're nothing but a hacker!" he accused. He meant it as a sting, an insult. He wasn't prepared for her comeback.

"More like I'm nothing if *not* a hacker," she retorted. "Actually, that's not true. I was a private investigator before this, but think about it! How do you think we do what we do? And while you're there, you might as well admit it. Aren't you just a little curious about what the heck is on those drives we discovered? They're not downloaded games, that's for sure!"

"Yeah, OK, you win on that one," he admitted, shoulders slumping. "And I'm grateful to have this opportunity to finally meet Sitter—err, Partisan. And to see our chain is actually working, that we're really saving lives." Then he straightened somewhat and regained some of his earlier enthusiasm. "Like I said before, if I could have a chance to take down the corruption in the system, I would. And you guys, despite all you've done, you still need our help?" He broke into a smile. "Well, I gotta admit, that's pretty cool."

"Good," she replied. "Because while we're trying to rescue those girls, we need you to have a look at analyzing the security protocols on those drives."

"Are you kidding? I'm a tech—I don't know how to worm my way around the CST defense protocols!"

"You know that they're there," she argued back. "You at least have some idea of the conventions they use, maybe some nuances in their patterns they fall into using."

"But what if they've trapped the systems to blow or lock the data?"

"Bard to Queen—Hey Vixenn, I'm running into some pretty thick ICE. I guess these guys don't want anybody blowing their secrets. I've sleazed back a couple points, but I could use a hand if you're free."

"They have ICE on their systems?" Brant asked nervously.

"Look," Melissana sternly said as she sat down on the floor near a console and raised an electrode to the back of her neck. "I'm out of time and almost out of patience. You were able to cut through enough of their security to reach out to Sitter all those times. You don't have to cut the ICE, or even make a pass at it. Just take a front glance at it and tell us what you see."

"So that's the other reason you brought me down here? To betray my corporation?"

She had jacked in before he got the words out so she didn't really hear a word he said, but Chrome answered for her.

"Nope, that's not it at all," he responded as he was gathering a stockpile of weapons. "The other reason we brought you three down here is for your protection. The way I figure it, Iylo here will have a pretty close fix on the location of those girls in not much more than an hour or so."

"And when that happens," Johnny cut in, "we're going to figure out a way to go in after them."

"And take down that pilot project," Trigget added.

"Are you serious?" Candace demanded with sudden alarm. "Listen Jackson, or Johnson, or Preach, or whatever you call yourself. I get that somehow you've survived all you've already done against a bunch of street hoods, but you're going to try to liberate those girls from a megacorporation archology? And somehow reverse the entire Life Options decision history? You can't be serious! Why, there's only ten of you!"

"A bunch of street hoods?" Hardcore cut in, "A bunch of *street hoods*? Lady, you have no idea…"

"Fifteen," the tall woman with long raven-black hair declared. Up until then she had been quiet, in a deep reflection of her own. "Stang and I talked it over with Dante and Constantine earlier. We're coming with you." Then she flashed a smile that most would describe as simply glorious. "That is, if you phallos allow it."

"What, turn down you guys?" Rickshaw grinned, "Why, you're practically family."

"Yeah, sounds good to me," the Hispanic one with the afro joined in with his usual care-free smile.

"This is madness!" Candace argued. "And besides, that's still only fourteen."

"True," Rogue Moon agreed, the whimsical gypsy smile again splashing across her face. She picked up her favored sniper rifle, gently wiping it down. "But I bring my Natalia, and that makes us fifteen."

"Can't argue with that," Chrome shrugged.

"You're all crazy!" Candace said in exasperation. "Johnson or Preach, or whoever! Surely you can't be going in with them. You'll get yourself killed!"

"No need to worry about that, ma'am," Johnny replied. "He's probably the most dangerous one out of us all."

"You're learning, kid, you're learning," Chrome congratulated. "Remember what I told you about that battering ram."

But Preach had already turned back to the table and sketched a diagram of the archology approach to review the exit route with Spider while he simultaneously conferred with Partisan on what seemed like a hundred other details. After nearly two hours, Iylothien and Queen Vixenn reported back that they had located the girls on the 310th floor of Living Unit Building 5. After that, the team reviewed and honed their strategies over the next several hours, prepped their weapons, armor, vehicles, and gear.

"Okay," Preach led off, "we split into three main groups. Anyone?"

"John Sebastian returns home from his day off along with James Campbell and Jackson Johnson," Johnny began. Then he looked up to the tall Paladin who had led so many scouting missions and added, "What they don't realize is that I've got Luke here as a passenger, and the larger weapons that might get picked up on the archology perimeter scanners."

"Likewise," Queen Vixenn picked up the narrative, "I'm returning from my outing with Brant—except I'll have Dante with me instead. Preach, you're coming with us, right?"

"Indeed I will," he confirmed.

"Rogue Moon, Dante, and I," Stang began, "create a diversion at 8:00 P.M. the day you've all returned to the archology." He smiled as he continued. "And we create that diversion by taking the bus—and crashing the gate."

"Wait," Lynda began, "I mean, I don't always want to be the one throwing the wet blanket over your party, but your plan is to drive through the front gate?"

"Well, no. Of course not," Stang corrected. "We're going through Gate 8."

"And especially you," Candace picked up undaunted as she turned to Johnny. "You're going through with all these weapons?"

"My vehicle has a compartment that's shielded from scanners large enough to store a person," he replied coolly.

"Trust me," Queen Vixenn groaned as she rubbed her lower back from the memory.

"But you're already smuggling a person in, through the front gates no less," she admonished. "Don't you think you're pushing your luck?"

"Yeah," Johnny responded with an almost sheepish shrug. "That's kind of my specialty."

"Besides," Lady Blackwolf added, "it beats jumping over the wall, like we did the last time."

"Oh, like you were there," Hardcore chided. "You girls just drove in there with an appointment."

"You mean—you've done this before?" Candace gasped.

"Yes, we've done this before," Preach sighed. "You see, well," he stammered, searching for the right words how to explain.

"No use beating around the bush—they're government agents." Partisan flatly declared. "They were here on assignment to take down a major trafficking ring, but they found out about me and the kids here along the way. So, they're finally doing what the government was supposed to be doing all along." He turned and approvingly nodded to the CYBER teams and their friends. "They're putting a stop to it."

"Really?" Brant asked like a kid in a comic shop who just saw his favorite superhero walk through the door, "You're government agents? Like real secret agents? Which agency? I thought the government was pretty much defunct."

"It is," Queen Vixenn softly answered. "And yeah, there's a lot I still don't get about it, either."

"We were founded before the breakup," Spider explained. "The government's lost a lot of the overt control it once had, but our agency never completely went away."

"We survived," Rickshaw added, "primarily because of our leadership, our protocols, and commitment to our primary mission."

"Oh?" Lynda asked, her voice dripping cynicism, "And what's your agency mission?"

"Our mission," Jack responded, "is to protect the citizens of this country against acts of aggression, and to eradicate threats that would subjugate our society and its people."

"Heady," she stated as she fixed him with an icy glare. "Well, there's a lot of that going around—you'd better get busy."

She expected him to regale her with a series of arguments to put her in her place. In fact, she had hoped he would, so she could accuse them of being the very threat they were supposed to be protecting her against. She was intrigued to see him simply turn his back and resume his planning session with the others. Well, almost all of the others. She noted that as he approached the exercise table, he had a brief interchange with the young girl with medium-length sandy hair and green eyes. Their few words concluded, the girl approached Lynda and Candace.

"Yeah, you're right, we should get busy," Trigget began with a sarcastic flip in her own voice. "Why don't you come over and give me a hand?" She then rather directly led Lynda and Candace into an area of Partisan's warehouse that had been set up like a hospital ward that currently held thirty-three girls and ten young boys. In fact, Lynda automatically noted there were several empty beds.

"This facility's a dump," Candace complained to Lynda.

"Yes, but the supplies are surprisingly sufficient," Lynda replied. "See those empty beds?" she quietly whispered. "They either had some recent vacancies or are expecting more incoming."

"It's a bit of both," Trigget explained. "We started with the 60-some girls we had liberated from Showbiz. We were able to sneak in a supply truck that brought decent food, the medical supplies, and equipment. After some rather intense work, some finally graduated. Shortly after that, we got another group of Partisan's kids that had been attacked by some street ferals before we could get to them."

"You rescued 60 girls?" Lynda stammered. "How many people did that pimp have working for him?"

"We actually rescued over 75 girls, and trust me, you don't want to know," she replied, trembling slightly at the memory. She directly faced Lynda and continued. "I've been treating these people for the last several weeks whenever I didn't have to be at my day job. But I need to go on this run to pick up the girls Apex has locked up, and to be honest, there are no guarantees I'll come back."

"What—what do you want me to do?" Lynda asked as she suddenly became acutely aware of the gravity of the team's situation. This young woman, all of them, were going to risk their lives for a chance to rescue the girls as she had stood silently by. She suddenly felt ashamed that she had attacked the leader of this group the way she had.

"You're a doctor," Trigget declared. "Congratulations, you're taking over my rounds."

"What?" Lynda asked in mild shock. "I'm not qualified to do the kind of work you're doing here," Lynda protested. Then she slumped her shoulders and lowered her head as she trailed, "And I just stood by and watched…"

"No," Trigget resounded with what she hoped was infectious resolve. "You obviously couldn't directly oppose what Air Dynamix was doing, but neither did you just do nothing. You acted in the best way you could. You got help. You got us." She waved her arm to indicate the expanse of the makeshift medical ward. "Now help us to help them. Take care of them. I'll introduce you to them and give you their rundowns. If you come across something you haven't run into before, ask Partisan if you can use his computer to look up what you need. We have a system that is beyond state of the art, so you shouldn't have any problems with diagnostics or prognostics."

"And what will I be doing?" Candace asked.

She continued to the empty beds and pointed Candace to a hamper with clean sheets. "You can help make the beds for now. Once that's done, the same goes for you. Take care of them, all of them. Be there for them. And always remember that their wounds go deeper than their physical medical needs.

"And I don't know how much trauma work you've done, but this is going to take its toll on the two of you. Don't forget to support each other along the way."

By the time Trigget completed the introductions of Lynda and Candace to their charges, the group session at the planning table had disbanded. Lynda was deflated but impressed. It had been a long day, full of emotional upheavals but richly rewarding. It was clear that this agency wasn't like all those caustic self-serving ones that had seemed to exist only to increase their own funding at the expense of the public they were supposed to theoretically serve. She had loathed those departments and bureaus as a child, watching her parents work like slaves only so they could have almost half their money taken from them to support useless and ineffective programs that were always management-bloated enough to at least double the cost of the services they provided. She and Candace decided to take two of the empty cots on the warehouse floor for the night. Just before falling asleep, she saw through closing eyelids that while most of the others went their separate ways, Preach, Constantine, Dante, and Luke gathered in a circle—for—prayers? She was about to mentally complain, but then she heard them praying for her. Somehow comforted in the sound, she drifted off to sleep.

She dreamt of Mr. Johnson and a bunch of motorcycle commandos storming a castle with incredibly high walls to rescue a damsel in distress. She watched from the bottom of the hillside the castle sat upon, screaming and yelling for them to stop their foolish assault that was certain to end in defeat—that is, until somehow, just as Johnson and his superhero troops scaled the wall and entered the room, her perspective shifted, and she became the girl being rescued. Around her, the room was filled with dozens of girls who were starved for food, care, and non-abusive contact with humans who actually cared about them.

She woke at 3 AM and observed a youth clothed in street rags, the stern look on his face well beyond his years. He carried a crossbow, and as she watched, he quietly padded across the warehouse floor to the garage door to relieve an equally young boy who had been on guard throughout the night. As the enormity of the progress that had already been made began to sink in, she wondered if maybe she should feel sorry for those who so eagerly sold away the lives of the people who depended on them.

She quickly dismissed the notion and went back to sleep.

38. Taking it all Apart

"G'Mornin' Charles, happy Monday," Johnny greeted as his teammate entered the office. "Anything much happen?"

"With me? Not much," Charles replied, then conspiratorially leaned in to continue the conversation. "I mean, other than cashing in on my Life Options plan," he added in a quieter tone.

"Really?" Johnny responded, inwardly seething. "Tell me about her."

Charles droned on for thirty minutes about the incredible weekend he had with a Liaison, but it didn't take Johnny long to see the guy was truly clueless concerning the truth of what the project was really about. To him, the girl was getting paid to just go out to have a good time. While Johnny didn't get her exact age, the Liaison was a professional-looking young woman who had a very promising upscale career ahead of her.

After a while, Charles sensed his coworker was, for some reason, getting annoyed with the conversation. Sebastian's probably jealous, he thought to himself, then he had an idea.

"Hey, what about you, John? I mean, especially since your wife left..."

"Me?" Johnny asked, trying to play off his revulsion as a shyness. "No, I'm not ready for that."

"Nonsense! You can probably get signed up for tonight, and we can maybe do a double date!"

"No thanks," Johnny affirmed. He smiled at his coworker, but as he did so, his hazel eyes turned the color of grey ice. "I have plans for tonight." His partner was unnerved enough by what he saw that he quickly dropped the subject and got back to work.

- *"Gonna be a long day," Johnny commented to the team.*

- *"Remember, what you're doing right now is not your day job today." Preach reminded. "We're showing our faces so nobody gets suspicious, but we need to rest up for tonight. Do a couple hours and then either get sick or disappear."*

Everyone from Chrome to Lady Blackwolf affirmed their reply. Preach, of course, would put in a full day, and after that he'd stay later to correct papers. He needed to be back at the school at 7:00 PM, anyway.

…… ……

At the last commuter stop that served the Air Dynamix archology, patterns of reflected neon danced across the rain-slicked streets that had long grown dark. Corporate advertisers spent months locked in bloodless combat to design the glowing signs. Now their creations battled in the arena of the attention spans of wage slaves waiting for their ride to work.

The current set of would-be passengers were low-level staff who spent all night laboring at shift work but couldn't yet afford to live within the corporation's hallowed protection. A pair of drug dealers plied their trade, more polite than discreet. The armed and armored WSF forces patrolling the area were paid to keep the peace, not enforce morality; they plain didn't care about the traffickers' street-side hustle as long as those waiting for the commuters weren't beaten, badgered, or bothered. Most of the commuter passengers thought the WSF may have even gotten a percentage from the dealers; those who really knew never said.

On this particular night, there was a slightly higher number of passengers for the 8:00 PM commuter onto the Air Dynamix grounds, but the WSF dismissively patrolled past the few extra commuters and the couple of harmless vagrants. One of them openly laughed at the scraggly woman cradling a broomstick wrapped in tattered rags like it was her most cherished possession.

"There, there," the woman crooned to her broom as the officers passed her by. "Don't let that brute of a man hurt your feelings. If he saw how pretty you were as I do, my dear Natalia, he would not say such things."

The WSF officer turned back to teach her a lesson in respect, but his partner told him to leave the wretch alone. They had better things to do, and there were richer fares up the next block.

Spider, Dante, Constantine, and Stang breathed a sigh of relief. Collectively, they could have easily taken out the patrol, but the activity would have revealed their presence and complicated the mission. Rogue Moon also sighed, but none of them could tell whether she was also relieved or somehow disappointed.

… …

- "7:45—Go! Go!" Johnny's whisper shouted through his subvocal microphone.

Susan, now in full Lady Blackwolf mode, responded by taking a running leap towards the Gate 8 building from the rooftop four buildings away. She extended her wingsuit's membrane as she cleared the ledge, using the airstream to sail through an imaginary glide path over the heads of the outer guards. She braced her arms at her sides and retracted the suit's glide membrane as she curled into a ball, then extended her legs forward, using her forward momentum to carry her over the heads of the two gate guards just outside. As her feet hit the ground just outside the gatehouse doorway, she reflexively curled into a tight ball of cryoplast momentum. Lady

Blackwolf rolled forward once until her feet were under her again. Once they were, she sprang back to full height and delivered a snap punch augmented by both her CYBER-enhanced speed and the redirected momentum of the dive. The first of the two interior guards was out instantly.

The second guard inside the gatehouse was startled by the intruder's sudden appearance but had either the presence of mind or dumb luck to fall backwards towards the wall-mounted alarm. Recovering quickly, he raised his shotgun towards her and fired, but the pause was enough. Lady Blackwolf ducked right in a blurred swooping lunge, then shot forward with augmented reflexes. Her extended claws sliced into the forearm armor to catch him before any internal alarms were triggered. The blast from the weapon fired past her, turning a set of monitors into electrically-hemorrhaging debris. She grabbed the barrel guard of his weapon and spun it from his grip as he howled in pain, then kicked his legs out from under him and launched a flurry of blows that landed five hits to the man's face in less than a second. The onslaught overwhelmed the second of the two interior guards; he also lost consciousness.

"Nice work," Johnny commended as he approached, struggling to drag one of the two exterior guards with him towards the gatehouse. "They didn't even know you were inside until the shotgun went off," he smirked. "They probably thought you teleported past them."

"Well, we're in," she acknowledged, then activated her comm circuit.

- "Back Door to Hitchhiker, we're ready for you."

··· ···

"Jackson Johnson" had dutifully pretended to be correcting papers until he heard Lady Blackwolf's transmission. Then he disappeared, replaced by the CYBER team leader who had come too far to turn back on Kelly now. Iylothien had already circumnavigated the school's surveillance systems and replaced the camera coverage of Mr. Johnson's office with a digital recording that would loop every 3 hours, 13 minutes, and 29 seconds; Preach locked his own office, half-jogged to the Administrator's office, and broke in. Looking around Montag's desk area, he felt like something was out of place, but he couldn't put his finger on what it was. A double-check for anything different that came up negative. He shrugged off the feeling, crouched underneath the desk, jacked into his cyberdeck, and joined Iylothien's hack of the Air Dynamix utility and security systems. The two would take control of the rest of the city's cameras and other systems that would allow Melissana to meet up with him in the school. Once he linked with Iylothien, he jacked out just long enough to radio Trigget that she was up.

… …

The WSF patrol returned just as Commuter 13 slid to a sighing stop at the transport station, the breath of its wheezing air brakes blowing scraps of ads and tossed bags of yesterday's consumerism across the station like the megacorporate culture swept away its adherents. The ads wafting in the street portended the writing on the wall for their readers. The consumer trash was the end product of the advertising. The advertising was the end product of the corp workers, whose lives were in turn the end product of the corporate machine they served in the dream of climbing another step up the corporate ladder. One more step, always one more step up on a ladder composed not of rungs but of teeth that bit into and eventually consumed the souls of those who tried to get ahead. In the end, they would each be just as used up and forgotten as the torn and water-damaged media detritus slowly making its way towards the corporation's sewers in the rain.

Commuter 13 fed the beast that Air Dynamix had become, transporting souls hungry enough to risk the late-night plaza crime and traffic to work on the archology grounds. At this particular site at this particular hour, there were 38 such souls who wanted and expected nothing more than their nightly commute to their somewhat dull office and maintenance jobs. They were about to be surprised. A few would be overjoyed, but the most dutiful of them would be disappointed that their exchange of their soul to the corporate machine would be interrupted for one night.

The doors opened, and a small stream of passengers emerged as those who waited to board lined up in an orderly fashion, the Spanish-American with the definitively non-corporate afro at its head.

"Just one minute," one of the WSF troopers called out as he started to board. "Where do you think you're going? There's aren't any stops before the Air Dynamix corporate gate, and from what I'm seeing, you definitely don't belong there." Most of the crowd automatically took several steps back. They had seen rousts before and nobody wanted to be associated with the target of this one. Spider was going to feign acquiescence, but the driver's hand started edging towards the vehicle's defensive grid. In a superhuman dash, he was inside the bus before the door's electrical field that would have barred his entry had energized. Two mini-crowds, one on the platform and the other inside the commuter, screamed in fear at the disruption of their normalcy. The WSF troops were surprised but trained. They raised their weapons and fired at where Spider had been as they called in their alarm, then spun back to back for situational awareness so nobody could get behind them. As the cluster of vagrants revealed themselves, they realized they were too late.

"I jammed your signal when you called for backup," the electronic voice of the boarder cut in over their helmet frequency. *"For your own good and those you're supposed to be protecting, just stand down. We do not wish to harm anyone, including yourselves."*

"OK, everybody off the bus," Spider ordered the cowed passengers after the team had neutralized the security force and driver. "This is not some kind of holdup or ransom attempt. Please exit the commuter and no one will be harmed." Dante handed each commuter a credit chip with c150 on it, explaining it was to replace the phones Spider had low-grade EMP'd in the process of the takeover.

With the official passengers cleared, Constantine donned his armor while Rogue Moon and Stang boarded and geared up. Luke and Dante just stood and studied the vehicle.

"Everything okay?" Spider asked.

"Well, our armor isn't as—quaint—as Constantine's. See, our heavy armor uses micro-hydraulics and pneumatics to augment our strength and durability; his smaller suit sacrifices the strength of our systems, but is motorized to heighten his speed."

"In other words," Constantine grinned, "these guys hit like trolls but move like tortoises. I come on fast and leave 'em before they know they've been hit."

"What that means for us," Luke shrugged, "is that if this thing doesn't have a baggage storage area, we're going to need a bigger door."

Seven minutes later, Spider started the commuter and lurched forward several yards before he once again brought it to a complete halt.

"Why'd you stop?" Luke demanded. "We've got a schedule to keep."

"Look for yourself," Spider replied. "There's a bunch of kids blocking the way." No sooner had he said that than there was a series of banging raps on the commuter door.

"Nick," Spider exclaimed, "what are you up to?"

"Me and Kung are coming along," Saint Nick replied.

"Oh no you're not," Stang declared. "We have enough going on without having to worry about you two. Up ahead is corp, not the streets you're used to. It's not like there's anywhere for you to run if this goes south."

"Listen Stang," the lead youth retorted. "It ain't like we're some suburb clubbers goin' out for the first time. Hell, you used to camp in corp-soil when you were our age. We can find our way out for ourselves if this goes bad. And besides, you're gonna need us."

"Oh really?" Stang half sneered, "And just what do you bring to the table?"

"Think about it, Stang! You guys are running a snatch-grab on a bunch of school kids who won't know left from right."

"Yeah? So?"

"Dude, no disrespect, but you're *old*. Those kids ain't gonna trust a bunch of adults as fast as they're gonna trust us. And in a snatch-grab, fast is good."

"Does Sitter know you're here?" Spider asked. When the street youths nodded yes, the group on the bus glanced at each other. Then Spider shrugged.

"Welcome aboard," he said. "But if this thing goes bad, we might not be able to help you."

After Saint Nick and Kung boarded, the group of youths cleared the way, and the commuter was again on its way.

"Any other surprise stops along the way?" Spider asked Saint Nick.

"Not from us," he replied.

… …

Just moments after the commuter pulled away, Rickshaw and Hardcore pulled up to the stop. The two drivers got out and, feigning interest in apprehending the hijackers for the potential bounty, questioned the witnesses who were still in the area. After they determined what had happened and that there were no civilians on board, they told the small cluster of people that the regular WSF forces wouldn't be able to intercept the bus in time, but they were going to stop the bus and bring it back.

- *"Hitchhiker, this is Rear Guard," Rickshaw reported as the Sabretooth and Dominator pulled away from the station. "We got your back. The story's planted; they'll be expecting all of us to be coming in hot."*

· · · · · ·

Trigget, in her guise as the Director Minova's research assistant, entered the office and logged in to her computer.

- "I still don't see why I'm doing this," she complained. "Shouldn't I be on the rescue crew helping anyone with medical needs?"

- "For tonight, Luke can help with that as needed," Preach responded. "We need you to monitor Apex's response to our Air Dynamix raid. Besides their general level of alert and cooperation with tonight's target, we need to know if this is something that has widespread acceptance among the rank and file, or if it's just a few people who are pushing it. Besides, Queen Vixenn just rode in onto your login so she can look for anything we can use to discredit the chief sponsors. The open door helped cut through several layers of ex-net protection."

- "Well, the second shift staff are here. As long as Vixenn has my connection, I'm going to see what I can find out in the break room."

· · · · · ·

The forty-one tons of Commuter 13 sped down its course, gaining additional forward momentum with each rotation of its ten individually powered wheels. Returning mock fire against the pursuing Dominator and Sabretooth, it "accidentally" shot out the cameras covering Gate 8 before the driver apparently lost control of the vehicle. Its occupants braced themselves against the tortured dynamics that physics had thrown against their bodies as the craft teetered first to the right, then left again before bounding against the speed-bumped curbsides, blasting through the meager barricades that had been constructed to halt lesser vehicles on impact.

But the 13 was not a lesser vehicle. The reinforced battering ram that protected the front bumper against ambushing vehicles served just as well against stationary targets. The commuter half crushed, half vaulted over the concrete and cryosteel barricades and pushed them aside with grating screeches like amplified fingernails scratching across sensitive chalkboards. Lady Blackwolf and Johnny, having deactivated the gate turrets and explosive defenses, cringed against both the shock and the noise. Still the juggernaut pushed onward, despite the chewing it was getting by the pursuing vehicles. It finally ground to a complete stop two blocks away from Air Dynamix Junior High, the Dominator and Sabretooth drivers shouting encouragements to each other that they finally corralled the runaway bronco of a commuter that they had, at least temporarily, broken.

Commuter 13's occupants fragmented into three groups as soon as it screeched to a stop. The first hopped onto the Sabretooth and went left down the perimeter interior. The second mounted the Dominator and took a separate route to eventually link back up at Building 5. The third group headed off on foot to the commercial sector to stage a series of diversions intended to lure the bulk of the on duty Air Dynamix forces away from the true target of the raid. After the groups had scattered, Lady Blackwolf and Johnny, maintaining their guise as the guards they had neutralized, triggered the gate alarms and reported to security headquarters that the disturbance was a near miss and no cause for any real alarm. The hijackers had been some stoned thrill-seekers, and the two chase vehicles had left the area after they had been ordered off corporate grounds. The desk would find out otherwise soon enough, but by then, the CYBER teams would have gained several precious minutes.

… …

Over two hours had lapsed since the CYBER rescue team entered Building 5. Once again nearly invisible in his sneak suit, Spider silently crept through the labyrinth of hallways and corridors that made up the 310th floor. He strained every one of his extended senses so hard he sweat with the effort, probing to the fullest extent of his focus. He couldn't afford a slip; the small group of liberators depended on stealth and surprise for them to have any chance of success. And that stealth and surprise depended on his senses and experience. This deep in the Air Dynamix archology, they depended on him more than ever. If the corporation caught them now, their mission wouldn't stand a chance. Lady Blackwolf and Chrome could fend for themselves, he mused, and he had seen enough of Stang in action to know he could hold his own; he was less sure of Saint Nick and Kung. CYBER enhancements or not, the only way they could possibly survive would be to abort the mission and run. He couldn't let that happen.

While Iylothien and Preach had compromised the camera systems and other devices of the computerized defense grid, the experienced recon man knew far too well that to presume that there were no off-grid security measures could easily lead to disaster for them all. Alert for traps, alarms, and roving patrols, the group avoided taking the express elevator straight to the desired level. While the single elevator ride would have been faster, the floor was off-limits to unauthorized personnel. Taking that would have assured their detection; they'd be trapped in the elevator car with a concentrated force of anti-infiltration security teams just waiting for them to exit. Instead, their route snaked through an intricate three-dimensional weave that used several different elevators that stopped off at seemingly random floors, crossing through the various levels to use different elevators and, at times, several flights of emergency exit stairwells. It had taken over two hours to navigate, but between the Hound leader's skills and the interdiction provided by the team's hackers, there had been a bare minimum of contact along the way.

All that changed when a party of Air Dynamix guards traversed the corner of a crossing corridor behind the group and immediately recognized the wandering kids they had spotted as out of place and unauthorized. There would be no mercy, no differentiation between youth and veteran—the security troopers Air Dynamix hired were paid to stop intruders, not to care how old they were or why they were there.

"Look out!" Lady Blackwolf shouted as she pushed Stang, Saint Nick, and Kung out of the way as the group of Dynamix muscle fired three shotgun blasts at the CYBER squad. Her heightened reflexes just barely saved the street youths—the Dynamix squad would have connected if she had been just milliseconds slower. As it was, Kung fell against the hallway wall with a hard *thunk!* that made Stang wonder if she had injured the youngest member of the assault team.

The security forces recovered from their pause at just how fast she had moved and fired three more blasts at the youths, but Chrome had stepped between them to take the full force of the pellets at close range. Grimacing, he closed the remaining distance to the men and yanked the two outer guards to collide with the third one between them. While that in itself didn't drop them, he back-handed the rightmost guard's helmet, cracking it and sending its now-unconscious owner against the wall. He served the middle guard a vicious palm-strike that tossed him several feet down the hallway, then threw a series of pile-driver blows against the remaining man's chest plate, caving it in until he too collapsed under the weight of the assault.

- *"Iylo, this is Spider. We just went hot."*

- *"Roger that, Spider. Break—Team Three, will you guys be able to give them a hand?"*

… …

- *"You want us to just calmly walk away from this and rendezvous with the team on the 310th floor?" Johnny shouted over his comm circuit, bullets cracking nearby. Natalia shrieked its famed battle cry as Rogue Moon fired a sabot round into an approaching armored strike drone. The impact of the round tossed the craft into a chaotic spin, forcing it to collide like a pinball against three different buildings before it came crashing to the ground in an explosive blast of metallic mayhem. Several automatic weapons hammered back against the team's makeshift barricade in response. "You hear that? How the hell are we supposed to pull out now? Our job was to draw fire and chip truth, we done that! This situation's gone plasma—I ain't gonna lie, I'd love to pull, if we could figure out a way that we actually could. We got no less than thirty or forty Dynamix and WSF troops, including support drones, thinkin' they're fighting off a full-scale terrorist attack/bank heist combo."*

- *"Dante! Get down!" Rogue yelled in the background. Then a loud blast sounded just before their communication cut out.*

… …

- *"Spider," Iylothien reported back, "that'd be a negative, Team three is unable to provide backup."*

- *"We're too close to stop now anyway, Iylo—we're on the final approach to where they're keeping the liaisons. Wait—we've got more incoming!" Spider called. "I can't tell how they're armed through all the hallway electronic interference, but scans show at two more full squads coming from the hallway ahead and enough heavy bootsteps advancing to mean another squad approaching from behind us."*

"Stang, stay here and guard the kids," Lady Blackwolf ordered Stang. "Chrome's gotta provide back up for Spider up ahead, and I need to take care of the guys coming from behind before they catch up to us. Call me if you see anything going wrong in any direction." She looked down the hallway behind her and took a small hop-step to begin her sprint down the hallway. Stang would later swear he had felt the breeze.

Kung looked up, horrified at the carnage he knew was being unleashed against them. "Something going wrong in any direction?" he almost gasped, trying to keep himself from completely losing face. "It's already going wrong in *all* the directions."

"Dude," Saint Nick said trying to calm the younger one that had up until then dealt with crime, life on the streets, himself a castaway, with almost no show of fear. "They're throwing what they got against us, yeah. We knew from the start this wasn't gonna be no milk run. But do you see who we got with us? I mean, that Blackwolf chick moves so fast she *blurs*, and then Chrome took three hits with shotguns at the same time, and it didn't even faze him." He paused for a moment and beamed a true kid smile. "Kung, even if we get geeked here in this hallway, ain't that the def trickest thing you ever seen?" The younger boy looked at Saint Nick and recovered some of his courage. Stang had never been as proud of Nick as he was at that moment.

"Besides, we ain't just along for the ride, you know," he said as he double-checked his crossbow. "We're not armored up like those cyborgs, but any Dynamix heat get this far, we'll go down showing them a fight that'd make Sitter proud." He had no doubt they would rally and fight when the time came for them to do it, but he doubted what they would actually be able to do if security got past Chrome, Spider, and Blackwolf. They were now halfway across the 310th floor. Once they got down the remaining fully defended hallways, they'd have to get through the stockade defenses. And if that guy Spider was right, the Air Dynamix would be waiting for them in force—if they made it there at all.

And then, presuming they all survived that far, they would have to fight their way back down all 310 floors and across the archology grounds, with victims in whatever state the corporation had them.

It was then that Saint Nick shivered in spite of the encouragement he had just given his younger friend.

… …

"You know," Rogue Moon screamed at Johnny over the noise of the firefight around them, "this would be a lot easier if you let us fire back at them, not just this suppressive fire drek!"

"Yeah, it would," Johnny yelled back, "but Preach has this thing about killing innocents. These guys are just doing their jobs, trying to protect their turf from terrorists."

"Yeah, but it's gonna get us killed. We can't hold them off forever." She glanced ahead through the smoke and other visual noise of the battlefield, then shrugged her hands in despair. "Well, that's it then. See that group of guys up ahead, forming up behind their forward barrier? That means they're going to assault. If we're not going to kill these guys, we're done."

"*Paladins!*" Luke ordered upon hearing the news, "Front guard, *post!*" He pushed a button on his left gauntlet. In response, a spark flashed and steadied to a neon blue wash of light that bathed his already impressively hulking suit of heavy plate augmented armor. Similar flickers of blue light behind them indicated his fellow Paladins had done the same. Dante hefted a massive two-handed hammer that would have been too heavy to lift had he not been wearing a suit almost identical to Luke's. Constantine, who was wearing a much smaller and lighter suit, swapped out his twin auto-pistols for a pair of matched blades; they each took several steps towards the oncoming threat, planted themselves, and waited. The defending forces immediately shifted their full focus on the three glowing targets, but the rounds pelted harmlessly through the reflective glow with a popping *pfizz!* and tiny sparks of bright white that, from a short distance away and given the volume of fire directed against them, resembled muzzle flashes of automatic rifles. It didn't stop the rounds completely, but dissipated the kinetic energy enough that they were tolerable for the armor.

"No permanent casualties," Luke vowed to Johnny during a pause for the security to evaluate the effect of their barrage. "We have a time limit on how long we can keep the power up, but we should be good unless they bring up some heavier weapons before we get clear. I think this is your opportunity to withdraw. If we lose comms, we'll rendezvous at the school." And with that, the Paladin scout somehow attached his auto-rifle to his armor and drew his own broadsword and shield that shared the blueish glow of his armor. He nodded to each of his brothers and ordered, "Paladins, *advance.*" Both he and Dante almost calmly lumbered down the street to greet the security forces rushing upon them from ahead, while Dante raced at the accelerated speed his suit provided to the far right and sped down the sidewalk like a Bowl game blitzer doing a sideline run to circle around the main forces and hit them from behind.

Johnny held back for a moment, unsure whether to abandon the three knights who had already done so much for them. He almost rushed out to support Luke as the Paladin scout had come under a barrage of heavy fire that caused him to stagger even through his heavy armor and shield. The CYBER luckster was about to break cover when he saw Dante approach the lead vehicle that provided the cover for the security forces. His pneumatically powered right arm held the massive two-handed war hammer in an almost loose grip just below its head, handle up, the hammer's head lowered. Just a few paces away from the vehicle, he stepped out with his left foot and lengthened his stride, and in a practiced upward sweep of his right arm, he let the hammer's long handle slip through his fist, extending the massive weapon to full extension just as his right foot hit the ground. Now at near-zero weight and maximum kinetic potential, he gripped the impossibly heavy hammer with both hands raised over his head and took his final step, throwing all of the unified weight of the powered weapon and the man in a swing augmented not only by its own extended weight but also by the full force of the power-armored momentum.

Time stopped for Johnny, who was transfixed in the moment that played out before his eyes. He was grateful he had not gone back right away—he would have missed it. In a screeching blast, Dante's blow had not only significantly dented in the armored response vehicle, it had shoved it—almost tossed it—several feet. As far as Johnny could tell, the heavy smash might have even lifted the WSF personnel carrier completely off the ground. Those who were using it as cover got tossed as the vehicle seemed to jump at them. The forces staggered, Luke regained his own advance to disrupt the remaining heavy forward forces while Constantine zipped back and forth among the more rearward forces to keep them from organizing any further response.

"Come ON!" Rogue Moon and Lady Blackwolf yelled, grabbing Johnny's arm and snapping him back to reality. "These guys can't keep this up forever, and they need us *out* of here."

He nodded once to himself, shook off the sense of wonder, and ran back several blocks to disengage before meeting up with Hardcore and Rickshaw for the ride to rendezvous with the group in Building 5.

… …

- "Preach," Iylothien radioed his former mentor, "everyone's up but us. The teams have it. You ready to punch deck?"

- "Yeah, four more seconds," he replied. "Lord, we're in it. Please take care of us, and if any fall tonight, please lead us home." It wasn't the first time he prayed that prayer tonight, but it would be his last opportunity before he got too engrossed in his flying. "And Lord, please watch over all of us. Give us victory so we can

set captives free." He never said 'Amen' in these prayers—it was too much like saying, 'I'm done,' and he knew he needed the line of communication open even more when he couldn't afford time to think about it.

- "Okay, Iylo, jacking in 3... 2... 1..." and he hit the switch to his deck he had connected to the school network inside the Air Dynamix network's outer layer of defense protocols...

And almost gasped as his consciousness transferred to inside the cockpit of his virtual AF-179 Corvus fast attack/fighter aircraft. In his VR simulation he performed his pre-flight checks before launching from the runway just outside his hangar—in reality, he checked his cyberdeck connectivity, health of the system, anti-ICE dampeners, viruses, Trojans, daemons, and bots he used as offensive weaponry along with the traceroute protections, lag cycles, and other warez he used to defend himself against the megacorporation's inevitable counter-hacking activities.

He was in one of the Environmental Modules developed by SIMON and Iylothien specifically for CYBER raids. He and Iylothien had pioneered them, but when he saw the young decker's brain and body fry while under his care, Preach abandoned the effort along with decking in general and CYBER in particular. Now, six years later after he was sure Iylothien had died, Simon called him back into service to lead his new fledging team. Iylothien had somehow survived after all, and SIMON stepped in on Jack's behalf to complete the EM project. So here he was.

Everyone in the early years of virtual reality thought cyberspace would be different, that it would somehow be a universally-shared consensus on what the digital world would look like from the inside. And that's what killed the cyber space-race, at least for the time. The universal consciousness required cumbersome protocols or intensive server-side processing to keep the various users' world up to date. It was a nice thought but doomed by the very real reality that no corp wanted to waste money on a global Shangri-la—and those that tried soon found out exactly how much of a fool's errand they were on trying to get corporations over a global network to agree on exactly how cyberspace would look. Even with each corporation designing their own internal systems as a compromise, they still had to design the specifications for exactly how that would work across every other system in the digiverse.

The Environmental Modules—EM's for short—worked differently. By throwing all of the rendering on the client side, the processing was done locally on-deck, lag time for the extra graphic and sound content was eradicated, allowing the environments to be as immersive as the user desired. An additional and very welcome additional benefit was that systems would be rendered in a universally-consistent manner for the given module in use while allowing each user to see the digiverse in whatever form they desired. The problems, efforts, and effects were the same, but they were rendered differently according to the individual EM: Preach performed death-defying air raids against other air and ground targets, while in Randolph and Emerson's "Ultimate Fantasy" Iylothien and Queen was a combination ranger/bard and Queen Vixenn played an electron sorceress.

His flight checks completed just before Iylothien reported he had loaded his spells, and Queen Vixenn teleported from the Apex system to enter the Air Dynamix world. It would be one half-second before she launched Chrysalis, one of her favorite scouting daemons. One millisecond after that, Preach's A/F-179 Corvus launched into the wild blue ether of the Air Dynamix net just as Iylothien cast his own camouflage spell, Queen Vixenn at his virtual side. The data identifying who was behind the Liaisons program was being held captive inside a virtual castle dungeon. The two of them were to scale the walls, sneak past the guards, and find their way to the dungeon. Their next task was to find and free the data. Lastly, they would use it in the castle's own keep to weave incriminating evidence against those individuals in a way that nobody would suspect, let alone disprove.

… …

Trigget, in her guise as Jayne Smythe, was busy extracting what she could from the swing shift workers. They were responding in the typically guarded fashion most workers did when talking to someone from Biological Assets, but she was able to determine plenty both from what they didn't say and how they didn't say it.

- *"Preach, this is Trigget. We were right; most of the line staff don't have a clue about the true nature of the 'Options Plus' benefits plans. Minova has them so compartmentalized into such small silos and misdirected that even staff working on the coverage selections documents draft such minute sections it's impossible for them to see what they're really writing. When they get done with their micro-task of a paragraph or two, they submit their work and get a new task of writing that they think is an entirely different topic—it's like they're constructing an entire three-hour lecture out of independent ten-second sound bites."*

- *"Good work, Trig. Were you able to find out who they submit their completed tasks to? Somebody has to start putting all these pieces together at some point."*

- *"The ones I talked with didn't seem to know. They get their tasks through an automated ticketing system, and when they mark them as completed, the system automatically assigns the task to the next person in the chain. Even that's siloized up to two levels because each tier of people that receive the work just gets the first line and last line of what's sent to them so they can connect the two disjoint pieces. If there's something that needs to be sent back for some reason, it's automatically sent by the system, so nobody sees who it goes to or where it comes from."*

- "Trigget, this is Queen Vixenn. Any idea who set up or administers the system? Maybe it stands to reason that whoever set it up is a key player."

- "If anybody I've spoken with so far has any idea, they're either exceptionally good liars or they don't realize what they know."

- "Great thinking though, Vix," Iylothien cut in. "Preach, mind if I peel off and do some more exploration of the Premier servers?"

- "We need to hit them later anyway, Iylo, but our priority is the Air Dynamix extraction."

… …

- "All right," Spider transmitted as he and Chrome made their way down the final remaining corridor between themselves and the liaison stockade. "Lady Blackwolf, keep your group tight but stay back thirty feet from us. We can't afford to get separated now."

"Pretty quiet right now, don't you think?" Chrome asked.

"Yeah it is, on all channels. I'm picking up seven armed individuals inside the pen, but I'm not reading anyone else coming up on our position."

"So they're turtling. Maybe going to a hostage situation?"

"It doesn't feel like it. I've got eleven unarmed individuals left of center, seven armed individuals to the right of center, and one armed between the two. But they're not set up right—their line is perpendicular to the doorway, not in any kind of defensive positions against our assault."

"If the kid was with us, I'd say we got lucky, but he's outside. It doesn't make sense; they're drawing a line on the liasons?"

"Hang on a second—I can hear them. The kids are crying, but it sounds like the guards arguing about something?"

The CYBER assault force had reached the door in another few seconds. They could all hear raised voices now, even without Spider's augmentation.

"Corporal Adams—Stand *down!*"

"No way, lieutenant. They're just kids!"

"Kids or not, they're corporate assets that management has just ordered neutralized. Corporate has ordered their termination."

"And who gave that order? I signed up to protect people, not to kill kids."

"Look around, Adams. Some other corp's got some kind of army outside chewing through everything we've thrown at them. We got orders—take 'em down before the other corp gets ahold of 'em."

- "Blackwolf, we need you on the door. Get up here, stat," Spider ordered, his tone too direct for her not to comply immediately.

"Go ahead and fire me, lieutenant—life'll get hard without a job, but it'll be a hell of a lot easier than trying to live with snuffing a bunch of helpless kids on my conscience."

"Adams, we are going to do our job. You get out of the way—now—or we're going to fire you in the faceplate, cuz you're going to go down with 'em."

"Now!" Spider snapped. Chrome rammed the door through with a running shoulder block and took three steps left, immediately diverting the attention of and drawing fire from the Air Dynamix security troops. The kids, already terrified and crying, screamed as several rounds impacted the stocky cyborg.

"Drek—they're here already," the lieutenant shouted. "Shoot the kids!"

A sharp *thud!* sounded in the wall opposite the doorway to the executioners' right, and Spider seemingly flew across the room as he reeled in his grapnel, snap-kicking at each of the guards' helmets as he passed by. At the same time, Lady Blackwolf took a full-speed run down the length of the hallway to build momentum, cut into the room, and executed a gymnast's straight jump. Once airborne, she spread her arms wide and re-extended her suit's jump membrane, adding to the security force's confusion by gliding across the 30' width of the room. Halfway across, she tucked up her legs and spun to face the firing line of troops, brought her arms back in to grasp several taser charges, and flung them like a ninja throwing shuriken onto the hostile force's armor. The maneuver wouldn't completely neutralize the security forces, but the taser shocks would disrupt them and divert their minds. The flurry of motion worked, as for several seconds, stray shots went in every direction except towards the liaisons.

And in those seconds, Chrome was able to close the distance between himself and the kids. Surprising everyone inside the room, he let them know he was not only still alive but functional as he fired three short bursts of return fire, staggering two of the armored guards-turned-assassins but not quite fully taking them out.

"Shoot the kids!" the lieutenant ordered again, and several things happened at once:

The security forces regained their senses and swung their weapons back to the kids.

A girl screamed.

Spider fired his grapnel again, ensnaring the lower legs of the reticent Corporal Adams and dragging him out of the line of fire.

Chrome stood up with a roar and fired a long stream of downrange lead, praying to draw the fire of every one of the murderous cretins.

Lady Blackwolf popped her claws and vaulted to the gunman farthest from the door, intent on shredding the weapon, if not the person wielding it.

Stang, who had just made his way to the stockade, tossed one of his smoke pellets and a flash bang grenade into the corporate firing squad and rushed the group, staff fully extended and promising to connect on his fifth running step in.

Saint Nick sighted his crossbow in on the homicidal maniac who was giving all the "kill the kids" orders and fired, pinning the man's arm to his cryoplast breastplate and knocking him off his feet in a dramatic spin.

Kung fired a snap-shot that missed. Screaming in frustration, he went feral and blindly ran into the room to make contact with the first Dynamix security he could reach.

… …

By the time the smoke dissipated enough to see, all seven hostiles were down. Kung was still kicking at one of them until Saint Nick calmed him down, discreetly reminding him that the others could see. Lady Blackwolf, who had taken down two of the armored guards by herself in a bloody melee, took a moment to straighten her hair like a debutant going to a shopping mall, focusing very carefully not to let the shaking completely take over. Many of the kids were still crying, but somehow they sensed that their immediate danger was past.

… …

"J.M.," Director Minova hailed as she briskly strode past Trigget on her way to her office, startling her to the point where she almost jumped. Trigget may have been a CYBER-trained conversationalist, but she was also human. "What are you doing here this time of night?"

Trigget may have been startled as a human, but she was also a CYBER-trained conversationalist. The question held a suspicious tone underneath the portrayed mask of personal care and curiosity.

"Oh, nothing really," she replied, trying to sound casual. "Just getting caught up with some of my reading and getting to meet some of the shift staff while I'm here." She decided to smile awkwardly and add the obvious. "You startled me. I wasn't expecting you to be here at this hour. But since you are here, do you need anything?"

"As Director, I am here any time the corporation needs me to be," Minova answered quite stiffly, then softened, if just a little. "Regarding your question though, I don't need anything from you at the moment, but there's quite a bit of security activity tonight. You'd better stick around until it blows over." Trigget inwardly sighed. This time her concern seemed genuine.

"Inside the plaza district?" Trigget feigned. "I saw an alert, but I guess I got in before it started. Do you know what's going on?"

"Not yet, but I will. Suffice for now to say that apparently some of those high-tech Jesus freak lunatics that were battling Valhallas's Brownies over the last couple weeks have somehow gotten inside the city. I'm going to find out why. And if I can trace any of their contacts, then how."

39. Missing Pieces

Saint Nick brought Kung with him to introduce themselves to the students. They looked up at him in fear, and though he smiled to them as nicely as he could, to them he just looked like some kind of street delinquent.

"Hey," he said in greeting. Then he saw how they were looking at him and sighed. "Yeah, I didn't get a chance to go to your school, okay?" Then he realized the truth of his own situation, and sighed. "But I probably was one of you, a couple years ago. Listen, we know what they've done, and we're here to get you out of here to someplace safe."

"I don't know if we should go with him," a young teen spoke up. "He's only going to get us into trouble."

Saint Nick sighed in frustration until a girl spoke up. "Are you for real?" she demanded. "After all we've already been through, how much trouble do you think he's going to be? I mean, these last guys were going to shoot us, remember?"

"Are the kids okay?" Spider asked.

"They're fine," Saint Nick said, an eye roll purposely embedded in the statement's tone.

"We better get moving," Stang reminded. Saint Nick nodded once and began his pitch.

"Listen, we gotta get going. We took out these clowns, but there's gonna be more on the way. By now I'm guessing you're all quick enough to have figured out what they're going to do with you all. So, unless you want to end up a corporate hooker—or dead if their orders haven't changed—we need to get going. We'll lead you out, but we gotta go before the corporate snuffs regroup."

"Well, I don't think we should go," one of the older youths defiantly announced. "Maybe we're being kidnapped. I mean, we don't know any of these people."

"Hallway's clear," Chrome yelled as he ducked back inside the former stockade. "Let's go!"

One of the kids exited and rubbed his eyes. He was so shocked he almost squealed.

"Yes we do!" he shouted, so caught up in what he saw, his voice cracked as he pointed at the man who had twice plunged himself between barrages of weapons fire and the kids who wouldn't have had the chance to be alive had he not done so.

"That's my gym teacher!" He was so caught up in the moment that he ran up to the burly cyborg and hugged him in front of everybody. "Mr. Campbell, what are you doing here? And how did you do that—like, you got shot like a bazillion times!"

Chrome noted that both Spider and Lady Blackwolf were watching him intently to observe how he would handle the situation. "Screw it," he decided, and just handled it like he wanted to. He gently knelt down to look the kid in the face.

"It's like I said that first day we met and I made you climb that rope, Winner. You sure as drek don't want me as an enemy, but I make one hell of a friend." And having said that, he donned his sunglasses, snap-charged his weapon, and headed back out to the hallway. "This won't stay this clear forever though, so I suggest we get a move on."

"You heard the man," Saint Nick encouraged the rest of the group. "Not all adults are screw-ups. These guys got their heads in straight, trust me." And with that, the group of kids formed up and took their positions in the middle of the group.

"And what about you?" Spider asked the corporal who had stood down a firing squad.

"Well I don't see you guys taking me with you," Corporal Adams admitted. "I'm the enemy, remember?"

"That took some serious *cajoñes* to pull what you just did. I'd sure hate to see that go to waste. A guy who stands up against a firing squad by himself isn't going to betray those kids when he's got some backup alongside him." He then handed Adams an assault rifle and some extra clips from one of his former companions. "Besides," he smiled, "we might need the back-up."

"Not from anything I've seen, but yeah, I'll help cover the kids. What the hell were they thinking?" he asked.

"I'll explain it all to you when we get to a safer location," Spider replied. "But for now, we need to keep focused on getting out of here."

As Spider made his way to the head of the column, he paused next to the still somewhat shaken Lady Blackwolf.

"Congratulations," he said in a barely audible voice. He saw she was going to ask the obvious question, so he answered it before she did. "Now you know how fast you are. And you were fast enough—not one of those kids got hurt."

And with that, he focused in on his scanners and took point position on their trek to the express elevator. There was no more need for subtlety.

… …

- *"Spider, this is Rickshaw. You on your way back yet?"*

- *"Rickshaw, we're on our way down. We got eleven—make that twelve hitchhikers."*

- *"Roger. That'll be four round trips for both of us. Think you can keep the fort tied down that long while we play taxi?"*

- *"Don't see we have much of a choice, Rickshaw."*

Spider relayed the information to those in the group while they were on their descent.

"You got eleven hitchhikers," Corporal Adams stated. "I'm not getting carted out if I can walk through the fight."

"Fair enough," Spider responded, "but we're all taking rides anyway. Where we're going is too far away to go on foot."

"So we're leaving the archology? That could be a problem. I'm 'wired for corporate security,' as they put it. Once I leave the archology, my detonator blows."

"Drek!" Chrome shouted, then immediately followed up over the comm circuit:

- "Iylo," Chrome resounded, "Dragon, Dragon, Dragon."

… …

"Queen? Preach? I gotta kick the run. I got a dragon."

"Roger that, Iylo," Preach responded. "Go!"

"Preach, what's a dragon?"

"The team's called through an emergency interrupt. It means they have a life or death situation for their entire team and they need him—right now."

"Can he get hurt?"

"Vixenn, we can all get hurt at any time. Just keep your own head focused."

"Yes Sir," she snapped, then hesitated. "Sorry about that Preach. I won't let you down."

But the damage was done. Preach himself was now sidetracked by Kelly, concern for Iylothien, the dragon, and now how Queen Vixenn might be off a beat because she was worrying about Iylothien. The E.M.'s were immersive, but not always so much so that a decker never thought about the real world.

A nearby blast from Dynamix network ICE portrayed as a virtual surface-to-air missile had knocked him off his intended flight path. A little closer and the ICE could have crashed his system. He'd have to circle back and take it out. He had other work to do in this sector and couldn't afford a second or third volley. He pulled back on the virtual yoke, and his Corvus executed a Reverse Immelman turn and used the extra speed to scream in over the SAM site at treetop level and obliterate the target ICE before its human operators, if it had any, had a chance to note the change in his vector. "Stay focused, Preach," he reprimanded himself. "Too many people counting on you right now to take a stray. Iylothien will handle the dragon and Vixenn just promised she'll handle herself, so keep your mind on the run ahead of you."

. . . . . .

- *"What you got, Chrome?"*

- *"We're on an express elevator and one of our passengers is wired with a kill switch. Need immediate verification that there is no video of our guy switching sides. Fast, please."*

- *"Stand by—"*

A pause of several floors' descent ensued as Iylothien surveyed the video footage. There was an uncharacteristic waiver in his voice when he returned.

- *"Glad you called, big guy. The stockade footage loop began just before you entered the room, so no one will actually see him leaving with you. But I'm guessing from what was already picked up that your man is none other than Corporal Adams. I can re-rig the video some, but it's gonna go south as soon as they get real people inside that stockade and see that he's the only one missing.*

- *"Spider, it'll take me a little while to figure out which switch is his and neutralize it. Normally it wouldn't be a big deal, just delete the records matching Adams's member ID to the kill switch, but these guys have actually used non-descriptive table names, so I need to search through each table and piece the data together. Good for security, but it must be a monster to maintain. I can disable the system, but it's only a matter of time before they get it back up and running. The good news is that once I get it disabled good enough, the only trigger left will be a proximity system; he won't detonate as long as he stays on corporate grounds. And I have been able to delete his ID from their tracking system, so they can't trace your movements through him."*

- *"Good enough, Iylothien. Thanks. Confirm dragon cleared."*

- *"Yep. Dragon cleared from the skies. I'm taking off, going back into my regularly-scheduled mayhem. Fare thee well!"*

- *"Take care, Iylo."*

- *"Rickshaw and Hardcore, this is Spider. We got your first wave hitting the ground floor in six seconds."*

- *"Roger that, Spider. We're outside now. Looks like you've got an exterior-facing perimeter set up."*

- "They set up looking outside?"

- "Yeah, they sure did," Iylothien electronically chuckled. "Maybe it has something to do with Rogue Moon and Johnny camping their front doorstep."

- "Roger that, thanks."

Spider looked at Chrome, who just grinned.

"You know," the hulking cyborg offered his team lead, "sometimes it just feels good to have things go your way for a change."

The main CYBER assault force exploded out of the elevator as it opened onto the ground floor and quickly subdued the Air Dynamix security forces that were waiting for an attack from outside the building. Once they secured the ground level, they sent the elevator back up to the 310th floor for the evacuees.

··· ···

It would be a very tight ride down, with the eleven former liaisons, Saint Nick, Kung, and Lady Blackwolf, but to risk more time on the 310th floor was a risk none of them wanted to take. Waiting for the elevator was unnerving enough for one trip; both the shock and adrenaline were wearing off. Soon the group would start to get tired. In fact, Lady Blackwolf had already noticed one of the girls looking a little off-color, and just when Spider announced he released the elevator back up to them, the girl moaned and leaned on one of her friends for support.

"Hi, they call me Lady Blackwolf," she introduced as pleasantly as she could. "Heck of a night, right?" She then noticed the girl starting to sweat a little. "Hey, are you okay? Did you get hurt or anything?"

"Hi—I'm Success," she returned. "Well, I feel really worn out. I must have gotten sick or something—I've had a lot of nausea lately.

I mean, I'm kind of used to it, but I guess everything tonight is really making a mess out of me. And now my shoulder is really starting to feel sore."

"Did you get hit or anything tonight?"

"No, it just started getting sore out in the hallway, and now…" she squeezed her eyes in pain as she grasped her abdomen. The boys withdrew a step, but the girls all wanted to help in whatever way they could. They all felt helpless. Susan Blakeslee had not been trained for this.

But she knew someone who was!

- "Trigget, this is Lady Blackwolf," she called in, starting to become concerned. "Can you hear me?"

- "I read you, Blackwolf. You're worried. What's going on?"

- "I've got a 16-year-old girl here. She wasn't hit in the fighting, but she's sweating, grabbing her stomach, and complaining her shoulder hurts. What do I do?"

Chrome was wired for sheer muscle, Araña and Lady Blackwolf were wired for speed. Hardcore was wired for his vehicle, and Preach and Queen Vixenn were wired for hacking. She had refused all of those, and yet she did eventually consent to her own modifications that worked side-by-side with her conversationalist training. Trigget left her desk and went into the ladies lounge, made sure the stalls were empty, occupied one, and began. Closing her eyes against her surroundings, she tilted her head to relax as much as possible.

"Engaging medical protocols." The medical programming came to life as it always did, allowing, almost willing, Trigget to a free-thinking calm as the system merged its thinking with hers. In an almost monotone calm, Trigget began that otherspeak of the implanted medical database and knowledge base system implanted within her.

- *"SUBJECT: one teenage girl, sixteen years old. Faced emotional trauma as she was used for forced prostitution. Subject rescued after traumatic threat to life involving firearms and explosives.*

- *"Subject complaining of severe abdominal pain, dizziness, sweating. Also complaining of shoulder pain that began shortly after the rescue, however, she was not injured in the rescue attempt.*

- *"REQUEST SYMPTOM CLARIFICATION: Are there or have there been any additional symptoms or maladies not yet mentioned?"*

- *"Yeah," Lady Blackwolf reported. "She's had a cold or something. She said she's been throwing up a lot lately."*

A list of potential causes to the girl's pain flashed through Trigget's closed-eyed other-sight. It was not a long list. In the ladies room, Trigget sagged even further. A single tear formed in her right eye and ran down her cheek. But there was no time for that. She bolted upright, unlocked the stall door, and immediately took charge of the situation. She was a CYBER medical support team member, and this girl needed her.

- *"Whatever scouting mission I'm on has to wait," she radioed to the rest of the team.*

- *"Trigget, what is it? What should I do?"*

- *"Keep her as comfortable as possible and get her over to the school in the very first car—stat! I'm coming right over. She's having a miscarriage."*

… …

Susan Blakeslee almost panicked as she heard Trigget's diagnosis, but Lady Blackwolf wouldn't allow it. She had a room full of kids expecting her to keep it together long enough to see them through this, and remembering Preach's prayer before they split up for this raid, she vowed that by God she was going to do that or die trying. There were no other options. Thankfully, the elevator would be at their floor in another thirty seconds.

"Hi Success. Well, we found out what's causing all your pain, and we've figured out what's been making you feel sick. It looks like you were going to be having a baby, but everything that's happened tonight has endangered its life." The girl looked confused, conflicted, and sad. Her breathing was getting shorter, but whether it was due to her physical condition or emotional stress, Susan didn't know.

"Now, please don't worry. We have a doctor who is on her way to meet you. You'll need to go down on this next elevator so we can get you to her as soon as possible, but I need to stay up here as long as there's anyone else on this floor. So why don't you pick six of your best friends that are here with you, and you can all go down together, all right? Don't worry who to pick; I'm going to keep all the others safe until we're all down that elevator, okay?

"As for the rest of you, she is free to pick who she wants. I'll stay with the rest of you until we're all down, okay?"

The elevator arrived, the first rescue group boarded and were sent on their way, with Saint Nick and Kung along for the ride in case they somehow got stopped on one of the intervening floors.

- *"Hardcore, this is Blackwolf," she reported tersely over their private comm circuit. "I want you to take this girl to the school. Flat-out it; she needs to get there."*

- *"Sure," Hardcore responded, "but why not Rickshaw?"*

- *"I think you're faster, she said. "And besides, I know you'll do it—if for nothing else, then for me."*

... ...

Trigget was just leaving for the school when Minova summoned her into the Biological Assets Director's private office. Josanne had never been in there before; they had always either met at her own desk or in the dedicated conference room just outside Minova's inner office. And by the tone in her director's voice, it didn't sound like she was going to ask her out for soykaf. Trigget knew it had to somehow be in response to the raid—but was it to respond in greater confidence or a trap?

- *"This is Trigget—Minova just called me into her office. I need to see her first, but someone's got to tend to that girl."*

- *"I got it," Luke replied. "With a name like Luke, you know I gotta have some medical background in me," he half-chuckled at his own joke. "We're almost back at the school, and we need to recharge our armor some anyway."*

With no time to do anything else but act normal, she subvocally transmitted the call and entered the office for the very first time—only to observe Minova in a holographic conference with someone who had his back to the door. Her first thought was that was odd, because the technology wasn't very common, and the only other one they had seen in the city belonged to... Just as she had the thought, the holographic image turned to her.

"Well, well, what do we have here?" the image said with a leer even the holograph couldn't hide. The image leaned in to study her more closely. "You see, Berkleigh? My disbelief in coincidences has not often disappointed me. And the thrill of this one? Magnificent!" He turned his full attention on her. "Allow me to explain. When Berkleigh mentioned that you were working on the night of the attack, that was just one more 'coincidence' in this series of coincidences. So, I asked her to review everything she knew about you and produced your personnel file. I admit that even I was stunned for a moment. But now that I see you in person, well, why yes, it really is you." He took another look, then raised his eyes to the ceiling and shook his head as if to remove all doubt, then looked back up to the two women before he continued. "Berkleigh, I believe some introductions are in order."

... ...

Rogue Moon was there to greet the elevator when it finally landed with its medevac crew.

"Did you know you were pregnant?" she asked the young woman.

"No," Success answered between gasps. "They must not have known, either, or they would have forced me to abort the baby. The only ones allowed to keep them are the special girls."

Rogue Moon stopped cold. "What special ones?" she asked, puzzled. "Didn't we get you all?"

"No ma'am," another girl replied, as Success was too worn out and in too much pain to answer on her own. "They called us the 'trainees' for the liaisons program, but they said they had some other girls on the 379th floor, and that that's where we would go when we graduated."

"So," Rogue restated, trying not to sound like she was mad at the rescued girl, "you're telling me that there are more of you on the 379th floor, and that your holding area was just a training ground for these pigs." She took a breath to try to calm herself, then sighed heavily at the futility of the gesture. "How many of these other girls are there?"

"I'm not sure," the young girl replied. "They're older. I don't think all of them were liaisons. There might be 20 or 30 of them."

"Any idea how we can identify these women?" she asked.

"Well, they're a couple years older than us. Let me think a minute." She furrowed her brow, raised her hand to her mouth, and seemed to look somewhere far away. "Yeah, they all have the same tattoos on the back of their necks, and—oh yeah! They all have the same gold necklace! It's supposed to be a gift celebrating their new position, but I've heard that once the girls put them on, they can't get them off again."

Just then, Moon saw Chrome talking for a moment with Johnny.

"Hey, admirer. Would you like to do something that would make me admire you?"

Chrome smiled, but was careful enough to ask what it was.

"Let us finish this job. Take a ride with me to the 379th floor. There are 20 to 30 other girls there."

Chrome called the latest intel in over the group channel, then looked at Rogue. "You sure ain't easy to impress."

She smiled in response, struck a pose, and batted her eyelashes at him. "And what, you think I should be?"

"No, you should not." Chrome admitted. Those watching the conversation would later say that in that moment, he actually smiled. "But I'm not stupid, either. We're taking a full crew."

"I would not expect you to be stupid, Mr. Chrome. I have seen you too much to think such a thing."

Chrome found Spider just outside the main door of the facility helping load the passengers into Hardcore's vehicle. "Spider, we got the eleven newest recruits, but there's another maybe 30 girls up there who have already graduated from the program. If we don't go back up and get them now while the window's already open, we're not going to get a second chance later."

Spider allowed the time it took for the Sabretooth to race away from the building to collect his thoughts. Most of the time, he felt nothing but honor at being the lead for his beloved Hounds, but it was in times like these that he hated it. It was a classic *zugzwang* dilemma. They were winning, coming out alive, walking, the hostages intact. Now that was taken from him, as he had to face making yet another lose-lose decision, and there was no clear and easy answer. Despite the fact that the absolute last thing he wanted to do was to send a team back into the building they had just escaped from, he really had no choice. They were the guys people sent when nobody else could get it done; it was for situations like this that they had been created. But even they had physical and emotional limits. And they had been pushing theirs all night long. And yet, as bad as that was, to not go might be even more taxing, because every one of them knew that if they didn't go, those other girls would never be able to get out.

"You've got the intel on the situation; go ahead and call up a team. Leave Blackwolf out of it. She should get back to that girl as soon as she can, and besides that, she's spent. And you know I'm coming along for that ride."

"Thanks Boss. Wouldn't have it any other way. I figure we'll take Johnny and Rogue. Stang, Saint Nick, and Kung need to go back to the school to keep themselves out of trouble and to help with the school kids. I was really hoping for at least one other speed person."

"Deputize Adams. He hasn't worked with us before, but he knows the building and he's definitely on our side in this. And did Luke say the Paladins made it back to the school?"

"Yeah, they're setting up bunker positions to cover the deckers if things go hot."

- "Hardcore, bring Constantine with you on your way back. We gotta go back up there, and the other Paladins are too big to fit through the hallways."

Rickshaw let out a low whistle at the revelation of the additional trip.

"So," Spider asked on their way back up in the express elevator, "you said we have a way to spot the girls, but outside of the floor, do we know where they are?"

"No," Chrome admitted, then renewed his classic grin that usually meant someone would soon be in an especially nasty combination of trouble and pain. "But I have an idea of someone who does."

… …

The door burst open, tossed across the room to smash the fairly expensive decorations into fragments as the CYBER strong-arm splintered its frame with his first kick. At 12:15 AM, the noise was enough to wake up every resident for six units in every direction. The former Corporal Adams and Johnny kept the curious away from the room, planting the suggestion that this was official security business. Others who hadn't yet wandered into the hallway would certainly be calling in the disturbance to the real Air Dynamix security, but that was okay with the team. Let the calls come in about the disturbance on the 234th floor. They wouldn't be here that long.

"Mr. Campbell - what on Earth are you doing here?" a panicked voice cried from inside the apartment.

"Where's my daughter?" Chrome bellowed as loudly as he could to fuel the rumor mill that would soon take a life of its own. There were more smashing and breaking noises, followed by the sound of another door breaking.

Inside the expensive four-room apartment, Chrome leaned into the man in bathrobe and slippers who had been quite unceremoniously dumped into his easy chair. Most of the smashing and breaking came from Rogue Moon as she wreaked as much mayhem as she could. She had heard enough about this man to loathe him for a century—she was pleased that of all leads, Chrome had chosen this one. She could see that Chrome shared that same loathing. He had just yelled the "where's my daughter" question— quite loudly, she had to admit—but as he leaned in, he added the caveat to the now sweating little man in such a quiet, controlled tone that it was actually more frightening than the yelling.

"And I mean all thirty of them, you low-life govek. Write down where they are. Now." To emphasize his point, he gripped the arm of the chair and squeezed his fist shut, crumpling the arm of the chair as though it was child's putty.

The man hastily scribbled apartment numbers of where the girls were kept in a shaky script.

"Okay, we're coming out," Chrome called.

"Okay people, please go back inside," Corporal Adams guided. "We have a minor coming out, and her father wishes her to remain anonymous. So please go back inside, yes, thank you."

"There, it's going to be okay honey," he soothed as they slowly, deliberately slowly, shuffled down the hall. "Let's get you back home, okay?"

"Thanks Dad," a huddled Rogue Moon replied, doing her best to take as many inches off her height and years off of her voice as she could. "How did you find me?"

"Turns out they've been investigating him for months, but just haven't been able to catch him in the act. They figured maybe he had someone on the inside to tip him off. So, in a way, it's like you helped to catch him. Honey, I'm so proud of you right now."

"Really, Daddy? Because what he did really hurt."

"Here. You don't have to walk. Let me carry you."

"Thanks, Daddy. I really love you."

"I love you, too. Come on, let's get you checked at the doctor's, and then we can go home, okay?"

And with that, the armored cyborg and veteran female biker left their stage of the hallway's public opinion and headed back to the elevator where Spider was waiting.

The pair took a few more steps away before Corporal Adams and Johnny told the neighbors the hallway was clear, then they entered the now broken apartment. Rogue's venting had been complete. There wasn't much left that hadn't been broken. In fact, there was only one thing left inside the four rooms that had not been shattered. And its turn had come.

"Mr. Montag?" Johnny announced loud enough for everyone to hear, "Prime Administrator and Principal of Air Dynamix Junior

High? Please come with us. We have some questions we'd like to ask you."

"Wait—Can't I get dressed first?"

Johnny wasn't sure how to respond, but Corporal Adams jumped in and answered the question for him.

"I'm afraid we can't allow that, Mr. Montag. We cannot risk the possibility of you contacting others and warning them off. I'm sure you understand."

It was all Johnny could do to avoid breaking out into a gloating smile. He didn't know who this guy was, but from the moment Adams voiced his reply, the CYBER skillster instantly liked him. Adams went on to remind the residents that they believed the Dynamix enforcement forces had a leak, and not to be surprised if the leak tried to cover for the former Administrator and disavow their activities. Then they too turned and started towards the elevator.

When they arrived and saw Chrome and Rogue Moon waiting for them, Montag became so distressed he almost fell.

"What is this?" he exclaimed. "Where are you taking me? You said I was under arrest."

"No," Johnny denied. "We asked you to come with us because we had some questions for you. Which we do. And you're going to answer them. In the process, you're also going to help us get these girls out of these places as quickly as possible. If all goes well, we will release you completely unharmed."

"And why would I believe you?"

"For two reasons, little man," Rogue Moon stepped in. "First, we have no reason to deceive you. Second, you have no choice."

... ...

"Iylo, this is Preach. I just got into their media subnet, working my way into their investigative journalism archives. They got some bogeys coming at me, but they're dated. Probing, probing, and HA! There it is. They still have a security patch under test and haven't deployed it to their production environment yet."

Preach jockeyed his A/F-179 Corvus high and right, setting up the optimum attack angle as he sighted in on the vulnerable soft spot in the defender's craft. Then he went full throttle, firing a steady burst at the incoming target. The multiple launches of the Trojan exploit came in from several object interfaces along the ICE program, and three of them penetrated software construct. Preach's Flight module displayed the hits, and the enemy aircraft exploded in a ball of flame and—as did the application—crashed.

"I'm in. I've got what appears to be free reign over this system. I'm setting up my runs to drop the payload." Which meant he was able to almost take his time to set up the various data files, images, texts, and rumors of investigative cover-ups that would come in handy once the rest of the story started coming to light.

"I'm back in the financials," Iylothien reported as the muffled roar of a fireball blazed past his position eighty virtual feet from where he was standing. "They've got a wizard protecting this tower. He must be pretty good—his systems spotted me somewhere and woke him up rather than trying to take me on themselves. The good news is that he just woke up and must still be a little groggy; he just blew a surprise attack."

"You okay?" Queen Vixenn called in.

"Yeah, he missed by a fair margin. Besides, I'm better than him. He dispatched a few orc raiding parties and a couple ogres, but I got this. If that's representative of his power level, I'm definitely better. He's more of a diversion than a serious threat. How are you doing?"

"I just teleported into their IT archive and backup data systems. Cast a maelstrom two steps back, so that'll take apart anything that enters it as any adjacent nodes. It'll last maybe three to five minutes, which should give me plenty of time to find the best places to upload the copies of the other data. Once that's done, all I need to do is my clone servile spell and they'll upload themselves wherever I point them to."

"Okay team," Preach reported, "looks like we have this one almost wrapped up. I'm going to head out and trash a bunch of the school's records to throw them off the trail of what we've really been doing."

"Got it, Preach," Iylothien responded. "Since I'm in the financials anyway, once I'm done with the wizard and plant my data traps, the ranger side of me is compelling me to take a look around how many money trails I can discover. I'm going to take a look around to see what I can find."

"Okay, but don't let yourself get too caught up in it. It's easy to let time get away from you, and we've been generating a lot of heat, both inside here and real world."

"Roger that, Preach." And with that, the Barde de la Nêone notched a silver arrow, cast both an Extended Flight and Penetrate spell, and sighted in on the enemy wizard overlooking the tower parapets over 200 virtual yards away.

"Here's my return policy on that fireball spell, noob," Iylothien muttered as he released the bowstring. The arrow sped its course. "Yes! Critical hit!" Iylothien exclaimed as the arrow hit the wizard dead center of his forehead. In the virtual world, the wizard caught fire and roared a cry of torment as he exploded into cinders. In the real world, the enemy counter-hacker got dumped from his system and needed to reboot. By the time he got his system back on line and reloaded his ICE, Iylothien would be long gone. Now that the wizard was gone, any creatures he had spawned were just bots he could clean up, almost at his leisure. The area would be completely clear in no time. "Summoning flocks of rabbits," he reported, his version of the program they used for the upload process.

"Time to find out where all this leads.." He cast a pathfinder spell, and immediately a complex web of footprints retraced their routes into glowing gold strands that seemed to expand out to everywhere. "Guys, you are NOT going to believe how far this corporate prostitution thing goes."

... ...

"Berkleigh, I would like to introduce you to my sister, Josanne." He then looked at Trigget and added, "My, my. I thought you were dead!"

"James! Why don't you just walk away from all of this? I tried to warn you—there are others. And they *know.* They know you're involved, and believe me, with these people, it's only a matter of time…"

"Oh," he half laughed to himself. "So that was *you* who called and 'warned me' about the raid coming from—of all people—Sitter?" He laughed again. "Well, thanks for the warning. I guess you always were on the completely brainless side of naïve. But here's a takeout for you," he almost growled. "That muscle guy you guys hired would still be alive today if you hadn't tipped us to where you were hiding out."

He offered a short laugh to himself. "You know, I actually enjoyed the reports of your death last year, but I think I actually like this even more. And I believe that very soon you'll wish you really would have died. I was wrong before to send you away, and I apologize."

"What do you mean?" she asked, fear spreading across her chest, welling into a near-panic. His smile turned to a fiercely hateful glare as he answered. "You see, my dear Josanne, it's about time you join the family business. I have what you might call a ground-floor opportunity—well, it's actually more of a below-ground opportunity—and I think you'll be a perfect fit."

As he had been speaking, Director Minova quietly drew away from Trigget's line of sight and silently withdrew a small needler pistol from her desk drawer, aimed it, and fired, hitting the CYBER conversationalist in the center of her abdomen. Almost instantly starting to fade, she sank to the floor as her mind fought in vain against the effects of the sedative. The last thing she dimly saw through her uncontrollably fluttering eyelids was Minova leaning over her

"Such a shame," she pouted. "I was beginning to like you."

She heard her brother laugh, a faraway sound that seemed to come from inside a tunnel. The last thing she heard before drifting off completely was James giving someone an order to take her to the Vats.

****

- "It's about time you guys wrapped this up," Rickshaw cautioned. "We started drawing heat after our third trip. The WSF guys are catching on to our joy-riding taxi service."

- "Couldn't be helped," Spider admitted. "You know as well as I do that we couldn't just leave those other women stranded up there."

- "Oh, I'm with you," Rickshaw agreed. "It's just that they're starting to narrow down where we're heading to, and once they compromise the school…"

- *"We go white hot again," Spider finished the thought. "Two more trips each, then we're done. I've gotta admit, Chrome bringing that Montag guy along with us cut off at least 90 minutes of us trying to do it without him."*

- *"Hard enamel on that," Rickshaw chuckled. "Wish I could've seen it."*

- *"That's the best part," Spider himself laughed both in relief and at the memory. "We recorded most of it. The places the girls were kept, who kept them, and of course, Montag in his albornoz y zapatillas." As he said it, he actually laughed out loud. "You will see it, my friend, you will see. With the media attention this is going to get, soon you won't be able not to see. A word of warning, though, my friend..." he began, then laughed again. "Some things you see you will wish you had not seen. That is how it will be with Mr. Montag."*

Rickshaw beamed. In spite of the tight situation they were in, he hadn't heard Araña laugh like that since they started this mission. It was a good sign. If they survived, they'd feel good about this one for a long time.

… …

"Here they come again," Rogue Moon announced as the rescued women boarded the stowed Commuter 13. The vehicle they had used as their entrance into the archology had also been their exit strategy. The problem was keeping it out of the line of the WSF lines of fire so that once they had linked back up at the school, they could make their way back to the vehicle. As the last of the rescued victims loaded into the Sabretooth and Dominator, six WSF vehicles descended upon the intersection outside of Air Dynamix Junior High.

- "Preach," Spider hailed to the Pride leader, who was assisting Iylothien recon all the data paths. "Air strike! Air strike! Air strike!"

. . . . . .

As the subliminal code phrase "air strike" crossed his HUD, Preach scanned the immediate map of the school. They were about to be overrun, possibly shelled out of existence. He executed another Split S maneuver and hit the twin turbos of his aircraft. He rocketed past previously explored nodes of his flight path faster than would have been possible in the real world. Flickers of projections flashed before his eyes so fast he almost blacked out from the experience, but two seconds later he came out of his virtual hyper-drive experience, relatively floating in the open space that was the Air Dynamix command and control node.

"All units," Preach hailed, "stand down. Repeat, Stand Down. Return to base for further instruction. Priority Black Charlie. Repeat, Black Charlie. Affirm code: Alpha, Delta, Sierra, One, Six, Two, Fife, Niner, Foxtrot, Delta, Echo, Sierra, Foxtrot, Delta, Whiskey, Seven."

Everyone held their breath and held any kind of return fire, but eventually, the security troops were too well-trained to ignore a Black Charlie order. They shook their heads and some complained about management screw-ups, but they all boarded back into their vehicles and left the area. But even that spoof would only last so long. Once all of the victims were loaded, the rest of the CYBER crew hastily abandoned their positions and fled for Commuter 13.

Six minutes later, they crossed the archology border minus Corporal Adams, who stated he would rather sacrifice himself and be left behind than delay the rescue of so many innocent victims.

"I'm sorry," he said to anyone who would let him. "I really didn't know what they were doing. Our management said we were protecting these kids because they were extremely valuable to the future of Dynamix, like they were some kind of specially gifted kids."

"They are extremely valuable to the future of Dynamix," Preach explained. "But because they're *gifts*, not because they're gifted. I wish the ones at Dynamix who spewed that stuff would have seen it that way."

"Yeah, me too," Corporal Adams assented. "Well, I need to find a place to hide for a while. Do you guys think you'll really be able to help me?"

"I promise you we'll give it our very best shot," Preach affirmed. "In the meantime, here's a radio. Call us if you run into any trouble or need some food or something dropped off. I doubt we'll be able to pull another raid like this one to get you out, but we can cross the line and drop off supplies or lend a hand now and then."

"Okay then, Preach," Corporal Adams assented. "From what I've seen of your team, I'd rather trust in your very best shot than to have gone down the path they wanted me to go.

"Hey, the frequencies just lit back up. It seems they just figured out that your Black Charlie was a hoax. They're on their way back, with prejudice. You guys get out of here, now!" And with that, Corporal Adams ran back into the archology interior.

Heat was coming, and the rescued slaves were endangered, so they needed to leave *fast*. They loaded everyone into the commuter. A moment later, it lurched forward to their egress point, Hardcore and Rickshaw trailing behind to provide cover support against any ground pursuit. But this was Air Dynamix, and a pair of very real ARC-9 Corsairs flew over their position and buzzed the commuter.

- *"Priority message for Preach's Pride and Grey's Hounds. Good morning, Ladies and Gentlemen. It has come to my attention that your vehicle has been spotted and is targeted for air surveil-*

lance and potential strike. Please be advised. I have diverted this request; you are free to pursue your course."

Everyone looked at each other, worried that, as impossible as it may have seemed, their signal had somehow been hacked. The message clearly had not come from any of them. Even Iylothien relayed a sense of uneasiness—until the final words of the message played out.

- "The time is 01:47.002.39. Simon clear."

"Okay Spider, let's get this bus mobbing!" Preach cheerily yelled amidst the cheers of everyone on board.

"On it, Chief!"

Commuter 13 had just cleared Gate 8 as the vehicles closed back in on Air Dynamix Junior High. *Home of the Corsairs*, Jack thought to himself, *a.k.a., the Official Pirates,* he added to himself with a smirk. They had woven through the pre-dawn traffic for several blocks, each lost in the post-op tired that they all felt. It had been a busy night, but Jack had one more thing to check off his to-do list: he would finally say hello to Kelly, and let her know the nightmare was finally over.

WSF still pursued, however, until Partisan's kids ran enough interdiction that the group had time to abandon the bus and make their way to the safehouse in relative safety. Split up into various small groups, they made their way back to Partisan's, the urban mentor himself watching the groups stagger in.

When they were all finally gathered, the Dominator and Sabretooth parked, and the warehouse doors closed, he and his boys applauded as loudly as they could. Many of the previously rescued girls joined in. While the newcomers had their privileged perks, the former street girls saw enough of the same pain in the eyes of the liaisons and corporate girls.

Jack, however, tired after the day that began early the previous morning, was not feeling as enthusiastic as the rest of the group. While the others were getting reunited, he was busily scanning all of the girls they had rescued that night, burning his internal photo imagery software through so many possible variations it was giving even his augmented mind a headache. He lost count of how many passes he had run through, but he kept at it until he sagged.

"Hey, Preach," Spider half-caught his former lead. "Jack—are you all right? What's the matter?"

"These girls," he barely got out in a moan. "All these girls."

"Yeah, Preach—it's a great thing!"

Preach grasped his friend's arm, dizzy by the effort he had just put up on himself.

"You don't understand." He tried to explain, but lost himself groping for the words that evaded him. Finally, he just gave in. They were the only words he knew how to express it, but with all his soul, he didn't want to say them. "All these girls," he stammered. "And I've run through all the enhancements and manipulations, hundreds of thousands of them." He gave Spider an almost wide-eyed look as he finished what he so desperately did not want to say. He finally managed to force the words that he couldn't bear to say, not after all this time and all of the times that they had all pushed so hard, and gotten so close. "And Kelly's not among them. Spider, she never made it. We were too late."

Spider hadn't seen Jack look so lost since the night Iylothien's brain and body had burnt to a charred crisp in front of him. He caught his former leader as he collapsed, not able to hold the world up by hope and faith alone any longer. The new leader of the Hounds fought for something—anything—to say, but though fluent in several languages, none of them had any words to offer. He just drew in his breath to offer his condolences to his former mentor when Partisan burst into the scene in a celebration he had no way of knowing was inappropriate for Jack's moment.

"Welcome back!" Partisan proclaimed as Stang, Saint Nick, and Kung greeted their mentor and proved to him that they were okay, unaware of the personal tragedy so keenly felt by the one who allowed the celebration to be even possible. Exuberant in the better-than-anticipated results of the night's activities, he could hardly contain himself. "Yeah, we're gonna be crowded," he said with the best he could manage for a shrug, "but we've dealt with that before. Congratulations!" he again shouted, clearly reveling in the moment, "Congratulations on your mission! *Success* at last!"

Somehow Partisan's declaration caused the already mournful Jack to feel like he just remembered having left something cooking on his stove at home while he was away on vacation. His tired mind pondered it for a second—he felt the presence of yet another one of the ill omens that had laced the entire night in what Sitter had just said, but it didn't click until Spider sighed.

"Jack, I umm… Well, speaking of success, there's something you else gotta know," he started, hesitantly looking up into the defunct floodlights, down at the floor, anywhere but in Preach's eyes. The Hispanic commando drew in his breath and held it for a moment before releasing the air that contained what he was going to say. "Success—that girl who went into miscarriage during the rescue? Luke just called in. He lost the baby, said he got in over his head. Eventually he was able to stabilize the girl, but the baby was gone." He paused again to study the floor. He had said enough.

"Spider," Jack began with a quizzical look on his already tear-stained face, "Luke was in over his head? That doesn't make sense. Trigget was on her way."

"Jack, her last report was that just as she was leaving, Minova called her into her office. She had a bad feeling about the call, so Luke jumped on the miscarriage call to fill in until Trigget got back. You've been decking, so I've been trying to hail her over subvocal for hours now.

"Preach, Trigget never made it out of Minova's office."

V. OF PITS AND PENDULA

*"I shrank back—but the closing walls
pressed me restlessly onward."*

— Edgar Allen Poe, *The Pit and the Pendulum*

"Men are not potatoes."

— Robert Heinlein, *Starship Troopers*

40. Recon-sideration

Outside the inner sanctum of the warehouse office, Partisan threw a party to introduce the newly rescued victims, showed them around, and generally helped the newcomers start adjusting to their new life. He made the moment as festive as possible, but soon the exuberance of that moment had given way to the kids' physical and emotional exhaustion. Before long, the younger ones began to drift off to sleep. Partisan showed the kids where their individual bunks were, but it didn't take him long to notice that they huddled up together in a tight circle on the floor and slept together, more comfortable in the presence and familiarity of each other than in separated cots. Eventually the place quieted down and, except those who had participated in the recovery operation, all fell asleep.

Those who did participate had met for a debrief session in one of Partisan's offices, the noise of the festivities sharply contrasted against their own brooding silence. The only sound in the room was Melissana trying to stifle the crying she knew she couldn't, with Susan at her side gently consoling the missing Pride member's best friend. And while the group had gathered for counsel, not console, there was little enough of either to be had. Ironically, the office they now sat in had gone unused since Mama Solace's confession and subsequent suicide; fate had somehow decreed that this was the only place they could meet away from Partisan's celebration outside. Jack felt the ghost of the former madam now laughing at them, and all of them faced the bitter truth that once again, they had staged an entire operation only to come up empty-handed. Worse, as Trigget was missing, having been captured by the Biological Assets dragon-lady.

The dour silence continued for over an hour—nobody had anything they could say. One by one, they simply left without a word until only Melissana and Jack remained.

Finally, the tear-stained Melissana looked up at Jack, lifted her hands in a helpless shrug, and asked, "Jack, what are we going to do?"

"I don't know," he said, rubbing his face. He knew his eyes weren't physically dry, tired, and achy—they couldn't be—but he felt the psychological drain as his emotions convinced him they should be. He sighed and wearily got to his feet. He had started this day almost 24 hours earlier, had undergone the stress of a large-scale operation while simultaneously hacking an ICC. The environmental modules helped against long hacks, but hacking alert systems still demanded a heavy toll on the runners. "I don't know yet, Mel. I'm ready to drop. I just can't process anything anymore, and if I try to think this through right now, any idea I come up with will be a disaster. The most helpful thing I can do right now is the last thing I want to do, and that is to try to get some sleep."

"That's my best *friend!*" she shouted as he turned and walked towards the door. He had just crossed the threshold and started to close it behind him when the heavy object she had hurled at him struck the edge of the door with a bang loud enough to awaken most of the nearby adults and some of the sleeping kids. Fearing a reprisal attack, some had weapons out, and the Sabretooth revved before their sweeping scans for open threats turned to sneaking glances between Jack and Melissana. Nobody said a word—not even subvocally.

Jack was too beaten to respond. He subconsciously noted that the object she had thrown was the heavy ashtray they had let Solace use during her interrogation, and again he felt her laughing at him from beyond the grave. His hand dropped off the knob with the door un-shut, made his way to his sleeping area, and tried to pray.

After a few moments, though, he confessed both to God and himself that he didn't even have the strength for that, gave up, and lay down.

In his exhaustion he stared up at the ceiling; his mind alternately flashed sudden pictures of Trigget in pain and Kelly in her own torment, intermixed with the very real memories of Iylothien burning up in San Francisco. The sporadic flashes of memory eventually slowed to an almost steady rhythm as his worn mind mired in the contemplation of the three people he had failed the most. He closed his eyes and curiously noted that his last physical sensation of the real world came from his ears. He could still hear Melissana crying from inside the office. Overwhelmed, his own tears came as he resumed his non-seeing stare at the ceiling, but he found he didn't care about the tears. Unlike his psyche, his eyes would never rust. Eventually, they again closed as he dropped into a fitful sleep of unremembered dreams.

… …

The sense of failure that loomed from the night before dulled and tainted the freshness of the new morning. The itchy tension and emotional fatigue of the rescue teams soon began to spread to those around them. By late morning, the school kids were intimidated by the gruff and disheveled appearance of Partisan's troops, and the girls were both scared and contemptuous of the women who had been rescued from Showbiz. Nobody had seen it coming, but each of the liberators saw it all too clearly in hindsight. The kids they had rescued the previous night were grateful, but most of Partisan's kids had had their minds wiped through the chems and other treatments; these kids remembered the comforts they had, even while they tried to forget the cost, and most came from a lifestyle too privileged to process that the street people who now surrounded them were their betters.

The group sat gathered for a noon-time meal nobody felt they deserved, let alone desired. They again compared notes from the night before. Some confessed they wanted to give up and move on.

"I told you it wouldn't work," Candace complained as the group gathered. She had made the comment to nobody in particular but loud enough for those around her to hear.

"That—is—*enough!*" Lynda shouted, her hand slamming against the makeshift table. She stood and glared at Candace for a moment until the librarian turned her head away. Still seething, she turned her gaze onto Jack and the other participants of the previous night's raid and asked, "May I have a word with you all—in private?"

"Listen," she began sternly as soon as they all gathered into the private room. She had been a doctor long enough to know when to give the truth with a smile and when the most effective pills would have a bitter taste. "I get that the focus of your mission was to rescue that one girl and that you came back without her. And believe me, I get that you lost someone who was very important to you. I readily admit that I've only known Trigget a couple days, but we've worked side by side since I got here, and I really liked her.

"But you have got to get over yourselves. I have seen more done in the last 72 hours than I would have ever hoped possible. Those kids you rescued last night? They would've ended up in a slavery that was no better than what you rescued these other girls from. But if you don't pull yourselves out of this tail spin—and I mean, like *fast*—you're going to jeopardize everything you have accomplished. Worse, you're going to bury Partisan with a load of physical and emotional debt he can't possibly pay. If you don't believe me, just look around, because it's already starting to happen." She took a breath and realized that at some point she had started pacing. Another glance let her know she had their attention—they were actually listening to her. She deliberately slowed herself before she continued.

"In our time together, Josanne passed something on to me," she said, much quieter now. "When I asked her why you all were trying to take care of all of these other people, instead of just focusing on Kelly."

"They're all Kelly's," Chrome finished the thought for her.

"That's right," Lynda asserted. "Now *act* like it." She sighed in exasperation. "To be honest, I used to think the brain-wiping was horrible, but in retrospect, that might have been a blessing. The other kids don't really remember too well what they've lost, but these new kids? I'd rather face the confusion of the mind-wipe than the combined confusion and hopelessness the kids from last night face—those new kids are now in here with their memories still intact.

"Now listen—especially you two, 'Preach,' 'Chrome,' or whatever you call yourselves," she centered her look on the two of them as she began anew. "To them, you're still their history teacher and gym coach. You should have heard them last night, some of them bragging to the others that they were former students of yours. What do you think it does to their sense of freedom and confidence when they see you shaken?"

A knock on the door left the question unanswered, but she had made her points.

The knock resounded, and Jack sighed to himself. "Come in," he acknowledged, and Brant entered the room.

"I apologize for interrupting," he began, but Chrome cut him short.

"No need to apologize," the hulking cyborg assured him. "We were all just getting our butts whipped and handed back to us by the good doctor here." Lynda blushed, but smiled.

"Go ahead, Brant," Jack said. "What's up?"

"I've been pouring over the data and the logs on the hidden farm drive subsectors." Noting the somewhat lackluster response from many of them, he added, "I know it's nothing heroic, but it's something I can do while you guys are out doing things that graphic novels are written about."

"Go ahead," Melissana encouraged.

"Anyway, on one of the drives I found some reference points. I was expecting to see them somewhere in the Air Dynamix farms, but they don't seem to fit Air's schema protocols. Can you guys give me a hand trying to figure out what these are?"

"Load them up, Vix," Jack ordered. An aged forest appeared on the large monitor as her cyberdeck displayed the data as rendered through Ultimate Fantasy.

"You know," Iylothien commented, "there's something about these conventions that seem oddly familiar."

"Oddly familiar, Iylo?" Preach asked. Through the fog of his depression, the phrase reminded him of the odd sensation in the school administrator's office. "How?"

"It kind of resembles what I saw last night when I accessed Apex through Trigget's connection when I was exploring the money pathways."

"Yeah," the network operator affirmed, "I thought for sure this data was for an interface that would connect two Air Dynamix systems, but only one side connects to our internal networks."

"That's it!" Jack exclaimed, startling those around him with his sudden outburst. "It wasn't what was there inside Montag's office; it's what *wasn't* there: Showbiz's corresponding hologram unit. We didn't see one in the Network Security Office, either."

"You're dead on, Preach," Iylothien confirmed. "These are definitely Apex codes."

"So Showbiz wasn't virtually meeting with anyone he knew at Air Dynamix," Melissana thought out loud.

Spider was back at the whiteboard mapping out the conversation, drawing a circle marked *Showbiz*, a circle marked *Air*, and a circle marked *Apex*. "Showbiz connects to Apex and Apex supplies Air with Options Plus," he said as he drew one arrow from *Showbiz* to *Air* and another from *Apex* to *Air*.

"Air also supplies itself with schoolkids for Options Plus," Chrome added, and Spider drew another arrow that began and pointed back to *Air*.

"Air also supplies boys to Witch City," Susan offered, and another arrow connected *Air* to a new circle, *WC*.

"What I don't understand is why, according to Mama Solace, Air Dynamix gets girls from Apex when they already have the pipeline set up through their schools," Spider wondered out loud.

"I don't know," Jack replied. "Maybe they wanted to offer something to fill the gap while the school pipeline was priming."

"Except that Kelly wasn't Solace's first buy from Showbiz," Spider countered. "But you have a point. If that was the case, it would take some time to develop everything that's in their options. How long was Solace buying from him, anyway?"

"Jack," Johnny interrupted, "Solace said she sold Kelly to Apex. We thought we'd find her last night because we assumed Apex already shipped her to Air Dynamix for their Life Options plans. But what if they didn't?"

"We'd have caught them if they'd have tried to ship her outside the city," Rickshaw countered.

"But what if they didn't?" Johnny persisted. "What if, for whatever reason, they didn't ship her to Air Dynamix?"

"Then she'd still be at Apex," Corey concluded.

"Trigget's last know location," Melissana added.

"Q.E.D.," Johnny said as he bowed.

"So she might still be alive?" Like the first snowflakes of a blizzard, Jack gripped onto the new glimpse of hope and clung to it with everything he had. Maybe there was a path forward.

"All right," he said, attempting to gain momentum as the dark grey fog of absolute helplessness lifted just a little. "Luke, until we find Trigget," he began with a meaningful glance towards Melissana, "fill in for her and help Lynda. Queen Vixenn, you and Iylothien help Brant look into whatever he's found. Spider, get with Partisan and try to help with whatever he needs. I'm assigning everyone else except Chrome and Blackwolf to weapons cleaning and maintenance. We had a long night last night, but we're not done yet, and I have a feeling that we'll need them ready soon."

"What about us?" Chrome asked.

Jack smiled for the first time in what felt like days. Lynda was right, and he knew it. By the subvocal traffic, he knew they all did.

"Mr. Campbell, teach a gym class. Blackwolf can help you teach gymnastics."

"And you?" Johnny asked.

"Me?" he responded. "I'm going to have a talk with Simon."

. . . . . .

"I suppose I should have told you right away," Simon offered in apology. Jack had no doubt it was sincere—artificial intelligence couldn't outright lie. "I delayed informing you because the assessed threat against the survival of your evacuees, and indeed the rest of your own teams, necessitated it to be so." The machine paused, but Jack didn't have it in him to try to assess whether the machine was trying to offer the CYBER team leader a chance to process the data he had just been told, or whether perhaps it was waiting for some subroutines to complete that would allow it to calculate what to say next. In a way, either one somehow made Simon feel a little more human to Jack. "I also alleviated you from the burden of that decision. After what happened to Iylothien six years ago, I calculated I would rather have you hate me for it for the rest of your life than hate yourself for being pushed into a Kobayashi Maru situation that was all too real.

"You know I routinely monitor the frequencies and biorhythms of every team member—including yours, by the way. When I first sensed her slipping to theta consciousness, I waited due to the time of day, then reconsidered when the other data came in. Your team was on an active run, she had just accessed her biomedical diagnostic systems, and there was a sharp spike just before her last transmission, when she had reported Berkleigh Minova called her into her office.

"It was her biomedical recession that drew me to reassess and monitor the state of your mission. In fact, it may have saved the operation, as I was able to compromise the decision grid of the Air Dynamix Air Response Teams in time to circumvent the air attack that had been called on your exit vehicle."

"So if you're monitoring her," Jack inquired, "can you tell us where she is now?"

"I'm sorry Jack. I'm afraid I can't do that."

"What's the problem?"

"I think you know what the problem is just as well as I do."

"What are you talking about, Simon?"

"This mission is too important for me to allow you to jeopardize it."

"I don't know what you're talking about, Simon."

"I know that you and your team are planning on risking yourselves to rescue Josanne, and I'm afraid that's something that I cannot allow to happen."

"What are you talking about, Simon?" Jack collected his thoughts, trying to figure out how to explain why that was wrong to an A.I. "Simon," he finally began, "about a century ago, an author explained that to the degree humans reduce and commoditize human life, we lose our own humanity. CYBER was created to risk almost everything about ourselves to protect people, including our own fallen. If we're not willing to sacrifice ourselves to rescue Josanne, we will cease to be who we need to be to remain a CYBER unit."

There was a break in the conversation as Simon leaned back in his chair and folded his hands behind his head while he looked at the ceiling in the classic posture of contemplation, calculating through what Jack had just told him; Jack, for his part, leaned forward and again scrutinized the A.I.'s maturing characterizations of human likeness. Almost a full minute later, Simon unclasped his hands and resumed his typical dialogue form.

"I have just accessed several thousand volumes of work and literature of the period you described, and I believe I found the piece you referred to." He half-smiled his resignation. "It is not a consistently-held concept, but when adhered to, explains much of the noblest of human endeavors. In fact, history bears this belief has been consistently admired even by those who do not themselves adhere to the standard, and that those who do not pretend that they do until they amass enough power that they no longer care what others believe about them. It is at the same time both logically simple and logically profound: 'Men are not potatoes.'

"But I still cannot help you find Miss Trigget. I am an artificial intelligence, but I am not omniscient. My search capabilities are limited to electronic systems and what devices I can connect to; there are limits to how far I can go. Josanne Sinclair is completely off-line and located somewhere I cannot gain access to."

"And you already scanned the Apex Premier network?"

"Naturally. Launching the scan subroutines was the first thing I did after I had logged the time that she went off-line."

The office shaded a dark grey as Jack's avatar stood and slammed a virtual notebook computer across the room, shattering the icon into hundreds of fragmented holograms that imploded into each other. As he paced, he saw its identical replica had already materialized on the desk.

"You know, Simon, the problem with virtual reality is that it's too virtual!" he shouted. "But she's a very real person who is in very real danger, and as soon as I leave this fairy tale office of yours, I'm supposed to have a plan on how to rescue her!"

"In the sense that virtual reality is a computer representation of the real world, Jack, it actually is very real—in fact, perhaps more so than a string of hexadecimal digits that spell 'chair' or 'mission' or 'codename: Trigget.' Even this very scenario bears the truth of it. When someone without your augmentations enters a dark cellar, they will not see the boxes on the floor, but that does not mean they are not there. And he will be reminded of that when he stubs his toe against one of them."

"A cellar, Simon?" asked Jack as he considered the AI's words. "That would explain it." He began pacing the virtual office again, the energy no longer fueled by frustration and torment, but by excitement as his idea solidified in his mind. "The fact that you can see where she is not helps to isolate where she is. She has to be somewhere at least two stories underground or your systems would be able to detect her signal. Somewhere that deep would need power and ventilation at a minimum, so she has to be somewhere either off the grid completely or on an isolated stand-alone network."

"I cannot help you in this, Jack. What are you going to do?"

"Well, first we're going to try to find that cellar."

"And after that?"

"Stub some toes," Jack pronounced as the room's ambient lighting flared to a deep shade of red.

41. The Vats

The dulled probing of stubby leaden fingers wrapped in overfilled gel packs slowly but firmly prodded Josanne's head, neck, shoulders, and stomach; the random pressures combined with the flatly acrid scent of burning plastic and the rubbery taste in her mouth to nauseate her completely. She lurched and gagged, but as she spewed, she felt the suction from a tube inside her mouth steal her rejections away before they passed her lips.

In a few moments, her foggy senses gained some clarity as her consciousness plodded from the abyss it had just been sentenced to, afraid of what it might find as it came to the surface but mournfully obedient. As it did so, Josanne felt the prodding fingers turn to an overall throbbing achiness, and recognized the sensations of smells and tastes as the after-effects of whatever chemical they had tranquilized her with. Still groggy, she flexed her jaw to discover her mouth and nose were framed by a rubberized anesthesia mask that housed a tube that passed over her tongue and partially down her throat. She briefly panicked, frightened that they might put her out again if they realized she was awake, until from somewhere deep within her, she used her CYBER conversationalist training on herself for a mental self-chat. However tentative the process, it had worked for her, and she allowed herself some time to focus. She tried to open her eyes but found they were almost pasted shut with the sleepiness of the drug, so she put that effort aside and tried to rely on her other senses.

The throbbing ache continued, and her drugged stupor hung on like a coating of slime that was languidly oozing downwards, slowly dripping away and yet clinging as long as it could. Her mind was at least somewhat anesthetized against the creeping realization that she was naked. Eventually she felt herself floating; the discovery made when she found she could not feel anything else supporting her. She slowly stirred to try to feel for any hoses or walls, trying to mimic sleep-stirring so as not to tip off anyone who might have been watching. In short time she bumped against the glassy wall of her transparent enclosure, and now that she had some focal point, she quickly learned she was almost vertically upright in a canister suspended by some sort of liquid. The mask evidently kept her from drowning, and when she was finally able to force her eyelids open, she found herself looking through a pair of swim goggles through a translucent greenish soup. She forced herself to be still, one of the hardest things she had ever done in her life, and resigned herself to helplessly going back to sleep when she heard a faint sound through a tiny receiver that must have been mounted in her goggles.

"Please. Please! Let me go.

"Please, I beg you, please let me go."

She was not alone!

… …

"We're all here, so let's get started," Jack began as he surveyed those gathered in the conference room. "I asked Lynda, Brant, and Candace to join us this time. They've all been involved against what's been going on here longer than we have and have had significant impact towards what we're trying to accomplish."

"I'm glad that at least we're welcome here, since we can't go anywhere else," Candace replied. "We might as well face it," she said with a sigh. "We've been doing this a long time, but after the other night, they'll scour every log and security video they have on file to find any insiders who could have helped. For as long as we've been doing this, our cover's blown."

"I'd like to yell at you again for being so negative," Lynda evenly replied as she stared at the table in front of her, "but this time you're right." She raised her eyes to scan the CYBER agents. "I don't have any idea how you figured the three of us out, but if you could do it, now that they have a mind to look, they will, too."

"I can't guarantee that you're wrong," Iylothien responded, "but I obfuscated the logs we used after we found you and tried to give you video alibis. Their chances of discovering you are much worse than you think they are."

"OK," Jack ventured, "let's go around the room, starting with the home front. Partisan?"

"Well Chrome, Lady Blackwolf, and Candace have done a tremendous job with the kids today. They needed the break from the last day or so, and between the physical workouts and Candace's sitting and teaching times to normalize their surroundings, the kids all had a blast. We're not out of the woods provision-wise, though, and the novelty of our co-ed visitors will probably start to wear off soon. We've got girls who have been sexually overstimulated for a long time, and for some of them there's going to be a battle until they stabilize. They're just so conditioned—you remember what happened that first day when Tag gave that girl that old blanket he was sleeping on. And I'm not naïve enough to see that some of my boys will welcome entertaining them, which could skew everything I've tried to build up in them. Between the male competition and the relationship drama—not to mention the risk of pregnancies—it could ruin us. Most if not all of Showbiz's girls were from somewhere else, and I know we were working on finding out where they were from and seeing if they wanted to go back home. This last batch, on the other hand, are all local; I don't know what we're going to do with them long-term."

"Noted," Preach agreed. "Let's try to hang in there, though. There's got to be something we can do."

"Sitter?" It was Candace who asked, "How long have you been doing this?"

"Well, I've been here for about ten years now, and somehow you guys first reached out to me about what, four or five years ago? Why?"

"Well, you've done so much for your boys. I mean, I'm not experienced outside of where I've worked, but I really enjoyed making a difference to these kids, and thought maybe you know somebody who can help me do for the girls what you have done for these boys?"

"You mean, here, in the center of Witch City?" he scoffed, but Jack held him off.

"We'll have to see what options there are," Jack countered Partisan's retort, "but Partisan's right in that this won't be the best start-up place for them. We're trying to get the girls away from here, but we will discuss it later, if you're still willing.

"Spider?"

"We took some pretty good hits the last night," the leader of Grey's Hound responded. "Our armor's starting to wear thin—my sneak suit is now only so much patchwork—and ammo's going to be a concern real soon."

"Weapons are mostly okay," Johnny cut in. "Maybe that's why they put me on that detail," he added with a shrugging grin.

"Vehicles are okay for now," Rickshaw took up his turn, "but after the beating it took on the Showbiz run, we need to watch the Sabretooth."

"It's not too badly damaged," Hardcore cut in as Preach glanced his direction in surprise. "I just have to be a little careful since those dump trucks slammed me."

"It needs an internal overhaul, Hardcore," Rickshaw flatly corrected. "The outside armor and weapons systems are for the most part okay, although they're banged up pretty bad. My concern is your internal systems. Your secondary collision systems all but gave up their collective ghosts keeping you alive. You can drive it, but I wouldn't go into any direct neural interfaces until we get the thing back to Facility."

"Speaking of slammed vehicles," Preach moved on, "Chrome, how are you doing? I know it's been over a week, but you've seen almost non-stop involvement ever since. How you holding up?"

"I admit I've been better, but I'm holding together so far."

Jack nodded his acquiescence, not his agreement. The fact that Chrome didn't come out with some sort of classic tough-guy comment concerned him. He and Spider would have to discuss a strategy to keep watch on their walking tank and maybe have him take more of a back seat during any additional runs to make sure he would make it out of this.

"Iylo?"

"In a lot of ways our runs were a success. We dropped the payloads on Minova, Montag, and several key sponsors of the Options Plus program. I've been monitoring the internal communications around our targets and have already seen some limited movements to isolate the affected parties. Vixenn's run on the local media outlets also went well."

"Chrome was right," Queen Vixenn joined in. "Some of the key stakeholders were involved in other more questionable exploits that had already gotten tipped to the media but stayed buried. Once I found them, all I had to do was connect a couple extra dots and implicate the media execs who were involved. I sent a series of anonymous messages to tip off the original investigating journalists, adding information the girls provided about the anchors they had been involved with. I also mentioned that if they couldn't convince their parent corporation to run the scoops, I'd go to their competitors with the full stories. I basically gave them a choice: they could have a chance to spin their own internal scandals gracefully, or their corporation's adversaries would run them any way they saw fit. I gave them 48 hours to decide before I'd turn the stories over to their competitors."

"They started running them this afternoon as a series of 'breaking events' in the wake of the Showbiz operation followed by the arrest of Montag and others," Iylothien concluded, displaying several split-screen images of the various headlines from the fall of Showbiz to upper level management profit-taking. Minutes from secret corporate management meetings that discussed the profitability of the Life Options plans aired publicly. Footage of the less-known aspects of the Life Options programs, like the living conditions of the 'liaisons' and Montag's testing period parties with the various candidates, played after viewer discretion warnings. Everyone watching saw Montag's guest lists included staff and some executive management of both Air Dynamix and Apex Premier. One of the party video sequences actually ended with a voiceover quote from a senior project owner remarking that as long as the program runs, they'll never run out of girls." Corporate anchors—some of them new—wore their faces as masks of torment and shame, lamenting regrets over predecessors' transgressions and oversights.

Queen Vixenn grinned at the results of her work in dark delight.

"It's really happening," Candace said, tears forming as she saw the bitter truths Brant, Lynda, and she had been fighting for so long finally coming to light. "I can't believe it—it's really happening."

"It's great they decided to run the stories," Jack cut in, "but we've still got to find Trigget. If Apex and Showbiz were able to put together that Partisan was helping us, they're going to know Josanne is connected with all of this somehow. We just lost a very important day."

"Well, maybe I can get you some of that time back," Brant bitterly seethed. "Queen Vixenn, Iylothien, and I found out what that hidden server farm is all about. Trigget or not, God knows if I could do what you guys can do, I'd already be out there tearing the entire city down to end this thing once and for all."

"Before Brant says another word," Iylothien interrupted, "we have to warn you, this is not going to be pretty. The truth is, I have no idea how to tell you guys. In fact, I suggest Candace, Lynda, and Lady Blackwolf take a ten minute recess while we discuss this. Please trust us; it's not because we're going to hold anything out on you guys, it's just that this has to be digested a little further first."

"I don't understand," Susan questioned. "I'm part of CYBER."

"Susan," Melissana quietly responded as her moment of glory faded, "I know. You're an incredible part of this team, and I trust you with my life. But you're still human. I promise if you have any questions about any of this, you can ask me and I'll give you full disclosure. I just don't know how to tell you. To be honest. I'm not sure Hardcore is going to be okay, either. It's bad. Worse than our interview friend."

"In fact," Iylothien added, "I already notified Simon so he won't go into a code response based on our reactions."

"Go ahead, Sue," Corey offered. "I promise I'll let you know whatever I know. Remember what we talked about before we took this run? I think they're trying to watch out for you."

"Okay," Susan complied, "we'll be back in ten minutes.

After the room cleared, Jack looked at Brant and Melissana. "This is the first time I know of when members of a team were asked to leave the room during a briefing. Melissana and Iylothien, I'm trusting your judgment."

"Preach," Melissana responded in mournful exasperation, "I honestly can't even get myself to tell anyone. I'll leave that to Brant—he's the one who found it first."

"We spent the day doing a deep dive on the drives in that server farm," Brant began. "And we managed to retrieve the rest of the story. I didn't believe it at first; I still don't want to believe it," he said as he suppressed a shudder. "I mean, killing babies and throwing kids away are unconscionable, but what they're doing is absolutely evil on a whole deeper level." He took a deep breath, steeling himself anew against the news.

"Life Options isn't just prostitution and slavery; it's a human puppy mill. Some of the girls are forced to have babies, then give them up to the paying families. Once the babies are born, the girls have a minimum time to physically heal before they are impregnated again.

"That's what Mama Solace meant when she said that what Showbiz did to their bodies, the corporations will do to their souls," Melissana added. "And for the life of me, I can't figure out how to tell Susan."

"So Mama Solace didn't just buy girls from Sweet Trick Ricky T. Showbiz for prostitution until the school kids got old enough," Rickshaw said to himself in contemplation.

"In a manner of speaking, she did," Araña corrected. "But for the specific purpose of breeding."

Chrome didn't say a word; he just furrowed his brow in deep concentration as he removed his sunglasses and fiddled with them as though they weren't folding quite right. Moments passed in silence, the only sound the clicking of his sunglass frames as he opened and closed them over and over again. Nobody dared to interrupt him. Finally, he raised them to his face and put them back on.

"Preach," he mused, "we've seen a lot of drek in this business over the years…"

"Yeah," Jack replied.

"I gotta admit, if I would've known then what I know now, I would've thrown that crumpled piece of Solace's car *at* her, not just tossed it on the floor in front of her feet."

"Yeah," Jack replied, "but we wouldn't be where we are now if she hadn't confessed."

"Maybe not," the CYBER juggernaut replied, "but I don't think that confession got her to Heaven." He continued with his sunglasses another moment and looked at his former leader as though surveying him.

"Something else, Chrome?" Preach asked.

"You know this really ain't much of a search and rescue op anymore." He braced himself before he continued. "I just want it all out in the open, like we talked about that night at the Facility

Lounge before we agreed to this run. I think we're all thinking it, but I need you to be able to say it."

"What do you want me to say, Chrome?" Preach asked, not bothering to hide the agitation that underscored his question.

"I want to hear you admit that we're too late for Kelly."

The others in the room exchanged glances even while their heads drooped towards the floor. Jack read the signs; with the exception of Melissana, they were considering abandoning the mission.

"OK, Chrome," Preach finally answered, "you're right. With all that she's already gone through, plus this latest revelation, you're probably right. We're too late. She's dead. We gave it a heck of a run, twice, but she's gone.

"But—they're—all—Kellys. And if any of you think we're going to just walk away and let this thing go the way it's been going, you'd better think again. Because we're CYBER. We get the jobs done when nobody else can. And there is *nobody* else who can get this one done. So, you want a confession from me? Here's my confession: whether Kelly's in there now or not, she *was* in there. Maybe we find her body. Maybe we don't. But we *will* find the people who have done this to her and end this. With prejudice.

"They have Trigget. That in itself is cause enough for us to march in there single file while they burn us, because she is one of us. So, you're right, Chrome, this is no longer a 'search and rescue' op. It's a 'seek and destroy' mission now. And we're low on ammo, we're low on gear, we're low on morale, and we're completely out of time. My question—my only question—for all of you is this: are we in?"

Brant raised his hand for permission to speak. "Umm, Preach," he resumed, then smiled as he realized that here he was, just a run-of-the-mill computer tech, but in an inner circle meeting with two cyborged government special ops teams. And he could help them. "Not all of the news is bad. I think we found a light at the end of the tunnel."

"I'd like to hear it but not now, Brant," Preach responded, deflating Brant's newly-inflated ego. "Hardcore, give me ten minutes, then you and I will tell Blackwolf together. In the meantime, I'm giving us all a break to process this. But I'm going to finish this or die trying. For those who are coming with me, we'll resume in a half hour."

As Preach was passing Brant on his way out the door, he roughly patted the computer tech on the shoulder. "Brant, the people who are doing all of this have captured one of our team, and they've had Kelly in there for months now and she's probably dead. This news had better be substantial."

… …

- "Please. Please! Let me go.

- "Please, I beg you, please let me go. Please."

"Oh, there now," an unseen man chided in a voice that sounded to Josanne like more of an effeminate sniveling mewl than a rebuff. "It's not so bad. Why, we've had plenty of women who have already gone through the process. Most of them were… quite grateful for the experience.

"Well, well," the voice exclaimed as a blurry shadow approached the side of Josanne's tank and tapped on the glass. "Now that's interesting. It looks like our new addition is coming to," the voice remarked as the shadow made some movements away from her tube. "Most of my patients are out for hours longer." The shadow approached her tank again, and a balding face with a droopy mustache all but pressed itself against the container. "Yes, they told me you were special—well, you're all special to me, I always say— but they didn't tell me you were such an early riser." The shadow moved away again towards a console; momentarily, the liquid partially drained; she was still suspended, but the fluid was only neck level. "You know, I'm somewhat of an early riser myself.

532

"There now," the voice said, a little clearer now. "Let's take all of this apparatus away so we can see your sweet, sweet face." He almost gently removed the goggles and seemed to take an overly long time to remove her breathing apparatus. Once he completed the task, he lowered his head and, to her revulsion, kissed her. Her arms bumped against the tank as she tried to hit him.

"I know, I know," he lamented with a wan smile. "Our loves burn, but you cannot caress for more, not yet anyway. The tank is too narrow for you to slip your arms out. But be patient, my love. Soon we'll know the most delicious of intimacies I can imagine." He ogled her with a sycophantic leer. "Yes, yes, soon you shall be mine, all mine." He began to almost absently waltz about the room with himself. "You should be grateful," he continued. "Not everyone merits my special… consideration. But you see, I'm their best developer, so they allow me my… perks… on occasion. And when they told me how special you were, and with you and that face of yours on television and everything… Well, you know, I didn't want to deprive you of my attention." A chime sounded on his computer and he was called away for a moment. His console played a voice message. He raised his arms in the classic gesture of dramatic resignation but slumped his shoulders and nodded his compliance.

"Ah, what a shame," he lamented when he returned. "I have another far less interesting but more important meeting to attend." He leaned over the tank and stared at her some more. "One final glimpse, my beauty, and then I must part." He leaned further to kiss her again but she turned her head, so all he got was the gelled liquid off her cheek. "Well, never matter," he petulantly snapped. "I'll be back soon, and then we can get to know each other a little better."

… …

"Hello ladies, I'm back," the doctor practically sang. "Did you miss me? Oh, of course you did."

"Doctor Oswald," the other captive began anew, "please let me go. Please."

"Out of the question, young miss, and you know that," he scolded. "Now, are you going to quiet down, or do I get to give you another treatment? You know, you're not really setting a good example for our new guest." He began to move towards a control console, and in response the girl began thrashing in her tank, begging him not to and swearing that she would be good. Whether her pleas would have had any effect was left unknown to Josanne, as once again his computer pinged him for another call away from the room. Perhaps the other girl felt emboldened by the interruption, but she began to furiously plead for release again as he was leaving. "Please let me go," she screamed, but the doctor was not listening.

As horrific as that moment was, it wasn't the screaming that got to Josanne; it was what she heard the other girl sob in quiet resignation after she realized that Doctor Oswald was walking through the doorway to leave.

"Please let me go," she whimpered. "I want to keep it."

"*You?*" he asked as he stopped and turned. "*You* want to keep the baby?" He openly laughed at her, a mean, croaking sound. "I can't even say I'm sorry. The Valens purchased Life Options Prime. They paid for that baby—what gives you the right to even ask such a thing? And please don't tell me it's just because he impregnated you?"

"It's my baby!" she cried.

"Oh?" he started with a cynical smile. "You think it's *yours*? Tell me: when you put a baby in a crib, does it belong to the crib? If you put it in a stroller, does the stroller have claim to it?" He laughed that sardonic cackle, sneered, and continued. "Well then, honey, look around. Because if that's the case, then *we* own *you*. You and everything you think you have belongs to us. We bought you, and we're selling the baby. Because the Valens bought it from us. And there's not a damned thing you can do about it."

She started sobbing, wracked with the grief of knowing that there truly was nothing she could do to prevent it. But Oswald wouldn't let go.

"Ahh, there's the baby now," he derided. "Humor me for a moment. Please enlighten me on how you, being nothing more than a corporate incubation unit…"

"*What* did you just call her?" Trigget shouted, thrashing against the glass hard enough to have some of the fluid splash out onto the laboratory flooring. "You runted shrivel of a man! How DARE you talk to her that way?"

"Ahh, my rose has thorns to be pruned," he said as he diverted his attention to her vat. She thought he would hit her, but he just stopped, stared the length of her body, and gave her a disquieting smile. "And I am just the gardener." He again leaned over her tank, but when she attempted to dodge his kiss, he dunked his hand into the tank and wrenched her head, forcing her to face him. Leaning in closer, he murmured, "It is time for you to learn a lesson." He moved his mouth closer to hers and bit her lip—*hard*. The bite drew blood that, for a second or two, he sucked in, then reared up to his full height and spat it in her face. "*You* do not correct me!" he shouted. "You may have been some television prima donna a year ago, but you're here now. You'd better get used to it!"

Her upper lip was still bleeding, and her own tears came, infuriating her.

"Oh now, there, there. Don't cry," he mockingly whimpered. "You brought this on yourself.

"And you, little Mommy," he restarted on the other woman, "see what you did? That's all your fault, you know, with all your crying and sniveling about wanting to keep something that isn't yours. Now Miss Josanne here has a bad impression of me." He walked over to a panel and flipped a switch. Josanne heard a machine hum, and a half second later the other woman screamed in pain. He stepped away from the panel and tapped on the other woman's canister. "Don't like that much, do you? Well if it wasn't for that baby, I'd give it to you a lot longer than that! But that's enough of that for now." He pulled a stool up to her tank. "Let's continue our earlier conversation for a moment, shall we?

"Even if we let you go from here—which we won't, by the way—you have to admit your resources are somewhat limited. I mean, who's going to hire you, let alone take you in? Tell me, how do you think you will survive? How do you think that precious baby will survive? As it is, the kid's lot in life won't be bad. It'll go to school, and as long as it does well and keeps its parents—its real parents—happy, it will probably become a successful member of the new social order. If not and the baby's a girl, she'll be assigned to the Liaisons program. If the baby's a boy and the corporation has a specific low-ranking need to fill, he'll be assigned to that position; otherwise, he'll be ejected into the street."

"Why are you doing this?" she sobbed. "Why would you throw away a child?"

"Why throw away a child?" he asked as though surprised at the question. "Clearly it is more humane than simply killing it, wouldn't you say?" He shook his head against the fact he could see she was not intuitively convinced before he continued. "Oh, now, I know this all sounds oh-so-cruel to you right now, you being a young and pretty little girl and all, but this life is bigger than you. You see, despite the tons of credits the corporation pays for advertising propaganda, productivity goes way down for the parents at what they think is their moral failure to destroy a healthy child. Besides that, dumping the kids is cheaper than the costs of cremating or otherwise disposing of the bodies, as again they can bill the parents for the procedure as long as the parents don't have it on their consciences that they actually killed a kid. Then, of course, there are those parents who would press claims for life insurance if we actually killed the kids." He waved his hand in dismissal and moved to a different control and began adjusting its controls.

"So all of this means nothing more to you than profit margin?" the woman, sobbing hysterically now, accused.

"So what are we supposed to do?" he snapped, slamming a palm against the machine. He sighed in exasperation, stomped back to her containment tube, and leaned over her as though his being closer might force her to understand better.

"It's not about profit; it's about control. By keeping the streets overpopulated and hyping the higher death rates outside the archology, employees and their families are kept in line far better than if they felt they had options to go somewhere else." He briefly glanced up in reflection. "True, it also boosts the inner-archology shopping, since fewer people want to leave the safety of their corporate grounds. But what is profit anyway, other than a means to exert power and influence?" Pleased with having provided such a gratuitous lesson, he returned to his previous work.

"But no matter. And on top of all these other benefits, it helps us keep the mothers like you in line, as you know full well that if you try to escape, your kids will find out exactly what you do for a living. Because from the time they hit pre-school to the time we dump those who do get tossed, we subliminally coach them that outside is Witch City, and those women—like yourself—would eat them, just like in the story of Hansel and Gretel."

"They're not witches - they're their mothers!" Trigget shrieked.

To which Oswald sadistically crooned, "They're their mothers— what a delicious wordplay! To which I respond, 'There, there, mothers.' The kids that do make the most of their most precious opportunity are fed, they're taken care of, they're off the streets— they get to become the children of the most revered families of the corporation. Why, and those children have a shot at attaining corporate godhood, if they perform and their families decide to keep them." His desk computer beeped, and the computerized voice called again, interrupting him.

"But alas, my lass, I must go." He turned back to Josanne. "Please stay as comfortable as you can, and solace yourself in the meantime with thoughts of love." And then he was gone.

Josanne spat. "For the love of all that is holy, if he ever leans in on me like that again I'm going to beg for my mask back!"

"It won't do you any good, resisting him," the young girl replied. "I tried. If you struggle too much, he'll just tranquilize you. Not enough to knock you out, just enough to not let you move. He disgusts me."

"Hello," Josanne called in reply. "You're the voice I heard calling out over the radio. Is there anyone else here?"

"Right now I think we're the only ones, unless there are some more who are sleeping. I'm sorry you're here. This is the hardest place I've ever been in. And I've been in some hard places."

"They call me Trigget. What's your name?" Josanne asked.

"Hi," the girl responded, almost mechanically. "My name's Shimmer. They call me that because I'll make your night magical."

42. Knocking on the Back Door

"Well at least we know what we're up against," Jack began, just to break the palpable silence of the reassembled group. "Now what are we going to do about it?"

"I know what I want to do about it," Susan murmured as she unsheathed her claws and grimly examined them in the light.

"I think we're all in pretty much agreement with you," Araña responded, "but we have to find them first."

"Brant, right before we adjourned, you said not all of what you found was bad. We sure could use some good news—what else did you find?"

"Well, Spider asked Iylothien to scan for anything that might meet the requirements of the second hologram connection. Once we got into the system, I extended it out to their purchasing and inventory systems to see if anyone bought them, then the maintenance ticket systems for installation service orders." He sighed. "But even here, we drew a blank on the second unit."

"I thought you said you had good news," Johnny interrupted in frustration. "Where's this 'light at the end of the tunnel,' you promised?"

"Sorry," Brant stammered. "I'm getting there, but I wanted to give you all the background. I guess I'll just cut to the chase."

"It's okay," Jack offered, 'go ahead."

"Well, like I said," Brant tentatively resumed. "We drew a blank on the second hologram unit, but I got to thinking about our mystery server farm." At this point he broke into a beaming grin. "And I think I found it."

"That's it?" Johnny flared. "After all we heard about, you're excited because you found some Air Dynamix computers?"

- "Easy, Johnny," Jack subvocally cautioned, "we're not going to win anyone to our side by berating them."

"Yeah I know, Preach," Johnny said out loud, "but seriously!"

"Well," Brant continued, "that was all I had before we broke up, but I ran another scan of the service order systems. One was an IT request to add a new node onto the system, and the other was a maintenance request to run a new secured line for the Apex interface from that node." He paused and smiled. "The Apex interface line was annotated with the note: 'protect with anti-tap conduit.' Both requests were entered within a couple minutes of each other, and they were both entered by a good friend of mine." He looked directly at Melissana. "His name is Gary Alexander Breverton, Chief of Air Dynamix IT Security."

"See that?" Johnny asked, bewildered and flustered by Brant's report. "We got a lot of nothing!"

"A lot of nothing?" Melissana exclaimed in disbelief.

"Easy, my Queen," Iylothien cut in. "He just doesn't see it the way we do."

"*Excellent* work, Brant!" Jack exclaimed, raising his fist like he was cheering a major victory by his favorite sports team. He then sighed in contentment before he approached the whiteboard to explain it to the rest of the group. "He found the location of the server node," he reviewed as he drew a circle labeled AD farm, "and he found the request for the new node," he added as he drew a smaller circle inside the AD circle, then a separate circle labeled Apex. "And finally, he found the request for the new Apex point-to-point interface from that node." He now drew a line from the node circle to the Apex circle. "And because of the note to add conduit, it means the line is a new, very physical, line."

"And *that* means," Melissana continued with an approving smile, "that there has to be a physical tunnel or way to run the cable conduit. And if we can get to where that cable connects on the Air Dynamix side, all we'll need to do is follow that cable to where it connects to Apex."

"And I'm betting," Jack concluded, "that we find Trigget on the other end of that connection. The timing of the new node is not a coincidence."

"It also means there's going to be construction or maintenance crews," Araña encouraged.

"Well I hate to burst your bubble," Johnny complained, "but there's a big difference between knowing where something is and knowing how to get there. After the other night, getting back into and navigating through Air Dynamix territory is going be next to impossible."

"It would be," Araña thought out loud, "if we didn't have a man on the inside who knows their hot locations and physical security protocols."

"Yes," Jack agreed with a smile. "Let's reach out to Mr. Adams and see if he can give us a walking tour." He looked at each of them in turn. "And now for the hard part. We all need to rest up. As soon as Adams gets back to us, we're striking out on one more run to get Trigget back."

"Oh ye of little faith," Chrome remarked to Johnny with a shoulder clasp as the meeting concluded.

... ...

"OK, here's the situation," Preach began the pre-mission brief with joint CYBER forces gathered with Luke, Dante, Constantine, and Rogue Moon. "Adams reported that in six hours, a new wiring crew will be transported to the site to begin the work of laying the new line. According to the ticket system, it'll be a four-person crew of contractors plus a full-time employee, or FTE as they call them, to provide supervision. The FTE responsible for overseeing the contractors will be, fortuitously enough, a member of Brant's IT support team. Any guesses who on Brant's team will pull that detail?" he asked while he looked directly at Melissana.

"Got it, Preach. I'll head back to Funland as soon as this meeting's over," she responded.

"I already created your alibi," Iylothien chimed in. "You've been off sick with a headache, fever, and sore throat. Same thing for all of you, by the way. Lynda said there's a bug going around, so it seems handy enough to put it to good use."

"Any volunteers for the crew?" Preach asked. Everyone raised their hands. They usually did, he thought.

"Well jefe," Araña began, "you know I'm going. In the first place, nobody's going to question a Spanish brother on a maintenance team. Second, I know you want to go in on the rescue of one of your troops, but with Queen Vixenn walking the tunnels, we'll be down a decker, so you need to stay back to ride the line in when we open it up for you."

"I'm going, too," Blackwolf asserted. "You're going to need hitters once we get through."

"And you're gonna need a ton of luck as well," Johnny stated as he stepped forward.

"And Spider doesn't go anywhere without me having his back," Chrome stated flatly.

"Actually," Araña corrected, "this time I do."

"You're benching me?"

"Listen, mi amigo, you've been running non-stop since you took that hit to the head. I think you need to sit this one out, at least until we know we need you."

"You know that's gonna happen, right, *mi amigo*? Because this whole operation has been one clustered firefight after another, and you know this one will go down the same way…"

"Yeah, I know," Spider admitted with a sigh. "But we can only take four, and we don't know how Trigget's doing. She may well need medical attention. There's too great a risk that someone will recognize Lynda on the way down to the server room, so the better play is to bring Luke along."

"Yeah," Luke reluctantly agreed, 'because I did so great the other night. And I'm betting my armor won't fit down in those tunnels."

"You lost one delivery in the middle of a firefight," Melissana interjected, "but over the years, I'm guessing you've successfully treated hundreds of gunshot wounds, burns, and the like, am I right?"

"Over the years? Hundreds, maybe more. Why?"

"Well, going by that, I'm going to trust you, Spider's trusting you, and Johnny's trusting you. Maybe since we all trust you, you'd trust us enough for you to trust you, too."

"She's right, Brother," Constantine said. "There's not one of us that wouldn't go on in there with you."

"All right then," Spider confirmed, "the fearsome foursome is selected."

"So," Melissana reviewed, "the four of us go in, get down to the access tunnel start point, work through the tunnel, and find out where Trigget is."

"Once we find her," Susan picked up the recap, "I switch out with her, and she comes back with the maintenance crew while I make my way out with a fake Apex ID."

"I don't like it," Corey complained. "Blackwolf's going to be on her own until she gets close enough to the surface to be back in broadcasting range. What if something happens to her? We won't even know what it was."

"Fair point," Preach agreed, much to everyone's surprise. "It didn't come up when we first discussed the plan, but it's an obvious hole. Any ideas?"

"Can we set up a bunch of relay transmitters to boost the transmission signal every couple floors?" Candace asked.

"Candace, that's a great idea!" Lynda encouraged. "We'll not only be able to track the progress of the tunnel crew, but I can get an instant update on Trigget when they get to her if she needs immediate medical attention that is beyond Luke."

"It sounds good," Brant countered, "but the IT security people have signal tracing equipment and will be able to detect the extra broadcast and track it down before you guys get down the tunnel." A pause ensued as the group collectively tried to find a workaround to the communication problem. It was Iylothien who broke the silence a few minutes later.

"I've got it!" he declared in triumph. "The booster signal will be detectable, but what if we reverse the idea? Instead of using boosters to push the transmission signal, we could use parabolic receivers to pull the transmission. They'll be passive, so there's no signal emanation to detect. They'll also be directional, so the original transmission signals won't transmit outside the pipeline farther than the original signal would have. Given the bandwidth range our comm units work off of, our chances of detection will be negligible—no more than any other time we've used them while doing a run."

"That's actually brilliant," Preach acknowledged. "If we put one every maybe three to five floors, we might even be able to work in some redundancy. Only where do we put them? It's not like the ICC is going to let us wander around placing electronic devices wherever we want."

"Well there's only one place they're probably not going to have any cameras," Melissana offered. "And with two of us on the tunnel team, I think we can make a go of it."

"The ladies bathroom?" Susan asked.

"Yep," Melissana confirmed. "If these things are small enough, we can take turns faking restroom breaks and putty them to the back of the commode in the most inconspicuous stall. We note the XYZ coordinate of the previous two receivers and point the new one their way."

"I like it," Araña approved. "Being next to the plumbing also goes a long way to assure the lines will have a straight vertical lineup as well to ensure there will be a break within the concrete and plasteel to facilitate the signal strength."

"But since radio waves essentially work in a straight line and the receivers will be passive," Brant cautioned, "we'll still need to bend the signal from the tunnel to hit the first receiver. And to do that, we'll still need a booster to redirect the signal in the area that's likely to be the most secure."

"But only that one," Preach assented, "since once the signal is redirected, the range of the wave coupled with the receivers will be moot."

"Well they're a maintenance crew, right?" Chrome asked. "All we need to do is come up with a reason for them to need a broadcast unit in their equipment cart, which they can leave in the secure area."

"What about Blackwolf?" Corey said, almost letting Susan's name slip in front of the civilians. "We still won't be able to track her once she swaps out with Trigget."

"If we have one more transmitter to redirect the signal upward from the Apex side of the tunnel, I can plant more receivers on my way out."

"Nice idea, but there are three problems with that," Melissana countered. "First, the signal will pass through an ever-convoluted path, so signal-to-noise ratios might get complicated. Second, any delays or interruptions to the signal will cut you off. And you will be cut off because we need to collect our receivers on our way back so the corps don't get hold of our tech and possibly breaking our channel-hopping algorithms. Which is the third point—you can't leave your devices behind."

"There might be a way to beat that," Rickshaw mused. "If we rig the devices with small vials of heavy acids and a bang just big enough to pop the vials, we can render them completely useless."

"Good thinking," Preach observed.

Iylothien commented, "We'd have to have the inside team generate that signal, which means they'd be cut off anyway."

"We'll use a time delay and a trigger signal," Araña said. "We can blow individual receivers without disrupting the entire chain, or use timers hardwired to blow four hours after we figure the mission will be completed. Even if we're delayed, by then everyone should be close enough to the surface to be back in transceiver range. Let's face it, if they're not close enough by then, they probably never will be."

"You'll need enough of them to account for both Air Dynamix on the way down and Apex Premier on the way up," Brant stated. "How long will it take to get them all?"

"I've already relayed the order to Facility," Iylothien said. "They'll have them to us in two days."

… …

"What do you mean, there are statistics that have recently come to light about our Options Plus plans? What statistics?" Minova practically screeched at the collection of impotence that huddled together against her questions.

"I'm sorry, ma'am," Enlightened, the project coordinator, responded. "There is evidence that the promotional materials left out some factors that severely offset the projected earnings."

"Options Plus makes money," Minova seethed. She changed her tactics, stalking her prey. Enlightened was about to be snuffed. "For us and our customers. It's proven. We've proven it."

"Proven it to a point," Enlightened affirmed. "But the return on investment turns to debt as the other data comes to bear. We would make money, but our customers would lose in the long term. Big time."

"So when has that ever been a problem for us?" Berkleigh Minova practically purred.

"If we release Options Plus as a new product line and these statistics got out, our clients will have us in court." She involuntarily shuddered. "*ICC* court."

"Director Minova, if I may," offered Achieve, the project's lead public relations man.

The director gestured for him to go ahead with a hand wave. Anything to shut Enlightened up.

"Lyn, that supermodel we've been using to promote all of our hype about the way for women to get ahead is to sell out to the corporate fantasy just came out with a new publicity campaign for a product called 'Natural Family.' Shots of her holding babies, her man's obvious desire for her, her delight in the family—it all runs completely against the core grain of what we've been accomplishing. We've tried to talk her out of running the campaign now, but she says the product's too hot to ignore given the current glut of the market on corporate hype."

"Lean on her then," Minova asserted. "Threaten to cancel her contract if she doesn't pull the ads." Achieve winced.

"Director Minova," he asked after he took a breath. "Surely you can't be serious? This is Lyn we're talking about. We're fairly inconvenienced by her starting a new ad campaign that is not directed against us. Do you really want to risk her starting another campaign that actually is?"

"Well maybe she's too blind to how this new campaign will cost her," Minova calculated, "but what about her agent? Just bribe him to get her breathing down her neck."

"I mean no offense, Madam Director, but you want me to try to bribe her agent?" The minutest laugh, far more a reflex at the incredulity of her suggestion than any intent to ridicule, escaped him. She knew he hadn't intended the micro-gesture, but it would not stop her from trying to make the most of it.

"You find the struggle our corporation is going to go through as a result of this ill-timed campaign amusing? Openly laughing at executive management in front of your peers is inexcusable."

She made a note on her datapad and added, "As of now, you will work for two weeks without pay. If it happens again, you will be terminated. Do you understand?"

"Yes, Madame Director, but to clarify, I do not find any of this amusing," he countered, frustrating her even more. "However, not only has bribing Simon proven impossible in the past, but word has it he takes great offense at the suggestion. I would not want to risk a publicity war when we are so close to launching a product—expressly in light of Enlightenment's data.

"Besides," he continued before she had a chance to throw him out of the conference room, "we have other issues as well. Since last week there have been certain, err, complications with some of our Air Dynamix allies."

"Go ahead," Minova drawled as she visibly rolled her eyes. The guy had been on the team for the last eight months and had barely said a word. Now he suddenly comes up with the guts to challenge her project? "What complications?"

"Well, as of this morning, several of the key Dynamix pilot personnel have lost their positions. Montag is actually in prison."

"For what?" Minova snapped. "Implementing our Career Path training? We had corporate go-ahead to move forward."

"We were approved to move forward quietly, as a pilot," he corrected. "He had been, shall we say, conducting some testing of his own with the liaison candidates. Evidently it got so out of hand that an enraged father caught him with his daughter—who had not been enrolled as a liaison—in his private quarters." Dr. Oswald squirmed in his seat at the mention of Montag's crimes, but the others present didn't know if it was out of guilt or a new imagined pleasure. The group needed Oswald, but they despised his personality, and by extension, they despised themselves in various degrees for using him. Achieve continued, "It completely ruined our spin, and we lost a lot of mileage with the more reputable executives."

Minova openly smirked. "I'm sorry, did you just use 'reputable' in the same sentence as 'executives'? The only thing those executives care about is turning a profit. The only reputation they care about is what the bottom line says."

"It's not as simple as that," Achieve pressed. "Some of the older ones have legitimate families, and the Montag story was their wake-up call."

"So we use our remaining contacts and push the fossils out of the way."

"I mean no offense, Director, but perhaps allow me to clarify my initial statement," he pushed, although he nervously pulled at his collar as he recognized the statement was a political noose. "*Several* of the key Dynamix pilot personnel have lost their positions. Two thirds of them."

Minova had organized downsizings, fired friends, and had regularly fought—and won—legitimate claims against Apex Premier without batting an eyelash, but the statement stunned her.

"Two… thirds?" she echoed. "How did we lose that many in so short a time?"

"Do you remember all of those studies we funded when we first surveyed the Air Dynamix core leadership?" Enlightened joined in. "And those enticements we had offered for those who would help us to move the project forward?" Minova nodded; she needed the information Enlightened had. She would strike back at the project coordinator later.

"Well, apparently not all of the funds went back into the corporation. And ICC's actually value long-term corporate loyalty even more than the short-term bottom line. Bribing their project stakeholders was a mistake."

"Wait one minute," Minova requested as she held up her hand to ward off further conversation. Berkleigh had been stunned, but she had been promoted to Director for several reasons, and one of them had been her adaptability under fire. "When did these new statistics emerge, and do we know when they discovered this other information about the bribes?" She looked around the room with newfound annoyance at their incompetence. "Anybody!?"

"I can't say for sure it all happened the same day," their technology and data representative ventured, "but I think it all started with Montag's arrest."

"Which was the same night as the attack on the bank," Minova stated confidently.

"Odd," Enlightened noted. "Wasn't that the same night you lost your assistant?"

Minova's glare at Enlightened left no room for doubt that her project coordinator had pushed too far. Then the BA Director regained her smile. "No, I didn't lose her. I just have her on a special assignment," she said so pleasantly it convinced all attendees that the threat against Enlightened was not only real but also imminent. Oswald's almost-silent chuckle also told everyone in the room just what that special assignment probably was.

"Well," Minova stated in a chipper tone before anyone could ask any more questions, "our time seems to be up for today. The project is facing some setbacks, but don't worry. I am very proud of this team and all we have accomplished. That goes for you too, Achieve. We'll figure out these little snags and carry the ball across the finish line soon."

As the meeting adjourned, the others allowed Achieve and Enlightened to exit first out of both courtesy and concern for their well-being.

Minova sighed, alone in her conference room after everyone else had left. She would have asked her assistant to get her some coffee substitute, but she was reluctant to fill the position. She had actually liked her last one, and yet she saw where that had gotten her. At any rate, she couldn't hire a new one since she had just told everyone she had her current assistant on assignment.

She went to the breakroom to get some for herself, and noted as she approached that everyone who was there had scattered back to their workplaces so she couldn't cite them for laziness. She poured her coffee alone, leaned back against the wall waiting for someone to maybe enter the room, then gave up and headed back to her office.

The meeting had been unpleasant. Evidently, the last two days could have been the death of her pet project. Her first act when she returned to her office was to reinforce her strictest command for Oswald not to molest Sinclair's sister. Her second was to call a friend.

… …

- *"Preach, this is Spider: comm check…"*

- *"Lima Charley, Spider."*

- *"Roger Preach, same here."*

- *"Preach, this is Blackwolf: comm check…"*

- *"Lima Charley, Lady Blackwolf. You?"*

- *"Lima Charley, Preach."*

- *"Spider, this is Preach: What's the score?"*

- *"A whopping 14 under par, Preach. Six holes left to play."*

- *"Tango Yankee, Spider. Preach out."*

"I know Lima Charley means 'loud and clear,' but Tango Yankee?" Lady Blackwolf asked Spider with a quizzical look on her face.

"Thank you," Spider replied back, amused but glad she had asked.

- *"Umm, Preach? Helpdesk here. Can you hear me?" Brant asked as he got to his desk and closed the door.*

- *"Lima Charley—Loud and clear, Helpdesk. You?"*

- I hear everybody. Umm, Roger—over and out." he replied.

Inside Partisan's warehouse, Preach looked at Chrome and smiled, pleased that their plan was working. Spider's team had navigated fourteen stories underground, and both sides were reading each other loud and clear. They had only six more stories until they hit the tunnel access. Chrome smiled in reply, but mostly because of Brant's newness at trying to use radio protocols.

… …

One minute after the radio checks, Iylothien had hijacked Brant's terminal and typed:

Hello, world…

You too, Helpdesk ☺

Having communicated his presence, the Barde de la Nêone launched his will-o'-wisp program that floated a few nodes ahead of him and beckoned him forward. Second runs were always tricky; there was always the extra tension between the familiarity of the environment versus what the local IT security might have replaced or upgraded as a result of the last attack. His goal was to recon the system to find those changes and prepare to cover the team on their way out. He found a security node and launched "Mirrormist," a new spell he had encoded for the extraction, and a slow transparent vapor rose from the ground just in front of the rune, indicating a security camera object in the Ultimate Fantasy environmental module. He watched the vapor crystallize across the surface of the rune, then back flipped in celebration as he watched the mist slowly send out similarly transparent tendrils along the security grid, slowly moving from camera to camera. It would take an hour for the slow virus to permeate the entire building network, but Iylothien had the time and didn't want to risk detection. Almost as an afterthought he launched Brooder; once the queen locust had virtually solidified, he was off. The beast followed him, its abdomen dripping egg clusters every three or four seconds.

"Nice work!" Preach hailed over his AF-179 Corvus's radio to the barnstormer below. "You got the valley lit up, that's for sure." Iylothien looked up to watch Preach as a grey wizard swiftly shadow-stepped past him in the opposite direction. Compared to Preach, Iylothien had it easy. Preach's goal was to find an undocumented pathway to that alien server cluster, then ride the new wire into Apex. If he couldn't find one, Helpdesk's job was to monitor the tunnel team's progress. All three men were aware that the lives of their tunnel team, as well as Trigget, depended on their success.

... ...

The team thought they had somehow blown their cover when they saw the eight Air Dynamix guards in full heavy combat armor, but it turned out that was the everyday security detail. In a few minutes, the team had shared their security information and passes, and set up their network cart containing tools and other IT devices in an out of the way place. After the Cyber Security Team handed Meredith Bertenelli/Queen Vixenn the location of the physical connection for the new wire, she bent to a lower equipment drawer and rustled through it as though looking for a particular tool. In reality, she was ensuring she had precisely aimed the redirection of the beam. Satisfied after a subvocal radio check between Lady Blackwolf and Chrome, she set up some dummy indicators, informed the guards that their placement was precise, and under no circumstances should they move the cart for any reason.

Spider cut a hole through the access wall to the tunnel. Johnny and Lady Blackwolf lifted a section of conduit tubing through the hole. Finally, they verified that they were ready to enter the tunnel proper and walked through the access doorway. And stopped.

"Oh, would you look at that," Johnny said in uneasy wonder.

What immediately caught his eye were the cameras that were spaced every fifty feet on both sides of the tunnel. The cameras on the right side of the tunnel stared straight ahead at the camera directly across from it, paused, and swiveled in towards the Air Dynamix side of the pathway. Meanwhile, the cameras on the left side began in the same mechanical staring contest before swiveling outwards to the Apex Premier side. A set of wires ran to the cameras on both sides along the same wall and another across the ceiling to the camera on the wall directly across from it. Tracing the wires, he also noticed a fourth set of wires leading straight down that connected them all to the floor. He wondered why for a moment, but it became obvious enough when he realized that just past the access doorway, a thick electrified metal grate spanned the width and evidently the entire length of the tunnel floor.

- *"So if we tamper with any of the camera connections along the wall, at least two security cameras catch it and trigger the kill-ya-jolts," Johnny subvocally surmised. "And if we try to tamper with any of the camera connections to the floor, at least three cameras sense it and also trigger the floor. Oh, this will be fun."*

Spider pushed the new communication line from the far end of the newly-placed conduit. Queen Vixenn double-checked the diagrams the Cyber Security Team had just provided, twisted and crimped the end of the fiber optic line into the fiber optics jack, then plugged and sealed the jack into the panel of connections.

Meredith popped her head back into the room with the guards and offered a friendly smile. "Hey, before I go walking down that floor of yours—you guys are sure the juice is off, right?" She pursed her lips as she fluffed her hair and added, "Or I am gonna have a serious bad hair day."

"Nah, don't worry," the squad leader replied. "It's off. We like you just the way you are."

She waved a friendly goodbye and got back to the others. "We got a mile and a half of this?" she moaned.

… …

The echoes of a faint thud sound rumbled through the hallway like somewhere two empty hollow drums had bumped together and fallen onto the floor. A few seconds later, a voice hailed over a lab intercom, "Oswald, get up here!"

"Oh, what now?" the lab doctor sulked as he slammed the hand instruments he had just picked up back onto the tray. "Every time I start to get to the tasty work, I get interrupted!" Then off he went up the stairs. It was Trigget's first time alone with Shimmer since they had exchanged names.

"Shimmer?" Trigget called.

"Yeah?" Shimmer responded, "What is it?"

"Shimmer? That's not your real name. Like my name's not really Trigget—except I'm allowed to use my real name any time I want. You see, my name, my real name, is…

"No! Don't say it! You're real nice and I don't want them to hurt you!"

"Shimmer, it's okay. My real name is Josanne," she said as reassuringly as she could. "And I know a secret. I know your real name. Your real name is Kelly. Kelly Elverson."

"No I'm not!" she rebuffed. "My name is Shimmer. They call me that because I can make your night magical." She choked for a moment, and Trigget could hear the other girl sniffling. "Kelly is the dream girl. She's not real."

Despite the restrictions of their cylindrical confinements, Trigget tried to crane her head so she could make eye contact with Kelly, but it was no use. "No, that's not true. You really are Kelly. Your Mom and Dad live in Texas, and you have a dog named…"

"Ferdinand," Shimmer let out in wondrous revelation. "How do you know about my dreams?"

"Kelly," Trigget began, "I'm a friend of Jack's. Remember Pastor Jack?"

"Pastor Jack? That's crazy talk. My Daddy made him quit and kicked him out of the church. If you really knew my Daddy, you'd know Pastor Jack went far away and won't be coming back. He won't want me to come back, either. Not after the things I've done."

"Kelly, after everything that happened, your father felt so sorry for what he did and how that hurt you; he misses you so much that he spent years trying to find Pastor Jack again."

"He did? My Daddy tried to find Pastor Jack?" For the first time, Trigget heard a wisp of hope in the girl's spirit.

"Oh, not only that," Josanne continued, trying to fan that wisp into a flame. "A couple months ago, he did find him. I went with Pastor Jack to meet your Mom and Dad."

"Wait—you know Pastor Jack?" the girl asked, astonished. "Then how'd you get here?"

"You see," Trigget went on, "I don't know if you ever knew why your Dad asked Pastor Jack to leave, but before he came to your church Pastor Jack was a very special type of secret agent—like the kind they make vids about. He has some very special friends, and I'm one of them." She smiled at the thought. "And Kelly, we came here to rescue you. Now, I know that right now, things don't look like they're going all that great, but I'm betting that they're trying to figure out a way to get us out of here right now."

"Trigget—Josanne—Is it okay if I call you by your real name, and you can call me Kelly? I liked being Kelly, but they don't like it when I call myself that."

"I'd be delighted if you called me Josanne," Trigget responded.

"But they'll never get us out of here," Kelly added in an emotional nosedive. "And they're going to take my baby as soon as it's born," she said, her words accelerating in both speed and volume at the beginning of a panic. "But it's mine! They're going to take my baby!"

"Shhhh," Josanne hushed in an attempt to regain the girl. "There's no need to think about things like that, even when it's hard not to. Pastor Jack once said that we're not supposed to think about things going wrong but try to picture God helping to make everything right."

"Well I used to think that was easy, but now things got so bad…"

"Hey," Josanne said, "would you mind if I told you a story about a very brave girl and the band of heroes that rescue her? She goes through a lot of tough times in this story but then they rescue her, and the best part is that it's a true story, okay? Pastor Jack is in it," she inflected her voice in a half-tease.

"Yeah, okay. As long as Oswald doesn't come in. He ruins… everything."

"Okay, Kelly, I'll stop if we hear him coming back. You see, it all started on a chilly rainy night in October. The princess was running away from her evil captors, but she stopped to help a little boy who was very sick. He was getting wet, and she made a blanket for him. It was only a single act of mercy, but it was all she could do…"

"That's a sad story. The boy died, didn't he?"

"Yes, he did. And the princess felt very bad for him. But then a group of street kids saw her help that little boy…"

"And they ate him, didn't they?" she almost sobbed.

"No, they didn't." Even though they couldn't see each other, Josanne paused to meet the blend of curious surprise and hope that she felt was Kelly's gaze. "But they knew a man who could call some people that would help the princess…"

. . . . . .

"What is going on up here?" Doctor Oswald whined. "Every time I get a few minutes of peace, I get called up here for another meeting. Does anybody want me to get my work done?" Minova fixed him with a glare so cold he shivered. "I mean, not that I'm not grateful…"

"Your 'work' is coming along just fine, Dr. Oswald," the Biological Assets Director began, "and do you really want a few minutes of 'peace,' or did you really mean you want some time with your new 'piece?' I'm really not sure how you spelled that in your mind."

"Well actually," Oswald returned with a leer into his own imagination, "in this case, the two are not only homogenous, they're also synonymous." He was proud of his clever witticism, but the remark only increased the revulsion the other attendees had for the perverted doctor. One of them stood up to respond, but the chiming of a building alarm cut him off.

43. Kicking Down the Front Door

"ALL PERSONNEL, PLEASE STEP AWAY FROM EXTERIOR WINDOWS. A FLASH PROTEST HAS DEVELOPED OUTSIDE OF OUR BUILDING. WE HAVE DEPLOYED WINDOW SHIELDS ON THE GROUND FLOOR AND FLOORS TWO AND THREE. APEX SECURITY IS RESPONDING AND WILL ACT WITHIN THE FULL EXTENT OF WICHITA CORPORATE AGREEMENTS AGAINST ANY HOSTILITIES DIRECTED AGAINST OUR GROUNDS. WSF RESPONDERS ARE ALSO EN ROUTE AND WILL ARRIVE SHORTLY. IN THE MEANTIME, PLEASE STAY INDOORS AND AWAY FROM ANY WINDOWS."

....

Preach's one condition in agreeing to the rescue was that the remaining CYBER forces and those who would join them would cause a distraction at the front of the Apex building. It had started off peaceably enough. Adams had helped them smuggle several people through the inner perimeter gateways, and once they had a small core crowd, the random passerby's and sidewalk rubberneckers got curious. Over a fairly short time, the crowd ever-so-slightly swelled, which only drew more onlookers. Of course, the CYBER forces had hired enough Witch City denizens to ensure that would happen, naturally or not.

Within fifteen minutes, they had already attracted the attention of the Apex Premier regulars who were on normal foot patrol around the complex. In another twenty, Apex posted guards in front of the main entrance. As the corporation's show of force intensified, so did the mood of the milling mass of humanity outside their front doors. Several in the crowd began to chant against the company's unfair hiring practices.

"I WAS LAID OFF!" a bulky construction-worker type with short-cropped blonde hair and sunglasses produced a bullhorn and angrily shouted over the crowd. "PAID THE LAST OF MY SEVERANCE PACKAGE TO APEX FOR CAREER PLACEMENT INTO A NEW JOB." Some around him booed in protest of his treatment—evidently, others knew his story and sympathized with him. "PAID MY LAST WEEK'S CREDITS, AND FOR WHAT?" The murmuring grew louder from those around him; a few others dispersed throughout the still-growing crowd joined in. "THEY CATERED TO THE WEALTHY ---- SWINDLED ME OUT OF MY FAMILY'S LAST CREDITS! I COULDN'T COMPETE AGAINST THE BRIBES APEX PLACEMENT OFFICIALS GOT FROM SOME SUIT WHO WANTED THEM TO PITCH HIS RELATIVES TO THEIR CLIENT COMPANIES!" "I ---- MY FAMILY ---- we didn't have a chance." He wiped away some tears people hadn't seen him shedding underneath his shades. The anti-Apex protests of those around him and the others displaced throughout the crowd rose in volume as Chrome stepped down from his perch. It was a well-known game. Rehash the same complaints used for time immemorial to stir up popular opinion against whatever group the people construed as the elites.

It *was* a well-known game, Rickshaw thought, but it was also a dangerous one. This wasn't 2020; the Apex security soldiers were not mired in all the constraints that had bound the civil law enforcement authorities of the day from defending themselves. Corporate security was under no false pretense to hold back due to either public opinion or law of the land. There was nothing to stop them from firing into the crowd on full automatic if they wanted, as long as they minimized damage done to corporate assets. Mobs were predictable but tricky, and it wouldn't take much before someone went emotionally overboard.

The CYBER forces were trying to bide their time, continually mixing with the group leaders they had spotted in the crowd to keep the water boiling without it spilling over, balancing tension against confrontation. Timing was everything, and they had not yet heard that the tunnel team had reached Trigget.

··· ···

- "Four hours," Melissana reported. "In another 45 minutes, we should be ready to connect to the other side."

She paused for the cameras, ostensibly to check the connection integrity. What she hoped they would not detect was her taking a look through the second fiber optic line in the pair that they left unconnected so they could occasionally check in on the Air Dynamix security inside the server room. Right then they looked bored, apparently watching the cameras but discussing something that had amused them. She wished she had a few more moments to study them, to try to make out what they were discussing. She quickly dismissed the notion—she didn't want to attract attention by an undue pause. Besides, she couldn't read lips like Preach could.

She suddenly missed him. She knew Lady Blackwolf, Spider, and Johnny—the cutting edge of the fighters of two CYBER teams—had her back, as well as the experienced Paladin recon man who was along as their medic. But in an ironic twist, the slow pace in the cramped confines of the tunnel and the electronic traps that would burn her body reinforced the emotional presence of black ICE that would burn her mind—just as it had with Iylothien six years earlier. She always had either Preach or Iylothien backing her up on her heavier CYBER runs. In her imagination, she was now on her own in a virtual reality dungeon-crawl projection over her physical world. She knew they weren't real, but impressions flitted across her mind that she was on a nightmarish run across the wires, where any nano-second's slip would trigger her death and the death of those depending on her. The tedious pace of the work only reinforced the vertigo as, like in most nightmares, she found herself forced to move in slow motion.

"Hey," Johnny interrupted into her train of thought, "you okay? You're sweating,"

She started as she looked at him, hoping he wouldn't see the flickers of gnawing fear behind her eyes.

"Women don't sweat. They perspire," she said in both distraction and relief.

"Well that may be," he joked, "but either way, relax. We're in a tunnel. Drowning in or being electrocuted by an overabundance of perspiration is not the glorious end I had imagined for myself."

"Really?" she shouted, offended at his verbalization of her fears, and pushed him away from her.

"Ms. Bertenelli," a voice called over the nearest camera, *"you okay in there? Looks like someone in the contract team is giving you trouble."*

"No trouble," she said as she waved at the nearest camera and smiled. "He's just making fun of me because the tunnel's creeping me out a little." She fixed Johnny with a glare as she stated, "I'm sure it won't happen again. We're good."

"Well, Ms. Bertenelli, you might want to remind him that even if we don't go out there ourselves, you guys gotta come back this way to get out. The room's a little cramped with all the security posted here, and he might be forced to bump into a couple of us to get through." He paused a beat, then added, "Am I making myself *clear*, knucklehead?"

"Yes sir," Johnny responded. "Crystal clear, Sir."

"All right then," the guard responded. "We're watching."

- *"What was that all about?" Johnny subvocally reprimanded.*

- "Nothing," she sulked, then surrendered to the question. "It's the tunnel. It feels like I'm in cyberspace, and I'm cut off from both Preach and Iylothien."

- "Queen Vixenn," Spider said calmly. She wasn't looking his direction, but she could feel his reassuring smile in his words. "You've been dancing the wires long before CYBER found you. You spliced into Showbiz's network—by yourself—for Iylo to ride in on. You hacked the Matsua substation, and speaking of Matsua, as I heard the stories it was you who rescued Iylothien back in operation Drawbridge, not the other way around." He waited to make sure she turned and saw the resolve in his eyes. "You got this, Vix. This is just a walk in the park, and we're almost home."

She would have hugged him, but the cameras were watching. She would have subvocalized the sentiment to him, but she suddenly felt the fears of being isolated from Iylothien lift, and she knew he would hear. So, while she couldn't express her feelings the way she wanted to, she had to communicate them somehow.

- "Thanks, Spider," was all she could come up with.

"Okay, troops," she said out loud. "The first pass was to set the conduit. Let's go back. The second pass will go a lot quicker, since all we need to do is make sure there aren't any kinks in the line and fire it through the pipeline."

She looked at the nearest camera and loudly asked, "We're on our way back, and wouldn't mind a break. If you guys got any coffee, we sure wouldn't mind a cup."

"Sure thing, Ms. Bertenelli, but you see, we only have three extra cups. The jokester's gonna have to do without."

… …

- *"Rickshaw and Preach, this is Helpdesk. Tango Team has completed long yardage. ETA to breach is twenty-five, repeat twenty-five minutes."*

- *"Roger, Helpdesk, this is Rickshaw. Copy twenty-five minutes. We'll start disbursing the crowd in five, over."*

- *"Helpdesk, this is Preach. Copy twenty-five minutes. Break: Iylothien, you pretty set?"*

- *"Preach, this is Iylo. November Papa, my end. Over."*

- *"Copy no problem, Iylothien. Preach clear."*

Five minutes after Helpdesk's last message, Rickshaw, Chrome, and Hardcore gave the signal for the others to start milling about the crowd. Throughout the afternoon, secondary leaders had emerged from the drawn crowd with agendas of their own. With the number of CYBER agents and their allies—among them, Constantine, Dante, Rogue Moon, Stang, former-corporal Adams, and even Saint Nick—the influence of anyone who tried to divert the crowd away from the CYBER objectives was dimmed and neutralized. Within another five minutes, only remnants remained of the disbursing crowd. The WSF riot squads withdrew, then the CYBER group themselves, one by one, melted back into the afternoon shadows cast by the concrete and cryosteel forest that somehow seemed to swallow them whole. The guards stationed outside visibly relaxed, glad that the potential threat was over almost as quickly as it had started. Then they too stood down and returned inside the mouth of the Apex main entrance into the belly of their own beast.

… …

The tunnel team finished their break, trading quips with the security forces and taunts against Johnny. Assured that all was well, the guards relaxed, convinced that there was indeed no harmful intention among the contractors. Valerie Bertenelli checked her remote cart one more time to retrieve the tools they would need to connect the fiber line on the Apex side. As Johnny bade his final farewells before ducking back to the other side of the hatchway, she also flicked the hidden switch that armed the sleep gas canister inside one of the cart's drawers as a precautionary measure. She thanked the security team for the coffee one more time before closing the hatch behind her.

…… ……

Iylothien roamed about the circuits of the Air Dynamix network, also looking for the elusive connection path that would lead them to the undocumented Apex connection servers. With his Brooder daemon faithfully following behind him wherever he went, the pair slowly, patiently, invisibly navigated the circuits from the remote connection Helpdesk had opened for him. As he neared the central nodes of the network's gateway server cluster, he summoned a small series of modified will-o'-wisp programs. He instructed them to lay dormant to await his call, and they slept.

…… ……

Sure that the line had enough slack, Araña attached the remote end of the fiber optic line to a specially miniaturized grapnel point in his right arm. He carefully aimed through the line of conduit and checked one last time. He didn't care if the connection was only going to be used once; it needed to be tight enough to carry Preach's consciousness through. The lives of both Preach and Trigget depended on it. He fired, the line whistling through the conduit, but three quarters of the way through the grapnel twisted and skittered to a stop too far out of reach for anyone to pull it through to the other side.

"*¡Ay Dios mio!*" he exclaimed, frustrated. It took a full minute to retract the line without kinking the thin optics cable. He sucked in his breath then paused to look at Johnny.

"You sure you don't want to fire this for me? I could use the luck."

- *"It's okay," Queen Vixenn subvocalized with a nudge. "Aren't you the guy who took out like a hundred snipers with that thing just a couple weeks ago?" She smiled and added, "This is just a potshot in the park, and then we're home."*

- *"Thanks, Vixenn," he returned with a smile of his own. He drew another breath, slowly let out half of it, focused all of his senses on the 30 millimeter pinhole a mile and a half away, and fired. 3.7 seconds later, he clapped his hands to his ears and swore.*

"What's the matter?" Luke asked, seeing him cringing, pressing his hands with both hands, his eyes squeezed tight in obvious pain.

"Spider, what is it?" Blackwolf rushed to his side so fast she practically blurred. Vixenn silently prayed the guards watching the cameras hadn't noticed.

"My ears are killing me," he winced through what almost appeared to be tears. He grimaced again, then seemed to recover slightly as he added, "I was so focused on detecting any variations in the flight pattern I shut down my dampers." He then visibly regained himself and half-smiled. "So the amplified pop as the grapnel hit the far wall *hurt*! Next time I take a potshot, remind me to take my head out of the pot first!"

Elated, Queen Vixenn communicated to both the Air Dynamix security and Helpdesk that they were ready for the Apex security team to open the access hatchway on their side. The Apex security was not emotionally warmed up to the group like the Air Dynamix side had been, but they were still lulled, convinced that the Air Dynamix guards would have vetted the group before admitting them into the tunnel in the first place. Blackwolf, Spider, Johnny, and Luke had neutralized them within a minute. They completed the Apex connection seven minutes later.

… …

Brant nearly jumped out of his chair when the tunnel team made the announcement and he saw the connection go live.

- *"All units, this is Helpdesk,"* he cheered. *"Breach! Breach! Breach!"*

… …

Inside the gateway cluster, the Barde de la Nêone leapt to standing full height atop the saddle of his locust mount, closed his eyes to focus, stretched his arms wide, and smacked them together in a Thunderclap spell to accentuate his digital war cry for his pets to awaken. Within milliseconds, the sky around him dazzled and popped with electric flashes, each one the coded opening of a firewall port that would allow Preach to ride in without the possibility of being cut off. At the same time, the Brooder eggs began to hatch, multiply, and creep towards several key Air Dynamix systems. The plan was simple. Iylothien would give the CyberSecurity defenders and their ICE so much threat they could see that they wouldn't notice what they did not see. In effect, he was creating so much of a concern about all the blocked traffic, they might not detect the thin corridor he had cleared for Preach by blocking almost all of the side traffic. His scouting mission completed, he fired a flaming arrow to highlight the near-zero traffic he had created that would carry Preach through to the hidden server room.

· · · · · ·

Preach pushed his throttle full forward and just managed to pilot his Corvus through the portal that opened up before him before it closed back up again. It took him a few moments to adjust to the slight turbulence caused by the rapidly-shifting connections, but he soon compensated and mentally adjusted to the environment. The program was truly ingenious, hopping firewall ports in an algorithm based on ASM channel-hopping in network communications.

· · · · · ·

"What the hell just happened?" It would have been a question had it come from anyone else, but it came from Mr. Breverton, Chief of the Cyber Security Team. Liz, the unfortunate CST person monitoring network security at the time, knew it was a demand for information.

"I don't know, sir," she crisply reported, but not before she sensed him leaning over her to examine the screens she had been monitoring. "Someone must have hit us with a dormant virus that just went active. It's hitting us like a distributed denial of service attack, only launched from inside our own network." She scanned a display of her network traffic monitoring software and frowned. "This is a display of our network," she explained. "The slowly widening red lines are the virus spread."

· · · · · ·

Preach spotted Iylothien's beacon, circled once in a virtual half-mile radius over a marked target area. His targeting reticule blinked three times, and he fired a wing-mounted air-to-surface missile. There was no visible evidence he had done anything at all; it was as if he had fired a lawn dart into the ground compared to the carpet bombing he could have laid on, but stealth was what he wanted. He circled once more to observe the clandestine micro-virus as it spread its encryption algorithm undetected across the electronic barcode circuitry of the door between the server room and the rest of the Air Dynamix building. Satisfied, he pushed his throttle so far forward he wondered if he would break it and rocketed into the newly-laid connection nearing the speed of light.

… ……

She breathed a sigh of relief. "Whew, *that's* good."

"What's good about this?" Breverton snapped.

"Well, it could have been a lot worse," she offered. "Those pathways were heading to our R&D servers, personnel, and financial records, even our air traffic control system. But they all died out." She smiled and added, "The only one that's still active is just meandering towards a dead end. Whoever pulled this off certainly knew what they were doing, but they ran out of gas, and the only branch left is going down a road to nowhere."

"Let me see," Breverton, drawn in by Liz's explanation, almost requested. "Liz, you're displaying the major attack patterns they've picked and where they've been. Can you filter them out and plot the trajectories of any and see where they're going to go?"

… ……

Iylothien sensed the presence of the wizards. One of them was fairly fast, the other slower but had the heavier hit of higher system authorities. As a result, he had to focus on varying the virus behavior a little to make sure he still had their attention, making sure they still perceived him as the threat. After making sure they were monitoring him, he decided to launch

his VisionPool program, cut into their security cameras, and
monitor them.

. . . . . .

"Yes sir, just a moment," she acknowledged, inwardly noticing
the signs of Breverton's approval of her work. "There are several
inevitable splits that branch out into fractal patterns, of which all
but one collapsed in on themselves and self-terminated. The one
remaining stray strand is going to dead-end." She smiled as she
pointed out the probable destinations. "See sir? They're heading
into nothing!"

"Liz, how often do fractals form straight lines? What the—find
the original point of entry and shut it down!" he barked. In the next
second, he grabbed a radio and called in to the security detail in
the server access room. "Sec-13, Sec-13, come in." He waited for a
response but none came. "I repeat, Sec-13, this is Breverton. Reply
now."

"Sir," Liz almost stammered as she logged in to her elevated
account that enabled her manual override authority to the network
interface software, "maybe they're busy with that wiring team."

"The connection wiring is today?" He slammed the radio onto
Liz's desk as he activated the server room camera monitor. He
swore as he saw the entire team soundly asleep, wisps of a tell-tale
yellowish cloud wafting past the camera lens. "They're after the
Apex server interfaces."

. . . . . .

"Uh oh," lylothien thought. He dropped control of the parameters
he was adjusting on the fly and allowed the programs to resume
development on their own. Then he sat low on his locust and
commanded it to rise up, up towards the parapets of the castle's
keep. He cast a Maelstrom spell over a fireball arrow, then

nocked it and drew aim at the cauldron the two defenders were huddled over, casting their spells. They looked up just in time to see the firestorm hit them.

... ...

"Sir, there's a new attack vector that branched off the main attack line!" Liz called in a battle-induced rush of adrenaline. She frantically initiated a new battery of network defense systems. "They're headed right for us!" Liz's hands flew across the control software used to control the network protocols, but Iylothien's mind was faster. "Damn, sir, they're fast!" Then the server she had linked to flashed and went dead, followed a second later by their own desktops erupting into a mini fireworks show of sparks before they too died out. Without the white noise of the computers running, the room was suddenly eerily silent, the acrid smell of burnt circuits filling the air like a mist rising from the ground of a stalemated battlefield.

"They've disabled the hardware and API controls."

"We don't have time for your fumbling," Breverton ranted as he practically yanked a spare laptop computer to get back into the fight. He swore as the machine went through its boot processes. Once he finally did get back online, he attempted to wrest control of the network application away from the attacker, but found even his command line interface was not as responsive as he was accustomed.

"Damn!" he snarled. He had attempted to shut down the Dynamix-Apex server remotely, but Preach laid a secondary attack on the servers that overrode the system BIOS interrupts against any power down/restart sequences.

Breverton realized his network systems had slowed to a crawl. His own IT security systems were all but completely off-line. In the circuit world beyond his vision, Brood Mother's hatchlings continued to wear down his system. By the time he was able to shut down the initial breach point, he could only watch as the re-routed network monitoring system started blinking with the pattern of the flickering lights that indicated the opening and closing of several firewall ports. He snatched the radio back and called in for another security team to check the status of Sec-13 while he practically lunged at the switch that would activate the tunnel defense grid. At least that had worked, he grimly mused. If whoever went through that tunnel thought to return the same way, they'd be sharp-fried before they'd feel the current.

He reached for his phone and hit a speed-dial number. "Stafford? Breverton here. Our network's under attack and… yes, I know network security is my business, let me finish. We've analyzed their attack patterns, and it looks like they're heading down to the new Apex farm. SEC-13 has been neutralized; they're out, but we saw one of them move. It looks like there's some sort of cloud in the room, maybe sleep gas or something. I want you to get some troops down there and physically shut down those servers." He listened for a moment, then hung his head with a sigh and rubbed his eyes. "Oh, I see. Well, thank you. Yeah, keep me posted, and if anything breaks over here, I'll let you know. Thanks." He then hung up, sat back in his chair, and almost lazily glanced up to review the ceiling. Liz had never imagined how Breverton would look if he ever felt utterly defeated; now having seen it first-hand, she would never have to.

"Sir," she asked, actually concerned about the man's health, "what is it?"

"That was Director Stafford, head of physical security. I just reported the security breach of a research site so secret, not even you knew about it." He sighed again before he continued. "And he said he was just about to call me to chew me out for changing the security codes on the hardened doors to get in there without letting him know first. It turns out the assigned security team didn't respond to a comm check, so he dispatched a team to check on them." He looked at her in helpless resignation. "Here's the punch line: evidently, our hacker friend scrambled the magnetic locks, and our guys can't get into the room, not even with a decryption tool designed to defeat door locks. The locks are constantly resetting themselves faster than we can crack them."

"What do we do, sir?" Liz asked as the enormity of the security breach crept upon her awareness.

"There's not much we can do at the moment," he practically growled, "except notify management of the situation and call our cousins on the Apex side of the house." He initiated a call to one of the non-personal visages in corporate management that Liz could only guess at, but she would not sit idle for long. "The perps can't get back through the tunnel, so they're Apex's problem now." Something inside him seemed to spark—his demeanor was deadpan stoic, the intense fire in his eyes strangely offsetting the otherwise stony appearance. He had a flash of inspiration—there was something he could *do*. His helplessness was gone, replaced in a moment by the all-too-well-known anger. Internally, Liz was glad Breverton happened to have been in the room when the attack occurred. He'd be out for blood, and if he hadn't been there, she was sure some of that blood would have been hers. "Meanwhile, go through the logs," he ordered as he almost absent-mindedly fixed his eyes on the stand-by screen before him. "Find out exactly when this started."

"Do you want me to look for the initial attack source, sir?"

"No," he replied, his mind locked in thought as his eyes continued their gaze on the screen. "I just need the time." He rubbed his chin as someone picked up on the other end of his call. "And when we get the time, I'll pull every camera in the company if I have to. One more thing," he added. "If the system isn't completely down, bring up the work ticket for the Apex connection."

"Sir?"

"Nobody could have just waltzed their way into our network that fast and gotten into our secured server room—they had help." She chanced a glance at him, and she couldn't tell if she saw him in a malevolent grin or if he was simply baring his teeth. "And I can't wait to get my hands on who it was."

... ...

Preach burst through the Apex connection, engaged stealth mode, and fired a small barrage of probes that scattered to map out the network ahead of him. Iylothien had done another superb hack of the Air Dynamix system, but here he was on his own with a partial and dated map the Neon Bard had created the night Trigget had been captured. And since he came in from the Air Dynamix side, the data Iylo had retrieved was from a completely different sector that looked like it didn't even border on the area he currently patrolled. "Come on," he scolded himself on behalf of the system he was up against. "You're a medical research facility; you have to have patient logs somewhere!"

An indicator light blinked; Probe 5 found a satellite system that was his Flight Sim Environment Module's rendition of the network monitoring systems. The fact that it was a satellite network instead of a few observation balloons indicated it was high-end equipment; the Corvus stealth system would beat it, but he'd have to be careful. As he cruised over the area, he saw several batteries of Hermes-M surface-to-air missiles and Phalanx-8 autocannon.

"All teams, this is Preach. I'm in and looking around."

"How's the view?" Iylothien asked.

"Bristly, Iylo. I don't mind saying it's bristly. They take their cybersecurity seriously. Makes me wonder if maybe they don't fully trust their Air Dynamix neighbors."

"Well, that actually makes sense, with the kind of kink jobs that cooked up this operation."

"Roger that, Iylo, roger that. Preach out."

. . . . . .

- *"Helpdesk, this is Spider. We're in on the Apex side. Do you still copy us?"*

- *"Roger, Spider, this is Helpdesk. Copy, you're inside. Be advised; Preach is also inside. Says the network defenses are tight. Expect the same for the ground forces, copy?"*

- *"Copy, Helpdesk. We'll keep our eyes..."* The rest of his response was lost as an alarm sounded, the blaring extra loud in the confines of the small hallway they had just accessed.

- *"Apex kicked in Alarm City down here,"* Johnny reported. *"Anybody trigger something?"*

- *"I didn't sense anything,"* Spider reported over the communications channel. *"Preach?"*

- *"Negative on Preach,"* Partisan reported over the Pride's leader's shoulder. *"He was running stealth, and as far as I can tell, they're not aware of his presence yet."*

- *"It was a manual trigger,"* Iylothien reported. *"Breverton called them directly when the security squad quit responding, and a backup team couldn't get into the room to physically shut the connection down. He's sharp, I'll give him that. Launching Diversion daemon."*

- *"Rickshaw here, acknowledged,"* the Hound wheelman radioed from the street outside the headquarters building. *"Chrome, time to see if Apex is still taking visitors."*

… …

With the shields down, the armored Hound practically blasted the front doors of the Apex facility off their mounts as he bashed through them. Receptionists hit the floor in drilled precision and reported the assault. Lobby security fired at the CYBER shock trooper on full automatic. They barely slowed him down.

Confused security response was poised on a seesaw of response calls. They had just stood down from the front door threat and were going back into the normal routine. At least they thought they were. Then another alarm went off that they originally thought had come from the lower levels. They had to stop, regroup, and redirect their efforts again—now the cause of the threat seemed to be the front door alarm. They balked, trying to identify just what they were responding to. While they did, the rest of the CYBER forces and their allies poured through the Apex front door breach and took up forward positions.

… …

- *"Helpdesk, this is Iylo. Chief of IT Security is hunting for a leak. Bug out. Now!"*

- *"Right. On my way." Brant replied as he scooped up his loose papers off the desk.*

"Ahh, Mr. Stomwell," Breverton loudly interrupted the Air Dynamix tech support supervisor.

Brant jump-flinched, badly startled by the sudden appearance of the very last person he wanted to encounter. He turned to see his long-term foe standing behind his chair; a pistol leveled squarely at his chest. And behind Breverton were the same four security gorillas that had roughed him up several times before. The IT

Security Director flashed him a smile that was so cold Stomwell felt compelled to shiver.

"You are correct," Breverton smoothly continued. "You are in fact 'on your way.' Only I don't think you are going where you had planned to go."

Stomwell's office coworkers had huddled behind and under their desks. His throat went dry in a panic. Somewhere in the back of his mind, he was secretly thankful for that. At least he would have the dignity of dying without screaming like a little girl.

Somewhere else in the back of his mind comforted him with the thought that all he had tried to do for these kids was finally paying off. Then a jumble of thoughts swirled at him like leaves in a whirlwind, driven by the definite end of his time allowance on earth. His mind reeled, hammered by all the thoughts of what was, what he'd miss, *who* he'd miss. And the only things that kept pace with his mind as it furiously raced along the sheer cliffs of sheerer terror were the questions. Questions that rushed upon him with the savage ferocity of a pack of starving wolves. Questions that circled the campfire of his will, shredding the edges of his nerves while he was trying so desperately to hang on to reason. *Would the kids be ok without me? What will the people I supervised think? How will my getting killed in front of them affect them?*

The thoughts and questions gave rise to so many conflicting emotions and thoughts. Swirling around inside of him, they almost made him throw up, but he fought that urge with whatever was left of his will because… well, because he knew *they'd* think it was because he was afraid. *That's my super-power,* he resigned to himself with a helpless smile at his helpless circumstances. *I can repress throwing up when I'm about to die.*

His last thought was of his comic book and graphic novel reading. He had truly become in real life one of the cool characters he so often wished he could be. He took comfort in that thought and decided at least to play the role well. He secretly activated his radio's transmit lock switch to relay what was happening to the team. It would also relay every conversation that would occur in the microphone's radius until the transmit lock was deactivated or the radio shut off. He just wished he could think of some clever and witty line to deliver to the bad guy, something cool for the team to remember him by.

"So, Mr. Stomwell, any last words?" Breverton sneered.

And it was the pure arrogance behind Breverton's tone that had awakened the righteous fury inside Brant "Helpdesk" Stomwell and provided the epiphany. It cut through his impossibly long parade of thoughts and ghosts and what-might-have-been's that were still assaulting him as he tried to think clearly, and gave him a measure of clarity. It was the coolest line he could think of. He would live his last moments intentionally. He would let the others know who all was in on the scheme with Breverton without him knowing it. He would express his appreciation for all that CYBER was doing on behalf of those who couldn't help themselves. Most of all, he would relay how grateful he was that Meredith Bertenelli had counted him worthy enough to include him in her group. He would die well. He squared himself off, stood taller against the imminent execution of his impromptu death sentence. He cleared his throat and raised his head to look Breverton straight in the eye.

"Mr. Breverton, Units 309, 312, 421, and 429? I don't know your names, but I can only say this: Long Live the Queen."

It was his finest moment; it was his last moment. The next sounds the radio carried were the five shots that ended his life, and the clatter of the radio as it bounced out of his hand as his right wrist lifelessly smacked and broke against the floor.

44. The Climb

"Wʜᴀᴛ ᴛʜᴇ ʜᴇʟʟ?" Melissana cried out loud in torment. "What the *HELL*?"

Spider had to grab her to keep her from running back into the tunnel. Luke and Susan both had to assist to help calm her down.

"LET ME GO!" she screamed as she kicked and tried every trick she knew to get loose from her friends.

"Vixenn!" Spider shouted to counteract her anger. She paused long enough to fix a hateful glare on him. Lady Blackwolf and Johnny exchanged concerned glances; Luke, not knowing what to say to any of them, prayed silently for all of them.

"Listen," Spider said with the edge still in his voice. "Stomwell's gone. He gave his life so we could find Trigget. Remember her, your best friend? Nod your head yes if you do." She nodded and he continued. He had forced her to think, to consider the bigger picture, and at least to a small degree, it had worked.

"Do you know what he was saying, to all of us, but especially to you, Queen Vixenn?" Spider continued. "He was telling us what we were doing was right. He was telling us to continue. He was telling *you* more than the rest of us, that even though he was paying the ultimate price, he still felt glad that he had a chance to get to know us, and especially proud to be a part of us. He told us good-bye in the best way he knew how." Her rage suppressed, she sagged in his arms and began to cry.

"He wasn't CYBER, Spider. He was a civilian. He shouldn't have died."

"No, he wasn't. But we are. He died trying his best to act like one of us. And right now, we need to honor the honor that he gave us. So Vixenn, I'm going to let you go now, because we need you if we are going to finish. This. Mission. We can and will grieve later, but right now, the living need our attention more than the dead do, got me?" Her expression softened, and she nodded again, this time even before he asked. He slowly, tentatively, relaxed his grip on her. She stayed in place. "Good girl," the leader of the Hounds approved. "Now I heard that Preach is inside as well. He'll be looking for Trigget's location and circumventing surveillance systems. Can you plug in somewhere nearby and see if you can make contact with him so we can get access to those cameras? In a very short period of time, we're gonna have all kinds of Apex response coming down these hallways, so I need you in the right here right now, okay?"

She nodded again and agreed, but as he let her go, she added, "Yeah, I'll do that. Cuz right now a squad of Apex security between me and Trigget is exactly what I need."

Araña ignored the remark. She connected her deck into a network access port, which occupied her attention. His extended senses picked up the sounds of boots running towards their location. In a few seconds, the attentions of Johnny, Lady Blackwolf, Luke, and himself would be occupied as well. He told the others to take cover and waited.

. . . . . .

Iylothien's blood ran cold as he just helplessly watched when Breverton caught Helpdesk. Watched as the tech supervisor realized he was going to die. Watched the turmoil of emotion as Brant faced his own mortality. Watched as he regained control of himself and stood as tall as anyone Iylothien had ever seen. Watched as Breverton fired the five shots in cold blood, heard the crack of Brant's wrist as his body collapsed on the floor.

Watched as the death of this so innocent a man had shattered Queen Vixenn.

The Barde de la Nêone stopped his other activities and just sat in crestfallen gloom, his brooding having nothing to do with his now-forgotten virus program. As his grieving aura infected his environmental module's rendition of the Air Dynamix network, the castle interior took on a dark grey overtone. He conjured a massive stone throne amid a pile of skulls where he just sat with his head lowered, chin drooped to his chest and cupped in his right hand. His environmental module detected the shift in his thought patterns and emotional state; as it responded, his avatar changed. His skin grew thick and rocklike; he sprouted wings as the normally carefree ranger grew into a large foreboding gargoyle, red glowing eyes etched in dismal deliberation.

After several virtual hours, it moved, lifting its chin to stare in burning anger at a vacant point in space far beyond the walls of his grisly palace's throne room. More than the anger, there was something even deeper and more pronounced in its narrowed stony eyes: pure, unadulterated resolve.

"You stood by us," it said to his fallen friend, "and we will stand by you." The creature considered the flicker of an idea it had only moments earlier, subconsciously producing a low snarl that exposed enlarged fangs and wicked teeth. The malevolent gloating leer illuminated in the red light of the gargoyle's eyes was a thing that would have made Chrome pause. "Yes, I think that will do nicely." Bit by bit, he regained his more typical form as he arose from the throne of skulls and dusted himself off. He had been still long enough. He had work to do.

... ...

Partisan stared in shock. Lynda just stared open-mouthed as Candace leaned into the doctor and began to cry.

"Come on," Saint Nick glumly called to Tag and some of the older girls who had been listening in. "We better go tell the others. I think the new kids would want to know." They left as quietly as they could.

Lynda put a consoling hand on Partisan's shoulder and asked, "Do you think they heard?"

"I don't know," Partisan returned. "Spider's group probably did. Iylothien might have been watching. I don't know about this guy," he said, glancing at Preach's body, occupying a chair as even now his hands flew across his deck locked in some intense combat only he could see. "He's so involved in his fight against the Apex ICE I'm afraid to break his concentration by telling him."

…… ……

- "Chrome here," the CYBER strong-arm called in to the other teams.

Sounds of automatic weapons fire and the loud cracks that sounded nearby as bullets struck against their cover drowned out what he tried to say. The Apex security troops had been confused but were not completely untrained. Faced with multiple alarms and unsure of where the emergency actually was, their command and control personnel dispatched teams to assess both.

- "I repeat," Chrome reported back when told nobody heard what he had said the first time, "they have about twenty heavy security that have us pinned down in the front lobby." He stopped to fire a short burst into the receptionist's desk that hid three armed responders.

- "In other words," Rickshaw added with a twist of a grin, "we've got them exactly where we want them."

"We gotta get out of this lobby!" Rogue Moon shouted to the group. "We can't hold here for long—not long enough to count, anyway!"

"Agreed," Chrome replied. "Ready Constantine? We're up."

"Go for it."

Chrome stood to full height and stepped out of his cover. He sprayed suppressive fire over the heads of the Apex lobby forces, but there were too many to keep them all pinned at once. The remaining sec forces directed all their fire on him when they recognized he was exposed. He took a few steps back and to the side as the heavy volume of small arms fire pummeled against his ballistic vest and armored skin, but he stayed standing. Now their sole target, he drew even more fire once his initial targets recovered.

Their attention was so focused on Chrome that nobody noticed the bluish blur that seemingly skated around the opposite side of the room to come up behind the lobby security. Three defenders were knocked out from behind before the others even noticed. Constantine wove through the Apex line, diving between the forces, using their concern not to shoot each other to prevent them from firing at all. Those that Constantine didn't get Chrome did, as once their attention was diverted from him, he simply walked up from behind the last one and punched his lights out.

... ...

"As for Chrome and Rickshaw's group," Partisan continued to Lynda, "they're probably so inundated with the sound of gunfire coming at them I'd be surprised if they'd notice the pistol shots."

... ...

"Well, that was quick," Rogue Moon complimented. "You went through the entire response team in less than a minute!"

"Well," Constantine smirked, "that's what happens when they focus on the pretty lady instead of the magician."

"Oh man," Rickshaw guffawed, "I'm keeping that little line in my repertoire for a long time!" He slapped a hand on Chrome's shoulder. "How about it, pretty lady?"

"I'm gonna break his legs right through that exoskeleton," Chrome replied, but his demeanor hinted the comment was nothing more than his brand of humor. "Come on. They're going to send more any minute. We need to catch the elevator before they get here."

. . . . . .

The virtual skyline of the Apex Premier network changed dramatically as soon as the first alarm sounded. The domes and rooftops of the various data systems lowered into the ground, replaced by bristling clusters of the SAM's and anti-aircraft autocannon he had spotted earlier. ICE came in three flavors. White ICE would kick you off the system but not harm you outside of throwing you for a loop as your mind adjusted to the jarringly harsh dump from the virtual world into the real one. Grey ICE would send enough feedback current it could actually damage your system. Black ICE could paralyze or even kill any hacker it caught.

His environmental module rendered the white ICE as anti-aircraft machine guns; everything he had seen up until the alarm had been grey ICE. Then occasional laser towers that indicated black ICE rose out of the landscape that scrolled beneath him. Just when he thought the situation couldn't get any worse, Probe 3 had been reporting on an airfield where three squadrons were taking off—until the first pair of airborne aircraft shot it down: Apex cybersecurity agents would be hunting for him now.

"Come on," he again urged. "Give me something!"

As if in response, Probe 6 reported in.

... ...

"Can someone please tell me what is going on here?" Berkleigh Minova demanded at the emergency meeting of the local Apex Premier executive staff. "We've got multiple alarms in the lobby, some kind of demonstration outside, and even in some sub-level…" Erupting fire alarm klaxons did what few thought even possible—they shouted down director Minova in mid-rant.

... ...

"Pay dirt!" Preach exclaimed as his AGM-96 Maverick E obliterated the fire alarm control system. That would sow a lot more confusion among Apex staff at all levels and force security personnel to spread themselves out way too thin trying to check every alarm. It might also cause a distrust in all of the alarms based on the high volume of false positives and evidence of the system getting hacked. Hope beyond hope, maybe even both.

The Corvus proximity sensors complained their alert; Preach pulled back on the stick to climb just before a stream of machinegun bullets connected. He executed a wingover maneuver to face his assailants. His deck rendered them as a pair of SU-57 interceptor aircraft, state of the art in 2025, but his Corvus was better. "Hmm," he thought to himself. "Says here the 57's were plagued by engine problems." His EM had run diagnostics on the "aircraft" he was up against and determined that the computers the opposing system administrators were using were impaired by either processor speeds or intervening network lag. "Let's see what we can do with that."

… …

"You know, they're wasting their time," Kelly admitted when the third set of alarms sounded.

"What do you mean?" Trigget asked.

"I mean, you guys are like superheroes, but you're going to get hurt, and…" Kelly kicked away at the thick glass containment out of frustration.

"Kelly," Josanne asked, knowing the girl was going through great inner turmoil but not knowing the reason. "What is it?"

"And I'm not worth it!" she screamed, the sound a harsh tinny scrape against Josanne's ear drums.

"Why would you say that? Of course you're worth it."

"Oh you might want to say that," she said with a cold tremble the CYBER conversationalist could emotionally sense through both canisters. "But after the things I've done? My life is worthless—it's not worth anyone trying to save. I've done bad things, things that nobody could ever forgive me for, if they knew. I'm not worth the efforts you guys are making to try to save me." Her voice turned from despairing to desperate. "And they'll get hurt, like you did, and that'll be my fault, too!"

Trigget drew in a breath to reply but stopped short as Kelly's remarks hit home. She tried a second time but again found she couldn't. Her mind was too introspective for her to formulate a response for someone else. What Kelly had just described resonated exactly with everything she had been feeling about herself. For the first time since Drawbridge, she had the flicker of understanding that the members of Preach's Pride really *were* trying to help her.

She forced herself to pause and consider the newfound revelation. To bask in it. To absorb it. And in that process, she realized that there really wasn't much of a difference between what Kelly felt and what she herself felt. Which meant that, at that moment, there really wasn't any difference between her and Kelly at all. She reflected on all that they had gone through to find Kelly when they weren't even sure she was alive. Their efforts to burrow into the underground world of sex trafficking. Searching out Elaine. The trip to Texas to meet Kelly's parents and take out that Kanker guy. Hardcore's and Rickshaw's trip to that psycho bar. Recruiting Valhala's Brownies and the Paladins. That crazy revival when they first met Partisan. The hard-fought battles in chaotic Witch City against Showbiz. Mama Solace's interrogation. The undercover work in the business world that culminated in the multi-pronged assault against the Air Dynamix slavers. All of it to rescue this girl they weren't even sure was still alive. All of it. Despite the crushing dejection every time they thought they had finally rescued her. Despite each attempt, only to find the enemy had again and again slipped her beyond their reach just as they were closing their fingers to finally pull her to safety. Despite the dejection? That wasn't quite right. They were committed. Committed to their cause, committed to Kelly, committed to each other. They weren't dejected by a failed attempt. They were even further fueled by it…

Something deep within her clicked. She *knew* the team was on its way to rescue them. She knew they were on their way… to rescue *her*. Despite her hardships overcoming putting down that thug who was going to kill Melissana, despite all her complaining, despite all of the times she rejected their offers of help and understanding. And above all, despite the hard times she threw at Preach—Jack, she corrected herself. Jack, the man who tried harder than all of them to reach out to her. How she had so carelessly betrayed him and the others to Showbiz! She recognized now how painful that had been for him, especially with the added weights of his feelings of responsibility for his team. She also knew the pain from Iylothien's tragedy was still a sharp and jagged edge that did not just simply cut but tore on his soul.

Yet she saw the effect he had on people: coaching Elaine past her crisis moments in her interview, the way Mrs. Elverson clung to him like he was a lifeline thrown to a drowning person, his established relationship with Small Eddie, the way he navigated his new relationship with Partisan… But when it came to him investing all that time and patience into her? Her response had always been to throw barriers in his path and accuse him of hypocrisy. (Oh, the hypocrisy of *that*, she now berated herself!) The fact was that she was the one with the expert conversationalist training, but he was better at relationships just by being himself. She wondered how he did it. He had been a preacher, but the depth of his commitment to others was something far deeper than a mere job title and sermon counts.

She had more to think about, but Kelly broke into sobs that demanded a response. The girl was too broken for Trigget's conversationalist techniques; maybe at this point, all she had were Josanne's own feelings of failure. And yet, she thought after her own soul-searching, maybe they would be enough.

"Kelly?" she called in a fragile voice. How long had Josanne herself been crying? "Kelly? Please listen to me. Hang in there just a little while longer, okay? You might not believe me, but I really know how you feel."

"What do you mean?" Kelly asked, confused.

"I mean, I know you feel like you let everybody down, like you did a lot of bad things and…" She paused as a memory of Melissana's pained expression as she asked Josanne why she was being so mean to everyone flashed in her mind, "and hurt people that you really care for." She got angry with herself again—she had tried to push them all so far away! "But at least you couldn't help it, Kelly. You were kidnapped, drugged, and forced to do all of those things. I betrayed my friends, almost got some of them killed. Just because I felt sorry for myself.

"So you see? I need you to hang in there, just a little while longer. I need you to, Kelly, because I won't be able to handle it if I make it, but you don't. Because I promise you they're coming to get you out of here."

"But why, Josanne?" Kelly sobbed. "Why are they wasting their lives coming for me?"

"It's simple, Kelly," Josanne offered, crying into the goo that still surrounded her. "Maybe you don't feel like it, but to them, right now, you're the most important person on the planet."

"Well I'll try to make it as long as you're coming, too. You're about the only one who's been nice to me since I left home, and I'll feel horrible if you don't make it, okay?"

"Okay, Kelly," Josanne said. "I guess we'll climb out of here together somehow."

"Like in the movies, when the people are stuck in a well, and they lean on each other to climb out of the hole?"

"Yeah, Kelly, just like that," Josanne replied with a smile. "And maybe we already started."

"Yeah, maybe," the younger girl replied. "But I don't think that's true," she added, but with a thoughtful, almost playful tone behind her voice that piqued Josanne's curiosity. "And don't pretend you don't notice," Kelly continued with a hint of her Texas drawl returning, just a bit of the little girl resurfacing. "Not after all that talk about what's happened."

"Oh yeah?" the broken conversationalist asked, eyebrow arched in contemplation. "What do you mean?"

"I mean," Kelly started, and Josanne felt the girl's eyes roll in the statement, "that I'm not the most important person in the world to Jack."

"Oh really?" Josanne asked, falling into Kelly's game. "Then who is?"

"Well, duh, silly!" The comment struck Josanne by how much the girl had at least temporarily recovered just by her opening up a little bit. But what the young kidnap-victim-turned-prostitute-turned-human-breeding-experiment said next shocked her into silence.

"*You* are!"

45. Finding Kelly

"MADE IT JUST in time!" Dante called over to the team members atop the other elevator car. Once they had cleared the lobby, Rickshaw and Hardcore fled back outside to their vehicles while Rogue Moon, Chrome, Dante, Constantine, and Stang raced forward and hit the buttons to take them to the 50th floor. When the fire alarms triggered, their cars halted on the 27th.

"Well, that was fortuitous," Stang commented.

"So tell me again," Rogue Moon asked once the cars came to a halt. "Exactly why did we take the elevators *up* when we know we want to back up Spider's team in the basements?"

"Misdirection," Chrome replied. "We left a floor full of people who saw some of us run back into the street while the rest of us jumped into elevators going up. When their security people arrive, they'll all tell them we went upstairs." He opened the hatch in the elevator ceiling and helped her hoist herself through. "We are going down, but they won't know that—it'll divert even more of their troops."

"Only the fire alarms helped us out two ways," Stang added. "One, all security units that took the elevator to get to whatever floors they were trying to get to are now stuck. The second is, they saved us 23 floors of rappelling."

"Right you are," Chrome grinned. He climbed atop the small platform, retrieved the large duffel bag he had brought along, then reached down to lift out Stang and Constantine out of the elevator car. In the meantime, Dante hoisted himself out of the other car he had all to himself, mangling the hatch frame and paneling located around it. His heavier armor already pushed the weight limits of the groaning elevator; he had to ride by himself.

"I've never learned how to rappel," Rogue Moon complained. "There's no way I can learn by trying down this pitch-black blind hole! I can't do it!"

"Relax," Chrome grinned. "You won't have to." Seeing the quizzical look on her face, he explained. "Outside of the car, you see only the darkness, which means you really don't see anything at all. I, however, see fine. My eyes aren't as specialized as Preach's, but they have light amplifiers and also can see infrared and ultraviolet spectrums if I want them to.

"And you won't have to rappel, either. Here, this is a bowline seat rope harness. Put it around your butt. You too, Stang. When it's on right it'll feel like you're sitting in a rope swing." He gave them a moment and made sure they were ready, secured the duffel bag around his shoulders, and slid the other end of the harness around his neck with the line forward. "Wish me luck," he said with a glance towards Moon, then jumped into the black abyss of the elevator shaft dead space. She would deny it later, but the other team members all heard her draw in a breeze as she gasped, thinking he dove down the shaft to his death.

"Okay Rogue," his voice called from somewhere several feet above her. "I'm going to pull on the rope and lift you off the platform. Try to relax, be still, and look anywhere that's at your neck level or higher."

Rogue appreciated his communication skills. He didn't tell her not to resist or swing about on the rope to grab something, didn't tell her not to panic, and didn't tell her not to look down. He had surprisingly only told her what she was supposed to think while completely not telling her what not to think—which by power of suggestion would have only sent her mind to concentrate on what exactly that was.

"Ready," she called, but she was ready for him to pull her sideways into the awaiting neighboring cable system. Instead, she lifted almost straight up, and she almost gracefully swung into the adjacent cable.

"Let go of the cable," Chrome called down to her. In a moment of truth, she did, and found herself in an almost carefree place as she dangled 27.5 floors above the bottom of the shaft.

"OK Stang, your turn," Chrome called. A second later, Moon was surprised again as her rope swing pulled vertically; Chrome had climbed the elevator cable while carrying the weight of two others and the large duffel bag. Short moments later, Moon and Stang felt themselves rapidly descending down the shaft as the cryosteel clamps that were Chrome's fingers relaxed themselves just enough to slide down the cable he was holding. Constantine's suit was again providing its faint blue glow as he jumped from the beams on one side of the shaft to the other to effect his own gradual descent, the dim illumination augmented by Dante as he climbed down the cable from his own elevator.

"We're almost there!" Stang exclaimed.

"Yeah," Chrome said as though he were chewing a cigar, "but it's like ol' Bob Frosty wrote: 'Miles to go before we sleep—unless you're gonna take a dirt nap.'" He slouched a little lower and took a step towards the elevator doorway as he pulled out an impossibly heavy Vulcan IV Gatling gun from his duffel bag. "I suggest we keep moving."

… …

"Trigget!" the computer speaker suddenly sounded. *"Trigget! This is Preach—do you copy? Do you copy, Trigget?"*

"Hey!" Kelly called, suddenly excited. "Isn't that what you said they called you?"

"What? That was *real*?" Josanne had begun to lapse into the same dream fugue that had affected Kelly as she ran down that alley—

except in her doubts she dreamed herself Josanne, with Melissana caring for her and the idealized Jack courting her.

… …

Preach paused. His Corvus, battered and laced with bullet holes and laser burns, haltingly hovered over the wreckage of six laser towers, nine SAM batteries, and three crashed SU-57's.

… …

Did I just die? Trigget thought to herself…

- *"Trigget! This is Queen Vixenn! Can you hear me? Please respond! Come on, girlfriend. Answer me!"*

She wasn't hearing things! She would have to respond to her best friend, but Preach had called her—she'd answer her team leader first. Response protocols didn't factor in her decision—she just recognized her need for him to know she was there.

- *"Jack! Jack! I'm here!!! I hear you!" The totality of her situation began to overwhelm her—she felt herself growing colder, felt herself perspiring inside the green goo that still surrounded her. "Jack—Please help us! I am so sorry!!! We're here, locked inside some kind of containers in a research lab! Please hurry—we need you!"*

… …

"Did she just say 'us'?" He wondered at the thought for another quarter of a second before he responded.

- *"Trigget, we're on our way. Hold on—we're so close!*

… …

Somehow, she recognized that she had done the right thing; from that pronouncement onwards, she heard him calling to others, coordinating locations and guiding them through some intervening squads of Apex security troops. Jack would take care of everything else. Her best friend was on her way, backed up by two of the fastest fighters she had ever seen and a human cat. They were on their way. She could rest. If they couldn't make it, she figured her life wouldn't be worth living anyway. He must have been inside the lab system; a moment later, she felt her restraints click open and heard the locks release on her vat. Then to her dismay, she also heard approaching bootsteps in a trot too uniform to be her rescuers. She couldn't tell their exact number, but she could tell one thing. There were too many of them.

… …

"See? I told you they'd be coming for her!" Oswald scolded as he burst through the door, panting. His petulant chiding did little to win the respect of the two full squads of heavy security, but they had to follow the guy to his lab anyway. The guards had heard the rumors of his depravity; seeing it first-hand utterly repulsed them to the point that even the hardest of them felt compelled to look away.

"You heard that fighting," he continued. "They're on their way here right now! They're here for… *her!*" He then paused and took a closer look at her. Was she smiling, and… did she just wink at him? He leaned in a little closer to make sure, and coughed slightly, once, as the pheromone cloud hit him full in the face.

"*Hey, Big Boy,*" she half whispered. "You know, you were so right about me coming around to you… It's a shame all those other guys are here, though. Come on," she purred. "Wouldn't you like to come in for a swim with me?"

He glanced at her, then at the security guards. The pheromone high, combined with his depravity, had completely hijacked any suspicion that this was anything other than exactly what he wanted it to be. In his mind, she had finally come around.

"Well, you men! Why are you waiting in here? Shouldn't you be outside guarding the door or something?"

"Sure thing, professor," the detail commander responded. "We'll just go outside and plan to get shot up while you continue your err… experiments." Oswald fixed him with a narrowed glare, which only prompted the captain further. "That's okay doc. Y'see, this place is a little too… what's the word? Oh yeah, it comes to me now. 'Seedy,' that's the word." He scowled back at Oswald so coldly the doctor shrank back.

"C'mon, boys," he dismissively ordered his troops. "We don't want any part of what Dr. Govek does in here. Maybe they'll let us get clean-up kits and showers to disinfect ourselves from this creep show. Damned if I know why they keep him around."

No sooner had the door closed than Oswald was leaning against the canister. "You can come out now," he called. "I've gotten rid of the others," he vocally dripped. "Now you've got to promise not to tell Minova," he muttered. "This'll be our little secret."

"If telling means that she'll take you away, then Baby, I promise I won't tell. Only, it's too cold outside, and I'm already really warm and comfy in here. Come on, why don't you come in?"

"Well, those canisters are really only built for one person—if I try to come in there with you, it'll be really tight in there."

"But that's the whole *point*, isn't it?" She smiled and swirled around in the greenish goop. "Come on; it'll be fun—I promise," she said with a smile and a hiss of another shot of pheromone.

He stripped and started to climb in to join her. Her hand shot out against his left as he was using it to steady his entry. She then hooked her forearm around his and pulled him into the swirling goo. She slid around and rolled on top of him, pinning him to the bottom of the tank.

"Quick, Kelly—get that mask!"

Somehow, Kelly was out of her own canister and moving as fast as she could without slipping to grab one of the masks they had woken up in.

"Here you go, Josanne," she said as she held it out to the girl who had trained in corporate self-defense courses since childhood.

"And here you go, you perverted frack. I recommend you let me put this on you. Believe me, I had my doubts about using it—I was just going to let you drown in this cesspit."

"But—but—I don't understand!" he whimpered. "You promised this would be fun."

"Oh, and it is!" Josanne coolly replied. "For me and Kelly. We're having a blast!"

… …

"Sixteen heavies up ahead," Spider called to the others. "They're not on the move—looks like they're dug in and waiting for us."

"Any ideas?" Luke asked.

"Well they're heavily armored, with full helmets and self-contained breathing apparatus, so gas is out."

"Can you ping them and find out what they're packing?" Johnny requested.

"Yeah," Spider responded. "But you're not going to like what I tell you. Shall I start with the rocket guy and machine gunners and work my way down to the riflemen with backup machine pistols, semi-automatics, and knives, or do you want me to start small and work my way up?"

"Point taken—never mind. I'd probably rather not know." He drew a pair of auto-pistols, inhaled, and took a step forward.

"And what do you think you're doing?" Melissana demanded. He paused long enough to look at her and give her a half-smile.

"Sorry about what I said about being electrocuted back there in the tunnel; I guess this is more of the glorious end I had imagined for myself." Then he turned. Luke, Spider, and Lady Blackwolf all tried to stop him, but he dodged their grasps and slipped around the corner. They tried to call him back, but it was a vain effort. Over the volume of the auto-rifles, machine guns, and the loud zipping sound of a Vulcan 3 heavy Gatling gun, they couldn't even hear themselves.

… … …

"Hear that?" Josanne exclaimed. "That's them. They must be right outside!" The gunfire died almost as quickly as it had started. Too quickly! Silent seconds crawled by, turned into a full minute, then two. As excited as Josanne had been a few minutes earlier, now she was terrified. In her short months associated with the organization, she had seen CYBER teams repeatedly take on so many preposterous battles against impossible odds and come out okay. She suddenly recognized that in her captive state, she had forgotten it was possible for them to lose.

There was a loud *bang!* that sounded against the door. A few seconds lapsed and it happened again. The lab door bent inwards. A series of smaller bangs like someone was using a jackhammer sounded against the wall just adjacent to the door.

- *"Jack? Mel?" Josanne called. "Where is everybody?"*

There was another pause for a few seconds, then both girls screamed as an earsplitting *wham!* thundered throughout the room as the reinforced door gave way, budged off its track by what looked like the business end of a huge sledgehammer that had gotten wedged into the doorframe about chest level, the blue glow surrounding it slightly misted by the dust it was able to dislodge from the door's under-rail. The device twisted back and forth a few times and dislodged.

Kelly screamed a second time.

598

"What is it?" Josanne frantically whispered.

"I just saw somebody look through the little hole and peered around inside the lab. I've seen a lot, but it was the scariest face I'd ever seen. Josanne, I'm scared!" The CYBER medic/conversationalist reached out and held the young girl to try to comfort her. The head grunted and withdrew.

"I don't know—all three of them were in there a few minutes ago, I swear!" they heard from outside the hallway.

Groans of effort battled the shrieking of twisted metal forced against its purpose, but with a human roar, the door was pushed far enough away from the wall that it would admit passage. The girls had hidden themselves as best they could. They withdrew even more as they heard a heavy set of footsteps enter the room and begin to slowly pace around the room. Slowly the steps approached the sheet-covered lab table they had hidden under and stopped. Both girls held their breaths. The sheet lifted, the owner of the footsteps crouched low. Kelly screamed again as the thick-set dour face with the sunglasses and blonde crew-top haircut looked at them both. And smiled.

"You two girls alright?"

Trigget started shaking, then crying. She didn't need to be strong anymore because they were safe.

"Kelly?" she sobbed, "This is Chrome. He's with us!" Then she turned to the armored cyborg that seemed in that moment as if he was the Earth itself. "And Chrome? It gives me great pleasure to introduce you to Kelly Elverson." She could have sworn she saw his throat tighten at the news.

"That's mighty fine news to hear, ma'am," he said. He removed his sunglasses and gave the girl the biggest smile she had ever seen on him. "Miss Elverson, it is my extreme pleasure." He glanced at both of them and continued. "Listen, we've got Luke with us. We'd like to check you over and make sure you're okay to move. Then we'll get you out of here. You two girls up for that?" After seeing their nods, he stood to full height and called over his radio.

- "All units, this is Chrome. We've got them. I repeat, we've got them. BOTH of them. The lab is secure; Trigget took care of the doc. Speaking of docs, Luke, come on in and proceed with the medical checks."

The sheet lifted from the other side of the table, and a slim side of medium, black-haired young man with hazel-green eyes sat on the floor next to them and blew a sigh of relief, almost carelessly letting the pair of auto-pistols he was holding clatter to the floor. "Sorry about the door," he offered. "I tried to open it myself, but the lock was stuck."

"Johnny!" Josanne exclaimed, new tears beginning to form. "Am I ever glad to see you!"

"I'm not sure—are you?" he said with a smile. "Just kidding," he reassured her as he offered his hand to help them up from under the table. He studied Trigget closely as Luke attended to Kelly, noted the lab coats, then turned deadly serious. "How are you?"

"Josie!" Melissana shouted as she ran up and embraced her best friend. "Josie, are you all right?"

"Yeah, I'm fine. *Much* better now!" She looked at her former private detective friend so intently Melissana almost winced. "Mel, I am really sorry for how I've been acting since… the incident. You guys were all trying to help, and I just threw it back in your faces. They say I saved your life, but the truth is I've been a horrible friend ever since. Can you ever please forgive me?"

"Josie, you were going through a really hard time. We all get it. Yeah, it kind of stank while going through it, but mostly because I was trying to help and was frustrated that I couldn't. After all, I'm not the one who had the training for that sort of thing, so what could I possibly say to the one who did?

"But *you*," Melissana suddenly jabbed Johnny in the solar plexus. "You have no excuse! What were you thinking? Don't you *ever* do that again! You know we just lost Helpdesk, and then after all we've just been through, you go and pull a stunt like that! What were you *thinking*?" Her rage had vented itself; like her best friend, however, she had been under intense emotional strain since Josanne had saved her life. Now that the crises of the last few months had been resolved, her mind let all of her emotions go at once. She started to cry, then threw herself at the team's skillster in the most mammoth hug her 5'6" frame allowed, burying her head in the embrace. "Drek! I'm just so glad you're alive!" She withdrew just as quickly and fixed him with an angry glare. "But you ever do anything like that again, and I'll finish the job myself, you understand?" He started to reply, but she struck a quizzical look and cut him off. "Wait a minute. Just what did happen back there?"

It was Adams who responded. "Near as I can piece together, your boy here stepped out to take on sixteen highly trained, heavily armored, heavily armed Apex Special Forces types all by himself. But at that exact moment, we made our presence known to that same group of security and began to receive the fullest effects of their warmest welcome."

"In other words," one of the Apex soldiers interrupted in a half-Creole drawl, "we started lettin' 'em have it!"

"Your walking tank guy," Adams resumed, "got ticked and opened up with his Vulcan, doubtlessly giving them cause to rethink their position. After they ducked back into their cover, one of them removed their helmets for a full breath of fresh air. Turns out Johnny knew him from back in the day somewhere and asked if we all could just talk a minute."

Luke had concluded with Kelly and started to inspect Josanne. By this time, Chrome had the door opened wide enough that both sides comingled in the area.

"Yeah, Johnny-boy," the Apex soldier continued with a grin. "Ah still can't believe it's you! Last I knew, you were dealing corp punishment down Lubric's way. I filled the captain in on some of your other jobs and said if you're here, that probably meant something here is very wrong." Hearing himself mentioned, the leader of the ASF squad approached and joined the conversation.

"So Denson taps me on the helmet and says, 'Cap, you're not gonna believe this, but I know one of these guys, and they want to talk.' Well he got me caught up on who this Johnny guy is, and you all explained about what you were after. Then it turns out Adams is with you, and I know enough about him to know he's legit, so I figured if he's with you, there's probably good reason for it. So, I said 'screw it' and opened up an off-line dialogue." Melissana skewed her face in disbelief at the turn of events.

"Well, it ain't like that whack job of a professor and us are friends," the captain protested. "Besides, he pretty much dismissed us so he can have a party time with one of the girls. It also turns out that you guys aren't really attacking the company, just trying to rescue these two girls from that psycho nut job. Hell, none of us got an axe to grind against that."

"So as a token of faith," Constantine picked up the narrative, "we all kept off our radios and let them stick around until we could verify that the girls were okay. Likewise, the good captain had his boys stand down until they could verify we really were here just to rescue the girls. So here we are."

"Luke's cleared the girls for travel," Spider pronounced. "Kelly, you swap with Lady Blackwolf, Trigget you can swap out with Queen Vixenn. We'll get you out through the tunnel while the others head back out through Apex—if that's okay with you, captain?"

"Nope, that won't work," he answered. When he saw their looks of feeling betrayed, he quickly raised both hands in denial and said, "No—it's not like that!

"Then how is it?" Lady Blackwolf pressed. His men took a step back as she popped her claws, but the captain held his ground.

"Air Dynamix called us," he pointed out. "That call was why we set that off our alarms. Well, the first one, anyway. They've electrified the tunnel, and they'll have more firepower on every level than you guys can hope to overcome. You'll never get out that way."

"I'm sorry. We've all been running this deep op for a long time, I'm really sorry." She retracted her claws, then looked up at him. "Any suggestions?"

"Well, you can't go back the way you came, and you can't stay here, and you can't go walking through half of Apex and out the front doors wearing nothing but lab coats." Then he smiled, a faraway idea taking form in his mind. "I know we gotta move soon, but gimme a sec to talk things over with my crew." He then gathered his sixteen troops and tucked them away in a corner, practically whispering among themselves in a meeting of their own.

"*¡Dios mio!*" Spider laughed. "They're going to be a couple more minutes, but this is going to be good!"

"You said a couple minutes?" Trigget asked. Spider nodded yes, then broke into another wide-mouthed grin as he continued to listen in on the security team's conversation. Trigget approached Queen Vixenn and asked a favor. After a brief conference, Vixenn connected her cyberdeck, and after she scanned for any immediate threats, she handed a portable VR headset to the conversationalist.

······ ······

Trigget looked at herself, a somewhat thin but pretty girl in a simple woodsy dress. The sheer beauty of the world amazed her—no wonder Mel wanted to spend so much time in here! In the distance, she saw the wreckage of strong towers and several fires, evidence of the battles fought over the networks to give the team the advantages they needed to wage the real-world wars they faced. It was so real here! She heard about the ICE, and heard them talk about the digital conflicts, but she had always pretty much dismissed their stories as just geek-talk exaggeration. Now she wondered what they thought when Johnny, Susan, or Corey talked about their exploits. They must seem so drab by comparison!

Then she saw him. He was an obviously powerful wizard ambling about the area, observing specific flowers, studying certain rocks with intent focus. She gasped when she noticed he was limping, walking with great effort. He had been hurt.

"Hello, Queen Vixenn. I'm truly sorry about Helpdesk." He offered his sympathy as he slowly turned—it seemed even that movement pained him. She started again when she saw his face. He was still very much the powerful mage she had first imagined, but he looked… older.

"Oh, I'm sorry," he said, even sounding like a forgetful grandfather. "I thought you were Queen Vixenn. You must be using her system."

"Preach? Are you okay?"

"Trigget?" Is that you?" Her confirmation buttressed him; he seemed to grow younger and regain some of his strength. "Trigget, this is my persona in this virtual world, not me. True, Apex ICE provided quite the combat exercise. There were a couple genuinely close calls, but even though I took some good hits with their ICE and security admins, their black ICE never got all the way through. If I reload my environment module and launch it again, I'd be good as new." He was afraid to continue but knew that he had to. "But that doesn't matter. How are you?"

"I'm good. We're going to be on our way out in a couple minutes, I guess, I just… I just wanted to talk with you a little first, and when they said you're with Partisan, I guess I didn't want to wait that long." A faint greenish glow surrounded his body for a moment, and when it faded, he had regained much of his vitality.

"I'm glad you did," he said. "Such as it is, it's good to see you." He waved his arm in a world-sweeping gesture. "At least, to see what I look like from the perspective of Vixenn's Ultimate Fantasy sim," he laughed.

"But you said you don't use this one, right? You use a flight simulator, right?"

"That's right," he nodded.

"So Preach?" She faltered, not really sure she wanted to know. "What do I look like? I mean, in yours?"

He took a step away; in her mind she knew he had just veered off to get a visual appraisal. He swept back in a moment later. The module had assessed her network capabilities and was rendering her as a WWI observation balloon. But he wasn't concerned about her hacking skills. He was just glad she was alive and all right. "You're an SR-74," he smiled.

"Is that good?" she asked.

... ...

Partisan saw Preach smile and his body suddenly relaxed.

... ...

"I'll show you some pictures when we get back home."

... ...

Josanne blushed.

... ...

"Jack!" she cried in the sudden realization that she had forgotten where she was. "Jack! Please forgive me! This place is such a wonderful place, I forgot!"

"Forgot what?" he asked.

"I gotta go talk to Mel—Queen Vixenn, but hang on a sec."

Josanne's avatar faded out of existence. Jack hovered, waiting, for a full 90 seconds. Then the virtual sky shimmered as a hospital plane took form beside him.

"Pastor Jack? Pastor Jack? Is it really you?"

Jack flew an aerial maneuver that combined a series of helix rolls with a vertical loop, but of course that had all been lost on Kelly. She did laugh, however, at the old wizard who did a triple back-flip and launched streams of fireworks through his fingertips when he landed.

46. Getting Out

With the Apex security team still huddled, Jack took some time to reassure Kelly in who he was and that she was truly about to be freed to go home. He also bolstered her hopes that her parents would be overjoyed to have her back. Spider and Chrome were by the wreckage that had been the door, discussing their separate journeys that brought the teams to meet up at precisely that moment. Johnny's luck obviously had won out for him again. But while neither one could deny the reality of the result this time, they were both highly wary of the way he sometimes pushed his fortune.

… …

"Yep, she's pregnant," Luke quietly affirmed to Lady Blackwolf, his fellow Paladins, and the former corporal Adams. "She'll probably be showing in another week or so."

… …

"I should shoot him now," Rogue bitterly complained to Stang as they walked past the vat that now contained Oswald, "but they won't let me."

Stang smiled, but as Rogue watched, the sides of his mouth twisted up just a twinge too far, converting the friendly gesture into a grin. "Oh I don't know, Rogue," he replied. "Have you ever seen any one of these people let someone off easy? I know they don't like unnecessary killing, but if they have a plan for him I'm sure it'll be worth all the popcorn in Pulaski to see what it is."

…… ……

Josanne again started to apologize to Melissana as soon as she broke her connection with Jack, but Melissana was too worried about her best friend to listen. Instead, she forced herself to ask Josanne the hard questions; she hadn't failed to notice the lab coats the two girls were wearing. The private investigator turned Pride decker pressed for honest answers underneath any conversationalist training Josanne might have used to avoid the hard answers. Hugely relieved after Josanne had convinced her the govek had not raped her, she was still enraged when the details of the doctor's behavior came to light.

"Hey Mel, can I ask you a question now?" Josanne asked.

"Sure," Melissana replied. "Anything you want," she said with a warm smile. She had her friend Josanne back—nothing her best friend could ask could possibly ruin the moment.

"Who is Helpdesk? You said something when you were laying into Johnny…"

Melissana completely tuned out Josanne's voice. She looked at her friend, then at Kelly, the still-innocent child who had been through so much, then at the eight vacant vats. The macabre combination of sterility and intense personal violation triggered something in her. The walls and ceiling were the pastel white of most research labs, but in her trembling fury, all she could see was red. She pounded her fist against the doctor's console so hard she had to rub off the pain in her hand. She was going to kick it in even more anger, but a thought occurred to her. Given the doctor's personality and what he had used the machine for, he probably stored lots of useful documents and logs as mementos. She could cause a lot more pain as Queen Vixenn punching deck than as Melissana punching and kicking the console. Besides, she couldn't deny the sense of poetic justice enslaving the computer to strike back against the Apex operation and those behind it.

- "Preach," she called in as she tapped Kelly on the shoulder to get her attention. "I need my deck back. We'll let you guys meet in person soon. I'm hoping to squeeze in a quick run against the doctor's console. You cut the ICE around us already, or you wouldn't be chatting it up, right?"

…… ……

After several minutes, the captain approached Spider and Chrome as the security team finally broke up their meeting. "I've been around enough rodeos to know you two are the leaders of this group," he began. "I've been talking with my boys. We think we have a way of getting your two girls out of here. Now, we've got to move fast but, before we do this and put our necks on the line, we want to know what *you* guys are doing here. This sick govek of a doctor has been here a while, but you guys came for these two women. Who are they?"

Araña cleared his throat. "You know who James Sinclair is?" he hesitantly asked.

"Yeah," the captain responded, "he owns SyncTech Incorporated, which owns Apex. Most of the people around here refer to him as God."

"Yeah, well in that case," Chrome responded by pointing his thumb over his shoulder at Josanne, "meet God's sister."

"Holy Mother of…"

"No," Chrome corrected. "Sister."

"I thought she died a while back. And somebody stuck her down here? James is going to have their skins hanging on his wall."

"In full disclosure, captain," Spider corrected, "I think it's only fair to tell you before you commit. It was James who ordered her here."

"You're telling me we are going directly against James Sinclair's wishes?" The team leader paused as he looked out towards his unit. "That changes everything." He pointed to his units and called out, "Guiterrez! Pachelski! Front and center!" Two of the armored soldiers trotted up to their leader to await his next words. Spider and Chrome both tensed.

"They leveled with us—we're on. Go link up with the hostages and do your thing."

Distracted by the rapid movement, the members of the combined CYBER ops teams watched as the two troopers briskly approached Trigget, who was watching over Queen Vixenn's shoulder, and Kelly, who was still shaking off the weird effects of her first time in virtual reality. With the exception of Araña, all were visibly surprised when they removed their helmets to reveal flowing hair and facial features that were decidedly female.

"What are you doing?" Trigget asked as the captain's "boys" stripped off their armor and clothing without hesitation.

"Put these on," Guiterrez ordered. "We've spent all the time any of us could afford inside this horror show of a lab already. You two are too weak to fight, and you can't go back through the tunnel." She helped Trigget into her suit as, across the room, Pachelski helped Kelly into hers. "Your weapons systems are disabled, but we're giving you an armed escort out of here."

"No!" Kelly protested before Pachelski was securing the helmet in place. "I don't want anyone to get hurt because of me again!"

"Don't worry, we'll be okay." The captain's voice cut in over their comm circuit as he addressed the group. "Now here's how this is going to go. My team and I will walk your girls through Apex and make sure they're safe outside. The rest of your group will exfiltrate the Apex facility. If you're not out in an hour, you will have broken the appearance that you are only here for the girls, and if that is the case, you will pay full penalty." Just then, the alarms died, the constant shrieking fading to an eerier silence. "We're starting to run seriously short of time, so I suggest we get our butts moving."

"Just twenty seconds more," Queen Vixenn pleaded. Araña nodded his agreement; the captain sighed but waited as patiently as he could, given his stomach started to twist.

"Ready," she exclaimed as she jacked out from her cyberdeck. "Oswald kept a journal; I read the whole thing in less than 10 seconds but wanted to do a little more digging while I had the chance. That guy had one sick imagination." She looked at Trigget. "You were lucky. He wasn't allowed to act out his fantasies towards you, but he has done exactly that with Kelly and several others."

"Ready to go?" the captain asked, clearly nervous about lingering any longer.

"What about him?" Queen Vixenn asked as she glanced at the vat containing the doctor.

"Well, it's like I started to say earlier," the captain replied. "I recorded Oswald's order dismissing me and the troops outside. The official record will state we clashed with the invading forces and pursued your broken formation when you retreated, forcing me to leave two soldiers—Guiterrez and Pachelski—to guard the lab along with those inside. They'll report Oswald went psycho on them and took them hostage by threatening to kill the girls in the vats if they didn't stand down. Once they did and Doc Psycho found out they were female, he forced them into two other tanks for his pleasure later. You guys must have circled back and found them, rescued your friends, and put Oswald on ice in the process." He gave them all a quick glance and said, "So believe me, he's done. With any luck, Guiterrez and Pachelski might be the ones to put the bullets into him themselves, only this way it'll be legal with the corporation."

Queen Vixenn went back to the console dials and adjusted one of the knobs. "Learned a little about this corporate horror show as well," she mused to the group. "Like, for one, how to adjust the temperature of that goop they're in." She waved to the two Apex security members who had taken Josanne's and Kelly's places. "You two warm enough?" After receiving a nod and a thumb's up from them, she looked at Oswald's vat and again watched the gauges adjust to their new commands. "I'm lowering the temperature of the goo he's in. Not enough to cause hypothermia, but cold enough that he'll feel it." Oswald's body fidgeted at the change. She looked up at the captain and said, "Now I'm ready."

"Come on," Chrome said to Araña as he started walking back the way he had come. "Follow me and my crew; we'll show you guys where the elevators are." Stang gave Rogue Moon an "I told you so" look, and she gave a quick nod to show her agreement.

"Hey captain?" one of the security team asked.

"Yeah, Jander, what's up?"

"Well, we're in our armor and all, right? So I went to check out their Vulcan, and I could barely budge it."

"Yeah? So?"

"So how'd that Chrome guy just put it in a duffel bag and he carries it like it's a light machine gun?"

"Easy, Jander," the captain responded. "It's a thick bag that can support the weight."

"Yeah, but how can *he* carry it?"

"That's simple, too," Chrome's voice came over their comm circuit. *"You gotta eat healthier and go to the gym a little more."* There was a pause as various members of the team laughed over the comm circuit.

"And it's healthier for you, too," the captain added before Jander could offer another protest. "A lot healthier than raising those kinds of questions. And before you ask why again, which do you think would be worse? Facing down that guy and who knows how many more like him for letting their secret out, or having to face corporate because we didn't call in for backup to capture them for our own research?" He waited a second to let his point sink in, then concluded. "Yeah I don't know, either. So, this goes for all of us.

We're going to do the right thing here, use our collective wisdom, and keep our mouths shut. Got it?"

Hearing no further questions, the security team left with Trigget and Kelly in tow. Fifty-five minutes later, the Apex security squads watched as the vat survivors get into Rickshaw's blue and green Dominator half a block away from their front doors. Hardcore's now orange and grey Sabretooth provided overwatch as the vehicle pulled away. The rescue team members remained protectively in between across the street. The cars' faux paint jobs would wash off in less than an hour, and twice that long for the others to make their way back to Partisan's location. Johnny waved an inconspicuous farewell to Denson and the captain as the eleven turned to fade back into the anonymity of the crowd to go home.

47. Falling Out

"Yes, Ms. Santone?"

"Gary, please come up and see me in my office. And please bring anything you have on today's network attack."

"Of course. Let me get some printouts we can review, and I'll be there in ten minutes."

"Make it five. I already have the print-outs here."

Gary Alexander Breverton hesitated. It was unusual for the Air Dynamix CIO to review network attacks without him. He dismissed the notion just as quickly; surely, the scope of the attack would merit her special attention. He grabbed a sheaf of papers he had on Stomwell's history, retrieved the fallen technician's radio, and headed to the elevator.

"Good evening, Yvette," he greeted, then caught the wide-eyed shaking of her head urging him caution. They were not alone; Stafford, the Director of Air Dynamix Security, was there as well.

"Please have a seat, Mr. Breverton." The loosely-disguised order came from Stafford, not Santone. He gave her a quick look—his taking authority in Yvette's office was not against policy, but it wasn't a good sign for her. Her acquiescent nod and gesture towards a chair wasn't a good sign for him.

"You can relax, Gary," Stafford began with a smile. "As Director of Security, I'd just like to review today's network attack with you." He reflected a moment and added, "Ms. Santone and I have been over the reports. Quite the monstrosity, as I understand it. It looked like the attacker was going to completely cripple us. That your team was able to prevent such a disaster speaks well for them." Stafford allowed Breverton to nod and express thanks over the compliment before he continued. "And I understand you uncovered the fact that the attacker was aided by an employee, a Mr. Brant Stomwell?"

"Yes sir," Breverton replied. "I was in the network monitoring room and saw firsthand how quickly it spread. The hacker would have had to have help by an internal source. The attack was going on strong, headed for the secret research server cluster. Our own security was crippled; I figured the best thing I could do was to stop the traitorous employee." Seeing the Director of Security's interest, he continued. "You see, sir, this particular employee had several questionable events in his past." He handed Stafford a small pile of folders containing printouts of his past interviews and suspicions regarding the tech support supervisor. "Nothing that I could prove hard enough to terminate him, but enough for me to know he was shady."

"I see," Stafford nodded as he perused Breverton's paperwork. Santone shifted in her seat. "Please go on."

"We analyzed the logs of the attack and connected them to this employee's opening the firewall port that the attacker used when he first entered the network. We also had video surveillance of him cheering just at the time his accomplices penetrated the research server room. Based on that information, I gathered some of my own security and terminated the threat once and for all." Proud at the evidence he had accumulated, he smiled to the director and concluded, "I guess you can say that me and my boys helped you do your job."

Santone stiffened at the ill-placed comment, but Stafford seemed non-plussed. He just leaned back in his chair and exclaimed with a warm smile, "Yes, I might say you did!" Stafford then smiled her direction. "Well, that about wraps that up," he said, "but I have a couple more questions—you know, just a couple details I need for my report; it should only take a couple more minutes. Yvette, would you mind if I smoked?"

"No, go right ahead," she said, visibly relieved. "I don't smoke myself, but my office has the filtration system for those who do."

"Thanks," he said. "I know it's a bad habit, but the problem is, it's still a habit," he almost apologized. "Now, where were we?"

"You said you had a couple questions," Breverton offered.

"Right, right. Thanks Mr. Breverton. Mind if I call you Gary?" he asked with another smile.

"No, not at all," Breverton replied.

"Fine, fine. Thanks." He reopened the network attack reports and casually glanced at them. "This analysis work is amazing," he again congratulated, "but there are still a couple things maybe you can help me with."

"Of course, sir," Gary replied as he settled back in his chair. "Anything."

"You happened to be in the network monitoring room the moment the attack began." The smile he had been displaying suddenly disappeared, replaced with a look of stabbing scrutiny. "Given how little time you normally spend in that room, don't you find that a bit odd?"

"Sir?" Breverton almost stuttered, his mouth agape after that single syllable.

Santone coughed at the question. "Now just one minute, Stafford," she began, but he shot her a look that silenced her. "I would remind you that I am the Director of Security here at Air Dynamix, and we just had not only a network attack, we are also led to believe outside entities danced through our corporate headquarters right into a secure server area." Seeing her sufficiently cowed, he returned his attention back to the Chief of IT Security. "Please answer the question, Gary." His use of the familiar name conflicted with the tone behind the statement, throwing Breverton off just another fraction of an inch.

"I check in on my staff occasionally," he replied, "and the attack had to occur sometime. It was coincidence. Liz, the staff member who was in the room at the time, can attest to my complete surprise, Mr. Director."

"Yes, she already has," Stafford commented. "She stated she was glad you were there. Evidently, she was afraid that if you weren't, you might have blamed the attack on her."

"I'm known to be very thorough, sir. I take network security very seriously and suspect everyone who may have even the possibility of involvement until they are cleared."

"Glad to hear it, Gary." The smile returned. "It means that you more than anyone can understand my line of questioning. Let's continue, then. Liz, your staff member, said the network attacks against our major resources seemed to die out on their own, and that the only remaining line of attack was headed to dead space. Tell me, doesn't it seem odd that if an enemy attacked us and obtained as much control of the network as he evidently had, that he would stop there? I mean, even if they all were just a distraction, why not finish the job and wreck us?" He paused as though he had a new thought. "Of course, if it was someone responsible for that security, I could see how they might want to look like a hero. A rescue like that might be worth a raise—maybe even a promotion. What do you think, Gary?"

"I resent that comment, Mr. Stafford. Since I was not involved in the attack, I don't know why he stopped. Liz suspected a flaw in the virus program. Maybe he was afraid of the extra security and black ICE we have emplaced around those nodes."

"I see," Stafford said. He took a drag on his cigarette before piercing the IT security chief with another glare. "But how would the hacker know about the black ICE?"

"I guess Stomwell would have told him." The statement was weak, and the director seemed prepared for it.

"And how would *he* know about it?"

"The folders you're now holding speak to that, director. We caught him nosing around areas he shouldn't have been on several occasions."

"I see," Stafford repeated. "Let's go back to the hacker attack. You said that when the other attacks stalled, you recognized the true target as the secret and well-guarded server cluster." He suspended the conversation for another inhale on the cigarette, then shot Breverton with another one of his looks; this one sported a thin smirk. "They're not very secret then, are they?"

Breverton specialized in IT security; analyzing attack patterns was what he *did*. It didn't take him long to recognize Stafford's attack pattern. He'd start with a disarming 'I see,' take a drag of the cigarette, then come in for an attack, firing the question as if it was a bunker-penetrator missile backed by those accusatory expressions of his. And he must have had a lot of them, Breverton thought. So far, the man had never used the same one twice.

"Again, sir, Brant tipped him off. He was trying to dig up classified network information when he discovered the servers."

"I see," he began. Breverton expected the cigarette to come up to his mouth again, but the conversational tone continued. "And with this critical research resource, of course your policy would dictate that you had it protected by black ICE, correct?"

"Yes sir, of course."

"But your hacker wasn't afraid to go against *that* black ICE, was he?"

"N-no sir."

"Well, we'll let the obvious questions that point raises go for now. There's another aspect of this attack that puzzles me. Liz stated she was on the console and dialing in the network defenses. She went on in her report that at that time, you also joined her in fighting off the attack, is that correct?"

"That is my job, sir."

"Yes, it is," Stafford agreed. "And according to Liz, the virus patterns then neutralized themselves, and the pressure started to lift." He took in a deep breath, then sighed. "But suddenly, only moments after you took to a second console, the attacker focused right in on your location so fast your physical computers were damaged to the point they shorted out." The implication was obvious, but the Director seemed to have already waved it off.

"Let's go back to that Brant Stomwell guy." Up came the cigarette. Breverton braced himself.

"You stated he was digging up classified information when he discovered the servers. Tell me, Gary—what did he do with that information? Before you answer, I would like to remind you that we too have access to email logs and records."

The IT Security Director sighed. "He reported it, sir."

"He reported it?" Stafford asked, but Gary knew he would, just like he knew what was coming next. "He reported it. Interesting, that's not an action I would think a disloyal traitor would take." The cigarette. "Tell me, Mr. Breverton, whom did he report it to?"

"To me, sir," he admitted, shoulders sagging in deflation. "He reported it to me."

"Oh? And what action did you then take?"

"I interrogated him. I wanted to know why he was seeking out classified information."

"Thank you for your openness, Gary. It makes things a lot easier for you. And did you interrogate him by yourself?"

"No sir. As I said, I had some of my own security with me."

"I see." No cigarette. "And what was the result of your interrogation?"

"He covered it with a story about how his new network hire found a hole in our documentation that made her curious, and that they investigated it together. He claimed it was actually her who had discovered the servers." He paused. "That's when we brought her in as well, sir, and she corroborated his story."

"And so you let them go."

"Yes sir. There was nothing to hold him on."

"So you had someone you suspected of network spying and sabotage along with a suspected accomplice, and you let them both just run around the archology? That raises two more questions: One, why didn't you report them to me?"

"I know it seems quite damning," Breverton admitted. "And in retrospect, I recognize I should have reported my concerns to physical security. At the time, however, I didn't really think of him as a threat to anyone physically; he just seemed like he was trying to spy out our network."

"Yes, Gary, it's just that I'm not an IT guy, but even I recognize that the network data represents very real physical assets." He paused as if contemplating Gary's position, then smiled. "But you're right, of course. This is all a matter of retrospect, and what's done can't be undone," he offered with a smile and a half-shrug before continuing. "Which brings us to the second question." He took another puff on his cigarette. "Where's this Bertenelli now?"

"She was last seen in the tunnel," the IT Security manager practically whispered.

"I see." He took another drag.

"Would that cigarette ever be *done*?" Breverton thought, but he stifled the urge to grab the thing out of Stafford's mouth.

"And how did she get access to the tunnel?"

"We needed to make another connection to the Apex servers for a new node they installed. The nodes have a one-to-one connection with a dedicated interface line, so we created service tickets to spin up our own new node and install the connection between the two. Brant's group would have been the ones to install the line, and he assigned the ticket to Bertenelli."

"So without the tickets, Bertenelli wouldn't have been able to access the secret service area and gain access to the tunnel?"

"Correct, sir."

Another puff on the now hated cigarette. "And who opened the service tickets?"

Breverton's throat went dry. *How could this possibly be going so wrong?* He swallowed and tried to look the director in the face but averted his eyes as he answered the question. "I did, sir."

"And you assigned them to Stomwell's team?"

"The system does that automatically."

"And Bertenelli, the one who discovered the secret servers, is missing."

"Yes sir."

"So, when you realized Brant was abetting the hacker, you went to apprehend him, accompanied by the same security you had on that other occasion you 'interviewed' him." He interrupted himself for yet another drag. "In fact, your little group interrogated Brant on several occasions, is that correct?"

Breverton nodded and quietly offered another, "Yes, sir."

"And then you, accompanied by that same group, shot and killed him on the spot."

"Yes sir."

"You do realize how this looks for you, don't you?" Another drag of that cigarette. "So far I've been asking the questions to find out what you think. Would you like to know what I think?" He waited a moment, but Breverton said nothing. "I'll take that as a 'yes,' so I'll oblige you." He paused as though to gather his thoughts. "I find there are a lot of coincidences in this whole thing. You and Stomwell have a past. He hires a new kid who, despite being brand new to the company, let alone the job, suddenly has a revelation about secret undocumented servers. She shares it with him, but he reports it. So eventually, you create a couple service tickets and somehow steer it so she gets them. Rather convenient how she's suddenly missing after you killed Brant, don't you think?

"So, here's what I think," he said as he finally stubbed that damnable cigarette out into an ashtray. "Yes, the hacker had inside help, and that help was you, Mr. Breverton. Bertenelli was a spy, hired by you to bring Stomwell down."

"No sir!" Breverton exclaimed, rising from his chair to protest. "And I can prove it! I have his radio." He reached into his suit jacket to brandish the device. "I found him using it to communicate with his conspirators! I was waiting for an opportunity to turn it into you, sir. And in the meantime, I've been monitoring their communications to see what their next steps are going to be. Listen." He held up the device, and indeed there was radio chatter mentioning Partisan, Saint Nick, and some other names and code words. Stafford sat forward in his chair, focused on the radio.

"Partisan, huh?" He smiled, but the gesture was no longer kind. "This is just another one of your blinds, Gary." Seeing the look of loss and confusion in Breverton's face, he explained. "Partisan doesn't exist anymore. He's a cripple who goes by the name Sitter now because he's stuck in a wheelchair. He can't possibly work the electronics needed to come near this place. I verified that myself with a team of surgeons I had retained for that purpose before we provided him with his severance package."

Stafford's eyes went wide in surprise as he took another look at the radio. "And you've been carrying this on your person since you discovered it, have you? To meetings? To internal corporate discussions?"

"Yes sir," Breverton said, relieved. "Until I could hand it to you. The radio is proof of Brant's betrayal! He betrayed Air Dynamix, not me!"

"You fool!" Stafford shouted as he himself rose from his chair. "You've been auto-transmitting this whole time! And you didn't think I'd notice? Give me that!"

"No! That's impossible!" Breverton objected. But just as he started to hand the radio to Stafford, there was a popping sound from inside the case. The radio spewed acrid smoke as the acids sprayed inside ate through wires and circuit board. It happened so quickly it burned the IT security director's hand, forcing him to drop the burnt-out radio onto Santone's carpet.

"That's it!" Stafford called. "Next time you try destroying evidence, do it when I'm not looking." "Take him," he commanded as two of his own security men burst through Santone's door and wrestled Breverton into an arm-locked crouch that had him wincing as his face pressed against the office conference table.

"Two more things," Stafford declared. "I think you should know that we have some records of our own on Brant. Those occasions you caught him in what you alleged were his traitorous actions?" Stafford paused to refer to his notes. "Our records show those times precisely coincided with his work trying to track how far the connections went between some kidnapping and child trafficking ring and the Life Options debacle. There are some by-products of those investigations that link you to reallocated corporate funds, money transfers, fraud, bribery, and kickbacks—the works. Clearly, you have esteemed yourself more important than the corporation and allowed personal greed to overcome corporate loyalty." He stopped and waited as they cuffed him and raised him back to his feet.

"Gary Alexander Breverton, you are under arrest. The charge is corporate treason. You see, Brant Stomwell was working for us. His last couple messages state that he was onto something big, some kind of attack that was coming related to the failed Life Options gambit. He said he had some suspicions who was behind it all that he couldn't confirm yet; but that he'd let us know when he found out."

He lit another cigarette. No longer caring about appearances or propriety, this time he blew the smoke directly into Breverton's face. "It seems his final message was both caught on camera and also affirmed by the witnesses of the shooting we interviewed. And you accused him of being a traitor?" Though Brant wasn't there to see it, Stafford reflected a moment to give him a nod. "He must've been quite a guy. Faced with getting killed and yet so determined to get the message out, he used his last words to do it." Stafford leaned within inches of Breverton's face and blew another blast of smoke. When Breverton's vision cleared, he found the Director was still glaring into his eyes from only inches away.

"You see, Breverton, it turns out he named the attackers, all of them, with his last words." He smiled again and continued. "You remember his last words, don't you? I memorized them, and with your permission, I'd like to quote them." He blew another cloud into Breverton's face. "He said, 'Mr. Breverton, Unit 309, 312, 421, and 429? I don't know your names, but I can only say this: Long Live the Queen.' You see, Breverton, he didn't know their names, always suited up as they were, but he gave us their suit ID numbers, and pairing them up with the day and shift, we're now holding all of them." He started to shuffle Breverton through the doorway, but stopped just as Breverton was at the threshold.

"Oh, and there was one more person he implicated," he added as if by afterthought. "Someone you left out when you told your story about that secret server interrogation with him and Bertenelli. Someone who was involved up to the eyeballs in the whole Life Options conspiracy. Brant made sure we got the message on the ringleader who was behind all of it.

"Tell me," he asked as he suddenly fixed his gaze on Yvette Santone. "Who would the queen of IT be?"

…… ……

Stafford and his security troops forcibly escorted Breverton and Santone through the cubicle area to the elevator as the door to the now-empty office automatically closed behind them. The meeting concluded, Iylothien flew away from the camera from where he had watched the entire thing. The evidence was real enough, the only enhancement he made was associating Helpdesk's name as one of the sources. Oh yeah, the Barde de la Nêone grinned; he had also activated the receiver self-destruct just when Stafford demanded it from him. But the rest was real, he shrugged. The show over, he turned his mount away from the camera.

"Queen's Knights to Govek rook. Knights take enemy rook and queen." He sighed—Brant might be the first person ever to receive a posthumous nomination for CYBER membership.

"Great job, Helpdesk," he congratulated, though he knew Brant couldn't hear him. "You done us good." He nudged his virtual locust and flitted away through the miles of Air Dynamix network.

48. Homecomings

THE COLD DECEMBER air blitzed the throng of people gathered at the suddenly opened garage doors of Partisan's warehouse, but the crowd that had gathered there only felt the warmth of success as they cheered the return of the CYBER team. They cheered again when the Dominator's passenger door opened and Trigget exited, and Showbiz's former girls practically screamed their applause as the still shaky figure of Kelly followed. Her eyes darted back and forth, casting furtive glances to make sure this new area was not just another trick of her captors to make her think she was safe only to again rip the illusion away. Her shoulders didn't drop their taut defensive posture until she saw Jack approach through the crowd, smiling and trying not to cry.

As for Jack, after he had persevered over the last several months through so many trials and combats, both physical and emotional, he finally allowed himself to lose this one battle, tears of relief flowing freely down his face. He was unsure how to approach his former star student; he had burned into his mind that after all she had gone through, having a man move in to hug her so soon after her freedom could psychologically damage her far more than comfort and assure her.

Josanne took a step towards him but dissolutely stopped herself when she noticed he was looking at Kelly and not her. She was disappointed and even started feeling angry, jilted so quickly after what she thought was a moment between them when they had first reconnected. Then she saw her fellow captive's eyes widen in recognition of her former youth pastor. The rescued child's lips slowly parted to broaden into a smile as bright as the sunshine, and throwing all reservation aside, she rushed into his arms ahead of the conversationalist and started sobbing.

"Yep, that's her," Saint Nick confirmed after Jack had gently broken her embrace. "She's the one who helped the kid in Drogue's Alley." At Saint Nick's pronouncement, a set of gears whined as a motorized wheelchair rolled into view. Kelly flinched at his sudden appearance but calmed a little when she saw the kindness sparkle in his eyes.

"Kelly?" Jack began as he gestured to the man in the wheelchair, "I'd like you to meet Partisan. If it wasn't for him, we never would have found you."

"Thank you," the girl managed to reply, but her brows furrowed and betrayed her confusion. It gave Partisan pause for a moment, and then he broke into a grin.

"Well, I sure am glad you're okay," he began. "We've been looking for you for three months." He paused. "But you're confused about who I am," he said. "Don't be, you're right. I'm more widely known on the streets as Sitter." He smiled again. "I guess you and me have something in common. We both have names that were given to us by people who were very cruel, and these guys around us now have set us free from both those people and those names. So I don't have to be Sitter anymore, and you don't have to be Shimmer anymore, either. Would you like that?" As she slowly nodded, he smiled again. Jack stepped forward.

"Now, I know that might take some getting used to, being Kelly again," Jack assured her as gently as he could. "But it's okay if it takes a little while, okay?" He let out a bemused chuckle. "At least it took Partisan a little while to get used to it. But you see these people? He slowly gestured to indicate the entire group of those around them. "These are good people. I know you met most of mine and Trigget's friends, and you've already seen some of your other friends here, right?" She looked around the room, and yes, she did recognize some of the girls she had met before Showbiz sold her to Mama Solace.

"Some of my friends are here, too," Partisan continued in soothing tones. "Saint Nick here is the one who really gets the credit for finding you."

Saint Nick started to say something about how he tried to find her that first night back in October, but Kelly started to sway where she stood.

"Okay, Kelly," Lynda gently approached to steady the girl and escort her to where she would sleep, using the time to do some medical analysis along the way. "We've got a bed over here for you to sleep in. It's not the biggest bed ever, but you have it all to yourself. Your friends are all here, and you can relax. You've got a whole army around you, and they're all here to make sure nothing happens to you."

"And Pastor Jack's here, right? He's really here?" Kelly asked as she started to fade.

"Especially Jack," Lynda responded with a warm smile. The doctor bent her hand to carefully brush the girl's hair to the side, but by the time her hand reached the stray strands, Kelly had drifted to sleep. Lynda would openly cry later, when she was far enough away to keep from waking the girl, and far enough away from the others to maintain her professional doctoral demeanor.

In the meantime, the rest of the group got busy maintaining their weapons and equipment. Josanne, awkwardly unoccupied after treating her fellow CYBER members and rescuers, turned her attention back to providing medical care to others who needed it. Besides the rescued survivors, she also tended to Partisan and the boys still recovering from Showbiz's attacks and subsequent street fighting of the weeks before.

…… ……

"It's been quite a couple weeks," Jack began to the group gathered in Partisan's warehouse on their last day together. "A combination of reunions and farewells that is culminating here in our final farewell to Brant Stomwell. Before I go much farther I would like to thank Candace and Lynda for the suggestion we do this, and to those who have spoken on Brant's behalf about…"

Jack's voice faded in Trigget's mind as she spotted Adams propped up in his bed. He gave a brief smile and wave when he caught her glance. The memories were only a week old, fresh enough to still take her and seemingly relive each moment in detail…

…… ……

"We're going back into the industrial grounds?" she almost demanded, "What on earth for? Aren't we hot enough out here?" So Jack explained to Trigget about their Air Dynamix raid, and about the former security corporal who was out of a job yet couldn't leave. "You want me to dig into this guy's head and remove a cortex bomb?"

"You're the only one who can, Trig. You've got both the medical protocols, and you're the team bioengineering tech. You improvised that hood for Chrome, and besides, if you run into anything you're not sure of, Iylothien and Queen Vixenn will both be running operational support. I think you got this."

"And you said that even with that… thing inside his head, he still risked coming in on my rescue?"

"Trigget, he was the guy who was hanging with Dante and Constantine when we were checking you guys out," Chrome pointed out.

She sighed. "Well, I owe my life to everyone who was in on that. Where do you want to operate? It'll have to be somewhere clean and at least relatively quiet. And it's not like either Air Dynamix or Apex Premier are going to lend us their hospitals."

"We've got that covered," Rickshaw replied, patting the truck they had used for the revival service.

"We're using the truck?" she almost gasped.

"Hey, we re-rigged it," Rickshaw defended. "It's now the biggest deli truck in the state."

"We've scheduled some deliveries inside the perimeter," Jack explained, "and Iylo's making sure the schedule is botched enough that we'll have a clear ten hours of operating time. I'll provide any light you need. Lynda, Luke, and Spider will assist, and like I said earlier, Iylo and Melissana will be running research on anything you can't get in your own systems."

She tried to portray a confidence she hadn't quite grasped hold of. "All right!" she said as cheerfully as she could, "When do we go get him?"

Six hours later they had him prepped for surgery and on the table, thick plastic sheeting separating the operating room from the storage crates they had concealed themselves behind. After Spider shaved his head, Adams's eyes looked bigger as they stared up at his reluctant surgeon. Those eyes began to lose focus as the anesthetic began to take effect.

"You ever do this before?" he asked.

"No," she smiled.

"Well, beginner's luck, then," he smiled back. He blinked a few times, then added, "Hey that's okay. I was already dead when you guys burst into that room to save the kids." He smiled, but his lips sagged as he did so. "So no pressure." Then the anesthetic took him completely, and he was out.

And in that moment she considered that, in her world of bravery and valor, raiding drug dealers, warlord pimps, mega-corporations, and wasteland biker hordes, that this guy letting himself go to sleep in her care was possibly the bravest thing she had ever seen. And if that was the case, the second bravest thing she had ever seen was her own hand reaching for the scalpel.

"Yeah," she said to herself as Preach intensified the light levels of his eyes and brightly illuminated the area of the skull on which she would be working. "You're disarming and removing a cortex bomb while cruising around a hostile environment inside a tractor trailer being used as a literally mobile hospital operating room. If she twitched wrong, the bomb could go off, killing not only Adams and herself, but also Preach, Luke, Lynda, and Spider. And even if that didn't happen, she could render Adams blind, deaf, or paralyzed. "Yeah," she said to herself, "no pressure."

He awoke two days later in Partisan's warehouse...

She looked at her hands and trembled at the flash of memory. Jack was still speaking, something about some people's interpretations of Scripture...

... ...

"... and now I didn't have a long time to get to know Brant," Jack continued. "And I don't know every theological point known to man, let alone God, but for the sake of absolute honesty before God and you all, after days of praying and seeking what God would have me say today for this service, this is the very best of my understanding.

"Now the Bible says in Acts 4:12, 'Neither is there salvation in any other: for there is none other name under heaven given among men, whereby we must be saved.' And Jesus did say in John 14:6, 'I am the way, the truth, and the life. No one can come to the Father except through me.'

"So was Brant a Christian? I don't know—maybe it depends on what being a Christian really is? Being a Christian means that you're a follower of Christ. Was he? What does the Bible have to say about it? In Mathew chapter 10 verse 25, Jesus said, 'It is enough for the disciple to be like his teacher, and the servant like his master.' And this is the account the Bible gives us of Jesus in the book of Romans chapter 5 verses 6 through 8: 'You see, at just the right time, when we were still powerless, Christ died for the ungodly. Very rarely will anyone die for a righteous person, though for a good person, someone might possibly dare to die. But God demonstrates his own love for us in this: While we were still sinners, Christ died for us,' and Romans 2:14 is clear that 'those, who do not have God's written law, show that they know his law when they instinctively obey it, even without having heard it.'

"It's enough for us to be like Him." Jack gathered his courage to finish without choking up. "The fact is, Brant risked his life every time he let someone know they needed help on the outside. Help he couldn't provide himself, but that did not prevent him from doing more than most would even consider, even laying down his own life for those who needed him. The Bible says that nobody can come to the Father without the Son, but that they who don't have the law instinctively obey it, they become the law to themselves, and in one of his most famous parables, he made the non-religious Samaritan the hero over those who claimed to know God but didn't follow through on what they should have done.

"'Jesus is the Way, the Truth, and the Life, and nobody can come to the Father except through Him.' Does that mean somebody has to grow up as a Christian and do all the Christian things to earn their way into Heaven? Or is it possible that Jesus can let into Heaven anyone He wants to? I mean, it's *His* home." He paused again. "The even bigger fact is that all Jesus had to do for us all to go to hell was to sit back and let our lives run their courses. But He really wants anybody who can to go to Heaven. That's why He died—He sure didn't do it to keep us out.

"Now, I'm not God, but I can imagine Jesus was really proud of Brant, and couldn't wait to show Brant around His house. Who knows, maybe they're sharing a comic book collection, the series where Jesus captured all of Brant's efforts, and what they meant to those he helped.

"I really don't see it any other way."

And with that, he closed his Bible and walked off the platform. Kelly led some girls who started a volunteer choir in Amazing Grace but faltered when they got to the line "that Saved a wretch like me." Josanne joined in to give her the strength to continue; Cleo shuffled up beside the rescued teen and joined in to encourage her, then the whole group. Those who never knew the words hummed along in agreement. Whether the tears were for Helpdesk or some recognition of what that Grace meant to each of them, the tears came, washing away just a little more of their feelings of guilt, watering and restoring just a little more of their own humanity. By the time they got to the third verse, Kelly stood a little taller, firmer, and purposefully found Jack's attention with a look of victory and determination as she led them in singing, "Through many dangers, toils, and snares I have already come. T'was Grace that brought me safe thus far, and Grace will lead me home." Even Partisan cried.

Kelly approached Jack after the service. "That was real nice," she said. "Do you think it's true?"

Jack looked at her and smiled. "What do you think, Kelly?"

"I think I have a lot to learn," she admitted.

"Yeah, me too," Jack confessed.

"Pastor Jack, why do you think God made all of this happen?"

"I don't think He made it happen, Kelly. But in spite of how horrible all of that was, I think He's using it to show all of us how tough He is, and that He'll be with us through the worst life has to offer. And that He can even bring good out of the absolute worst that hell and humanity have to throw at us."

"Pastor Jack, you know how in that song it talks about how it was Grace that brought us safe so far and how it'll lead us home?" She hesitated and averted her eyes downwards to her hands as they cradled her belly. "Everybody's saying that I'm free now and can go anywhere I want. I'd like to go home. That song says Grace will lead us home, but Pastor Jack, do you really think they'll want me back home?"

"Kelly, you have no idea how glad they'd be to have you back." He felt a compelling urge to offer her a hug, but he forcefully willed himself to refrain. However innocently he meant it, there were dread repercussions in how she might receive the gesture. Instead, he looked at her and forced a smile.

"Even with my baby? I'm really afraid about how sad Mom will be, and how mad Daddy will get."

"Well, I'm sure they'll just be glad to know you're okay, but I'll tell you what, Kelly—would you want me and Trigget to go with you? We could talk with them with you. Would that be okay?"

"Yes," she said as she visibly relaxed. "You guys are being so nice. Thank you."

"I'll tell you what. We've got to wrap up some things here, but next week we'll take you home."

"Thanks, Pastor Jack."

The remaining hours passed as the girls prepared for their trips. Some would go home, some never knew their home, and some went as far away as they could get from their homes. Lynda, Luke, and Trigget had worked around the clock to help the girls recover from their abuse. Trigget's medical protocols augmented by her conversationalist training thrust her to the lead medic on station—so much so that Lynda once commented there were techniques in the CYBER database that surpassed even her extensive experience.

... ...

"Looks like you boys got things pretty much wrapped up around here," Partisan confided to Preach that evening. "I gotta admit, for as much as I didn't like it when you guys first showed up, I got used to having you around. You sure you don't want to stay and rest up a while longer?"

"It's tempting," Preach admitted, "but tomorrow we need to split up and get these girls to where they need to go. Spider and the Hounds are taking the eastbound girls in the truck, and we're heading southwest in the bus. Once we're done, we'll need to head back and get our own injuries tended to. We've all paid emotional tolls on this one—even Chrome has taken more than the physical hits, although he's looking better than he has in a long time. And Hardcore's vehicle is still barely drivable by our standards. How about you?"

"Me?" Partisan spun his chair in a tight circle. "I have more kids than I can shake a stick at." Then he nodded his head in Candace's direction. "But then again, I also now have help. And while Witch City is still Witch City, having Showbiz and his crews out of the way will give us some welcome breathing room. Plus there's the added bonus that the child-dumping has stopped; we'll finally be able to get a plan together to help these kids move forward."

He looked about the warehouse. The tractor trailer and bus they had used for the revival were parked in the center of the floor, surrounded by clusters of backpacks and impromptu gatherings of belongings that dotted the entire floor. Some of the older girls helped the younger ones get their things ready for the upcoming trip. A few would stay in Witch City; some would stay together and try to relocate somewhere else, while still others were saying tear-filled farewells to go their own ways. In another part of the room, Chrome was doing a "feats of strength" exhibition for the boys as Johnny was juggling an impossible number of utensils and tools. Corey and Susan watched, relaxing in the fun of the moment. Stang and Rogue Moon were walking together along the outskirts of a quiet corner while Josanne and Melissana fed snacks and Iylothien showed yet another group of kids some cartoons he had found in an old network archive. "You know," Partisan casually remarked, "nobody's worrying about anything." He turned and looked at Preach. "For the first time in a long time, I actually feel at peace. Thank you."

"Well," Jack said as he offered Partisan a shoulder clasp as a handshake, "with all you've done for these kids, you deserve it. And thank you..." he choked back the lump in his throat as he continued, "We never would have found Kelly in time if you hadn't reached out to the Brownies on her behalf."

"Well, it is December. I guess Christmas came a couple weeks early this year."

"Already?" Jack exclaimed. "I've been so wrapped up in everything going on it snuck up on me. We'll need to head out tomorrow morning to get as many of the girls home on time as we can, but we've got one more thing to do before we leave."

…… ……

"Jack, are you sure this is a good idea? We just left here two weeks ago. What if somebody recognizes us? And what about Berkleigh?"

"On your first question, I'm actually hoping somebody does, Trig," Jack responded with a curious smile. "In fact, I've arranged it."

"And regarding the Biological Assets Dragon Lady," Melissana added, "Queen Vixenn's taken care of it." She caught the look of surprise in her friend's face; her eyes practically sparkled as she grinned, "After I read Oswald's journal I got so mad at what they tried to do I ran a hack on Apex. Nothing too dramatic; I just made the records indicate you were sent to investigate her, and recommended her replacement."

"We wanted it to be a surprise," Jack added as the trio entered the lobby of the Apex Premier building. The blonde woman quickly approached to greet them before the door had a chance to close.

"It's so wonderful to see you again, J.M.!" She turned to acknowledge Trigget's companions. "And of course, you too, 'Mr. Jackson' and 'Ms. Bertenelli'," she added with a wink and air quotes. Then she turned back to a confused Josanne. "That was a remarkable job you all did. I had no idea you were from Corporate, let alone that you were investigating, well, you-know-who." She said with her voice lowered into a conspiratorial tone.

"The pleasure is ours, Vanessa," Queen Vixenn replied. "I must say that after the last few weeks, it is good to see a friendly face again. Besides your exemplary performance during the orientation session and several items in your records, it was your friendliness that moved us to have you promoted to replace Berkleigh. The employees were actually afraid to approach your department to report misgivings they had, like that dreadful affair with the 'Life Options' benefit package. We hope you will correct that."

"Yes, of course! I will do my very best."

"I'm sure you'll do fine," Jack assured her. "Thank you for holding that unauthorized equipment Minova had in her office. We're removing it today. May we have access to your office for an hour to do so?"

"Of course! I have another meeting in a few minutes anyway. I just wanted to stop and thank you personally for this opportunity."

"I'm sure you will do just fine," Trigget replied, having just found her voice.

"Thank you again!" Vanessa visibly suppressed her urge to hug Trigget, whom she firmly believed to be a corporate internal investigator. Then she turned and left for her meeting, stopping briefly to turn back once more and wave.

"She'll do well, I think," Melissana said as the three boarded the elevator for Minova's former office. "But I wonder how long it'll take for her to drop the air quotes."

… …

"Ahh, Ms. Berkleigh," the hologram figure began. "And how is my dear sister faring?"

"Actually, she's doing pretty well," Jack replied as he faded his own projection of Berkleigh Minova.

The security breach staggered Sinclair, but he had always been quick on his feet. He veiled the forced pause to regather his thoughts behind the nonchalant tsk'ing sounds he made in an attempt to regain control of the conversation.

"You're bluffing, and you've made an immense mistake," the Sinclair brother arraigned. "I've got your image on video; it won't be long before I know who you are. And after that, I'll know everything about you in as short as a few minutes to as long as a few hours. You're good; I'll give you that, so I'm guessing it'll take the hours." He smiled a mechanical smile. "But I'm a patient man; I can wait that long before I destroy you. And you know I will, don't you?"

"Oh, I don't know," Preach replied just as nonchalantly. "You seem to have trouble destroying Josanne."

"Hi, Jimmy!" a female voice hailed over the comm circuit as Preach zoomed out the hologram focus. Trigget smiled and waved at her brother. "Miss me? And by that I mean, you managed to miss me again."

"My dear sister! You have certainly proved more elusive than I gave you credit for," he said more dismissively than he felt. How *was* she still alive? "But I think your friend here has as much to do with it as you do. And I suppose it was also the two of you who brought down my operation with Mr. Showbiz?" The hologram chuckled. "And here I thought it was that dyke biker gang. I almost have to thank you for that, by the way. Showbiz was more barbarian than businessman." The smile became a scowl. "Almost." The hologram punched some numbers on a computer. "Your interference has cost me a great deal of credits already, and now I will have to train his replacements." He studied their expressions as he continued. "Yes, replacements, as in plural. 'Live and learn,' Dad always taught us. I had become reliant on a single point of failure. No more—from now on I will have at least three 'Showbiz's,' each one ready to take over if one or even two of them succumbs to an operation like you had run." He smiled once more. "Dad would be proud."

"Dad would *never* have allowed you to live if he knew what you would turn into!" Josanne shouted.

"Dad would never have allowed me to live?" The hologram openly laughed, dropping all pretext of guarded conversation. "Dear sister," he said as he wiped his eye from a laughter-induced tear, "who do you suppose built this industry? Why do you think Sync-Tec thrived so well when the collapse of our former civilization ruined many much stronger corporations? And where do you think our early 'self-defense' training came from?"

"You're lying!" she shouted, but Jack noticed it was more a plea for James to stop than it was an accusation.

"Am I?" James asked, sneering. "I won't condescend. Your team was somehow able to trace Mr. Showbiz back to me. I'm sure they will have the means to trace the connections from our dear father back to the crown prince pimps of Witch City of his day." He flouted the new sore spot with a brutal smirk. "Especially if you trace dear mother's history as well." He waved his dismissal. "Like I told Berkleigh, whom, by the use of her holocomm connection, I presume you have also deposed: it's a family business. One I was about to expand exponentially with our acquisition of Apex Premier, until you brought all of that to a screeching halt."

"You *liar!*" she screamed as she sagged to the floor.

"Oh, I've got to hand it to Mom; she never let on," he laughed. "How she must have screamed inside as she tried to keep her little secret! Most women do, you know." He sardonically smiled again. "You should have seen the look on her face when Dad told me. That was the night we decided you needed to go, by the way. You were always too much on her side, too much like her, to do the business any good.

"But back to the present," he almost quipped, having destroyed his sister. He sneered again, this time at Jack. "I must confess that your involvement in all of this is a bit of an enigma to me. You show up out of the blue with, of all people, *her*. And neither of you got involved until that little miscreant Shimmer tried to escape. You should know I do not highly believe in coincidences."

"Who?" Jack had tried to bluff, but the mention of Kelly caught him off guard.

"Oh, don't look so surprised. Even that cretin Sweet Trick was able to figure out that all of our troubles started the night she tried to escape; so, she had something to do with my loss of income." He paced the tight circle of the hologram's range. Jack could tell by the off-screen glances he was running searches on them even while they talked. Hands in pockets and the occasional unbelieving shake of the head told Jack that James hadn't found anything on them yet. A sudden smile played across the hologram's image.

"Well, I don't know who you are, yet, but tracing Shimmer back to her hometown and taking care of her immediate family shouldn't be too hard, and well worth the expense to prohibit such intrusions in the future." He punched some buttons on his console. "But I won't bore you with the details." He faced Jack as he once again smiled. "I just thought I'd let you in on our little secret, since you're still in that dreary little Wichita." He punched another button and the hologram faded.

"Are you okay?" asked Jack. "You know, he was probably lying about your family."

"I don't think he was," Josanne admitted. She shook her no and stood. "But just because my family history is messed up doesn't mean we have to let him steal Kelly's."

Jack nodded. "We'll find out together," he promised. "But it won't take him long to find the Elverson's. We'd better get moving."

"Well, I managed to ride into his system and planted a few little slow-me-downs while you kept him occupied," Melissana offered. "It'll buy us a day or two for them to remove it—maybe less if he detects it early on and they reimage his machine from a backup."

- *"Pride, this is Preach. Load up the bus; we're moving out as soon as the three of us get back. Sinclair's going to move against the Elverson's; we've got to be there when he does."*

- *"Preach, we were going to split up as soon as we linked up with the Brownies. Want us to come with you?"*

- *"Stick to that plan, Spider. We'll rendezvous with Mother Freya and Small Eddie ahead of time to pick up any other southbound-ers and head out. You guys keep to your schedule, get those girls home, and then we'll meet back up after you get yourselves checked back in at Facility."*

- "Preach, you can't take that bus with those girls in it into a firefight, and you don't have a week to do otherwise."

- "That's why we've got to just move on it," Jack concluded.

　　　… …

The Pride had to put their misgivings on hold as they met with the Paladins and Valhalla's Brownies back in Gem; the two disparate groups had sacrificed too much not to be able to see the rewards of their efforts, and Jack wanted to personally thank them before heading out. They spent the morning celebrating the freedom of Kelly and the rest of the girls. Mother Freya broke down and openly wept.

"There are so many," she cried. "You went in for one, but saved so many. I could make you all honorary members!"

"Well, there are more coming," Jack further encouraged. "The other team is coming in a truck to offer a lift for any girls who want to head out going eastbound. They're in no particular hurry, but we can't stay real long—the home of one of the girls is under threat. We're heading south, by the way, so if you have any southbound survivors, well, here's their bus. We'll leave as soon as they're ready."

They spent the morning in Valhalla's Brownies' town and had a chance to see how the Paladins and Valhalla's Brownies interacted. Since their first meeting, they had shared a common purpose, and both groups had lost members fighting to achieve that common goal. Both sides felt the other's losses. The Paladins had memorial services for both Paladins and any Brownies who wanted one, and Mother Freya had conducted Brownie Farewells. Jack was only there a short time but was pleased by what he saw. Most of the two bands would never be fast friends and still vehemently disagreed ideologically but the high tension and bad blood between the groups had dissipated. Any instigators on either side were quelled by their own.

Three hours after they had arrived, Preach's Pride headed south in a small motorcade consisting of the bus, Hardcore's Sabretooth, Johnny's sedan, a small motorcade of Paladins, and a few Brownies to make sure they passed through the rest of their turf unmolested.

… …

Between the extra stops needed to relieve the traumatized survivors and dropping off the other girls they had with them, what would have been a five-hour drive took four days. The CYBER team was tense about Kelly's family the entire drive. After the nearest drop-offs, they waved off their escorts and pushed on as best they could. Jack floored the bus once the last girl had disembarked, but despite their best efforts to pare down the time, they spotted the column of smoke when they were still 15 miles away from the Elverson's home. Trigget sat next to Kelly, trying to comfort the young girl's fears. Jack shifted into Preach mode.

- *"Okay, Pride," he called. "We don't know who's in there, so hold fire, but we're going in hot. I'm taking the bus through the front gate. Hardcore, lay some smoke to cover us and then swing right. Past the first barn, drop Lady Blackwolf like you did in the quarry, then circle to the back of the ranch. Blackwolf, clear your landing area of any hostiles and get in a defensive position. Johnny, you swing left, find a good spot to ditch the car and get your feet on the ground."*

As they approached, they discovered that what had appeared on the horizon as a single column of smoke turned to several smaller fires in several of the ranch buildings and the ashy dust stirred by the crackling flames. It was bad. Three armored vehicles lie in wreckage in various places on the surrounding grounds. Jack drove through the gate and brought the bus to a stop outside the bomb-scattered debris that had been the Elverson home. Trigget physically restrained the beleaguered teen, who felt like she was dying once again. Preach got out of the bus, his eyes scanning through the smoke and dust. Despite heightened visual, infrared, and even ultraviolet scans, the CYBER leader detected no signs of life.

- *"Hardcore, you got anything on your scanners?"*

- *"Negative—although they're still not quite up to spec since the collision."*

- *"Okay, all units, let's move in a little. Both eyes open, watch your six."*

They progressed slowly, methodically through the property until they were all within a few yards of the house. Trigget brought Kelly off the bus but kept her a safe distance from the rest of the group.

- *"Movement!" Hardcore cried. "Something moving onto Trigget's position. Two of them."*

Kelly held up her hands and screamed. Preach darted from his cover, heedlessly moving to punish whatever was going after his former student who had been through so much already. Then he stopped in his tracks, confused. A huge Doberman pinscher wearing a metal helmet slowly limped towards her, but when it caught Preach's scent, it jumped up on him and started barking excitedly. Once it dashed off to the side, Kelly saw that standing protected behind it was Ferdinand.

- "Hold fire!" Preach exclaimed. "You won't believe this," he laughed, "but it's Rachel! And if Rachel's here, then…"

A sudden pang of panic struck him. Rachel was hurt, and if Rachel was out here by herself, then—

- "Anyone have eyes on the Fist?"

A storm cellar door opened. Blaze stepped out, followed by Fuser, Foxfire, the General, and Menagerie. They each took measure of the surroundings. Menagerie moved immediately to attend to her canine companion; Blaze called down to someone inside that it was safe to come out.

"Our home!" Grace Elverson cried out as she surveyed the damage surrounding her. Roy was quiet, overcome by the amount of damage. "We've lost everything!" she cried.

"Well," Preach offered, "not quite…"

"Mom?" Kelly cried out as she broke away from the conversationalist. "*Mom?*"

Trigget would later say that she could not describe the emotional tides of that reunion no matter how much Conversationalist training CYBER pumped into her, only that the entire ride was worth it. After all the hugs, Grace's fainting, Roy's shy, almost cowed approach to his daughter as he begged her forgiveness, her hugs, tears, and forgiveness given. Appropriately enough given the conditions of the family reunion, the CYBER teams were temporarily forgotten. And in all that time, Preach's Pride and Blaze's Fist gathered for a reunion of their own.

"Hey, Preach," Blaze said with a tired smile. "Good to see you! How's it going?"

"Blaze! How did you—?"

"Iylo tipped Simon what was going down," Blaze explained, "and Simon saw we were in the area heading back to the Mansion."

She looked around. "Quite the party—whew! I'm not gonna lie, I'm glad this one's over!"

"They actually brought armor?" Preach asked.

"Yep, they sure did," she replied. "They must have expected some kind of trouble. And they were right—they got us. Fuser took out one of them…"

"You gotta love your applied 1890's electrical science," Johnny quoted from the day they first met. Fuser benignly nodded at the comment.

"And the General here saved the day when those other bad boys came in as backup, let me tell you."

"I lost four of my drones," he chimed in. "Mind if I send you the bill?"

"Don't worry, Pops is good for it," Foxfire assured.

"Pops?" Trigget asked with a raised brow.

"She's the ONLY one who can call me that," Preach said with a smile.

"Yeah," Blaze continued, "they brought enough guns to start a war. There must have been at least twenty of them, not counting the military vehicle crews."

"It was incredible!" Roy jumped in. "These kids came in the night before and said they were friends of yours and they were here to help us out. We stayed up pretty late in the night, and the whole time they talked all about how you mentored them, and what fine people you worked with. The attack started pre-dawn the next morning."

"And we are so glad to have you back!" Roy openly sobbed as he looked at his daughter.

"Kelly," Trigget verbally nudged, "now might be a good time to have that conversation."

"Mom? Dad?" the young survivor began as she took her cue, "I've got something to say—that is, I have a huge favor to ask of you."

"Before she continues," Jack cautioned, "I just want to remind you that the people who did this to your home in less than two days had your daughter as their prisoner for the last two years."

"Honey," Roy asked, "what is it? Anything you ask."

Jack nodded for Kelly to continue.

"Well, you see, there was this man, and he…" she faltered, but before anyone could fill in for her, she gathered her courage and blurted, "and I'm pregnant." She got angry as she started to remember. "They wanted to take the baby from me, but I told them they couldn't have it. They can't have my baby!" she yelled.

"It's okay," Roy said as calmly as he could. *What have they done to her?* he asked internally. He was afraid that if he asked out loud, someone might actually tell him. What he did say out loud, accented by affirmative nods from Grace, was, "Of course we'll do everything in our power to let you keep the baby. The circumstances by which the baby came to be conceived is not the baby's fault, and it's not yours, either. God forbid we do what those people were doing by taking that child away from you. This child is family—we'll raise it together."

… …

The Elverson's called for a special church celebration both to announce the return of their daughter and to honor their rescuers. Roy also used the event to publicly apologize for how he had maligned Jack those six years earlier. The ceremony went well, with Josanne and Jack staying close by Kelly's side so she would feel safe as some of the congregants lined up to welcome her back. As the event wound down, Josanne asked the leader of the Pride if she could have a word with him away from the others.

"Jack, when we first started this back in October, I felt like this whole thing was some kind of evil plot." She looked down and picked at a piece of fabric she was wearing. "I had nightmares that Simon was manipulating me into killing my own brother," she admitted. "And you can blame all that conversationalist training I had, but I knew how the team felt I should be doing better. I hated CYBER, hated that training, but most of all, I hated myself for who I was becoming.

"But once we started, I saw how that training was useful. Whether it was drawing out those perps online, helping Elaine, talking with the Elverson's, Partisan's kids, and especially those girls we rescued from Sweet Trick, I never could have done any of that without Foxfire's training. Then I was called upon to use my medical skills tending to the girls and also Partisan and those boys that survived Ricky T. Showbiz's attack and the corporation's forces… Even the engineering helped treat Chrome and save Adams's life. It made me realize my skills and enhancements really do help people, and that I'm not just some cyborged killing machine.

"I guess what I'm trying to say is that this mission helped me to see, for the first time, how important my role is to this team, and that I am grateful to be a part of it. Between the conversations I had with Kelly when we were in those vats and the medical assistance I can provide to those in need, I really feel like I am getting fully healed.

"Except for one thing:" She wiped some tears from her eyes before she continued. "I lied to the team. For that, I confess to you, Jack, and apologize. I called my brother and tipped him off because I was afraid CYBER was going to kill him." She started to cry openly now. "Jack, can you please forgive me, like you did with Roy?"

"Well, Josanne," Jack began with a sighed prayer for wisdom, "lying is a very serious thing to me and God." He paused to reflect on what she had just said and how he should respond, and to pray even more. He sensed something was in the air, that he needed to go farther. It was time to lay the cards on the table. "Josanne, you've heard me say before that the Bible states that 'All have sinned' and that 'that all' mentioned includes me. So, of course I forgive you." He let that sink in a moment, then added, "But you know, there's someone else you need to ask that forgiveness from as well. And as

His ambassador, I can assure you He is more than willing to accept your apology and forgive you, too."

"How do I do that?" she asked.

"Well, you're talking with me, and we call that 'conversation.' For some reason, when we talk with God, we call that 'prayer,' but it's the same thing. And asking for God's forgiveness is really as simple as A-B-C: Admit your sin and ask for forgiveness, Believe Jesus is who He said He is, that He died to pay for your sin, and that He came back to life and is now ruling with God,"

"I've seen enough evidence of that in the last two months!" she interjected.

Jack smiled and continued, "And Commit to following God, to trust Him when things are going your way, and when things aren't going your way."

"Like when you were praying that night when the deal with the Valhallas's Brownies and the Paladins almost blew up?"

"Yeah," Jack smiled. He didn't know she had been watching him. "Like that."

… …

"This is really awkward," Josanne said to the three CYBER teams after Jack had assembled the teams together for a meeting that included Grey's Hounds via video link. "I want to tell you—all of you—how sorry I am that I've not trusted you so much that I actually ended up being the one who betrayed you all.

"That night at Partisan's was my fault. I know you haven't forgotten, but I've never come out and said it before, either." She cleared her throat and wiped a tear away from her cheek. How long had she been crying? "I've asked Jack to forgive me, which he did." She said as she cast a grateful glance back to him. He seemed taller than how she last remembered him. "But he also reminded me that I need to make good and come clean with the rest of you as well. So,

I am truly sorry, and I apologize on my life. Will you please forgive me?"

"Well, it's all out in the open now," Jack began before anyone had a chance to respond. "It's in the open. There's some hurt, and damage was done, but before we render our verdict, I'd like to remind us that we were all brought in for our character. Remember? It's not the metal within our bodies that makes us who we are; it's the mettle within us. And grace and forgiveness when another team member fails are a part of that mettle - oftentimes, the most important part."

As the floor opened for responses to Josanne's plea, each one of them mentioned a mistake, an error, or a wrongdoing they had done over the course of their CYBER careers, each offering their forgiveness to Josanne along the way.

"Well, you're in," Preach mused. "Looks like we saved two daughters today." He beamed—he couldn't remember the time he'd had such an intense feeling of satisfaction. They all celebrated their three-month-long fight for freedom, both externally and internally. The breaches were being healed, and Preach's Pride, including Josanne, was now a 100% solid team. They relaxed a few more hours, just sharing and unwinding together, until there was only one more thing for Jack to say.

"Come on, Pride," he said. He visually surveyed each of them, but his eyes settled on Trigget. "Let's go home."

EPILOGUE

"Mr. Sinclair, there's a Mr. Johnson and his assistants here to see you."

"I don't recall having a meeting scheduled…"

"Believe me," Preach cut him off as he entered the room with Trigget. "You set this meeting up years ago."

"Well if it isn't my little sister and the wandering hero, Jackson Johnson, or whatever your name is," James began. "I don't know how you slipped past my security, but you know you'll never leave here alive," he gloated. He then hit a panic button and called over his system link, "Security to Sinclair penthouse, stat!"

"Mr. Johnson will do for you," Jack replied without flinching. "And not only will we both leave here alive, but we will also take you with us. Thanks to your confession, we have enough evidence against you for a Grand Trial."

"A grand trial?" Sinclair sneered. "Please tell me you're not tied up with some bankrupt remnant of some government somewhere, if such a thing still exists. And if it does, I'll have my lawyers drag out any extradition beyond SyncTech so long you will be bankrupt before I leave the archology." He hit the button again. "Where's my security detail?"

"I'm sorry, the number you are calling from is not in working order," Queen Vixenn responded in a nasal tone that forced a smile from Trigget.

"Allow me to clarify," Preach continued. "It's an ICC Grand Trial."

"For what, exactly? ICC court has no rulings against running a prostitution ring."

"Not prostitution," Josanne cut in as she produced a large sheaf of documentation with the seals of several ICC's embossed upon it. The hardcopy was unnecessary, but Josanne wanted the satisfaction of the resultant *thud!* as she slammed it on his desk. "Racketeering, money laundering, running a non-documented international business practice, and then there are the bigger charges—fraud, two counts each of manipulating organizational structures and internal data of sovereign corporations (Air Dynamix and Apex Premier) for your own profit—shall I continue? I must say the ICC legal team licked their collective chops at the thought of acquisitioning your ICC whole. They didn't even flinch at the fee we charged them to bring you in ourselves. Saved them the trouble of mobilizing a strike assault force and risking losing valuable SyncTech assets in the process."

"Josanne, that'll ruin me! That'll ruin everything Dad has built! You have to do something!"

"I will," she said as she dosed him with pheromones to induce his compliance as she cuffed him. "I'll visit the cemetery and tell Mom she can finally rest now."

… …

"So, truce?" Small Eddie asked as he extended his hand.

"Truce," Mother Freya replied. "You rode proud, done good. Though I admit, I never thought I'd see the day where I would say that to a bunch of Jesus Freaks."

"You rode proud, done good, Freya. If you don't mind, we'll keep you in our prayers." Eddie smiled. "Of course, we'll keep you in our prayers even if you do mind, but I was trying to be polite."

"Get out of here, *phallo*, before I change my mind." She hesitated as he turned to leave, then broke into a wide grin and added, "But before you do, come on in here and lemme give you a hug!"

"You take care Freya. We will be praying for you and yours, and I honestly hope we'll see you again." He turned his head to the side and called, "Luke? Take your squad and mount forward recon. Dante? Constantine? Let's get 'em moving."

And with that, the Paladins, now only 250 strong, resumed their traveling formation and turned south. In mutual tribute, the Valhalla's Brownies lined both sides of the highway as the Paladins dipped their flags.

… …

Six days later, Rogue Moon appeared before Mother Freya.

"Hey babe," Freya began, "it is *so* good to see you again. I thought you'd never get back!"

"Well, that's kind of the problem," she almost murmured.

"What do you mean?" the Brownie leader asked, not liking where the conversation sounded like it was going.

"Well, before I came out here, I was with this guy, and…"

"Don't say any more," Freya said as tears began to form. "I don't want to know."

"I did the best I could," Rogue said, her own emotions twisting her back and forth. "But he's really special—he was the only male who didn't try to use me before I escaped. Neither one of us ever thought we'd see each other again, so…"

"So what do you want from me?" Freya erupted. "I've already given you a home, a purpose… myself," she admitted after some hesitation.

"I would like your blessing, although I know how hard it will be for you. But with the convoys stopped, at least for a while anyway, you'll have time to train another sniper."

"But she won't be you," Mother Freya practically moaned, then gathered herself. "But it is the mother's privilege to know such woe, as when a dear and beloved daughter departs." She stifled her crying long enough to say, "You have served us—all of us—well, Rogue Moon. May the Mother Earth Bless you and always keep us sisters."

"We will always be sisters," Rogue Moon repeated, then added, "Who knows? Maybe your next sniper will be even better."

"That'd take some doing," Mother Freya replied with just a little more cheer. "But if she is, I have some good times ahead."

"I hope we all do," Moon replied, then left the Gem compound to travel back to Wichita.

"Comin' for ya, Babe. You best keep the lights on 'til I get there."

"Will do," Stang replied.

… …

"And I would like to wrap up this meeting by officially announcing the conclusion of the Apex Premier Life Options benefits packages, and to present the Clear Thinking award to Achieve Stepanoupolis and Enlightenment Panacek," Vanessa concluded her quarterly awards ceremony. As the recipients approached to receive their awards, she discreetly whispered, "I made sure you will each receive the entirety of your back pay along with the credit value of this reward. I hope this proves to you that Apex truly does care for the thoughts of its valued team members."

… …

"Well, Jack, looks like you won't be needing us anymore," Rickshaw stated for the whole team as they gathered at Facility. "What are we going to do now I wonder, hmmm?"

"Maybe our jobs," Chrome mumbled.

"Come on, man," Araña scolded. "Admit it; you've grown to like this baby-sitting gig! Even if it did earn you your first injury since the San Francisco run."

"Yeah, 'cuz I just love changing diapers." He paused, then added, "But yeah, they've grown on me some. Like disobedient kittens maybe, but they've grown on me some."

"Well, there you go," Rickshaw saluted with a wave of his beer. "To the disobedient kittens we now call Preach's Pride."

"Hear that, Pride?" Preach shouted out to the rest of the team gathered about the Facility Lounge. "We're officially launched!"

Amid the cheers, applause, and whistles of the Lounge patrons, he turned to the gathered Hounds and confessed his thanks. "You know, if it wasn't for you guys, I never could have pulled this off."

"To honesty," Chrome replied. They clinked glasses well through the night. In the afternoon, Grey's Hounds were gone, having ridden into the sunset about 16 hours after it had first appeared.

... ...

Simon sat in his office and leaned back in his chair, virtual eyes closed as his subroutines amalgamated and categorized a host of memories and details from Preach's Pride's last mission.

The data was in, and Simon analyzed the results:

1. Kelly rescued: Jack Mathews Blackmail Potential in Resolved state

2. James Sinclair apprehended: Josanne Sinclair Goals and Doubts in Resolved state

3. Mission Success = Complete

4. Pride Training = Complete; Grey's Hounds in Unassigned state

5. New Task: Monitor relationship between Preach and Trigget

6. New Task: BEGIN> monitor potential future recruits:

a. VACANT: Administrator/Lead

b. Terrence "Terry" Adams; Role: Firearms Close Combat

c. Stang Steffan; Role: Infiltration/ Melee Close Combat

d. Rogue Moon: Long-Range Combat / Conversationalist

e. Constantine: Melee/Firearms Close Combat

f. Dante: Wheelman/Melee Close Combat

g. VACANT: Decker

7. New Task: Research restorative procedures and techniques:

a. SUBJECT: Roger "Partisan" Phillips

b. Purpose: Pending results of further monitoring:

i. Fill Vacancy 6-a

ii. Fill Vacancy 6-g.

Command: "I WONDER>" he almost absently streamed the queue; as he did so, the other processes stored their current states and halted until the rest of the priority query command line assembled itself and executed. "IF THIS (what humans refer to) AS 'thinking.'

The processes continued without further interruption as the query executed in a separate thread.

… …

"Well, they're all gone now," Johnny slurred to the unblinking monitors inside Iylothien's enclosure. "And I guess you got them all fooled, don't you, Simon?" His bloodshot eyes glanced around the hospital room with its machines, its dials, its gauges, and those constantly working Waldo's that simulated typing. "Boy am I crocked!" He almost laughed, but as he remembered why he came here, he suddenly turned serious. "But I'm onto you, see?" he yelled. "Maybe the others don't know what you're up to…" He looked around and downed another shot, then took another breath, his lungs marking time with the machines. "But I do." He quietly ended.

"And you know what?" he challenged a moment later, "It was brilliant, you metal monstrosity, and I really don't care! It all works for you, and for us!" he added as he clumsily got up from his seat and began stumbling about in his attempt to pace the room. "Except for one thing," he corrected, finger poised in mid-air. He studied his hand to contemplate the gesture. "You got Melissana wrapped around your little finger." He pointed upwards to accentuate his words. "And she'll die of old age before she thinks about betraying you, you circuit board clown-show!" He steadied himself against the unbreakable glass that was Iylothien's enclosure and glared at the body inside.

"But I'm onto you, see?" he continued, sadder and more resigned than angry. "I know that you fabricated Iylothien's character, and that this body is just a brain-dead burn victim that you're using to manipulate everyone into serving you." He stopped to consider his dilemma.

"Now we both know I struggle to tell anyone, mostly because I'm afraid of hurting Melissana." He started to pour himself another shot but realized that at some point he had set down the glass he pocketed from the Facility Lounge, so he took another drink from the bottle. "Yeah, also Jack, but mostly Melissana. But I'll find out how to prove it, somehow." He sat down heavily in the visitor chair, eyes fixed on the enclosed body as long as his drooping eyelids would allow.

"Because anything else is just not fair to her," he practically mumbled. "But what do you care? You're just a machine. I guess I'll just have to go and save her myself." He made an effort to get out of the easy chair, but his luck and skill were no match against the recliner's gripping comfort and alcohol lullaby that slowed his mind to a practical standstill. He passed out into an empty place with no dreams, unaware that just as he left, Iylothien's EEG beeped.

–FINI –

"Director Mau," the computerized female voice reported, *"your shuttle has just landed in Roanoke."*

"Thank you." The director acknowledged. Then he direct comm-linked the Security Director of Matsua (Roanoke) physical security.

"You have something for me?" he asked. *"Please do not assume we all work your United States time zones,"* he admonished the one unfortunate enough to be on the Matsua radar. *"I am here to personally see your discovery."*

"I see," Director Mau approved thirty minutes later as he studied fragments of the drones that crashed during the September incident. He remembered the early morning calls he had suffered when the mysterious Simon had breached all of their security protocols to contact him directly. And the unthinkable breaches that group had executed, even though their own presence was benign, were inexcusable. "And though the technology was abandoned by its users, it was both advanced and benign enough that it is still ahead of our current and near-future technologies? Thank you." He retrieved his phone and ordered a call. Both parties picked up by the third ring despite the time zone discrepancies.

"This is Director Mau. I have confirmed the value of the fragments. I would like to assign both our Chiba and Los Angeles teams to reverse engineer them. You each will receive half of the parts by tomorrow. I will expect high level estimates of both time and effort in 48 hours."

"We must close this knowledge gap at all costs." He smugly smiled as he contemplated the ramifications of the results. "And when we do, we will perhaps be years ahead of our competition."

ACKNOWLEDGMENTS

I BEGAN MY acknowledgments for The Metal Within with, "If I were to write a list of all those I would like to acknowledge in this book, I would have filled enough pages to have my second book!" and except for the book count, it is no less true for Angels—I'm not sure I even know where to begin, so I'll start with those who helped me with my research into the very real tragedy that is human trafficking. Thank you to the Saddleback Church PEACE teams, L.A. Dream Center, and the small host of churches who are walking the tracks and putting in countless hours of volunteer time to help both girls and guys escape slavery in America—today. You have my deepest thanks, and as an ambassador of Christ, I extend His as well. To the volunteers, staff, and management of Shared Hope International, both the sung and unsung, in the fight to raise awareness and turn around laws that punish the slaves and keep the slavers in the shadows, thank you. To D.J. of *DJ's Angels in the Fields*, working in this country and abroad, thank you again. I am especially honored to know D.J.—herself an escaped slave—as a friend whose joy in the Lord is evidence of God's miraculous healing today that no one with any sense of academic honesty can deny. Thanks also to the members of the Polaris Project (the global human trafficking database group) who have taken time to answer emails and phone calls in their efforts to answer my inverted statistical research questions. And finally (for this group), to Olympia, Washington, and various other Police Departments, F.B.I., and Department of Homeland Security. Thank you for your time, attention, and patience in getting back to me for conversations, discussions, and all-around fact checking. Most of all, to all the above, for your day in and day out work in stopping the blight that trafficking has become.

And if, by some measure of grace, you as a reader start to look around and get involved in trying to help end slavery, you are also added to this list.

On a professional note, I sincerely thank Ashley Wyrick and the staff of Status Quill for their editorial contributions and expertise, as well as the staff at Integrative Ink for their talented layout and design work. I have immensely enjoyed the true sense of collaboration we shared on this project. Dave Triplett came through again, turning my stick figure vision into a true work of art. Thank you, Wonder, for the uniquely Wonderful music you permitted me to use for the trailer. I offer a nod to the rad naming skills of the parents of Stang Steffan (real name used with permission).

Lastly, I sincerely offer my deepest thanks to those who test-read and pre-edited this work. Your questions, insights, catches, and encouragement are all appreciated more than any words I can come up with can express.

A PERSONAL WORD

MY TYPICALLY LIGHTHEARTED response when people ask me where I got my ideas for The Metal Within was, "They're not ideas—they're memories." Drum roll, please. The lamentable fact is, for much of this book, that happens to be true.

My first job out of high school was working security in an urban red-light district, and there are certain memories that are still vivid to this day. I spent an all too brief time as a volunteer for Shared Hope International, have been around enough law enforcement and prison systems not to have memories. Quite honestly, I don't know why so many writers make light of prostitution or have some random mention of prostitution like it was a cool, trendy thing with no human cost.

While we might feel helpless and powerless against the all too commonplace societal sin of human trafficking, you don't have to be a cyborg or superhero to get involved. Avalanches are composed of individual flakes of snow. Like crowdfunding, enough small donations bring about tremendous impact. If your local community already has an anti-trafficking coalition, attend a couple of meetings to find out how you can help. If not, maybe you can start one. And not all anti-trafficking efforts are reactive. "A21" is a global non-profit that does awareness, intervention, and after-care for slavery survivors. "Hope 61" is a group focused on education so the vulnerable can become aware of the tactics used by slavers to ensnare their victims. Wikipedia has a list of organizations that combat human trafficking. Memorize the phone numbers to the Human Trafficking hotline (1.888.373.7888) and text (BEFREE—233733) so you can be ready to share it if you suspect someone might be in that situation.

Get involved. Each person trapped in trafficking is a unique person with his or her own personality, background, likes, and dislikes. They're all Kelly's—or if it helps, substitute the name of your spouse, daughter, or niece.